Aug, 2010

Dear John & Donna,

I hope you enjoy the "Locust Queen".

Thank you for your encouragement & support. Best Wishes.

Michael A Farrand

The Locust Queen's Feast
A Story of the Place Between the Worlds

Michael C. Glaviano

ISBN 1452895856

Acknowledgments

Susie Localio and David Blevins both provided wonderful input to the content, style and mechanics of *The Locust Queen's Feast*. Susie, a former English teacher, made sure that my grammar and punctuation were reasonably well-behaved. Dave, a trained engineer who possesses the sensibilities of top-notch musician, kept me from climbing too far out a limb with pruning shears. Susie and Dave both provided valuable input on my ensemble of characters and my story lines.

My venerable and excellent friend, Alex Stewart, guided & supported me through the daunting landscape of the printing technology wilderness. I shudder to think how this book would have looked without his expertise.

And Lyn Glaviano enthusiastically read iteration after iteration of the manuscript. She asked the tough questions. She told me what she liked and what she didn't like: more of this, less of that. That bit's confusing. That bit's better this time. From the start to the finish of this project, she was my unwavering source of encouragement.

Thank you all.

For my Beautiful Angel

One

According to the paperwork, the Riviera pulled to the right if you hit the brakes hard. Actually, it pulled to the left. Of course it had been Donny and Leon, the biggest stoners in the shop, who had done the checkout on the big Buick and signed off on the Drive Away contract, so Eddie wasn't surprised they got it backwards. Anyway, Eddie, AKA "hot-shot kid," almost stacked it up in the first hour of the trip because of that screw-up.

They said the car got ten miles per gallon too. Right. A '72 Sky-lark with a 350 might do that, but not a meaty, '66 Rivvie with the dealer-installed, dual-quad kit gulping high octane fuel into the maw of a 425 V8. Best case, hotshot figured he was getting somewhere south of eight.

Not that it mattered. This was a Drive Away delivery gig for Big Vin, and the Vinster would be picking up the gas tab. The pay Eddie earned for the delivery sucked, but it was cool to cruise the interstate in an old monster Buick. The hood on the thing went on forever. Big Vin would squawk like a kicked chicken when he got the gasoline bill, but hotshot was following the route that had been laid out for him. The odometer still worked. It'd verify that he'd stayed mostly on course. It wasn't Eddie's problem if the fuel cost cut into the Vinster's profit.

Since the Riviera was well over forty years old, the stereo sucked just as much as the pay, but he had his MP3 player plugged into the cigarette lighter and earbuds were cool. He had the tunes cranked. He had his foot on the pedal. The miles had been sliding past ever since he'd climbed into the cockpit of the Rivvie at Big Vin's shop outside of Buffalo the day before.

The car's body was straight and the interior was still nice. Somebody must've kept it garaged for most of its life. There was a shimmy in the front end at about 45 miles an hour, though. Eddie wouldn't admit it to anybody, but that was a little bit scary. He thought it might be the ball joints. After all, the car was twenty-and-change years older than he was, so it could easily be ball joints. He hoped not. Jesus Christ himself wouldn't be able to tell you where the beast would end up if a wheel fell off at highway speeds.

When he thought about it, hotshot kid liked the whole Drive Away thing. The big car's cockpit was his own private turf. His personal soundtrack added to the enjoyment, the insulation, the isolation. When he thought about how he was spending his time, he mostly thought it was cool that he had a gig where somebody paid him to tool around in expensive cars. Being cool factored heavily in the kid's priorities, so when they occurred at all, most of Eddie's conscious thoughts centered on being cool. It was cool to get around, cool to check things out, get laid, party.

It was hotshot's third or fourth cross-country stint. Unconsciously, he'd developed a pattern. He would pick up a car in town A, deliver it to some stiff in town B, and then work here and there at whatever jobs looked easy until the next car came along. In a way, Big Vin was one of Eddie's regular customers. The Vinster had a car restoration business. More often then not, when somebody – usually some old, rich dude with a fetish for the model in whose back seat he'd got his cherry popped – bought one of Big Vin's "restored" beauties, the car would need to be delivered.

Sometimes Vin would use a regular auto transport service, but the Drive Away people would get the call if Big Vin figured he could save a few bucks by having a kid like Eddie deliver the goods. Eddie was pretty good with the cars. At least he didn't abuse them too much. Anyway, he was one of the Drive Away outfit's better delivery boys.

Once he'd dropped off the product, Eddie would FedEx the paperwork back to the Drive Away office. Then he'd hang around in whatever town he landed. He'd get a cheap room and a minimum wage job and chill. He'd stop partying completely because nine times out of ten the Drive Away guys would have him go to a local lab for a drug test before the next run.

Anyway, usually within a week or a month at the longest, Eddie would get a call on his cell. Sometimes he'd have to hop on a bus for a day or two, but then he'd be off again, cool again, on-the-highway-cool. For three or four big, cross-country joyrides, the whole thing had been a sweet deal, a very sweet deal.

But then things went sour. Hotshot kid got stuck. Blind-sided, he went from cool to lame in the blink of an eye.

One minute everything was just fine. He had a nice set of wheels with his kit in the back. Somebody else was picking up the gas tab. The tunes were good, there was plenty of power under the hood and he was moving. As long as he stayed away from that front end shimmy at 45, it was all good.

His luck changed on a Thursday afternoon in May. Eddie had rolled into an anonymous Rust Belt town at the helm of the '66 Riviera. He was about a day's drive away from his destination outside Minneapolis. After he delivered the Rivvie to the straight in Minneapolis, Eddie would catch a bus to Bloomington. The Drive Away people had another car waiting there for him to pick up and drive down to Omaha, so he wouldn't have any down time. Sweet.

Eddie was feeling good as he cruised the town. He was on schedule, had his next few days mapped out, and he thought maybe he'd take a little break. Yeah. Like he was on a mission and he needed a little R&R. He had an image in mind, an excellent image. He planned to saunter into a bar and order himself a beer. When the straight at the bar carded him, hotshot would slap his driver's license on the bar. It'd be cool, seriously so. Today was his twenty-first birthday.

He had gotten off the main drag and driven slowly through one of the older neighborhoods. He rolled down the window, shut off the MP3 player, and let the mild air freshen the cockpit. There were big, heavy trees, not yet in full leaf, at the curbsides. Behind those massive sentinels were block after block of solid, three story brick houses. Everything was a little down at the heel but not too shabby.

Hotshot kid wasn't sure why, but he liked looking at this kind of neighborhood, this sort of place. It was so different from the ranch style subdivisions where he'd grown up. These houses looked as though they'd sprouted in place from saplings rooted when the town was young. Now the houses had grown and matured. A few had gone to seed, but most of them were still pruned and neat. Sometimes, when he saw neighborhoods like this one, the kid would wonder what stories went on inside the houses, but he'd soon shake off those thoughts. Thinking about shit like that was lame.

After checking out the cool old houses, hotshot kid drove on with his eyes and thoughts, such as they were, for company. Before long, the character of the place began to change for the worse. Crossing a big thoroughfare or two, Eddie found himself near what had once been the town's bustling business center. Without warning, the big Buick hit a pot hole, then another.

"Fuck!" Eddie heel-slammed the steering wheel and slowed down. Busting a tire or a shock wouldn't be cool. Catastrophic failure of a worn ball joint would be a total and complete bummer. Strictly speaking, he shouldn't be cruising this lame town in search of a brew. Strictly speaking, he should be back on the interstate. Of course, strictly speaking, he didn't really care about *should*. No one was there to tag him for it.

Idling along now, the hotshot kid began looking more seriously for a bar. Signs indicating the Interstate appeared. He decided that if he hit the interstate, he'd get back on and see about snagging a beer later in the day.

Eddie craned his neck as he drove through what remained of the city center. There was the obligatory town square sporting the obligatory rusted artillery piece and the obligatory statue of some long-forgotten figure of local, historical significance. All available surfaces were well-coated with beautifully-aged patina of grime and bird droppings.

Michael C. Glaviano

The few shops that weren't boarded up were anything but prosperous. Rundown railroad and Continental Trailways stations faced off
at opposite ends of the square. Each guarding its share of dwindling
commerce, the dilapidated stations glared suspiciously at each other.
Bingo! Predictably, the only business that was enjoying much
activity was a bar. There was music – not great, but not too terrible –
streaming from the dark cave of the bar's entrance. Tunes reached into
the open cockpit of the Buick, into the receptive ears of the hotshot kid
and grabbed his attention. Eddie often pictured himself enjoying a good
mug of beer and the easy camaraderie of a friendly local inn or tavern. Of
course he'd never actually managed to get past the "let's see some ID"
stage of the process, so there was little substance to his fancy. That was
about to change.
Now two words can aptly describe the sort of person who
would've mistaken that seedy dive for a friendly, local tavern: "young
fool." Or, to be a bit more charitable, perhaps just "hotshot kid." In any
case, Eddie was much less experienced in the ways of the world than he
thought himself. So, that was precisely his mistake. He pulled over and
parked the Buick right in front. Then he got out and sauntered into the
tepid darkness.
Eddie could tell the place was wrong from the instant that he
squinted into the gloom, music, and smoke. Too many conversations
were interrupted while too many eyes sized up the newcomer. No welcome hail or nod from the bartender greeted him. The smart thing would
have been to do an about face, get back into the Riviera, and drive away.
But hotshot kid wasn't interested in doing the smart thing. It
wouldn't be cool to turn tail and run. Definitely not cool. It would be
cool to be confident, cocky, and to ignore the wrong feeling of the place.
With the single-minded stupidity of inexperience, he went right on in and
ordered a half pint of Bud. The bartender didn't bother to card him.
Naturally he was mugged. They didn't even have the decency to
let him finish his beer. A common enough technique was used: three locals surrounded Eddie at the bar. One pretended to be friendly. Another
watched silently. The third one picked a fight. The bartender insisted
they take it outside, and before you could say, "set up the home-boy," Eddie was lying face down in the stinking alley behind the bar.
Actually, he got off lucky. He was left with contusions and abra-
sions and a headache the size of the Oklahoma Panhandle. His wallet lay
in the filth a few feet from him, sans cash. And, oh yes: they bagged the
keys to the Buick.
Eddie reeled down the alley and around the side of the building
to the street. There he found his worst fears realized: the 1966 Buick
Riviera was gone and with it his gear. After staring for a while, open
mouthed, at the spot that was no longer occupied by his transportation,
livelihood, and sum total of his worldly possessions, Eddie began to

4

curse. After a while he cried tears of frustrated rage. At least he was smart enough not to go back into the bar and demand help.

Instead he staggered back across the town square in roughly the direction from which he'd come. After a few blocks, he reached a busier street. At that point, his pounding head would allow him to go no further. Woozy, he hunkered down on the curb and held his head. Eventually, a couple of cops in a patrol car pulled over and stopped. His sorry appearance corroborated his pathetic story sufficiently so that the officers helped (as opposed to stuffed) Eddie into the back of their patrol car and took him to the local station.

There, while she took down a cursory report, a bored desk sergeant made no discernible attempt to hide her opinion of Eddie's mental abilities and general competence. She had short gray hair, very little neck, and her range of facial expressions spanned the distance that lay between disinterest and mild hostility. A badge pinned to her uniform read, "Driscoll."

Eddie figured her to be in her mid-to-late fifties... sort of your generic Middle-aged Aunt From Hell-type. Probably had a heart of gold. Well, maybe. She did begrudge Eddie a cup of coffee. Sour and strong though it was, the coffee soothed him. The first sip scalded his tongue. Even so, the brew felt wonderful going down. The kid relished the feel of the chipped, stained mug. Coolness notably absent for the moment, he clutched the mug as though he'd stumbled upon the Sacred Grail.

Sipping his coffee, he sat in a stale, unwashed room in the rundown police station. He sat in a hard, wooden chair that was worn and scuffed and sticky on the arms with the residue of decades' worth of sweaty palms. The chair squatted in front of the sergeant's desk. Desk, chair, mug, and sergeant all admirably matched the cracked, yellowed linoleum floor. Eventually, in that unpleasant place, Eddie managed to collect his thoughts. He actually chuckled a little. It kind of hurt, but that was okay. A bit of the coolness, the cockiness of the hotshot kid seeped back.

Sergeant Driscoll didn't share his improving mood. She looked at him as though he were a species of congenitally-deranged insect.

"What's so funny? You like gettin' mugged, huh? You know you're damn lucky those guys didn't cut you up for a little extra fun," she growled at him. "They probably figured you weren't worth getting their knives messy."

The sergeant glanced down at her paperwork for a moment. Then she looked back at Eddie. "I see today's your twenty-first birthday," she continued in a slightly less hostile tone. "You might want to consider your survival a birthday present from this beat-to-crap town."

Eddie decided that she was trying to reassure him.

"Er, uh, sorry," he mumbled. "Um, I just now remembered that I've got a few bucks stashed in my shoe. So I'm cool. It's not much, but maybe you know a place where I could rent a room for a couple of days? ...nothing fancy, just a place to hang out while I figure out my next move."

"Humph. Nothin' fancy. Yeah, well maybe. Let's just get these reports done first. If that meets with your approval. Shall we?"

So they filled out the auto theft report. And they filled out the stolen property report, and the robbery and assault reports. Then they notified the Drive Away folks, Eddie's erstwhile employers.

The Drive Away people asked one question: where did the assault and auto theft take place? When informed that Eddie had gotten into an altercation in a bar, they were not pleased. They were seriously displeased, in fact. Hence the term, "erstwhile."

Since lack of good judgment does not by itself constitute a crime, the police weren't overjoyed at having Eddie on their hands. They weren't particularly inclined to want to put him up (not that he was all that keen on spending the night in the tank, even without it being a forced stay).

The Red Cross will generally try to find a spot for a distressed citizen to spend the night, and to her credit Sergeant Driscoll did offer to contact that worthy organization. By now though, Eddie had calmed down a bit more and wanted to appear at least slightly under control. He wanted to reassert his persona as "hotshot kid," so he decided to give his earlier request a second try.

"Uh, sergeant?"

"Yeah, what?"

"You mentioned earlier that you knew a place where I could maybe rent a room? That'd be a lot cooler than going to a shelter."

"Well, now. We wouldn't want to detract from your coolness, would we? I said, 'maybe.' You know Painter Avenue? No, I guess not," she answered her own question. Then she paused a minute and regarded Eddie with that look cops are able to invoke on demand. She kept it up until, coolness retreating, he squirmed a little.

"Look," she continued, "I guess you're basically okay for a dumb kid. You stick around for about another half hour 'til I get off shift. I'll drop you off someplace where you can stay."

"Hey, thanks."

"It's on my way. In the meantime, why don't you make yourself useful? You can grab a broom and sweep up around here. We got no regular janitor since the last round of budget cuts. There's the broom closet over there." She gestured with her chin at a narrow, beat up door across the room.

This suggestion further deflated Eddie's coolness level, but he knew that he needed help from this cranky cop, so he swallowed the wise remark that had jumped to his lips. "Uh, sure. Yeah. That's cool," he muttered.

He wouldn't have admitted it to himself, but by then he was seriously in need of doing *something*. And maybe it'd get him on the old broad's good side, assuming she had one. So he got a broom and dust pan and went at the dingy, old room.

The half hour turned out to be more like an hour and a quarter. The station got busy for a while, and the sergeant got surlier as her shift dragged on. Eddie just kept at it and tried to stay more-or-less invisible. Eventually, there was a lull in the fun and the sergeant's replacement – who, except for gender looked as though he'd been pulled from the same mold as Sergeant Driscoll – could take over by himself.

In the meantime, Eddie had swept the floor and emptied the trash. He even found some Windex and clean rags and reduced the grime level on the room's only window. While the place definitely needed more than a cursory cleaning, he imagined that the perceptive connoisseur of police station chic could just make out the results of his efforts. Finally, the sergeant caught his eye and once more employing that expressive chin of hers, indicated a side exit. Relieved, Eddie put away his tools and followed her outside.

Relieved, that is, until the instant he left the building. The sun had long since set and taken with it the lovely spring afternoon. He shivered as a blast of cold air hit him. Kicking at the cracked blacktop, he recalled that his jacket was likely now the possession of some low-life, car-thief scum. Worse yet, it was probably just tossed out. This brought the events of the day back into sharp focus and dealt Eddie's young self-esteem another blow. Coolness was definitely not happening.

Sergeant Driscoll pointed her chin at a beat up Ford pickup, and Eddie wasted no time hopping in and slamming the door. He noticed that the interior light didn't work. The cab of the old Ford smelled faintly of dust and mildew. Sergeant Driscoll clomped around to her side and climbed in.

She cranked the starter. The battery sounded weak, but the engine caught on the second try. Deep inside the dashboard, a worn piece of metal began to squeak. They started off.

"Is it always so cold this time of year?"

"Not that cold if you're dressed for it. Place I'm taking you, Joe Tabs', it'll be warm enough."

"Joe Tabs?"

"Yeah. Joe Tabs. I think his real name is Giuseppi Tablarasa or something like that, but everybody calls him, 'Joe Tabs.' He's a strange old bird, but he's okay. And I know he's got a room for rent. Anyway, I drove past it every day the last two weeks goin' to and from the station."

"Sounds good to me. If it's not too much money."

"Yeah. That's good. Like I said back at the station, kid, you seem to be okay, but we're gonna want to keep track of you for a while on account of that being somebody else's expensive car you lost."

7

Michael C. Glaviano

"Hey, Sergeant, I didn't ask to get mugged," he whined.

"An' what exactly would you call goin' into a dive like that? By yourself, no less? A smart move? A good plan?"

"Yeah, well... I guess I sorta figured that out at this point..."

This earned him a snort that (by some stretch of the imagination) could almost be construed as an expression of amusement, so he decided to press his advantage, "Uh, say, Sergeant Driscoll, you know of any jobs? My money's not gonna last too long, and I'm gonna need to get some clothes and stuff."

"I dunno, kid. This town's not exactly boomin' right now, in case you didn't happen to notice. In fact, I don't remember a time when it was boomin'. We don't even know down at the station when we'll be able to hire a new janitor. Or if. Maybe Joe'll have some ideas. He always knows what's up around town. Can you do anything useful?"

Now that was quite a question. Just what could he do? As Eddie tried to answer, he realized what a paltry list of skills he could claim. This hardly matched the image of Cool, Independent Man that he was struggling to establish and maintain.

"Yeah, well, I worked at a deli making sandwiches, and I'm a good driver. Been back and forth across the country a couple of times now in Drive Aways. Done some semi-skilled labor. Short time work when I needed some extra cash... waitin' 'til the next car transport job came up.

"This is the first trouble I ever had," he finished lamely.

Sergeant Driscoll must've sensed Eddie's discomfort and decided not to follow up on his lack of prospects for gainful employment. She just drove on in silence for a space. Then, more gently than he'd thus far heard her speak, she repeated, "Maybe Joe'll have some ideas. Like I say, he's a strange old bird, but he sure seems on top of things."

Now this was the second time Sergeant Driscoll had mentioned the "strange old bird" thing. It made Eddie wonder just what he was signing up for. Not that he had much in the way of alternatives, but still, he could picture some nosy oldster with a lot of time on his hands. Time that he used to chew the ears off innocent bystanders (as Eddie imagined himself).

Eddie squirmed in silence. Finally, he couldn't help asking, "Uh, just how old is this guy? What's he do, anyway?"

The sergeant shrugged as she made a left turn into a residential neighborhood. By their looks, these houses were of the same vintage as those Eddie had admired in the trouble-free warmth of his afternoon swing through town.

"You know, kid, I got no idea. Seems like he's been here forever, but he doesn't ever lose his spunk. When you talk to him, you just don't feel like you're talkin' to an old guy."

Lose his spunk? What the fuck did that mean? Again the image of a peppy, chatty senior citizen swam into the hotshot kid's thoughts. Eddie was still searching for an appropriate response to this tidbit when conversation, such as it was, was cut off by their arrival.

"Tell you what, kid. You wait here 'til I see if it's gonna be okay with Joe. And look. Tomorrow, you call down at the station and ask for me. I go on shift at noon. We'll want to make sure you and Joe get things sorted out okay, and besides we'll..."

"Yeah, I know, you'll want to keep an eye on me anyway. Thanks. I'll be sure to check in. Maybe we'll all get lucky and somebody will turn in the Buick."

"Hmmph. Don't count on it." came the reply. With that she opened her side of the Ford and got out. Eddie watched his gruff benefactor make her way up the walk to the front door of the house.

This house was very much like those he'd noticed earlier in the day. The walls were constructed of bricks with heavy stone blocks at the corners of the building. Long, flat stones braced the tops of the window openings. The roofs were pitched somewhat steeply. There were two, main levels. In addition, dormer windows hinted at a smaller living space on the third floor. Four or five steps led up to a covered front porch. The front yard was neat but unassuming, with minimal landscaping beyond a small lawn and a few shrubs that were trimmed below the level of the first floor windows.

After a minute the light came on, and he watched her back while the sergeant talked to someone inside. She gestured as the conversation progressed, and more than once, she pointed back towards the truck where Eddie waited. Abruptly, she turned and motioned for him to join her on the porch.

Sergeant Driscoll waited until he got to the step. She stayed just long enough to make introductions. Eddie's new landlord, who in the dim light of the porch looked to be in his mid-sixties, offered a surprisingly firm handshake. When introduced, he nodded and said, "Call me Joe... Joe Tabs."

The Sergeant admonished Eddie once more to be on his best behavior and returned to the pickup. From there she waved off his thanks as she got back inside the battered Ford. Then she pulled onto the quiet street and drove into the darkness. Eddie was left standing on the porch step, his arms crossed across his chest for warmth while Joe Tabs regarded him for the space of a dozen heartbeats.

"Well then," he stated mildly enough, just as Eddie was beginning to get uncomfortable, "we can't have you out here freezing, can we? The good sergeant says you appear to be a decent sort, and I believe that is quite a recommendation coming from her. Come in. Come in."

While he certainly wasn't going to disagree with Joe Tabs, Eddie thought at the time that the old man made up his mind about him a bit on the quick side. He followed Joe inside, glad to get out of the cold. As would any polite school boy, he remembered to wipe he feet on the mat and close the door softly behind him.

The front door opened on a short hallway. There was a worn Persian carpet on the floor. Several doors led off from this entry hall into other parts of the house. Joe gestured brusquely to the left, back, and right at the closed doors. "Parlor – that's only for special occasions. Stairs up. Straight back is the main part of the house. There's a dining room behind the parlor. That door opens on the stairs to the basement.

"I understand from Sergeant Driscoll that you haven't had any supper," Joe continued.

"Yeah, well, it's been a long day. I guess I haven't thought about it much."

"Would you care for something to eat?"

Eddie realized that he was actually very hungry. "Well, yeah. Thanks... I'd like something. That'd be cool... Uh... I mean, if it's not too much trouble."

"No trouble at all. I'll just get some things out, and you can serve yourself. Please follow me." With that, the old man turned and went through the doorway and into the living room.

As he followed the old man, Eddie noticed for the first time the smell of the house. Lingering in the air was the aroma of a hearty meal. Beneath that were the scents of dried herbs and polished wood. They passed through the main living area, and the young man had time to notice comfortable furniture arranged around a large fireplace.

A small fire burned on the grate, and this, together with one reading lamp, provided all of the illumination in the room. By the dim light, Eddie could make out that the walls were rough plastered and then wainscoted to just above waist height. There were pictures above the wainscoting, but his host was moving too fast for Eddie to stop and examine the surroundings carefully. At the back of the living room, they turned left through a swinging door into the kitchen.

While the parts of the house he'd seen so far had looked old to Eddie, the kitchen had obviously been remodeled. Without being trendy, the kitchen was modern in its clean functionality. The appliances were new and, to Eddie's untrained eye at least, appeared expensive. The back-splash was tile, but the countertops were fashioned from a medium-tan stone.

With an economy of motion that he was to learn was one of Joe's characteristics, the older man set out some leftovers while Eddie washed up at the sink. Eddie put some of the food on a plate and popped it into the microwave.

The food heated while Joe pointed out features of the kitchen area. "In the back there's a service porch, a pantry, and a half bath. The whole back of the house faces south and opens into a greenhouse. It's fine now, but soon we'll need to put up the shades or it'll heat up the place unmercifully and kill all my plants."

He gestured in the opposite direction – toward the front of the house. "Through that door is the dining room. There's a door connecting that to the parlor. I already pointed out the parlor door leading directly from the entry hall. Again, I don't use either of those rooms much except when I have guests. I prefer to eat most of my meals in here."

The place was homey even to a stranger, and Joe's quiet descriptions of the house had helped to put Eddie at some ease. For the moment, after what had been far from the best of days, he felt safe and relaxed. By now the food was hot, so Eddie carried his plate to a small table on which Joe had set out two glasses of plain tableware and a bottle of red wine.

Throughout Eddie's meal, Joe kept up what one might term "genteel conversation." He asked just the right number and degree of questions. He listened to Eddie's answers, and his tone and manner encouraged the young man to speak candidly and openly. Unlike most oldsters in Eddie's limited experience, Joe talked very little about himself.

To attempt any detailed description of Giuseppi Tablarasa would be more than a little futile. His appearance did have some constancy to it, but it had a great variability as well. Often Eddie could imagine him as an uncle or an older cousin, but then Joe would say or do something that made him seem more a contemporary than someone of Eddie's parents' – perhaps even his grandparents' – generation. Then, other times, the old man would look at Eddie from such a distance and with such a strange expression that Eddie was sure he must be the oldest man on earth. Ancient, he looked at those times – ancient but never frail or weak.

As the young man was eventually to learn, Joe habitually dressed in sturdy work pants – often khaki or navy blue. In cool weather, he tended towards flannel plaid shirts; sometimes he varied the wardrobe to the extent he'd wear a sweater over a lighter shirt. In warmer weather, he favored plain T-shirts in solid colors. Sometimes he'd wear basic work shirts too, but of course Eddie did not see all this at first. That first night, Joe wore work pants and a light flannel shirt.

His hair had probably once been dark; now it was mostly gray and white. It was thick and wavy. His skin was creased with sun lines, frown lines, and many, many laugh lines. Despite his apparent age, Joe was still fairly heavily muscled.

In the days to come, Eddie was to witness ample demonstration of the older man's strength and stamina. Eddie was to realize that the old man had had nothing to fear from the strange youngster he had invited into his house. In fact, the hotshot kid eventually came to understand that very few people would trouble Joe Tabs at all.

At the same time, there was no bravado about him. He was always quiet and polite and friendly, and he loved his food and drink. He loved a good story or a joke – even if it was on him. He had no patience with pettiness or cruelty, and he was capable of a state of awesome fury. In such cases, Eddie learned that it was best to step back and do his best to follow instructions. Fortunately, those cases were rare.

After his meal, Eddie cleaned up as Joe directed. By then Eddie felt more energetic and more himself; although he still looked as beat up as he was. The two men, one in the first resilience of youth, the other old and tough, left the kitchen.

Each with a glass of heavy red wine, they moved to the living room and took up stations in the pair of great chairs that were pulled up in front of the fireplace. Despite the fact that it had been unattended throughout Eddie's meal, the fire continued to cheer the room.

They stared into the flames for a time. Joe broke the silence before the atmosphere grew too weighty. "So... the good sergeant says that this is your twenty-first birthday. *Salud!*" Joe raised his glass slightly and took a small sip of his wine before continuing. "In any event, you've lost the better part of both your funds and your possessions, and you haven't a job."

"Well, yeah, I guess that's right," Eddie replied with some reluctance. He felt that this statement was somehow incomplete, too much a bald-faced admission of vulnerability. He was also feeling pretty sorry for himself at this point, but he didn't intend to let this old guy know it. "I really enjoyed traveling," he offered. "Seeing the country, different people and all, but I'm not worried about sticking around and working and getting set up again. I've done okay in strange towns before."

Joe regarded Eddie again for a few seconds before he turned back to the fire and continued. "An old man such as myself could do with a bit of company from time-to-time. Also, I sometimes find that I must attend to... interests... elsewhere. At such times it would be helpful to have someone who is trustworthy watch over my home until my return. Finally, if you prove to have the requisite aptitude you could possibly help me in my work."

"Uh, which is?"

"I'd rather not get into that right now; it's nothing illegal of course. But it might seem slightly boring to someone your age. Tell me, Eddie, are you handy with tools?"

"Well, I've painted, done a little plumbing and rough carpentry. I've done a little car repair, but I don't like it much. I'd rather drive 'em than work on 'em. I guess I'm not all that great at any of it. Like I told Sergeant Driscoll, I've done some deli work and some semi-skilled labor."

After a moment's reflection, Joe appeared to reach a decision. He looked directly at Eddie and held the young man's gaze. "Well, then. Here's my proposal. I'll hire you to help me with the work around here –

real work that needs doing... maintenance of the house and grounds, help with the gardening, cooking. Further, as I mentioned, if I find that I am comfortable leaving you here alone, I'll need you as a house sitter from time-to-time.

"I expect this will average approximately four full days of work each week, occasionally more. I can afford to give you room and board and a small sum. If you give it a solid try, you will be able to pick up any skills you require. I'm patient in most things."

He named an amount. It was better than Eddie could have hoped. "Whoa, that's really cool. I..."

Joe held up his hand. "Mind you, this isn't charity or make-work. And I don't need anybody hanging around who can't or won't work steadily and consistently. Much of what I'll have you doing I'd have to hire someone to do anyway. Your help will allow me more free time to pursue my studies. I'll expect good, honest work, and I'd like you to promise me you'll stay on at least three months – say well into August. After that we can negotiate."

This was just too lucky. After a couple of seconds, Eddie couldn't contain himself and he finally blurted out what bothered him the most about the whole deal. "But why me, Joe? I mean, you don't know anything about me. I'm grateful for the chance and all, and I think it'd be cool to stay here and work and all..." He finally ran down under the old man's steady look.

"I am not often wrong about people, young man. We've talked while you've had a meal. You've recovered your composure fairly quickly after what must have been an unpleasant incident this afternoon. You're well-enough spoken considering your age and the time of the world. I'd bet you come from a good family – people who tried to do right by you. I wouldn't be surprised to find that you're a bit more educated than you let on."

Something about the old man's tone found a crack in the hotshot kid's armor. Eddie felt a wave of emotion hit him. He started to speak but found that his voice had a decidedly uncool quiver. He tried to cover it by clearing his throat and taking a sip of his wine.

"Yeah, well... my dad was a good guy. Educated and all that. He did his best."

"Was?" Joe prompted.

"Um... Yeah... Dad and my younger brother, Willy, got killed by a drunk driver."

"Sorry to hear that. How old were you when that happened?"

"Seventeen. Senior year of high school."

"And your mother?"

"Yeah, well. Mom tried, but..." here Eddie had to pause again for a several heartbeats. "...she kind of lost it. Afterwards," he finished raggedly.

"I see. So, did you graduate from high school?"

"Oh, sure. Piece of cake. I was a real smart guy, for what good it did. Had a shot at class valedictorian; the whole thing, man. Was studying for an AP test the night of the accident. Otherwise it'd been me driving Willy to the dance. His first high school dance. That motherfucking drunk..."

Eddie fell silent again. Then, surprised at himself for opening up to the old guy, he took another deep breath and finished the story. "Anyway, after... after they got killed, uh, well, I just coasted through the rest of my senior year. Grades fell, but... yeah, I graduated. By summer, Mom stopped getting out of bed most days. Just stayed in her room. I ended up cooking, shopping, all that crap. It was okay, I guess, for a while. But, well, she... just... fell apart."

"What's she doing now, if you don't mind my asking?"

"Doing? State hospital. Dad had decent insurance, but medical bills and the house payment sucked it all up in a year. She's all drugged out. The place smells bad."

"Ahhh... so you decided not to go to college then?"

"Oh, I went to the local community college for a couple of semesters, but it all just seemed like bullshit. Then I heard about the Drive Away gig and jumped on that."

"I see. And you liked that, evidently."

"Yeah. It was cool. Easy." Despite himself, Eddie laughed a little. "At least until today it was."

"Indeed. Well, young man, I'm sorry you've had such a lousy time of it. Of course I can't do or say anything to make things better. Except to offer you the job, of course."

"Yeah. I could use the job, man. Thanks."

Joe stood and offered his hand. "So we have an agreement?" Eddie nodded and stood as well. They shook hands, and the deal was done.

Joe then suggested a brief tour of his home. This included a brief visit to the second floor which consisted mostly of Joe's private rooms. These included his library with adjoining study, a bath, an incredibly cluttered workshop, and his bedroom.

He asked that Eddie refrain from entering his rooms without permission. The other rooms on the second floor were not used unless guests were visiting. They functioned as guest bedrooms. There was also a hall bath.

From the second floor landing, a narrow stair led upwards to a garret apartment. Tucked beneath the pitched ceilings were a small bedroom with an attached bathroom and a tiny den or sitting room. These rooms were paneled in a light colored wood to waist height. The walls above the wainscoting and the ceilings were painted a warm, cream color. The den had a small desk tucked into a south-facing dormer and a whole wall of built-in shelves – now mostly empty. The bedroom also sported a generous closet that was lined with aromatic cedar.

"Let's see here. Yes, here we go." Joe rummaged through a chest that lay at the foot of the bed.

"Here are some clothes that you can use until you have time and funds to purchase things that suit you better. There are clean linens on the bed and towels in the cupboard on your left as you go into the closet. I happened to buy some fresh toiletries yesterday. I'll drop them by while you get cleaned up. There are some basics already in the bath.

Tomorrow, after breakfast, your first task can be to freshen up your rooms. I noticed that they could use a good turning out. I've cleaned them recently, since I'd planned on renting the apartment if the right person showed up. Yet it's always best if the occupant takes charge of his own space."

Joe hesitated for a moment. Looking off into the distance, he quietly observed, "I'm fairly optimistic that this will work out well for both of us."

Then, closing the door behind him, he made his way out. Eddie looked around again. After cheap hotels and sleeping in the backs of cars, these small rooms underneath the rafters looked just fine. He wasted no time in getting into a hot shower.

Afterwards, Eddie felt much better but was extremely wrung out. The day's events had taken their toll. True to his word, Joe had left a bag of personal supplies just inside the door. Evening rituals complete, Eddie got into bed. Despite his fatigue, it was some time before the young man could relax and get to sleep. A great deal had happened to change his life in the space of a single day. It looked to be a change that had some interesting possibilities. He would wait and see.

Joe was indeed a strange one, but his strangeness was not in any way a negative thing. He was merely, completely his own person. Eddie considered it a little farfetched that the old man actually needed anyone to help him. Hotshot kid resurfaced a little and resolved to check it out. Promise or no promise, he thought, if he couldn't stand it, if it turned out to be lame or weird, he could always bail.

As Eddie relaxed, he noticed that the house was very still. The darkness around him gradually assumed a strange property. He had the sense that it... *watched*. Not inwards at him, but outwards: outside and around the house, the grounds, the quiet streets. It was disquieting and creepy at first, but Eddie shrugged it off as some kind of reaction from the day's events.

He wouldn't have admitted it, but he felt secure and protected in a way that was reminiscent of homecoming. Gradually, his eyes became heavy and he dropped into a deep, dreamless rest.

Michael C. Glaviano

Two

After the kid turned in, Joe Tabs sat in his chair downstairs and watched the fire. He had much to think upon. Was this young man, barely past his teens, the helper whose arrival he had foreseen? If so, there must be more to him than was visible at first meeting. He appeared to be a good enough lad, but much more than "good enough" would be required of him if he were called.

What lay at his core? Was there nascent strength there? Indeed, the young man had suffered at the hands of ill-fortune, had been badly bruised in fact. It spoke well of him that he'd pulled himself together to the extent that he'd been able. So there was some strength. That much was clear.

And the old man's skills assured him that there was no evil in the lad, no subterfuge or deception. The young one was no more than what he had appeared.

He must *become* more, however. He must become much more. If he were to succeed, even to survive, he must develop. He must learn. Could he do that?

The kid was young. That much was in his favor. He'd started out on a good path but had been sidetracked. Perhaps his personality was still susceptible to constructive influences. Or, perhaps not.

Well, nothing need be decided tonight. For a time Joe would play only the most superficial aspects of his own role and see how the young one responded to physical work... observe how his youthful mind responded to knowledge.

But time was fleeting. Time had become an unseen adversary for this young man, as it was for all young people. More to the point, time was running down for this very world.

And against that grim backdrop, there was the matter of his own, long life. Joe couldn't keep on like this forever. Well, strictly speaking, he probably could... as good as forever, anyway. But people notice after a while when someone doesn't get any older. People notice when they remember you from their childhood even as their own middle age leans on their shoulders, makes their knees ache. They notice. They talk. Word gets around.

It used to be simpler in the old times. Move to a new village, set up shop, and in a few years you were part of the landscape. In the world today – *this* world anyway – it was harder to remain anonymous. Oh, he could do it. He knew how; he had the resources. What he lacked was the will.

Indeed, his active participation was overdue, but still he missed her, and missing her, he brooded. He had let his feelings dull his edge, and now this whole world was in pain. And the world's suffering folded back upon him, drained him. A bad feedback loop, this, but it was the nature of his being.

Some, a very few, of his former associates still lived. They could help. They would, as countless others had over the years, step forward. They would, if need be, sacrifice. He knew that he must reestablish those connections, but he was tired. He knew that he must shrug off his lethargy and respond to the growing threat.

Joe was well aware that the Locusts had taken advantage of his own lack of enthusiasm for the struggle. They had stepped into the vacuum engendered by his apathy and were abroad again. All the signs were there. For the hundredth time, he cursed his own inaction, his brooding inattention.

Finally, underlying this listlessness were the memories. She and he had parted on... unfortunate terms. He, born of the bones of this world, could be stubborn and impatient. She, an ephemeral creature of another, had been strong and proud. And she had been far wiser, far more intelligent than many of the ancients. He knew that she still lived, but she was old now and tired in the way of mortals.

The ancient warrior shook his head sadly. He must take up the fight very soon, or what actions he could muster would amount to nothing. He also knew that, having once in his long, long life found his heart's desire, only to lose it, to lose her, his chances for happiness were vanishingly small.

With an effort, he pulled himself away from those pointless regrets, sighed and got up from his chair. Absently, out of habit, he waved a hand in the direction of the fire and the flames died. Silently he made his way up to his rooms where he worked and wrote and studied until an hour or so before dawn.

As he worked and planned, he drew energy from the deep well that underlay the physical plane. That energy sustained him and kept him strong and vital. That energy, as well as other sources of strength, lay always at his fingertips. Finally, in the predawn silence, he rested for a short while and was awake and up, refreshed, well before the youngster stirred from his garret bed.

Three

The next day, after breakfast and a tour of the yard. Eddie returned upstairs and aired out his rooms. Housework wasn't cool, was in fact extremely uncool, but the kid got it that he had a sweet deal, so he vacuumed and cleaned until the rooms were fresh. He was surprised at the result. As Joe had promised, the result was not only a more pleasant space. Despite himself, Eddie saw that his efforts also imparted a slight sense of ownership and identity. They were now "his rooms" as opposed to the place where he crashed.

When Eddie came back downstairs, Joe told him that they would start with spring gardening work. They began implementing a plot plan that Joe had sketched. They broke for lunch around noon, and Eddie remembered that Sergeant Driscoll had wanted him to check in. He mentioned it to Joe.

"Good. I'm glad you remembered," the old man remarked. "The good sergeant cares about such details."

So, right after lunch, Eddie checked in with Sergeant Driscoll. While she didn't sound particularly glad to hear from him, she did at least let him off the phone with a single, "Stay outta trouble, kid. You hear me?" admonishment. That obligation out of the way, Eddie spent his first afternoon helping with Joe's garden.

Working side-by-side, they prepared the earth. First, they turned over the soil and broke the clods with their shovels. The earth was rich and loamy from many years of care, but they added compost from large bins near the back wall of the yard. Joe brought a few more bags of other garden nutrients from the garage. They mixed and turned these into the soil.

At dinner that night, Eddie was so exhausted that he was barely able to sit up and eat his food. In contrast, Joe was cheery and full of plans for the upcoming growing season. After cleaning up the kitchen, the old man gently suggested that Eddie might want to go upstairs and relax. Eddie dragged himself up the stairs and took a hot shower. As the young man got ready for bed, he felt another wave of tiredness hit him. When he finally lay down, sleep found him instantly.

Eddie's days quickly fell into a routine. Joe took pains to keep him busy, to set tasks that lay right at the limits of his charge's abilities. As a result, the young man never felt taken advantage of, and true to his employer's word, he did learn a great deal of gardening, maintenance, and the pleasure that derives from hard work.

Work in the garden and the yard continued. The old man was totally unaffected by the physical labor, but by the third day the younger man found himself sore in his back and arms. He tried, with precious little success, to ignore how his hamstrings felt. If Eddie's host/mentor/landlord experienced any discomfort, it never showed.

In fact, it was at first his landlord's stamina that kept Eddie from bailing on the deal. The hotshot kid didn't think that all the physical labor was cool. It was definitely not cool, but even less cool would be admitting that some oldster, probably forty years his senior, could outwork him day after day. The fact that the old man made nothing of it increased Eddie's awareness of his own lack of conditioning.

Shades went up on the greenhouse. Seedlings that had been started earlier in the year went either into larger pots or else into places they'd prepared in the garden. This allowed the men to start some other, more delicate plants that would make up a second crop later in the summer. There were hedges to be trimmed and other basic yard work to be done.

It wasn't all physical labor, however. Without discussing it at all, Joe assumed that Eddie wanted or needed to learn about plants, their growth and uses. Often during the yard work, Joe would stop and call Eddie's attention to some characteristic of a nearby plant, tree, or shrub.

"Look at this," he'd demand in a quiet voice. "How often have you stepped on or ignored the humble dandelion? Did you know that every part of the plant is edible? You can make tea of the roots or roast it and grind it for a coffee substitute. The uncooked leaves can go into a salad.

"Then there's the rose. All roses are edible. The flowers are tasty as well as fragrant. The rose hips – the parts left after the flowers die – are a great source of vitamin C. You can eat them raw or brew them in tea. The seeds have a hairy skin that's a bit irritating, so it's best to cut open the pods and remove the seeds before eating the rose hips.

"Just don't eat anything that has been sprayed with pesticides by your typical, avid, suburban gardener," the old man added with a short laugh.

Frequently he'd show Eddie a cutting or sample of a plant that he'd discussed previously and ask the young man its name and common uses. Before long Eddie felt comfortable in the garden and knew more than he'd ever thought possible about the plants, trees, and shrubs that surrounded them.

Except for the fact that Joe often had to teach the young man how to perform various tasks, and that he usually set the day's agenda, Eddie sometimes felt that they were housemates whose job it was to maintain and restore a fine old home. As the days passed, with little awareness of the change, Eddie grew stronger. His muscles lengthened and got used to hours of steady work. Discomfort receded, and more gradually, so did the obsession with being cool.

As Eddie became more familiar with the old house on Painter Avenue, his appreciation for it grew. It had been designed for the long term, and Joe clearly did his best to care for it. Still, some restoration work on the old place was in order. Caulking, patching, painting, all the maintenance that older homes require, comprised many of their projects.

Even though it was stoutly built, the wall around the back and sides of the property required frequent attention. There was also what looked to be a burn mark near the southwest corner of the house. Near this, the masonry had been chipped and cracked – as if by a forceful impact. Under Joe's guidance, Eddie learned how to repair this damage and many other things besides.

There were regular trips to the neighborhood stores. In food, hardware, and clothing, Joe's purchases inevitably ran to basic necessities. He most often purchased staples and such items that he could not supply from his own labors. The old man was well-known and well-liked at the stores where they shopped. Although they were seldom idle, Joe invariably had a few minutes to spend commiserating with a shopkeeper who's business wasn't doing well or to inquire regarding a relative or friend who had been away. His concern appeared genuine; yet he was never sucked into the dramas.

The young man didn't notice it at first of course, but gradually, Eddie realized that Joe never contributed any nasty gossip, negative comments, or ill-will. When negative things came up, Joe would change the subject and casually wrap up the conversation by paying his bill and gathering his purchases to leave.

Over time, Eddie decided that this unobtrusive but consistent unwillingness to engage with negativity was why everyone confided in the old man. Perhaps with the tough economic times and poor business conditions, the people around him were comforted by this strong, good-natured oldster who was always okay, always attending to his own business.

At first Joe took pains to introduce the young man to the merchants. Gradually, they began to acknowledge Eddie and include him in their daily greetings. It began to feel good to be recognized and acknowledged as part of a community. This was a far cry from the attitude of detachment he'd previously cultivated during his "Drive-Away Days."

Before long he was able to restore his wardrobe, and although he did not emulate Joe in his dress, Eddie too began to favor more practical basics. Shortly thereafter, he felt himself fitting in, just a little, with his surroundings. While he continued to think of himself as a free agent, he also enjoyed the transition from "the strange kid that Joe's taken in," to "Joe's helper."

What felt best of all was when Eddie began to learn enough so that he could take care of part of the errands himself. It was just a few weeks after he'd started working for Joe.

"Er, Joe?"

"Yes?"

"Suppose you go on ahead and pick up that stuff at the hardware store. I can do the groceries and you can swing back by. It'll save time."

"You know what to get?"

"I think so."

"Good. I need to go to the library this afternoon. It'd be a help to save that half hour."

And so it went. Little things, these victories were, but without realizing it, Eddie began to feel more like someone making his way on his own. His carefully cultivated self-image of the hotshot kid, the cool, independent smart guy faded. Even though he was totally dependent on a single employer for his livelihood, the young man was, nevertheless gaining some confidence and developing some real skills.

Two weeks later they received a message from Sergeant Driscoll. They'd found the Buick – or what was left of it – behind a deserted warehouse on the river a little more than ten miles south of town. The car had been stripped. Even a few of the Riviera's body panels had been removed, and what was left behind hadn't evidently been treated kindly. Some of Eddie's stuff was still in the trunk, but what'd been left was pretty trashed.

On one of their shopping excursions, Joe dropped Eddie off at the station and the young man collected what items were worth the trouble. Sergeant Driscoll was there. She was cheerful as ever.

"So, this your stuff?"

"Yeah. It looks like my stuff. What'd they do light it on fire and run over it to put it out? Most of it is totally ruined."

"Well, these aren't exactly solid citizens we're dealing with here."

"Got any idea who did it?"

"Kid, we got plenty of ideas. It's just that this is a property crime. We got enough worse crap to deal with. So unless one of these creeps comes in here and sez, 'Hey, I mugged a kid, ripped off his Buick and trashed it, can I go to jail, please?' we're just not too likely to get to it. See?"

"Is it that bad around here? Joe's neighborhood is pretty peaceful."

"You don't know how lucky you are, kid. There's damn few decent jobs or even prospects of 'em in this town. Most smart folks who

22

could figure a way out have left already. The ones still here are too stupid or too lazy to leave."

"C'mon, Sergeant, it's not that bad, is it?"

She looked at him hard for perhaps fifteen seconds, and then her face softened, just a little at the edges. Eddie thought that her eyes acquired just the tiniest hint of sadness, but then the sergeant looked down and blinked once. When she looked back up her face was as stony as ever, but her voice was a little kinder.

"Naw, kid, it's not really that bad. It just seems like it today. It's been a lousy week. Hell, it's been a lousy year."

She continued, "So anyways, to change the subject. I don't think we'll be needing to get in touch now. From what I can tell, Joe likes you and you're keeping your nose clean. So you can take off any time."

"Well, okay. But I gave Joe my word that I'd stick around until sometime in August at least, and things are going pretty good, so I won't be leaving any time soon. Joe says that he's going to have to go on a short trip before long, and he's going to need me to stay around and watch his place."

"So you're going to become a regular citizen of our little burg, eh?"

"Can't say for sure, but I'll be around for a while anyway."

"Well, then. You landed pretty good, stayin' with Joe Tabs and all. Stay out of trouble, kid, and you'll do fine."

"Uh, okay... well, thanks, Sergeant. I better go meet Joe now."

"Right."

He signed the receipt for what was left of his possessions. Most of his stuff had been so abused that he put all but a small notebook and a belt into the trash. Sergeant Driscoll lifted her chin at him in a half-nod and then turned back to the pile of papers on her desk. Eddie tucked the notebook and belt into the pocket of his borrowed jacket and went outside to wait for his landlord and employer.

Michael C. Glaviano

Four

Wrapped in yet another stunningly sheer and revealing gown, the beautiful figure of the Locust Queen sat unmoving in the cold, blue room. Her graceful hands held, caressed a sphere of polished lapis that was inlaid with an intricate filigree of ivory, platinum, and diamonds. The featureless, blue orbs that were her eyes easily penetrated the dim corners of the throne room. What visible light she permitted within her throne room was directed upon her form to highlight its loveliness.

A world, manipulated, twisted by her efforts, lurched toward ripeness. It approached that stage of dissolution at which it might be consumed, its fabric added to her greatness. Never sated, her hunger would be, for a brief time, appeased. Her glory would be duly celebrated.

Yet she brooded among her treasures, her beauty, her power. Her unbridled pleasure was perturbed by timid reports of... ripples, of disturbances. This annoyed the great Queen. Furrows played briefly upon the pristine expanse of her brow. A sigh lifted the perfect fullness of her breasts.

Messengers and agents, weaklings all of them, were brought forth. They were questioned, chastised. Some were severely interrogated, and even their suffering held limited ability to restore her serenity. To the end, however, they assured her that all was well with the program. The dissolution of a world was proceeding apace. Nothing would delay her feast.

Then for a time, assured that these annoying ripples would come to nought, she turned away from the irritation. The Queen sought solace in pleasure, in the admiration lavished upon her, in the fear she engendered among her admirers. Even so, after a brief interlude, the reports returned to disturb her reverie. She was displeased at the notion of an impediment to the next installment of her fulfillment.

Her ire simmered. Reclining upon her icy throne, the beautiful Queen frowned ever so slightly. Her ministers feared this, as well they should. The courtiers shrank back, trembled in their corners. The featureless eyes probed the furthest reaches of the throne room. Murmurs

Michael C. Glaviano

trailed off in the shadows, ceased in the corners of that cold, blue room. Fear, deliciously palpable fear, permeated the frigid hall.

Enough. The Locust Queen reached a decision. These ripples must be identified, damped, these irritants erased. She leaned forward and, with a single gesture, summoned another probe, an agent capable of independent action, an agent with some real talent and intelligence. The agent was kept ignorant of course, tormented, naturally. Yet this one still retained a desire to advance in the Queen's service. This agent was still able to function autonomously, to take initiative.

Calm restored for the moment, the Queen again reclined as she awaited a more detailed report, anticipated more effective action. The chill of the room surrounded all, wrapped all those present in a reminder of their monarch's power. The Locust Queen gazed through the shadows upon the fear of her subjects and drew joy from the reminders of her strength.

Five

Not long after the meeting with Sergeant Driscoll, an event oc-curred to crack Eddie's tranquil existence and very nearly precipitate his departure. It happened on a Friday – his nominal day off. He'd taken to hanging out at a park near Joe's house and reading. He'd met no one near his own age as yet, at least no one with whom he'd made any kind of connection. Naturally he was interested in making some friends of his own.

As is typical of early summer in the mid-west, the weather was humid. Several shaded paths ran beneath spreading poplar, maple, and oak trees. The air was always milder beneath these trees. Traffic sounds withdrew to be replaced by birdcalls. Browsing a book that Joe had loaned him, Eddie sat on a bench in the shade. The book was a history of magic in medieval England (not exactly a hot topic for the young man), so he was sort of half reading and half dozing in the afternoon warmth, when an incredibly sexy voice spoke from a short distance away.

"So, I haven't seen you around here before. You just passing through?"

Eddie looked up and promptly dropped the book from his lap. Before he could recover, the woman standing in front of him stooped, re-vealing significant, barely confined decolletage, to gather his book from its resting place on the path. She brushed it off with a well-manicured hand and, after a quick glance, extended the book.

"Oh, are you a student of magic?"

"Well, no, not really. A... friend just loaned it to me."

The silence lengthened, and Eddie felt as if he had to say some-thing. Her eyes enjoyed no small similarity with a laser targeting system as they locked on his. Those pretty eyes were dark and full of promise, full of anticipation. Eddie stammered out an awkward introduction and she responded with a smooth, first-name-only response. Her name, she said, was Alicia.

Afterwards, try as he might, Eddie could not recall the conversa-tion that ensued, but he did remember that he had been torn between de-siring it to continue and wanting nothing more than to escape from the presence of those eyes and that figure and that face. Or perhaps he was torn between desiring what he saw (or thought he saw) and wondering what the hell to do with it if he actually were presented with the opportunity he imagined. Or maybe he couldn't decide whether he felt like a virile young man or a bird staring at a hungry snake.

And, like the conversation, Eddie could only dimly recall her actual appearance. All that got through the fog of desire and fear was that she said that she was visiting some friends for a few weeks. She added that she was from "farther north, originally."

Somehow, she stayed and chatted, and that chatting lengthened and grew more intimate. Eventually, Eddie gained some modicum of confidence and actually tried to keep up his end of the conversation. She was, he recalled later, so *receptive* to everything, no matter how inane, that he managed to say. After a time, they started walking together along the path, and before Eddie knew it they had left the park and were walking down the street and Alicia had her arm in his.

This felt wonderful, and his thoughts – a generous term at this point – were decidedly limited in their scope and mostly devoted to some very graphic fantasies that were beginning to form. What little he said was invariably greeted with a musical laugh and a gentle pressure on his arm. He could feel the shape of her along his side, and her scent was in his head.

Seemingly of their own volition, Eddie's feet trod the familiar path towards his recently adopted home. The strollers quickly reached the doorstep. It was so completely natural and easy to invite Alicia inside. She accepted so... willingly.

As he stepped across the threshold, Eddie called out to Joe, but then recalled the old man's plans to spend the afternoon with some of his cronies across town. Eddie figured that Joe wouldn't return for hours yet and said so to Alicia. Bliss. They made their way into the living room and sat in the cool dimness of that inner room. Their conversation began to have further, significant gaps, and then suddenly they were in each other's arms. She melted into him for a time, but then she pulled back.

"Wait," she breathed into Eddie's ear, "I don't want to rush. This is very sweet."

"Um, sure. Would you... like uh, something to drink?"

"Suppose you show me around your house." She was somehow biting his ear at the same time she was suggesting the tour.

So they got up and began walking around the first floor. They took frequent breaks during which they embraced, snuggled, and generally acted even younger than Eddie was. He showed her the first floor rooms, and then they reached the stairs.

"You want to go upstairs?"

"I'd love to."

He followed her hips, legs, and spiked heels up the stairs. They reached the landing outside Joe's rooms. Eddie was continuing on to the narrow stairway that led to his rooms, when she pulled up short.

"What's in here?" came the musical query.

"Those are my landlord's rooms."

"Can we see?"

"Nah, I don't think so. Joe, that's my landlord. He wouldn't like it."

"But *I'd* like it. I'd like it... very much."

Alarm bells started, dimly at first. Something was going wrong with this perfect encounter. Why on earth would she insist on this? As if through a fog or mist, the thought came to Eddie that maybe she wanted to do something unusual (in an erotic sense), and he started to waver. She smeared herself against him and reached her arms around to pull him firmly against her. The alarm bells grew faint; so did he.

Alicia stepped back and looked imploringly at the young man. With his right arm around her waist, Eddie reached for the door to Joe's shop. With an audible *snap*, a sharp blue spark jumped from the doorknob to his hand when he got to within a foot of the knob. Startled, Eddie jerked his hand back. The door flew open, and there was Joe. His face was full of thunder and his eyes flashed with real anger.

Joe stared intently past the young man towards Alicia, and Eddie followed his look. The young man cried out and stepped back involuntarily. Beautiful she still was, but now her beauty was hard and threatening. Where before she appeared to be Eddie's age or just slightly older, now she had the appearance of a beautiful but cold-faced woman ten or fifteen years his senior.

Joe spoke first, tilting his head in the young man's direction, "This little one is not for you. I've sensed you nosing around the town for days, and I suggest that this be the last we see of you. Go! On your peril, do not return here." His words were strangely clipped and full of menace.

Alicia threw back her head and laughed – a wild, almost hysterical sound. Then she shouted a complex collection of syllables that hurt Eddie's ears. She seemed to throw something from her empty hand at Joe. The old man stepped aside slightly, but the skin on his cheek split as from a sharp blow. Blood began to well, but almost casually, Joe brushed his hand across the wound and the flow was staunched.

He glanced at the blood on his fingers and then flicked a drop at Alicia. It struck her and sizzled and she screamed in pain and rage. Joe lifted his hand as though to reach toward the woman, but with unnatural strength and grace, she leapt back a dozen feet and turned half away from them.

Alicia held her left hand, thumb extended, out at the end of a stiff arm. Reaching up high, she quickly jerked her arm down. There was a

Michael C. Glaviano

ripping sound and the air beyond her hand peeled back to reveal a murky landscape of gray shadows and indistinct shapes.

Just before she jumped through the gap, Alicia looked over her shoulder at Eddie and made a kissing motion with her lovely, frightening mouth. He felt a sudden, sharp pain and then wet warmth flowing down the side of his face. Suddenly, she was gone, and the rent in the air snapped closed behind her.

Reeling from what he had just witnessed, Eddie spun to face Joe. The old man was holding a handkerchief to his cheek and regarding Eddie with solemn but unsurprised eyes. Eddie felt very small and confused, and he knew without being told that he'd done something terribly wrong by bringing Alicia into the house. Eddie suspected that had she actually gained free access to Joe's rooms, the results would have been much worse.

Again Joe spoke. Far from appearing to be a kindly, mild-tempered old man, he looked both powerful and dangerous. His voice no longer held rage, but he was still angry, "Go upstairs and compose yourself. Wash the smell of that bitch off you, and meet me downstairs in fifteen minutes."

Eddie had never heard this tone, this anger in Joe's voice. It was obvious, however, that the only adequate, the only safe response was complete compliance. On weak knees, the young man made his way up to his rooms. It was impossible for him to climb the stairs without gripping the rail, and even with that support the muscles in his thighs and calves were watery. Once in his rooms, Eddie stripped out of his clothes and got into a shower that was as hot as he could stand.

Although the bleeding had stopped, his face throbbed with pain as he dried and dressed. Reluctant for some reason, to touch the clothes he'd removed, Eddie wrapped them in a damp towel and brought them with him downstairs. Instinctively, he held the bundle away from his body as, on still wobbling knees, he worked his way to the first floor of the old house. Joe was waiting in the kitchen. The old man's right cheek had a small bandage taped in place.

There were two tumblers of scotch sitting on the kitchen counter as well. The amber liquid caught the afternoon light, and the aroma of the liquor was sharp in the still, warm, summer air. In the time it had taken to walk from his garret apartment to the kitchen, the throbbing in Eddie's cheek had extended its reach to wrap a tight, painful band around the young man's head.

Joe had already started hot water with bleach and detergent running in the washing machine. Without a word, he took Eddie's bundle of clothes and dumped them into the washer. He closed the lid and the machine began its work.

Still silent, the old man stepped to the sink and scrubbed his hands. Then he set to work and gathered several herbs from among those resting in baskets and in jars on shelves near the pantry. He ground these to a fine, aromatic powder using a mortar and pestle. The powder became an astringent-smelling paste when mixed with some water and a splash of scotch.

"Now," he said, speaking for the first time since Eddie had come into the kitchen, "hold still while I smear some of this on your wound. It will hurt."

Eddie's face was already very sore, and the first touch of Joe's paste made him draw his breath in through his teeth. It was as cold as ice and burned like fire. Eddie took a deep breath, held it for a moment, and released it. Some of the pain and tension flowed out with his breath, and his face began to feel better. The throbbing band around his head receded slightly.

"I think that she actually liked you... a little bit... as much as she can like anyone," Joe spoke quietly, almost to himself. "You'll have a scar of course, but she could have done so much more to you than this little bit of damage. I'll check you over in a few minutes to see what else she left behind; there will almost certainly be something. We'll need to keep an eye on you for a few days, but clearly she's not really all that adept at more than relatively minor mischief."

"Uh, who was she, Joe?"

"A player. Not even a major one. From the other side. What'd she call herself?"

"Alicia."

"That's as good a name as any. You and I will refer to her as 'Alicia' – unless we're somehow lucky enough to learn her real name at some point."

"What the hell's going on, Joe?"

"Take a sip of your scotch. It's past time I explained some things. Of course I blame myself for not protecting you better, but if I'd said anything to you before now, you'd probably not have believed me. I'm just glad that I sensed her presence and was able to lie in wait for her. Despite her tough act, that fancy exit will have taken a lot out of her. If we take reasonable precautions, she will not trouble us for some time."

"So was I some kind of bait in a trap or something?"

"No. She could not be trapped that easily. All I could do was to lie in wait with neutral intentions. If she hadn't tried to violate my home, I would have – *could have* – done nothing. Since I would not attack unless pressed, she could not detect my presence. If I had intended to attack her with no warning, she would have sensed my intent. Mere waiting, observing can be neutral and extremely difficult to sense. There is a certain balance yet in this world, for all the damage that's been done to it."

"I'm really confused, man, and I don't think I like what's going on. Maybe I should just get the fuck out of here."

Michael C. Glaviano

Eddie was feeling better physically, but he was embarrassed at being taken in by this woman and being treated like some kind of incompetent ward by Joe. The implied insults to his young manhood combined with the damage inflicted on his youthful pride. He was left feeling surly and petulant.

"That would be... unwise. She's marked you. She will be able to find you for some time. You're susceptible to her, and she could surely think of other uses for you. Further, even if she were to leave you alone, you've seen just enough to torment you for the rest of your days."

"Enough of what? What exactly have I seen?"

"Suppose you tell me."

"Well... I'm not exactly sure. She threw something at us that scratched our faces, I guess; although I didn't see what it was. Then somehow... she... left. I'm a little bit fuzzy on that part. It looked like she tore a *hole* in the air and jumped through... into some dark, foggy place. But that's crazy. It must've been a trick."

"So that's how you explain it to yourself? You attempt to rationalize what you saw as some sort of trick?"

Eddie was getting angry again. He couldn't accept what he'd just experienced. Yet he had no explanation for it. This was frustrating, frightening beyond his abilities to manage. "Well, the only other choice would be to say that she did those things by some kind of magic or super powers or other kind of lame shit. Does it matter? I'm gonna pack my stuff and get out of this weird-fucking little town. I don't need it. I'm outta here."

Joe didn't respond directly. He merely stood there, calmly, mildly. "Take a sip of your drink," he suggested, "a small one. It's strong."

Glaring at the older man, Eddie picked up the glass, downed the entire contents. It felt like silken lava. With his eyes bugging out, he began wheezing and coughing. Joe stepped over and pounded him on the back and held his arm until Eddie could breathe again. Then Joe released his arm and sat down at the kitchen table.

The old man sat there and looked at Eddie with just the tiniest twinkle in his eye. For a couple of moments the young man glared back at him, but then Joe started to chuckle. Eddie couldn't help it and after a minute's struggle joined in, albeit somewhat ruefully. The tension was broken, Eddie felt sheepish, but no longer humiliated. The kitchen was warm, comfortable, and familiar.

After they settled down, Joe poured Eddie another drink and added another splash to his. Then he suggested that they move from the kitchen to the living room. They each took one of the huge chairs that faced the now-dark fireplace. They were silent for a time. Eddie knew without being told that Joe was working through his thoughts and deciding how to proceed. The silence was companionable, and the drink was warming his belly, soothing his head. Eddie felt no need to talk just then. He was returning to his equilibrium, or moving to a new one. He waited through the silence.

Eventually Joe spoke up. "So, my young friend, do you have a mind to listen to a fantastic but true story? Or would you rather end our association? I've been pleased with the things you've learned, and I believe that you could be of real help in my work. It is possible that you may someday take a major role, but that cannot be decided yet. What say you? Stay and learn, or go? I promise you that I bear you no ill-will and will think none the less of you if you choose to lead a life more typical, more normal for a young man in this time of the world. But I do promise some very interesting times if you choose to stay.

"What I cannot promise is real safety," he added, "but like most people of your age and temperament, you have not felt the chill of your own mortality to any real extent. Thus words offering safety or safe-haven have little attraction to you. Yet I say that you should consider the possibility of danger to yourself and to those with whom you have contact.

"What say you then, 'go' or 'stay?'"

Eddie took a deep breath and let it out with a long sigh. "Well, Joe, you said that it would be – what was it? – *unwise* to leave. What's that mean?"

"Oh, you'll need to stick around for a little while. Not too long. And I'd have to contact a few associates, call in a few favors. We'd spend a few weeks setting up a new identity for you and then get you settled somewhere else. I've done it before. There's no magic in it, just work. In, say, four to six weeks you'd have a new identity, a new place to stay in another part of the country, and a new line of work.

"Is that what you want?" the old man finished. His eyebrows went up a little at the question, but he waited patiently for a response.

"Well, uh, I... I guess I'd like to hear more. I gotta tell you, Joe. On the very first night I wondered why you needed me. Like, I was glad and all, but I couldn't see what was in it for you. So, in the back of my head, I've been wondering all along what was really goin' on.

"So, anyway," Eddie continued, "are you gonna explain what happened today? In words that make sense? Like I said, it's not a surprise that there's more going on here than learning about plants and cooking and woodcraft and home-repairs, but I never dreamed..."

Joe laughed a quick snort through his nose, "Indeed there is more going on. If you'll promise to hear me out, I can tell you a story. It will be true, but it will also be strange. And the telling of it will leave you marked. Not as marked as some, but marked nonetheless. You'll not be overly satisfied with selling shoes or studying history or driving for hire afterwards. Not that there's anything wrong with any of those jobs or a hundred others like them, but once you've heard this story it will call you.

Michael C. Glaviano

And if you act on my words and take your part in it, why then to the end of your days you'll be part of the work, the story; and not much else will do.

"So think long and hard before you answer," Joe finished. "...before you tell me whether you will go or you will stay."

Now this was a fairly long speech, one of the longest Eddie had ever heard Joe make. Further, the young man couldn't recall ever seeing the old man so serious. He resolved to try. Whatever he was going to hear, it promised to be interesting, perhaps exciting, but surely, the old man spoke in metaphors. Surely.

Six

The old man was mostly pleased. He had not wanted to test the kid so soon, but the Locust Queen had made a move, and he'd been forced to respond. Clearly, his adversaries were aware, or at least suspected, that he had roused himself from his passive brooding. Why trouble him otherwise? In any case, the youngster had shown resilience. He'd been shocked of course, and he'd reacted in a manner consistent with his age and experience. Even so, the kid had recovered quickly enough. He was curious, open to hearing more.

Still, they were likely to test the barriers around this place once again. While he was confident that he could repel them, he was also sure that he needed to get Eddie – he sometimes thought of the kid by name now – out of harm's way... or at least off the front lines. The kid needed a little time to learn and grow and become more able to survive.

And Joe had to go out to the boundaries again. Most of the portals to the Place had fallen into disuse, had been forgotten and lost. Many more should be open and permeable if this world were to survive, let alone recover. It was a constant back-and-forth, this battle for the flowering or desiccation and evanescence of the worlds.

Someday, perhaps, the kid could become an independent actor, but not now. He had too much to learn. Was too vulnerable.

Joe thought back across the years. He recalled the names and faces of some of those who had helped him. Over the long years, many good people had lent their strength and sometimes their lives to the struggle for this world, for other worlds. There were so many faces, and the burden of those lost lives was a weight around the ancient warrior's own soul. And the memory of the woman he'd loved but could not hold was a weight with barbed hooks in his heart.

It was hard to ask another to step up. It was hard to say the words that would surely entrap, would surely ensnare the young, idealistic heart. At the same time, Joe knew he had to do this; the life and death of worlds hung in the balance. Countless battles and threats without measure lay ahead. Still, it was so much to ask. And however much they gave, in the end, Joe would have to ask others to take up the battle. It went on and on.

He stirred himself and once again prepared to tell the story.

Seven

The light had now grown dim in the living room. Despite the season, a chill had crept into the air. Settling back into the deep recesses of the comfortable, overstuffed chair in which he rested, Eddie pulled his feet from his shoes and tucked his legs beneath him. Once again, as on his first night beneath its roof, the house emanated that feeling of being on-guard. It watched out into the evening as something prowled nearby, something menacing, something of which the strange, frightening woman, Alicia was a part.

Joe got up from his chair and moved softly around the room. At a glance, candles that rested in sconces on either side of the fireplace flamed to life. At a gesture, a fire leapt into being. Flames crackled and danced along the logs. A small circle of warmth and golden light formed to push back the larger darkness.

As the old man called fire into being before his eyes, Eddie sat up straighter but then forced himself to sit back and observe. He looked around the room. The heavy plaster on the walls, the clear pine floors aged to a deep amber, the worn Persian carpet upon which the chairs rested, the casual display of abilities that were the stuff of stories, these all combined to promise something unprecedented.

Joe returned to his chair and settled in. Eventually, he tossed back a slug of his drink, cleared his throat softly, and began speaking. His voice was quiet but clear in the dim light. His tone was no longer one of conversation. He spoke as if reciting, almost chanting some traditional history that had been passed down through generations of faithful custodians.

"Tears of laughter, tears of joy, tears of compassion and sorrow and rage all rain down upon the misty place between the worlds. The ground in this place is mostly boggy, mostly wet and shrouded in mist. A diffuse light washes out shadows and makes distances hard to judge. Tiny rivulets feed streams that meander in a hopelessly complicated maze of interconnected waterways. It is quiet there, with muted sounds and far-off cries.

"The place between the worlds is a most useful and perilous place, for it is drenched by the tears of the gods. And because it is so watered, it is infinite. Why infinite? How could it be otherwise? If it were not infinite, the tears of the gods would surely wash it away. It is the Great Hub of the Cosmos, and all the myriad worlds spin and dance around the Hub as on an immense wheel. All the infinity of living worlds touch it – all the worlds that may be found within the dreams of the gods."

Joe fell silent. He stared into the middle distance and provided Eddie with an opportunity for questions.

"So... this Great Wheel? Where is it?"

"Where? Why, it is elsewhere, everywhere. It is one of the realms."

"One of? There's more than one?"

"An infinity of infinities, young man. Beneath, around, above, whatever... let us say 'near' the Great Hub lie other planes. There are the realms of bliss that fan out in an ever-changing array of light. At the base – another useless term – lie the hell realms and the realms of chaos where the elder gods still cavort, still feed, still struggle in their fevered madness. And beneath all that... the Abyss, the Void. Whatever you want to call it. Without end, without light or hope or life, the Abyss... extends... outward."

"Damn. That's real? I mean... it's not, like, a story or something? That's a lot to take in, man. A lot to accept. It's... I dunno. Overwhelming?"

"Oh, it's real enough. And indeed it is overwhelming, Eddie. Indeed it is. You don't need to believe it all now. For now, just learn, help as you're able. I'll never ask you to do anything evil. I can promise you that."

"So what side is Alicia on?"

"Her own, ultimately. For now, she and those she serves – I call them 'the Locusts' for the destruction they leave in their wake – try to seal off this world. By severing the connections with the Great Hub, they cause magic to fail. Imagination will die. Art will whither. The people will soon forget their own dreams."

"So they want to... to kill off magic in this world?"

"They're far along in their project, but yes, basically."

"Sorry, man. I'm pretty fuzzy on this. So what does killing off magic do for them?"

"At the start, the locusts skim wealth and power. They are clever and ruthless. With magic gone from the world, the people become easy to manipulate. People no longer question their place in the world, nor do they desire romance or mystery.

"Scurrying to and fro' to accomplish their allotted tasks, the people become little more than angry, fearful ants," Joe added. "Wealth and power move up a steep pyramid. And at the apex of that pyramid, largely invisible to the multitudes working to support it, dwell a very few, extremely powerful beings."

"Bummer. So they end up owning everything, huh?"

"Yes. Everything that they consider to be of value at any rate. But once a world is cut off from the Great Hub it begins to shrivel and die, and as that world begins to dry up, to fail, the locusts make their way to another and begin again.

"And at the very end, the Queen herself feeds upon the stuff of the failing world. She gorges on the life force of the multitudes. What is left is barren, dead."

Joe paused and stared silently ahead for so long, that Eddie thought he was done, but then the old man spoke once more, and his voice sounded tired. "A few of them are very old... and very strong. The Locust Queen is the strongest of all. Yes. She is literally able to consume the stuff of weakened worlds. She draws upon, drinks the life from them and weaves it into the twisted matrix of power that she has become."

Joe fell silent again. This time he was obviously done with his narrative, but Eddie wanted the conversation to keep going. "But what do you do?" he asked. "How do you fight them?"

With a discernible effort, Joe pulled himself from his reverie. "Soon I will need to make one of my trips. Quietly, unobtrusively, I intend to reopen an ancient portal. I had hoped to go and return before any of the Queen's servants became aware of it. Now, that may not be possible.

"This portal dates from prehistory and is found on an island in the Caribbean. If I am successful, a few people from the region will notice a slight return of the old magic. The effects will be local but real nonetheless. Eventually, we may remake the portal completely so that those who know the way could use it to move to and from the Great Hub. For now, however, merely restoring the connection will suffice to bring a little more magic back into the world. Art will be created. Perhaps music will return, music that will help soothe and heal some of the damage that's been done of late."

"So do I go with you to help?"

"Ahhh. I take it by your question that you've decided to stay."

"Totally. I mean, yeah. Of course. How could I do anything else? This sounds totally cool, awesome even."

"'Awesome' it is, indeed. But there is more danger than I could describe to you in a month of little chats such as this. To answer your question, however, no. You won't go with me on this trip. Hopefully, some day you will. For now, you will stay behind and guard my home. You will make sure that it is safe upon my return. Now that they know of your existence, they will likely try to use you to gain entrance. This will occupy at least a handful of them and thus enhance my chances of success."

"So I'll just stay here? I want to do something more."

"You will. At least that is my hope. But you must learn a great deal before you can assume a more active role. Recall, please, what happened today. We must spend the next few weeks teaching you how to avoid being deceived. I will not have you sacrifice yourself needlessly. Mark my words. Now that they know you are here and that you are vulnerable to that woman, their forces will be divided. Some will try to track me and impede my plans. Others will try to gain admission here."

"What's so great about getting into your house? I mean it's a cool place and all, but it's just a house. What would they do, leave a trap of some kind?"

Joe chuckled, "Indeed. It is a 'cool' place. Actually, it's far more than 'just a house.' It stands over another ancient portal. Beneath this house lies a fully-functioning portal that gives access to the Place – the Great Hub. If you are strong enough, if you know enough, magic works here. Real magic.

"I moved here some years ago and had the house built in just the right spot and in just such a manner to allow me to protect and strengthen this portal. In the past, I've used elaborate trickery to make them unsure of whether I was in residence or not," he continued. "This, plus certain protections I've installed over the years, has deterred them, but they grow bolder. With the general failure of magic in this world, with its slow slide toward dissolution, the Locust Queen grows impatient and hungry.

"I have invested a great deal of my time and energies in this house. If they could gain unhampered access, they could undo much of what I have accomplished. This would leave me greatly weakened. In a sense, I am now more vulnerable than in the past. If I leave my home un-attended by human watchers, there is no one to trick, no one to make an error in judgment that could render me less protected than I might other-wise be."

"Then why not take me with you?"

"Frankly, because you would be more of a liability than an asset at this point."

This stung, and Eddie started to react. But then he thought better of it and bit his tongue. Joe was, of course, correct in his reasoning. The young man was disappointed, but he could see that his host was right. Another thought occurred to him, however.

"Uhh, Joe...you said you had this house *built*? This place is old, man. How long ago was that?"

Joe just glanced at the young man with a faraway look in his eyes. That remote look shriveled up trivial questions. He shook his head ever so slightly and whispered, "a long time, son. A long time."

After a few minutes of silence, Eddie tried to pick up the thread of conversation again.

"So if I'm a liability in your company and a vulnerability if left behind, then why have you given me a job helping you? You'd be better off by yourself." Eddie tried, with partial success, to keep the testiness from his voice. The older man's mild answer surprised, but did not reassure him.

"You are correct. In some ways I would be better off. Yet alone I can only do so much. Those of us who do this work must recruit assistants who can eventually expand our efforts on this and other worlds. A few months back I roused myself to action. I decided to start looking for a helper... one with the potential to become a protégé and, if we're both skillful and lucky, eventually a partner in the enterprise. If you prove able, you will add your strengths to our efforts. We might, perhaps, find another portal for you to protect and nurture."

"Like maybe on that island in the Caribbean? That might not be too bad."

Joe's eyes crinkled at the corners and his mouth quirked up a bit, "Well, perhaps, but we'd probably do better to find you a place where you'd fit in and not be noticed too much. That could be somewhere on this world. Could be on another. We can't say yet.

"And it may be that your natural aptitudes would indicate a different role. Something less tied to place. I cannot say. We will see how things unfold."

Eddie started to comment, but Joe was not finished. He held up his hand and Eddie kept silent. The old man took a final sip of his drink and cleared his throat one more time before continuing.

"At any rate, some time ago, when I first learned that the island gate might be restored, I made several trips. I needed to observe its immediate surroundings and determine what shape the portal itself was in. Eventually, I recruited someone whose family has lived in the region for generations. This made it plausible, unremarkable when she suddenly inherited a small estate from a 'distant cousin.'

"Now, this woman is not particularly young. She will be occupied in the coming years with finding someone to carry on, someone to help her. Again, that should be someone from the area. Someone who will blend in. In the meantime, I must correspond with her, visit occasionally, and help her learn. My upcoming trip will mark a turning point for her, perhaps a small turning point for this world as well. If all goes well, she will become the guardian of that portal. As such, she will be invaluable, but she will be tied to that place. She will not take a role as a wide-ranging force in this world."

"Okay, so I don't get to move to the Caribbean, but it was worth a try, right? Anyway, like it or not, it looks like I'm returning to my life as a student. I suppose all the stuff about plants and tools and so on has been some kind of prep work?"

"In part, yes. This has also helped me to learn what sort of a person you are. You have an affinity for living, growing things. You don't mind hard work, and, despite the vast differences between our ages and backgrounds, I believe that we can work together. You are even learning to control your temper a little. These are reasonably important qualities. If we can get you some basic skills, run through some scenarios, make some progress in shoring up this house's protections, I'll perhaps be able to make my trip to the Caribbean before hurricane season. I'd just as soon do that, believe me."

"So when would that be. How long do we have?"

"Let's see how much we can get done in the next couple of weeks."

Joe stood up and stretched. Eddie realized that the old man looked tired and felt a pang that he'd not even considered what the encounter with Alicia had cost him. The young man tried to make some sort of apology, which was waved off.

"Thank you. You didn't know. Now you do. And truthfully, it is the long distance preparations that I have been performing these past several months that have taken their toll. That woman we encountered today contributed little to my fatigue.

"Still, I am tired. Fortunately, it is in my nature to recover quickly. I will set some protections so that I can really and truly rest tonight. It would be simpler for me if you were to remain in your rooms until morning."

That night as he lay in bed in his quiet garret rooms, Eddie resolved to himself that he'd do everything possible to move from the liability column to the asset column in Joe's accounting of his skills. He'd already seen and experienced first hand the stuff of the imagination, and he was certain that he wanted more of it. While Eddie was sobered by Joe's description of the fabric of reality, he was also enticed by the mystery and beauty to which the old man had alluded. Although he thought that he'd be much too wired up to sleep, Eddie drifted off while mulling over the events of the day.

* * *

So now the young man entered a new phase of his life in the Painter Avenue house. Where Joe had been his landlord, boss, and sometimes teacher before, now the old man became a mentor in earnest. A real sense of urgency underlay each day. Never before in his life had Eddie experienced such stress. It was like some kind of never-ending, life-and-death finals week. The "next couple of weeks" estimate that Joe had made on that fateful night extended itself by a factor of three, but the changes this period wrought in the young man were remarkable.

Now that the pretense of being a simple caretaker or mainten- ance assistant could be dropped, Eddie's days quickly took on a routine of intense study and exercise. Each day he arose at dawn. At Joe's request, breakfast was taken in silence. After breakfast, there would usually be a pile of readings for Eddie to pore over until ten o'clock at which time he'd meet Joe in the back yard for some serious calisthenics. These physical workouts lasted an hour and a half. Then the young man would wash up just a little and practice various, prescribed meditative techniques until some time after noon. There would be an extremely light lunch – just enough to take the edge off the hunger really – and then Joe would set studies that lasted through most of the afternoon.

There was always another workout late in the day. This one in- volved strength-building exercises. Although he'd fancied that his spring and early summer work with Joe had improved his physical condition, this was a whole new level of activity. Eddie hurt a lot, nearly every- where. Joe was always there to offer encouragement and to keep his stu- dent moving forward.

It was hard work, true, but it was all interesting and eclectic. Boredom was never a factor – even with the exercise program. Joe had little charts made up, and it was amazing to see the progress as Eddie fol- lowed the strange program outlined by his mentor. After the second daily workout, he showered while Joe made dinner. After dinner, Eddie cleaned up the kitchen and the two men would spend an hour or two re- viewing the day's work. Then the young man would limp up to his rooms and, for all intents and purposes, collapse.

A portion of Eddie's studies touched on philosophy and psycho- logy. He encountered Jungian psychology, with a special focus on the concepts of archetypes and historical images. He studied several branches of magic from weird old texts that obviously assumed that ma- gic was real and worked. Some of the language was all but impossible to decipher, but Joe was invariably nearby to answer questions and discuss concepts that presented insurmountable problems. As with any excellent guide, the old man pointed out the path ahead of his student and waited at the start of each difficult climb to make sure that Eddie got a good foothold.

Eddie's studies of plants, native and exotic, continued until he could identify and recite the preparation and use of a handful of species including dandelion, daylily, foxtail grass, nettle, plantain, and wild rose. He actually learned to make a fire using flint and steel. He learned to throw a knife (and hit what he intended to hit, sometimes). He medit- ated. He learned to focus his attention and keep the mantra going while Joe ran a wood chipper 6 feet away or rototilled part of the garden. He read the first three of Castenada's *Don Juan* books, and they talked a lot about "seeing." Joe was really big on seeing. He said that if Eddie learned how to see what was in front of him, Alicia and her crew would have a much harder time deceiving him.

Eddie studied first aid, cardiopulmonary resuscitation, and hypnosis. It went on and on. The young man was nearly always tired, often frustrated, but somehow each tidbit of knowledge wove its way into a larger fabric, and this helped motivate him.

And then there were the weekly exams. Each Saturday afternoon, Joe grilled his student mercilessly for hours on end. Without warning, he'd go back and review material they'd covered in previous lessons. It was a true mentor-student relationship, but with a highly varied and bizarre curriculum.

The notion of mastery became familiar. Joe made it clear that he expected Eddie, over time, to master a significant body of knowledge. An intense, six week program, no matter how well done, will not produce mastery, but it can certainly introduce a wealth of things to study. After the first couple of weeks, the young man could feel his body and mind responding to the work. While not a master of any discipline, Eddie became stronger, more flexible, more alert, and most of all, more able to learn.

Early on, Joe had Eddie fill out some forms. Apparently, Joe had contacts in the university system of the young man's native California. Essays were submitted for review. Telephone interviews were conducted. Eventually, somehow, his mentor convinced the administrators that what his student was doing was worth another semester's worth of college credits.

Although this wasn't what he'd intended or even thought of, Eddie was pleased as well as a little surprised when he received his updated transcript some six weeks after he'd started this "program." When Eddie questioned Joe, the old man said, in typical fashion, that a degree might come in handy later. It hurt nothing and could possibly help at some point to accumulate the units.

Finally, at breakfast one morning, Joe broke their habitual silence to state that he couldn't put off his trip much longer. He intended to leave within three weeks. Eddie put down his fork and was silent for a moment more.

"But I don't know anything yet. What am I supposed to do while you're gone?"

With a touch of amusement in his eye, Joe stood up. "Stay there," he ordered and walked out of the kitchen. He returned almost immediately and stopped in the doorway to the living room. Still smiling, he locked eyes with Eddie and said, "Here, catch," as he threw a small paperweight in his direction. Almost without thinking, the young man stood and held his teacher's gaze while he tracked the trajectory of the paperweight in his peripheral vision. Eddie snatched the object from the air as it sailed past.

"Think you could have done that a month and a half ago?"

"Well, probably not." He paused for a minute and thought. When Eddie continued, he was speaking as much to himself as to Joe.

"It's true that I'm in better shape, and I'm beginning to focus my attention better, but there's got to be lots more that I'll need to know than how to catch a paperweight."

"Indeed there is. It won't stop; there will always be more to learn, but you are now in a position to act as a caretaker for me. You are more alert than you were. You are stronger, much more focused, and you are blessed with the reflexes and resilience of youth. You have a basic understanding of the principles of magic – as it used to work in this world in the old times, and as it can be forced to work for brief intervals even yet. I will provide detailed instructions and set powerful wards on the environs. My trip should not last longer than two weeks, three at the outside. We will lay in supplies for you so that you can play the recluse for that period. I'll let a few people know that you'll be house sitting for me so they won't get worried when I don't show my face around."

By this point in his studies, Eddie had a rough grasp of the forces arrayed against them. He was overwhelmed and a little frightened and no longer minded admitting it, but he also had a lot of faith in his teacher. If Joe said that he'd be okay, then he figured that he had a chance. The young man smiled a half smile and nodded in acquiescence.

If the previous weeks had been busy, most of the time remaining before Joe's departure was pure madness. They continued to cover herbcraft and lore, wilderness survival skills, and physical conditioning, but now European history, and ancient Greek history were added to the mix. The pace was amazing; yet with a week remaining before his mentor's departure, it finally dawned on Eddie that the old man was keeping pace with him and more!

Joe always mastered in advance the studies he set the young man to learn. He had always prepared the lessons, was consistently able to answer questions without hesitation. At the same time, he took over most of Eddie's usual chores and did nearly all of the food preparation. He often led the young man in his workouts, and Eddie was amazed over and over at the old man's strength and stamina.

The magic studies were especially problematic, as Joe admitted readily enough that magic barely worked at all in this world. Because of the functioning portal in the basement of the Painter Avenue house, Joe could demonstrate some spells indoors. Since he assumed that they would be under observation, he was reluctant to do anything outside.

He showed Eddie, or tried to show him, several, simple spells. These were mostly centered on woodcraft – how to see where game hid, how to call game to a snare that you'd set, how to find water or call up a breeze. Eddie practiced these and others until he could recite the words and make the hand motions ("passes," Joe called them) that went along with each. Joe insisted that he get them right, even though the most he ever was able to get out of any of them was a slight tingling in the arms and fingers that could just as well been attributed to excessive muscle tension.

Apart from all the theoretical exercises in magic, there was one spell that Joe insisted Eddie learn. He said that if Eddie had only one, this should be it, and he drilled his student mercilessly until the young man got it. Joe claimed that it was one of the few that would work in nearly any world, no matter how isolated or damaged. This was a basic spell of seeing. He claimed that with it, Eddie could see if someone bore him ill will or good. Joe claimed that the spell could also be used to tell whether someone had recently traveled between worlds.

If Eddie performed the spell properly, Joe promised that he would be able to see a bloody red halo or aura surrounding anyone who intended to harm him. If someone had a clear, white light surrounding him, it meant that he was basically positive in his regard towards the person casting the spell. If the nimbus surrounding a person was brilliant violet, it meant that he or she had recently traveled between worlds.

After a solid afternoon of working and practicing, Eddie had a blazing headache. Even so, he was excited to see a clear light surrounding Joe when he called out the words in the darkened living room. His teacher promised that this would become more pronounced as the young man practiced, and that Eddie should practice it almost continually, until it was nearly habitual. Once the spell was mastered, the words to invoke it could be spoken sotto voce, and Joe suggested that this was the eventual goal of the practice.

Then with mere days until he had to leave, Joe abruptly called a halt to the routine. They discussed various strategies that Eddie would follow if someone tried to gain entrance to the house in the days ahead. They did a final shopping excursion. Finally, asking that he not be disturbed unless "wolves were truly at the door," Joe handed Eddie a list of tasks to complete and then retired to his rooms.

Eddie's tasks mostly involved getting himself organized for the time ahead. Of course Joe also expected that the young man would continue his studies and had set assignments. Working quickly, Eddie was able to complete his list of preparatory work. Then, as per the instructions, he spent most of the remaining time sitting in meditation.

On the evening of his departure, Joe emerged from his rooms. He looked refreshed and relaxed. The craggy map of his face had smoothed, and he looked to be perhaps in his early to mid 50's. His hair had darkened and he wore a neatly trimmed mustache. He had substituted a sports shirt and slacks for his usual work clothes and presented very much the image of a trim, middle-aged businessman on vacation in (for example) the Bahamas. The change in his teacher unsettled the young man.

They had a light, vegetarian supper that Eddie prepared according to the instructions Joe had provided. There was little conversation, and this dealt with mostly mundane topics such as what was happening with the garden and which books Eddie had most enjoyed reading recently – just surface talk.

Just before 7:30 PM, the front door bell rang. Startled, Eddie began to get up. Joe put out a restraining hand, "That'll be my cab. You can walk me to the front door. No words now. Here, read this once I've left." He held out a folded piece of paper, and the young man slipped it into his shirt pocket.

They walked to the front door. Two battered but rugged suitcases waited. They reminded Eddie of their owner, and he guessed that Joe must have brought them down from his rooms before dinner.

Joe opened the front door and handed one suitcase to the waiting cab driver. He picked up the remaining case in his left hand and offered Eddie his right. "Take care of my house... and yourself. I'll see you soon." A brisk handshake, then he was at the cab and gone.

As he looked after the departing vehicle, Eddie was suddenly aware of the silent house at his back and an unseasonably cold wind from the street. The house was again alert, watching. And it felt as though something *out there* looked back as well. With an involuntary shiver, he closed and locked the door. As the bolt slid into place, the snick of the heavy, old lock added a finality to his mentor's departure.

Eddie returned to the back of the house. It was not until after he'd finished cleaning the kitchen, that he remembered Joe's note. Unfolding it, he sat at the kitchen table and pored over his final instructions.

You've done well, lad. At this point, you should be fine as long as you don't allow yourself to be rattled. Tend the garden each day, but alternate among the various paths there and back. Walk the property boundary each day around noon. They are weakest when the sun is at its peak. Look for any change in the wall around the property. Use a small broom to sweep off anything you see sprinkled on the top of the wall. Sweep it away from the property.

47

Do this even for trivial things such as leaves or twigs. Hose down the broom each time you use it.

Avoid letting anyone in the house - especially anyone you don't know well. Continue your studies, and I'll see you in two or three weeks.

If for some reason things get seriously out of hand, try to get out. Don't be a hero. Leave a message with Sergeant Driscoll saying that you've got a sick grandmother in California and get on a bus. Go to Omaha and get a room at the DeAnza Hotel under your mother's maiden name.

-J

P.S. Head for the basement if things get really bad. Try to leave a glass turned upside down on the top of the refrigerator as a signal to me. Bar the door from the inside of the basement. The bottom three steps of the basement stairs fold up. Follow the tunnel. Take a pack with supplies and light camping gear. Bring your knife and a compass. Don't forget a water bottle. If you make it through, head for higher ground. <u>Do not tarry in the Place Between!</u> As you walk, hold the thought: "Head for higher ground." Repeat it over and over until you *emerge. Afterwards, try to reach the Inn at Three Corners. I'll meet you there when I can.*

Eddie barely slept at all that night. Every time he dozed off, he heard (or thought he heard) a bump or a scrape, and his heart would pound and he would be sure that someone was breaking in. Finally around dawn, he got up, went downstairs and made himself something to eat. Eddie went from room-to-room, drew the curtains back slightly, and peeked from all the windows. As one might expect, the neighborhood was quiet. By the time he'd finished cleaning up the breakfast things, the sun was fully up, so he went out into the backyard.

There was a heavy feeling to the air and a lot of dark clouds were forming in the east. It looked as though a thunderstorm might develop later in the day, so Eddie decided to walk the property line first thing. He picked up a broom from the garden shed and headed to the west side of the yard. Approximately 2/3 of the way along the east wall, some leaves had fallen. As per Joe's instructions, he swept them over the wall and continued on his way. He noticed nothing else – certainly nothing suspicious – and started to feel a bit better. Still, he remembered to hose off the broom and put it back in the shed.

With the chance of some heavy weather in the afternoon, Eddie decided that it would be a good idea to tend the garden first thing. The garden was substantial and, at this point in the summer, was developing rapidly. Weeding, watering, pest management, and generally checking things out took about half an hour's worth of work each day.

Before solstice, they'd been harvesting radishes and salad greens. From then on, the garden had supplied all of their fresh herbs and vegetables and, Joe claimed, would continue to do so through late October. Onions, garlic, and potatoes would keep in the basement well into January. Joe dried about three-quarters of the herbs and used them throughout the year.

Eddie decided to water a little less than usual in case the rain really happened and he did that first. Then he weeded the parts of the garden that needed it most. The exercise and fresh air, even with the oppressive feeling of an impending storm, made him feel better. By the time the garden was tidy the clouds had gotten heavier. The young man returned indoors.

The phone was ringing when he walked in the kitchen door. Whoever it was hung up as soon as he answered. So much for feeling better. Eddie thought that maybe getting more vigorous exercise than garden maintenance had provided might calm him down, so the young man launched into his conditioning routine with a real vengeance. By

Michael C. Glaviano

the time he'd finished, he was hungry again, so he made a grilled cheese and mortadella sandwich. Then he walked the perimeter of the property again, but nothing had changed since his early morning circuit. He returned to the house, got cleaned up and tried to study for a while.

Even though he was interested in the material (survival camping, wild edibles) it was hard to focus. He kept putting down the book and pacing the room. After an hour or so of non-progress, Eddie closed his books, went outside, and began practicing his knife throwing. He'd leaned a quarter sheet of scrap plywood against the wall behind his target so that he wouldn't break the blade against the wall when he missed. After weeks of practice, he was finally getting better at sticking the blade into the target.

When he first started throwing the knife he couldn't hit anything, but over the weeks, he'd gradually improved. Now he could stand nearly 20 feet from the target and have his knife hit where he wanted at least half the time. Eddie wasn't sure if it was useful, but it was at least calming.

The phone rang several more times in the afternoon. Each time was the same. He'd pick up, there would be a pause, and then a click as the caller disconnected. The tension level ratcheted up with each call. Eddie must have peeked out the windows at least 20 times that first day. He tried to do his breathing practice, and maybe it helped calm him slightly, but he couldn't tell for sure.

It was almost a relief when, sometime in the mid afternoon, he heard the first rumble of thunder. By then the sky was completely overcast. He ran upstairs and looked out his windows. The lightning strokes were still off to the east, but he could tell they were coming closer. The intervals between the flashes and the thunder got shorter, the booms of the thunder louder. Then the rain started. Within a quarter hour, it was pelting down. It rained hard for most of an hour. As the peak of the storm passed, the lightning and thunder came every five seconds or so. It was a great, mid-western downpour! Gradually, the rain began to taper off.

For some reason the storm functioned to isolate Eddie from the external world. It made him more aware of the shelter the house provided. After all, Joe had told him repeatedly that he stood a good chance of being okay if he stayed on the property. And what could the hang-up calls really do apart from rattle him as much as he'd allow them to? Eddie resolved to be less wimpy about the situation. When the rain stopped, he walked the property boundary again and found nothing atop the wall but a few puddles standing in the old concrete.

The phone rang again. This time he picked it up and answered, with a bit of sarcasm in his voice, "Still here." Of course this time it was Sergeant Driscoll.

"Driscoll here. So that's kind of a strange greeting, kid."

"Oh, Sergeant. Sorry. I've had maybe a dozen prank calls today."

"Really? I guess people don't have much else to do. Pathetic. Hey. Did Joe get off okay?"

"Yeah. A cab picked him up late yesterday. Why?"

"Nothin'. Just checking. He mentioned he was going out of town, so I thought I'd check. You must be getting along okay if he feels like leaving you there to take care of the place. So don't screw up, right?"

"Uh, sure, Sergeant. I've got a routine, and I'm doing my best to follow it."

"Well that sounds real good. You just do like Joe says and things should be fine. Gotta run now. Keep your nose clean, kid. Hear me?"

"Yeah. I will."

She hung up. Eddie felt a mixture of gratitude and resentment: gratitude that she felt like checking up on him, resentment that she felt the need to. After thinking about it, he decided that Joe had probably asked her to check. It certainly didn't hurt. He hated to admit it, but he was actually more than a little grateful for the brief contact with a familiar voice, even Sergeant Driscoll's.

By then the afternoon was well on towards evening. Eddie wasn't hungry yet, so he picked up some books and sat beneath the windows in the living room and started reading. After a while he dozed off and was startled when the book fell in his lap. The room had gotten dark during his impromptu nap. The moon was in its last quarter and cast a weak, flickering light as clouds rushed past. The sky continued to clear. He flicked on the light, stood up and stretched. Now he was getting hungry, so after one more circuit of the windows, Eddie decided to get going on his regular evening activities.

Later that evening, he began to feel the effects of his previous, poor night's sleep. Pretty soon he was yawning. Remembering the hang-up calls that had punctuated his day, Eddie unplugged the phone and went upstairs.

The house began to exhibit that watchful feeling again. Now that he was used to it, Eddie found it more comforting than strange. He left the lights off upstairs and went from window to window to look around. The clouds had gone and the sky was completely clear. The crescent moon shone on quiet streets and yards. Even from his higher vantage point, everything looked as it should. No real difference from the ground floor view.

He tried to read for a while, but again he fell asleep. This time, Eddie was seriously out. He barely moved all night and didn't wake until the sun was streaming in the east windows of his room.

After the first day, Eddie's role as a house-sitter settled into a regular flow. He stuck to his activities as best he could; although it was definitely harder doing all the chores alone. He left a note for himself as a reminder, and first thing in the morning, he plugged in the phone. Last thing before turning in, he unplugged it. That way the prank calls couldn't keep him from resting.

Joe kept a small pack on a hook by the back door. Following his mentor's precautionary suggestion, Eddie threw a few things into the knapsack and left it in the front hall. Having basic stuff at hand, either for a bolt out the front door or a more serious one down the basement stairs, seemed like a good idea, and it made him feel slightly better.

But then he considered his preparations. "Throwing a few things" in a pack wasn't at all how Joe would prepare. That was more like the Eddie who'd blown into town in a Drive Away Buick last May. That was more like the hotshot kid.

Joe's note had said to pack supplies and light camping gear. The implication was that Eddie might be spending some time outdoors. From Joe's instructions, it was unlikely that the young man would face the possibility of a trek through the Himalayas, but it didn't sound like an afternoon at the Santa Barbara Hilton was in the offing either. Eddie dumped everything out and took stock of what he'd packed. He looked at the scattered items, clicked his tongue at the careless assortment, and re-solved to start over, to do it right.

The extra, long-sleeved shirt was fine, so were a couple of changes of socks and underwear, but what if it got cold? Eddie dashed upstairs and got a set of long underwear.

Next he went down to the basement to where Joe kept the camp-ing gear. Just as Joe had said in his note, there was a heavy bar just in-side the door to the basement. It fit into some metal brackets that were bolted into the frame and screwed into the door. The bar looked plenty stout: if it were dropped in place the door wouldn't open out into the hall. Neither could it be forced inward. There were switches for the basement lights at both the top and at the bottom of the stairs.

The camping gear was on a free-standing shelf right near the foot of the basement stairs. Neatly coiled on the top shelf, he found several lengths of stout cord. There were some bungee cords there too. The second shelf held some good quality, waterproofed ground cloths. Even if the weather were mild, he'd want to have something underneath him. Eddie found a waterproof ground cloth that had heavy grommets all around the edges. It was a sturdy, eight foot by ten foot tarp that could double as a small tent if need be. Finally, he selected a slightly larger pack that was mounted on a rigid pack frame.

Eddie brought his finds up to the entry hall and set them next to his pack. Then he ran back upstairs. He rummaged in the hall linen closet until he found a light thermal blanket. Neither heavy nor bulky, it was made of a modern fabric that looked like it would retain heat.

He carried the blanket back down and then remembered seeing some hats in the coat closet near the front door. Yes. On the top shelf there was a collection of wide-brimmed hats. He found one that fit okay and which wasn't too badly worn. It might be good to have something to keep his head warm or to keep the sun off his face. Either way, a hat would be good if he were going to be outdoors for a couple of days.

He rolled some cord, the thermal blanket, and the ground cloth together in a tight bundle and hooked it onto the bottom of his pack frame with the bungees. Now he had a compact bedroll that could provide shelter if the need arose.

Next he went out to the pantry to see what he could find in the way of nonperishable food. There was one unopened pack of food bars and part of another. There were also some dried apricots and some jerky. This was all good, light food that could keep him going. It went into the pack.

Eddie set aside some of the nonessentials that he'd put in the pack first time around. A toilet kit made of up of toothbrush, toothpaste, a bar of soap, and a small towel were fine, but he didn't need anything more than that – certainly not the beach towel, wash cloth, metal mirror and shaving kit that he'd started with.

At the end of all this, he had a pack that wasn't too heavy or bulky. His compass was in one side pocket, his sheath knife in another. The knife could be transferred to his belt later. The water bottle was filled and resting on the floor next to the pack. The hat lay on top. He could wear his jacket or tie it to the pack. This felt right. This felt like what Joe probably had in mind.

His packing complete, Eddie decided to check out the sub-basement stairs Joe had mentioned in his note. The big basement was pretty typical of older, midwest homes. It was large, nearly equal to the footprint of the house. Besides the camping gear, there was lots of old stuff around. Tall, metal shelves and steel cabinets lined three of the exterior walls. There were big trunks and boxes. Most of them had labels with Joe's writing on them. There was also a separate, closed off area where Joe had his wine cellar. As basements go, it was okay, but still it was a little creepy, full of shadows and years. Of course Eddie was expecting creepy.

Eddie knelt on the unfinished planks of the basement floor and looked at the stairs. It took some fumbling around, but after a bit, he figured out the trick to get the bottom six stairs to fold up. There was a counterweight, so once the latch was released it was easy to lift them.

Supporting the stairs, he ducked into the small space. Right away, he noticed a bare bulb light fixture mounted farther up the underside of the stairs, so after making sure that he could work the latch from the inside, he let the stairs drop behind him. It was dim, with just the tiniest glimmer of light filtering through the gaps between the stairs.

He reached up and felt around for the bulb and chain. The sudden glare brought the small space beneath the stairs into sharp relief. A passage, sort of half hallway-half tunnel led down and turned left into darkness. Eddie took a few steps down the tunnel, but he couldn't see much and didn't feel like exploring. To the left of the tunnel entrance stood a small, rough, wooden table that looked as though it'd been resting there for a couple of geologic ages. On the table, lay a bunch of candles, some stick matches, and a lantern-sort of a thing to put the candles in.

Satisfied that he could get to the tunnel and follow Joe's instructions if he needed to, Eddie returned upstairs. He thought that further preparations were in order, so he moved to the kitchen next. He got a glass out and left it on the counter next to the refrigerator. In his mind, he called it "his signal glass." Just in case, he told himself. Then he went outside and walked the perimeter again. Nothing was out of place; nothing lay atop the wall.

By then, he was starting to feeling slightly stupid. After all, apart from a few hang-up phone calls and a strange feeling outside, absolutely nothing out of the ordinary had happened. Still, he told himself that his preparations couldn't do any harm.

After that, every day or two, he'd get a real phone call. Most were from Sergeant Driscoll. Once or twice a librarian friend of Joe's called. Also, neighbors and friends, all known to the young man checked in occasionally. It made Eddie feel better to know that people would take a minute to call.

He began to settle in, to feel more secure and sure of himself. After all, almost a week had passed. It wouldn't be that much longer until Joe was scheduled to return. Nothing much had happened, certainly nothing that he hadn't been able to handle. Then he noticed the cars.

In addition to doing all the stuff that Joe had listed, Eddie had gotten into the habit of peering from all the windows at various times, day and night. He hadn't seen much of anything, just a car parked here and there on the street across from the house. These were mostly over near the road that led to the park where he'd had his encounter with Alicia. At first he thought that there was a random selection of parked cars, but gradually he began to notice a pattern. There were three different cars. One was a late model Ford; one was a white van, the other a nondescript gray sedan – some kind of old Chrysler.

Eddie realized that one of those three vehicles was always parked across the street, about halfway up the block. Of course he tried to shrug it off for a while, but by the end of the first week, he was pretty sure that the house was under a 24 hour watch. This made him redouble his efforts to be careful and to follow to the letter the routine Joe had laid out for him.

By now, the moon had become a tiny sliver. Soon it would be completely dark at night, and it would be hard to see much on the street beyond the light cast by the few street lamps that still worked. Still, nothing of real substance had happened, so he just tried to watch carefully. By the beginning of the second week, the calls started again in earnest. Eddie realized that "They" (whoever they were) were trying to rattle him. They were succeeding, and his realization of that fact helped him focus his attention.

He started seeing a lot more stuff on the walls around the property. Besides the usual bits of yard debris, occasionally he noticed some things that looked like bread crumbs sprinkled across the top of the wall. He carefully swept these away from the property and just as carefully rinsed the broom. Sometimes there were chalk marks too. These, he wiped off with a rag which he then rinsed carefully. Afterwards, he washed his hands in hot, soapy water.

Finally, when he woke up on the first morning of the dark of the moon, there were some markings on the top of the wall that didn't wipe off easily. They looked as though they were drawn in blood, and he felt his heart pound when he saw them. The once-substantial wall appeared old and decayed in the areas near the marks. He got a hose and squirted the water at the top of the wall. The water hit the markings, and they sizzled and gave off a nasty smell that made him gag. He kept squirting water on the area, and little-by-little the markings dissolved. When they were completely gone, he leaned over and washed down the outside edge of the wall. Later in the afternoon, when Eddie went back out to check, the wall looked strong again, as though the effects of the markings had worn off.

The pressure was building, but he was coping with it. Then the front doorbell rang, and heart in his throat, the young man went to answer it. No one was on the porch, but on the sidewalk across the street was the woman who'd called herself Alicia. She leaned on a cane as she stared intently at the house.

The woman was still beautiful, but now he could also see a haggard and hungry look about her. When she saw Eddie open the door, she met his eyes and smiled. The worn look melted away, tiredness left her face, and the cane became an umbrella that hung from her forearm. She appeared once again as attractive as she had on their first encounter. Now his heart was really pounding.

"Invite me over?" she called from her position across the street. Her voice was once again full of music and promise.

He swayed and leaned against the doorway while a wave of vertigo crashed over him. His will nearly crumbled. If she'd been closer, he probably would have given in. At the same time, he dimly realized that the warding that Joe had set around the house must be keeping her and her friends at bay. This helped Eddie regain his wits. He took a deep breath.

"No way, lady. Why don't you just go away and leave me alone?"

She was still smiling, but now her smile held more menace than beauty as she replied, "You'd do well to invite me in. With you or without

Michael C. Glaviano

you, we're going to break past the old man's barriers before he returns. If you help us, we'll let you go. Just leave the door open and invite me in before you leave."

"Like I said, Alicia, or whatever your name is. Get lost." This was pure "hotshot kid:" all bravado with nothing to back it up, and Eddie was sure she knew it. Even so, the gesture felt good.

Then he had a thought. He uttered the words of the seeing spell, and even across the street, he fancied that could see a red glow spring up around her. It was dimmed by the afternoon light and barely visible, but it was definitely there. This was the first time he'd actually used a spell as opposed to practice it. Despite his fear, he was grimly pleased to get results. That crimson glow helped harden his resolve.

Deliberately, slowly, Eddie closed the door. He fastened the stout old lock. Inside, with his back to the heavy door, he leaned against the wood and tried to get control of his heart. Things had changed, the tension had increased, events moved from the realm of possibility to reality. He recalled her assertion regarding Joe's barriers to their entry. Was she bluffing? The wall had definitely looked bad this morning, but then she looked more than a little worn herself.

For a while, he remained where he stood. Eventually, he shook himself loose from his uncertainty and went through the motions of his daily routine. Nothing happened for several hours, and he realized that with Joe's protections in place, the woman was probably hard-pressed to come any closer to the house. He pondered that for a while without anything much coming of it, then slowly an idea began to form. Surely they had tried Joe's defenses in the past and hadn't been able to break in.

Eddie realized that they were probably counting on panicking him enough so that he did something stupid such as trying to bargain with Alicia for his own safety. Given his response to her appearance and voice, he wasn't sure they were wrong about this. He wondered if it might help to do something to confuse things a little – to get some of the pressure off.

Could he make them think that he'd left? That he'd run for it? If so, then there'd be no reason for them to keep up the pressure. On the other hand, Joe had said that all he had to do was sit tight for two or three weeks and all would be well. He knew that were he to leave the property, he'd be unprotected. Still, he fretted about the phone calls, the cars, Alicia's brazenly aggressive attitude.

After giving it some thought, he decided to risk leaving the property for a short time. He would try to fake a run for it. His success would depend on how specific Joe's defenses were. If Alicia's real goal was to frighten him so much that he let her into the house, and if Joe's defenses were specific enough to recognize him, to let him back in once he'd left, then his plan might work. Eddie knew that those were some big "ifs" but it still felt better to be doing something besides waiting.

56

With an idea for action finally in mind, Eddie got calmer, got busy. The first thing was to check the barriers. He ran out the back and over to the west wall of the property. There was an alley behind the property, on the south side, and he guessed that Joe would have his strongest protection there. The neighbor on the west had a seldom-used, overgrown back yard, and Eddie was pretty sure that he'd be able to slip into that yard and then to the alley without being seen. Surely, that path would be less intensely protected than the alley itself. If it were bad, he'd just have to walk around the block and back in the front door. If he couldn't get in, well, he'd head for Omaha like Joe had said.

When he put his bare hands on top of the wall and pressed himself up, there was an unpleasant tingling, but he could tolerate it. He scrambled over and dropped down into the tall weeds and overgrown shrubbery of the neighbor's yard. Nobody was around, and it was quiet with the hot, heavy stillness of a midwestern summer afternoon.

Before trying for the alley, Eddie inched back to the wall and swung a leg over. The unpleasant feeling was stronger moving this way, but still not too bad. He dropped back into Joe's back yard and, bent low to the ground, crept to the wall at the alley. There was a different sort of feeling waiting for him at this, the southern boundary of the property. A feeling of dizziness and intense nausea assaulted him as he made his way over the back wall. Still, he could manage it.

So without hesitating, he retraced his steps. It seemed that the warding had been specifically set to allow him to pass. Once he was back within the confines of Joe's yard, he turned and again swept the top of the wall, just in case his scrambling had had some effects. So far so good. Returning to the house, he called a cab and made arrangements to get a ride to the bus station early in the evening.

The next few hours crawled along. Now that he had his plan set, Eddie wanted to get on with it, but of course he needed at least the cover of dusk to help him avoid discovery. He tried to spend the remaining hours following his routine, but eventually he went to his pack, got out his knife and returned to the back yard to throw the knife against the target. Repeatedly, he threw the blade, walked over and pulled it from the target (or, picked it up when he missed). He got into a steady, calm rhythm: throw, walk back, and throw again. Just before five o'clock, he went in, put his knife & sheath back in his pack, had a glass of water and checked the house again.

Finally, around five-thirty, he heard a car honk in front of the house. He looked out the curtained window and it was indeed the cab. Of course it was possible that his phone call had been intercepted and that this guy was not what he seemed. Again, Eddie tried the seeing spell. The guy didn't have much of a halo around him, good, bad, or indifferent. Eddie supposed that the driver was indeed nothing more or less than a tired cabby.

Grabbing his pack from near the basement door, Eddie locked the house and ran down to the waiting cab. As he reached for the door handle, Eddie glanced up the street. The white van was parked in its usual place. He was afraid to stare at the vehicle, and his brief glance didn't reveal whether or not anyone was sitting behind the wheel, but he assumed that he'd been observed. With a deep breath, he got into the back seat of the cab.

The cabbie wasn't particularly talkative, and of course that suited Eddie. The driver verified that the destination was the Greyhound station and, basically retracing the journey from a few months previous, they headed across town. Of course the young man hoped this ride ended more successfully than his last visit to the old town center. They reached the bus station without incident. Eddie paid the driver, got out, and went into the station.

It was desolate inside. People, many of them as worn and shabby as their surroundings, milled around as they waited for departing buses. Others sat listlessly, with no luggage or packs, as if the bus station were a safe haven, a place to rest before wandering elsewhere. Compared with the bus station, the police station where Sergeant Driscoll toiled was right out of Architectural Digest.

After waiting for about ten minutes, Eddie went back outside and looked for the cabstand. He found the waiting area, but there were no cabs. Of course a lot more people left than returned to this town, and it made sense that the local cab company wouldn't have a bunch of cabs waiting around at the bus station. Eddie went over and asked the guy lounging at the stand if he could get him a cab into town. The man nodded and picked up his phone to call the dispatcher.

Eddie felt exposed, but he didn't want to miss his cab. There wasn't anything he could do but pace back and forth. After 30 minutes of torment, a taxi finally showed up. Luckily, it wasn't the same driver who'd brought him. Just to be safe, Eddie checked again – another neutral nimbus.

The young man glanced at the clock above the cabstand. It was around quarter to seven. He got into the cab. Evidently, all the good cabs were reserved for outbound patrons. This one was seriously filthy. The back seat was redolent with scents he tried hard not to identify. In addition, the driver was obviously taking his time and adding more than a few unnecessary turns on the way to his destination.

Now usually, that would trigger a complaint or, if Eddie was feeling in his "hotshot kid mode" some wise-ass remarks. This time, however, it suited him fine. It was well after seven thirty by the time they reached Joe's neighborhood.

Eddie asked the driver to pull over several blocks from Joe's place. He grabbed his pack and, glad to be free from the smelly interior, got out. He paid the driver, who accelerated into the warm evening without a "thanks" – much less a glance. Eddie looked around. He was apparently unobserved. The sun was well to the west; although it being the summer, the evening was far from full dark. The shadows were long and the light gold and orange. It was still hot and humid. He moved into the shadows and put a lot of effort into being small and invisible as he footed it back to Joe's house.

The alley was deserted, and he made a dash for it. For a minute he was tempted to try to scale the back wall of Joe's yard, but it felt smarter to stick to the plan. Eddie stood still and listened. No neighbors were outdoors. He could hear their air conditioner going full blast. Barely audible beneath the roar of the air conditioner, Eddie could make out a television that blared gunshots and explosions.

Quickly, he scrambled over the back fence and into the neighbors' yard. The unpleasant sensation was definitely stronger. Maybe the fact that he was taking such a circuitous route back to the house had something to do with it. Belatedly, he wondered if Joe's protections might not recognize him so well after dark.

Eddie crouched low and made his way from shadow to shadow in the overgrown yard. Once he reached the spot he'd climbed over before, he jumped up and put his hands on the wall. This was different! This time it really hurt. His hands burned, and he couldn't breathe. He could barely see as he swung his leg over and dropped into Joe's back yard. It made sense that Joe's protections would work this way, that they would be stronger after dark, but it was bad. Eddie landed wrong, twisted his ankle slightly, and fell to his knees. His vision gradually cleared, and he could breathe again. It took him several minutes to feel more-or-less normal. Finally he limped back into the house.

Once inside, he locked the back door and glanced at the glowing numerals on the oven. Not even eight thirty. Eddie was pretty beat, but he also felt really good – as though he'd truly accomplished something with his subterfuge. He noticed that he was sweaty and sticky. It was as if he'd done a major workout while wearing his street clothes. Moving softly, he brought his pack into the entry hall and returned it to its spot near the door to the basement.

Now it was nearly dark, and Eddie barely caught himself before he flicked on a light. Great, he thought: go to all that trouble and then signal to whoever was watching that he was back. Limping slightly in the semidarkness, he climbed the three flights to his rooms. Then he showered and changed. His ankle was a little bit sore but not too bad. He grabbed his hiking boots and carried them back downstairs.

By this time it was fully dark. There was no moon, so he made himself a snack and ate it in the darkness. He was still nervous and keyed up and decided to leave the glass upside down on the 'fridge in the signal Joe had mentioned. If everything was okay, he could remove it later in the week.

Michael C. Glaviano

An hour later there was still no sign that anything was going to happen, so he crept upstairs once again. He sat in his rooms. Eddie was too wound up to try to sleep, and he couldn't turn on a light to read. For a while, he tried to sit and meditate, but stillness and focus eluded him. He got up, paced, looked tentatively out of the windows. Finally, he decided to go back downstairs. By then, it was nearly eleven.

As he tiptoed down the stairs, Eddie sensed that the house once again had that watchful feeling. It was strong, more powerful than before. It made him feel a little better, as though he had some backup, as though he weren't completely alone and vulnerable. It felt better still to be on the ground floor, and he pulled his jacket from the hall closet and went into the living room.

Despite the heat of the summer night, he wished for a fire in the fireplace and the warm glow of the candles in the sconces, but of course those comforts were out of the question. Eddie went over to the back wall of the living room and lay on the sofa with his jacket spread across his chest. He didn't think he'd fall asleep, but now that he'd given up trying, he did eventually doze off.

A few hours later, he came groggily awake. He had a kink in his neck from the way he was lying on the sofa. His jacket had slipped to the floor and despite the season, he felt slightly cool in this small, still hour. He stood up and stretched and then, his jacket over his shoulders, went into the kitchen to get a drink of water. The house was extremely quiet. It still had that vigilant feeling, and by this point he was starting to feel as though he'd successfully pulled off his deception. Surely they'd seen the cab. Perhaps they'd followed it to the bus station and decided he'd made a run for it. In any case, they were no longer trying to rattle him.

Determined to get some real rest, Eddie headed for the stairs. Before he reached them, however, he paused to take a quick peek out the front windows. Ever so slightly, he drew aside the curtain to the right of the door. He jumped back with a gasp. His heart hammered in his chest. Alicia had her hands pressed against the outside of the glass, waiting, waiting! Her face was contorted into a false smile; her eyes glowed with a strange, feral light. Even as Eddie thought the spell of seeing, she blazed with an angry, fiery corona. He hadn't fooled anyone but himself, and she was closer than ever to breaking Joe's defenses. She was closer than ever to reaching him.

At that point, Eddie went on autopilot. His jacket had fallen when he jumped back, and he bent to scoop it from the floor. He shrugged into the jacket as he darted across the hall. He jammed on his hat, swung his pack over his shoulder, stooped and grabbed his boots. Eddie shoved the water bottle into a boot so he'd have a hand free.

He reached for the basement door. Flinging the door open, he scrambled inside and slammed the door behind him. Then he flicked on the light to illuminate the basement stairs. Hands sweaty, he grappled

60

with the heavy beam as he slid it in place to bar further entry. He fumbled and dropped his knife as he tried to slide the sheath onto his belt. Fortunately, rather than falling into the shadows of the basement, the knife came to rest on the tread just below.

"C'mon, c'mon, c'mon, Eddie!" he muttered and took a shuddering breath. He stooped, retrieved his knife and carefully threaded the sheath onto his belt. Finally, the water bottle went into the top of the pack. He wiggled his feet into his boots, tucked the laces into the tops so he wouldn't trip, and clattered down the stairs.

Once he reached the floor at the base of the stairs, Eddie flicked off the basement light and groped for the bottom of the steps. He lifted the hinged steps over his head and let them fall as he stepped inside the low space. It took some feeling around in the darkness, but finally, a quick pull of the chain overhead returned light and sight. Squinting against the bare-bulbed glare, he stopped and listened. There was nothing to hear besides his panting breath. He worked to slow his breathing, to get some kind of control.

Moving more deliberately now, he stooped and with shaky fingers, laced and tied his boots. Then he checked his knife to make sure it was accessible but secure in its sheath. He took a deep breath, held it and let it out. Another. Another. He wasn't really any calmer, but Eddie could at least pretend to think. He tried to come up with other alternatives, but in the end, he decided that there was nothing to do except try to move through this "place" Joe had described.

Eddie lit a candle and put it into the lantern. He also pocketed a few extra matches. Then he shut off the light. Shouldering his pack once again, he took another shaky breath and looked around one last time before setting off down the descending passageway. The flickering light of the candle lantern showed him the way. His feet on the stones and his ragged breathing were the only sounds.

The young man hadn't given much thought to how long the passage would be or how it would actually feel to be inside it. Joe hadn't described it at all, and the young man hadn't thought to ask about it either. Walking slowly, tentatively at the center of a flickering pool of illumination, Eddie tried to observe the passage. It appeared to be of relatively recent construction. The walls and floors were unworn, modern-looking brick; although the masonry was a bit smaller in dimension than what he was used to seeing. The ceiling was only a foot or so above his head and was constructed of some kind of heavily enameled iron or steel plate. It looked like armor and reflected the candlelight with a diffuse glow.

The passage kept turning to the left as it sloped down at a fairly steep incline. Luckily, the floor was completely dry, and the bricks provided good traction; otherwise the footing would have been difficult. He turned around and looked back over his shoulder. The dimly lit tunnel curved up into darkness. He faced forward. The tunnel curved

Michael C. Glaviano

downward into darkness. With no reference point, his situation was very disorienting – almost as though he were walking on some kind of moving belt. He tamped down a surge of panic at the thought. Disturbed only by his tentative advance, the air was dry and still.

After creeping ahead slowly for several minutes, he noticed that the passage had become narrower and that if he were to stretch his arms out from his sides, his hands would easily touch the walls of the passage. This was better: something was changing, indicating progress. He picked up his pace. The passage continued to narrow and a little farther on it ended abruptly at the mouth of a tunnel.

This tunnel was obviously from a much earlier time. Roughly ovoid in cross section, the tunnel was significantly narrower than the passage had been. The floor was made of rough stones. The walls were hewn from larger stones and fitted very closely. Keystones, a few inches above his head, gave the tunnel an arched effect. Eddie wondered how far below the surface he had gone. He had to be at least 40 or 50 feet beneath the street level. The air was cool, and, apart from the sounds he made, the silence was complete.

The tunnel also had the same watcher-like feeling that had occasionally been palpable inside Joe's house, but here it was much stronger. He definitely felt that he was being observed. There was no hostility, merely observation and awareness. Eddie was glad that he had grown used to the feeling from Joe's house. Even so, it stood the hairs of his neck on end. His footfalls were muted, deadened, as though the sounds his feet made were absorbed by the surrounding stone. He kept catching himself holding his breath.

Now no longer curving, the tunnel led steeply downward. After a few minutes, it did a sharp switchback and, continuing downward, reversed its direction. He imagined that it led back towards a spot directly beneath Joe's house. Eddie tried not to think about all the earth and rock above his head and kept reminding himself that the tunnel had been there for a long, long time. Surely it would last well beyond the few minutes his steps would take to traverse it.

Eventually, the tunnel opened out into a circular room that was slightly more than a dozen feet in diameter. The walls of the room were of the same construction as the tunnel, large and tightly-fitted stones. The roof of the room had the appearance of a dome of perfectly fused stone that had been polished so that it reflected the dim candlelight and made the whole space shimmer.

In the center of the room, a little more than two feet out from the walls, the floor dropped to form a cylindrical pit that was about eight feet in diameter. Eddie leaned out carefully and was relieved to see that the bare, stone floor of this smaller space was only four or five feet below the path around the room's periphery. The floor of the smaller space was dry.

The air was very still and cool. Eddie looked around. A sconce with a fresh candle was bolted to the stone wall at the right of the tunnel mouth. Eddie lost no time in striking a match and lighting the candle. It added to the light a little and to the feeling of flickering stillness even more. To the left of the entrance, was a niche large enough to hold the candle lantern he'd carried with him, and in that niche was a folded piece of paper.

He withdrew the paper and replaced it with the lantern. Unfolding the paper, the young man saw right away that it was another, hand-printed note from Joe:

Well, if you're reading this, I can only assume you've decided that you must try to transit the Place Between. With your hands free of encumbrance, stand to the left of the tunnel entrance with your left hand touching the wall and your right extended out over the space. Walk carefully, slowly, and backwards around the room in this manner. If nothing happens, do it again until it does. When the room changes, face the tunnel opening with both arms out, your back to the space. At the right time, step back and drop into the portal.

If you reach the Place, do not linger. Hold in your mind the phrase: "head for higher ground." Repeat it. Make it a mantra, and keep at it. Again, you must not linger in the Place. Hold the mantra. Eventually, you will find yourself in another world. Make for the Inn at Three Corners.

So that was it? By "portal" Eddie assumed that Joe meant the smaller pit in the center of the room. That made sense of a sort. But

Michael C. Glaviano

walk around the room backwards? Widdershins, they used to call that. He felt sheepish and creepy at the same time. Joe had obviously been serious in his instructions, but this mumbo-jumbo was silly. Suddenly he caught that sense of watchfulness again and imagined that underlying it was the tiniest hint of amusement. The young man started to sweat a little then. "Okay, okay. I'll try this," he muttered to himself – or perhaps to the air around him – and took another deep breath.

Keeping near the wall, he backed slowly around the room. Nothing. He tried it a second time, a third; still nothing. He fought against a rising sense of anxiety. Suddenly, Eddie felt disoriented. Stretching out a hand to steady himself on the wall, he noticed that the flickering was stronger.

Now there was brighter light and a strange, keening sound that emanated from the stones and flowed down the tunnel. The sound and the light grew in intensity. He had no idea of the source of either of these phenomena, but he figured that these were the changes to which Joe had referred in his note. Still, it was with reluctance that the young man faced the mouth of the tunnel with his arms extended.

The sound and the light were both getting stronger, and he unconsciously took a step backward, off the edge and into the pit. His mind flashed that it was going to hurt when he hit that stone floor. Then there was the briefest, faintest sense of resistance and intense cold, and he fell *through*. Eddie landed on his backside on very soft, damp ground. Moisture immediately began soaking into his trousers, and he scrambled to his feet. The circular room was gone, and Eddie appeared to be outdoors, surrounded by a dimly lit, misty landscape.

Eight

Apart from the brilliantly illuminated throne and the beautiful, still figure resting at ease upon it, the cold, blue room was shrouded in shadows. The contrast made the throne room seem empty as Alicia stepped across the threshold. Even through the haze of her fatigue and weakness, however, she immediately knew the impression to be false. Whispered comments and occasional laughter, soft and vicious, reached her ears. All things in the Blue World were cold, were blue, and this room lay at its center.

As always, this world was locked in an attempt to displace the place between the worlds, the Great Hub as the Center of All. The figure on the throne admitted no other hub, no other cosmos, but that which radiated from her own being. Devourer of worlds, she was the Locust Queen.

Alicia supposed that the room was precisely this shade of blue to accentuate the cold of that shadowed place, and that the cold was, apart from the obvious display of power, perhaps merely an artifice, a window-dressing intended to push the reluctant visitor further off balance. Whatever the reason, it certainly had that effect on her. Alicia tried to hold her head up as she approached the throne of the Queen, but her knees were soft and it was all that she could do to keep from stumbling.

The woman resting upon the throne was beautiful – very beautiful and very still. Wrapped in a glistening, diaphanous gown, the Queen's icy body radiated the inhuman perfection of a goddess, or perhaps her own idealized fantasy of one. Alicia had heard whispered stories that the woman had been born as human as she. The stories asserted that, over a great period of time, this woman had drawn more and more power to her and that now she could maintain any form she chose. So she chose to assume a face and form that were stunningly beautiful.

Although perfectly proportioned, the woman appeared to be somewhat larger than the human norm. No hint of line or blemish marred that porcelain display. Despite the sheer fabric of the Queen's gown, there was not the slightest hint that the cold of the room had an effect on her. By contrast, Alicia felt chilled, puny and imperfect. This

65

powerful woman's form may well have been carved and polished from a block of flawless stone. Only the eyes were fully present and alive, and they looked nothing like the eyes of a living, human woman. The power that radiated from those featureless blue orbs licked the edges of Alicia's heart and made it quake.

At a dozen paces from the throne, Alicia halted. At an unspoken command, she dropped to the floor and crossed the remaining distance on her hands and knees. She was simultaneously furious, humiliated, and terrified. The woman on the throne noticed and transmitted the impression that she found Alicia's discomfiture distantly amusing. As if comprised of small, living things, the floor beneath Alicia's hands and knees squirmed, and she suppressed a shudder.

As Alicia reached the throne, the Queen gestured with her strange, frightening eyes, and Alicia bent to kiss each elegant foot. Awash in power, the great porcelain figure shifted slightly on the throne, and Alicia prostrated herself fully on the icy, squirming floor.

From the distant shadows of the throne room, further, whispered comments and haughty laughter reached her ears. Despite her fear and the cold, Alicia burned inside. She did her best to bury that anger deeply.

Her initial humiliation complete, Alicia was wordlessly and painfully instructed to lie at the foot of the throne with her arms at her sides and her legs extended behind her. Adding to her embarrassment, the short shift that all supplicants were expected to wear at such times hiked up revealing her to those lurking in the shadows. There were more giggles and muttered comments from that quarter. The Locust Queen rested her feet, heavy, heavy and cold on Alicia's head and shoulders. Hurting Alicia's cheek, her breasts and belly, the floor squirmed and bit and scratched revoltingly through the thin fabric.

Now that the niceties of introduction were over, the real interview commenced. A series of painful questions – images really – appeared inside Alicia's mind. In her thoughts, Alicia tried to answer, to explain what she had attempted and why she had thought her actions were the proper course. Her explanations were found wanting, painfully so.

New instructions were given, and Alicia assented readily, without hesitation. It was then that she made her error. Hoping against hope that she would be released then, she let slip just the tiniest thought that she didn't really understand why the complete destruction of the two men, one so young and earnest the other so very old was absolutely required. It was such a tiny, infinitesimal slip. She damped it immediately. Surely, it escaped notice.

There was a sudden, malevolent silence and Alicia's sight grew terrifyingly dark. Invisible bands encircled her chest and she found herself barely able to breathe. Something coiled up from the cold, biting floor to gather her wrists and draw them straight out from her sides. Then some *things*, some gibbering, damp things encircled her ankles and drew them further, painfully apart. Something lashed fire across her back, arms, and legs, and she caught her breath. The flimsy material of the shift shredded and fell away.

The things that bound Alicia to the cruel floor pulled more strongly, and the side of her face, her breasts, her belly and thighs began to feel as though they were being scratched and bitten more aggressively by some*thing* that dwelt within the floor itself. Her hair was being pulled down around her face, almost pulled into the floor. With her thick hair pulled so, it became even more difficult to breathe. The lashing continued, now punctuated by her screams. Her voice grew harsh and hoarse in her own ears.

A thought insinuated itself into what was left of her mind then. It was simple. It offered a trade, a precious gift: an end to this torment. The price demanded for this treasure was little enough. It was merely her unwavering, undoubting acceptance of all instructions. Three times, this bargain was offered, and three times, Alicia accepted it, painfully at first, then desperately, and finally hysterically.

The pain withdrew then, and Alicia sank, terrified, through the floor to land painfully on a hard surface. The tattered remnants of her garment hung from her. She was apparently alone in a dark, silent place. Still cold, it was nevertheless not quite so cold a place as the throne room, and it was a place where the floor did not bite and scratch. At first she shuddered and sobbed uncontrollably. She shook with a violence that was itself torture, and she could feel wetness seeping out of the cuts left behind by the lash. Gradually, gradually, the violent shudders subsided and became merely shivering.

Alicia still hurt. The welts on her back and legs would leave scars. She could not yet see it, but in the aftermath of her torment, her once pretty face was now lined and careworn. Later, she would notice that her eyes held a haunted, terrified look. These confirmations would come later, but already, she knew instinctively that she was marred, indelibly marked. At a fundamental level, she believed that she was no longer beautiful. She had been taught beyond hope that she was a weak and flawed creature.

There would be worse scars that would not be visible, but she was already growing hazy as to why she hurt. She knew with surety only that her present, miserable state had something to do with those men. That nasty, strong old man and his callow protégé had caused this hurt. They were the reason she cowered here so painfully injured. The blame for her humiliation lay squarely upon their heads. Unbidden, an image rose in her mind: an image of the two men. They sat feasting at a heavily laden table in a warm room. They could see her and they pointed at her, laughed at her pain and humiliation, laughed at the loss of her beauty. They ate and drank and laughed as she lay before them and suffered.

Michael C. Glaviano

Alicia lost consciousness again, and, entrapped by terror and pain, her mind orbited a stark resolution. She would devote all her skill, all of her power and intelligence to hunting down these men. The old one would be difficult and dangerous, but the young one had escaped so far only because she had been stupid and weak. She would take him easily and painfully and use him as bait to snare the old man. Then, slowly, painfully, and utterly, she would destroy them both. She would draw from their broken bodies all the power they had accumulated in their silly, hateful lives.

Only that power would restore her, make her whole and strong and beautiful.

Nine

Until this moment, Eddie hadn't really believed in his gut that the things Joe had told him were real. Stories, yeah. And some of the things he'd seen with his own eyes – Alicia and all – were pretty strange. Now, however, the undeniable reality of standing, with the seat of his pants damp, in the middle of this unnamed swamp had left him dumfounded. Water trickled around him and tendrils of fog drifted past. He remembered to close his mouth. He swallowed and then looked around.

Visibility was limited to twenty or thirty yards in every direction. There were some boulders or perhaps some large, pale shrubs off to his left. In the fog, it was impossible to tell which. Eddie followed the sound of trickling water and in a dozen paces or so came to a tiny stream. He could have easily stepped over it, but looking around with wide eyes, he merely stood there, unsure as to what he should do next. The harsh cry of a bird, or bird-like animal behind him made Eddie start from his reverie, and he suddenly felt vulnerable and exposed as he lingered, rooted to that swampy ground.

Alert now, the young man recalled Joe's instructions. He fished the crumpled note from his jacket pocket. "Head for higher ground," Joe had written. That and, "make for the Inn at Three Corners." Now the tone of the note took on more urgency, and Eddie decided that it would be a good idea to follow Joe's instructions right away. He was supposed to make that intention, heading for high ground, the focus of his thoughts. Okay, he could do that, but with the fog and all, it was hard to see which way led up hill.

He looked back down at the stream. It was flowing gently from left to right. "Well, water flows downhill," he muttered, and trying very hard to hold the thought in mind that he should be heading for higher ground, Eddie adjusted the weight of his pack and headed upstream.

After five minutes or so of walking, the stream petered out, but now there was a definite slope to the damp ground, so while running the thought to "head for higher ground" in his mind, over and over, Eddie kept moving. Every time his thoughts wandered, he noticed that the fog drew around him more thickly. As he held the thought, he imagined that the mist thinned slightly and was encouraged to be able to see a little farther around him. The air was definitely fresher smelling, less boggy now, and there was a hint of a game trail ahead.

When he'd first fallen into this place, it had been warm and damp and he'd thought briefly about taking off his jacket. At the time, however, he would have needed to remove his pack, then his jacket, and then re-shoulder his pack, and this amount of delay had felt dangerously excessive. The foreboding surroundings, the threat implicit in the misty shapes and strange sounds impelled him to keep moving. Now it was markedly cooler, and he was slightly more comfortable. He stumbled over a root or a rock or something and realized he'd once again lost his mental focus. This time, however, the fog hadn't closed in quite so much. Shifting his pack on his shoulders again, Eddie continued up the now obvious incline.

Another twenty or so minutes passed and Eddie finally crested the top of a small rise. Blowing down slope from still higher terrain at his left, cooler air hit him, and despite the modest exercise, he was suddenly glad for his jacket. He turned to face back down the way he'd come. The game trail he'd been following, at this point really just an absence of larger rocks and shrubs, appeared to descend into a fog bank some seventy-five or a hundred yards back. Now the ground sloped away to his left and joined up with similar rises in the ground in the middle distance. He wondered if he needed to keep repeating his instructions over and over, and decided to keep it up for a while yet. It was as though he'd somehow hiked out of the Place and into the countryside of another world.

"Head for higher ground. Head for higher ground. Head for higher ground," he repeated softly as he walked uphill. Now he was timing it with his steps as he walked. The rhythm, together with the audible repetitions, kept him from losing the mantra.

So it went for some time – Eddie lost track completely – and finally, the path of his footsteps intersected with a definite trail. He paused and once again looked back the way he'd come. The land sloped very gradually into the distance, and from this perspective, the fog appeared almost solid, as though it were a jumbled landscape of small hills and boulders. As Eddie watched, the illusion of solidity became more and more pronounced, until to his amazement, the illusion became reality and the foggy way back into the Place was gone. It was as though a slightly out of focus lens had been adjusted to crystal sharpness to reveal a clearly defined landscape.

Even though he had no idea how to use the Place to return to Joe's house, until this point, he had at least imagined that he knew roughly where the portal had deposited him. Now that feeling was gone, and Eddie was completely cut off from his old world and his life there. If he were ever to return, it would be through the assistance of some other agency or person. He could only hope that Joe would get back safely, understand what had transpired, and figure out what to do next. In the meantime, all he could do was follow Joe's remaining instructions and try to find this Inn at Three Corners place. It was a very lonely feeling.

Taking in the countryside, Eddie did a slow turn. Now there was a very definite change to his surroundings. The Place had felt enclosed, a locality unto itself. It had been swampy and dreamlike, hard to see even in the midst of it. Where he stood now reminded him of the rolling hills near the coast of his childhood Southern California. Only these hills had more vegetation, and the native trees were clearly more varied than eucalyptus and scrub oak.

The air was now crisp and clear, and Eddie could see that the path continued ahead for a good distance. There were more game trails, and the land was more alive. There were birds chirping and twittering ahead. He continued up the path at a leisurely pace and, while trying to decide his next move, attempted to take more careful note of his surroundings. There were no signs of human habitation, and even though the day was gentle, Eddie kept in mind that this was wilderness and that he was alone. He knew that he must be watchful, that any kind of serious injury would likely prove to be fatal.

In particular, Eddie began to realize that wherever he was, he was going to have to feed himself from what he could glean from his surroundings. He tried to recall what Joe had tried to teach him about camping in the wilderness. While he had some snack food in his pack, he wasn't prepared for a long trek. He wondered how far away this Inn at Three Corners was, and he hoped he'd find the kinds of forage that Joe had patiently explained to him over the last months. At that time, the lessons and even the trips to the countryside had been little more than interesting, challenging activities. Now he could only wish that he'd paid more attention than Joe had demanded.

When he'd fallen through, into the Place, it had been in the still, pre-dawn hours of the day. He felt as though he'd been walking for a long time, and of course he had no idea how long he'd tarried in the Place while he tried to collect and focus his thoughts.

Wherever he was now, the shadows suggested that it was mid to late afternoon, and Eddie began to look for a place to camp for the night. He needed shelter of some kind. He realized that he was thirsty as well, and he was beginning to feel the first pangs of hunger.

He got out his water bottle and took a few sips. Fortunately, this land was green and fresh, and Eddie had some optimism that there would be water nearby. Even so he resolved to limit his intake until he found a source to replenish his meager store. The trees he'd noticed earlier were getting closer and now resolved into a sizable grove, and near the trees, to one side, the foliage was very dense – a good sign if he hoped to find fresh water.

The grove was hushed as he approached. He paused, stood motionless, and listened. He could indeed hear the sound of running water off to the left of the trail, so he veered in that direction and after a moment's search, found a cool stream that flowed beneath some overhanging bushes. He worked his way through the plants to the edge of the stream and got down on the ground to drink. It was cool and refreshing and made him very much aware of how empty his stomach felt and how little food he'd brought with him in his pack.

All the same, he had a few things to eat, so he rummaged in his pack and pulled out a food bar, which he unwrapped and devoured in two bites. That did little to sate his appetite, but it took a tiny bit of the edge off. Stuffing the wrapper back in his pack, he topped off his water bottle. He figured that the bottle held enough for a day, if he didn't mind being a little thirsty and didn't exert himself too much... and it didn't get too hot. "That's a lot of 'ifs,' he mumbled to himself."

The next order of business was to find shelter. He also wanted to get a better look at the grove, so he headed back towards the trail. A few moments later, the trail opened into the grove. It was really quite beautiful.

He didn't recognize the types of trees, but he stared appreciatively at them nonetheless. The bark was smooth and light. The trunks were slender and straight, and the bottom branches flared out from the trunks eight or ten feet above the floor of the grove. The trees were gathered around a small clearing. There was a little bit of underbrush here and there near the periphery of the clearing, but the overall effect was symmetric and peaceful.

Eddie walked softly around the perimeter of the grove. Halfway around, he noticed that he could see more water through the trees, this time off to the right. He wove through the trees to find a small pond that appeared to be fed by a spring near its opposite shore. Between the trees and the pond there were some large rocks and he wandered over. After a couple of minutes, he identified a possible campsite. There were three boulders in a cluster with a small amount of space between. While no real cave, there was a good overhang between two of them, and the earth was soft and dry. Eddie searched around for a few more minutes and couldn't find anything better, so he resolved to make that cleft between the rocks his camp for the night.

As it had been at home, it was early summer in this part of the country, so there were a few hours of light remaining. Eddie decided to make the most of the light and explore the grove and its immediate surroundings more fully. He retraced his steps and reentered the grove to continue his walk around its perimeter. Once again the natural beauty of the place drew his attention.

Then he stopped and frowned. There was something wrong with some of the trees in this part of the grove. Several of the largest and loveliest among them had ugly gashes in their trunks. The bark of one had been peeled, chewed, it appeared, nearly halfway around the base. Eddie stood and looked at the damaged trees. During one of their walks in the park near his home, Joe had explained how there was a way to repair certain kinds of damage. Eddie tried to recall just what Joe had said. Facing the trees, he dropped to sit cross-legged on the ground. After a few moments of deep, careful thought, he was pretty sure that he had it.

The context of Joe's lesson had been repair of kids' carvings in the bark of trees, but Eddie figured this was close enough. He knew that there was supposed to be a little bit of magic involved and he felt sheepish reciting "magic words" over mud, moss, and leaves. Nevertheless, he figured that whether the magic part were real or not, the other ingredients might at least protect the trees in the areas where their bark had been injured.

Once more, Eddie left the grove and returned to the pond. The shore of the pond supplied some moss and mud, and there were plenty of leaves scattered around the grove. It took him a couple more trips to the pond to gather what he figured would be enough material. He knelt down and kneaded the mixture together. After a little hesitation, Eddie decided that since there was no one around, there was no need to be embarrassed, and he repeated the words he'd been taught. It didn't make any detectable difference, and he couldn't decide for sure whether that relieved or disappointed him.

When the mixture felt right, he smeared it on the gashes. It stuck okay, and it looked like it might protect the trees until the bark could be replaced naturally. He stood and brushed his hands together somewhat absently and then returned to the pond to wash off the worst of the mud. Coming back to the grove, Eddie was surprised to see that a few of the smaller marks were fading right in front of his eyes, and that even the worst gashes were a little smaller!

"Whoa! Now that's pretty cool," he said to himself. "Sorta looks like magic to me." Now of course he wished he'd paid more attention when Joe had tried to get him to memorize various spells and incantations. Then he shrugged. There hadn't been that much that Joe had tried to show him about magic anyway. Maybe he'd remember a few more things or maybe meet up with someone who'd be willing to teach him some stuff. Maybe this was a one-time deal, and it wouldn't make any difference one way or the other.

Continuing around the grove, Eddie found no more signs of damage, but he did notice that his surroundings had become quieter than he thought normal. Earlier, before he reached the grove there had been birds flying around, and more than a few butterflies and other insects had been visible. But now the place was deathly quiet. Even the gentle breeze had died.

Once he noticed the stillness, he decided it was kind of creepy, unnatural for a summer afternoon in a forest. The hairs on the back of his neck rose a little and he shivered involuntarily. He felt that he was being observed. Eddie glanced around, but he didn't see anything. More watchful now, he continued walking. As he circuited the clearing, some-times the feeling was stronger and other times weaker, and he imagined a dim hostility in it, but he still couldn't pinpoint the source of the feeling. Finally, he looked up and saw a strange creature, sort of a cross between a beaver and a gigantic squirrel, crouched on one of the branches. Its eyes glowed red and it glared angrily at him.

Eddie took an involuntary step back and of course stumbled over his feet and sat down hard. This broke the silence. Displaying large, blunt incisors, the beast began to chatter furiously. It was obvious that this creature had been the source of the damage. Eddie picked up a rock and heaved it at the thing.

"Buzz off! Go on," he yelled.

The rock flew harmlessly past the animal, but Eddie's action en-raged it. Now chattering loudly, it ran and leapt from branch to branch. Without warning, a limb gave way and the angry beast tumbled to the ground 20 feet away. It was stunned, and for a moment, Eddie wondered if it had been seriously hurt or killed, but just as he was thinking about walking closer to check it out, the creature sprang to its feet and charged him!

There was no time to pull his knife and throw it (not that he could have hit the thing as it ran at him), and he began to back up. Then a strange calm came over him, and Eddie leaned slightly forward on the balls of his feet. When he didn't retreat, he expected the beast to back off, but instead it launched itself at him. Reflexively, Eddie brought his hiking boot up in a sharp kick. The creature fell back, stunned. Before it could recover, Eddie stepped forward and put his boot on the thing's neck. He leaned into it, and there was a sharp snap. Silence returned to the grove.

He stood staring down at the beast, and as he looked, the animal changed. It became smaller and its head and mouth shrank. No longer the size of a large badger, the proportions of the creature's body shifted. At his feet lay a dead rabbit. "Eddie, the rabbit slayer," he muttered to himself, both bewildered and chagrined. Why had it attacked him? Why had it been so much larger than a rabbit and so fierce in its behavior? Above all, why had it been chewing on the trees?

Well, one thing for certain, if he could get a fire together, he'd have something better to eat for dinner than he'd had any reason to hope for. Without warning, a large dead branch crashed down to land 10 feet from him. He jumped, startled at the sudden noise but then noticed that the fall had broken the wood into very convenient pieces. Eddie looked between the dead rabbit and the pile of wood and shook his head.

"Thanks!" he called to no one in particular – or maybe to the grove as a whole.

As if in response, he noticed that a few birds had returned to the trees and begun to sing. A butterfly meandered across the clearing, and he thought he could hear some bees. He bent and picked up the rabbit by its hind legs.

Now Joe had explained how to skin and cook small game, but Eddie had never done it himself. Joe had assured him that skinning a rabbit was easy. "Almost like removing a sweater," the old man had claimed.

"No time like the present to learn," his stomach rumbled. Eddie set to his task, and found that with the help of a sharp knife it was, while slightly grisly, not too difficult. When he was done, he skewered the carcass on a stick and rolled up the pelt. Using a sharp stick to dig a hole, he buried the offal at the base of the tree that the beast, in its earlier form, had damaged most extensively. It seemed like the right thing to do.

He scrubbed his hands in the mud at the bottom of the pond to remove the worst of the rabbit guts. Then he pulled his soap from his pack and went to the stream to wash his hands and knife.

Eddie went to the clearing and gathered an armload of firewood. Then he returned to his campsite to make dinner. Once he had a small fire going in the shelter of the boulders, he propped the rabbit up on a long stick to roast. He tended his fire carefully and paid a lot of attention to the roasting rabbit. It took real willpower for him to take his time and avoid burning it on the outside while leaving it raw in the middle, but eventually, three-quarters of an hour later, it looked perfectly done and smelled great.

He tried to eat it as slowly as he could, but all too soon he was finished. Now he felt pretty well fed – mostly full at least. It was hardly a balanced diet, one roast rabbit. Still it was far better than a food bar and a sip of water. By the time he was finished eating and had cleaned up, it was beginning to get dark, so he made several more trips to the grove and gathered as much firewood as possible in the waning light.

Using a stick, he made a separate, smaller fire pit near his main campfire. He dug a bunch of coals out of his fire and put them in the pit and covered them with a few inches of leaves stripped from the bushes near the stream. The leaves immediately gave off a thick, aromatic and astringent smoke. Over this Eddie placed the unrolled rabbit pelt, fur-side up. Finally, he covered the whole thing with more green leaves and a good-sized pile of stones. Hopefully, by morning time, the pelt would be mostly dried and preserved.

It had been a long and stressful day, but before turning in, Eddie wanted to relax and enjoy the tranquil surroundings and the pleasure of a full, warm belly. He clambered to the top of the boulders and sat in the twilight of the darkening sky. In this place, it was past the time of the new moon. Silvery and bright, a first quarter crescent was inching above the horizon. He could hear the birds and animals doing whatever they do at dusk. Day timers were seeking shelter for the night. Looking for un-wary tidbits, the hunter-types went abroad with sharp senses and sharper teeth. Eddie did not yet feel a part of it all, not by any means, but he did feel slightly more optimistic than he had for several days.

Scrabbling back to his camp, Eddie straightened up his things. He scooped out his sleeping place. He thought it might get cold later that night, so he sat for some time and fed his fire. Once he felt the rocks warming around him and had a good bed of coals, he used a stick to sweep most of these into the shallow ditch he'd dug beneath the over-hanging boulder. Then he piled dirt over the coals, several inches of it. He knew that the coals would warm the earth and allow him to sleep in relative comfort even without much in the way of blankets.

Next he needed to fashion a bed. He pulled the tarp from his pack and re-folded the material along its longer side. Then, he lay the tarp over his sleeping place. Finally, he added his blanket.

Eddie surveyed his camp with some satisfaction. He was fed, he was comfortable, and he was pretty sure he'd sleep warmly. For a time, as he began to feel slightly drowsy, he fed the fire and stared into the flames.

Suddenly, he sat bolt upright. There was a girl, a young woman standing on the other side of his campfire! She was tan, and in the fire-light, her skin glowed with good health. Her dark hair was wavy and more than a little wild. She wore a plain white shift and was barefoot. Her eyes reflected the firelight in an unusual way, but she flashed Eddie a warm, relaxed smile.

Instinctively, Eddie tried the seeing spell on the strange young woman. Thankfully, a clear light, with no hint of red in it, glowed happily around her. She obviously recognized what he'd just done, and her smile got even brighter.

Embarrassed, Eddie struggled to his feet and promptly smacked his head on the rocky overhang. Stunned, he dropped to his knees, and she leapt past the fire to grab his arm and steady him. "Are you hurt?" she asked.

"Who? Where? Uhh, ow," Eddie managed. Great start, he thought, head still spinning.

"I am so sorry, my friend. It was not my intention to startle you. I came only to thank you for your kindness."

"Kindness?" Eddie struggled to get a grip on himself. "I'm sorry. I don't think I follow you."

"Follow me? I did not intend to leave so soon – unless, of course you wish it." The tiniest note of disappointment in her voice accompan-ied this last bit; although her unusual eyes had lost none of their smile.

"Whoa. Let's slow down. I think maybe you've got me confused with somebody else. I'm just camping here for the night."

"But you took care to tend my trees, and you dispatched the poor, twisted creature that had done such damage!"

"Those are your trees?"

"Indeed, they are. My trees, my grove, my forest. Is it not lovely?"

"Um... so am I on your land? Is this private property, or something? I mean, I didn't see any fence or sign or anything."

"Once again, I confess that I understand each of the words that you say, but the way you weave them together makes no sense to me."

Eddie took a deep breath and struggled for simple clarity in his speech. "Do you object to my being here?" he asked.

"Most certainly, I do not. I am glad of it."

"Okay – I mean, 'good.' If those are your trees, and that animal was hurting them, why didn't you drive it away yourself?"

She lowered her gaze and fixed her oddly glowing eyes on the fire. Her voice took on more than a hint of sadness. "I have not the magic. Perhaps some day, if I survive these times and live to become the mistress of a great, world-spanning forest, I will be better able to protect all creatures in my care, but for now I am young, with but a single forest to nurture."

Now this was the longest speech either of them had made, and a weighty silence followed. At last Eddie spoke up.

"Well, okay – I mean, 'I guess I understand,' but I didn't use magic. I just stunned it and then broke its neck with my boot. Why couldn't you have trapped it or something?"

She looked up, and now there were tears in her eyes. "Do you not know? If my trees are hurt, so am I. My grove and I are indeed one. I thought everyone knew that. I could scarcely move for the pain, and I feared that I would languish. Look!"

Here she stepped back and gently hiked up the side of her shift. By the glow of the fire, Eddie could see that her leg, tanned and beautiful as it was, was marred by newly healed scars. One such ran halfway around her thigh.

She smoothed the shift back into place. "So, when you happened by, I did what I could. The creature had no little magic in it, but while its anger was focused upon you, I could act."

Here she looked up and met Eddie's eyes, an irrepressible spark in her own. "And so, through your actions, I am quickly healing. ... Tell me... are you a wizard? You seem young to be a wizard. Yet you used spells to help my trees, and you buried the creature's entrails where they will speed the process further. I am already taking back the energy that was robbed from my grove."

For a moment, Eddie was tempted to say something or to make a claim to try to impress the young woman, but he caught himself and laughed ruefully. "No. I'm not a wizard. My teacher, my friend... Well, this old man that I stay with and try to help... he taught me a few things, but I'm afraid I'm not much into the wizard-stuff.

"Hey," he continued. "So why'd that animal attack you, anyway? What'd it have against you? Oh, and what's your name? Mine's Eddie." Here he stuck out his hand.

She hesitated for a second as if unsure of his intentions and then she brightened. "I think that is part of your true name, sir," she replied, taking his hand in hers. "That removes all doubt. You are surely a stranger here. You had best keep your true name to yourself. Have you another name that you can offer to those you meet?"

Eddie was more than a little distracted by her hand, which he couldn't help but notice was strong and warm. And as shapely as her leg had been. "Another name? Uh, I don't know. Lemme think... Sheesh, I don't know. I'm drawing a blank here. Hey. What should I call you?"

"You may call me, 'Maia,' for goddess of the month in which my trees blossom."

"Maia. That's pretty nice."

She dimpled and then spoke again. "You are young in your own way, as I am in mine. We both have much to learn. It will be important that you learn to bend when the wind blows strongly. May I call you 'Reed?'"

Eddie tried out the sound, "Reed? Reed. Yeah, I like that. It'll work fine. Now I need to remember to use it. Uh, do I need a last name too?"

"Perhaps. Although most times a single name will suffice. You have been a friend to me and my trees. I owe you what help I may give. Let me think."

Maia closed her eyes for a moment and inhaled the redolent bouquet that swirled around the grove. She opened her eyes and pointed to a small plant nearby. It grew in the shade of the trees. The shrub was close to the ground and had bright green leaves and its small, white, star-shaped flowers reflected the glow of the campfire.

"There," Maia announced. "That fragrant plant is sweet woodruff. It demands little, not even strong sun. Its fresh leaves may be used to heal wounds. This reminds me of you, my friend, who made a poultice, spoke words over it, and thereby healed the wounds to my bark. I name you 'Woodruff.'"

"Reed Woodruff, huh? Well, that's sort of cool. Er, I mean, thank you, Maia. That will more than suffice."

Maia laughed and clapped her hands as he tried to match the cadence of her voice and her use of language. "I had been of a mind to grant some small boon to you in return for your kindness. Yes. The Gift of Tongues, plus some measure of woodcraft would be most appropriate."

'Woodcraft' Eddie understood, and he agreed completely. He knew that he'd need all the camper's skills he could get to survive in the wilderness, but what was this 'Gift of Tongues' thing? He had to ask. "So what is the Gift of Tongues?"

"Once imparted, you will be able to communicate with any sensible creature. Your dialect is strange enough to draw attention, and in these times, that is perhaps not a good thing."

"Hey, that's at least the second time you mentioned 'these times.' What about these times? And you never said why that animal was trying to hurt you. Or your trees."

"Sadly, Reed, these things are all knit together." Here Maia dropped her voice and leaned close. "The agents of the Locust Queen are abroad. Such a one passed some months ago, and twisted that poor rabbit into a creature bent on hurting my trees. Now, the power he put into that spell has flowed into you and, due to your kindness, back to me."

"But why?"

"Why did he wish to harm me? It is simple. The boundary between this world and the place between worlds is thin. Magic is still strong here. There are some, although not as many as one would hope, who still practice the old ways. The Queen knows well that healthy forests are a source of life, beauty, and magic. A great forest is a threat to her power. Even a small one is an affront to her.

"Moreover, if the right person were to help me start another grove in a neighboring world, why both worlds would grow the richer. Good magic would be exchanged, would grow in both. For all of these reasons, if a creature of hers passes, it sees my trees and thinks only to scar and weaken them."

"Oh... so you know about the Place, huh?" The fire was dying slightly, and Eddie moved to add a few more branches and stir the coals. The night was mild and the moon's crescent was bright in the clear sky.

"Yes, I know. My magic is different from the magic of men, but it is in my nature to know, deeply, certain things of the worlds, and this I do understand."

"So they don't want your forest to grow. Or to expand to another world. Mine, for instance."

"Ah, so I am correct in my suspicion. You do come from a nearby world!"

"Well, yeah. I guess I do."

"This you must also keep secret. Think carefully upon the intentions of those whom you meet. The evil ones are abroad and they will harm you if they find you."

"Well, I'd pretty much figured out that part." Eddie – he was trying to think of himself as "Reed" now – paused and thought for another minute. "You said something, something about the right person help-ing you extend your grove to a neighboring world. How would that work? Could I do that?"

At this, the young woman looked sharply at him. Her face, while still open, had a sudden stillness to it, a deep focus. Despite the warmth of the fire and the mild evening, Eddie felt a chill on his arms, his neck. He gave a slight, involuntary shudder. As he met that sharp, glowing gaze, the young man knew beyond question that Maia was nothing re-motely like a human girl.

Yes, she had a pretty, impish face, and the plain shift she wore highlighted rather than concealed the curves of her body. Her voice was sweet, pleasing to the ears. But there was nothing human in those eyes. The smile still touched the corners of her lips, but her voice held a hint of the wind that foretells a storm.

"You would do this, Reed?"

Afraid to back down now, Eddie swallowed and nodded. "Yeah. I'd help if I could," he croaked.

"That would truly be a great boon to me, to this world, and to yours. Yet by your actions, by your own admission, it is obvious that you know little of the ways of magic. I would not take advantage of your in-nocence. Therefore I ask you clearly, would you help me establish my forest on your world?"

One more time, Eddie invoked the spell of seeing. The aura sur-rounding Maia remained clear and bright, without the slightest hint of crimson. Despite no small nervousness, he made up his mind then.

"Yeah, Maia. I'll help you."

A subtle tension, noticeable by its sudden absence, withdrew then from the grove. Maia's smile warmed – ever-so-slightly – those strange, beautiful, inhuman eyes. Her voice was full of music.

"I thank you, Reed Woodruff. I thank you. Now rest. I will watch over you. No harm shall come to you while you shelter within my forest. When you wake, you will possess the gift of tongues. You will carry it all of your days. When you wake, woodcraft will begin to come alive in your heart and mind.

"And finally, tomorrow, we will do what is needed that you might someday carry my forest to your world. Now rest, sleep."

With those final words, Maia faded from view. Eddie looked around the suddenly still campsite. He stooped, added a few more sticks to the fire. As he straightened, Eddie felt a wave of fatigue wash over him. Barely able to stand then, he moved to his bedroll, undressed and tucked himself into his blanket. The bed was warm, the ground soft. As he drifted into slumber, he felt safer than he had since the afternoon Joe had climbed into the cab in front of the house on Painter Avenue.

* * *

The sun came up early. Eddie felt warmth on his face and opened his eyes. Nearby, watching, Maia sat at the fire. She must have kept it going all night. She smiled as she saw him wake.

"You rested well. Eat now, refresh yourself. I will return shortly," she spoke softly. The sound of her voice blended with the calls of the birds and she again faded from Eddie's sight.

Eddie threw back his blanket and climbed from his warm bed. As he stood, he looked around the neat campsite. He fancied that he could see the area around him more clearly, slightly more coherently.

The thought of the nearby pond came to him and he walked to the shore. It was colder away from the warmth of the campsite, but the water beckoned him. He stripped and dove into the clear water. Eddie came up gasping and laughing in the chilly morning air. He swam around until he felt refreshed and then returned to his camp.

He dried himself off and got dressed. Then he rummaged in his pack for another food bar and broke his fast. Perhaps twenty minutes later, he'd cleaned up the camp. He drank some water and poured the rest of his supply over the campfire. Then he made two more trips to the stream so he could be sure that the fire was completely out. Finally he made a trip to top off his water bottle for the walk ahead.

Eddie was just finishing up when, smiling, Maia walked around a tree. She looked around the camp and gave an approving nod.

"Yes, my welcome guest. You have left this place in order. Now let me show you a few things that you may find useful," she offered and began to indicate details of the forest around him.

As Maia pointed out plants that were good to eat and which he must avoid, he began to understand more deeply how his lessons with Joe had been put together, and much that had he had barely noted at the time came back to his mind and fit into larger and more complete patterns. Eddie saw that Maia's gift of woodcraft couldn't by itself make him knowledgeable. Rather, she had given him a small talent for learning the workings of the natural world. It would be up to him to develop the talent, but what before had been random and bewildering now had some sense and structure.

An hour or so later, the grove grew quiet. Maia stopped in mid-sentence and suddenly became alert and watchful and then obviously nervous. With eyes again alien and sharp, she scanned the sky and the forest and appeared to look into some great distance. Eddie began to ask what was going on, but with a tense look and a tiny back-and-forth movement of her head, she drew him back into the space where he'd sheltered for the night.

"Move beneath the overhang as far as you can," she whispered, "I did not think that they would be out so soon, but perhaps they have de-

Michael C. Glaviano

tected the change in my forest, or perhaps they sense your presence. Either way, the hounds will soon be abroad."

"Hounds?" Eddie repeated. This didn't sound so good.

"Yes. And, for all one knows, other things. I must go into deep hiding and you must get as far away from this place as you can."

"I've got to leave? I don't want to leave yet!" he argued.

The forest goddess became very quiet. Very still. And as she looked deeply into his eyes, Eddie saw clearly for the first time, the centuries, the vast span of years, the mystery and goodness of her.

Eddie felt a sharp pang in his heart, but he did not pull back or retreat from her gaze. Maia smiled just a little. It was a wistful and slightly distant smile, but a smile nonetheless.

He realized he'd been holding his breath and released it with a soft sigh. "Okay," he said. "I get it. Do you have any idea of a good way out of here... a good direction to take? Or what to do next? My friend – the old man I've been staying with – said that if I came through the Place, I should try to make for the Inn at Three Corners. Do you know of it?"

"Not directly. I do not leave my forest, but from the few other good beings who have come this way, I have heard rumor of this Inn. As I watched you sleep last night, I thought upon these times and upon the agents of the Locust Queen. I had hoped it would not be needed so soon, but I know how to hide you and, for a time, protect you as you travel.

"To the southeast, my forest has its greatest extent and that is the direction you must go. You will travel for four days within the shelter of my trees and for three more in the open country beyond. While you are within my forest, there are things that I can do to confound those who may follow.

"Within the forest, you will encounter trails and small paths. Do not follow these as they will make you too easy to track... and no few of them will wind back and forth in a tangled web to lead the unwary traveller far from his goal.

"Near the point where you emerge from my forest, you will encounter a trade road that comes up from the south and swings east. Parallel that for two days until it turns north again. If you see good folk on the road, you may ask to join them – approach them slowly and in plain sight – but do not travel by yourself on the road.

"Once you leave my forest, you will be beyond my protection and must travel as rapidly as you can, for you will be exposed on all sides and visible at great distances from the sky above. There will be outcroppings of large rocks and small groves of trees here and there and you must use these to your advantage: from the shelter of each, spy the next that is closest to an easterly direction. Try to catch some glimpse of potential shelters that lie farther ahead so that you keep moving towards your goal, which will be directly east of where you emerge from my forest."

82

Here she paused and looked at him as if she were not sure how to choose her next words.

"What is it, Maia?"

"It is only... do you know how to navigate across open country using the sun as a guide?"

"Oh, well probably not. But my teacher... He said to bring this." Here, Eddie opened a pouch at the side of his pack and brought out his compass. He looked at it and, relieved to see that this world had a magnetic north just as his own did, held it out to her.

She took it, turned it over in her hand, and looked at the needle and the dial. Then she looked up, clearly puzzled.

"Turn it. The needle – the pointer – always points to the same direction, see?"

Immediately a light dawned in her uncanny eyes and she smiled again.

"Yes, I can see how this will work! And the magic behind it is reliable?"

"Yeah. It's reliable," Eddie replied with a slight smile of his own.

Maia turned so that she faced in the direction that the needle pointed. Then she pointed her right arm straight out from her side.

"This is the direction you must follow after you exit from my forest. The trade road will go this way for a time, but you must continue this direction when the road curves north."

This confirmed that in Maia's world's directions were consistent with those of his own.

"And my goal is the Inn?"

"No. Sadly, the Inn is much further and somewhat south of your first truly safe resting place."

"Which is?"

"The Old One. Call her my aunt, if you will; although that is not truly the way in which we are related. You will be safe at her holding. It is near the sea and has the appearance of a small farm. There will be a friendly dog to greet you, a few sheep and some chickens that stay close by. Perhaps a goat or two. The walls of her cottage will be fresh-plastered. It will be roofed with a thick thatch.

"She is powerful and ancient, Reed, although she will not necessarily appear so. I think that she is as old as the bones of this world... and as strong. If anyone can confound pursuers it will be she. She will be able to help you reach your goal. I have sent word to her to expect you in seven days."

"Seven days, huh?" Eddie mused aloud.

Maia looked sharply at him. "What is wrong?"

"Well I'll give it my best shot, but that's a long time to go with such small rations as I packed when I left my world."

"Oh, yes. I sometimes forget. I can help in that realm as well."

Michael C. Glaviano

She looked up into the nearby trees and life practically exploded from the branches. Squirrels and birds appeared and dropped nuts on the ground.

"Wow! Thanks!" Eddie got up and quickly began gathering nuts and stuffing them in his pockets.

"This will supplement what you have brought. As you eat them, leave the shells where they fall. My creatures will carry them and scatter your scent far and wide.

"Also, you now have some knowledge of what plants are safe to consume and which you must avoid. You will learn more from Auntie and you will learn more from the forest as you travel. Streams will cross your path and give you water, but you must avoid cooking fires, and..." here her voice trailed off.

"What?"

"Each day you must travel as far as you are able. And each night you must sleep quietly, hidden from view. You will do all of this in the arms of the trees."

"You're kidding! Joking, I mean."

"No, Reed. You can do this. It will be difficult, but I have asked my trees to help you. Look!"

Here she pointed up to the trees nearby.

"See the large, lower branches?"

Eddie swallowed. The branches she indicated were at least twelve feet above the ground. "Well, yeah. I see them."

"Look at the next tree to the east. See how the branches of one tree reach to the next?"

"Wow! Yeah, I see that now. How'd you do that?"

"It is as I said. I have asked my trees to help you. The placement of their branches will be your path. If you follow them you will not go astray."

Secretly, Eddie wasn't all that keen on scrambling from branch to branch a dozen feet off the ground for four days, but it was very clear that she thought this a necessary precaution. He kept his misgivings to himself.

"Well, thanks. I'll do as you say. And thank you... for... all that you've done."

But Maia wasn't quite done, "I've also taken a small piece of the fabric from the bottom of your shirt. I have given the scent that I found there to the animals of my forest. Even now, they fan out from this grove. They will carry your scent from place to place in ever widening circles. Their trails will cross and re-cross. This should further confound and slow those who follow."

"You've thought of everything. That's really cool," Eddie was thinking that this whole thing just might be possible. Difficult and dangerous, yes, but perhaps possible.

"And now, Reed, there is one more thing that is important to me. It may be important to you and your world as well. We spoke of it last night."

Here she looked down for a moment. Then she again met his eyes with that lovely, inhuman gaze. She brought forth – from where, he could not see – a small packet, an open package made of leaves. She held it forward.

"Look upon this, Reed," she demanded softly, seriously.

He looked. There were seeds and bits of moss and some feath-ers. A tiny pebble, some leaves and pine needles, something shiny as the scales of a brook trout, and other things as well lay there. He met her eyes again.

"And I am to carry that to my world?" he guessed.

"Yes, but first we must quicken it... I would ask you now: how did you come by that scar?"

"Scar?"

"Indeed. The scar upon your right cheek," she gestured.

"Ah. Well. One of the Queen's... um, agents, well, she did some-thing and I ended up with that scar."

"As I thought. I would erase it. I would replace it with a subtler mark of my own. May I?"

Now Eddie was very puzzled. They'd been talking about the seed packet. Now they seemed to be on a completely different subject. He gave up trying to figure it out.

"Sure, Maia. If you want to, that's fine, but..."

"Quiet then, Reed. We have little time. We begin. Watch. Do not flinch."

If Maia's beautiful eyes had seemed inhuman before, now they assumed a completely mystifying character. Her voice came again. It came from her lips and throat but also from the rocks, the soil, the trees, and the air around them:

> Eyes, talons of the falcon, strength of the bear.
> These are mine.
> Wiles of the crow and fox.
> These as well, I possess.
> Stealth of the cat.
> Gentleness of the mother wolf with her cubs.
> All these are mine.
> And beneath all, the memory of the world resides, lives,
breathes.

Without warning she lashed out with her left hand. The move-ment was a blur, much faster than human eyes could follow. Eddie felt a

Michael C. Glaviano

sharp pain on his cheek where Alica's hateful kiss had struck. He felt blood trickle from a newer, deeper wound.

"Now, dear Reed, bend forward. Quicken the life of this packet with the blood of your world!" Maia demanded.

Eddie bit his lip at the sudden pain. Now he understood the strange turn of conversation that had preceded Maia's action. He bent forward and saw blood drip from his face into the small, leaf-wrapped parcel that she held. A profound sense of strangeness enveloped him.

Again moving too fast to see, Maia's hands blurred and she held a tightly wrapped package. She extended it to him.

"Wrap this in the rabbit fur to protect it further. Guard it that you might bring it safely to your world."

He straightened, took the package, cradled it in his hands. It seemed small. It seemed weighty. He sensed how precious it was to her, how it might be to his world.

"Now, I must finish this and you must hasten away. Be still a moment. Do not move!" she ordered.

Holding his eyes now, she moved her hand slowly, gently toward the cuts on his cheek. Blood still welled there, and there was no small pain. He made as if to draw back, but she smiled and shook her head.

"No claws now, dear friend. Let me heal this."

She drew her small, pretty hand across the injury. He expected it to hurt, but after the first touch there was no discomfort. Replaced with a sense of warmth and well-being, the pain flew away and was gone.

"I hope that you are not angry, but there is no other way. Blood must be taken, given. Wounds must be healed. That is the way of life.

"Now," she continued, "if you are able to place that packet in a safe place in your world, my forest will grow there... I will see the earth, the sky, the water of your world. My forest will do its part to heal and restore the life there. Magic will return.

"That is, if you still wish it." She finished, looked away.

Eddie took a deep breath and let it out. Mindful now of her power and magic, he reached gently toward her and took her hand. "Of course I wish it. I can't think of anything that I'd want more."

"That must be enough for now. There is a bond between you and me. But know this, Reed Woodruff: you must keep the deepest places in your soul open to the love of a human woman. My forest and I are one. Although I feel close to you in this time and although my memory of you will last as long as my forest survives, from my perspective a human life is but a few seasons of joy and sorrow. This does not mean that I do not care, but the boundaries of time are definite and severe."

She gazed far off for a moment, and Eddie thought that perhaps what she saw in that great distance brought the tiniest of smiles to her lips. Then she shook herself and refocused her attention on him. "Now

86

you must secure this precious parcel at the bottom of your pack and be on your way."

Eddie looked down at the pack that lay at his feet. He knelt and pulled everything out. He wrapped Maia's parcel within the dried rabbit skin and tucked it at the bottom of his pack. It took only a minute to replace his few possessions.

As he moved, he realized that the nuts he'd gathered and stuffed in his pockets would be uncomfortable in a long hike, so he emptied his pockets and distributed the nuts here and there in his pack. He was glad to have them. The nuts did not constitute a balanced diet, but if he were able to supplement it with a few other plant edibles, he'd be fine for a week or so.

Quickly, too quickly, he was ready. Eddie stood still, looked around the camp one last time. He glanced back at Maia.

"You must go now," Maia insisted. "There is no more time. Reed, know this. If somehow things work out, we will see each other again. And no matter what lies ahead, we part friends. If the worlds – at least some of them – can heal, there will be much joy. But now you must go somewhere else and I must move into the deep, secret places where the creatures of the Locust Queen cannot follow."

He imagined that he felt a cold wind rising. "Okay. I guess I'll try to shinny up the trunk of the tree."

"There is no need. Here. I will lift you to the first branch."

She leaned back against the nearby tree and held out her hands. He was again struck by their beauty. They seemed so small, delicate.

"Are you sure? I don't want to hurt you," Eddie said.

Despite the tension in the air, she laughed hard. For an instant, the animals in the branches echoed her laughter and Eddie remembered for the hundredth time that she was not truly as she appeared. Slightly embarrassed, he placed a hiking boot in her right hand and leaned forward to rest his hands on the tree trunk above her head.

"Are you ready?" she asked.

"I guess."

Then, lifting him and his gear as easily has he'd lift a kitten, she raised her hand slowly and carefully over her head. She used her left hand to brace his ankle, to steady him. As she did this, he walked his hands up the trunk to keep his balance. He was just able to reach the bottom branch and pull himself up.

"Now stand and reach above you. There will be branches nearby that you can use to keep your balance. If you are careful, you will be able to walk from tree to tree. Trust to the path of the branches and you will not go astray."

"What will I do when I need to come down to get water and to rest?"

"Along the way you will find branches placed to help, but you must stay in the trees as much as you can! And when night falls, you must look for a place where you can nest in the branches."

The reality of what lay before him was becoming clearer and Eddie's confidence was wilting in equal measure. Not wanting to betray his feelings, he nodded his assent and Maia continued.

"Farewell, my human friend. Move quickly but carefully. Be wary. Use your second sight when you can but be careful of that as well. There are those who will find it easy to detect."

He couldn't think of anything else to say but "Farewell, Maia. Thank you. I..." here his voice trailed off.

Despite his lack of words, she understood. She smiled an almost-human smile then and made a shooing motion with her hands. He turned his attention to the branches and the way southeast. As he set out, he looked back once, but she had already vanished into the mystery of her forest.

Ten

Still haunted, still hungering for revenge, Alicia was abroad again. Bruised far beyond her physical injuries, she wrapped herself in what preparations she could and entered the Place to cast about for her quarry. She dodged and hid from those dwellers whom she wished to avoid. She hurt and drove away those who were weaker. As she searched, she came across sights, images in the mists of the Great Hub that held the potential to confuse or distract her. These she avoided as well. All the while, she sought a trail. With all her skill and a malevolence that strayed well beyond the jagged borders of madness, she sought her prey.

Eventually, she found the path the young one had likely taken. Of the old man there was no sign. She paused near the tenuous boundaries of the boundary-less Place and flung her awareness outward into a world that was only beginning to draw the hungry attention of the Queen. Excited then, she called forth more power than was wise in her fragile state. She was rewarded. Alicia perceived the young one in a grove of trees. The grove lay at the edge of a forest near a portal to the Place. Now that Alicia had located the young one, he would be easy to run down.

Alicia descended back into the Place, shrouded herself in the mists and shadows to ponder her next move. Hours or seconds or centuries later, she transited back to the Blue World and begged some means of driving the young one to ground. The sincerity of her plea was made obvious by her pain, and she was granted three of the Queen's hounds. These were a cross between large wolves and true hounds. They were bred and cross-bread to produce specimens that were strong and fearsome to behold. They were also intelligent, savage creatures that would barely obey Alicia's commands. When the time came, it would be difficult to keep them from rending their quarry, but that was acceptable.

The injured agent had some ability to alter weather patterns in the worlds and it was her plan to use this skill to slow the young one and make him easy to run down. The exercise of this ability would cost her dearly, but that did not matter now. All would be well once Alicia brought the young one – or some identifiable parts of him anyway – back to the Queen. Success would bring with it reward: Alicia's torment would be salved; she would be restored.

The hounds near, bound by her will, she again used the gate in the Queen's palace to return to the Place. From there she began to track the young one in earnest. The path of his flight was clear, but the ministrations of the the Locust Queen had weakened her, and she could not move rapidly while simultaneously holding the Queen's hounds to heel.

After some hours, she reached a forest – one that was a danger to her and those who trod the same path as she. This forest was too healthy, too strong. It had the potential of spanning worlds and making them accessible to the dreams of the gods and, thus, the potential of fostering the kinds of thinking that made the denizens of the worlds hard to control, hard to crush and consume.

This forest should have been weakened by a changed beast that had been let loose here some time back, yet the forest was vigorous and alive and very much aware of Alicia and the hounds. This awareness wore upon them as they reluctantly entered the living maze of the forest. The hounds howled and snapped, fought against her control. The beasts of the forest were nowhere to be seen.

The forest was silent all around them. The great hounds were confused and pulled in different directions. It was as though their quarry had left no clear scent to follow. Angry, frustrated, fearful, Alicia was tempted to burn the forest, but this was early summer. Everything was green, moist, and alive. There was little underbrush, none of it dry.

And, worst of all, this place was full of a magic she could not fathom, much less overcome. She hadn't the strength to burn such a forest; she could barely abide here, barely walk here. In her current, fragile state, it would be complete folly to do more than move ahead in search of the young one. He bore half of the responsibility for her sorry condition. Bringing him down might half-way restore her.

But how to track him? She had expected a clear trail. The dwellers of the forest were completely hidden. They watched. She knew they watched! But she could not grip them, could not see them. She did not want to be in this forest, but she knew she must stay. The Queen would accept nothing less than the fulfillment of her wishes, the consummation of her desires.

An idea surfaced. Alicia would range back-and-forth. It would take time, but she could go boldly and quickly. She would send storms before her to harry her prey, a different storm each day in a different part of the forest. The youngster was not an experienced woodsman. He might go to ground, hole up and seek shelter. He might lose his way. Surely, he would make a mistake and leave a trail. Then she and the hounds would be upon him.

Traveling northeast, they set out. They loped to the border of the forest, turned to follow the border and scan the open terrain beyond the woodland. Then they reversed direction and travelled southeast. Once they reached the southern extent, they again turned. This zig-zag march formed their search pattern. Alicia and the hounds burned energy at a frightful rate, but they did not stop. She was hollow with hunger; they were ravenous with it. Bending the hounds to her will, she drove them and herself onward.

Michael C. Glaviano

Eleven

It took some time and no few bruises, scrapes, and bumps to get used to following an elevated highway of living tree branches, but gradually Eddie learned. The trick was to use a hand-over-hand motion on the branches above while keeping his eyes on the larger branches below. He grew sensitive to the size of what he began to think of as his "balance branches" and paused for a second to look up as they tapered and became too small to be safe.

Each time he looked up, he could see another branch within reach. Then he was able to return his attention to the placement of his feet.

After the first half-hour or so, the young man grew tired and irritable. His shuffling gate didn't cover much distance, and holding his arms above his head wasn't any fun. Still, he kept at it. Little-by-little, he developed a rhythm to his movements and made decent progress through the rest of the morning.

When, by the light filtering through the tree canopy, Eddie finally sensed that the sun was nearly overhead, he decided to take a short break. Carefully, he picked his way over to the nearest tree trunk and sat down. His arms, his neck, and his upper back felt tired. It was good to lean against the bark and rest.

He rolled his shoulders and neck and stretched as best he could. Using the handle of his knife, he broke open a few nuts and snacked on them. Trusting Maia's instructions, he let the shells fall for her animals to collect. As he ate and rested, he looked around the forest floor but recognized none of the plants nearby as edible.

After resting for a few minutes, Eddie sipped from his water bottle, replaced it in his pack, and got to his feet. His arms and legs, neck and back protested as he set off, but here his youth was on his side. Within a few minutes he was back into his rhythm and the discomfort retreated.

A soft breeze came up and this, plus the shade of the tree canopy, kept him comfortable. The trees were as reliable a guide as anyone could hope to find. The small forest animals and birds went about their business largely undisturbed by his passage.

As he moved along his arboreal path, he occasionally paused to look around. He wasn't yet comfortable enough to change his focus away from hands and feet while he moved, but when he stopped to take a breath and stretch, he tried to notice his surroundings.

There were four, perhaps five regular birdcalls within earshot. Once in a while he saw a rabbit dart from rocks to bush to shadow on the forest floor. Squirrels kept an eye on him from a safe distance, but they were obviously curious about this big creature that was making his way through their territory. In a way that he'd never before experienced, Eddie felt himself woven into the life of the forest.

The forest contained several different types of trees; although Eddie wasn't yet enough of an outdoorsman to match them with real certainty against those he'd studied with Joe. He thought that there were sycamores and maybe some kind of elm. Occasionally, he'd encounter something that looked like an oak. There were few conifers, so clearly this was a seasonal forest rather than an evergreen forest. There were also clusters of birch scattered here and there. He'd read that diversity was a sign of a healthy forest and this forest certainly looked healthy.

There were signs of game trails and from time to time, Eddie came across small groups of animals that looked very much like white-tailed deer. Just once, a fox poked its head from a thicket and watched Eddie as he passed. From time-to-time, the trees Eddie followed skirted the edges of grassy clearings.

Mid-afternoon came and went, and when his path crossed a gently flowing stream, Eddie decided that another break was in order. He stopped and looked around. Just a few feet away, a rough-barked tree had fallen against another, and he thought that this could provide an easy path to and from the forest floor. On his left, one of the occasional clearings held some bushes that contained berries.

Carefully, Eddie made his way to the ground. It felt strange after so many hours of travel on the resilient branches to set his feet on the unyielding earth. It felt strange, but good.

Eddie stretched and took off his pack near the stream. He drank a little and refilled his water bottle. Then he turned his attention to the clearing and the bushes it held. Remembering Maia's words of caution, Eddie crouched down as he reached the edge of the clearing. He got as still as he could and waited and watched.

After several minutes of watching, Eddie had seen or heard nothing out of the ordinary, but just to be safe, he circled about a quarter of the way around the clearing without leaving the shelter of the trees. At this point the wild blueberry bushes were about ten feet away from him. They shone invitingly in the afternoon sunlight.

Slowly, tentatively, he edged into the open. All remained good, bright, and safe. Still, Eddie caught himself holding his breath as he made his way to the bushes. The berries were ripe and sweet and there were plenty of them, but he didn't want to eat too many berries all at once. With some regret, Eddie turned his back on the sweet fruit and returned to the edge of the clearing. Finally, he retraced his steps to where he'd left his pack.

When he reached his pack, Eddie turned to look across the sunny clearing at the heavily laden bushes. Was there a way he could gather more berries for later? After a moment's thought Eddie had the idea that he might make a pouch by tying a knot in the sleeve of his spare shirt. He could fill it with berries and tie it to the outside of his pack! It took only a minute to get the shirt out of his pack and tie a knot near the cuff. He turned back to face the clearing. Since he'd made one trip out and back without incident, Eddie thought that it would probably be fine simply to walk out to the bush this time.

He'd walked no more than half a dozen paces from the sheltering trees when a cold wind came at him from the north. The previously bright, blue sky darkened. Instinctively, Eddie crouched down. The wind turned icy, and a distant howling reached his ears. Blueberries forgotten, he threw himself on his belly and wiggled back to the trees as quickly as he could. To the west, the first howl was answered by another.

No sooner had Eddie reached the shelter of the trees when the sky darkened even more and the air began to pulse as if some gigantic, exposed heart were beating, pounding somewhere to the north. Immediately around him, the forest had fallen silent, but Eddie felt that his own heart was pounding hard enough to be heard from the other side of the clearing.

As quickly and as quietly as he possibly could, Eddie shouldered his pack and made his way up the fallen tree to the lower branches of his "highway." At the lower branches, he paused, looked around, and wondered if there were a way to dislodge the tree that had provided his way down and then back up to the branches. Almost immediately, however, he discarded that notion. If trackers came this way, they'd figure out where he was with or without that tree in place. Even if it were possible, knocking that tree loose would take up time better spent getting away.

Now his hours of practice earlier in the day began to pay dividends. Following the path provided by the trees, Eddie moved quickly and efficiently away from the clearing. As he put more distance behind him, the forest around him gradually returned to normal.

After perhaps an hour of steady progress, Eddie's heart had stopped pounding and he decided it was safe – as safe as it was going to get anyway – to pause and reflect on what had happened. What had that been? One minute the clearing had been warm and sunny, and then within a matter of seconds, the pleasant atmosphere had changed to one of cold and hostility. What at first had been safe and welcoming had become dangerous, charged with fear.

If there had been any doubt in Eddie's mind that he was the object of a search by someone who meant him ill, that doubt had been put to rest. His life was different than it had ever been. As Joe had warned, it was indeed as if he had been marked in some indelible way.

Eddie thought back to Maia. She was strange, inhuman, yet she was also kind, full of warmth, and plain goodness. He wondered when – or if – he would again feel that sense of connection. He hoped it would return but could afford to spend little time on the memory of it. The young man shrugged his pack into a more comfortable position and turned his attention to the path. He continued on his way with all the speed and care he could muster.

* * *

As the afternoon wore on, Eddie was convinced that he'd escaped notice this time. He'd been lucky and quick... mostly lucky. His world shrank down to his immediate surroundings: the life close by in the forest. The next handhold. The next branch. The next spot to place his foot. Sounds. Changes in temperature. The gradual lengthening of the shadows.

His arms and legs were tired and he itched from a million tiny scratches on his hands, neck, and face. The thought of six more days of hard travel was daunting, and he did his best to push that thought away. He paused more and more to rest and sip from his water bottle. The bottle was now only half full, and Eddie was glad that he'd crossed that stream and been able to drink there and then fill the bottle.

Just how far did the forest goddess expect him to travel in a single day? Did she understand the limits of human strength and agility? How good was her estimate of four days to the edge of her forest? Again, he pushed those thoughts aside and tried his best to focus on his movements.

Clearly he was becoming dangerously fatigued. With a start, Eddie pulled himself from a daydream. He barely caught himself as his balance wavered on a branch that was more than adequately wide and flat. Peering ahead into the gathering shadows, he reminded himself that if he fell he would probably be seriously injured. And even if he were not the object of pursuit, being seriously injured in a forest was pretty much the end of the line for a lone traveler.

So, Eddie began looking around for an appropriate tree. He needed something that would shelter and support him for the night. As he approached each trunk, he looked around for a way that he might construct, from his tarp, ropes, and blanket, a place to sleep. He'd never slept in a hammock and was worried that he might turn over in his slumber and be dumped to the ground, so his thought was to use the tarp to fashion a kind of pouch that would hold him while he slept.

Eventually, he found some stout branches on neighboring trees. Each branch pointed almost directly to the opposing tree. This was just what he needed. First, Eddie used a spare bungee cord to attach his pack to the nearest tree. He unfastened his tarp from the bottom of the pack and folded the waterproof material in half to make an envelope five feet wide and eight feet long. To form the foot of his nest, he laced one edge together and tied it to a branch. For the head, he fastened only the bottom half of the tarp to the opposite branch. Finally, he laced the side closed for two-thirds of its length and thereby created a sort of bag that could keep him safe. He put his thermal blanket inside this.

Nest secure, he rummaged through his pack and took inventory of his supplies. Then he went through all the nuts that Maia's creatures had gathered for him. When organized more carefully, he had enough to fill the two, largest pockets on his pack. So he figured that his rations would be light for the next few days, but as long as he made it to Maia's "aunt's" farm, he'd be fine. If he were able to gather some more wild berries or other plant edibles along the way, it would be even better.

Now that he had his food organized, he looked through his other things. There wasn't much, but so far it had proven adequate. Reflecting back on that night when he packed, he was very glad that he'd taken the time to pay attention to what he was doing.

At the very bottom of his pack he saw the bundle that Maia had given him for safekeeping. For a little while, Eddie toyed with the thought of unwrapping it and looking it over, but it didn't feel right, so he left it there and hoped that someday, somehow, he'd be able to plant it in his own world. He wanted to do at least that much for her, but at that moment the goal seemed far away.

Eddie replaced most of the things in his pack and made a sketchy meal from his stores. Next, he carefully unlaced his boots and put them and his socks inside the pack. He pulled out his thermal underwear and crawled into his little pouch in the branches. Once safely ensconced, he changed into his thermal underwear and rolled his pants and shirt up. His jacket could be a pillow. If the weather stayed mild he knew that he'd be comfortable. At first he thought that he'd have a hard time falling asleep in such strange surroundings, but he felt reasonably good and was very tired. As he lay back, the shadows were dark and the forest was in deep twilight.

"End of day one," he muttered to himself as he drifted off to sleep.

* * *

Even though it stayed warm and mild for most of the night, a combination of cool, moist pre-dawn air, empty stomach, and sore muscles woke Eddie at first light. For a few minutes, he tried to get comfortable and go back to sleep but he could tell that it wasn't going to happen, so he sat up and stretched. His ground-cloth/tent/pouch had kept the dew off and his things were dry. He looked around and prepared to emerge into the early morning.

The limbs of the trees made darker shadows in the deep twilight surrounding him. Night animals were heading back to their dens. Day animals had not yet emerged from their burrows. Here and there, high in the treetops, Eddie could hear the few birds who could see the sky lightening to the east. He shivered as he gingerly crawled from his nest to get ready for the day.

A few swallows of water followed by a food bar, a little dried fruit and some jerky constituted breakfast. This would be the first of many mornings when Eddie thought wistfully about lingering over a hot cup of coffee. His meager breakfast was just enough to wake his stomach fully, but he knew that once he got moving the empty feeling would diminish – at least for a while.

Despite the cold and the discomfort, Eddie was actually in decent spirits. He'd made it through a day of travel and a night of treetop camping. Collecting his thoughts, he sat with his back to the trunk of the tree and breathed in the cool air.

After half an hour or so, light had penetrated the forest canopy sufficiently to make it safe for Eddie to gather his gear, untie and roll his tarp, and stow everything in his pack. His back and shoulders ached a little as he put on the pack, but he was young and healthy and easily able to shrug that off.

By this time there was enough light to see his way, so Eddie started out. The branches were slippery with dew and he knew that he was stiff and still somewhat sleepy, so he moved with deliberate caution as he warmed up. Also, he needed to stop at the next source of drinking water to refill his bottle, so he often paused to peer into the dim light of the forest floor.

As he shuffled carefully along the damp branches, Eddie was struck by the quiet that lay behind the sounds. He could sense the daytime forest coming alive. More birds were out. Although it did not penetrate very far into the lower branches, a breeze stirred the treetops. The forest skills that Joe in his way and Maia in hers had tried to give him verged upon awakening. He looked at the world around him and was aware of its richness, its complexity, and its balance.

The subtle interplay of scents that characterize a living forest reached his nostrils. Leaves, flowers, animals, the mouldering detritus that lay beneath the trees and shrubs, scents of life and death, growth and decay, all swirled through the cool, morning dampness. Eddie breathed it all in and felt himself immersed, peacefully enveloped within the atmosphere of the woodland.

He was getting better at recognizing the types of trees and other plants. Yes, those definitely were sycamores, elms, and scrub oaks. Yes, that clearly was a birch grove. The sun touched the topmost branches of a huge live oak off in a clearing to the right. That bush was obviously poisonous hemlock, that one nettle. There was great burdock and wild rose, both edible.

Just being able to recognize some edible plants with confidence allayed Eddie's concerns regarding food. By the time he heard the sound of running water, it was light enough to climb down safely, drink some water, and gather some food.

As Eddie neared the little stream, he started moving very slowly and looking around even more carefully. He found a good place to climb down from the branches, but he waited there, motionless for several minutes, to make sure that he was alone and unobserved.

Eventually, he decided that it was safe, so he worked his way down from the trees and onto the forest floor. The first order of business was to get his water bottle filled and stowed. Then he had a long drink and a few more nuts from his supply.

He saw dandelion and remembered that the root could be boiled to make a tea-like drink, but he'd brought no utensils, and anyway he recalled Maia's insistence that he avoid cooking fires. He picked some of the leaves, however, and enjoyed the intense, fresh flavor. Eddie also noticed some wild roses to add to his breakfast. Careful to avoid the sharp thorns, he picked some and enjoyed these as well.

Then he realized that he was stalling. He stretched one last time and returned to the tree for the climb up to the branches. With one final look around, he started off. Again, the trees provided a pathway that was manageable as long as he paid attention.

Eddie's second day on the elevated treeway passed uneventfully. He remained careful and alert and established a good, steady rhythm to his movements. His muscles adjusted to the work and he found himself able to relax and enjoy the beauty of the woodland. As he adapted to his mode of travel, Eddie found that the day flowed easily, swiftly, and he made solid progress towards the southeast edge of Maia's forest.

The young man stopped at a couple of streams for water and to eat and continued to find here and there, a few plants about which he felt sufficiently confident to add to his diet. At the end of the day, Eddie again built himself a nest and settled in to sleep. As on his first night aloft, sleep came easily.

Again he woke at first light, repeated his morning routine. He stretched and felt his sore muscles loosen as they anticipated the work that lay before them. Eddie slipped his arms into his pack. It was beginning to feel familiar and he rolled his shoulders a little to get the straps

Michael C. Glaviano

right. A deep breath brought the ever-changing tapestry of scents to him; his ears were again attuned to the birds, the wind in the trees.

"Okay, Maia" he whispered to the forest around him. "Here goes day three."

100

Twelve

After two days and two nights of searching, of chasing the youngster's scent only to find that it led nowhere, Alicia had some sense of what was going on. He must be traveling downwind from her and her hounds, and somehow he was managing to scatter his scent. Doggedly, Alicia continued her search, but both she and the hounds were raw and tired. They chased here and there through the hateful forest to find trails that tapered off into nothing. It was clear that the woods conspired with her quarry to confound her and hamper her movements.

Frequently, the scent of their quarry led through dense thickets. She and the hounds forced their way through only to find that the trail had evaporated. She was scratched and filthy. Her feet hurt terribly. Her once beautiful hair was tangled and full of leaves, twigs, and only the gods knew what vermin.

The hounds were hungry, irritable, barely controllable. They whirled and snapped at each other continually. Several times she caught one or more of them staring at her, as if weighing her ability to fight them off. Each time she noticed this appraisal, she hurt them. Inflicting pain used a little more of her waning power, but it kept the hounds focused on her commands. Pain kept them afraid and bent to her will.

As they moved through the forest, she sent out tendrils of storm. This too cost her, but she was sure that it would also confuse and weaken a youngster who was traveling alone through an unknown forest. She imagined him herded by the storms. She pictured him huddled and afraid. Still he eluded them.

The afternoon wore on. Finally, the hounds sensed something in the air. Alicia thought it likely that her quarry was southeast of her, so she summoned much of her remaining power and sent an intense winter storm careening through the forest in that direction.

They continued their zigzag course but reduced the amplitude of their swings through the woodland. Reluctantly, she and the hounds stayed nearer the mid-line of the forest. It was hard for Alicia to imagine anyone – even her quarry – wanting to stay near the center of such a watchful, alive place, but apparently he was doing just that.

Michael C. Glaviano

Her fatigue and irritation grew. The animals strained and pulled. At some basic level, Alicia knew that she should stop and rest, but there was no shelter. And she could not risk sleep with the hounds near. That was certain. She was hungry too, but there was nothing to eat. Nothing. She pushed away the feelings of hunger and exhaustion. She pushed away all thoughts but those of the hunt. With grim excitement, she anticipated the release that revenge would bring.

Thirteen

The first part of the day was largely a repeat of the previous two. By this time, Eddie had a rhythm firmly established and was making good time. He continued to find wild edibles and his supplies were holding out well. With the exception of the frightening incident at the clearing on the first day, there was no sign of pursuit. He began to think, to hope that this trip would be easy and uneventful.

Late in the third afternoon, however, the temperature started to drop. The sky darkened drastically, and what light that filtered through the canopy became dull and gray. Rain pattered its way through the multitude of leaves that comprised the upper reaches of the forest.

The leaves sheltered Eddie from the direct effects of the storm, but eventually his hands became wet and cold. The world around him was muted and close. The sound of the rain muffled everything else. The birds grew still. The branches became slippery, but Eddie pressed on.

Without warning, he lost footing and clutched at the branch above him. His hands, now stiff with cold, missed their grip and he slipped. He banged his left knee hard as his foot came off the branch. He managed to arrest his fall on the broad branch – mainly by crashing against it with his ribs and the side of his face. His hat came off, but he snatched it from the air before it fluttered to the ground.

Panting, he lay there, left arm wrapped over the branch, right hand crushing his battered hat. He hurt in three places and could feel that he'd cut his face on the rough bark. He took a deep breath and thought that although his ribs were surely bruised, they probably weren't broken.

Slowly, carefully, Eddie pulled himself together on the branch and replaced his hat. He half slid, half crawled to the nearest trunk and lay back against it. Secure for the moment, he hugged his arms against his sides and shivered – from the cold, yes, but also from the adrenaline rush. Eddie knew beyond a doubt that if he'd hit his head on the way down or if he'd fallen to the forest floor and landed wrong, he'd now be dead or unconscious.

Michael C. Glaviano

Now that he was sitting still, Eddie could hear distant, ominous sounds. Neither baying nor howling, but some evil, frantic mixture of both, sounds of pursuit reached his ears. Were these the hounds that Maia had mentioned? If so, they could be nothing much like a normal hound.

Again a pulsing, beating sound reached his ears and brought a shiver that had nothing to do with the cold rain. That pulsing sound reminded him of drums – or the beating of a gigantic heart. Eddie thought back to the incident in the clearing. On that first day of the trek, these sounds had come from the north, now they were more directly behind him.

The temperature continued to fall, and the raindrops were icy on his skin. Eddie knew that he was in trouble and needed to set up his shelter. He looked around. The trees were more trackless here, but above Eddie's head was another branch. He pulled himself up. As he put weight on his left leg, his knee gave a twinge, and, afraid of doing more damage, he backed off immediately. His shifted most of his weight to his uninjured right leg.

Carefully, slowly, painfully, Eddie pulled himself up to the next level of branches. Here, now over sixteen feet above the forest floor, he spied a place where he might set up his camp and hide from the weather and whatever might be tracking him.

The first order of business was the pack. He got it off his shoulders and carefully fastened it to the branch with a spare bungee cord. Eddie checked and rechecked that his pack was secure. Losing it now would be a disaster. He crammed his hat into the top of the pack. Trying to control his breathing and shivering, he unpacked the tarp and blanket and set up what he now called his nest. He stowed some food and his water bottle inside the nest and checked his pack one more time to make sure that it was secured to the branch and tightly closed.

Then, sitting on top of his nest, he got out of his damp clothes and pulled on his long underwear and his extra socks. He added his spare shirt. Then he crawled inside his makeshift tent and pulled the flap over himself. The rain continued to fall and the temperature continued to drop. Eddie continued to shiver, but as he huddled, wrapped in his blanket, he gradually grew warmer.

His left knee throbbed and he probed the sore area. The tenderness was centered on the outside of the knee. He noted with relief that there was little swelling but couldn't tell whether he'd merely bruised the area or whether he had suffered a more serious injury to the joint itself. Carefully, slowly, he brought the injured leg up as he bent the knee. Then just as slowly, he straightened the leg. The knee joint moved easily and the pain held steady. In the absence of any other information, Eddie decided that this was a good sign.

The hounds or wolves or whatever they were continued to howl in the distance. Their baying calls grew louder, then softer, then louder again, but he could tell they were trending nearer. The pulse of the huge heart, the pounding, the cold rain, all continued. He wondered how cold it would get and if his improvised nest would be adequate.

After some time, in the midst of his fretting, Eddie dropped into a deep sleep. He dreamed of pursuers. He dreamed of food. Finally, he dreamed that Maia was telling him to awake, and he struggled from the dream.

As he folded back a corner of the cold-stiffened tarp, Eddie saw that the rain had turned to sleet and then to snow. The tarp had kept him dry, and he was actually warm. The air was icy cold, but he could feel warmth radiating from the forest floor. Carefully, gingerly, he peeked over the edge of his tarp and was astounded to see 35 or 40 female elk, gathered on the ground immediately below him.

The great animals were amazing to see (and to smell) by the leaf-filtered, silvery light of the waxing moon, and Eddie could hear them chewing, farting, and rustling as they huddled together beneath the trees. It was far too early in the season for calves, and the largest, strongest cows stood at the boundary of the herd.

In the dim light, Eddie could also make out a much smaller group that consisted of a few, massive bulls. Separate from the larger herd of cows, the huge males were arrayed in an arc that faced west and north. As Eddie watched and listened, the animals became agitated and called to one another. The bugles were neither a mating call nor the challenge of rutting season but something else, something that conveyed a sense of urgency and warning.

Then Eddie heard the howling bay of his pursuers. They were very close. In the dim, silvery light, he made out three large shapes in the lead and another, smaller one behind. These newcomers emerged from the shadows of the forest. He thought that the one in the back looked human. Those in the front were the source of the baying. Clearly, these were the hounds.

Michael C. Glaviano

Fourteen

Now that the scent of the elk was in the noses of the hounds, the trackers were uncontrollable. Driven beyond command by the smell of the herbivores, they lunged toward the herd in the moonlight. Alicia called to them, punished them, but they ignored her and snapped at the places where she stung them.

Standing antler-to-antler, huge bulls formed a living wall between the hounds and the much larger herd of females. The powerful bull elk were having none of this attack. Alicia watched, aghast, as the maddened hounds lunged and were caught and tossed by those great antlers. Oh, they dodged, and they struck with wide, ravenous jaws, and they certainly injured one or more of the males – perhaps seriously – but they were only three, and the end of the battle was sure at the outset.

Only one of the three hounds made it past the bulls. Wounded, the hound leapt at the line of females and was met with a deadly kick from a powerful foreleg. There was a snap, a yelp of pain, and the final hound was hurled backwards. For a few seconds it struggled to rise, but then it fell back and was still.

What Alicia did not realize until it was too late was that the enraged elk also sensed her presence. When they finished stomping the remains of the hounds into the forest floor, they turned towards her and came on fast. She barely had time to use the last of her energy, her power, to find refuge in a tree some twenty-five yards from the herd's western boundary.

Even so, she was not quite fast enough. One of the great elk gored her leg before she could swing it out of his way. Her wild cry of fear and pain, rang out in the icy darkness.

Alicia's cry caught Eddie's attention, but in the moonlight, shadows and trees, he could see little and recognize less. Even so, he was sure that he knew the source of that cry, and he went wide awake. His arms and legs twitched with fear and adrenalin. His own hurts were forgotten and, thankful for the warmth around him, Eddie settled back into his nest to watch and wait.

"Thank you for the elk, Maia," he whispered.

Michael C. Glaviano

The great animals milled around for perhaps another hour. Then the elk once again divided into separate, male and female herds. Quietly, as the moonlight dimmed, the two groups moved in different directions, off into the night.

Fifteen

Despite the fear and wild events of the night, sometime around dawn, Eddie must have dozed off, because he woke to more seasonal temperature. The immediate vicinity was shrouded in a dense fog. The vanished herds left a huge quantity of elk droppings, the crushed and trampled bodies of the hounds, and almost total silence in their wake.

In the first light of the morning, Eddie felt better than he thought he would after his near-fall the previous day. He rubbed his face in the silence. Then he pulled himself together and began to make plans for the day. He decided that before he left, he had to check the area to try to see at close hand what had happened.

His ribs were tender to the touch. On the other hand, the pain in his left knee had subsided, and the joint was still flexible. Huddled inside his nest, Eddie changed into his clothes. They were still damp from the previous day's rain, but they were at least warm. Moving very carefully, Eddie emerged from his nest and reached his pack. He pulled out his shoes and socks.

After repacking, he worked his way gingerly from his high perch. It took a long time. At each step, he was conscious of his bruised knee and did his best to support his weight with his arms. This convinced him that his ribs, while bruised, were not broken. The immediate area remained silent, still deserted, but the fog was lifting in the warmth of an early summer's morning.

Slowly and carefully, he followed fifteen or more trees before he finally found a way from the branches to the ground. Once down, he limped back to the site of the night's battle. Eddie could see, even gored and crushed as they had been, that the hounds had been huge, ferocious creatures. The reek of their trampled carcasses, the blood, the scattered contents of their bowels, made him gag, and he backed away from the grisly scene.

He tried flexing his knee again and imagined that it was beginning to limber with movement. He was gazing up at the branches and dreading the day ahead when his reverie was interrupted. Eddie's heart

Michael C. Glaviano

practically jumped from his chest as the sound of weeping reached his ears.

Trembling, crouching, limping, he made his way toward the sound. It took only a minute to find her. It was indeed Alicia. She was skinny, dirty and, clearly mad with fear, but she was still recognizable. She clung to a tree trunk twenty feet above the forest floor.

As Eddie approached, she first heard and then saw him. Her weeping stopped and she hissed like some bizarre, hunting reptile. Then she scrambled down to the bottom branches and leapt from the tree at him. Her hands were outstretched like claws.

She looked surprised as she fell straight down and hit the ground hard. Even though he knew she meant him ill and that she was dangerous, on the ground, huddled and shivering, she looked frail and pathetic. Her right leg was scored by a huge gash. Eddie saw that it had stopped bleeding some hours ago but had reopened with the impact.

Her painful fall had, for the moment, taken the will to attack out of her. Panting and weeping, she ignored him as he drew near. Despite himself, Eddie crouched beside her and looked at her leg. The bleeding wasn't serious but the gash looked painful. Eddie had no bandages, but he had one fresh tee shirt left in his pack.

Unloading his pack, he rummaged around and pulled out the shirt. It was a simple matter for him to cut some strips of cloth, to brush some dirt from the wound, and to improvise a dressing. He offered her some water from his bottle and one of his precious food bars, but she hissed at him, knocked the food from his hands and tried to claw him again.

"Okay, lady, I guess that's enough. Even though I know that you were after me, I can't leave you here."

Eddie didn't know what to do with her though. He couldn't carry her. His ribs and knee wouldn't stand for that, and anyway, he knew she'd try to hurt him (or worse) if she got the chance.

Wondering what he could do, he once again looked around his immediate vicinity. He reasoned that it was probably safe to travel this last day on the ground. Had there been more than one party close after him, they'd almost certainly have been here by now. He could make good time on the forest floor. Besides, he didn't want to risk his knee on the arboreal path.

In the end, he decided to try to make a travois for her and bring her to the edge of the forest at least. As soon as he made that decision, there came the sound of cracking in the trees above and he looked up in time to see two long, straight limbs and four or five smaller ones, tumble to the forest floor. Several of the limbs were festooned with vines. Evidently Maia, in some sense anyway, approved of the decision.

It took Eddie nearly an hour to cobble together a travois and to get Alicia tied to it. She kept trying to bite and scratch him, but she was very weak. He felt strangely calm and rested, however – as if he'd had an infusion of strength. As he worked, he recalled what Maia had told him right after he'd dispatched the creature that had been hurting her trees. Something about the energy flowing back into her. He wondered if somehow the events of last night had similarly helped him.

He shrugged off the thought. Glad to feel good and happy to be moving, he lifted the ends of his makeshift litter and set off. By then, the crows had found the carcasses of the hounds. The shiny black birds squawked and argued in the morning sun as they spread the news of the feast. Soon, the bodies of the hounds would add to the nourishment and rich life of the forest. The ugliness of the scene would be erased.

Eddie used the trees above his head as a guide and, even walking around the trunks of large trees and trying to avoid bumping his unhappy passenger, he made excellent time. He was careful of his footing and his knee loosened up as he walked along the smooth forest floor. His arms and legs were strong with the steady exercise of his trip and, earlier, his mentor's strenuous fitness regimen. Even with the weight the travois behind him, even with bruised ribs and a sore leg, it felt fine to stride along the firm ground.

Eddie's heart lifted still further when, by mid-morning, the trees began to thin and he could see the edge of the forest. "Good-bye, Maia!" he called. "I hope we see each other again!" This elicited an inarticulate shriek from Alicia, but birds sang and butterflies flitted among the branches as he left the forest.

Ahead the ground became a gentle, grassy slope that was dotted here and there with outlying trees and shrubs. In one of the final, shady spots, Eddie spied another example of sweet woodruff, the plant that Maia had used to name him. Perhaps five hundred yards ahead, he could make out the line of the trade road that Maia had told him to look for, and he walked in that direction. Dragging the travois down the gentle slope was easier than winding among the trees, and he moved along quickly.

Soon, he reached the trade road. It was a well-graded, dirt track a dozen feet wide. The way was dusty, but not overly so. Visibility was good, and the early summer temperature continued to be mild. The road followed the natural contours of the terrain. Gentle hills fanned up on both sides of the track. The vegetation was mostly tall grasses, here and there broken with stands of taller plants. Rocky outcrops, small and large, added further variety to the landscape.

Eddie remembered Maia's warning about traveling the road alone, but he was unwilling to leave Alicia behind. It was much easier to pull the travois along the smooth surface than it would be through the undisturbed ground on either side. And Eddie couldn't think of a way to move quickly from shelter to shelter as he dragged the litter behind him. He knew that he was exposed, visible at a distance, but he sensed that with the hounds gone and Alicia's whereabouts known, the danger he faced was much reduced. At least he hoped that was the case.

With constant movement, his injured knee had begun to ache, so he kept his pace slow and deliberate. Frequently, the young man stopped to rest, and each time, he offered his passenger some food or water. Alicia was, however, beyond reason or communication. Eddie was worried that she would do herself serious harm by refusing nourishment, but he didn't know how to get through to her.

The woman's hair was tangled and wild. Her once perfectly manicured hands were scratched and cut, her nails torn and broken. Her clothing was ripped and, most frightening of all, she had a sickly, hollow look. Over and over, he tried to speak to her, to make some kind of connection. Over and over, his efforts were rebuffed or ignored.

As he walked, Eddie kept an eye out ahead, and, from time to time, he looked over his shoulder to see what might overtake him on the trade road. He was slightly surprised, therefore when a train of merchants hove suddenly into view. They'd had ample time to see him first, so he decided that it was pointless, or worse, to try to hide. He tried the seeing spell, but with Alicia's malignant glow on the litter behind him, he couldn't see much. He just kept walking as they gradually overtook him and his unpleasant burden.

The train consisted of four wagons. One was obviously meant to serve as a place to sleep and prepare food. It was pulled by a team of two horses. The other three wagons contained boxed cargo and their teams were twice as large. There were also six, well-armed outriders. They could see that, with the exception of the sheath knife at his belt, Eddie was unarmed, and they were watchful but not belligerent as they pulled up next to him. Once he had an unobstructed view of the outriders, he quickly tried his seeing spell and was relieved to see no telltale red nimbus.

As the wagons drew closer, Eddie could tell that they were of modern design and construction. The metal parts were well-machined and both wood and metal were finished professionally, even beautifully. The camper wagon had glass in its windows. The horse-drawn vehicles obviously had good suspensions and featured modern-looking, metal wheels.

Everything about the wagons was well-designed and stout. The tack was also modern looking. The teams of horses looked well-fed and healthy.

Even though he was trying not to stare too much, Eddie couldn't help but notice that the weapons that the riders carried were also fairly modern – perhaps mid-20th century in Eddie's world. In addition to the firearms, some of the riders (there were three men and three women) had recurved bows and quivers of arrows with modern fletching.

As they pulled up next to him, Eddie slowly set down the poles of the litter and made sure that his hands were in plain view. The lead rider called to him.

"Hello, young man. What do you call yourself?"

Eddie almost blurted out his name but then remembered Maia's warning. "I call myself 'Reed,' sir," he answered.

"The 'sir' isn't necessary, Reed. I am called 'Tam.'" He looked down at Alicia.

"What happened to her?"

Eddie had rehearsed this part earlier in the morning and had what he hoped would be a plausible explanation ready.

"She is a mad-woman that I found in the forest. You know where I mean?" He pointed back the way they'd come.

"She set her dogs on me where I camped."

"What happened to the dogs and why do you think her mad?" Tam asked.

"Well, she will not speak but only shriek and try to bite and claw. She will accept neither food nor water... as for the dogs, well, I camped near a herd of elk. The dogs made the mistake of going for the elk before going for me. The dogs are no more and her injuries would have been worse had she not gotten up a tree.

"Still, I could not leave her there, injured as she was, so I brought her out of the forest and hope to find someone who will care for her."

Tam considered this for a few moments. Then he said something that surprised Eddie.

"Elk do not normally stay within the confines of that wood – especially not in these warm months when the grass is plentiful on the plains to the north and south. Soon it will be mating season and the bulls will be focused on building and defending their harems. If you could camp there and have the elk protect you, why then you are either a great wizard or else you meant the place no harm and were rewarded for it. That forest is a place of no little magic.

"And no offense, young man, but looking at you I doubt that 'great wizard' is the most likely explanation."

Eddie looked down at himself. He was filthy and scratched up and clearly minimally provisioned. He slapped at his pant legs, raised a cloud of dust, and laughed.

"None taken, Tam. Indeed I meant the place no harm and liked being there."

Here he paused and indicated the ragged, muttering figure on the litter, "Although I didn't much like being chased by her and her dogs," he added.

This got a few chuckles from Tam and the other riders.

"We have heard little from the lady of the forest for several seasons. Did you chance upon her?"

"Well, I believe I did, Tam."

"Is she well?"

"She had been injured. Her trees were attacked, but she is better now and the creature that hurt her trees is gone."

"Gone?"

"Well, it's dead. It attacked me and I killed it."

"Was it a large beast?"

"No," Eddie laughed ruefully, "It was actually small, but it had been altered in some way, and... the lady wasn't able to defend herself. I did nothing of consequence and was just lucky to be able to help." Eddie was reluctant even to use the name "Maia" and thought it would be a good idea to understate his role in anything that had happened.

Even so, the riders seemed to accept his story and they relaxed a little bit. The atmosphere changed subtly and became more welcoming.

"We cannot take responsibility for the madwoman, but we can let her ride on one of the wagons, and you, if you'd like, can also ride."

"Well, thanks, Tam. I'd really appreciate a ride. I slipped last night and banged my knee. A rest would be very welcome."

It was a few minutes' work to get Alicia stowed in the back of a wagon. She huddled there and refused to speak or even look at anyone. Tam made introductions around. Eddie caught some of the names but apologized that it'd take him multiple introductions to learn them.

One of the other riders – Luke, Eddie thought – looked at Alicia. "The woman could be pretty if she weren't so worn and cross looking... and if she were cleaned up a bit."

Alicia obviously heard this and was enraged by it. She hissed and pulled against her bonds and slammed her body against the side of the wagon.

"Stop, woman! I meant no offense or no harm to you! Calm yourself before you injure yourself further. No one here will trouble you."

Slowly, Alicia's fit of rage passed. For a few seconds she looked warily at those around her, then abruptly sat back down in the wagon and stared into the distance. Everyone else looked uncomfortable at this outburst. Finally, Eddie spoke up.

"I apologize for bringing her into your midst, but I really did not know what else to do. I didn't want to leave her there... both because she was injured and because I wanted to keep track of her whereabouts. I'll understand if you'd prefer to leave us here; I'll just continue along the road for a time. I'd really understand."

Nate, one of the older outriders, appeared to be the leader of the group. He spoke with a quiet confidence, "No, no, lad. It will be fine. We will watch ourselves around her. Now, we should be moving."

And with that, the train got rolling again. This was the first time in several days that Eddie had traveled other than by foot, and he was very glad to sit and rest for a while. As he leaned back in the seat and felt the warm sun on him. The pain in his knee receded.

The driver next to Eddie nodded to him as he sat down. If he re-membered right, her name was Isabel. Beneath her hat, Eddie could see that she had red-brown hair, which was liberally streaked with gray around the temples and pulled back into a braid. She looked to be in her middle 40's and was obviously in excellent condition. Her hands gripped the reins confidently and her forearms looked capable and strong. Seem-ingly, she had spent a good deal of time outdoors. She didn't look at all weather-beaten, though, so Eddie guessed that her outdoor time was sea-sonal.

Once the wagon train was moving again, Isabel asked Eddie if he was comfortable and if he needed anything. He was just glad to be sitting down and not dragging a litter and said so. Isabel chuckled at this, a con-fident and friendly tone.

"So, Reed, where are you bound?"

"My plan is to follow this road until it turns north. At that point I'll head due east."

"Oh, so you intend to visit the Old One. Interesting."

Eddie remembered that the forest goddess had also used the term "Old One" to refer to the being she called "her aunt," so he nodded.

"Yeah, um I mean 'yes.' The, uh, lady of the forest suggested that I stop there and rest before continuing to the south. Now that I have the madwoman with me... well, I guess I'll just try to bring her along."

"If the lady has recommended that you go there, she must think well of you."

Eddie didn't want to dwell very much on his time in the forest, so he nodded again and smiled just a little. "I guess so," he acknowledged. "She said that she was grateful for my help, but we didn't speak all that much."

"And, if you don't mind my asking, Reed, where do you come from?" Isabel lowered her voice, as if reluctant to be overheard by the glowering cargo who crouched at the back of the wagon.

Eddie started to answer and then paused. He'd already decided that if at all possible he should gamble on the truth with these people, but first he'd try to get a sense of them and their world view.

"Um, well, I'm not sure how to answer that. I'm... from the other side of the forest."

Isabel was quiet for the space of a minute. A slight smile crept into her kind features. "Your clothes, dirty as they are, give you away, young man. I can tell that they were not made in this world. In winter I make clothes, you see."

"So you people know about other worlds? About the Place?"

"Aye, we do. Although these days, few know how to come and go freely."

"I don't know how to do that either. A friend, my teacher, gave me instructions in case certain things happened. I felt that the situation was getting beyond what I could handle and, somewhat in a panic, decided to flee here."

Isabel paused and looked at him. "And did she have something to do with that? With your decision to flee?" she nodded back at Alicia, who was glaring at them and muttering.

"Well, yeah. I mean yes. My teacher warned me to get out if the situation got to be more than I thought I could handle, and it certainly felt dangerous. But it was more than her. She got those hounds from somewhere. I have no idea where. There were people that I'm sure that she works with observing the house where I was staying... I'm not sure what the relationship is. Just that they're hostile."

Isabel said, "Listen, my young friend. You should try to keep all this to yourself as much as you can."

She gestured to the riders and the rest of the caravan. "These folk? They all understand and know of the Place and the worlds and much more besides, but there are others who deny this and who might try to do you harm were they to learn of your origins. There are changes afoot in this world, and it is difficult to see how those changes could be for the best.

"Tonight, the senior members of our trading cooperative will talk on this. I'll let them know. Perhaps they will have questions for you. For now, though, just relax. If you would like, you can tell me a little of your world. I'll reciprocate and tell you something of ours. And perhaps I can give you some sense of how to get along here."

Eddie agreed readily to the exchange of information. Then he sat for a while and thought about "his" world. "Uh, it's hard to know where to start," he said after a minute.

Isabel tried to help by asking a few, more specific questions. "Well, let's start simply, with big things. What are the major countries and regional groups? How do they interact? How does your government work?"

Being young and not particularly experienced, Eddie knew little about the subtle forces that govern the interplay between giant corporations, countries, and alliances. Still, as best he could, Eddie described modern geopolitics and some of the relationships between nations. The woman was obviously taken aback at some of the things he revealed, but Isabel's attitude and demeanor continued to be friendly.

As he warmed up, Eddie realized that his Drive Away days had provided him with a wealth of information about cities, towns, and highways. He was able to describe the places he'd visited and the differences he'd noticed between parts of the country and between rich and poor people. He moved on to some of the aspects of popular culture and more than once drew good-natured laughter from his friendly host.

Finally, he ran down. Eddie leaned back against the wagon's bench seat. "Is that more-or-less what you wanted to know?"

Isabel was silent for a moment. Then, as if choosing her words carefully, she merely said, "That's very different from this world."

"Different? How so?"

"We may speak more on this with the others tonight, but tell me, when did your country come into existence? And what about this group of older countries, Yur-up, you called it?"

Eddie related a little bit of American history. Then he talked more about what he remembered of European history. He was suddenly glad for Joe's insistence that he study the histories of Europe and ancient Greece.

Again Isabel was silent for a time as she collected her thoughts. "That is drastically different. And the other continents?"

Eddie tried to elaborate and give more information about various regions and the interactions between them and the Europeans.

Now Isabel nodded. "Yes, I am getting a rough picture. It appears that the histories of our worlds diverged significantly around the time of the Greek city-states. In our world, Greece never collapsed catastrophically but instead coalesced into a stronger federation. The library at Alexandria was never destroyed. Rome never rose as a dominant force and the ideas of the ancient Greeks dominated early cultural development and scientific thought.

"There were no 'dark ages' as you call them. Instead, the preservation and propagation of knowledge allowed the science and technology of sailing ships to arise over two thousand years ago. Trade expanded knowledge further.

"When, about fifteen hundred years ago, explorers reached this continent, they found it to be very sparsely settled. Over the subsequent centuries, the indigenous people interbred with people from what we call the 'First World.' The mixture of cultures synthesized something that many of us consider to be the work of the Old One. We believe that she wove all this into her great tapestry.

"But whether it was through the skill of the Old One's design or merely good fortune, our world culture has developed a great reverence for the natural world combined with the ancient Greek ideals of personal liberty and self government."

"Wow, that's 'way different!"

Once more she nodded, "Yes. Indeed it is. From what we have gathered, there is a great variety of worlds that touch and are nourished by the Great Hub and the tears of the gods. Ours is but one in a multitude. Some are fortunate; others less so."

She continued, "Again, I am sure that the others will want to hear more of this. I will share your story with them."

"Uh, okay," Eddie replied but then continued, "Could I ask you some other things though? Right now?"

Isabel nodded. "I'll answer what I can and tell you plainly if I'd rather not go into a subject. Does that suit you?"

Now it was Eddie's turn to nod. Then he picked up his thread of the conversation.

"If it's okay, I'd like to ask about your technology. What you know and use in your world."

"Yes, that would be interesting to discuss, to compare what you have on your world. What would you like to know?" Isabel responded.

"Well, let's start with these wagons. They are obviously modern and well developed. Do you use them by choice? Is there another trans-portation technology available? You see in my world, transportation of goods in significant quantities via horses and wagons stopped a long time ago."

"We have other modes of transportation, but we favor this tech-nology," came the reply. "I confess that I have not given much thought to the reasons, but I suppose they stem from some basic cultural differ-ences. Recall that the Greeks stayed in the city-state phase for several centuries. This continues to have an influence on our world-view, our culture and decisions."

She stopped for a few seconds to consider something and then continued, "we tend to emphasize regional economies and regional-scale enterprises... although we do have some inter-regional and even inter-continental trade."

"So, do you have internal combustion engines?"

"Yes, but we limit their use." She wrinkled her nose. "They smell bad. For intermediate distances, where time is not terribly important, we enjoy moving trade goods around in the manner you see here." She ges-tured around them at the wagon train.

"For long distances we favor rail or sea travel. Those modes are most efficient and provide the most benefit to the greatest number of cit-izens."

"Aircraft?"

"Yes, we have aircraft, both fixed wing and rotary, but again we try to apply that technology where it makes the greatest sense. Is your world similar?"

"Oh, we use cars and trucks, mostly. Those all have internal combustion engines. I've heard a little about electric cars, but I've never really seen one. Trains are used some. Mostly for freight, I think. If people can afford it, they usually fly on commercial airlines. That's the quickest way to get any distance. Some people like to drive on the high-ways though."

"Does this mean paved roads?"

"Yeah. Sure. We have lots and lots of pavement."

"That is too bad."

"Well, I'd never really thought about it much, growing up with it and all, but I suppose you're right. If your people can make this work, it'd probably be a lot less... I don't know... have a lot less impact, I guess?"

Warming to the subject, she gestured at the wagon train. "So my guess is that our development along these lines varies from yours by a wide margin."

"Yeah, I expect so. There's talk about changing the way we move things and people, but there's not much real change. Not to where you'd notice it."

"What of other areas of the society? Other applications of knowledge and technology?" she wanted to know.

"Well, there is the whole computer thing? Do you have that?"

"Ah, yes, we have computers and digital electronics, and have put significant effort into optimizing the ways we store information and move it around; although we find sub-molecular technology, we call it 'SMT,' more efficient. In our cities and towns we make use of electronics – primarily in the way we generate and use electricity. You'll even see examples of it at the rest stations along the trade roads."

"Really?"

She continued, with a smile. "Excuse me, Reed, but why would you be surprised? We have universities and various scales of enterprise. We have made choices regarding technology, its cost, and how its use may give the most benefit to all."

"Well, there's not much evidence of modern technology here, I guess. But I admit that we're not in the city... what's so funny?"

Isabel had burst out laughing. At first Eddie had felt himself redden, but Isabel's laugh was good natured and friendly. She saw that he was embarrassed and quickly composed her features. "I apologize for laughing. You merely surprised me. You are surrounded by our technology. Look at the wagons. Not the trim, but the wagons themselves. Look carefully and tell me what you see!"

Eddie had only glanced at the wagons before this. Yes, he'd noticed that they were sophisticated and that the woodwork was both attractive and practical. Upon closer look, he saw that the wagon shells weren't actually made of anything he could identify.

"What is this stuff? Is it some kind of plastic?" he wanted to know.

"No indeed, Reed. It is a rigid, high-strength, low-weight composite material. We grow the shells of the wagons as a single piece. The wheels are similarly grown to size. Then we add purpose-grown wood as trim and accessories. The wagons are light and extremely strong. Why should we haul around a heavy wagon? It would..."

"Grow?! You *grow* the wagon wheels and the bodies?"

Michael C. Glaviano

"Yes, we do. Not in the sense of growing plants, of course. When I say 'grow' I mean that we grow them in tanks, using SMT. Think of it as something like directed crystal growth. These wagons have a high carbon content, combined with traces of other elements. We optimize most of our transportation for strength, weight characteristics, energy efficiency, stability, and so on."

"What do you mean 'energy efficiency?' Aren't these horse-drawn wagons?"

"Well, yes, but there are also very light, efficient hub motors at each wheel. Energy from regenerative breaking is stored between layers of material in the beds of the wagon. When we climb hills, we supplement horse power with electrical power."

This information made Eddie stop and think, and he looked at the artifacts around him more carefully and with greater interest. After riding in silence for a few more minutes, Eddie returned to an earlier thread of conversation.

"So... how big are your cities, Isabel?"

She answered this readily and confidently. "Along the coasts, we have some very large cities – well over a million people – but the world is a big place. Our population peaked a little over a hundred years ago at around one and a half billion and has stayed fairly constant since then, so there's really not much need to cluster too densely."

"That's a huge difference. We are on track to have 8 billion people before long!"

Now it was Isabel's turn to be surprised. "Billion? With a 'B'?!" she wondered.

"Yeah, I am sad to say. Our population is only leveling off in certain areas that have wealth and education. Population continues to explode elsewhere."

"That is serious. You should keep that very quiet. It could be used to support the position of those who favor sealing our world from the Place."

"Yeah, I can imagine... but... but, well, I've heard that if a world is sealed off it withers and dies!"

"Yes, young man. My friends and I have heard this as well. In fact, it is seldom far from our thoughts. It makes us very worried about the influence of those who deny the existence of other worlds or who would try to seal us off from the Great Hub."

Here Isabel was quiet again for a moment. When she spoke again it was only to suggest that they postpone their conversation until later in the evening when more could participate.

Eddie had a lot to think about, and, after his days of hard travel, he was happy to relax on the comfortable seat as the wagon train traveled through the countryside. The day was bright and mild. The rolling hills and grasslands were lovely to watch as they rolled past. His stomach rumbled a reminder that it was past time for lunch.

"Hey, I've got some nuts from the forest. I've also got some trail rations that I brought. I can share this stuff. Would like to, in fact... as long as I keep enough so that I can reach my next stop."

"You have nuts gathered from that forest?" Isabel wanted to know.

"Well, yeah. The lady gave 'em to me. To make sure I had enough supplies to make it."

Isabel smiled and said that she'd like to try one of the food bars. "It is very gracious of you to offer to share the nuts you have gathered. They constitute a precious gift from the lady of the forest. She must have been very grateful to you for dispatching that creature! You might want to save your offer of sharing the lady's harvest until dinner time."

Eddie was glad to have something that he could contribute to the general supplies of the wagon train. He rummaged in his pack and brought out food bars and dried fruit from his world. They snacked as they traveled in the mild sunshine. The sky was a bright, clear blue. The air was warm and fresh. Their conversation eased back to more trivial matters.

Michael C. Glaviano

Sixteen

From where she crouched at the back of the wagon, Alicia struggled to listen to the young one and the woman. Muttering to herself, she hung her head, hid her face with the matted tangles of her hair. Unconsciously, spasmodically, of their own volition, her hands clenched and unclenched. She was filthy after the futile chase through that hateful forest. Her leg hurt terribly, and her thirst and hunger were nearly beyond bearing, but she channeled her discomforts, converted them to rage at her captors.

Even with the morning's enforced rest, she remained so weak and drained that she could not eavesdrop effectively. It was both difficult and painful to cooperate with those whom she should dominate and control. Still, she must rest and, perhaps, accept nourishment. She must appear docile so that when she finally did make a move, it would be more of a surprise and, thus, more likely to succeed.

But what kind of move? What would gain her the most? What would be most effective, most likely to succeed? What did she most *need*?

She needed revenge. For her hurts, she wanted to injure. For her degradation, her humiliation, she craved to subjugate. She was mad with the desire for revenge. It drove all other needs before it.

But there were too many of them and they were armed. Weakly, tentatively, she tried to send her mind out. Just to see. Each mind she brushed was healthy, aware, calm. In her present condition she could not overpower even one of them. And now, even the young one knew her touch. He too was wary and difficult to manipulate.

With a harsh sob, she accepted that she could do nothing here. She must escape, get away from her captors, regain some strength. Her easiest bet would be to escape tonight. Perhaps she could muster enough strength to do two things: bring in cloud cover to make things darker and then weaken her bonds.

But then where would she go? What would she do? Was there a way that she could return to the Blue World? A way to claim that she had driven the young one to ground and needed only more rest and resources

Michael C. Glaviano

to finish her task? That would be risky in the extreme. The Locust Queen was difficult to deceive, impossible to deny. Alicia had already fallen from the Queen's favor. If she returned empty-handed, she would surely suffer even worse punishments than she had already endured.

Curse these people! Curse them! She almost gave herself over to rage again, but then she gained some measure of control and drew herself inward. What should she do? She must watch. She must rest while she waited for an opportunity to act.

Seventeen

After several hours of traveling, the road rose slightly and the terrain became somewhat more varied. While nothing like the forest behind them, there were a few more oak trees, an occasional manzanita, and larger clusters of boulders. Small herds of antelope could be seen grazing on gentle hillsides. Riding the thermal currents, hawks soared far above. There was a slight breeze. Eddie could smell the country around him. He could also smell himself.

"Uh, Isabel..."

"Yes?"

"I am so incredibly filthy. Will we get to a place where I can wash?"

She laughed, "Indeed, you would benefit from a serious application of soap and water, young man! At any rate, you are in luck, Reed. We will reach Salter's Bridge before much longer. Nate will call a rest there. We will water the horses and you can bathe. There is a facility that travelers have built for that purpose.

"And I have another idea," she continued after a thoughtful interval.

"What's that?"

"Your speech is much like ours, and that is a good thing, but your clothes – your boots and especially the cut of your trousers – mark you as an outlander. If your way eventually takes you to a town, it would be best if you blended in as much as possible."

Eddie chose not to remark on his speech or Maia's "gift of tongues." He merely nodded to see what Isabel would say next.

"Now I cannot do anything about your boots, but as I mentioned, I am a tailor."

She gestured to the containers fastened to the bed of the wagon. "Among the garments stored in my trunks, I have trousers that will fit you and which will cause no second looks."

"Well, thanks, Isabel. That would be really great, but I don't have any money... anything to pay you for new clothes."

"Ah, but you do! I would like to see what I can learn from your garments. I would take them apart and see what design features I might incorporate into my own work. If you agree, I will trade you a new pair of trousers for those that you now wear."

Eddie looked down at his pants. They were a mess.

"Well that's hardly fair," he said. "These pants are trashed. They're filthy and they've got holes poked in them from my trek through the forest and all."

"I do not intend to wear them, Reed. The way the front of them is built is very different. Did you notice our men's trousers? The whole front fastens with visible buttons. That is the most obvious difference, but there may be others that I could study to advance my craft. So, if you are agreeable, I will put yours in a bag and take them apart when I return home. That will be interesting and, longer term, perhaps profitable."

"Cool! I mean, that sounds great to me, if you're sure it's okay," Eddie agreed. "I also have another shirt in my pack if you'd like to take a look at it."

"Yes, perhaps I will. Thank you, Reed."

They rode through the bright sunshine. Isabel pointed out more of the features of the wagon. She described in detail the wagon's sophisticated power train and proudly explained the way the suspension helped manage the load and keep the wagon stable. It was obviously a finely engineered machine that provided a reliable, if slow way of transporting goods across short to medium distances.

Before long, they topped a rise in the road and they could see, a short distance ahead, a minor river that was spanned by a viaduct consisting of two spans. As they drew close, Eddie could see that the bridge was constructed of beautifully fitted stone. In fact the stonework was so well fitted, that Eddie could scarcely see the seams between the massive blocks. He mentioned this to Isabel and she raised her eyebrows as she turned to answer.

"You cannot see many seams because the only seams that we put in our stone structures are those that we add to make the overall form more stable in the event of an earthquake. Most of the stone is grown in-situ. Do you not do this in your building?"

"In-situ... you mean that you somehow grow the stone *here*?" Eddie wondered. "We have nothing like that technology."

"It is closely related to SMT. Done correctly, it is so much stronger than most other forms," came the reply, "and we can make our buildings efficient, attractive, and no more obtrusive than necessary. This is something we have known how to do for quite some time. You will see many examples in our towns and cities; although you may not notice it because over the last half-century, this form has evolved to some degree of subtlety."

"It's beautiful. I'm looking forward to seeing a good-sized town."

"But first, that bath," she laughed.

"Uh, yeah. You bet. Where do I do that?"

Isabel and the others had pulled their wagons and their horses off to the right side of the roadway into what was clearly a rest area. The woman jumped down and went around to the side of the wagon where she pulled a stepladder from a storage area between the front and rear wheels. She set this next to the wagon and climbed up. Then she opened a stout chest by undoing a simple latch and swinging back the lid.

She rummaged inside for a few minutes and then straightened. She held up a pair of functional looking work pants. Besides the button front, Eddie noticed that it had cargo pockets and some loops along the side seams.

"I think that these will fit you. Do you find them acceptable?" she wanted to know.

"Sure. They look fine."

Eddie grabbed his pack. "If you'll show me where I can bathe, I'll go try to make myself presentable and bring back the pants." Here he opened the top of the pack and rummaged inside for his spare shirt.

"Do you want my shirt too? I have a spare, but it's no cleaner than the one I'm wearing."

"Here, let's take a closer look at it," came the reply as Isabel held out her hands. Eddie balled up the shirt and tossed it to her.

"Yes. Do you see the way the collar is cut? And the yoke is different. It is not so noticeable as the trousers, but I would like to compare. Here," she pulled out a shirt that was a few shades lighter than the pants. "I will trade this shirt for yours. Does it suit?"

This was a long-sleeved shirt made from a canvas-like material that had been processed to make it soft. It looked very strong but comfortable.

"Sure thing. Thanks! It's a cool... I mean a good shirt," Eddie replied, glad to have some help from someone who knew how the locals dressed.

Isabel pointed to the edge of the parking area where a trail led off towards the river. "If you follow that down, you'll see a bath house. Feel free to make use of the facilities. We'll probably be here for at least an hour."

Eddie gathered up his new clothes and his pack and, happy at the prospect of washing off more than four days' worth of grime, hurried down the trail.

When he neared the river, Eddie found a rustic bathhouse perched on the shore. It was built of rough-hewn stone and heavy timber and blended beautifully with the surroundings. He walked all the way around the small structure and saw that there was only one entrance, so, hoping he was following the proper social customs, he entered the building. There he saw some cubbies in a changing area where he could put his belongings. There were also some benches. Slatted floors let water drain away. Beyond the dressing room, there was a large, open shower area.

Eddie lost no time in stripping down and getting into the shower. A few seconds later, he was standing under the spray, enjoying a steaming hot shower. He was tempted to linger, but he also thought that he should get back outside and offer to help with the horses, so he dried off and worked his way into his new clothes. They fit well and were as comfortable as he'd hoped. He was glad to see that the people in this world also used belts, and he threaded his sheath knife onto the belt.

He put on his last clean pair of socks and his boots and looked down at his hands. They were stained and scratched from the time in the trees but they were now mostly clean. He noticed that he missed a significant amount of dirt under a nail on his left hand, so after he shouldered his pack, he pulled out his knife and started to tidy up that nail.

As he was finishing his manicure, he heard some voices outside. One voice was much louder than the others. There was anger in the voice, anger and urgency.

"Listen, woman. You keep arguing with me, you're dead. This gun here gives me all the right I need. You're gonna walk slow up that hill and then we're gonna get on that fancy wagon of yours and head over the bridge right now. You just make up an excuse, because this gun is gonna be shoved in your friend's back until we get across that bridge!"

Eddie let his pack slide softly to the floor. Holding the knife in throwing position, Eddie eased open the door just a crack. He could see Isabel and one of the men from the wagon train – Ben, he thought – facing a man whom Eddie hadn't seen before. The man had a gun pointed at them.

Of course Eddie had never actually thrown a knife at anyone before, and his heart was hammering in his chest. Targets were one thing. Someone holding a gun was very different. He took a deep breath and let it out slowly. He tried to recapture that centered feeling he'd found when the animal had charged him in Maia's forest.

In one motion, Eddie kicked open the door to the bath house and threw the knife hard. The man heard the sound and began to turn towards Eddie, but before he could get off a shot, the knife hit him. It wasn't a great throw but the blade embedded itself in the man's arm and he yelled in outrage and pain. The gun slipped from the man's grasp and clattered to the stone pathway. Ben kicked the man's feet out from under him and the gunman hit the ground. Isabel scrambled around and retrieved the gun.

In a second, it was over. Ben had their erstwhile attacker face down in the dirt with his hands bent sharply behind him. Ben's left knee pressed on the guy's back. It looked painful, but Eddie's friends from the wagon train weren't taking any chances. Isabel ran back up the path and in a minute was back with several others from the train and a piece of stout rope.

They got the man on his feet and tied his hands behind him. Eyes glassy and unfocused, the man was obviously semi-conscious. His breath was ragged and uneven.

Ben reached over with his free hand and jerked the knife from his captive's arm. The man screamed, and quite a bit of blood began flowing down the man's sleeve and onto the dirt. Ben wiped the blade on the man's clothes and offered it to Eddie handle first.

"Here you go. Nice work, kid," he said.

Eddie took the knife and re-sheathed it. He felt woozy. Ben glanced his way. "Hey, kid! Stay with us, hear? It's okay. Take a deep breath."

Isabel came around and had Eddie lean back against the wall of the bath house.

"Sorry... It's just... that I've never actually thrown a knife *at* any-body... It's just been targets... 'til now." Eddie's voice tapered off. His limbs were twitchy with adrenaline and his stomach was clearly not happy.

"That is fine, Reed. No one expects you to feel relaxed and calm after something like this. Just breathe slowly. Oh, and we have another problem."

"What's that?"

"The madwoman has escaped."

"What?"

"She must have used the excitement as cover. In any case, she has slipped her bonds and gone. The whole area around the wagon stop is filled with footprints, so tracking her will be difficult."

Eddie looked over at the man they had subdued. Blood was still seeping from the wound and the man was shaking his head and mutter-ing. Now he started looking around and focusing his eyes.

"What's going on? How in hell did I get here? Who are you people?!" he called suddenly. He struggled against his bonds and those holding him and then gasped when he put strain on his injured arm.

Eddie began to realize what had probably happened. He spoke up.

"You can probably let this man go. My guess is that Alicia — that's the madwoman's name — did something to his mind to make him attack you. I haven't seen her try this trick exactly, but I think it's just the sort of thing she might do. I really doubt that the attack and her escape are only a coincidence."

Now Nate, who had been watching the whole scene quietly, spoke up.

"Young man, I think we need to have a more detailed discussion concerning all this, but not right now," he looked around, "and certainly not right here."

Nate paused and looked back up towards the wagons. "Tad!" he called.

"Right here, Nate!" Tad was up at the edge of the wagon stop.

"Can you give this man some medical attention and see if it's likely that young Reed here is correct? Isabel will explain."

"Sure thing, boss!" Isabel and Ben led the injured man up the trail.

"Good. Let's get the horses watered and get out of here. Reed, you're with me."

Eddie grabbed his pack and followed in the older man's wake as they returned to the wagons. Obviously mulling things over, Nate was silent as they walked. Eddie stowed his pack in the wagon and then turned back. Nate's first question was surprising.

"So, are you good with horses, Reed?"

"I've ridden a few times, but I don't know much about them."

"Okay. We'll change the arrangements accordingly. Why don't you go see if you can help the others? I'd like us to get back on the road as quickly as we can."

So Eddie walked back down to the river to where the others had gathered with the horses. There was a trough near the rest area that could be flushed clean and refilled. The others were unhitching horses and walking them over to the trough to let the animals drink. Then they walked the horses over to a shady spot and let them graze for a few minutes before taking them back to the trough for another taste.

Eddie walked over to the tree and was handed the lead of a large bay. The horse was docile and well-trained. Eddie led the horse over to the trough and let the horse drink until the next horse, this one led by Ben, arrived for a turn. Eddie tugged gently on the lead and the bay followed him back to the shade.

Letting them rest in the shade and then have a little water, they cycled through all the horses three times. Ben checked hooves and eyes and legs. He spoke to all the big animals in a soothing voice. It was relaxing, calming work, quite a contrast from the earlier excitement, and Eddie was glad for the chance to collect his thoughts.

Eventually, all the horses had been tended. The day continued to be mild, and the animals were not stressed. With a minimum of fuss, the horses were returned to the wagons. Eddie saw Nate and Isabel engaged in what looked like a serious conversation. She looked over towards Eddie and waved. Then she went over to where the outriders' horses were gathered and adjusted the stirrups on Nate's horse. She swung easily into the saddle.

As Eddie came up to the wagon, Nate motioned him to board and the older man climbed up next to him. Then the wagon train pulled out of the rest stop and back onto the road.

Michael C. Glaviano

Eighteen

Alicia had rested for as long as she could stand to be passive. Her obsession with revenge burned in her. Her fear of the Queen haunted her. She was terrified, furious, frustrated. She had scarcely begun to heal, but she feared what might happen if she lingered with these people, so she resolved to escape.

Although she was weak, magic was alive in this world. Tentatively at first, but then with more confidence, she willed herself into a deep place that lay far from her hurts and weakness. Sitting very still in the warm afternoon sunlight, she drew on the living energy around her as she prepared to act.

First she must slip the bonds that held her. The knots were well-tied, the ropes strong, but there was no magic in either. As soon as she was left alone she began applying various spells of release. The ropes fell at the fourth try, but she did not move. Instead, she opened her eyes to tiny slits and looked around her. No one was near. She quickly wrapped the ropes around her ankles and wrists so that a casual inspection would detect nothing amiss.

Once she had loosened the ropes that bound her to the side of the wagon, Alicia sought to create a diversion. She cast her mind in the direction of the rest area and before long, detected someone napping in the shade. She probed deeper. Even when awake, he was not terribly bright, and best of all, he was armed. His dozing mind was easy to invade, manipulate. He was thus a perfect instrument, a tool she could use to cause a distraction.

The puppet-mistress made him stand and then had him turn to face the road. Carefully, she poked her head up and looked around. There! She could see him. Staring vacantly, arms slack at his sides, the man stood near that building by the river. Even in her weakened state, it was a simple matter to enrage him, direct him, and launch him at those gathered nearby.

She inflamed the man's temper and compelled him to seek escape. She continued to feed the man's fear. Alicia could sense that he was about to crack under the strain. She could feel the sweat on his face, his sides, his hands. As the man struggled to breathe, she could feel the tightness in his chest, hear the fear pulsing in his ears. Soon he would fire the weapon. The ensuing chaos would cover her escape.

All was proceeding according to her intent, but the young one, curse him, had at the last moment intervened – with a knife, no less! At the same time, the ensuing struggle had been enough to distract everyone nearby. Alicia made herself unobtrusive, easy to miss. In this bright light, she was too weak to summon true invisibility, but she managed to avoid detection as she scrambled from the wagon.

The first ten yards were the hardest. She had to keep her puppet disoriented and keep herself unnoticed as she made for a large boulder near the rest area. Once shielded from view, she relinquished control of her subject. Then she devoted what remained of her limited energies to getting away undetected.

As it was, she barely escaped the notice of the wagon driver. Had the foolish woman not been in such a hurry to alert the others and get back to the scene of the action, Alicia might have been discovered. For once, however, fortune favored her. She could hear her erstwhile tool yelling in pain and confusion, and she took advantage of that to claw her way up the hill to the next outcrop, and the next, and the next.

By the time the scene had settled down and the horses were be-ing tended, Alicia was several hundred yards away. She crouched down low. Her heart pounded, her breath was ragged, her vision dim and spotty. Once again, she had pushed herself to her limits. Slowly, slowly, the world came back into focus. Breathing better now, Alicia eased her-self into a more comfortable position to watch and wait. A scrub oak provided some shade and she hunkered in the dirt to peer out between small granite boulders.

She was still very weak, so she stayed where she was until the wagons and the outriders had pulled away. She rested and watched and waited. And while she waited, she planned.

Nineteen

Apart from the footfalls of the horses and the sounds of the wagons, it was quiet as Eddie and Nate rode along. Eddie could see how the outriders, on alert now, ranged all around the wagon train. They circled out in different patterns, fell back, looped to the side, and then overtook the train. They were practiced, and they were excellent with their horses. Eddie was a little envious of their grace and skill.

Before long, however, Nate broke the silence.

"So, Reed, suppose you go back to the start and tell me more of this whole situation."

"Uh, okay, Nate. I will, but..."

"What?"

"Well... That man. Will he be okay? What will happen to him?"

"Oh, he'll be fine enough. Tad is a good healer and even our field medicines are more than adequate to address his injuries.

"As far as we could tell, no one but Isabel and Ben – and you of course – actually saw what happened. The man himself recalled nothing of the incident, so Isabel told him that he appeared to have some kind of seizure and fell and hurt himself. Tad bandaged his arm and told him to favor it for a day or two.

"We take your word that the madwoman was the cause of all this. We agree that her escape was otherwise an unlikely coincidence. Indeed, I inspected her bonds myself. A normal person would not have been able to slip away as she did.

"But, again, I think it is time you gave a more complete accounting of yourself. How did you come to be in our world? Oh, and, yes." Here Nate answered the question in Eddie's mind, "Isabel has already confirmed what we all guessed when we first saw you. We know that you come from a parallel world – most likely a nearby spoke on the Great Hub.

"So," he repeated, "So suppose you go back as far as you need to in your story and tell me how today's events came to be."

And then, with some raggedness getting started, Eddie did exactly that. As best he could, he described the world he came from. He mentioned Joe, Alicia, and his own trip through the Place. Eddie omitted the mention of Maia's seed packet, but with that exception, he tried to give as complete an account as he could. From time-to-time, Nate asked questions, but the older man displayed no surprise at the story. Eddie thought that Nate's reaction was mostly one of faint regret or perhaps sadness.

As Eddie wrapped up his narrative, he wondered how else he could have proceeded. Could he have prevented Alicia's escape and an innocent bystander's injury? He asked Nate for his opinion. The older man was quiet for a few moments before answering.

"Well, Reed, obviously you could have been more forthcoming about this woman, Alicia. That's the main thing. Still, Isabel tells me that you answered her questions candidly enough and that she believes you were willing to give us a more complete picture had we thought to ask. And we realize that you didn't know us and therefore could not be expected to volunteer all details at first meeting.

"...So, I suppose, we must consider this unfortunate event to be mostly a sign of the times. We will be more careful going forward," the older man finished with an unhappy sigh.

It was a measure of Eddie's growth beyond the "hotshot kid" persona that he felt real regret at bringing trouble to the wagon train.

"Uh, I guess I owe you people an apology," he admitted. "I didn't intend to bring trouble to you or into this world. I know that's a lame excuse, but I'm still sorry about it."

"Thank you for the sentiment, young man. The circumstances are unfortunate, but considered from another point of view, perhaps we have become somewhat complacent."

"Complacent? You guys sure don't look complacent!" Eddie scanned the well-armed outriders. They were watchful and active. The work looked exhausting and hardly the product of complacency.

Nate followed Eddie's gaze, nodded. "Oh, in recent years, we've had a few incidents, a few problems along our route. In a few, remote villages, we received cooler welcomes than we expected, but beyond rumor, there was nothing so actively disturbing about this trip. And nothing that smacked so directly of the Queen's interference. So we will share what we have learned with others in our traders' cooperative and hope that the net effect will be beneficial."

The horses pulled the wagon along the road and Nate sat in silence for a time. Eddie had just about decided that the older man was done talking, when Nate continued.

"You see, we've struck a pretty good balance in this world. We're aware of the infinity of the worlds around us. There is much creativity. Art and science are mostly in a dynamic balance. What your people call 'magic' is recognized as a natural force that emanates from the Great Hub.

"Educated people, as well as many who are not formally educated but who remain intellectually active, know something of the worlds that have sunk into chaos and something of the fates of those worlds that have lost their connection with the Great Hub."

"Educated people? Intellectually active people? That implies..." Eddie began.

"Sadly, yes. This is a very good world, Reed, but it is not a perfect world. In most cultures, there are those who either through limited abilities or intellectual laziness do not avail themselves of the opportunity to learn. Is it not that way in your world?"

"Yeah, yes. I guess it's just like that in my world," Eddie admitted. Now he tried to choose his words with caution. "Lots of people... well, it's considered acceptable, desirable even... to care little about learning."

"Such people are easy to manipulate," Nate nodded, sighed. "Sadly, in recent years, we've seen a well-funded effort at such manipulation. Self-styled 'experts' of questionable credentials somehow have access to unlimited funds, which they use to propagate points of view that have no basis in fact and no credibility within the scientific community. At the same time, a growing number of popular media outlets are bent on reporting a controversy where none truly exists – a controversy between non-science and self-serving ignorance on one side and peer-reviewed work on the other."

"Yeah, that sounds familiar. I see stuff like that in my world too. Lots of it," Eddie agreed.

Nate continued, "It is a familiar pattern. Those who would drain this world of its life are abroad. They are powerful. One of their tactics is to denigrate learning. They acquire wealth and power. Yet they never have enough to suit them, do they, Reed?"

"Well, um, I guess they don't." Eddie's voice drifted off. He thought back to his many conversations with Joe. He wondered how he was going to locate and reconnect with his mentor. The young man experienced a sharp jolt of isolation, a momentary pang of worry, but he forced it down and pressed himself to stay engaged in the conversation.

"So, what do you do? About all this," Eddie wanted to know.

"Do? Well, we are traders. Ambassadors among the cities and towns. We try to live lives of good example. We try to be productive, to share knowledge, and to be as open and forthright as we possibly can. Thus far, keeping knowledge alive in our world has proven to be the most effective action available to us. As traders, our role emphasizes the mixing of cultures, of goods, and peoples. Since the cosmology of the Great Wheel is still largely accepted, we share stories about it. We try hard to keep thought alive about our place among the infinity of worlds."

"So it sounds like there are a lot of connections to the place between worlds here? In this world?" Eddie asked.

Nate nodded vigorously. "Yes, of course!" Then he paused, and frowned. "but now that you mention it, perhaps not as many as in the old days. And that is worrisome. I haven't thought about it for a long time, but the stories of my grandparents were... very rich..."

"In my world, the world I came from, I got the sense that there are very few."

"That is too bad. The old stories told of people steeped in ancient lore. They could open portals anywhere and admit the tears of the gods to nourish a thirsty world."

"The old man that I stay with in my world – my teacher..." Eddie began and then tapered off.

"Yes?"

"Well, I think he knows how to do that. Anyway, I'm supposed to meet up with him at a place called 'The Inn at Three Corners,' but the forest lady said that first I should stop off with someone she called her aunt.... but, have you met him? My teacher? Do you know him? Do you think it's a good idea to make that detour?"

Nate laughed. "You ask questions faster than I can answer!"

"Sorry... I just... I dunno..."

"Don't worry, young friend. I sense your confusion and will try to help. As to your teacher, well, without knowing more regarding him, I cannot say if our paths have crossed," replied Nate.

"I will say that you should be wary of mentioning him to those whom you do not know. Again, the Queen's agents are abroad! As to my own role, well, I am a trader. My father and my grandfather were traders as well. I know the old stories that have been passed down through my family but little else. I believe in the Great Wheel and think that the cosmology of it makes a certain sense.

"I love this world," he gestured around him, "but have never had an affinity for dusty tomes and ancient spells. Instead I have done my best to memorize stories of the old times. Stories of magic and mystery, stories that excite and entertain. I share these stories in towns and around campfires. Perhaps I should do more, but this is what I know. I suppose that in this, I am nearly as guilty as those who do not lift a finger to preserve the old ways."

"As to your last question," he continued after another short pause, "I am convinced of the forest spirit's goodness. If she told you to visit the Old One to the east, then I think that you should. We will let you know when we are at our closest approach to her lands and you may set out from there.

"The Old One has great power. If she chooses to get involved, she can help you," he added. "Surely, if the forest spirit sent you there, you will be well-received."

Now, Nate fell silent for a moment. Eddie glanced his way and saw that the older man's craggy features were furrowed in serious thought.

"You realize, Reed, that we will follow this trade road as it turns north?" Nate asked.

"Yes, I understand that."

"Know this: After you leave us, it will take us eight more days to reach our destination. Depending on trade, we will remain in the north for perhaps twice that long before saying good-bye to these wagons and horses. Then, bringing what small amount of goods remain, we plan to sail down the coast to Soapstone Bay... That is the name of the town where you may find this 'Inn at Three Corners.'"

"Oh, so then maybe I should stay with you?"

"No. Again, I think that you should follow the suggestion of the forest spirit, but depending on how long you stay with the Old One, and the manner in which she sends you hence, we may well reach Soapstone Bay at nearly the same time. Perhaps our paths will again cross yours. If not, well, it is always good to meet a fellow-traveller... especially an out-worlder."

Nate continued after another short pause. "I may try to weave your story into the tales that I share... but... to come to the point, I would give you some small advice."

"Sure, Nate. I could use any help I can get."

The older man nodded, smiled slightly. "It is only this. You will be safer if you try to fit in. Approach this stage in your journey as if you intended to take up residence in Soapstone Bay. You should try to secure some form of employment and regular lodging in town. Establish friend-ships. Live among residents rather than travelers. Choose a place near, but not *too* near the Inn. This will allow you to settle into your search without attracting attention."

"What kind of work?" Eddie wondered aloud.

"That will depend on your skills. There are many shops and there are always places that need kitchen help. There is a local newspa-per. Soapstone is not a big, expensive town and there is a modest, yet busy harbor there. There is trade. Most of the people are decent, honest folk. If you walk the town for half a day, I am sure you will find some-thing."

Eddie easily agreed to this. Sketchy as it was, it was the closest thing to a plan that he'd had since he had set out from Joe's house. "Um, Nate, may I say that I know you if I think it might help me find work and and a place to stay?"

"You are a good sort, young man. Thank you for asking. Yes, if it is appropriate, you may say that you have lately travelled with Nate the Trader and his band and that I suggested that you spend some time living in Soapstone Bay."

Michael C. Glaviano

"Now, let us set all this aside and enjoy the ride, shall we? We have several miles ahead of us before we reach our stopping place. If you will, I will share such local knowledge that comes to mind. This will help you fit in, which is to your benefit."

"Yes, thank you. That would be good." Even though Isabel had remarked that his speech was not overly foreign, Eddie was now consciously trying to learn the cadence and rhythm of Nate's speech so that he would fit in better in the days ahead.

Twenty

Alicia squatted in the lee of a boulder. She was hungry and cold but well pleased with the success of her escape. What's more, she had the germ of a plan in mind.

Now that she'd had some time to think, she knew that it would be impossible to return to the Blue World. No, that would not do. It would not do at all. She had already lost favor. The consequences of failure at this point were too great. The Queen would not listen; she would merely punish.

There were debts to be collected in the Blue World, surely, but collecting upon those debts must be set aside – for now. First she must regain strength. She must restore her abilities. Alicia thought that if she could find a power center in these hills, she might reach the Place. Even if she were forced to reverse her course, she could work her way back to the portal through which she had first reached this world. She would, of course, skirt the edge of that hateful forest, but she knew the portal that lay to the west of it.

And once in the Place there were many options open to her. For one, she might find a sparsely inhabited world where she could rest and gain strength. She would have to hide from the minions of the Locust Queen, but in the infinity of worlds, she might manage that. This was a passive course, she thought, but perhaps the safest.

In time she might heal, but she was loath to take that time. And she was sure that she had been marked. She believed herself no longer beautiful and this belief underlay and stoked her rage. The loss, the theft of her beauty was a sore that could not heal unless it were burned away by vengeance. As she dwelt upon this, thoughts of vengeance drove away rational considerations of safety.

There was another possibility. She might try to find another exile and ally herself. Surely there were others who had been wronged, and together they might plan and coordinate their efforts at revenge.

Unfortunately, there were issues of trust and betrayal with which to contend if she followed this course. Whom would she trust? She could think of no one. Whom would she betray? Why, anyone who had something she wanted, anyone whose betrayal could further her goals. She had, after all, cut her teeth at the feet of the mistress of betrayal. She set this notion aside: allies were not possible.

Finally, and most dangerously, she might remain in the Place. There, if she could survive and find a lair, she would more quickly grow in power and strength. She could kill small, weak creatures and absorb their power. If she accumulated enough power, she might invoke a Transformation that would give her great strength and the capacity to track her quarry. Yes, there was a risk of madness in this course, and such Transformations were themselves risky. She might end up with a form that was too terrible or too strange for her to move freely in the worlds without drawing undue attention.

Yes, that was a risk, indeed. And in her heart of hearts, Alicia knew that she was already very nearly mad: mad with hurt, with loss, with rage. It would take little to push her beyond the brink. It would take little to erase what little remained of her humanity, her ability to reason, to plan.

But the power! Hidden within the shadows and shrouding mists of the Great Hub, she could lie in wait. And when the unwary came near, she could consume them... consume their power. In her lair, she would wax strong. In her lair, she might eventually gain enough power to collect on the debts owed her, to redress the wrongs done her.

Previously she had hated the old man most of all, and indeed she hated him still. He had found her out, had immediately seen through her disguise. When she had invaded the old man's house, he had lain in wait and with precious little effort, bested her in combat. That defeat had cost her favor with the Queen. That moment had marked the turning point in her fortunes.

But the young one had humiliated her and in so doing had displaced the old man as the primary object of her hatred. She had been hurt and weak when he captured her in the forest. He could have killed her then, but what did he do? He had looked past the ugliness, the torture that marked her. He had pretended not to notice what she had become, and with no hint of revulsion, he had offered her food... food and water.

How he had mocked her! Surely he reveled in her misery, her twisted form, her beauty lost. She looked down at her once pretty hands. Scratched and torn, they now were more claws than the hands of a beautiful woman. He had seen at once that she was no longer powerful, that she was no longer a force to be feared.

Yes, he had hidden his feelings behind a mask, but how he must have gloated! She clenched, shook her fists at the memory of the young man and the way he had humiliated her. She was consumed with rage and scarcely noticed as the ragged nails bit her palms.

The anger in her burned, but she was weak. Again she grew faint. She trembled and again struggled for breath. Slowly, with a great effort, she regained a small measure of self control. Pulling into herself, she breathed in the cool air of the summer evening. She attempted to nurture the tiny flame of power that still lay at her core. Eventually, she opened her eyes and stared across the hills.

The young one was now the focus of her capacity for obsession. And perhaps, if she bided her time, she might snare him... or the old man. Ideally she would have both. What a feast that would be.

But first, she must gain strength. Then she must find a center of power or a portal. Finally, she must tear her way through to the Place. That could prove difficult, but she would prevail. Patience and focus, patience and focus were the keys.

Alicia rested and fed upon a few small, hapless creatures that she was able to snare with the dregs of her power. Next, she cast about and found a tiny spring. Slowly, painfully, she limped to it and finally slaked her terrible thirst. She felt a few grains of strength return to her core. Shivering through the night, glaring at the bright moon, she continued to rest and wait and brood.

Michael C. Glaviano

Twenty One

Afternoon shadows lengthened in front of the wagons. The road pressed on, but the horses and people of the wagon train required water, rest and food. As the clouds reddened and the sky beyond the clouds drifted towards twilight, the wagon train reached a way station.

There was a barn, a place to stable the horses. There was a place to take on simple provisions and a place of refreshment. For the more well-heeled travelers, there were even lodgings to be had. For the rest, and this surely included Eddie, there was a good camping place with fresh water and basic facilities.

Those who rode the wagons were uniformly glad to pull into camp and to stretch their legs. Even more road-weary, the outriders eased themselves from their mounts, saw to the tired horses, and then took their turns at rest and refreshment. Eddie learned that most of the people on the wagon train would either sleep under the stars or in the camper wagon. Ben mentioned that this was the best way to keep tabs on their cargo and to ensure an early start. He laughingly referred to those who slept in lodgings while on the road as "layabeds."

Isabel and Nate both invited Eddie to share meals with them, and Eddie gratefully accepted. He handed off his original trousers to Isabel. Nate raised an eyebrow at that, but Isabel just waved her hand back and forth at him cheerfully and put Eddie's ratty garment in a drawstring bag and then into a chest on the wagon.

"I'm going over to settle up with the campsite owner," remarked Nate. He noticed that Eddie looked up sharply at this. "No, please do not concern yourself, Reed. Your added expense is not a problem. You may help with chores, and the others may want to ask you questions this evening. I consider this, together with what you have already told me, compensation enough and bid you welcome to our camp."

Even so, Eddie showed the others what remained in his pack and offered to contribute to the communal meal. Isabel remarked aloud that the lady of the forest had given him the gathered nuts, and this revelation resulted in more enthusiasm than such modest contributions would ordinarily deserve.

One of the younger women walked over and introduced herself. Her hair was still damp from a visit to the bath house. "Hello. We have not met. My name is Helena Graysmith, but nearly everyone calls me 'Lena.'"

"Hi. My name's, um, Reed. Reed Woodruff. I kind of saw you... on that wagon with the windows. When we started up after the... break at, what was it? Salter's Bridge?"

"Yes. I drive that wagon. In addition to providing bunk space, it also carries our supplies. Anyway, today was my turn to eat dust at the back of the wagon train.

"So," she continued, "go wash the trail dust from your hands and face and then meet me at the supply wagon. We will shell these nuts, crush them, and add them to the tart I am planning to make for dessert. In fact, you can help me with dinner!" she laughed and smiled engagingly at Eddie.

Standing nearby, Isabel raised an eyebrow as she overheard the young woman's overture, but then she smiled gently and nodded. Eddie followed the others to an outdoor sink where they all washed their hands and faces. Isabel tossed him a spare towel and said, "Keep it for tomorrow."

Cleaned up slightly, Eddie realized that he was hungry and hurried over to where Lena was setting up dinner.

There was a large, outdoor cook-top and oven at the campsite. At first he was surprised to see that it was electrically powered, but then Eddie saw that photovoltaic arrays covered the south-facing roofs of all the nearby structures. He noticed a sizable stone building off to one side. The building had no windows but featured obvious vent stacks.

"Is that for batteries?" he wondered aloud.

"Yes, indeed it is," Lena replied. "All the camping facilities in the traders' cooperative have electric cooking facilities. Most of the wagon trains come through during good weather, so there is nearly always plenty of sun to charge the batteries and give us some power after dark. And of course they use solar collectors for their hot water supply."

Eddie thought that solar energy applications, coupled with horse-drawn transport, represented a strange combination of technologies, but it obviously worked. He supposed that the whole system could be practical depending on the cost of the technology and its availability.

"All right, Reed," Lena called, laughing. "The battery house will not go anywhere. You can stop staring at it and shell these nuts. I must start working on the main dish."

She provided him with a nutcracker and a bowl to hold the nutmeats. While Eddie worked, Lena made several trips into the interior of the camper wagon and returned with supplies. It turned out that the main dish was going to be a huge casserole... actually three huge casseroles – there were after all eleven of them in camp. There would also be fresh baked bread and some kind of braised greens. And dessert.

After he shelled the nuts, Eddie was assigned to wash and cut up the greens. These leafy vegetables resembled chard in both color and shape. It looked like there was a whole bushel of greens, but Lena assured him that they would "cook down to nothing." Eddie carried the basket over to the wash station and rinsed the greens. Then he brought them back and she had him slice the greens into a big pot. Lena had put a splash of oil, a little broth, herbs, and diced onions in the bottom of the pot.

"Just cut the greens into strips and dump them in there. Go ahead. When it gets full you can push down on the greens and jam the lid on. Once they start cooking, they will be fine."

The young woman had started bread rising that morning. She punched down the dough, rolled it, and made four braided loaves. When the loaves were formed, she brushed them with olive oil and sprinkled them with something that looked like sesame seeds.

While Eddie had been struggling with the greens, Lena had constructed three giant casseroles. Eddie thought she must have cut everything in advance, but he had to admit that she was very quick and efficient in her movements. She had the casseroles in the big oven well before he had the chard sliced and into the pot.

Lena Graysmith was a trim, athletic young woman. Her plain trousers and her work shirt somehow showed off her figure to good advantage. She wore a bright blue bandana around her neck, and the young man couldn't help but notice that it matched the shade of her eyes exactly. Her eyes stood out against smooth olive skin and hair that was neither blond nor brown nor red but had the appearance of some deep, rich mixture of all three.

Eddie figured they were close to the same age. He also decided that she was very attractive. Lena had a lively laugh, and she teased him in a way that was slightly sexy without being overtly provocative.

What with one thing and another, dinner preparations were over all too soon, but Eddie was pretty sure that he'd made a new friend before it was done. Lena was a good conversationalist. She was bright and had opinions about her world – opinions that obviously had real thought and study behind them. Like nearly everyone he'd met in the wagon train, she was self-confident without being arrogant, interested without being nosy.

Lena volunteered that she was taking a summer off from studies at her university to "enjoy some fresh air and outdoor living." As far as Eddie could tell, she was a serious student who had started advanced studies at an early age. He sensed that she was well ahead of most people her age. At one point, Lena mentioned that she was nearly finished with her university work and was thinking about what she wanted to do next.

From her remarks it was obvious that she'd had a conversation with Isabel about his origins, but she only asked a few questions and those were not deeply prying. She was naturally interested in the fact that Eddie came from a parallel world, but she had grown up with this idea so it was not the focus of the dialogue.

Oh, and without saying so directly, somewhere in the conversation, she let Eddie know that she was single.

For his part, Eddie was interested. Naturally, he was very attracted to Lena, but he surprised himself by thinking, in a quiet moment when she'd run back to the camper wagon for something, that she was a young woman worth getting to know, worth being friends with. These thoughts would have been dismissed as totally uncool by the hotshot kid who had turned up on Joe Tabs' doorstep on a cold, May night just a few months' earlier.

When Lena returned to the stove, Eddie asked where her university was located.

She raised her eyebrows and then smiled, "Of course, you would not... could not know that, could you? Soapstone Bay is a university town. It is the start and end of the trading loop we have followed this summer."

"You're kidding! That's where I'm headed; although I have to make a detour first. I'll be leaving the wagon train some time tomorrow. Hey, Lena," here Eddie felt suddenly nervous and self-conscious, "I was wondering if we might get together. When we both get back to town."

Lena's smile grew and the corners of her eyes crinkled. "Well, should I hope so!" she exclaimed. She took a deep breath and added, "Yes, I think I would like that."

And just like that, the feeling between the young people changed. Each could tell that something good was stirring and that perhaps, if circumstances and time and plain old luck smiled on them, something precious might blossom.

Now dinner was ready, everyone sat down to eat. The food was plentiful and satisfying. Although some of the spices and herbs were exotic to Eddie's taste, none was unpleasant and most were delicious.

Conversation died out while they took the edge off their hunger, but gradually the members of the wagon train began to chat. There was good-natured banter, laughter, and a few stories of other trading trips. Eddie heard descriptions of travelers met on the trade roads. He heard about remote villages and big towns, about sandstorms and horses gone lame. Occasionally, someone asked Eddie a question, but by unspoken agreement or general caution, none asked any question whose answer, if overheard by others, might let the hearer deduce something of the young man's origins.

That was fine with Eddie, who never liked being the focus of a group's attention and in any case was delighted to have Lena sitting next to him. To his credit, Eddie made the effort to be sociable and be part of the group. It was not natural or second-nature for him to speak up among strangers, but these people were so warm and welcoming that it was easy to participate.

Dinner, and every other mundane activity that evening became somehow more significant. It was obvious to all the others that something had passed between the two young people, but all the members of the wagon train had been young and they all retained the memory of youthful feelings. They were kind in the way they treated the situation.

After the meal, Eddie offered to help Lena clean up, but she said that clean-up was on someone else's chore list. She paused then, smiled, and invited Eddie to walk around the campsite and talk some more.

Now they walked a little closer together. Sometimes she took his arm. The night was warm and still. They could hear the voices of the others and, farther away, some music and laughter from other campsites.

There was something on Eddie's mind. His heart beat a little harder with nervousness, and he swallowed as he tried to organize his thoughts into coherent words, "Lena, uh, I need to tell you something... a couple of things, actually."

"What? You are not betrothed, are you? Or married?" she pulled back a bit, humor on the surface, but watchful beneath.

"Oh, no. Nothing like married, but... well, you know I was befriended by the lady of the forest. But it wasn't because of any great skill or strength on my part. I just happened to be there and helped her by getting rid of the animal that was hurting her trees."

Holding his eyes in the dim light, Lena nodded at him but said nothing, and Eddie continued. "Your friends here on the wagon train seemed so impressed with the nuts I brought from that forest and all... and, um, I didn't want you to think that I'm some great woodsman or that I'm fearless or anything... like that.

"What little I know about surviving in the wilderness comes from what the forest goddess – and my teacher back on my world, of course – shared with me," he continued. "Even my ability to speak in a way that's not too different from you... even that is a gift from her... a gift in return for killing that little beast."

Lena nodded and smiled, and a weight lifted in Eddie's heart.

"Thank you for your honesty, Reed. It engenders respect... and affection. I had already noticed you took pains to avoid inflating your abilities."

She paused for a moment. "You said that there was something else?" Lena prompted.

"Oh, yeah. Yes. I just wanted to let you know that Reed isn't my real name. My name is ..."

In a flash, Lena put her hand up and covered Eddie's mouth. "Not now! Not here!" she whispered. Later, perhaps. If things work out, we will share our true names, but we keep our true names to ourselves until there is a lifelong commitment. That is our way, our tradition, and it is a good one... especially in these times."

"Now," Lena continued, "it is late. Walk me back to the camper. We have another long day ahead of us tomorrow. I promise that we will have another chance to talk before our paths separate. Also, I am very glad that you shared that part of your story with me. It makes me respect you all the more, and I will keep what you have shared to myself. You should do the same, for your own sake."

They reached the camper wagon, and Lena turned to face Eddie. Slowly, holding his eyes with hers, she reached her arms around his neck. She was not very tall, and she had to press up against him to do it, "Good night, my friend," she murmured.

"Good night, Lena," Eddie whispered back.

He was pretty sure that this was supposed to be a friendly, casual good-night kiss and had every intention of keeping it low key. As their lips touched, however, something changed. Unplanned and unexpected by either, a deep, ancient magic rose around them. No longer low key, the friendly kiss became full of portent and power.

Lena stepped back, eyes wide, "Oh, my," she breathed. Then she smiled the smile that Eddie was already beginning to love. "That was very nice. I do believe that I am looking forward to the end of this trip more than I had anticipated."

In a flash, the young woman vanished up the stairs and into the darkness of the camper. Glad for the deep twilight and the chance to compose himself, Eddie turned away and walked back to where he'd left his gear.

The camp was quiet. The moon, now approaching its second quarter, hung in the clear summer sky. Slowly, Eddie changed into his long underwear and got into his makeshift but familiar bed. He was comfortable and he felt safer than he had in days. His mind spun with all manner of thoughts and he wondered where things would lead.

Naturally, his thoughts orbited around his budding relationship with Lena. In the quiet of the moonlit campground, Eddie suddenly realized that he hadn't had a friend his own age in years. The sad events of his senior year in high school had been sufficiently traumatic that he had withdrawn from all social activities. During his abbreviated college career, he'd had few close friends, and he had stayed in touch with none of them after he left. The Drive Away business had, by its nature, kept him from establishing any kind of lasting relationships.

He felt gratitude towards Joe, of course, but Joe was his teacher, his mentor – more of a parent figure than a friend. And Eddie was begin-ning to realize that Joe was ancient. Oh, maybe not ancient in the sense that Maia was, but Eddie suspected that Joe had seen far more years pass than those found in three or even four human life spans.

And, regarding Maia, well, as she had been careful to point out, the forest goddess was not human. She was good. Eddie was sure that her actions proved her innate goodness, but she was not human. She had even referred to Eddie as her "human friend." So, in some sense, a friend she was, but not at all in the way that another human could be. And Eddie guessed that, whatever form she chose to adopt, she was essentially as old as her forest.

Eddie's mind flitted briefly over the people he'd met in Joe's town. Sergeant Driscoll and the others. Many were decent, kind people, but Eddie had not found a close connection with any of them.

And, deep inside, Eddie realized that for several years he'd held people off. Even people who wanted to get close to him. That was why he'd been mostly a loner at college and why he'd taken the Drive Away job in the first place. The experiences of the past few months had changed him in some fundamental way. Maybe he had just not been ready until now.

Eddie was both happy and nervous about what might lie ahead. He thought that trying to make things better was worth the risk, worth the effort. Somewhere in these ruminations, the day's events caught up with him. He realized that he was tired and so, with the ease of youth, Eddie fell asleep on the ground in a camp on a strange world.

* * *

Birds in the nearby trees heralded the sun and Eddie rose at first light. He stretched and gathered some clothes and his borrowed towel and made for the main building. Yesterday he'd seen that there was a bathhouse and, since he'd learned that he couldn't depend on the availability of warm water and a safe place to bathe, he wanted to make use of it while he was able.

Returning to his campsite, Eddie packed and prepared for the day. This was becoming automatic and efficient. The pack was now a familiar weight. His knee felt a little better this morning. He thought that it would carry him without trouble when the time came. As he hung the towel on a bush to dry, Ben came up.

"Morning, Reed. We could use a hand pulling the teams together."

Eddie nodded and followed the big man toward the horse barn and wagons. They collected harnesses and other gear and began working. They spoke to the horses and patted the powerful necks as the animals were brought out. The horses stamped and nickered as if they knew that their road would be long. Despite Eddie's lack of expertise in the ways of wagon trains and horses, he was able to help Ben get the well-trained teams harnessed and attached to their wagons.

By the time the teams were ready, the camp around them was fully awake and everyone was busy with well-understood tasks. Across the camp, Eddie could see that Lena was in the midst of a serious conversation with the leader of the wagon train, Nate. At one point she caught his eye, smiled and waved, but she continued talking to the older man.

Isabel and Tad came by with plates of food. Ben and Eddie had just finished with the horses and then washed at the outdoor sink. They sat on a couple of wooden benches and enjoyed fruit, scrambled eggs, and a heavy dark bread. After the simple meal, the two men brought their plates to the field kitchen and took their turn washing up.

The wagon train was ready to pull out. He heard Lena's voice call out to him. She waved Eddie over to the camper wagon and invited him to ride with her. He happily joined her on the high seat of the wagon. Today they were the second wagon in the train.

At this point, the road was heading nearly due east and steadily uphill, so the sun was in their faces. Eddie had his hat pulled down low to shield his eyes. Lena also had a hat and likewise had it pulled down low.

"I do not like driving directly toward the sun like this," she remarked. "I do not know if any of the others mentioned it, but we have heard about more highjacking and robberies in recent times. Still, we benefit from excellent support, and as soon as the sun is higher in the sky, we shall have fine visibility all around."

Again Eddie noticed that the outriders were engaged in a complex, mounted dance. The escort rode in intersecting loops that took them out to the sides and back in. There were always riders facing different directions. It must have been very tiring to both horses and riders, but it must also represent a good deterrence to attack.

"Nate said that this train hadn't been attacked," Eddie remarked.

"Not on this trip, but last year they were. Ben was badly wounded. Thank the gods' happy dreams that the traders have adopted some of the new fabrics. Mother told me that she thinks that is what saved Ben. After that trip, Father decided to add Tad. He is a trained field doctor."

"Uh... 'Mother' and 'Father?'"

"Yes, Isabel and Nate are my parents. Even though I have tried to move through my university studies rapidly, I still enjoy spending time with them on the trade routes. We are close, and, quite beyond that, I respect the roles they have chosen for themselves. Traders are very well-regarded in our society."

"Well, gosh. I, uh, had no idea that they were your folks. I mean, I liked them both and all..."

Lena laughed gently. "There was no way that you could know that, Reed; although if you look closely, you will see that I do resemble my mother in coloring. And my eyes are the same color as my fathers.

"At any rate, they thought well of you too, Reed," she continued. "My mother and father both mentioned it to me, earlier this morning."

"Oh, well, that's good. That's really good, in fact." Eddie was relieved but was still slightly flustered by this new information. He decided to return to the earlier subject.

"Yeah, well... uh, Nate, uh your father, told me that Tad patched up that guy... yesterday... at the bridge."

She nodded solemnly and continued, "Father says that as recently as five years ago, it was not this way. Something has changed in our world. We think that it is not accidental that traders are coming under pressure."

"Why is that?"

"The wagon trains carry more than goods within a region. They also propagate culture and information. They provide tangible contact between communities. Sometimes people from a village will join a wagon train for one leg of a journey. That provides them with security as they go to see friends and relatives in neighboring villages. People look forward to the visits as much as to the trade. If the wagons stopped, we would have to rely on more technological solutions to maintain cohesion. While that is possible to do, less face-to-face visiting is not as satisfactory."

The young woman drove silently for a time. Then her voice darkened as she added, "And there is another thing."

"Which is?" Eddie prompted.

"Well, we have heard rumors of a few wagon trains that are playing the role of traders but are in actuality sowing seeds of discord and fear among the towns and villages. They are subtle, but we have all noticed that sometimes we are met with more suspicion than welcome when we first pull into a remote village. My parents are well-known on this trade route, so it has been possible to overcome these ill-feelings with little trouble. Even so, it is... disquieting."

"That could evolve into a real problem if it keeps going. Or gets worse."

"Indeed it could. That is one more reason why I decided to take this summer off. I want to see how I can help preserve this system, and how we might even strengthen it."

"Do you think it's been good? Worthwhile for you, I mean?" he wondered.

Lena looked his way and nodded. She turned back and was quiet for a few moments as she squinted into the sun, but then she smiled again and quietly added, "And now... now that you and I have met, I must say that I am very happy that I decided to join my parents and the others for this trip."

"Me too," Eddie agreed. "Me too, Lena."

Michael C. Glaviano

As the sun rose toward midmorning, they continued talking. Beyond the enjoyment of company their own age, both sensed that this time together was precious. Each tried to get to know the other to the degree possible. Eddie, at Lena's prompting, shared a little about his previous few years. He talked more about Joe – he now referred to him more consistently as his "teacher" or "mentor" – and some of the things that Joe had tried to teach him.

Eddie spoke just a little about Alicia and what Joe had said concerning the people she served. Lena saw that he was uncomfortable and did not press him for any details. Although neither of them spoke of it aloud, both young people sensed that they now had more to lose than ever before in their short lives.

Eventually Eddie got around to mentioning his family tragedy, and naturally Lena responded with kindness. She also expressed a kind of undramatic sympathy that the young man hugely appreciated. Then Eddie described his aborted college career and how Joe had gotten him enrolled for remote classes. Lena brightened visibly at this and said that she was happy to see that they had education and a desire to learn in common.

"So, how much of your studies have you completed?" she wondered.

"Well, I guess I've got about two and a half years' worth of credits now. Usually basic college degrees in my country are roughly a four year process. My studies have been sort of unfocused though."

"Do you think you will want to finish a university program?"

"Well, to be honest, six months ago, I'd have shrugged off that question, but after studying with Joe... and learning just a tiny bit of the things he knows, yeah, I'm pretty sure that I'll go back as soon as I can. I need to settle on a specialty though."

When the sun was near its zenith, Nate called a halt near some trees. Although there were no buildings, there was a well and a tank so that the horses could have water. They posted sentries, but now visibility was good and the risk of ambush lower.

After a short break, the train resumed its way along the trade road. As they pulled out, Nate rode by and called to them, "You two young folks had better start saying your good-byes. The road turns north in two hours, and Reed's way takes him due east."

Eddie and Lena nodded solemnly and Nate rode off to join the others.

Wheels turned in their heads. Neither knew what to say for a time. Eventually, Eddie shook off this funk and asked, "How will I find you when I reach Soapstone Bay?"

"You can ask for me at the university. Go to the student recreation building. I will leave word with my friends there. They will know where to find me. And you? Where can I find you if you arrive first?"

"I don't really know. Your father said that I should look for work and some lodgings in town. I'll be spending some time in a place called 'The Inn at Three Corners.' That's where my mentor told me to go."

"Oh. I have heard of that place," Lena admitted quietly. "It does not exactly have the greatest reputation as a spot for young women to go unaccompanied."

"Well, when you arrive, just wait to hear from me. I'll get to the university as soon as I'm able. Can you tell me how to find it?"

Now she laughed a hearty, happy sound. "Soapstone Bay has been a seaport for over a thousand years, but for the past five hundred it has also been a university town. When it was founded, the university was placed in a logged area west of town. Over the years, the school and Soapstone have expanded toward each other. You will find the university at the west side of town."

"Do you know where the inn is relative to the university?" Eddie wondered.

"The inn lies in the oldest part of town, down nearer the harbor. The land slopes steadily up from the bay and then levels off. The Inn at Three Corners lies just past the slope. It is remarkably tall for such an old building... and it is noteworthy because of an unusual architectural feature. It has a sort of bell tower – or perhaps a watchtower – in the center.

"I have only seen it riding past and do not know how the tower was incorporated into the building, but it looks as if the inn were built around it. For all I know, the inn might be one of the oldest buildings in Soapstone. Certainly, the central tower must date from a very early time. I suspect that if you get anywhere near it, you'll be able to identify the inn and find your way to it.

"And here is a thought," she added after a short pause. "It seems to me, that given your errand and the times in which we find ourselves, you might want to do your best to find your way there without asking for directions. And, if you can do so, you might even want to appear as though you wandered there quite at random."

"Yeah, that's a good idea," Eddie agreed. "I think that for the first few days, I'll focus most of my attention on getting a means of support and a place to stay. I'll try to fit into the background as much as I can. Once I'm established in a neighborhood, I'll be able to move around and gradually extend my range and acquaintances to include the inn and those who live and work near it."

"That is fine, Reed. Just make sure those acquaintances do not include any pretty barmaids!"

"Not a chance, Lena. Not a chance."

They laughed and talked a while longer – too short it was. Then Nate rode up to say that it would soon be time for Eddie to go his own way. Eddie nodded and when Nate rode ahead, Eddie reached his left hand to cover Lena's where she held the reins. He carefully and gently placed his right arm over her shoulders and she snuggled in as best she could without neglecting the horses. They rode this way for a few minutes longer.

Up ahead, Nate called a halt. Not wanting to delay his hosts, Eddie quickly pulled Lena to him and kissed her. He drew back and said, "Until Soapstone, then." His voice was husky.

"Until Soapstone," she replied, and Eddie thought that her eyes looked ready to spill over, so he grabbed his pack and jumped off the wagon.

Once down, Eddie swung the pack over his right shoulder and slid his left into the strap, as he'd done a hundred times, but of course this time it felt different. They smiled at each other and Eddie turned and jogged to the front of the train where Nate waited.

The older man had dismounted and stood with his horse's reins in his left hand. The road turned sharply to the left here and headed more steeply upwards to the north. Directly east, the land rose more gradually.

"Take care of yourself, young man. We are glad to have you as an ally and would welcome it if our paths were to cross again. Head due east from here. If you travel quickly and encounter no impediment, you will reach the Old One's holdings by mid-morning tomorrow."

"Thank you, Nate. Please thank the others for me. I know that I'm lucky to have met you, and I... well, I'm glad to know that you and Isabel are Lena's parents. Safe journey to you!"

The two men, one young, the other in the full prime of his strength, shook hands. Nate looked deep into Eddie's eyes for a few moments. He seemed to accept what he saw there, for he nodded and his strong features softened for an instant with a faint smile. Then he swung easily into the saddle. Lena's father raised his hand and swept it forward.

Now passing in front of Eddie, the wagon train started up again. He watched Lena's wagon approach and draw near. She was still teary-eyed but she was also smiling. Then she passed along, as did the others one-by-one. Isabel rode past and called a brief farewell. Eddie stood still until they had all passed, and then he crossed the road. There he paused and took in the scene for a moment longer.

Not sure if they could see, he waved his arm and set off. He had rehearsed this transition in his mind and picked out his first cover two or three hundred yards ahead. He moved as quickly as he could in that direction.

* * *

The first available cover was up a slight rise from the roadbed. Eddie could see a scrub oak, a few shrubs that looked, at a distance, reminiscent of sage, and a cluster of rocks. By the time Eddie had made it over the intervening ground, the wagon train was no longer visible. He silently wished them all well and hoped that whatever goodness that existed would watch over Lena. Then he fished out his compass and pinpointed the next significant cover that was east of him.

Before leaving his hiding place under the tree, Eddie looked all around. The land provided limited shelter. It was undeniable that a hiker moving across the gently rolling grassland would be visible for a great distance. Raptors soared in the bright sky overhead, but none were near. Carefully, Eddie identified some intermediate landmarks. Then, moving as quickly as he could, his next stop fixed firmly in view, he set out.

This pattern that Maia had suggested, this darting between areas of relative cover and safety, had good side effects. It helped Eddie focus his mind and keep him engaged in the task at hand. It helped him stay aware of his surroundings. He made good time as the afternoon wore on. It was warm in the direct sunlight, but there was a hint of a breeze, and he had his hat to shade his face.

Once, he moved too quickly and slipped on some talus near the base of a small cliff. When his foot went out from under him, he was reminded vividly and forcefully of his recently bruised ribs, his banged up knee. More importantly, he was reminded that he was alone and that even a twisted ankle would be very serious. Maia's "aunt," or as the wagon train people had called her, "the Old One," might very well be expecting him, but he still had to reach her holding. Once more, Eddie resolved to be as careful as he could and to move slowly when he encountered broken ground.

As he continued to put distance between himself and the trade road, Eddie began to sense the extent of the grassland. Most grasses were still green but a few had shaded to light brown and were already going to seed. The stalks waved in the gentle breeze. Here and there, stands of lupine, with its tiny blue and pink flowers, were entering the last phase of their bloom. The tall stalks were heavily laden with pea-shaped flowers.

Monarch and painted lady butterflies drifted on the gentle breezes. Grasshoppers jumped from his path. Once, he flushed a sage grouse that leapt into the air in a flurry of feathers and glided a new hiding place in the tall grasses. Momentarily as startled as the bird, Eddie froze in his tracks before laughing and continuing on.

In this way, he passed the afternoon. From cover to cover, always moving east, he progressed. After the first rise from the roadway, the land sloped gently, gradually downwards as he went. The general downward trend was punctuated here and there with small ridges that ran roughly north-south – perpendicularly to his course. Eddie paused for a short rest in the shade of more scrub oak. He snacked and, careful of how much he took, sipped a little of his water. As the day wore on, his shadow preceded him and grew longer.

Eddie kept moving for as long as he thought safe and then began to seek shelter. Obviously, it would be unwise to camp completely in the open. At the same time Eddie didn't want to crawl into a cluster of rocks and find that some other creature had already set up housekeeping. Finally, he sighted a small grove of willows in a depression 100 yards to the left of his trail.

He set up some stones as a marker and in the gathering twilight, used his compass to identify a point at the edge of the grove that was as near to due north as possible. Then he hiked over to that spot and set up another small pile of stones to mark his exit point for the next morning.

Eddie saw no need to move deep into the grove, so once he felt that he was shielded from view he set up his spartan camp. The air was cooler here, with just the tiniest tang of salt when the wind blew hard from the east. It made him glad to think that he had half a day or less travel ahead of him to reach his goal.

As he set up his camp, the air temperature continued to drop and Eddie wondered just how cold the night would get. Sheltered as he was by the grove, he thought that he might risk a fire. There were a lot of dead, dry twigs around, so as he'd done on his first night in this world, Eddie scooped a patch of soft soil to one side and laid a small fire in the center of the cleared space.

He fed the fire mostly small pieces of wood that caught easily and this kept smoke to a minimum. In between tending the fire, Eddie continued to get organized. He wanted to be able to leave at first light, so after some thought, he decided to sleep in his clothes. He kept the fire going while he snacked on his waning supplies. He repacked everything so that all he'd have to do before heading out in the morning would be to put on his shoes, roll up his bedding and hook it to his pack.

After a couple of hours of tending the fire, Eddie became sleepy and uncomfortably cold. By then he had a good bed of coals, so he used a flat rock to spread those in an even layer across the area he'd cleared. He carefully replaced the soil and scooped some more from around the camp so that he had several inches of dirt covering the hot coals. He checked all around this mound to make sure there were no hot spots. Then, without disturbing the soil, he laid half the width of his tarp over it and wrapped himself in his blanket.

He lay there, glad finally to be out of the cold. Then, reaching out into the chilly night air, he pulled the other half of the tarp over the top. Now he'd be warm and dry. The air on his face grew colder but the warm coals beneath his bed were doing their job and he was more comfortable.

Eddie drifted off to sleep wondering what tomorrow's meeting with the Old One would be like.

For several hours, Eddie slept peacefully, but gradually his dreams took on a nightmarish quality. They were strange, sinister, and full of half-seen images, shouted but indistinct warnings. A beautiful woman hovered nearby and spoke to him, but Eddie couldn't make out what she said. She kept asking him for something, but he wasn't sure what it was. The air was cold in his lungs. The woman drew closer and began caressing his face. He tried but found that he could not pull away from her hand when she laid it on his cheek. The touch of her hand burned, but he was paralyzed, unable to move his arms and legs. Her questioning grew more and more insistent.

Suddenly, a voice sounded in Eddie's head, "*Remember the face of your beloved!*" It was a strong voice, strong and clear. The woman with the icy hands drew back at this, and her murmuring ceased.

"*Remember her!*" the clear voice sounded again, and now Lena's face – kind, and full of love and acceptance – swam into view. At once, the woman with the icy hands screamed, and Eddie opened his eyes. It was near dawn. Lingering nearby was a hideous creature with long fangs and scaly skin. It stared hungrily at him in the gray light.

Still sleepy, Eddie locked eyes with the creature and his vision swam. He sensed the image of the beautiful woman superimposed on it. He began to drift off, to lose consciousness.

"*Remember your beloved!*" the clear voice sounded in his head a third time, and again Eddie remembered Helena Graysmith. Now he came full awake but he still could not move. He was unable to break his eyes away from those of the thing that had invaded his dreams. Suddenly, the light from the first sliver of sunrise caught the creature on its shoulder as it hunched there, unsure of its prey.

When the light touched it, the creature screamed in pain and rage. It whirled. The light hit it full in the face and Eddie watched as the creature crumpled upon itself, turned to ashes, and blew away on the dawn breeze.

With the thing's disappearance, the paralysis that had gripped him suddenly lifted. Eddie's heart hammered in his chest, and he struggled to take a deep breath. Finally, he summoned enough presence of mind to fling the top of the tarp back and crawl from his bed. The grove around him was silent. Eddie could see that his pack had been pulled apart and its contents scattered.

The sight of his gear strewn all over the campsite drove the last bit of lethargy from his limbs. He struggled into his boots and gathered what remained of his things. His water bottle was empty and broken so that it could not be used. What remained of his food was scattered. His compass was smashed to pieces.

All that was left were some of the extra clothes and his minimal toilet kit. He'd kept his knife in the bedroll with him, so that was safe too, but he had no food, no water, and no navigation. For a moment, Eddie felt real despair, but as he idled there, he caught again the tang of salt air. The smell of the sea made him recall Nate's parting words. He had less than half a day's walk to reach his goal.

He'd been traveling due east. It was just minutes past dawn. If he got out into the open, he could at least start the first leg of his journey by the sun. And it was near enough to high summer that the sun would pass almost directly overhead. He knew that if he didn't panic, if he was careful and stayed focused, he would survive and reach his goal. Moving quickly now, Eddie repacked his things. Unwilling to leave them behind, he placed his broken compass and ruined water bottle in the top of the pack. He picked up the clothes that had been shredded to rags and gathered the torn wrappers of his ruined food bars. He found the bag that had held the last of his dried fruit. The refuse filled the side pockets of his pack.

One last time, Eddie scanned the campsite. There was nothing else he could salvage. Here and there he could make out a crumb of a food bar, but the campsite was about as clean as he could make it. Of its own accord, Lena's face came back to him and he recalled the end of his nightmare. The young man understood that in a real sense, the feelings he had for this young woman had saved his life. With that appreciation came a change. Something deep inside that had lain closed and dormant since the deaths of his father and brother finally relaxed completely and opened.

He threaded his arms through the straps of his pack and set out. Although Eddie did his best to exit the grove very near the place he'd come in, he couldn't find his rock marker. There were scattered stones all around, but no small pile of stones. Even so, looking out toward open ground, he was pretty sure that he could see, uphill, the marker he'd left last night on his main trail. He made for that as quickly as he could.

Yes. There it was. This marker at least was undisturbed. Squinting his eyes in the glare, he lay on his belly and sited toward the rising sun. The ground ahead first sloped down slightly and then climbed gradually to a distant ridge. At the crest of the ridge, right in front of the sun, Eddie could make out something. It looked like a cluster of three trees, some type of pine tree, he thought.

Standing carefully, Eddie could make out the trees more clearly. They stood very close to due east, so with a final glance around, he started out.

It took over an hour to reach the trees on the ridge. On the down-slope, in addition to more pines, he could make out manzanita and more scrub oak. The ground was rich and fertile. The low grasses and shrubs were greener here.

Now the sun was much higher in the sky and, perhaps, somewhat off to Eddie's right. He had no idea what the latitude was, but he thought that he was pretty far north because of how long the summer days were. This meant that true east would be somewhat to the left of a shadow cast by a vertical marker. He didn't have a wristwatch, so there was no way to decide just how far to the left of the sun he needed to walk.

Still, he could smell the salt air full on his face and he figured he had only an hour or two more of travel ahead of him, so he once again picked out a landmark that was as far away as he could practically see. Fortunately, the terrain continued to be dominated by gently rolling hills, and from where he stood, Eddie could make out another distant ridge and some distinct features to guide him.

Now, however, Eddie was starting to get thirsty. Intellectually, he knew that he'd be fine for another few hours at least. If it didn't get hot, he could certainly last more than a day without water; although hiking up and down hills without a trail in such conditions would be miserable.

He sighed, knowing that the best thing he could do was to keep moving. So he headed for the next ridge. He tried to pace himself so that he could breathe through his nose and thus retain as much water as possible.

As he reached the bottom of the gentle slope, Eddie could see some bushes just off his way, perhaps 20 or 30 feet to the right. He looked closer and whooped out loud when he saw that they were wild blackberries. Although it was a little early in the season for blackberries, he lost no time in jogging over. He reached carefully among the sharp thorns to find the ripest berries.

The easy, sunny slopes were ideal for them and the bushes were loaded with fruit. In addition to providing some welcome moisture and an energy boost, this was further evidence that Eddie was near the coast. After he spent perhaps a quarter of an hour, Eddie's fingertips were stained a deep burgundy. He was no longer quite so thirsty and decided that he should get moving again.

He looked toward the ridge and picked out his landmark again. Then, moving with renewed energy and confidence, he began working his way up the gradual slope. As he neared the top, he could see more wild blackberry bushes and the crowns of aromatic eucalyptus trees. A short time later, Eddie topped a rise and could see, far ahead, the blue of the ocean.

Between where he stood on the ridge and the sea was a shallow, sheltered valley. The far, north end was occupied by a sizable cultivated field – perhaps a grain crop. The middle of the valley nourished and sustained a tidy orchard. Near the south end of the valley stood a modest farmhouse. Its sides were indeed white-plastered and fresh and the roof

Michael C. Glaviano

was crowned with a thick thatch just as Maia had said. Near the house was an extensive vegetable garden.

Even at this distance he could hear chickens. Behind the house there was an elevated cistern fed by a windmill that was perched near the top of the opposite rise. The whole scene was so tranquil and beautiful, that, unwilling to disturb any part of it, Eddie halted and breathed it into his being.

A porch spread across the front of the house, and this commanded a view of the valley and the rise upon which he stood. From his vantage point, Eddie could see that he had already been observed. Someone sat in a chair in the shadow of the porch. As the young man contemplated the scene, the figure rose, walked to the edge of the porch and waved. Eddie hastened to return the gesture. He had been acknowledged and, apparently welcomed, so he strode directly towards the house.

He'd covered half the 500 yards or so to the house when he was greeted by a medium sized farm dog. It looked to be some kind of border collie. Ordinarily, Eddie was a little nervous around strange animals, but after a couple of happy barks, this one was content to wag his tail and hop around in an excited dance as he accompanied the young man the rest of the way to the house.

The figure resolved itself into a short, middle-aged woman. At first her general appearance recalled that of Eddie's own great-aunt, his grandmother's sister, who'd long since passed away. Then the ancient map of her face broke into a warm and welcoming smile, and he felt as though he were a lost child being led home after a tiring, dusty adventure.

Eddie's reverie was interrupted by the dog. Asking to be acknowledged and patted, he licked the young man's hand and ducked his head beneath it. The woman's eyes were bright and kind. She spoke for the first time, "Welcome, Laddie. Welcome to my home. There's food in plenty and a safe place to rest and gain strength for the next part of your journey. I've spied you from afar and guided your steps, but you've done well in your own way. Now come in. Come in and rest. My name is Lillith, and I am daughter to the world, care-giver to its creatures."

Eddie recognized the clear voice that had reached into his dream the previous night, called up the image of Lena's face, and thereby saved him from the creature.

"It was you!" he blurted. "Your voice, this morning... in the dream!"

A brief shadow flickered across the radiant face to be chased away in an instant by a smile. "Yes, Laddie. In the old times, a harpy would never have dared come so close to my holdings, but there is much damage that needs undoing in the world today. We'll talk more of this later, but for now, come inside and be welcome."

So Eddie made his slow way up the few steps and into the Old One's safe, safe home.

Michael C. Glaviano

Twenty Two

For one whole cycle of the moon he dwelt beneath her roof, and six days out of seven he worked the long, summer daylight hours on her farmstead. Each morning he awoke to the smell of a hearty breakfast. Each night, after a simple, filling dinner, he made his way to a room tucked beneath the eaves on the east side of her house. There, he slept like a contented child until dawn.

The house was small. There were Eddie's tiny attic quarters. Downstairs there was one main room that served as kitchen, dining room, workroom. In one corner, a spinning wheel stood next to a huge basket of roving. The wheel glimmered in the dim light. On the opposite wall was a small doorway that led to Lillith's private room or rooms. Eddie never ventured there.

The tiny home was perfectly organized. And it was beautiful. Everything shone with polishing, strength, and good use. Oh, and amazingly enough, this anachronistic wonder had indoor plumbing.

Lillith's words were few; mostly small-talk concerning the garden, the animals, the crops. Eddie hung on each sentence and found within her words the tasks which she most wanted him to accomplish each day.

And each day as he went about the labors required to complete his tasks, he would recall the dream of the night before. These were dreams like no others he'd experienced before, and in his later years, Eddie saw that those nights were unique among all the nights of his life. Eddie came to understand that those dreams were Lillith's way of imparting the knowledge and understanding that she believed would most benefit him and the world under her care.

In the evenings, Eddie would return to the tiny house. He would wash and find food set out for him. Lillith, the Old One, would sometimes watch him eat, would sometimes speak a few kind words to the young man. Perhaps she would card wool or clean and putter around the single room. Eventually, she would make her way to the spinning wheel. Then, it was as if Eddie had vanished from her sight.

The great wheel would spin. Never faltering, the fiber would whisper in the Old One's fingers. Sometimes Eddie watched her spin, but he could never see the results of her work. The yarn trailed off to vanish into the shadows. Before long, he would move as softly as he could up the narrow stairs to his cot in the attic. Then, the sound of the wheel in his head, the young man would drop into a deep slumber.

On occasion, he would be drawn during the day back to the house, and he would sit in a chair on her porch or at her kitchen table and she would play the part of the kind grandmother and he that of the contented youngster. Sometimes she would speak a few phrases that would call to mind the dream of the previous night. The result would be that Eddie would remember and more clearly understand her sense and meaning and how it might apply to his situation.

In those weeks of hard physical labor, Eddie grew strong and steady. The work and the food created strength deep in his core. And in all those nights of dreams, he grew in knowledge that he thought might someday ripen into wisdom. He lost none of his humanity in that cottage and only a tiny bit of his youth. All the wheat remained but much chaff fell away.

On the morning of the twenty-ninth day, the young man came downstairs to find his pack waiting. On top of his pack lay his compass, miraculously mended. Next to the pack were his water bottle, now whole and filled to the brim, and his sheath knife, which he was later to find had received a razor sharp edge. For as long as he owned that knife, the blade retained its perfect edge.

He put the compass in a side-pocket and fastened the knife to his belt. The water bottle fit inside the pack, atop his clean, neatly folded clothes.

Lillith, the Old One, stood off to one side, waiting.

"It is time, Laddie. It is time for you to make your way down the coast and from there back into the worlds. Walk now, down to the shore from here. You'll find a boat. Row out beyond the breakers and you'll find a ship anchored. Climb aboard. Leave my boat; it will make its own way back to my beach."

"Thank you, Lillith. Thank you for your kindness and your teaching. I will do my best to put things right."

"I know you will, Laddie. You came well recommended by my niece... and by your actions in reaching this far. Now off with you. The captain knows to wait for you to board, but he does not enjoy the wait-ing."

She paused for a heartbeat, and then continued with a twinkle in her eye, "And mark this! When you come across that old scoundrel – you know him as 'Joe,' but he has other names... Well, you just tell him it's past time he came by for a visit."

So Eddie left that safe, happy place and moved again into the world. Now he had more resources, but he also had a greater understanding of what challenges lay ahead. Once more, he swung the familiar feel of his pack over his shoulder and threaded his arms through the straps. Once again he moved under the sky and sensed the ground beneath his feet.

The young man followed a well-marked trail that, tracing the contours of the land, meandered among gentle hills. The trail sloped steadily downwards. Within moments, Lillith's home was hidden from view. An hour more, and the land had changed from fertile, tended farmland to sandy shore land with scraggly plants and a windblown look.

Had Eddie glanced over his shoulder, he might also have noticed that the path behind him faded, the trail erased by blowing sand. But his eyes were on the way ahead and Lillith's words were as true as the stars in the desert night, true as the waves in the sea, and as the songbird's melody. The path in front of him remained clear, and the young man spied the beach and the water soon enough.

When Eddie reached the shore, he found that there was indeed a small boat waiting just at the line of the waves. Out in deeper water, Eddie could see a much larger vessel anchored. The sun was bright and the air smelled crisp.

Chasing fish that leapt from the water, gulls called to each other and boasted of their catch. Sandpipers scampered on the wet sand as the waves retreated. Plovers darted here and there, and Eddie was a young man with a new adventure facing him. He'd never ridden on an ocean going vessel before and was excited to get on with it.

Quickly, he tossed his pack in the boat. There were a pair of oars in the bottom. It took only seconds to unlace his boots, remove them and roll up his pant legs. Anticipating a climb onto a much larger boat, Eddie stuffed his socks deep inside his boots and then tied the boots together with some care. He grabbed the bow of the tiny craft and hauled it around to point into the foam. Then, when a wave came in, he pushed hard on the stern of the boat.

The boat rose with the water and began to float away from Eddie's hands. He almost lost his balance and had to wade farther into the water as he pushed once more. Now he was wet, but he was also invigorated and excited. He managed to get himself over the side of the boat as the next wave bore the tiny craft out.

Eddie grabbed an oar and, choking up on it like a baseball bat, used it as a paddle to get past the shore break. He flailed a little but managed to push the boat into position. After a brief struggle with the unfamiliar hardware, he got both oars into the oar locks. Using his legs as well as his back, he dipped the oars and tried to pull evenly against the water.

With half a dozen strong pulls Eddie had the boat resting in deeper water. He turned around and could see, perhaps a half mile out, a beautiful, three-masted ship that was anchored in what Eddie could now see was a sheltered cove. A natural breakwater curved out from the north. The mouth of the cove opened to the south, and in the clear, bright light he could see, a few miles beyond the opening, an island that stood well away from the shore.

Eddie put his legs into it and rowed for the ship. The breeze was coming from offshore, but it was not too strong while he was close in, so at first he made good time. The seagulls wheeled overhead. They swooped and dove.

Once he was halfway to the vessel, Eddie came out of the lee of the tallest part of the breakwater and had to adjust his course more to the north. This was a lot more work than pulling across a pond or sheltered lake and he began to breathe hard.

Still, a short time later, he pulled the little boat to the side of the much larger craft. Lillith had admonished him to be on his best behavior, so he put his hands to either side of his mouth and called out, "Hello! May I have permission to board?!"

A second later this was answered from an unseen speaker far overhead. "Aye! Permission granted! Board and be welcome!"

Eddie pulled in the oars and placed them in the bottom of the boat. A rope ladder was tossed down and the young man grabbed his pack and swung it onto his back. In a flash, he draped his boots over his left shoulder, one in front, one behind. Then he clutched the rope ladder and made his ascent.

It was the first time he'd ever tried to climb a rope ladder, and Eddie was not prepared for the way it moved. Before he'd reached a dozen rungs, he succeeded in banging his knuckles and stubbing his bare toes on the side of the ship. Once he thought he might slip and had to grasp the swaying ladder tightly for a few seconds.

He looked down and saw that he was already well above the water. The little boat had silently moved a hundred yards closer to the shore. His heart was racing with excitement, and Eddie laughed. Moving with care, he continued to the top. A strong hand reached over the side and helped him over the rail.

The hand was attached to an equally powerful arm. The arm's owner was a physically imposing man who stood well over six feet in height. The man's unruly mane of hair had been coerced into a ponytail and secured by a spiral thong of leather. The hair had once been dark; now it was sun-bleached and shot with gray.

The man wore a one-piece coverall that came to his knees. His feet were adorned with boat shoes that could be kicked off quickly if the need arose. His weathered face was strong and symmetrical, his smile wide and easy. His eyes, a striking and vivid green, were intense and alive.

"Welcome to the *Mother Rose*, young man! I am the captain. You may call me Thomas, Thomas Wyndham, and I am at your service... and that of our Elder on shore."

Here the captain nodded respectfully towards Lillith's homestead. Eddie followed the big man's look and saw that he could just make out the top of the thatched roof behind a hill that had blocked the view at sea level. Eddie could also make out that the little boat was again beached. It had obviously taken far less time to return than it had on the outward trip with Eddie at the oars.

Standing in silence, they looked toward shore for a few moments. A cloud blew across the sun, and when it had passed, Eddie could no longer see even that hint of Lillith's cottage. Likewise the little boat had faded, vanished. The shore was now trackless and empty.

He turned questioningly back to the big man who nodded solemnly, "Aye, lad, the Old One does love her privacy as she tends to the needs of the world." Then he brightened. "It is an honor to have aboard this humble vessel one who has been her guest!"

Again Eddie almost blurted out his name, but quickly he recovered and replied, "Sir, please call me Reed, Reed Woodruff." He paused for a second and then, with unaccustomed grace, continued, "And may I address you as 'Captain Thomas?' Your ship is far from humble, and in my mind, it is fitting to show due respect to one who makes his way over the waves at the bidding of the Old One."

This heartfelt observation clearly pleased the big man. Captain Thomas grinned even more broadly and covered Eddie's hand with his own massive one. The intense eyes flashed with good will.

"Aye, Reed, and I acknowledge your respect and thank you for it...."

Now that first introductions were out of the way, Eddie could look around the deck of the *Mother Rose*. The ship was as beautiful and as graceful as only a wind-powered vessel can be. It looked to Eddie's untutored eye to be some kind of great bird that had, for love of the sea, taken on the form of a ship.

The big man followed Eddie's gaze. "Would you like a tour of my ship, Reed?"

"Yes, sir. I would like that a lot!"

"Then let's get you settled into a cabin. I'll see about getting us underway. Once we're on course, I'd be delighted to show you around. What do you know of modern sailing ships?"

"Sad to say, I know next to nothing, but I'm eager to learn and look forward to the tour."

The captain chuckled. "You'll learn soon enough, Laddie. Soon enough. For now, the directions you need to know are 'fore,' 'aft,' 'port,' and 'starboard.' They're all fixed – defined relative to the ship herself, rather than the points of the compass or some shore-dweller's prefer-ence. The foremost end of the ship is the 'bow.' The aft-most is the 'stern.' A 'bulkhead' is a wall within the ship. The floor, here, is 'the deck.' You'll catch on." The big man gestured with his left hand as he spoke.

Now he indicated a structure that occupied a good fraction of the rear of the sailing ship. "For example, there's an empty cabin in the aft castle."

Eddie accompanied him to a door near the center of the struc-ture. A short hall gave access to four small cabins. The captain opened the first on the starboard side and gestured Eddie inside.

"Here you go, lad. You can stow your gear in here. Best you leave those land-boots in your cabin. I'll have one of the crew leave you some boat shoes to wear while you're on board."

Eddie could hardly contain himself. "This is great!" he said.

The big man laughed heartily, a sound that Eddie was to hear of-ten in the days ahead. "Indeed it is, Laddie. Indeed it is."

"That's your 'birth,'" he indicated the bunk-like bed in the cabin, "and down the hall is the 'head.' Shore dwellers call it 'a toilet.'" Captain Thomas pronounced the word as if he'd rarely heard it.

Now the Captain's voice took on a more businesslike tone. "We'll be busy readying the ship, weighing anchor, unfurling the sails and set-ting course. Even with all the modern capabilities the *Mother Rose* pos-sesses, it'll be a bustling hour. Once you're settled in, feel free to come out and sit on the ledge just outside the door to the aft castle. You'll be out of the way there but you'll be able to witness many marvels."

Eddie nodded and thanked the captain, who nodded in return, stepped back to fill the corridor, and retraced his steps to the deck.

Alone in his cabin, Eddie looked more carefully at his surround-ings. There was a berth built into the starboard bulkhead of the cabin. Beneath the berth were three drawers with a latch above each. Above the berth was an open porthole that let in the breeze. To the bow side of the door, there were a couple of hooks where one could hang foul weather gear. Eddie noticed grating on the floor beneath the hooks. The grating would permit water to drip off without puddling.

A stout wooden locker was fastened to the floor just aft of the exit. This had a lid with a latch. The bottom of the box was fashioned of heavy, parallel slats – a perfect place to leave his boots.

A small chair was in the aft corner nearest the corridor. It was secured to the bulkhead with something very like a bungee cord. A writ-ing desk was fastened about midway on the forward bulkhead. Opposite the desk was a compact, built-in wardrobe.

All the latches and exposed fasteners were bronze. Most surfaces were some kind of light colored wood – teak, he was eventually to learn – that had received the benefit of many coats of hand-rubbed oil.

Eddie noticed a switch above the locker by the cabin door, and when he tried it, he was happy to see a ceiling mounted light turn on in response. There was also a small reading lamp at the head of the berth and a similar light near the desk.

Both pleased and impressed with what he saw, Eddie stowed his few possessions. When he opened the door, Eddie found some boat shoes waiting just outside his cabin. With one last look around his cabin, he closed the door, slipped on the shoes, and made his way to the exterior door of the aft castle. Exiting there, he found on the starboard side of the door, the ledge that Captain Thomas had mentioned. In the warmth of the sun, the young man settled back on the ledge and enjoyed his view of the main deck.

The day continued to be bright and beautiful. The ship became a bustle of activity as the crew unfurled the sails and set a course south down the coast. Crewmembers carried out orders cheerfully and efficiently.

As he sat on the ledge and observed the activity, Eddie struggled to remember what little he knew or had heard about ships. He had to admit to himself that there wasn't a lot that he knew, but he guessed that he'd pick up what he'd need. He could hear orders being called out. The captain yelled occasionally, and once or twice, Eddie heard his great laugh booming across the ship.

The structure that Captain Thomas had called the "aft castle" rose eight or ten feet above the main deck. At the front, "the bow" of the ship, Eddie remembered, there was a corresponding, somewhat shorter structure. A "forecastle," he guessed.

Just as he observed with the wagon train, Eddie could see a mix of old and new technology aboard the ship. Besides the electric lights in his cabin, Eddie could see that there were motorized winches. Some of the ship's structures – especially those subject to great stress – were fabricated from modern, albeit unfamiliar materials. There were three masts, for instance, and the one closest to Eddie, the rearmost, was obviously made of something other than wood. It didn't appear to be made of metal either.

In addition, there were four, sturdy pedestals distributed around the main deck. Each pedestal supported a control console of sorts, and a sailor stood at each and operated controls. At a command, a small sail automatically unfurled near the bow. A large, triangular sail ran up the nearest mast. The sail on the largest, center mast remained furled. The sails sparkled and glistened in the brilliant sunlight.

At the captain's command, the ship weighed anchor. The *Mother Rose* swung gracefully before the wind, and the sails filled. The ship headed for the outlet of the cove. Birds called overhead.

Once the *Mother Rose* cleared the mouth of the cove, Eddie heard another command and the great, square mainsail was hoisted on the largest mast near the center of the ship. The vessel surged ahead.

Now the level of activity lessened. A sailor remained stationed at each console but mostly appeared to monitor instruments and only occasionally make small adjustments. The rest of the crew huddled for a few moments in small groups before breaking off to take on other tasks. A few moments later, Captain Thomas appeared at Eddie's side.

"Are you ready for the tour now, Laddie?"

"Yes, I am, Captain Thomas," he replied.

"Let's begin with a stroll around the deck. Then I'll check status with my first mate. If all is well, we can move to a more detailed inspection of the vessel. She is a marvel."

As they walked slowly around the deck, the captain introduced Eddie to various crew members. Eddie doubted that he'd remember most of their names and hoped they'd be patient as he learned.

"The *Mother Rose* is a modern variation on the caravelle or carack style of ships from several hundred years ago," the captain explained. "Those were some of the first effective cargo and warships to be designed in the western world. Early designs had tall aft and fore castles, and these caused problems with the cross section they presented to the wind. Since we have modern instrumentation, we don't need to be perched so high. This lets us keep the general shape of a caravelle but with a lower, more stable profile.

"Of course all the stress bearing parts of her are modern composites, most of them purpose grown. Notice the cross section of the main mast here: see the teardrop shape? A good airfoil effect. The same is true of the yards that support the main sail," here the captain gestured aloft at the big, square sail.

"What do you call the rearmost – aft-most," Eddie corrected himself, "mast?"

"That's the mizzen mast. We have her rigged with a lateen sail – triangular. Lateen rigging lets us travel close on to the wind."

Eddie looked up at the sails again and remarked on their shiny, almost oily appearance. The captain beamed at this.

"Yes, indeed. Yes, indeed! Do you know what those are? The fabric is completely waterproof, is lighter than silk, and produces electricity when the sun shines on it!

"But there's more: Did you notice the hull as you climbed aboard? It is also made of a special composite that is capable of holding an electric potential. The salt water is an electrolyte. In strong winds, we can pile on the sail. We don't go any faster than our maximum stable hull speed because eddy currents in the hull increase drag, but we can use the effect to charge capacitors and batteries.

"All the communications, cabin climate control, mechanical control systems aboard the *Mother Rose* are powered by the sun and the wind! A huge battery bank along the keel provides ballast and storage for many days' worth of electrical energy."

Eddie thought that Captain Thomas could barely contain his pride, his enthusiasm, his love for the ship. Even though he wasn't following the details and had no knowledge of exotic, composite materials, he got the idea and could see that a sailing ship able to generate plenty of electrical energy would be a marvel of comfort and efficiency.

"How many people are in the crew?" he asked, more to keep up his end of the conversation than anything else.

"We have 20 sailors, a ship's surgeon, two pilots, a bookkeeper, a maintenance technician, a steward, a cook and a cook's helper. I have a staff of three: the chief mate and two assistant mates."

Here, for the first time, Eddie heard the captain's voice darken. "We also have six gunners and a gunnery officer."

"Gunners?"

"Sadly, Laddie, the *Mother Rose* has of necessity become something of a warship in recent years. For sixty years she has plied these waters. Now we are frequently targeted by thieves and – gods save us – mischief makers. Those who seek nothing but to disrupt trade."

Eddie nodded. "I have heard similar stories elsewhere in my travels."

Captain Thomas quickly brightened again, though, "of course with the amount of energy we can store up and rapidly discharge – ultracapacitors, you know – we can blow any miscreants out of the water handily enough!" Here he elbowed Eddie in the ribs so hard that the younger man had to grab a handrail to maintain his balance.

"And of course there's the hull itself!" the captain was warming to his topic again, "The hull can withstand terrific impacts. It has a level nine self-repair factor! That's near theoretical maximum!"

Now the captain leaned in close and his voice dropped to something in the order of an 80 decibel "stage whisper." "And if things really got bad, we can collapse – reverse telescope the masts – and armor the entire superstructure... all under voice control by either me or the first mate. Worst case, we could completely seal the vessel. In that state we'd be blind and deaf, but we'd be impervious to most anything in the natural or unnatural world."

They walked in silence for a few minutes. Then Captain Thomas called a halt so that he could check in with his first mate. All was well, and the tour continued. Eddie was treated to views of the bridge, the galley, the mess hall, the officers' mess, the armory, the computer and network center, the energy storage and distribution systems, the infirmary, and many other sites. Captain Thomas wrapped things up in the main hold. Here Eddie could see shipping crates that interlocked and fastened to the walls of the hold to prevent cargo from shifting.

Eddie had never seen anything remotely like the *Mother Rose* and he said as much to Captain Thomas. Aloud, he recalled his first impression – that of some great bird that had taken the form of a sailing vessel – and shared that with the captain. The metaphor obviously pleased the big man. Eddie continued, "And I suppose she is in some ways similar to how I would imagine a ship would be if it sailed the depths of space. Powerful and self-sufficient and at the same time graceful."

"Aye, she is that," the captain agreed. "She is that."

Eddie asked about the dimensions of the ship and how fast it could travel under full sail and found that he could easily translate measurements into units of his own world. He learned that the *Mother Rose* was 125 feet long at the water line. She had a 28 foot beam. Under ideal conditions she could, due to the slickness of her hull and her computer-controlled sails, travel slightly faster than 10 nautical miles per hour – quite respectable for a fully-laden cargo ship.

The tour completed, their talk returned to more practical matters. "How long do you expect the voyage to last?" Eddie asked.

"Oh, with a fair wind we can make port in five or six days," came the reply. We'll have to sail out to sea a wee tad to avoid the shallows and some islands from which attacks have been launched at us in past voyages."

This made Eddie worry about Lena, Nate, Isabel, Ben, and the others from the wagon train who also had to travel this way. He asked if Captain Thomas happened to know of them and if they were in front of the *Mother Rose* or behind.

"I share information with most of the other captains in the coastal waters, and I believe that I know the ones of whom you speak. They are scheduled to be picked up eight days hence.

"Since they are so far north, their course will be different. Because of the coastline and the currents in that region, they will swing out far to sea. This takes longer, but is a route less likely to be harried than ours. Once they near the latitude of Soapstone Bay, they will pile on sail and head downwind at full speed. They are not likely to be molested."

Eddie breathed a silent sigh of relief at this. Then, another thought came to him. "One last question, Captain Thomas. If I am to be on your ship for five or six days, is there some work that I could do? It is hard for me to sit around – especially when the people around me are working. Again, I know nothing of ships and sailing, but I am young and healthy. I can cook and scrub and lift and carry."

The captain thought on this for a moment. Then, his weather-beaten face creased into one of its wide smiles. "Yes, Laddie. I believe you can be of help. Cook's helper wants to try his hand learning the navigational systems. If you work for your passage in his stead, he can have an opportunity that would otherwise not come easily. He is a good lad, but his family is poor. This could be a real boon to him."

The captain motioned for Eddie to follow him back to the galley. Here, without preamble, he announced the change of assignment to the cook and his assistant. The assistant, a young man named Liam, who appeared to be in his late teens, was pleased and excited at his sudden good fortune. He shook Eddie's hand over and over with repeated thanks.

The cook – "Old Davey" was how the captain introduced him – was less sanguine with the arrangement. He was a tough, grizzled specimen of a sailor, but hardly old. Clearly he'd been working aboard ship for his entire adult life. He didn't like unplanned changes in his routine and he let his feelings on the matter be known to all. His language was colorful and hard to follow in the extreme, but Eddie could tell that nothing he said was flattering to his new assistant.

Captain Thomas just laughed his booming laugh and clapped the cook hard on the shoulder. In another deafening stage whisper he said to Eddie, "Just let me hear of it if this old flounder gives you any trouble. Or feed him to the sharks yourself, for all I care."

Then he set off down the corridor with young Liam, who was still thunderstruck at his good fortune, in tow.

In the sudden silence of the galley, Eddie could hear the cook muttering to himself, and the man appeared dangerously close to boiling over. He decided to try to smooth things out a bit.

"Um, Cook? Davey?"

"That be Mister Cook to you, pissant," the cook interrupted.

"Indeed. Mister Cook then. I'm sorry to have disrupted things, but..."

"You're na' sorry. Ye' volunteered. Ye' ha' free passage on thi' scow – which be bonny for ye' by-the-way – but ye' be too much a girlie t' stick t' yer cabin like decent supercargo. So ye' come down here an' rattle Cook's cage wi' your airs."

"Well, then I apologize, Cook, for causing you inconvenience."

"That be Mister Cook, pissant. Hear me on yer life, girlie! Stay clear o' me sight," the cook turned away muttering.

At this point Eddie felt that he'd been more than polite in the face of rudeness, but he was determined to make the best of the situation.

"Have it your own way, Cook. I'd rather we got along, but it's not required. Just give me a job to do, and I'll stay out of your way as best I can."

Eddie, who already had a strange feeling about the man, called up the seeing spell. He saw the space around the cook pulse redly as the man tensed. Eddie took a step back and balanced on the balls of his feet. All of a sudden the cook turned around and brandished a very large butcher knife in his left hand. He lunged at Eddie, but the younger man was ready, and his reflexes had improved dramatically in the previous weeks. It was almost as though the cook were moving in slow motion.

Eddie stepped aside and grabbed the cook's wrist as the man came close. He slammed the wrist down on a stone counter top and heard the bones crack. The cook gasped but pulled away, and using his uninjured right hand, snatched up a meat tenderizing mallet from a rack. As he swung wildly at Eddie's head, the young man ducked and then dropped the cook with a sharp blow at the back of the man's neck.

The cook lay gasping and cursing on the floor. Eddie kicked the butcher knife away. He was barely breathing hard.

"Well done, Laddie! The Old One spoke well of you. She navigates right as always," came a booming voice from the galley entrance. "I've had my eyes on this one for weeks. First time he's shipped with us, and he's not been right the whole voyage. Mean, secretive and such. I do believe that he's been passing information concerning our route to the brigands who've harassed us.

"I'll clap him in irons in the brig... so I suppose you're now Chief Cook for the duration of the voyage."

Eddie's jaw dropped at this cheerful announcement. "Chief Cook?!"

But the captain wasn't done. "Now don't look like some gaffed sunfish! You've just disarmed a man twice in less than 30 seconds. You can surely figure out how to feed 40 hungry friends and neighbors for a few days!"

"Look here!" The captain helpfully pointed out. "Here's the larder. It's well stocked. And we'll see you're supplied with several large fresh fish every day.

"And see these?" Captain Thomas continued, indicating two enormous kettles. Fill those with good, hearty food three times a day. That'll be just right. That'll keep the crew fit and happy."

Finally, the captain's weather beaten face split into another gigantic grin and the big man's laugh boomed out again. Captain Thomas' laugh filled the room and sucked all the badness out of the world, replaced it with joy.

"Don't look so worried, Laddie! You have the visage of an old maid as she signs on to crew in a brothel! I'm only having a bit o' fun with you!" He motioned to someone out in the corridor. Two large crewmen came in and pulled the cook off the floor. Eddie watched blandly while the former cook cursed him.

"Take this one to the brig and make sure he's stowed nicely. I'll be along to have a chat with him later. And tell First Mate that he's in charge for the next two hours!"

The captain turned back to Eddie. "Now roll up your sleeves, Laddie. Captain Thomas was not always a master seaman. I started my career as a cook's helper. We've got a hungry crew to feed."

* * *

If Eddie had worked hard at Lillith's holding, he worked doubly hard in the following days. The captain was an able teacher, but he expected Eddie to learn fast and then take initiative to improve and build on what he'd learned.

As a result, Eddie was up before dawn each day to make porridge, slice fruit and put out bread. After breakfast cleanup, he started bread – a dozen loaves each day. While the bread rose, he began lunch, which was usually some kind of seafood chowder served with the previous day's bread. Dinner preparation started immediately after lunch cleanup.

After supper cleanup, the next day's bread went into the oven. Forty-five minutes later, he'd take it out and place it on cooling racks in the pantry while he finished stowing everything against the possibility of rough seas. Sometimes he'd set out a giant pot of beans to soak overnight. He'd rest the pot in the deep sink so that it couldn't tip in the event that the *Mother Rose* encountered heavy weather.

The larder was huge and well-stocked. There was a walk-in refrigerator and a separate freezer. There were whole goats, dressed and ready to roast. There were shelves of roasts and other cuts of beef. There were baskets and baskets of vegetables and herbs. There were many burlap sacks of grain and beans. And of course there was fresh fish.

Eddie learned that part of crew duty included fishing, and with the human population of this world at a reasonable level, the bounty that the sea could provide was tremendous. Eddie had learned how to clean fish from Joe, but those had been small river fish. These were great saltwater specimens, each weighing well over 50 pounds.

Even though it was far from gourmet, the food Eddie prepared was good and was well-received by the officers and crew. After lunch cleanup each day, Eddie would take a half hour "break" during which he looked over his supplies and decided what to make for that night's dinner.

After two days, Eddie was on his own. It was exhausting, but he found that he loved it. It was more satisfying to him than turning out deli sandwiches at a fast food joint. Hard working people depended on him to feed them, and it felt good to meet that need.

Throughout the voyage, the captain checked in with Eddie. He'd look over the supplies and discuss the menus. Occasionally, the big man offered suggestions for simple, easy to make meals. Captain Thomas also made sure that the crew was assigned a rotating kitchen duty to help with cleanup. They were a good lot and were plainly happy to be rid of the former cook. Eddie learned from the crew that the cook's surly attitude had been reflected in his food, which wasn't exactly prepared with love.

In the evenings, alone in his cabin, Eddie recorded his menu for the day and listed the supplies he'd used. He passed this off to John Hastings, the bookkeeper. Mr. Hastings, a solemn, thin-faced man, would be responsible for replacing the supplies when they reached port.

Eddie learned from Mr. Hastings that with freshly caught fish supplementing supplies stored onboard, the *Mother Rose* could easily stay out to sea for four to six weeks; although since this voyage was inten-ded to be only five or six days long, the ship carried only half its maxim-um supplies. This was to minimize waste and to keep the supplies fresh.

This was a happy time. Tiring, yes, but interesting and satisfy-ing. Eddie thought that he would be a little sad when the voyage ended. Then, on their fourth day, they came under attack. A klaxon sounded, and the lighting in many areas, including the galley, changed to a deep red hue.

The crew, Eddie included, had drilled in what to do in such cir-cumstances. Personnel not involved in direct combat went to their battle stations. For Eddie, this meant that he shut down and secured the galley and then made his way directly to the infirmary. Evidently, tradition had it that the cook lent a hand in the treatment of battle-related injuries.

Eddie thought back on the aftermath of the attack at the rest stop, when he'd thrown his knife and injured the man who had been threatening Ben and Isabel. He hoped that he wouldn't pass out at some critical time.

Because the surgeon might be called upon to treat serious injur-ies, the infirmary was brightly lit. Upon reaching the infirmary, Eddie stood for a moment while his eyes adjusted to the glare. The ship's sur-geon, Doctor Lutz, nodded to Eddie and helped the young man scrub and get ready.

As they waited, they could hear deeply muffled thuds and distant impacts that shook the ship. Occasionally, the air would become charged, electrified in some strange way. This feeling would build and pulse and then a few moments later the cycle would repeat.

Within minutes they received their first casualty. One of their six gunners had been injured by an incendiary device that had impacted the hull near a gun port. She was burnt along her left side and face, and she cradled her right arm in her left as she was helped into the infirmary by a crew member. Eddie swallowed as the doctor checked her over and ad-ministered a kind of hypo-spray.

Doctor Lutz turned to Eddie. "The burns are painful, but not ter-ribly serious. Some second degree. Her right radius is broken and the ulna is cracked from the impact, but neither bone is out of place. Here is a splint to protect her arm. Put this salve on her burns and splint the right forearm. Then have the crewman escort her back to her quarters. She may not return to her battle station."

The woman looked up sharply at this and started to argue, but then she gasped as she forgot and tried to raise herself using her injured arm.

Eddie swallowed again. He was suddenly grateful for Joe's first aid training. He decided that if he stayed calm he could handle this. The woman had obviously been sedated by whatever the doctor had given her. He put on what he hoped was a confident look and helped her lie back. Then he used the supplies that Doctor Lutz had indicated to immobilize and protect the arm and to salve the burns.

No other injuries came in while Eddie worked, and Doctor Lutz observed his assistant the whole time. Finally, Eddie motioned to the waiting crewman who helped the gunner back to her quarters.

"Good. I wanted to make sure you could follow instructions. Now, as other cases come in I will know what I can ask you to do. Stay alert and calm, and all will be as well as we can hope."

From start to finish, the battle lasted for perhaps three hours. Later, Eddie was to learn that the *Mother Rose* had hoisted all available sails and run far out to sea at her maximum hull speed. The crew used the ship's high tech weapons systems to charge and fire directed energy weapons that disabled and sunk the pirate craft.

There were seven more injuries in the space of the next few hours. Some were fairly serious; others had been minor enough to wait until the danger had passed. As he worked, Eddie became too busy to worry or fret. He just did what he could to help and tried to stay out of the way otherwise. The doctor was brusque but very good at his profession.

Eventually, the klaxon sounded an all clear, and, as quickly as he could, Eddie stripped off his surgical gear and returned to his galley. He was exhausted, but he knew that he had a crew to feed. They'd been under stress and they would be hungry and on-edge. He took stock of what he had that he could cook quickly but which would satisfy and give comfort to the crew. Then he set to work.

Dinner was a success. Already popular aboard ship for taking the place of his unpleasant predecessor, Eddie's efforts to feed them in the aftermath of the battle earned him a new place in the crew's hearts. When word got around that he'd also done well helping their injured comrades during the battle, Eddie found that he was met in the corridors with many a clap on the shoulder or firm handshake and heartfelt thanks.

These simple gestures had a strong impact on the young man. They helped him gain a more vivid sense of shipboard life and what it meant to be part of a crew. At night, in the solitude of his cabin, he thought long on this and saw that the ship was an apt metaphor for the world – for all the worlds.

In the days that followed, word travelled through the crew regarding the details of the attack. Previously, the pirates had been pathetic, poorly organized brigands. They looked for easy prey and they usually shied away from the *Mother Rose's* synthetic armor and energy weapons.

This time, however, the pirates had been better organized and better equipped. Captain Thomas' crew had never before suffered so many casualties, and even though none of the injuries were life-threatening, they were still a sobering reminder of what might happen. This battle reminded the crew of their vulnerability as they sailed a lone ship.

The captain considered this situation carefully and on the morning of the fifth day announced that they would continue out to sea for two more days and then gradually adjust course to the south. This would double the length of the voyage, but it would take them out of reach of any brigands who infested the coastal waters.

They would merge with the courses of the ships that sailed from more northern ports. Captain Thomas also sent word, via secure communications, to all the other captains concerning the new strength and determination that they were seeing on the part of the brigands.

Eddie was dismayed to hear some of the comments from the crewmembers. Of course he expected the change in plans to bother people. What he hadn't expected was to hear from many people that this would be their last voyage. Several experienced sailors offered the unsolicited opinion that the coastal trading routes had become dangerous and not worth the risk or trouble. Many professed to be saddened at the prospect of seeking a new livelihood on shore but mentioned families waiting at home. The attack had burdened too many sailors with dark thoughts.

The young man recalled his conversations with Lena and her parents in his brief, happy time with the wagon train. Slow, steady trade between the settlements, villages, and towns provided much of the fabric that knit this society together. If families stopped allowing their youngsters to travel aboard ship or on land, if the trade routes dried up, then that fabric might well unravel.

When Eddie heard comments to the effect that "Somebody needs to form a real navy... like in the old days," he wondered if these events might, in fact, be part of an overall strategy to disrupt and weaken a culture and not the actions of individual brigands or criminals. He sensed the scope of the battle that was being waged across this world. It was difficult not to be worried.

* * *

After the attack and the subsequent course adjustment, life on the *Mother Rose* returned to its usual rhythms. The ship was sailing close to the wind on the way out, so the square mainsail was replaced by another lateen rig. They made good time; although the seas were rough and the crew members were often drenched by wind and waves.

Eddie continued as ship's cook. He inventoried their supplies and let it be known that a few more dinners that centered on big salt-water fish would be a good idea. Fortunately for everyone on board, the sea's harvest was bountiful, and Eddie became confident that if there were no more delays or side-trips, they would reach their destination without having to resort to reduced rations. He experimented with bread recipes and occasionally produced some breads that were laced with sweet herbs, honey, and finely chopped dried fruit. These were popular and helped to raise spirits that had been dampened by both the attack and the detour.

Although he was happy with the job he'd found and the camaraderie he'd earned with the crew, Eddie regretted the way it had come to him and tried to visit the former cook in the brig. The man was consistently hostile and insulting. Old Davey obviously had no sense of his own responsibility for what had befallen him and continued to blame Eddie. Now he raged that from the start it had been the young man's intent to displace him.

Eddie tried to question the cook with the hope of determining whether the man had been manipulated or controlled in some way. While he couldn't be completely confident of it, Eddie eventually reached the conclusion that Old Davey was just an angry person. It was too bad that he had focused his anger on Eddie, but there was no obvious way to remedy the situation.

Eventually, after being rebuffed two or three times, Eddie gave up trying to smooth things over and stopped his visits. He had plenty of work to do and, along with everyone else onboard, was ready for the voyage to be over. It only made things more difficult to be cursed and verbally abused by the former cook.

As they entered the last leg of their voyage, the ship came about and ran before the wind with full sails. Since the ship travelled with the wind, those on deck could feel little air movement. Their work was often hot and monotonous.

They engaged all the electrical energy-gathering systems and ran consistently at maximum hull speed. The weapons were fully charged. All but the two most seriously injured crew members were back at their posts. The communications links were up and staffed full time.

Less than a day out from Soapstone Bay, men in three fast, light craft rushed around the shoulder of a small island. These attackers fired small arms at the *Mother Rose*, but what few rounds reached the ship bounced harmlessly off the composite hull. The captain put the ship on alert but did not order full battle stations. After he saw that the would-be pirates were bent on closing, Captain Thomas ordered one shot from an energy cannon off the bow of the lead pursuer. The weapon's shock wave capsized the closest boat and the other two vessels throttled back to res-cue their partners and salvage their gear. Shortly thereafter, the captain gave the order to stand down.

That was the last of the problems they encountered and several hours later, they caught sight of the mainland. Another hour brought them close enough to glimpse some of the waterfront. Finally, late in the afternoon of the eleventh day of a voyage that should have taken only five, they landed at Soapstone Bay. The beautiful vessel was secured to the wharf with hawsers as thick as a man's arm, and final, dockside as-signments were completed. At last, as evening approached, a tired, somewhat dispirited crew disembarked the *Mother Rose*.

Old Davey, the former cook, was brought out in irons and led away by the town constabulary. He cursed and spat on the deck as he left the ship. The captain's usually cheerful visage took on the aspect of a thunderstorm at this affront, but the authorities hustled their prisoner away before the situation could escalate.

Captain Thomas was heard to say that he'd swear out a formal complaint the next day. Attacking a fellow seaman with a knife was a ser-ious offense. Insulting the *Mother Rose* was an unforgivable one. Cap-tain Thomas was a well-regarded master seaman and his testimony – as well as his word – would carry weight. Not only would Old Davey face criminal charges, it was unlikely that he would find another captain in this port willing to take him on.

Eddie asked if he could stay one more night on-board so that he'd have a full day to seek work and lodging. The captain was agreeable to this; although in return he asked Eddie to stand first watch and then to cook breakfast for the remaining crew before setting off the next morn-ing.

The first watch passed uneventfully. The quay was well-lighted and well-ordered. Small teams of guards patrolled the docks of the busy, prosperous seaport. Secure and serene at its moorage, the vessel rested. No one approached. The night was mild and Eddie was comfortable as he paced the deck in the quiet.

At the end of his watch, however, Eddie was glad to turn in. He lay awake for a few minutes and mulled over the events of the voyage. The ship shifted about differently when it was tied up. The weight of the great hawsers drew the vessel toward the edge of the dock where wharf fenders cushioned the hull. Gentle waves contributed a subtle movement of their own. Eddie thought he might miss the feel of the ship beneath him.

It came to him that he could now approach an innkeeper or res-tauranteur and say with a straight face that he'd been chief cook during the *Mother Rose's* most recent voyage. This was obviously better than re-ferring to his food preparation experience as "making some deli sandwiches" and a vast improvement over simply saying that he'd traveled with "Nate the Trader" for a couple of days.

Early the next morning, his final morning aboard the *Mother Rose*, Eddie served his last meal as chief cook. After cleaning the galley and saying a few farewells to the Captain, Mr. Hastings, and others, Eddie shouldered his pack in preparation to disembark. His hiking boots, abandoned for the better part of a fortnight, felt heavy and stiff on feet that had become used to boat shoes.

Captain Thomas drew him aside. "Here, Laddie, you've earned this," the big man confided as he held out a small purse.

Eddie instinctively knew that he was being offered pay for his services as cook and surgeon's assistant. His first thought was to refuse, but knowing what he did of the captain and his ways, Eddie realized that it would offend the big man were he to turn away without accepting what was offered.

So Eddie accepted the purse and expressed heartfelt thanks for the Captain's generosity. They shook hands, a firm grip of shared experience, and Eddie left the Mother Rose. Once on the wharf, the young man turned for a final look at the beautiful ship. Haranguing the crew and yelling at the stevedores as they began unloading the ship's cargo, Captain Thomas' booming voice rang across the quay.

Michael C. Glaviano

Twenty Three

Eddie's first task upon reaching the shore was to get used to standing on solid ground. After an eleven day voyage, his sea legs expected all the fluid movements of the ship. It was a strange feeling, but it was also sort of pleasant – a tiny reminder that he knew would soon fade.

He looked across the bustling wharf and tried to identify all the various roles of people in his immediate view. Stevedores, seamen, women who entertained seamen, officials of various sorts, fishwives, scruffy children, scrappy cats, and more all conspired to assault the young man's senses. The riot of smells, sounds, and sights was very different from the feeling of being on board an efficient and well-organized sailing ship.

After strolling up the wharf for ten minutes, Eddie saw two policemen who stood together and observed the chaos of the docks. "Excuse me officers." Their heads swiveled as he called out. Silently, they tracked his approach and appraised him. They were watchful and, Eddie thought, more than a little edgy. He was glad that he'd gone over in his mind what he wanted to say.

"I am just off the *Mother Rose*, and I would like to find work and lodging here in town. I know no one who lives here, but people have told me that this is a good place. I do not want anything fancy, but I would like to live in a decent part of town. Any ideas?"

They looked him over. The smaller of the two said, "So you're lately of the *Mother Rose*, are you? Who's her captain, then?"

"That would be Thomas Wyndham, officer."

"And the bookkeeper?"

"John Hastings."

The constables relaxed slightly at this point, but they asked the names of two more of the officers before they were satisfied that Eddie had indeed just come ashore from the well-regarded ship. This suspicion reminded Eddie of his own world and the image of Sergeant Driscoll and her worn-down cynicism came briefly to mind. It was sad and uncomfortable, but he did his best to keep his attitude positive.

After a little chit-chat among themselves, the two officers gave Eddie directions. They informed him that they were standing at the foot of Prince's Wharf Road. Eddie should follow the Wharf Road west and pass Park. They said that the town got a little less "waterfront-like" beyond Park. After Park, Eddie would cross LeRoy. Prince's Wharf ended at Turnbull, and Eddie should turn left there. He'd then be heading south. Eventually he would encounter University. Anywhere around Turnbull and University should be good. It was a shopping district with street-side cafes – sort of neutral turf between the rich neighborhoods south of University Avenue and poor ones down near the docks.

Eddie thanked the officers and went on his way. Even though they had been polite enough and willing to help him, he sensed that they followed his passage for as long as they could make him out on the busy street.

It was a twenty minute stroll up the busy thoroughfare that was called Prince's Wharf Road. Eddie moved steadily along and kept alert to his surroundings. This district, "the Warrens" was what the policemen had called it, was clearly a rough part of town, and he was glad that he'd stayed aboard the ship one last night rather than trying to walk these unfamiliar streets at dusk.

As the officers predicted, the character of the shops and the appearance of the people on the street improved slightly around Park and got steadily better as he made his way past LeRoy. He could see another big cross street up ahead, which he assumed would be Turnbull. Eddie scanned the buildings around him and saw something that made him pause. Poking its head above the nearby buildings was a tall tower.

Eddie kept moving and when he reached Turnbull, he could see that to the right – the opposite direction from that suggested by the policemen – another road came slanting in from the north to intersect the street. Just beyond the intersection, at the vertex of the angle formed by the two streets, Eddie could make out a stone building. The tower he had spied a few minutes earlier rose from the midst of it.

This building and all those nearby looked ancient. The old, close-packed structures were formed from heavy blocks of rough-quarried stone. Walls were stained dark near the road but bleached by sun, rain, and wind above. There were very few thatched roofs in the district. Instead, various types of tile graced the tops of the majority of the buildings. The tiles came in a wide range of shapes and colors, and this lent a fanciful air to this old quarter of the town.

Embrasures punctuated the massive stone walls, and each opening featured glass windows. It was impossible to tell if the glazing had been there from the beginning or if it were a recent addition. Doors in this district were invariably made of heavy, dark wood - oak, Eddie guessed - and were bound with iron. A few of the buildings still possessed thick shutters that the young man supposed could be pulled closed to protect against violent storms, or perhaps, violence of other kinds.

Signage, where present, hung above the sidewalks on wrought iron brackets that were fastened to the walls of the buildings. Some signs featured names of proprietors or types of commerce. Others displayed only graphics. The sign on the building with the tower showed a simple, white triangle on a field of forest green.

The street coming down from the north to intersect Turnbull was called Longview. Eddie turned right on Turnbull and continued to the next intersecting street. This street was called "Landfall" and to the right it led back down to the wharf district. Instead he turned left and walked along Landfall until he again encountered Longview. Once again he turned left and followed the third side of the property that held the old stone building to return to the intersection of Longview and Turnbull. This meant that the building occupied a triangular piece of land.

So, this ancient stone structure was on a triangular – a three-cornered – piece of land in the heart of the old city. It fit Lena's description perfectly. It must be the place that Eddie sought, the Inn at Three Corners. He felt lucky to have found it but decided not to press his luck. He deliberately gave the Inn no more than a cursory glance and, finally heading in the direction recommended by the patrolmen, walked briskly south, down Turnbull.

Another fifteen minutes of walking brought Eddie to University Avenue. There he turned right and soon found himself in a shopping district. True to the policemen's claims, this area appeared to be far more prosperous than the twisty, narrow streets near the waterfront. Eddie walked up and down both sides of the street for three blocks. He encountered various shops that would probably be more than adequate to meet his needs. In particular, there were several moderately busy restaurants. A few of these were fancy, imposing places. More appeared to be casual eateries.

After a few near-misses, he found a Help Wanted sign in the window of a decent looking place near the corner of Wells and University. The restaurant was called the "Dancing Orca."

They specialized in fresh caught seafood. The decor wasn't much: mostly round cafe tables just big enough for four diners. There were some small tables at the front windows and two, larger tables at the back of the dining room, near the kitchen. The walls were whitewashed above dark, old-looking wainscoting.

The manager was there and after talking with Eddie for a while, hired him as second cook. In the interview it came out that "The Orca's" first cook had moved to a "swanky place uptown" and the second cook, who was very skilled and overdue for a promotion, had moved up. Eddie thought that both of these were good signs. During the process, Eddie asked for a tour of the restaurant.

The dining room, the kitchen, and the rest of the facility were all clean and well-cared-for. No "Old Daveys" were in evidence, and the kitchen help and wait-staff were happy and pleasant enough. A dishwasher and a busboy were both university students. Some of the others were slightly older, close to Eddie's age. It all looked good.

He'd be expected to arrive for work at noon, when the lunch crowds peaked. Eddie would assist the main cook through the noon rush. He'd help clean up and begin prep for dinner. He had a break at 4:00 PM and would have the kitchen to himself when the restaurant re-opened for dinner at five. The main cook's break was from 5:00 PM to 6:00 PM. Eddie's shift ended at 8 o'clock and he had Mondays and Tuesdays off. Today was Thursday. He was to start the next day.

Eddie had no idea if what he was offered was good pay or not, but the manager had an open, friendly face and he thought that she was probably honest enough. Her name was Mabel, and she was a skinny, talkative woman in her late 40's or early 50's.

After they'd settled the terms of his employment, Eddie asked her if she knew of a place nearby where he might rent a place to stay. Visibly pleased at being consulted, the woman smiled and asked Eddie what he was looking for in the way of accommodations.

"Well, I guess I'd like a small apartment in a reasonably quiet area. It should be in good shape, but my taste leans more towards basic and functional than fancy and expensive," Eddie explained.

Mabel thought for a few minutes and then scribbled down some addresses. "If you want to be close by, you should look at these places. The first two are actual rooming houses; the others are stores that have some little places above to let. I know the owners and they're all good people."

"Which place is the closest?" Eddie asked. He was hoping that she'd give him a complete rundown on locations, landlords, distances, and points of interest. He wasn't disappointed. By the time she was done, Mabel had given him a complete picture of each place – down to the hair color of the owner of the bookshop and the fact that the manager of the larger of the apartment buildings wore a toupee and sang badly.

"Thanks, Mabel. That's great information. It'll really help me," Eddie remarked when the manager finally paused for a breath. "Do you have time for one more question?"

"Sure thing, honey," she replied. "I'll need to get busy in another ten minutes or so, but you prob'ly noticed that I like to gab," she added with a laugh.

Eddie smiled and asked, "Since I just landed here, I don't know what to expect for basic living costs or how much money I should plan to pay for rent. Can you help me out a little?"

Here Eddie pulled out the purse that Captain Thomas had given him. He opened the drawstrings and poured out the contents. A substantial pile of heavy, silvery-looking coins, each slightly larger than a quarter in Eddie's world, lay on the manager's cluttered desk.

Mabel drew her breath in through her teeth and whispered. "Honey, those are half-plats – platinums. That's over two month's wages... *my* wages... and I've worked here for eight years. What'd you do on that ship?"

Eddie had already mentioned to her that due to some unforeseen problems in the crew, he'd been drafted as chief cook. Now he let her know about the pirates and having to assist in surgery and the fact that the voyage had turned out to last more than twice as long as it should have. Eddie said he figured that the captain had bumped up his pay accordingly. He decided it would be better to leave out the part of having to disarm the angry, knife-brandishing cook.

"Well, first of all, don't wave that around too much, hear? This isn't a bad neighborhood, but still... you don't want to tempt the gods. Now, you ought to be able to rent a real' nice place for one of these each month. And you should go to a bank and get this cash put away safe."

Here she smiled a sort of half smile and added, "You sure you even want to work here, honey?"

Eddie had no idea what other expenses he would have or how long he would need to wait before Joe turned up. When Lena returned, he would want to spend some time with her, and maybe take some time to do some fun things – things that other people his age would do. And he hadn't forgotten Nate the trader's advice to find a job and blend into the surroundings.

On the practical side, he wanted to get some other clothes and some shoes. Also, he had no household articles. Finally, summer was edging its way towards autumn and he expected cool nights soon. Without going into too much detail, he assured his new boss that he planned to stick around for a while and that he hoped to settle into Soapstone Bay. He mentioned having a girlfriend at the University and wanting to have a real place for a while.

At the mention of the word "girlfriend," Mabel's eyebrows went up and her half smile finished forming. Eddie's explanation satisfied her.

"That's good, honey. I think you'll fit in fine. But you really do need to get that cash put away. Here's the name and address of the bank I use. You go there next, hear?"

Thanking Mabel and promising to return the next day by noon, Eddie made straight for the bank.

He wondered what he could do for identification, but this world's notions of identity were very different from what he'd grown up with. Here, they based ID on finger and retinal prints, so he needn't have worried about official papers. In fact, this culture was very sensitive regarding citizens' "true names," so names and paper documentation were considered an imposition.

Finally, being a thousand year old seaport, Soapstone Bay merchants were accustomed to sailors coming and going and had developed a whole process to accommodate people like Eddie. The bank scanned his retinas and his right and left thumbprints. They gave him a receipt for his deposit and a little book that he could use to keep track of his account status. The whole procedure was efficient and took under an hour.

Eddie's stomach was starting to make its presence known, but he wanted to secure lodging before he did anything else. Once more thankful that Maia's "Gift of Tongues" extended to the written word, he pulled out Mabel's list and looked it over.

After walking the neighborhoods around University and looking at the outside of most of the places, Eddie thought the bookstore was the best choice. It was located on the south side of Center Street a little more than halfway back down towards Turnbull. There, Center Street formed a corner with a tiny side street called "St. Tolemy's." It would be less than a 15 minute walk from the restaurant. He estimated that it would take no more than twice that to reach the Inn at Three Corners – probably less.

Eddie went into the bookstore, "Tolemy's Cats," and looked around. Shelves lined the walls. There were tall rows of shelves that ran to the back of the store. Near the front of the store were some sale tables and racks that held postcards and greeting cards. It reminded Eddie of bookstores from his childhood.

Even without Mabel's description of the landlady, the woman would have been impossible to miss. She looked to be in her late 70's or perhaps early 80's, and it appeared that the years she had lived had taken their toll. Her hair color was such that one might term it "red," but it was a shade of red that Eddie had never before seen on anyone. It also looked as though the stooped, elderly woman had slept on her hair, straightened it by standing crosswise to a strong wind and then slept on it again. She wore a pink sweater, shiny, lime-green slacks, and white high-heels. The overall effect was breathtaking.

She looked up from whatever it was she was doing when Eddie paused, just inside the doorway. "Are you looking for something, or do you just want to block the door for real customers?" she called. Her voice was pitched high and loud – as though she were hard of hearing but unwilling to wear a hearing aid.

As he stepped closer, Eddie instinctively raised his voice while putting on what he hoped was his best face.

"Hello. I heard that you had a room to rent?"

"Did you now?" came the loud reply. "Who wants to know? And what makes you think I'd want to rent it to you?"

Eddie didn't know exactly how to reply to this, and he stammered a little, "Well... I, uh, just got off a, er, a ship and was hired as a cook nearby... My name is Reed."

"Your name's 'Reed' you say? Speak up! I can't stand it when people mumble. Everybody mumbles these days!" his potential landlady yelled.

Eddie looked around again. The bookstore was neat and tidy and well-stocked. Those were good signs, and he needed a good sign just then. Speaking at a volume level that would have done Captain Thomas proud, Eddie tried another tack."

"Mabel at the 'Dancing Orca' recommended you. I'll be working there."

"Mabel, eh? Why didn't you say so? Just wait there. Not *there*, you're blocking the door!" Eddie jumped to one side of the door. Wild, scarlet hair flying, the woman strode to the register counter. She picked up the handset of what Eddie supposed to be a land line and stabbed at some buttons. Eddie, at this point, noticed that her fingernails were purple, a perfect grappa.

"Mabel?! Well, don't just stand there. Get me Mabel! Mabel? Is that you? This is Iris Abellona at 'The Cats.' There's a kid here. He's kind of cute. He says he's working for you and wants to rent a room. Yeah, that's his name, or anyway, that's what he said it was. What? Speak up! Okay. I'll do that. Come by soon. We'll have tea. Or a drink."

The woman looked up at Eddie. Her face was still a little bit fierce, but she'd been sufficiently placated by whatever Mabel had said.

"Okay. Mabel says you're all right. My name's Iris Abellona. You can call me 'Mrs. Abellona.' I suppose you want to see the rooms?"

Eddie was getting into the sprit of the dialogue, "Yes, please, Mrs. Abellona. I would like to see the apartment!" he yelled in response.

"I'm too old to go up and down the stairs every time somebody wants to see something. I'll buzz you into the stairway. Just next door. On the right as you go out. The vacant apartment is the first one. There's only two, and the second one's only a storeroom at present, so you ought to be able to find it. Door's open. Just look around. Don't break anything."

"Thanks, Mrs. Abellona. I'll be right back!" Eddie called. He walked out of the shop. He saw a separate street entrance that opened onto a small foyer with two mailboxes and stairs leading up. Access to the stairs was granted via a thumb scanner, but as he approached it he heard a buzz and a click. The door opened at his pull and he faced a single flight of steps to the second floor of the building.

The stairs were tiled with a rough-surfaced ceramic material. It looked tough, and Eddie figured it would provide decent traction in wet weather. The stairway was nearly four feet wide and, like many of the buildings he'd seen so far was wainscoted in dark, oiled wood. The plaster above the paneling was painted a pleasant, warm yellow color. At both head and foot of the stairs, heavy wall sconces on either side, provided light. The wrought iron sconces looked very old. Eddie suspected that they had been designed to hold candles, but at some point in their history had been refitted for electric lights.

He climbed the stairs and found that they terminated in a short, rectangular landing. Unlike the stairs, this space was floored with hardwood. It appeared to be oak. The walls, however, continued the treatments of the stairway: dark, oiled wainscoting below, sunny yellow above. There were sconces on the walls next to each door. An overhead skylight made the hallway bright. The place was obviously old but was seemingly in good repair. The air was fresh, seasoned with an undercurrent of furniture polish.

As Mrs. Abellona had promised, the door to the first apartment was unlatched. The door was heavy and finished in the same manner as the wainscoting. Eddie pushed the door open and stepped inside to encounter a compact, but pleasant space.

The door opened directly into a small kitchen. In the back, jutting from the wall facing him, was a tiny, built in "nook." A tiled counter with a sink and some cupboards, ran along the right side. A small stove stood next to the counter.

There was a window above the stove that looked out over the roof of the bookstore towards the street and a smaller window with the same view above the sink. A short, wide window up high over the nook brought in light as well. This window was bordered, wrapped along its entire boundary, by small panes that were stained red, deep yellow, green, and cobalt blue. Eddie imagined that when the sun shone on the glass, the kitchen would be filled with color. Close to the door, a tiny refrigerator rested atop another counter of its own. The kitchen was painted turquoise and had a red and yellow linoleum floor.

Turning left from the kitchen, the young man entered the main room. A blank wall faced him, but the wall to the right featured two, large windows. Three small rows of stained glass ran along the tops of these. It was a good sized room. In the middle of the wall to his left was an opening and to the right of the opening were double doors. Eddie stepped over to the opening and found that it gave access to a short hall. On the left of the hall was a narrow walk-in closet; on the right, a plain but functional bathroom.

Returning to the main room, Eddie tried the double doors in the right half of the wall. These doors opened to reveal an old-fashioned pull down bed – a "Murphy bed," the words surfaced from a deep crevice in Eddie's memory. The bed was mounted on a spring-assisted hinge so that the metal frame and mattress were easy to lift into place or pull down for sleeping.

Like the space at the top of the stairs, the floors were made of very old oak. They had aged to a deep, tobacco brown and glowed beneath decades of buffed wax. There was a small sofa in the space between the two windows opposite the wall containing the Murphy bed, and there were some built-in bookshelves on the wall between the kitchen and the main room. The bookshelves were again a dark oak, but unlike the hallway outside, the walls in the apartment's main room were painted from baseboard to ceiling in a warm off-white that balanced the dark woodwork.

In addition to the small sofa, there were two wooden chairs in the main room. The chairs were placed with their backs to the bookcase. Eddie looked around and decided that the room and furnishings would be adequate to a gathering of perhaps four adults. Any more than that would get crowded, but that suited him fine.

Nothing was new or modern, but the place was clean and bright. Eddie tried all the appliances and fixtures. Everything functioned properly and the water pressure was fine. This would be perfect. Now all he needed to do was to close the deal with Mrs. Abellona. He hurried downstairs and reentered the bookstore.

"Well, does it suit you?" she wanted to know as soon as he'd stepped inside.

"Yes, it does, Mrs. Abellona. How much is the rent?"

"You say you're just off ship and new in town?" she asked.

"Yes, ma'am. We just got into port yesterday. Today is my first day in Soapstone Bay."

Mrs. Abellona made a great show of sighing as if the weight of the world rested on her. "I suppose you want to pay by the week?"

"Actually, I'd prefer to pay by the month. I am hoping to stay here for a while."

"Yes. That's what Mabel told me when I called her. She also said I should be nice to you... as if I'm not nice to everyone who walks into my shop!"

Once again Eddie wasn't quite sure what the best response should be, so he replied, "Um, thank you, Mrs. Abellona. How much would you like for rent?"

"What I'd 'like' and what I can get are two different things, young man. But I'll settle for a quarter-plat per month. I want first and last rent, up-front. No loud music or wild parties. Don't leave your things on the stairs and don't bother my customers."

"A quarter-plat per month would be fine, ma'am." When he'd set up his bank account Eddie had kept a couple of coins for cash money, and now he placed one on the counter."

The sight of cash on the counter appeased Mrs. Abellona. Eddie wasn't completely sure, but he thought that she almost smiled at him. Then, she wrote out a receipt and the coin vanished from the countertop. She held out her right hand. Eddie took it and was surprised at how firm her grip was.

"Now, let me set up access for you. She poked a few keys with her grappa-nailed fingers. Here! Give me your thumb. No, your left thumb!"

So Eddie reached out his left hand, and she grabbed it and held it firmly onto the face of a scanner. There was a brief chirp, and a light blinked green to the left of the scanner.

"Suppose you run out and check the stairway and the apartment to make sure the locks recognize you. And here. Take this!" She fumbled beneath the counter and produced an old-fashioned key. It looked ancient and had a very complex pattern of wards cut into the bit – a filigree of angles and whorls.

"I don't want you trying to track me down some rainy night just so I can let you into your apartment. I'm still not convinced these auto-mated scanners are reliable. This key will work no matter what happens to the electricity!"

Eddie accepted the large key. Then he nodded to his landlady and went next door to see if the scanners recognized him. Both the stair-way lock and the lock on his apartment worked perfectly. Now he had a place to stay! He returned to the bookstore and told Mrs. Abellona that all was well with the locks.

She nodded and turned her attention to whatever she'd been do-ing when he came in. Before he left, Eddie told his landlady good-bye, but he doubted that she heard him.

Twenty Four

She'd consumed no few small creatures since her return to the Place. Now she was stronger. She needed a lair. Someplace where she could feed securely, ideally someplace from which she could spring quickly to attack.

Alicia's face was still recognizably human, but it had developed a stiff, frozen look. Once slender and shapely, her body had begun to bloat with her strange diet – based as it was upon the life energies of weaker creatures.

Naturally she ate other things as well. Pale, fleshy plants and mysterious fungi attracted her. Sometimes these made her violently ill, but more and more she was able to ignore minor inconveniences such as myco-toxins. But most of all, whenever the opportunity presented itself, she preyed on weaker things. She knew, without understanding how, that her diet was changing her irreversibly. She was becoming something other than human, but that was no longer important.

When she first arrived in the place between worlds, she had been very weak, barely able to consume insects. As she grew in strength, she took on bigger creatures, long time denizens of that misty Place. She guessed, from the surges of strange energies that she felt just after some of her kills, that no few of her victims were natives.

Now that she was stronger, she slid back and forth between the Place and some of the soft, chaotic boundary worlds. Physical laws were weak in these worlds and it was easy to enter them, easy to return. She tracked and consumed prey in those places as well. She was in one such boundary world now.

She supposed, by the pulsing orange light that illuminated the alien landscape around her, that it might be day in this world. Today, she tracked something larger, something the size of a dog, but with bigger teeth and a wiry, bristly coat. These things were all teeth with jaws to match. They must have some senses, for they detected her and snarled when she approached. They had no discernible eyes, though, nor externally-visible ears.

She climbed far up and lay very still, and when one of these things scuttled beneath her perch, she hurled a large rock upon its back. There was a satisfying crunch and a hoarse, hissing yelp.

Alicia neared her prey. It still lived. Still had teeth. But it could not move its hind legs. She inched forward. The thing snarled, but it could not reach her. She found another large rock and threw it hard at the injured creature's head. The thing yelped again, fell. With a spasmodic lunge, her prey tried to rise, but then it fell back, unconscious. She struck again with a fist-sized rock. Long past sensing any life in the thing, she struck over and over.

Then she began to feed. It had little power, but it was meat. It was blood and bone and gristle. She fed for a short time, and then, clutching what was left to her like some hideous doll, she slipped back across the boundary into the Place.

She wandered long but eventually found what she sought: a place in the rocks where she might fashion her lair. Of course it was already inhabited, but she would lure out its current tenant, something long and sinuous, with the smell of the prey she had brought from the boundary world.

If Alicia retained any capacity for love or enjoyment, it was love of the hunt – especially the ambush. She made her way around and above the entrance to the rocky jumble that she had determined would be hers and there she waited. Barely breathing, unaware of the rank smell that surrounded her, forgetful of what she had become, Alicia waited.

The long, sinuous thing nosed from its place in the rocks. It could smell the carrion Alicia had left and it was hungry, but it was also cautious. It moved out and then darted back at some shift in the misty light, at some distant sound. Alicia waited. Two times, three times, the sinuous thing almost reached the rent carcass before it retreated.

Eventually, the thing's hunger overcame its caution and it emerged fully. It was at least seven feet long. Easily the biggest prey she'd attempted, it was a risk, but a worthwhile one for what it might bring her. Alicia waited until a split second before the thing's jaws closed on the bait. And then, committing herself fully to the attack, she sprang from her perch.

Somehow, the thing sensed her movement, and turned so that its belly faced upwards. Alicia had enough time to see that its belly featured barbs – probably venomous – that protruded several inches and then she landed full on its exposed neck.

Her initial blow did not kill the thing, but the impact stunned it. It tried to recover, tried to bring those barbs to bear on its tormentor, but Alicia had already sunk her teeth into the flesh just below the jaw. She reached underneath the thing with her right hand to hold the bottom of the jaw and force it back against her knee. She pressed down with all the strength of her left arm in concert with the pull of her right.

Still it struggled, but clearly it was weakening. Alicia bit harder. She buried her face in the soft flesh beneath the thing's neck. Fluids gushed around her, blinded her, filled her nose, coursed down the front of her once beautiful body. She continued to bite, continued to bend the thing's neck back and back and back until it finally snapped.

The long, sinuous thing shivered and lay still.

Although it could not overcome its attacker, the thing's life force was strong and as that life force flowed into the creature that Alicia was becoming, she rocked back and lay panting. She panted as one might expect a mother to pant in childbirth, but instead of birthing a child, Alicia was transforming into a twisted version of herself. Had another hunter come by just then, she would have been helpless, but the helplessness passed quickly enough.

As she recovered, she reveled in the energies that surged into her metamorphosizing body. She howled and rejoiced. And then she fed with abandon.

Michael C. Glaviano

Twenty Five

For Eddie, the next few days flew past. He'd gotten his apartment set up with basic necessities the very afternoon he'd rented it. That first day ashore had been a whirlwind, but, because his job at the restaurant commenced the following day, there was no avoiding it.

As soon as he closed the deal with Mrs. Abellona, he visited the shopping district. There he purchased bed linens, bathroom gear, and a pair of shoes for work. He spied a small cafe just down from the bookstore and, his parcels piled around him, he enjoyed an early, if solitary, dinner there.

After eating, he took his things home. Then he ran back out and bought a few groceries. Returning from the grocery trip, he opened the door to his apartment to realize that this was the first place he'd ever really felt was truly his. During his three semesters of college, he'd stayed in a dumpy apartment. It was a place to sleep, party, and occasionally study. After he'd dropped out of school, there'd been the whole Drive Away scene, and the persona that went with it. Then had come the changes that his encounter with Joe had wrought and then the circumstances that had brought him here. Now he was home. Be it ever so humble.

That first evening, he set things up and relaxed around his apartment. He organized his purchases in the kitchen cupboards and on the bathroom shelves. Over the course of the evening, he felt the inside of the unfamiliar refrigerator at least five times to assure himself that the milk he'd bought would stay fresh. When he finally turned in, he was both tired and excited. After tossing and turning on the unfamiliar bed for a short while, however, tired won and he fell deeply, happily asleep.

As had been his habit for weeks, he awoke at first light. It promised to be a beautiful summer day in Soapstone Bay. Eddie dressed lightly, had a little breakfast and went out to buy a few more basic necessities. He found a used goods store up at the west end of Central, near Meridian, and was able to purchase what he needed very reasonably.

Finally, well before noon, he prepared for his first day as assistant cook. He slipped into his new shoes and left the apartment. Happy and smiling, the young man strolled through the sunny streets to the Dancing Orca.

Michael C. Glaviano

The kitchen crew at the Orca was a great bunch, and Eddie fit right in. It was a welcome contrast to his experience upon arriving at the galley of the *Mother Rose*. Matt Walerian, the first chef, was a few years older than Eddie. Cooking was Matt's passion, and he loved to talk about food. Interestingly, although the first chef's thoughts were never far away from things gastronomical, the man was slender and fine-boned. He wore his dark hair cut very short.

Eddie and Matt maintained a running dialogue regarding menus and ideas for interesting dishes. When the kitchen got busy, they'd focus on their immediate tasks, but during the inevitable lulls, they'd ramp up their conversation and plan more good things to serve customers.

Although he'd been born farther south in one of the large towns on the coast, Matt had lived most of his adult life in Soapstone Bay. He'd never gone to sea or been in a wagon train, and he was interested in Eddie's experiences – especially the food-related ones. In particular, Matt wanted to hear what Eddie had done to improvise dinner menus on the *Mother Rose* when the cruise had been unexpectedly extended.

Eddie didn't think of what he'd done as especially creative, but in retrospect he recalled that everything had worked out with the meals. There'd been no disasters, no inedible messes served to hungry sailors at the end of a cold, wet day. Eddie had followed the basic premise of Captain Thomas: start with good, fresh things and don't mess with them too much. At one point, Eddie mentioned the breakfast bread in passing, and this led to a whole side exploration that evolved into some interesting dessert ideas.

The first week was mostly spent getting Eddie up to speed on the menu and the way Matt liked to run the kitchen. Everything made sense and Matt was patient and basically just a good soul, so this learning period was as low stress as a new job could be. Eddie could tell that he and the first chef would be a good team. They'd wow the customers at the Orca.

At the end of the first week, Matt suggested that Eddie join him and his girlfriend for an afternoon "just hanging around town." This suited Eddie perfectly and he readily agreed.

"Where do you want to meet? Here at the restaurant?" he asked.

"Hmmm. Well where do you live? Anna and I are over at the end of Spring Street... at Ochre, above the art gallery," Matt offered.

Eddie let Matt know that he lived over on Center Street above Tolemy's Cats.

"Oh, the 'Cat Lady.' She's quite a character around there. What's she like as a landlady?"

"She's okay. It was a little interesting at first, but basically she and I don't cross paths much. I think that as soon as Mabel told Mrs. Abellona that I was okay, she relaxed. Of course it hasn't even been a week."

Matt's girlfriend was a young woman named Anna Dymond, one of the waitresses at the Orca. She had heavy blond hair that she invariably wore in a braid. Anna was full-figured and had a husky voice that was occasionally pitched deeper than Matt's tenor. Matt and she had been seeing each other for a little more than a year-and-a-half.

Matt let Eddie know that in general, Mabel frowned on the staff becoming romantically involved, but that since he and Anna had thus far been able to "leave their relationship at the door," Mabel turned a blind eye. He confided to Eddie that he was thinking very seriously of asking Anna to marry him and wondered what Mabel would make of that.

They agreed to meet at noon in front of the bookstore on Monday. The plan was to get a bite to eat – Matt knew just the place – and then walk around town. Eddie was grateful for some company and excited to explore more of the town.

The next day, right at noon, Anna and Matt showed up in front of Tolemy's Cats. They laughed and talked and walked around the town and enjoyed the warmth of late summer. There were shoppers and strollers out. People young and old were taking advantage of the fine weather while it lasted.

The three young people enjoyed lunch at a tiny cafe located at the elbow of a bent street named "St. Zeno." The restaurant, "The Running Tortoise," was a favorite with the university crowd. Classes would start soon. Students, enjoying the last few days before the term started, surrounded Eddie and his new friends.

Matt knew the cook at the Tortoise and darted into the kitchen to say hello. He came back out and told the waitress that the cook was going to throw his choice at them for lunch. Despite the lunchtime rush, their food showed up quickly. It was a wonderful rice, seafood, and vegetable casserole that the cook had paired with a spinach and tomato salad. The casserole was full of flavor yet light. The greens were fresh and the tomatoes, whatever their origin, could have passed for homegrown.

Eddie was still sounding out a friendship with the other two, but he found them to be animated and easy to talk to and lunch went comfortably and quickly. They were interested in how Eddie came to Soapstone Bay. He told them some more about the wagon train and about Lena, of course. They already knew some of the details regarding his stint as a ship's cook. Eddie was vague about his life before joining the wagon train, saying only that he was from "further west." He offered the information that he'd run across the wagon train while hiking and had joined them.

Once they settled their bill and left, Matt asked Eddie what he'd like to do.

"Well, to tell you the truth, I'd like to go up to the university and try to leave word for my friend. I hope that she's back by now and that she didn't have any trouble on her voyage."

"We can do that, can't we, Anna?" said Matt. We'll take the streetcar up University and point out the sights for Reed."

Anna nodded and smiled, "Sure thing, boys," she agreed in her rich contralto. "We couldn't pick a better day for it."

They walked west up St. Zeno and then turned left at Anderson. Anderson took a slight jog at Shade Drive and then continued across Center. The sidewalks were wide and the breeze off the harbor was fresh and clean. Ambling along and looking in shop windows, it took the three young people just over twenty minutes to reach the corner where Anderson ended at University.

At University they turned right and walked about fifty feet to a trolley stop. They didn't have long to wait. An electric trolley showed up in under ten minutes. The trolley was fairly crowded, but they were able to find seats and they enjoyed the ride up University. Anna and Matt enthusiastically pointed out the sites.

Matt ran a nonstop, animated commentary on all the restaurants in town. As the trolley waited at another stop, Matt pointed out the upscale restaurant, La Mesa del Mar.

"That's where the Orca's old first cook, Galatea Fergusson, went. It's a very fancy, very expensive restaurant. Real top shelf stuff. Galatea – everybody called her "Taya" – anyway, she's a great chef. She went to a cooking school in one of the big, southern coastal cities. I learned a lot from her."

Anna slipped her arm around Matt's slender waist and squeezed him to her. "She's got nothing on you, honey," she protested huskily.

"Thanks, Anna, but she really is good! I think that eventually, she'll be the best in Soapstone. It was amazing that she hung around the Orca for as long as she did."

"Hmmphf. What-ever," Anna pouted slightly and turned to look out the window.

Oblivious to his girlfriend's pique, Matt continued to point out places that were good and places to avoid. Eddie was struck once again by his new friend's passion for the entire dining experience. It was fun to see someone so enthusiastic about his profession.

For a moment, Eddie forgot where he was. He unconsciously dropped into the rhythm and colloquialisms of his own school days.

"Man, Matt, I gotta say that it's cool how much you're into what you do," Eddie blurted.

"Excuse me?" Matt looked at him strangely. Anna's head swiveled around too.

"Oh, sorry, um. That's how I grew up talking. That small, western college town thing."

"What town did you say?"

"Oh, it's nowhere you've heard of, I'm sure."

Anna looked more directly at him. "Yes, you said that before. What town was it?"

Eddie thought fast. On a whim, he decided to use the name of a town on the west coast of his own world and risk that it would be unknown here. At least he'd be able to remember it.

"Well, it's called La Jolla."

"La Hoya?"

"Yeah. Heard of it?"

"Can't say that I have," Anna admitted. "Funny dialect though."

"Yeah. Uh, sorry... I try not to talk that way, but sometimes I forget. What I meant was that I admire and appreciate Matt's enthusiasm for his work as a chef."

This placated, or at least distracted, both of his friends. Matt, especially, broke into a smile at the obvious complement. Eddie followed up quickly.

"So was this Galatea woman, the former first cook at the Orca, was she a lot older? It sounded from how you described her that she knew a lot."

"No. That part was strange. I mean, she did know a lot. Taya was really, really good, but she was my age. Probably even a little bit younger. I guess she just stayed around to get more experience."

"Oh, she wanted experience all right. She hung around the Orca for so long because she liked you," Anna declared.

"Now *that's* funny, Anna," Matt laughed.

Anna wasn't laughing. "No it's not. In fact, she got that job at La Mesa after I warned her off you."

"You did what?!"

"I told Miss Galatea Fergusson to back off. Very clearly. In no uncertain terms."

Silence descended over the little party. Despite the embarrassment of the situation, Eddie was grateful that the focus had been shifted away from his own origins. He breathed a secret sigh of relief. Then, after a time, he resumed asking for more information regarding other shops, other features of the town. Gradually, the mood lifted and his new friends put their tension behind them.

Galleries, clothing shops, and other types of commerce rolled past. Soapstone Bay, in this transition time from late summer to early fall, was clean and bright. The shop-front awnings waved in a gentle breeze. The street-side sycamores hadn't yet begun to turn and the broad, green leaves dappled the sunlight on the sidewalks. For the most part, the people on the street appeared healthy and happy. The street cars were full and lively. Cyclists moved easily though the light traffic.

There were a few, slow-moving commercial vehicles on the street as well. Mostly, these took the form of open wagons and small, enclosed delivery trucks. They made little noise and produced no noxious fumes, so Eddie guessed that they, like the streetcar, were electrically powered. It was strange but pleasant to ride on a trolley with the windows open and to hear voices and birdcalls but very little in the way of traffic sounds.

Eddie, for his part, couldn't help but notice the difference between this town and the rundown city where Joe had his house. He thought back to the towns he'd passed or visited during his Drive Away days and couldn't call to mind any place that had looked so vibrant and, well, so upbeat. For a moment, he was saddened by the contrast and what he thought it probably meant for his world, but, with an effort, he shook off that feeling and resolved to make the most of the day.

The ride up to the university took a little over a quarter hour. When they neared the edge of the campus, Matt asked Eddie if he knew where he might find his friend.

"Not exactly," Eddie replied. "She said to leave word for her at the student union... No, the student *recreation* building."

Anna was a few years younger than Matt and had more friends at the university. "I know where that is. Pretty much the middle of campus. I'll just hop into the campus bookstore while you go to the rec. center, okay?"

"Just try not to spend all your money on magic books, Anna!" Matt laughed.

She laughed huskily and, eyes twinkling, tossed back, "No promises, darling! I haven't bought anything for over a month!"

Their earlier, tense exchange apparently forgotten, Anna and Matt went back and forth like this for another couple of minutes as the trolley neared the center of campus. Eddie already knew that Matt's passion was food. It appeared that Anna had recently become interested in magic. Not sleight-of-hand parlor tricks, he gathered, but the real thing.

Anna explained that she'd stumbled across some old books in a used bookstore. The archaic language was confusing and obscured as much as it explained, but the subject was fascinating to her. Later, she'd found a few, more contemporary texts, again used, but these had been written for children. Thus far she had been unable to find anything that was both modern and written for an adult student.

Eddie's initial reaction was reserved. He recognized that magic was much more alive and much more accepted in this world than in his own, but he was afraid that anything he'd say would further betray his status as an offworlder, so he just watched the back-and-forth with a slight smile and laughter at (he hoped) the right times during the good-humored dialogue.

They hopped off the trolley and Anna pointed out the student recreation building. "You go with Eddie, Matt. You get bored when I'm browsing in bookstores anyway. Let's meet back in, say, half hour or 45 minutes. Will that work for you?"

Without waiting for an answer, Anna waved and moved off to a long, low building a few yards past the trolley stop. Matt and Eddie crossed the street and headed towards the much larger student recreation center. Pushing through the doors into the lobby of the large, multistory building, they looked around and located a reception desk that was staffed by a security guard.

Eddie stepped up to the desk and said, "Hi. I'm looking for a student, her na-"

"Let's see your student ID," the guard interrupted.

"Well, I'm not a student. I..." Eddie started.

"We don't give out information to non-students." The guard fell silent and, offering no further information, looked down at some papers on the desk.

"Okay. Is there a place where I could leave a message for someone?" Eddie persisted.

"Upstairs. Room 404," came the minimal response.

"Thanks. Um, could you please direct us to the elevators?"

"Through those doors..."

Matt and Eddie turned away, but then the guard added, "But you can't go up there without a visitor's badge."

Eddie could tell that Matt was getting tense beside him, so he hurriedly asked the guard, "and can we get visitors' badges from you?"

"No."

Now, despite the fact that he really wanted to get in touch with Lena, Eddie was actually becoming amused. At least in some ways this world didn't differ so terribly much from his own. He persisted, putting on his best, friendly, earnest young face.

"Where can we obtain visitor's badges?"

"Administration."

"And could you please direct us to Administration?"

"That building." The guard pointed through the big exterior doors to another building perhaps two hundred yards down the road. It appeared that he had run out of ways to be unhelpful, so he looked back down at the desk.

Eddie thanked the guard very politely and motioned to Matt that they should leave.

"Reed, how could you stay so calm?" Matt wanted to know as they left. "That guy was just being a jerk."

"Well, yeah, he was, but I couldn't tell how far he wanted to take it, so I didn't want to give him any opportunity to make things harder. Let's just jog down there and see if we can get some badges."

A few minutes later they reached the indicated building. There they found a very helpful person at a desk that had "Information" displayed in large letters above it. He said that he could give them badges that would be good for the day. The transaction took about five minutes, and the young men were on their way.

Matt and Eddie both thanked him and left as quickly as they could. As they walked back to the recreation center, however, they noticed that they'd already spent nearly a half hour walking up and back. Anna might return soon, so Matt waited behind at the bus stop.

Eddie dashed back to the first building. Visitor's badge clipped prominently to his shirt collar, he ignored the guard at the desk and walked directly to the doors that led to the elevators. He could feel the guard's eyes on him and half expected the man to toss another obstacle in his path, but the guard must have exhausted all his talents. Without being stopped or challenged, Eddie pushed through the doors and found the elevators.

The building wasn't crowded and Eddie reached the fourth floor quickly. He followed some signs and found room 404 right away. This was some kind of lounge and student coffee bar. It was bright and lively and was obviously a popular on-campus hangout for the students. The chairs and tables were worn with hard use. Even though the weather outside was glorious, the room was over half full.

He didn't know anything else to try, so Eddie went up to the cashier and asked if there were a manager on duty that he could speak with. The young man at the register looked barely old enough to be away from home. He nodded and waved to a barista across the room and called, "Hey, could you get Phil? This guy wants to see the manager!"

Eddie thanked the cashier and backed away. In a couple of minutes a slightly older student walked up to him and asked if he could help. Eddie supposed that this was Phil.

"Yes. I hope so. I'd like to leave word for a friend. She said that the student recreation center would be the best place. The guard downstairs said to come to room 404."

"That one is a real shiny pebble, is he not?" Phil laughed.

"Well, it was a little difficult to get much out of him," Eddie replied.

"Anyway, this is not truly the right place. I suppose you could leave a note here, but there is no way to make sure it will reach your friend."

"Any ideas? I'd very much like to get in touch with her," Eddie persisted, making sure to keep his voice and body language friendly.

"Just a moment. Oh, of course! I should have thought of it right away... The guard should have too," Phil shook his head and laughed again. Eddie waited, eyebrows raised slightly. Phil continued.

"Yes. Just go down to the end of the hall. That is Student Services. Run by and for students. I'd wager that's what your friend was thinking."

Eddie thanked Phil and left. As promised, he found a room labeled "Student Services" at the end of the hall. He opened the door and saw another counter. This one was backed by a whole wall of pigeonholes. A young woman was at the front desk. She nodded to Eddie as he came in.

"Hi,..." and Eddie went through his story again. This time he struck gold. Yes, this was the right place. Yes, he could leave a message. The young woman was quick to add that they also had a few other services such as a clothing exchange and a book swap, but sure, he could leave a message.

"Sorry, I didn't think of it before now, but do you have a piece of paper and something to write with?" Eddie asked. He was relieved but at this point was feeling slightly frustrated by what he had thought would be a simple task.

"Oh, sure. These should work for you," she replied.

Eddie quickly jotted down the name and address of the "Orca" and the address of the bookstore. He added that he lived in an apartment above the store. Then he hesitated and wondered if it would be wise to leave detailed information of when he'd be away from his rooms. Eventually, he decided to add only that he had Mondays and Tuesdays off.

He folded the paper and printed, "Helena Graysmith" on the outside and slid it toward the young woman behind the counter. She brought out a roll of some kind of adhesive tape and taped the note shut. Then she turned and worked her way about a third of the way down the "G" column of the pigeonholes. Finally, she slid the note into an empty slot.

"Anything else?" she asked. Suddenly, Eddie had the distinct impression that the young woman intended to read his note as soon as he left the room. After a moment's thought, Eddie decided that he'd put nothing in the short message that could cause either Lena or him problems, so he just shook his head and smiled. Hoping for the best now, he thanked the young woman and left.

Eddie quickly retraced his steps. Upon reaching the lobby, the young man noted that there were now two guards at the desk. They were both watching the doors to the elevators and when he came out, they followed him closely with their eyes.

As fast as he could, he exited the building and made his way down the hill to the sidewalk where Anna and Matt waited. There was a trolley coming down the hill towards town. The two young men deposited their visitor's badges in an appropriately labeled drop box.

"Success?" Matt wondered.

"Of a sort," Eddie replied.

They swung onto the trolley. Eddie told the others that there had been two guards watching him as he'd left the student recreation building.

After a couple of moments, Anna said, "You know, it was weird in the bookstore too. I'll tell you more after we're out of here."

"Hey, if you don't mind, let's go back downtown by a different route," suggested Eddie. "It's probably nothing, but I can't see how it would do any harm to make things a little harder to trace us... just in case." Eyes suddenly wide, the others nodded silently.

"So," Eddie continued. "What's the first street that can get us downtown without a lot of hiking?"

Anna spoke up first. "Well, the trolley will cross Biscayne at the edge of the campus. The next street on the left would be Holmes. That's the street we want."

"Okay. I'll jump off here and wander around the edge of campus for a few minutes. In case anyone's watching, that will make it appear that we've split up. You and Matt stay on this trolley. I'll board another one in a little while. Let's meet up on Holmes."

"Holmes starts off going straight north, but after a couple of blocks it curves off to the east. Let's meet there. At that elbow," Anna suggested.

"Sounds good."

Eddie hopped off the trolley and looked around. He didn't see any security guards. He walked slowly back up the hill towards the administration building. On the surface at least, all was normal and calm. It could have been a lovely fall day on a university campus in his own world. Talking and laughing, students were walking or hanging around in groups. He wondered what Anna had experienced in the bookstore that had bothered her.

After loitering furtively in the vicinity of the trolley stop for several minutes, Eddie boarded another trolly and rode back towards the center of town. He kept track of the well-marked streets and had no trouble identifying the stop at Holmes. When the streetcar got close, Eddie left his seat and walked to the rear doors of the vehicle. At the stop, he got off and looked around. Then, as quickly as he thought prudent, he crossed University and jogged north on Holmes. A minute later, he saw Matt and Anna at the bend in the road.

"Clear?" Matt asked as Eddie jogged up.

"Yeah, I think so. You guys okay?"

They nodded. "We're fine," Anna added.

"Okay let's get out of here and get someplace crowded," Eddie suggested.

"We can do that, but we could probably get to our place faster," Matt countered.

"That sounds even better. You lead."

Holmes Street twisted and turned and then finally reached a larger thoroughfare called "Long's Peak." There they turned right and then right again at Meridian. Now they were heading back towards University, but within six blocks, they turned off into Anna and Matt's neighborhood.

A few minutes later they were in the young couple's upstairs flat. Matt immediately went to the kitchen sink and washed up. "Hey, you guys... Shall I throw together a little something to eat?" he offered.

Later, over a little chilled white wine and Matt's incredibly tasty "throw-together" stir-fry, Anna told the others that she'd been followed for the entire time she'd been in the bookstore. As soon as she had entered, a clerk had appeared and asked if he could help her. She had said, "no, thanks," but he had hovered nearby the whole time she browsed the books.

Despite being uncomfortable, Anna had found a few things she wanted. In addition to some notebooks and writing implements, she ran across a heavy, large-format textbook that seemed to be just what she had been looking for: a modern introduction, written for an adult audience, to the history and practice of magic. There were many copies available, and she noted that a hand-lettered sign taped to the shelf announced that the associated course had been canceled.

Anna had carried her items to the cashier. By then, the first clerk had been joined by another and they had flanked her as she made her purchases. The whole situation had been vaguely threatening, and Anna had wisely decided to use cash for her purchases. One of the clerks had actually stepped forward and said that they preferred she use a thumb-scan to pay. She'd ignored him and paid with coin anyway.

As she left the bookstore, she noticed that the second clerk had picked up a comm handset and was speaking into it while he watched her. "I know it sounds paranoid, but I felt like I was under surveillance," she added.

"I felt that way too when I left the student rec. building," Eddie agreed. "Up until then, I just thought that the security guard was having a bad day. Hopefully, that's all it was. Anyway, that was good thinking to insist that you pay cash for your books. Now unless they take pretty extraordinary measures, they'll have no way of tracking or identifying us."

Secretly, Eddie was hoping that Lena would get his note without any trouble. He didn't want to add to the general level of worry, so he kept his thoughts to himself. To lighten the mood, Eddie asked Anna more about the book she'd bought.

"Oh, it's just a more modern version of some of the old things I've found in the used shops," she replied. "These days it's not easy to get anything new. You know, written in a modern style. The RSM people put so much pressure on the commercial publishers that they shy away from any serious materials that deal with spells or any other skills relating to magic."

"RSM? What's that?" Eddie wondered. As soon as the words were out of his mouth, he mentally kicked himself.

Anna's eyebrows shot up. "Where have you been? Don't they have news broadcasts in your small, western college town?"

Eddie mumbled something about not paying much attention to the news. He wasn't sure that the other two bought it, but they were too polite to pursue the slip.

"Well, anyway," Anna answered, "It stands for 'Rational Science Movement.' It's really a bunch of desert religion people who say crazy things and claim that magic isn't real and that the pursuit of magical knowledge is evil. It's a fringe movement, but they are so well funded that they're always getting attention, and they're beginning to have an impact at the regional level – maybe even at the national level. Somehow, even though what they say is crazy and mean-spirited, they continue to gain strength. It's really creepy.

"So now, most of the companies who publish serious work are in the academic fields. The books are terribly expensive." Anna was quiet for a minute. Then she looked Eddie directly in the eye and said, "If you've lived in any city, anywhere, you'd have heard of the RSM's. So I guess you really haven't been paying attention, have you?"

Eddie felt his heart sink. He liked and trusted these two, but it was too soon to bring them into his confidence. Also, it might be dangerous to them. Maybe later, if things settled down and he got to know them better, he would confide in them. In as relaxed a way as he could, Eddie tried to shift the conversation away from himself.

"Well, La Jolla really is a small place. And, as for paying attention... I don't know; all I can say is that I've been on the road for quite a while now. I wanted to see the sites, travel around while I was young. That kind of thing. I traveled quickly at first and put a lot of distance between myself and the hometown. Later, I camped for a few days while hiking roughly east.

Eventually, I met up with the wagon train, and I liked those people. I stayed with them until they headed north. The guy who led the train called himself 'Nate the trader.' Maybe you heard of him?"

"Not me. I came up here from the south. I don't know any of the northern traders. Do you, Anna?" The young woman shook her head and Matt continued. "And you said you were on a ship later. That's where you got to exercise your cooking skills, right?"

"Right," Eddie replied. "That was after the wagon train. The wagon train people recommended a place where I could stay on the coast. For about a month, I stayed with an old woman who has a small farm that overlooks a cove where southbound ships sometimes anchor for a day. I told her that I wanted to go to Soapstone Bay, and she let me have room and board in return for chores."

"I stayed with her until the *Mother Rose* had anchored," he continued. "She knows the captain and got me on-board... People have been really nice to me. I guess they worry about a young guy like me traveling alone and want to help," he finished.

"Hey, Matt," Eddie added, gesturing at the dishes and wine glasses, "Let me give you a hand washing up, okay?"

Once again, Eddie thought that he'd managed to turn the conversation to safer topics. As they washed up, Eddie asked Anna to describe the spells that she was learning. Now that he was in a world where magic was more alive, he thought that it would be good to try to learn more than the single seeing spell that he'd mastered.

"You know, maybe I could to try to learn a few spells," he said as they were finishing in the kitchen. "How difficult is it?" he asked.

"Well, it all depends on the spell," she replied. "Some are easy, but others are too hard for me to figure out... and all the spoken spells require precise pronunciation. It's easiest to start with spells of perception – enhanced seeing or hearing spells where you're working on yourself."

"Oh, yeah," Eddie said. "That makes sense. That'd make me both the subject and object of each spell. So I'd be able to tell if I were doing it right."

The young woman nodded. Then she brightened. "Just a second," Anna called, dashing from the kitchen. She was back in a couple of minutes with a well-worn text.

"Here you go. Start with this one. It's basic and safe. It has some theory and then there are these little things you can try at home. They're real magic, but they aren't anything powerful or dangerous. If you decide you like these, we can talk some more."

"Hey, thanks, Anna. That's probably just right. It'll give me something to do when I'm hanging around the apartment."

Suddenly Anna looked serious, "Uh, Reed?"

"Yeah?"

"Listen, it would probably be a good idea if..." she trailed off.

"...if I didn't mention to anyone but you guys that I was trying to learn some of this stuff?" Eddie finished for her.

"Yes, that's pretty much what I was going to say. You know... the RSM people and all."

"Right. Okay, thanks, again. I'll keep it to myself. When I hook up with Lena again, I'll talk about it with her. And you and Matt, of course. But that's all. I'm getting it that these RSM people have their feelers spread all around. And I'm new in town and don't want any trouble."

Eddie thought that this might be a good time to head home, so he asked for directions. Then he thanked his friends again. Before leaving, he shook hands with Matt and got a hug from Anna. Then he headed into the gathering dusk.

It was evening by this time, and the late summer air was cool, so Eddie moved quickly through the quiet streets. Away from Matt and Anna's cheery apartment, the streets were empty and dark. Eddie was relieved when he started to recognize some landmarks in his neighborhood. After that he moved with more confidence and a short time later reached the Tolemy's Cats building.

He entered the little foyer and smiled as he noticed that Mrs. Abellona had inserted a tiny, carefully lettered card in the slot above his mailbox. The little label read "Reed Woodruff" – his alias on this world. Eddie thumbed the lock and ran up the stairs. Inside his little apartment it was warm and quiet. New as it was to him, it still felt good to be home.

*　　*　　*

Tuesday, the next day of his virtual weekend, was uneventful. Eddie resolved to stay as close to home as he could. As he settled in, he found that he needed a few more things for his apartment. He also wanted to stock his kitchen with basic staples, but he kept his shopping excursions short and focused. Each time he dashed out for an errand, Eddie made sure to check his mailbox, but it remained empty.

The weather was still beautiful, but almost overnight autumn had drawn nearer. Late in the afternoon, Eddie noticed a maple whose leaves were tinged with the slightest hint of red. He made a mental note to look for a warmer coat.

At the end of the day he still hadn't heard from Lena, and he settled down to another solitary meal. Afterwards, he cleaned up and opened the book that Anna had loaned him. He had another flash of gratitude for Maia and her gift that allowed him to read and write like a native of this world.

The book, "A Child's Garden of Spells," was very elementary. It started with a basic explanation of what magic was and how it worked. It repeated over and over that magic did not provide a way around hard work and that there was a strict accounting for tasks accomplished through magic.

Much of the text was taken up in a discussion of "good" and "bad" magic and emphasized the effects of each on the doer – or caster – of a given spell. Given the book's title and the writing style, Eddie was sure that the material was intended for a pre-teen audience but was nevertheless grateful for the clarity of the presentation. He was also glad to note the consistency between the material in the book and the things that Joe had explained.

According to the text, there was a kind of cosmic bank account that infallibly and automatically kept track of the cumulative effects of one's actions. Intention was important, and casting spells or invoking magical forces in an effort to harm someone else resulted in a sort of splash-back of harm on the caster. This reaction was reversed in cases of self-defense. Also, taking action that somehow undid harmful magic improved one's account balance.

The book also touched on other, more complex topics, but since this was an elementary text, none of these were covered in real detail. One advanced topic that was interesting, although presented superficially, involved a concept called "divine balance." Even the simplified treatment in *Child's Garden* was difficult to understand. The book seemed to be saying that all the worlds existed against a backdrop of growth and decay, good and evil, shadow and light.

This meant that small spells with local effects – say a spell to cast light under a sofa to see if that's where the cat's toy had ended up – were generally safe as long as they were applied for benign purposes. Stronger, more powerful spells could be performed safely too, but one had to be even more careful regarding one's intent in performing them. In general, the more local the effects of a given spell and the more innocent his or her intentions, the safer it was for the caster.

In contrast, there were so-called "great spells" that operated on the very fabric of the cosmos. One had to be extremely wise or extremely lucky to apply such a spell and live. The text only alluded to them, but it also implied that there were frightening potential consequences associated with performing great spells. These consequences were connected somehow with the realms of primordial chaos, the Great Abyss and the elder gods. Eddie wasn't sure what any of this meant, but it all sounded like things to avoid.

At the very end of the book, there was a small chapter that described some basic spells. Some were silly, the sort of spell that a ten-year-old might enjoy. Things like "funny hair" and "anywhere whoopie cushion" fell into this category. After careful reading, however, Eddie found a handful of spells that he thought might prove useful. He made a list:

1. Enhanced hearing
2. Distance vision
3. Casting a beam of light
4. Illumination of the path beneath one's feet

After thumbing through the book's spell chapter one last time, Eddie added:

5. Changing the color of an inanimate object

In each case, the general formula was the same: the person casting the spell focused his or her attention on the intent and recited, either aloud or sotto voce, a key phrase. When the object of the spell was something external, the recitation was often accompanied by one of several types of hand movement.

Anna's reassurances aside, Eddie thought it would probably be safer to begin his practice by directing his spells at something other than himself, so he experimented with the last three items on his list. After several false starts, he was able to walk around the room in the dark with just the area beneath his feet glowing softly. Casting a beam of light in a particular direction was much harder and Eddie tried for over an hour before he was able to create a fitful beam that was just barely bright enough to read by.

After working on his spells for a couple of hours, Eddie felt a profound sense of fatigue and also had a bad headache. Still, he had made some progress and felt pretty good about his efforts. The book suggested that the beginning student's best bet would be to spend a little bit of time each day at spell practice and try to build up strength and concentration. The text made it clear that spell casting – even simple, local-effect spells – involved developing skills and a certain conditioning regimen. Since Eddie's job left his mornings free, he decided that he'd devote an hour or two early in the day to work at this.

Finally, before going to bed, he copied out the spells into a notebook. Eddie thought that the act of writing might help him memorize the key phrases and hand movements. It would also allow him to return the book to Anna quickly.

Eddie liked Matt and Anna, but he still felt it wise to maintain a little bit of distance. When he'd been aboard ship or on the wagon train, there had been assigned tasks and definite roles. More importantly, each of these steps in Eddie's journey had a well-defined endpoint. Now that he was a resident of Soapstone Bay with a job and an apartment, he might need to stay here for some time. This argued for more caution in dealing with those he met.

Most of all, his intentions toward Lena were clear in his mind: he wanted a serious relationship with her. If that worked out it would mean that his connections in the town would impact not only his life but hers as well. So being friendly with his coworkers was great, but he felt it necessary, prudent at least, to move slowly in developing true friendships.

He turned in somewhat later than he'd intended. The old stone building was quiet. The weather outside was mild and the air was still. As he lay back and drifted toward sleep, he reflected on his travels. Linking somehow to his memory of Lillith's spinning wheel, the words from the *Child's Garden of Spells* echoed in his mind.

In the morning, Eddie fixed himself some breakfast and sat down with the book again. He thought that his subconscious must have been hard at work while he slept, because now he found that the spells made more sense and were a little easier to recall. He tried casting a beam of light and found that he could now produce light that was intense enough to shine on the wall even on this clear, bright morning.

Next he successfully changed the handle of one of his cooking utensils – a well-used, secondhand spatula – to a brilliant, fire-engine red. Then he turned his battered old hat black... and then back to brown.

Finally with a little bit of trepidation, he decided to try the distance vision spell. He rationalized that it was a child's magic book, so that the spells shouldn't be dangerous. Still, he reasoned that children would not try these things without guidance. He tried to balance potential risk against benefit and finally decided that it was worth the attempt.

Eddie went to the window and looked out. He saw some specks in the distance and focused his attention there. His first attempt was tentative, almost timid. The only result was a sort of visual distortion in the periphery of his sight. Then he recalled the fact that he had used the Spell of Seeing many times without ill effect. This spell wasn't terribly different.

He took a breath and committed himself to the attempt. Holding the Distance Vision spell in his mind and whispering the words, Eddie was startled to see an immense crow hurtling out of a gray sky toward him! The jet black feathers glistened in the morning light, the eyes gleamed, and the huge beak yawned as the great bird approached. Involuntarily, he stepped back from the window. He stumbled and barely caught his balance on the breakfast nook. Immediately his vision returned to normal, the giant crow was again a tiny dot in the distance.

Eddie relaxed a little. After experiencing the whole spell from start to finish, he knew better what to expect. He focused on the distant specks again, brought the soaring birds into focus, observed them, and then returned his perception to his room. He repeated the exercise several times and gained a small amount of control over the degree of enhancement.

Next he tried the Enhanced Hearing spell. It was still quiet in the building, and he wanted to take advantage of that quiet to avoid hurting his ears. He found this spell to be roughly the same level of difficulty as Distance Vision. He sat in his room and focused his attention. Then he practiced.

Eventually he was able to hear footsteps on the street and discern individual voices of passers by. He thought that eavesdropping would hardly qualify as an innocent use of magic, however, so he refrained from listening in on private conversations. Still, he could imagine using such a spell while in the wilderness. It could also prove valuable in detecting a stealthy approach.

Although his headache was starting to come back, Eddie was happy. He now had a grasp on six basic spells. The morning had passed

Michael C. Glaviano

quickly and he resolved to leave off practice until the next day. Eddie spent a few minutes straightening up his rooms and then headed out towards the Dancing Orca and work.

Twenty Six

The weather in this northern seaport marched quickly past the cusp of autumn. Leaves turned red and yellow. Strong winds surged up from the harbor and leaves fled from the trees to collect in great drifts. Farmers brought fall harvests to the grocers and there was wonderful produce available for the restaurant and for Eddie's tiny kitchen above the bookstore. The world paused and drew into itself before plunging toward harsher months.

More and more students filtered back into Soapstone Bay, and although they tended to congregate in the uptown area around University Avenue, their youth and energy contributed to the overall life of the beautiful little town. Their presence countered, in a way, the approaching darkness of the last quarter of the year. Their voices and laughter enlivened the sidewalks, shops, and restaurants.

The days stayed mostly mild, occasionally warm, but the nights were getting steadily colder. Eddie was glad that he'd acquired more substantial cold-weather clothes. He was certain that winter in Soapstone Bay would be a cold and wet time. Even so, he looked forward to the change of season.

The young man tried not to worry about Lena, but avoiding worry turned out to be a lot harder than his basic spell practice. More and more he found himself absorbed in consideration of her whereabouts. Wednesday passed without a word, and he had a difficult time sleeping that night. On Thursday morning, he awoke feeling muzzy in his head from lack of sleep. He shook this feeling off and followed his routine of spell practice before leaving for work. The concentration helped make him more alert and ready for his day at the Orca.

Upon his return home just after eight-thirty on Thursday night, Eddie saw that there was something in his mailbox in the foyer. His heart hammered in his chest as he fumbled with the thumb lock. Finally there was a note from Lena!

The note was short and scribbled, as if she'd been in a hurry:

So glad to find your note! Ship delayed. Arrived only yesterday and spent the day trying to add classes. Is good that seniors have priority in their last semester. Things are strange at the U. Keeping a low profile. Will meet you Friday night in front of the restaurant at closing time. Much to discuss.

-L

She was here. She'd made it, and he would see her the next evening! He reread the note and found the cryptic references to things not being right at the university more than a little disturbing. Of course, on his single visit to the school, the atmosphere had indeed been strange enough for him and his friends to notice. So he wasn't surprised that Lena had also noticed the presence of decidedly non-academic forces hovering around the fringes of university life.

He looked around his little apartment. He tried to picture her there with him. Would she like it? Eddie couldn't know yet where his relationship with Lena would go, but he had never felt this way about a woman, and he hoped that their relationship would develop into something special, something central to both of their lives.

He could hardly sit still. With all the pent up energy of his youth, Eddie paced his room. He adjusted his few pieces of furniture. He straightened and re-straightened his few belongings. His spartan furnishings were not fancy, but he'd become very conscious of order in his time under Joe's tutelage. This had been reinforced when he carried all his belongings in his pack and then again aboard ship. The little apartment was tidy and well-organized.

Even so, he felt compelled to do something. Eddie pulled cleaning supplies from beneath the kitchen sink. He scrubbed the floors. He cleaned the bathroom. He dusted. He couldn't stop until he'd burnt off some energy, some excitement. Eventually, his rooms above the bookstore on Center Street shone with polish and care.

Physically he was tired as he showered and got ready for bed. Even though Eddie was young and strong, he'd had a full day on his feet at the Orca and then spent three hours scrubbing his apartment from top to bottom. Yes, physically he was tired, but he was still excited and worried and hopeful all at the same time. He lay down and tried to read and eventually tried to sleep. If sleep had been hard to find on Wednesday evening, it was downright elusive that Thursday night.

He tossed and turned for what felt like hours. Slowly, he unwound. Slowly the day's work took hold of him. The strength and comfort of youth was on his side, and eventually, Eddie drifted off to sleep.

At first light, however, he was up and dressed. He tried to follow his regular routine, but he couldn't focus on his studies and he didn't feel like eating anything that he had on-hand. Further, he'd pretty much mastered his first six spells and intended to return the book to Anna when she came on shift that evening.

Neat as it was, Eddie felt a need to get out of the little apartment. He wanted to get some air and do something to occupy himself until his shift started at noon. He thrust his arms into the sleeves of his jacket and was out in front of the Tolemy's Cats bookstore before seven o'clock.

Of course few things were open. Hands jammed in pockets, breath fogging in the chilly air, the young man looked up and down the street. For the past few days, a man with a coffee cart had been up near the corner of Center and Anderson, but either he'd moved on or else wasn't out yet. Eddie looked back down the street and shrugged. He'd not returned to the Inn at Three Corners since his first day ashore. He'd considered going there, but hadn't felt that it had been the right time. Now, he had a couple of hours to kill and no real excuse not to pay a visit, so he turned around and headed east down Center Street.

At the corner, Eddie turned left and walked north at Turnbull Road. Even though this area wasn't as rough as the docks, it was clearly different from the environs of both his work and his residence. Eddie's watchfulness reasserted itself as he neared the Inn. Shops were opening, and he could see that the doors to the pubic room of the Inn stood wide. As he had done on his first day in town, he walked all the way around the triangular block that gave the Inn its name. He saw nothing amiss, nothing to warn him off.

"Well," he muttered to himself, "maybe I can at least get some breakfast and look the place over." He took a deep breath and entered, at long last, the Inn at Three Corners.

The day was overcast, but even so it took his eyes a moment to adjust to the dim light inside the public room. As he stepped inside, he instinctively stepped to one side of the open door. This let more light into the interior and gave him a better sense of the space.

Eddie's first impression was that the room was surprisingly clean and inviting. The floor was rough planking, but it had been swept and mopped. There were many trestle tables and a long bar. The bar was unoccupied at this early hour, but a couple of the tables had people at them. The smell of food wafted out from some swinging doors to the right of the bar. To the left of the bar, a wide doorway led deeper into the inn's interior.

No one at the tables gave him more than a passing glance as he walked in. Reflexively, Eddie thought back to the time when he walked

Michael C. Glaviano

into the bar in Joe's town and decided that this lack of interest was a fairly good omen... as was the smell of the food. He walked deeper into the dining room and stood for a moment at the bar. Within a minute, a waitress stuck her head out from the swinging doors and spied him.

"So. Be ye here for breakfast?" she wanted to know. She appeared to be roughly Mabel's age; although where Mabel was almost painfully thin, this woman was decidedly on the plump side.

Eddie nodded and tried to smile a little. His earlier excitement had veered more towards nervousness, but the woman smiled back, handed him a menu. She spoke in a dialect that he'd heard among the tradespeople who lived and worked in the older part of town.

"There be places enough a' this hour. Choose as ye like."

Eddie made his way over to a table near the wall and took a seat where he could watch the door. He looked over the menu. The breakfast offerings were plain, no-nonsense, and hearty. He realized that he was seriously hungry. In a few minutes, the waitress returned and took his order. She brought coffee and it was good. Eddie relaxed.

The food was ready before his nervousness came back. It was a fine, if simple breakfast, eggs done just right, potatoes cooked with onions and black pepper, good rye bread toast. Eddie decided that whatever nighttime events transpired, the early morning routine at the Inn was normal and not very different from that at any decent restaurant from his own world.

He finished, paid for his food, and pulled on his jacket. He felt that he'd crossed a kind of threshold by making an initial appearance at the Inn. Gradually he might work towards the status of a regular so that his comings and goings fit within the normal ebb and flow of the place. For now, he was satisfied that his initial foray had filled his stomach with warm food and had been without incident.

Eddie left the public room and took in the rough old streets before turning back down Turnbull. Now a chill wind blew up from the harbor. The gray overcast of early morning had given way to more serious looking clouds. He still had plenty of time, so he decided to walk back by his place and pick up a warmer coat.

By the time he reached Tolemy's Cats, Mrs. Abellona had the store open. On a whim, Eddie decided to see if she had any books on magic. He pulled the door open and entered the shop.

Mrs. Abellona was at the front counter. Her hair was still the wild shade of scarlet it had been the last time Eddie had seen her. Today, her outfit lurched in the general direction of bright turquoise. Eddie couldn't help but notice that his landlady had switched her nail color to something near the pink end of the spectrum. She looked up when Eddie entered.

"Good morning, Mrs. Abellona! Eddie called, "I was wondering if..."

220

"No. Your rent is due on the first of the month as we agreed. No extensions!" she interrupted loudly.

"Oh, I'm not here to ask for an extension, Mrs. Abellona!" Eddie replied. "You see, I was just interested in..."

"No parties either. I told you that when you moved in. No parties. I run a respectable place!"

Eddie decided that his only hope was a direct approach. "Mrs. Abellona, I'm looking for a book to buy!"

"Well, speak up, for goodness sake! What kind of book?"

"Do you carry any books on magic?" Eddie asked.

The young man was shocked at the effect this question had on his landlady. She looked as if she might faint. Her eyes darted from side to side and her voice dropped to a hoarse whisper.

"Well... I don't know about that. No. I don't know about that at all... I don't want any trouble. See here, young man... I... I don't carry any books on magic."

Eddie stepped close to the counter and lowered his voice a little. "Mrs. Abellona. Are you okay? Can you hear me?"

She nodded, and Eddie continued. "Has someone been bothering you? I don't want to cause you any trouble. I was just looking to learn some simple spells."

Slowly the old woman gained control of herself. She took a deep breath and, with some effort, stood straight. Now, for the first time, she truly engaged in a conversation with her young tenant. Her eyes bored into Eddie's as if she read his thoughts, as if she measured the blood coursing through his veins.

Reaching across the counter, she spoke firmly, clearly. "Give me your hand, young man," she demanded.

Bewildered, Eddie complied. As on their first meeting, he was struck by the strength of the old woman's grasp. She continued to look intently at him. Now, her voice changed, grew resonant with powerful undertones. He felt something like an electrical current in his hand and tried to pull back, found that he could not.

"So you are not one of those RSM jackals, are you?" she asked in this strange, new voice. "No, you are not. That much is clear," she answered her own question.

She fell silent for a few heartbeats. When she spoke again, her powerful voice shook him as he stood, unable to break away. "I see that you are very nearly as you appear, but not quite. Oh, No. Not quite. What am I not seeing? Oh! I hate being this old! I should be able to tell in the twitch of a cat's tail. But even now, even as feeble as I am, I can see the mark of the Lady upon you. And that of Lillith as well."

At this point, Eddie's knees began to buckle, and his head throbbed painfully. Afraid he might fall, he placed a hand on the counter. The pressure eased.

Michael C. Glaviano

Mrs. Abellona blinked, stood still, and considered him. She again had the appearance of an ordinary, elderly woman with questionable taste in color combinations. He noticed that she, too, steadied herself against the counter.

"Well, now. It is clear you mean no harm. But on your life, keep this to yourself. Do you hear me?" she demanded.

Not trusting his voice, Eddie swallowed, nodded. "Follow me!" she ordered. Her voice, pitched normally now, sounded almost relaxed, nearly calm.

Without waiting for Eddie's response, Mrs. Abellona lifted a hinged section at the back of her counter and left the cashier's area. She strode to the front door, locked it, and switched the sign to read "CLOSED." Then she turned and hurried toward the back of the store.

Perhaps halfway back, a perpendicular aisle cut the shelves. Beyond that intersection, the shelves were all shifted by half an aisle width. This meant that the shelves in the back of the store weren't visible from the front. Mrs. Abellona quickly negotiated the dogleg and continued to the rear of the store.

She stepped close to a tall bookcase at the back wall, and blocking Eddie's view with her body, fumbled with something near the floor. There was a click, and the whole bookcase swung out. Another set of shelves was sunk into the wall behind it.

Mrs. Abellona motioned Eddie forward and he stepped to her side. She gazed at the shelves.

"Have you read anything yet?" she asked, her voice still pitched normally.

"Yes. A... friend loaned me *A Child's Garden of Spells*."

"And you read it?"

"Yes, and I studied and learned some of the spells at the end."

"Show me!" the old woman commanded.

Eddie summoned the spell to cast a beam of light. This effectively illuminated the shelves that stood in front of them.

"Good," breathed Mrs. Abellona. "Now stop it. Can you do anything else?"

Eddie did as she ordered and extinguished the spell. Then he pointed down to the worn floor. He thought the spell and turned one plank white; then he turned it back.

The old woman gave him an appraising look. "Not a bad start... but it is only that: a start. How long have you been at it?"

Eddie told her he'd studied a little "here and there" but had only really tried to get organized in his studies since he'd moved to Soapstone Bay.

She looked thoughtful again and stepped up close to the bookcase. There she reached up and withdrew three texts. They comprised a three-volume set. She turned and handed them to Eddie.

She placed her hand on his arm. "Now help me close this," she whispered.

Eddie carefully swung the bookcase back and pressed it into the latch so that it was firmly fastened. Mrs. Abellona nodded once and marched back to the front of the store. Eddie followed, puzzled, but pleased.

When they reached the counter, Mrs. Abellona lifted the section and settled herself back at the cashier's station.

"How much? For the books?" Eddie asked.

She just waved her hands and shook her head, again looking directly at Eddie. Her voice was still quiet and steady. "Just study. And learn. Too few young people care for the old ways anymore. Remember! Say nothing regarding where you obtained those books. I mean it! Now go. Unlock the door and turn the sign around on your way out."

Eddie nodded. Meeting her eyes, he realized that they were clear and bright – hardly the eyes of an old woman. "Thank you, Mrs. Abellona," he said quietly.

She nodded to him and perched her glasses on her nose. Her face was serious, but he also thought he saw a tiny hint of smile in the corner of her mouth. The smile reminded him, just a little, of someone's, but he couldn't say who.

Eddie turned to go, but she called him back. As he turned, she added, "You may call me 'Mrs. A' when no one else is around." Eddie nodded again and left the store.

Once outside, Eddie glanced at the three texts, thumbed through the pages quickly. They certainly looked more advanced than the simple text he'd borrowed from Anna. He felt exposed on the street, so he dashed up to his rooms and put them in his bookcase.

He grabbed his warm coat and Anna's book. Then he hurried off to the Dancing Orca. The sky continued to darken. The smell of rain was in the air.

*   *   *

The morning had been eventful, but the afternoon crawled by. The evening was even worse. The change in the weather kept people home. Around six-thirty, there was one early bump in customers, but that was the only time they had to hustle. Even the usually ebullient Matt acted out of sorts and bored.

Anna came in for the dinner shift and Eddie returned her book. Given Anna's experience at the university bookstore and Eddie's own interaction with Mrs. A, Eddie decided not to make too much of the book that he'd been studying so carefully. He just thanked Anna, told her that it had been "interesting," and said that he hoped to spend more time studying in this area at some point.

His lukewarm response obviously disappointed Anna a little, but his recollection of Mrs. A's initial reaction had reinforced his sense of caution. Once more, Eddie resolved to remain cautious. He wanted to see what he could learn on his own from Mrs. A's books. And, he was focused on, hoping for, Lena's safe arrival in a matter of hours. He decided not to say anything to Matt and Anna about the note he'd received from Lena the night before. His hope was that Lena would show up and they'd be able to slip away unnoticed.

After the mini-rush at six-thirty, the rain that had been threatening for most of the day, finally arrived. This brought business to a standstill. There were only three small parties the rest of the evening. Matt remarked that once people got used to winter, they'd come back out, but the first, significant autumn storms were always received as though no one had ever experienced rain.

Matt suggested that Eddie begin cleanup at seven o'clock. This at least gave him something to do, but within a half hour he was almost done. The last half hour was painfully slow. By eight, Eddie was wound-up and tense. He struggled to keep up a cheerful, easy-going facade. At last his shift was done!

Matt took off his apron and tossed it into the laundry bag. Eddie's apron joined it along with a couple of cleaning towels. The two young men looked around the tidy kitchen. The dishwashers were still busy at their stations, but the activity was winding down. Anna came in from the dining room.

"Anna and I are going to get a drink before we head home. You want to join us?" Matt offered.

"Oh, thanks," Eddie replied. "I'd like to do that another time, but I'm feeling a little tired. Slept badly last night. I'd like to get some air and then head home."

"Okay," Matt nodded. "We can walk part way with you."

"No, you two go ahead. I'm going to sit under the awning outside and relax for a bit."

Eddie could tell that he'd put his new friends off by rejecting their invitation and he tried to smooth things over by being as open as he could. "I'm sorry guys. Ordinarily I'd jump at it, but not tonight. I hope you'll invite me again, but I have some things on my mind and I know I wouldn't be good company."

Anna looked at him closely then, and Eddie struggled to keep his face from revealing just how much he wanted to get outside. He shrugged and forced a half smile and then collected his coat. Stopping briefly to say good night to Mabel on his way out, he finally escaped from the restaurant. He moved slowly when all the time he wanted to rush into the evening.

Outside, Eddie found a spot on the bench under the awning. It was out of the rain, but it wasn't warm. A couple of minutes later, Matt and Anna left as well. Eddie thought that Anna again aimed a thoughtful look his way, but Matt had returned to his normal, upbeat self. The couple walked out to the street lamp and then into the darkness, arm-in-arm. The rain continued to fall gently. Moments later, the sounds of their voices and footsteps faded.

Eddie knew that Mabel would be inside closing up until at least nine o'clock. Then she, the dishwashers, and the custodian would all leave at the same time. For now he was alone. Trying to pierce the darkness of the storefronts, he looked around the deserted street. He thought that it might be better if Lena could see him more clearly, so he got up from the bench and went out to the rain-spattered pool of light beneath the street lamp. Once there he put on his battered hat and turned up his collar. And waited.

He paced back and forth for a while and wondered if Lena were going to show up. Was she okay? He didn't want to be hanging around when Mabel and the others finally finished and left. He paced some more. Eddie was starting to get worried when a voice called out behind him, "I am here, Reed. I needed to make sure you were alone, but I am here now."

Eddie spun around and Lena stepped from the shadows of a storefront across the street. She darted across the empty space, and then she was in his arms, pressed against him. All the feelings he'd experienced in those two days with the wagon train rushed back. It felt like coming home.

"I'm so glad you're here," he whispered.

"Me too. We need to talk. Can we go to your place?"

"If you want to. We could go to a club if you'd rather."

Lena laughed then, just a short giggle. "What? You don't want me in your apartment?"

"Right. That's it. Come on. Let's get out of the rain," Eddie laughed back.

They hurried through the wet streets. It was a long 15 minutes. They were both nervous, both happy, both self-conscious. They reached the building and scampered up the stairs to Eddie's room.

Eddie had wanted to take things slowly. She meant so much to him and he didn't want to rush her or push her. He tried to say what he felt, but she covered his mouth with hers. Then she pulled back and whispered, "I know. I know. But it is right. It really is right. I can tell."

And then they were consumed by youthful passion. Moments later they were in his bed, their clothes strewn around the room. They delighted in each other. The exploration, the touching, the intimacy, all of it. For his part, Eddie was amazed at the light in her eyes, at the intense beauty of her body, at the feel of her. For her part, Lena saw clearly that Eddie's experiences had left him changed, physically tougher and emotionally older than his years.

Later, they lay together as closely as they could. They listened to
the autumn rain for a time. He heard her breathing; she, his heart. Finally Eddie spoke softly, his voice barely above a whisper.

"Lena, I want to tell you something right away. Something that
happened the night after I left the wagon train. I... Well, it hasn't been
far from my thoughts ever since."

"What, my love?"

And so he described, as clearly and quickly as he could, what had
happened that night in the grove, when the harpy had descended on him,
had almost taken him. He told Lena that the Old One had pierced the
harpy's paralyzing spell and called to him, ordered him to remember the
face of his beloved. Haltingly, he told her that it was her face, Lena's
face, that had come to him, which had broken the harpy's spell and destroyed the creature.

"So in a very real way, you saved my life... And in that minute I
knew that you really were my beloved. Does that make sense?" he finished.

Her arms were strong and she held him, gripped him almost
fiercely. She slid her body along his and kissed him again.

"It makes sense enough to me," she whispered, "sense enough to
me."

And their passion was kindled again, and several more times that
first night. They were, after all, young and strong. They saw the divine
spark and blew upon it to make it flame.

* * *

There can be only one first night, but the one-and-only first
morning follows it, which can be a fine consolation. Eventually, the
young lovers drew themselves from the bed and made ready for the day.

Over breakfast, each in turn recounted the events since they'd
last seen each other. They sat across from each other in the tiny breakfast nook in Eddie's kitchen and talked. Their voices were quiet, their silences long. Each gazed into the eyes of the other and remembered the
night and the press of their bodies.

Lena's long trip north had been uneventful, but brigands had
been so active in the coastal waters that the ship captains in the northernmost ports decided to form an armed convoy. This delayed their departure but had been the right move. Those few ships that couldn't or
wouldn't wait and had set out alone had never reached their destinations.

Lena had returned to the university to find that for the first time
in the long history of the school, political action by well-funded ideo-
logues had resulted in censorship, restrictions on student activities, and
wholesale changes in curricula.

And even though it was one of the oldest and best respected in the university, Lena's own department had been impacted. The faculty had resisted, and several senior professors had been censured. All non-tenured faculty members who had stood against censorship had been summarily dismissed. Perhaps worst of all, those dismissed had been replaced with people chosen for their political stance rather than their academic credentials.

Lena could still receive her degree but none of the truly meaningful classes that she'd planned to take during her last semester were going to be offered. She and a few other senior students had met privately with the department head and had worked out a plan. They would keep a low profile and take electives to fill out their unit requirements. They would do independent study papers under titles with innocuous names. This would allow them to graduate. It was unsatisfactory and galling, but it was still the best strategy they had been able to identify.

Eddie realized that he didn't actually know what Lena was studying and said so.

"Oh, we discussed it just a little in the wagon train," she reminded him. "And I think you talked about it a little more with Mother and Father. You have a rough idea of how our world is organized. You know about the way we have structured our economy around semi-autonomous city-states, the importance of cultural exchange and regional trade, and how the wagon trains and the sailing ships all fit in. I study the socio-economics of all of that. I study what models work and how we can improve and advance without giving up what has been so good for so many generations."

"And they want to censor *that*?" Eddie was incredulous.

"It is those RSM people. They have an entire agenda. They deny the existence of the parallel worlds. They claim that the cosmology of the Great Wheel is superstition and that there is no objective evidence in support of it. They are lobbying for nothing short of the most severe censorship, and they use their media access to level vicious personal attacks against anyone who tries to engage in a serious discussion of the issues – let alone anyone who attempts to stand against them.

"Apparently, the group has intimidated or bribed representatives in the central government and those pawns are in turn sponsoring legislation with names such as the 'Information Protection and Accessibility Act' and the 'Academic Freedom Act.' These bills contain provisions that accomplish the exact opposite of what their titles suggest.

"Further, we are hearing unconfirmed rumors of an aggressive consolidation of populations in southern and western regions. They sound nightmarishly like forced relocation. In the universities, administrators are seeing funding connected to support of the RSM agenda. This is impacting all the curricula that touch on the concepts and practice of magic, regional economic models, and the like."

Lena continued, "And it gets worse and worse. There is a lot of talk around campus that big mining operations are ramping up in the west and that several major wind-farms and four solar thermal facilities have been decommissioned and replaced with fossil-fueled power plants... Truly, though, I think those are merely rumors. After all, you must ask why anyone would want to do that. It would be stupid."

Eddie was quiet for a while. Finally he spoke up. "I hate to say this, Lena, but it sounds like the people who were pursuing me – the people who drove me to flee to this world. That's an awful lot like their agenda in my world. If they're successful with it, their strategy results in tremendous concentration of power and wealth. My... my teacher calls these people 'locusts.' He says they move from world to world, destroying and consuming. They leave desolation behind them, and it doesn't take very many of them to do terrible damage to societies, worlds even."

Lena came around and sat next to Eddie on the little bench. He put his arm over her shoulder and they held each other. Eventually, she looked up at Eddie and he saw that she was crying.

"What is it? You're worried about all this, right?" Eddie asked.

"Well of course, but..." and she buried her face in his chest for a few moments. Then she pulled back and took a deep breath, "I realize I am being horribly selfish and irrational, but I was struck by my feelings for you and how we have only just now found each other. The world should be perfect, and it is not, and that makes me angry and sad."

"Yeah, it's just not right, is it?" Eddie added. "We're going to have to try to figure out what we can do. There must be something."

Lena cleared her throat and smiled, just a little. "In the meantime, I will have my studies, such as they are. And we will have each other."

Eddie joined in, "Yeah, and now that I'm settled in, I can start to understand more about your world. Oh, and yesterday I went to the Inn at Three Corners for breakfast. It was okay, not scary at all. I figure my best bet is to go there often, until I'm seen as a regular. That way I'll just blend into the crowd."

"Reed, that place does not have the best of reputations. Please be careful," Lena spoke softly.

"Oh, I will. Believe me, Lena, I will," he assured her. "I'll go there for breakfast a few times, and then, maybe next week I'll go there on my days off for lunch. Maybe hang around for a beer afterwards. I'm going to take it slow."

"When I can, I will accompany you," Lena added.

"Hey, you just said that it didn't have the best reputation. Now you want to go there?" Eddie laughed.

"Not 'want to,' particularly. What I want is to be with you," she smiled.

The previous night's rain had blown over, and the sky visible through the windows of the tiny kitchen was clear and bright. It was quiet and warm in the apartment. For a few minutes at least, they could pretend it was safe.

They cleaned up their breakfast things. The sky continued to be bright blue. Lena suggested that they go for a walk around the neighborhood. They collected their jackets and made their way down the stairs and out to the street. By then it was after ten o'clock.

"Let's go around the block and look at things, and then I want to walk you up to campus, okay?" Eddie suggested.

"Yes. Although with all the changes at the university – the increased security and such – I think we should meet off campus. I want to avoid anything that might draw attention to either of us."

Eddie nodded. "You really think it's that bad? Do you live on campus?"

"Yes, Reed, I do. Perhaps the changes will amount to little more than an annoyance, but I think that it is prudent for us to be cautious for now. My college, the College of Applied History, has a small residence hall for fourth and fifth year students. We each have our own room. The building is very old, one of the first buildings on campus, we are told. It is a real privilege to be chosen to live there. Or rather it was. As soon as I returned, I noticed some people slinking around the hallways and common rooms. Last year I knew nearly everyone who lived there – at least slightly. These were people I'd never seen around campus. Another unwelcome change," she finished.

"Well maybe we'd better stay at my place... oh, when you feel like it, I mean. Or if you want to," he added, suddenly self-conscious.

She squeezed his hand and then poked him in the ribs. Her laugh was the same musical laugh that he'd first noticed – was it only a few weeks ago?

"Do you in any way doubt that, Reed? After last night?"

A kiss seemed to be the only answer required, and he happily complied. Then, picking up the thread of their conversation, they walked a little further.

"But we will need a way to communicate," she said. "We will want to meet, yes, at your rooms, but also other places. How can we do that?"

"Is there anyone you can trust completely... or any place where we could leave messages?" Eddie wondered. "I'm pretty sure that the young woman at the student recreation center, where I left the note for you, intended to read what I'd written. My guess is that she barely counted to ten after I reached the elevators.

"Anyway I have a couple of new friends from work, and I think they're okay... am pretty sure anyway, but they aren't students and they live near me," he continued. "And I'm very confident about my landlady, but I have no idea where she lives, and leaving a message at her bookstore wouldn't be useful since my mailbox is right next door."

"And there is the restaurant where you work," she added. "That's right near the corner of University and Wells. Students are always down there."

"Well, maybe. I guess we could leave messages with Mabel. I mean, I'm sure she's okay and all, but I'd rather not rely on anyone..." his voice trailed off as he thought about the problem.

"Hey, wait. I have an idea," Eddie continued. He had real excitement in his voice. "Maybe we need a code. Something that we can remember without writing down. Something that doesn't even look like a code. Let me think some more. Since we're only trying to communicate a few things, basically a time and a place to meet, we should be able to come up with something that's pretty good."

"That might work," she agreed, "and in the meantime I will try to think of other places where we could leave messages... but I am hoping that we will always find it possible to decide when and where to meet next before we part."

By this time they'd walked to University Avenue and were halfway up the street towards the school, and Lena called a halt.

"I am going to go on alone from here, Reed," she said. "You need to get to work. I must get busy if I am to make something of my last semester at university."

Lena sighed and looked around, but then she perked up. They were walking past a busy tea and coffee house, and she indicated it with a slight tilt of her head as they continued up to the trolley stop. The place was full of students and was clearly a regular hangout.

"I have an idea for tonight," she said. "Most of the shops on University are open later on Saturday night, including that tea shop. I will come down with some friends. We will have dinner. That is something we often do. Afterwards, I will say that I want to be by myself and read. I will come here and wait until you get off work. How does that sound?"

"Yeah, that's pretty good," Eddie agreed. "Let's take it a little further, okay? I'll come here directly from work. Saturday nights can get busy, so it might be nearly nine by the time I get here. I'll come in and look for you, but I won't come over. Instead, I'll order something and once I've got it I'll stop near the front door."

Lena nodded as she listened. Eddie continued, "You leave and start walking up the street. I'll leave right after. Stay in sight. In a block or two, duck into the porch of a store front and wait 'til I catch up, okay?"

She smiled, "Yes, that will be fine, Reed. Now I will kiss you on the cheek as though you were a good friend but nothing more. Today will pass slowly, but it will pass... and we will be together again tonight."

She reached up and brushed her lips against his cheek. Then she smiled and turned with a casual wave. He tried to match her but thought that his motion probably looked as awkward as it felt. With a great exertion of will, he turned away and headed back down University to Wells. He was just in time for his shift.

*   *   *

When Eddie reached the Dancing Orca, the lunch rush was in full swing. The restaurant was loud and packed with people. Many in the crowd were university students who were enjoying the last Saturday before classes.

Matt had his hands full. He bugged his eyes out and pretended to be going crazy as Eddie walked in, and then he laughed at his own clowning and returned to his work. Eddie washed his hands and grabbed his apron. He took a deep breath, selected an order from the point-of-sale display, and began building a sandwich.

Even though his heart wasn't in it at the start, the familiar rhythms of prepping and cooking good food won Eddie's attention well before the rush tapered off. They did a good business all the way through the midday mealtime. Just once, Mabel ducked her head into the kitchen, grinned at them all, and let them know that business was great.

After lunch, Matt, Eddie, and their helpers started cleaning the kitchen. Once the kitchen was back in order, they began prepping side dishes for the Saturday dinner crowd. The weather continued to be fine, so they were hoping to recover from the previous night's poor showing.

When it was time for his break, Eddie had something to eat. It was still nice outside, so he left the confines of the kitchen for some fresh air while Matt wrapped things up. Anna showed up at quarter to five.

"Hey, Anna," Eddie called as she walked up.

"Hey, Reed. You doing all right?" she wondered.

"I'm fine." Eddie guessed the question had to do with his refusal to join them the previous evening, so he added, "I was just tired and wanted to get home. Sorry I didn't feel like going out last night. What'd you guys do?"

"Oh, we went for a drink and then headed home ourselves. The weather and all... Say, Reed, did you ever hear back from your girlfriend at the University?" Anna wanted to know.

"Uh, yeah. Yes, I did. Hear from her, that is." Eddie felt his face redden.

"Well, is everything okay? Are you going to be seeing each other?"

Eddie could feel his blush deepen. "Well, yeah. We will..." he admitted.

He tried to change the subject. "Uh, we had a really busy lunch today, and the weather's good. Maybe we'll have a better dinner crowd tonight. Think so?" he added, lamely.

Anna was having none of it. Again, Eddie thought that he noticed a trace of calculation in her look. "So when do we meet her?" she
asked.

"Well, uh, you know she's pretty busy with classes starting and
all. Her boat was delayed, so she just got back to town and has been trying to get her classes set up, so she's pretty busy. For a little while, anyway."

At this point, Anna was grinning broadly. She gave Eddie a
knowing look. He tried unsuccessfully to meet her eyes, sure that his face
was the color of a fire engine.

"Well... I guess I'd better go in and get, uh, set up," he added.

"Yes, I guess you should do that, Reed."

Eddie went inside. He and Matt crossed paths as the chief cook
left for his own break. He could just imagine Anna's and Matt's conversation. He sighed and started to get ready for the first few dinner orders.

Sure enough, when Matt returned after his break, his first question had to do with Eddie's love life. "Hey, Reed, so why didn't you tell
me your girlfriend was back? No wonder you wanted to stay close to
home last night! You going to see her tonight?"

"Well, yeah. After work," Eddie admitted.

"I guess you'd like to spend some time alone with her, huh?"

Eddie couldn't help but laugh at himself at this point. "Yeah. I
guess I would. I'll introduce you guys as soon as I can, okay?"

Tension broken, it was easier to dive into the dinner rush. It was
as though everyone in Soapstone Bay suddenly realized that autumn
wouldn't last forever. Winter would arrive after all, and people wanted to
go out while the weather was good. It was crazy-busy, but that was better
than Friday night's poor turnout.

As eight o'clock drew near, the crowds thinned significantly, and
Eddie started cleanup. Twenty minutes later, Matt told Eddie that he'd
stay to wrap things up. Gratefully, Eddie finished what he was doing, put
the finishing touches on his station, and took off. On the way out, Anna
caught his eye and smiled. Eddie waved at her as he left.

The air had turned colder and the wind was blowing in off the
bay. Eddie fastened his coat and was glad for his battered hat. He knew
that he faced a brisk ten minute walk up University.

Despite the weather, people were on the street. A celebratory
mood pervaded the uptown area. There were several bars on University
and perhaps half of them had live music. While the individual songs
were unfamiliar, Eddie was struck by the familiarity in styles and, from
the snatches of lyrics that reached his ears, themes in the popular music
of this locale.

The coffee house where he and Lena intended to meet was called
"Bean & Leaf." It was absolutely packed. There was a tiny stage area off
to one side and a duo was doggedly working through some acoustic

tunes. Eddie wondered why they bothered. Anyone who noticed the music simply talked louder to be heard over the general din.

He scanned the crowded room. At first Eddie didn't see Lena, but before he had a chance to get worried, he spied her sitting with a group of people near the back. She had already seen him and gave him a tiny nod before turning to say something to the young woman next to her.

Eddie looked around the room as he worked his way through the press. He imagined that he sensed an undercurrent of tension in the place but shrugged off the feeling as general nervousness. Eventually he reached the counter and placed his order. Careful not to look in Lena's direction any more than anywhere else, he watched the crowd while he waited for his tea.

He could not be sure, but he thought he recognized the security guards that he'd encountered in the student recreation building. Most likely the source of the tension the young man had sensed, the guards loitered near the musicians and, without trying to hide their actions, eyed the crowd intently. Eddie was sure that they'd looked in his direction, but he doubted that they remembered him. In any case, he was glad that he'd kept his hat on and had pulled it down low the moment that Lena saw him.

Eddie wanted to use the seeing spell, but decided against it and instead forced himself to look up at the specials menu that was posted above the counter. Before long, however, he was relieved to hear the barista call his order. Eddie wove through the pack near the counter and collected his drink. Next, carefully looking straight ahead, he started toward the door.

Near the exit was another counter with napkins, sugar, honey, and pitchers of milk and cream. Eddie added a little milk and fussed with his drink until he noticed that Lena had made her way to the door and exited the Bean & Leaf. Then he turned, discarded his stirrer, and took a napkin from a dispenser. Finally, he reached the door. The chill air was sharp in his face after the steamy, crowded coffee bar.

He could see Lena roughly half a block ahead. She glanced back at him and then kept walking. Sipping his tea, hands wrapped around the cup for warmth, he followed her slowly. He heard loud voices behind him and turned. The security guards had followed a group of four young men from the Bean & Leaf and were arguing with them.

For a few seconds Eddie was tempted to go over and try to see what was going on, but he decided that his first priority by far was to meet up with Lena. He turned back and could see that she had pulled ahead. The street was fairly well lit and there were small groups of people of all ages coming and going. He kept walking.

Nearly a block away, Eddie saw Lena turn and walk into a deep store front. Now she was out of sight. Glad for the distraction behind him, he quickened his pace slightly. She was waiting for him when he reached the storefront. Eddie felt a wave of relief wash over him. He realized that he'd been holding his breath and released it. Looking both ways to verify that they were unobserved, he moved to her and they embraced.

"Let us get away from here, Reed," she said quietly. "That was a difficult wait and the day has not been easy."

"Did you have trouble breaking away from your friends?"

"Yes. They insisted on accompanying me to the Bean & Leaf. They kept suggesting that we all go somewhere else, to listen to music or back to campus. It was stifling in there and I kept making excuses and telling them to go ahead." Here she chuckled.

"And then you walked in and suddenly I wanted to leave and go for a walk by myself. They must think I'm terribly antisocial... or simply strange," she ended with a another giggle.

"I had a grilling from my friends at the restaurant too," Eddie admitted.

Lena sighed just a little, "Well, I suppose that I should meet your friends; although I confess that I would prefer to have you all to myself for a while longer."

"Me too," he agreed. They walked along in silence. It felt comfortable, right. Even though they were in the first, passionate stages of their love, they enjoyed the simple feeling of being together and walking quietly.

"How's your schedule shaping up? Are you going to have something each day?" Eddie asked as they walked.

She was silent for a few steps. "Such as they are, my classes, are Monday, Wednesday, and Friday. None of them is challenging. Today I met with my advisor and we have agreed on two independent study papers. While you are at the restaurant, I can work on those papers and other assignments at the library and in my room. Our schedules don't line up perfectly, Love, but we will manage.

"But, Reed?" she continued.

"Yeah?"

"There is something more worrisome than juggling our schedules. I simply do not know whom to trust among my friends on campus. Oh, I feel that I can trust their intentions well enough as individuals, but all it would take would be the wrong word spoken at the wrong time, and then..." her voice trailed off.

"What could happen?" he wondered.

"Departments are under pressure. Campus security has become intrusive and rude. Students are being expelled on thin pretext and sent home. It is as though there is some kind of purge going on, and I do so want to finish."

"Well, I don't have to meet anyone from the university. I'm fine with that. I mean, it'd be great to meet your friends and all, but that can happen after... After things get back to normal."

"Oh, before I forget," Eddie continued, "I saw a couple of men at that coffee shop. Security guards. I'm pretty sure I encountered them last week when I left the message for you."

"Did they see you?"

"I don't think so. Or if they did, I don't think they recognized me. The coffee shop wasn't bright and I was wearing my hat. And when I left they were having some kind of shouting match with a few young guys from the school. So I doubt that they were thinking of me."

"Well, that is good," Lena nodded again, "but we still must establish a way of communicating and meeting that attracts little attention."

"I agree. The lower the profile the better. I have some ideas... Oh. Hi, um, Mrs. Abellona! Is everything okay?"

They'd reached Tolemy's Cats bookstore and Mrs. Abellona had sprung from the doors as they approached. Her hair was in its usual state of randomness. This evening, his landlady had selected a baggy, floral print pants suit for her attire. Her reading glasses had been perched on her nose. Now they fell, stopped by a chain, to dangle in front.

"As okay as it could be, waiting out here, freezing. An old woman could die out here from the cold!" she spoke loudly.

"Come inside. Now. Both of you," she ordered.

Eddie and Lena looked at each other. Eddie shrugged and they followed the old woman into the shop. She closed the door and locked it. The "Closed" sign was already turned out to the sidewalk. Then, without stopping, she motioned to them to follow her to the back of the shop. They turned right at the wall where the hidden bookshelf was located and walked along the back wall of the shop until they reached a narrow hall-way. There, Mrs. Abellona threw a switch and shut off the main lights in the store. Dim lights continued to provide a faint illumination.

She led the way down the hall to a door that opened onto a small living room. This was evidently Iris Abellona's apartment. Unlike the old woman who obviously lived there, the room was perfectly neat. Everything was orderly and pleasing to the eye. The furniture was old but well cared for.

"Sit down. Sit down," she said in a more normal tone of voice. I see you have something," she nodded at Eddie's tea.

Turning to Lena, she asked, "Would you like anything to drink, dear?"

"A glass of water would be good, please." The young woman looked completely bewildered. Eddie was sure he looked the same way.

The landlady moved spryly off and returned with a glass which she set on a coaster near a small sofa.

"You're still standing. Go on. Sit down," Mrs. Abellona told them again, making patting motions with her hands. This time they sat. The old woman glanced at an over-stuffed chair that stood near the door. The chair leaped to a spot opposite the sofa and the old woman settled herself comfortably.

"I suppose you are this man's sweetheart. From the university. Do you have a name? When no one else is around, you too may call me 'Mrs. A'" she said to Lena without preamble.

This was the first time Eddie had seen Lena so discomfited.

"Well, it is, um, a pleasure... to meet you, Mrs. A. My name is... Helena Graysmith. Please call me 'Lena.' But how do you know... did Reed...?"

"I spoke with Mabel. At the restaurant where your young man works. Mabel is a good sort, but she repeats anything she hears – if you know how to ask the proper questions.

We need to talk," she continued. "He's okay," here she nodded in Eddie's general direction, "Okay in a green sort of way, but he doesn't know much of this world, and without help he's going to draw attention to both of you."

"Mrs. A, how did you know that I'm not from...?" Eddie saw no point in denying it. He was still completely bewildered.

"It's as plain as the full moon on a summer's night. As plain as the ears on your head. If you are paying attention. Sadly, there are forces at work that are paying attention. Indeed, they are paying attention.

Today those RSM bullies were nosing around here. They couldn't find anything of course. But I had to confound them when they asked about the apartments upstairs. One of my oldest customers, poor Mr. Gaelen, had the misfortune to come inside just then and they started pestering him until I put a stop to it. They went away, but they'll be back at some point. Might even bring someone with a brain the next time.

I assume that you just left those books somewhere in plain sight in your rooms?" she added.

"Well, yes, Mrs. A. I put them in my bookshelves."

"That will not do. Not at all. Now listen. I am an old woman. I cannot keep this hearing spell up all night, and I am deaf as the bottom of the sea without it. There is a small secret space in the floor beneath your closet bed. What do you call it?"

"A Murphy bed," Eddie answered.

"See what I mean? Nobody but an outworlder would call it that! Anyway, press the back of the hinge, down near the floor. You won't see a latch, but you'll feel it. A little door will pop up. Put those books in there whenever you are not studying. Only remove one at a time, and leave the compartment open so that you can hide the book quickly. Keep anything relating to your studies or to magic hidden there."

"Are you studying yet?" she continued without a pause.

"Not yet, Mrs. A. Lena just... we...," Eddie could feel himself sweating a little.

The old woman's voice took on a slightly more gentle tone. "I know. I know, young man. Believe it or not, I was not always this old... No, indeed."

"But you need to start," she said, businesslike again. "Start at the first volume of the set. Practice every day. A minimum of two hours. Do it until you feel tired and then stop for the day. Each time you learn a new spell, loop back through those you've already mastered and review. When the review starts taking over a half hour, skip every other spell on alternate days. Then break the spells into three groups. Then four. Do you understand?"

She finally paused for a breath, but all Eddie could do was nod his head. He finally noticed that Mrs. Abellona's fingernails were now a shade that could only be described as "chrome yellow." The effect was stunning.

In the brief silence, Eddie sought, and finally found, something worth saying. "Lena and I are working on a way to set up meetings and communicate without establishing a pattern that's too easy to follow."

"Well, that's sensible. But the best thing you can do is decide where and when you will meet each time. Then nothing will be written down. Even so, you may need to leave a message at some point. Let me think," the old woman made a few hand gestures and whispered something under her breath.

"I have it," she said a few moments later. Now there was something almost like laughter in her voice.

"Yes, I have it," she repeated. "Baleen Park is at the southeast end of the town. In the center is a fountain with a sculpture. A whale chasing its own tail. Just to the south of that fountain are some stone benches that lie against an old brick wall. Now I haven't been down there in years, but in the old times, there was a brick directly behind the rightmost bench as you face the fountain. That brick is in the course that's just above the seat of the bench. Push on it and it will slide into the wall. Release it suddenly and it will pop out into your hand. Be ready! You can leave a note in the cavity behind the brick.

"There is no latch; no mechanism to rust. It is all done with a spell – a spell I cast at least forty years ago.

"Now be still for a moment and I will see if it still functions," she ordered.

The old woman closed her eyes and sank back into the deep cushions of her chair. Eddie thought that she looked frail. He glanced at Lena who met his look with a raised eyebrow.

Mrs. A cleared her throat. Her voice was tired, but she smiled.

"Yes. Even now I can walk the old ways with my mind. That is something, I suppose. At any rate, I just checked, and it's all still there at the park. Still waiting. If you both go down there and press the brick to-gether, then your messages to each other will be safe.

"It would take a witch of no small power to interfere," she fin-ished with just a hint of pride.

"Now, young man. Now you need to tell me why you're here. In our world. Quickly. I'm tiring."

So as quickly as he could, Eddie explained about his world, his relationship with Joe, and how he came to be in Soapstone Bay. Mrs. A asked Eddie to describe Joe, which Eddie tried to do as best he could. The old woman nodded. Now looking even more tired and drawn, she again leaned back in her chair. Her eyes were sad, her voice distant – as if she spoke more to herself than to her young guests.

"Yes, that would be him. I remember. From when I was younger than you are now. When I can, I may try to totter over to the Inn myself. Perhaps by myself; perhaps with you. I would speak with him... see him... one last time."

She brought herself back with a visible effort. She leaned for-ward and looked directly into Eddie's eyes. Her expression was again sharp and intent.

"So it appears that I was right about you, young man. A weight is upon you. You have not felt its full force yet, but I think that you might bear it. And your young woman friend. It is good that you have found each other. Well, perhaps you had help in that regard. At any rate, cher-ish each other."

The old woman fell silent. When she spoke again, her voice was barely above a whisper, "Now go, you two. Leave me to rest. Please see yourselves out. The doors will take care of themselves as you pass. Again, say nothing of this but between yourselves and then only where no one can hear."

Eyes wide, Eddie and Lena looked silently at each other. Lena held out her hand and Eddie took it. They made their way out through the dimly lit shop. Closing doors quietly, silently climbing the stairs to Eddie's rooms, they passed into the warm, safe apartment above the bookstore.

Twenty Seven

In a sense, the creature that had once been Alicia still remembered being human. After all, a very old person remembers being a child, remembers being young and strong, remembers milestones of a long life. But the memories are like photographs, and some elicit more of an emotional response than others. And, unlike the creature, the very old person is still, after all, a person, a human being.

Few memories of her humanity resonated with her, and most of those were images that produced rage and a desire for retribution. Most of the time, she was aware of little beyond the hunt, little beyond a hunger that couldn't be sated, a thirst that remained unslaked. Most of the time she prowled, hid, and attacked. When she was lucky, she fed.

The Alicia creature still had a face, but was a grotesque reminder of her lost beauty. The lovely mouth had become a tooth-filled muzzle. The once shapely body was still graceful, but now the grace was focused in one direction: that of the hunter.

After she had fed on the sinuous, serpent-like creature, she had lost consciousness. When she awoke, she was at first horrified to see what had become of her. Her body had metamorphosed into a long, roughly feline, shape. She was bigger, more powerful and found that she could no longer fit within the lair of the creature she had killed and consumed.

Quickly, however, that horror had faded, sloughed away with the remnants of her humanity. What had remained of her filthy clothing had shredded into rags during the transformation. When she had regained consciousness, she had clawed away the uncomfortable bits and pieces that had not already come off. The joints of her arms and legs had changed and she no longer walked upright. Her feet and hands continued to change and now resembled clawed paws more than anything else. She could still grasp things, but only with great difficulty. As if in echo of the serpent-thing she had consumed, her skin had become reptilian, scaled.

Gradually extending her territory, she prowled the region around the lair that she had outgrown. Less formidable denizens of the Place adjusted their behavior to avoid this new predator. She still killed and fed, but the hunting was not good. She was forced to range far and wide in search of nourishment, but she continued to return to the site of her metamorphosis.

Twenty Eight

The young lovers woke early. They lingered, a happy tangle of intimacies, in the warm bed, but both knew that they needed to be up and abroad. Sooner than either wished, they were up and dressed. If not fully ready for the day, they were at least determined to face it.

"You remember I mentioned that I'd like to be recognized at the Inn, right? You know, to have a kind of presence there. Get to where I sort of blend into the background any time I go in. Their breakfasts aren't bad. Do you feel up to walking over there?" Eddie asked as Lena came out of the bathroom.

"That will be fine, Reed, yes. We will be together. I will see for myself the landscape of the Inn."

Eddie looked around the rooms. He had stashed his books and his notes in the compartment beneath the closet bed last night, and he could see nothing else that might arouse suspicion. He looked out the window at another gray sky. Clouds opened briefly, and the light grew and then faded. He could look at an angle across the rooftop to see the sidewalk across Center Street. Now mostly devoid of foliage, the trees lining the street moved in response to a breeze.

"Do you think you'll be warm enough? I have an extra sweater you could wear under your jacket."

"Thank you, Reed, yes." She smiled then, and added with a small hesitation in her voice, "I realize that this is all so very fast, but would you feel comfortable if I brought a few things over? So that I can dress for the weather? And perhaps a few personal items...?"

"Oh, geez. I'm sorry... I should have invited you! Of course, Lena. Bring whatever you'd like. I want you to be completely comfortable, to feel at home. Somehow... even though it's very soon, I'd... I'd like this to be *our* home. Together."

The young woman's smile extended to the boundaries of her lovely face. "I do feel at home. It is silly to say that, I realize, after our second night together. Even so, that is how I feel."

It was still early. Even though no one was around to hear them, the lovers were unwilling to disturb the peace of the morning. They closed the door quietly and walked softly down the stairs. The air was cold and held more than a hint of rain when they reached the street. They walked as quickly as they could down Center street. The breeze marched directly up from the harbor, and the crisp salt air was refreshing. Screeching and diving, seagulls wheeled overhead. When the young couple reached Turnbull, they crossed the street and walked in the lee of the buildings. They hurried across each intersection as they emerged from the shelter of the sidewalk.

Moving quickly, they reached the Inn at Three Corners in well under twenty minutes. The Inn's door was closed against the cold but unlocked, and they were grateful to pass into the warmth of the public dining room. Eddie was pleased to see the same waitress and waved to her.

She gestured that they should seat themselves. A minute or two later, she came over, coffee cups and steaming pot in her hands, menus tucked under an arm. She smiled a warm welcome of recognition.

"Ah, ye were here last week, were ye no? So. An' Cook didn't kill ye wi' her breakfast so you be bringin' yer' darlin' in to sample our fare. Aren't ye both sweet?"

They smiled in return and thanked the waitress for the menus and coffee. Moments later, they ordered their food. Lena and Eddie sat together, each enjoying the warmth of the room and the closeness of the other.

"See. The place is pretty clean. And at least this time of day it doesn't feel the least bit threatening."

Lena agreed and remarked on the age and good state of repair of the woodwork. She speculated that the long, well-polished bar may have been put in place hundreds of years earlier. Eddie thought that it looked as if it might have been carved from a single piece of wood.

"Yes, that was a primitive time. SMT has been in widespread use for only the last half-century."

"SMT? Oh, right. I remember. Your mother mentioned that. Hey, how are your parents, and Ben, Tad, and the others? I'm sorry I didn't think to ask before now."

"Oh, they are fine. Originally, they had planned to stay down near the docks for a few days and look into the possibility of one more trade caravan this year, but in the end they decided to return home. You will remember that they do not live in Soapstone. My father's family is from well south of here and with all the troubles and rumors of troubles, they simply decided to wait out the autumn and winter months at home."

"Well, the next time you talk to them, please say hello for me... if that's appropriate, of course."

Lena laughed. "Yes, it is appropriate and I will be happy to do that. We have moved rather quickly, haven't we, my love?"

"Yeah, we have, but I'm glad."

"As am I."

They smiled their lovers' smiles in silence then. Eventually, they returned to their observation of the public room. "All this looks like a mix of very old and very new," he gestured around the room.

"Yes, these old buildings are usually retrofitted with newer technologies as they become available. Lighting, heating, energy sources, and so on in a place such as this may have been completely replaced six or more times since this building was new. My guess, however, is that some things which look old are probably modern. The rough plank floor is most-likely purpose grown, for example. It probably looks much the same as the original, but it will be resistant to rot and infestation."

Eddie scanned the room again, trying to figure out what was new and what was hundreds of years old. In some cases, the lighting for example, it was obvious. Just as in the rooms above the bookstore, the heavy wall sconces had probably once been used to hold candles or some type of oil lamp. There were two big chandeliers that had also been transformed to support electric lights.

In other instances, such as the window hardware, he thought he might guess, but often it was really impossible to say. How old, for example, was that long bar rail? The mirror behind the bar? In any case, he thought that the overall effect was good, and that, he decided, was what mattered most.

At this point their food arrived. Eddie thanked the waitress again and they focused their attention on breakfast. As before, the food was good and well-prepared, if simple.

Later, as they settled up their bill, Eddie asked the waitress about the hours that the public rooms were open for meals.

"Oh, Three Corners be open most-times. Drunks and bad-uns be shooed away three, maybe four o' the clock and the crew scrubs 'er down. Mother Henry be in 'fore five for to feed working folk. Ye live here-abouts?"

"Yes, we live nearby. I work in a restaurant in the uptown. 'The Dancing Orca.' Do you know it?"

"Aye, an' I do. It be a sweet place, true. All the schooled young 'uns go there. They come down to the Corners rare-times, which be fine. They be mostly a polite lot. An' there be commerce enough for all in Soapstone. What do ye at the Orca?"

"I'm an assistant cook. I'm just learning."

"I'd wager you be good at whatever you do." Here she gave Lena a huge wink and brought color to the young woman's cheeks, laughter to her lips.

"That he does, Mother, that he does," Lena agreed, slipping into the vernacular. Sensing an opening, she continued with, "I am called by Lena an' this be Reed." She nodded in Eddie's direction.

The waitress beamed and slid onto the bench across from them. "An' call me Margaret, children."

"Thank you, Margaret. Say then. An old friend o' his family's say on a visit tha' he sometime stop a' th' Corners. If we chose, be there a way to leave a message for one such?"

The Margaret nodded, and waved off to the left of the bar, to the opening that led further into the old building.

"Aye, through there. An' leave a message with who be at th' desk. It be Old Mel at this hour. Near all hours, true."

They both thanked her for the information and mentioned that they'd like to come back and try other meals at the inn.

The waitress cocked an eyebrow at this. "Well, Corners, she put on a decent spread. Most-times it be fine here for good, young folk as yerselves. I'd set a different course late nights... 'specially Friday, Sat'day. But most-times it be fine... Come as a couple an' stay close."

Then a bell sounded from the kitchen and Margaret jumped up. "That'd be me order. Thank ye, children, an' be safe."

"Thank you, Margaret."

Eddie and Lena collected their jackets and walked through the doorway to the left of the bar. The light was lower in this space, which they could now see functioned as a lobby for those staying at the inn. Heavy draperies, so deep a shade of green that they were almost black in the dim light, had been drawn over the windows. There was another door in what was probably the outside wall that faced on Longview Avenue.

Directly opposite that wall, perpendicular to the doorway through which they entered, was a reception desk that looked to be of similar vintage to the bar in the public room behind them. There was a lamp on the desk and two more fixtures in the ceiling directly above it that illuminated that space brightly. The rest of the room dimmed even further in contrast. Beyond the desk, in the amber glow of antique wall sconces, they saw stairs leading to upper floors.

The darkly-paneled stairs had a runner down the center of the treads and the heavy bannister rail terminated in a massive, ornately carved newell post. Everything had a well-maintained, if antediluvian appearance. Curtain rods, finials, and other metalwork were all of burnished brass and bronze, hammered tin, and heavy wrought iron.

Despite the apparent age of the furnishings and woodwork, everything glistened in the dim light. The scent of furniture polish mingled with the smells from the dining room. Eddie wondered what the upstairs rooms were like and what sort of client might favor a stay in the Inn.

An ancient looking man worked beneath the bright lights. With careful, deliberate movements, he placed slips of paper and hotel keys into pigeon holes that covered the wall behind the reception desk. He noticed the young couple entering from the public room and turned slowly around as they neared.

"An' what service can Old Mel be to ye?" the old man asked in the same dialect as Margaret.

Eddie spoke up, "Yes, sir. Margaret, the woman in the pub, said that we might leave a message here for someone."

"Aye, ye might. And he might find it. What be the name?"

"Well, I know him as 'Joe Tabs.'"

At this Mel looked sharply at them both. "An' what might two young 'uns such as ye be a-doin', that ye might seek one such as he?" he asked, his voice suddenly focused and serious.

"I... you could say that he's my great uncle."

"Could a' now? Tha' an' more, mos' like. But true, now! Would Old Mel wan' say tha'? Be it right?"

Eddie thought quickly, carefully. He took a deep breath and let it out slowly. "I have slept under his roof, shared his table, and worked by his side. He gave me to believe that I might find him here. More than that, I'd rather not say."

Old Mel looked levelly at Eddie. Briefly, he glanced over at Lena, and Eddie thought that perhaps his look softened just a little, but it was hard to tell for sure. In any case, when his gaze returned to the young man it was deep and still. The old man was silent for a long time, considering, worrying the thoughts in that ancient brain. Eddie resisted the urge to blurt out anything more. He resisted the urge to try the seeing spell as well.

Finally, the old man spoke. "Aye. An' whether ye meant him good or ill ye would not want to say overmuch. An' Old Mel canna' fathom that anything *ye* might put in a note cou' do one such as Joe Tabs bother or harm. Still..."

Lena placed a hand gently on Eddie's arm as if to say, "Let me try."

"Whatever our abilities or our age in years, we mean no ill. What if we wrote the note here, in front of you, so that you could see what it said?"

Mel absorbed this thought. He chewed on it a while, then took it out and looked at it. Then he processed it once more. Finally he nodded.

"Aye. Tha' wou' suit. Here."

The old man slid a piece of paper and a pen across the registration desk. Eddie considered what he might say, what he must not say. He wrote:

Joe: Long journey, but arrived as per your instructions.

Then he wrote the date at the top of the page and scribbled a deliberately illegible signature at the bottom. Eddie decided that would be enough. Joe would certainly be able to infer who had written the note.

Eddie reversed the paper and slid it back across the desk. Mel picked it up and looked closely at it. He held it up to the light and looked through the sheet. He brought the page close to his face and sniffed the ink as it dried. Firmly, steadily, the ancient man tapped three times on the page with the back end of the pen. Finally, he nodded again.

"That'll do, young 'uns. Aye, well enough to suit Old Mel... and most-like Joe Tabs, should he be of a mind to come a-seeking it. Not saying he be here, mind... or that he not be here. But if he – an' only he – ask, why then, Old Mel will give. Be tha' fair enou'?"

At this point, Eddie was sure that this was the best he could hope for. He nodded and thanked the old man. Lena chimed in as well.

"Does that door lead out to Longview Avenue? May we use it?"

"Aye an' aye."

"Thank you again, Mel. We will be on our way now."

The old man favored them with a minute nod and turned back to the work he had been doing when they'd first entered. Lena and Eddie walked to the door and pulled it open. They stepped out onto Longview. Even though it was still early, the day was now in full-swing.

They headed along the Longview side of the inn to the street's intersection with Turnbull. The earlier overcast had cleared, but it was still cold and crisp. Lena folded her arms in front against the chill. Eddie did his best to shield her from the wind.

* * *

"I should get back up to the university," Lena spoke softly. Unable to resist the attraction they felt for each other, they had gone back to Eddie's rooms and lain together for a time. Now they were again both up and dressed. It was nearly 11 o'clock. Eddie would have to be at work soon.

Eddie nodded. "Mrs. A will have the store open by now. If you're okay with it, I'll ask her if she'll add your ID to the lock. That way, if you want, you can come here in the afternoon and study. It's quiet and private. Soon it will be winter and it will be safer and more comfortable if we didn't have to meet after dark."

"Yes, I would like that. Thank you, Reed."

So they went downstairs and browsed in the bookstore until there was a break in the customers. They made their request (loudly) to Mrs. Abellona, who happily obliged. That accomplished, they left the shop and hurried down St. Tolemy's. The street was very narrow, really just a tiny bit wider than a sidewalk, but it cut through to University Avenue. Eddie had always turned off University at Anderson and walked over to Central and then down past the front of the bookstore. This was a slightly shorter path and provided an alternate way to and from home.

They walked up University to the Bean & Leaf where, as before, Lena placed a friendly peck on Eddie's cheek before boarding a trolley. She said that she'd gather a few things and some study materials and return. They agreed that she'd try to alter her route so that when she came to Eddie's there wouldn't be an obvious pattern to her movements. They also had the coffee house, the bookstore, the Orca and several other shops where they could meet.

Work at the Orca was routine. Sunday evening crowds were often small, especially in cold and wet weather, but this was the last evening before classes started at the university. Business was steady but moderate. He could tell that Matt and Anna wanted very much to meet "his girlfriend" and were trying hard to control their curiosity. The pressure was good-natured and tolerable, but he knew that he'd have to introduce them pretty soon. He wasn't sure when and how he wanted to make that happen.

After cleanup, Eddie said his goodbyes and dashed out. He moved quickly down University and turned left at St. Tolemy's. When he reached Central and the Cats building, he practically ran up the stairs to his apartment.

Lena was waiting and smiled warmly when he burst through the door. Eddie was struck by how it felt to come home to her. The sense of homecoming was strong, welcome. For her part, Lena was equally glad to see him. Eddie wanted to hear how things had gone on campus. Lena explained that the situation in and around the university was obviously deteriorating.

"They are continuing to cancel classes, Reed, but what is worse is that these security people are getting more and more aggressive. They are now going everywhere in pairs. They are carrying batons and they break up any group of students larger than three or four. Even worse, we have received notice that security officers will be present at all lectures. Students must sign in with security at the start of each class. This will shorten the lectures and will of course eliminate any substantive classroom discussion.

"As if that were not serious enough, these people are now patrolling well beyond the boundaries of the university."

"Yeah, they were out last night, remember? In front of the Bean & Leaf. I mentioned it later."

"Yes, I remember. I wondered about it at the time but could not see clearly what was happening. At any rate, they are definitely out in force today. They are walking up and down University, well beyond the B & L."

Eddie recalled the scene he'd witnessed the evening before: the four young men arguing with a couple of security guards. It had been slightly worrisome then, but now he wondered if there might be even more sinister overtones.

"This might sound paranoid, Lena, but I've got a bad feeling about this. It might be that whoever is behind these changes is trying to amp up the pressure. You know. Provoke a confrontation. Once that happens, they'll be able to justify a complete clampdown. I don't like to admit it, but I've seen this done in my world."

"Well, I can see how that might be a possibility, Reed. Remember, however, our history for the last few thousand years has diverged substantially from yours. We have a strong tradition of debate and discussion. From birth, children are taught that resorting to violence is a sign of either weakness or cowardice."

"I hope you're right, but..."

"What?"

"Well, those guys were pretty steamed up last night. If you hadn't been waiting alone up the street, I might have gone over there to see what was happening."

"I am glad that you didn't insert yourself into that situation, Reed. Apart from the possibility of immediate physical harm, which I think was small, such situations provide opportunities in which you might say something that would betray your origins."

"Oh," Eddie admitted, "yeah. And after what Mrs. A said, I guess I'd better watch that."

Lena nodded, "But you are right to be worried if you saw a heated exchange. What can we do?"

"I'm not sure, but if these RSM people – or whoever else is involved – are trying to provoke an incident, then the first thing to do is to let your friends know about it."

Eddie continued, "I remember you said that you weren't sure whom you could trust. You know that there are degrees of these things, right?"

"What do you mean, Reed?"

"Well, announcing to a whole roomful of strangers that you're on intimate terms with an outworlder you met last summer in the countryside is one thing, but telling a couple of people whom you know pretty well that you suspect a setup and then suggesting that each of them tells one or two others wouldn't be such a big deal."

"A 'setup?' A 'big deal?'"

"Oh, yeah. Right. I know I've got to watch language like that. A big deal is just a large or important event or opportunity. A setup can be lots of things, but here it would be where the authorities act to provoke a response that they then use as an excuse, a justification, for actions that they already intended to take. Oh, and there is one other thing about setups."

"I do not think that I am going to like this."

"Well, no, you probably won't. Some of these new 'students' that you're seeing around campus, are probably in on the plan. Some of them may act to inflame others' emotions. They might even instigate the violence that gets the ball rolling."

"Ball?... Oh, I understand. We would probably say something such as 'start the wagon.'"

Eddie smiled in response. "So do you have a small handful of friends that you could say something to along these lines? Really just warn that you 'heard' that there might be agitators posing as students and what they might be planning?"

"Well, yes. Yes, I do... and I agree that what you suggest is a prudent course of action."

"But, again, Lena, please be careful. Talk to the people you know best. Emphasize that you heard this from someone else – you can honestly say something like 'a friend in town heard that...,' right?"

"Yes, of course. I have friends I've known for my entire time at school. I will mention this to them while being as discreet as I can."

"I wish I could think of something else," Eddie continued, "but we don't have much information. I hope that Joe gets here soon. I'd bet he knows what to do."

"Well, I will start our own... 'ball rolling' tomorrow afternoon when I return to campus," Lena said, smiling.

"Sounds good to me. Oh, before I forget. My friends at the Orca? Matt and Anna? They really want to meet you. I should probably introduce you to Mabel too. She's the manager. You remember. Mrs. A mentioned her."

"Yes, I remember. And I am looking forward to meeting Matt and Anna too, Reed. When might we do that?"

"Well, we have tomorrow and Tuesday off, so I won't be seeing them for a couple of days to plan anything. Shall I suggest Wednesday evening, after work? I could mention it to them when I go in Wednesday at lunch. My guess is they'll jump at the chance to meet you."

"I am sure that will be fine. Suppose I come to the restaurant just before closing and we can all go out together after you get off work."

"Do you think it's safe?"

"Soapstone Bay is not a dangerous town, Reed. Especially on University Avenue before eight o'clock on a weeknight. There is a trolley stop at Spring Street. I will be alert and am sure that I will be fine."

"It's just that the situation around the university worries me."

"I am worried as well, Reed, but I will not be held prisoner by it. And remember, my love, I am not completely defenseless. A young woman learns things traveling summers with wagon trains and on-board sailing ships."

"I don't doubt that. Say, do you know the Seeing Spell?"

"I have learned few spells of any kind. In the instances where I have attempted actions in that realm, I have not been particularly successful. I attribute this mostly to a lack of real interest on my part."

Here she laid her hand on his arm and gazed deeply into his face, "Aside from the reproductive health spells that all young women are taught and a few things that deal with matters of the heart, I have focused my learning in other areas.

"But really, Reed, I think it will be safe. I will pay attention... and I am difficult to catch unawares. Trust me in this, please."

Eddie could tell he'd pushed the subject as far as he could, so he bit his tongue and tried his best to set his worries aside. Little by little, the mood changed in the tiny apartment. They shared stories from their times at school. Eddie made her laugh with some stories about his first few months working for Joe. For a time, they talked softly of childhood dreams and the places where they had lived as youngsters. Eventually, they passed the remainder of the evening wrapped in each other's arms.

* * *

Monday brought more rain and wind. The rooms were warm and cozy, and they stayed indoors for several hours. They used the quiet safety of their apartment to study. Lena focused on her university work, Eddie on his volumes of spells. Given their age and their circumstances, they also spent time studying each other in ways that gave pleasure to both.

Just before eleven they bundled up and walked to the Inn at Three Corners for an early lunch. Margaret wasn't there, but the two waitresses on duty were formed from a similar mold. They were cheerful and good-hearted. The lunch fare matched the style of the breakfast offerings: hearty, simple, and obviously made on-premises.

The crowd consisted mostly of tradesmen from the surrounding blocks. Many people were cold and wet from working out-of-doors. The common room was bustling and warm. Lena and Eddie had to wait for a few minutes to be seated, and they used the opportunity to check at the front desk for any response to Eddie's note. Old Mel was there and was his usual laconic self. He recognized them immediately and was willing to go so far as to indicate that their message had not yet been picked up.

"Naught as yet," he admitted before turning back to his work.

They returned to the common room and took their seats at one end of a big trestle table. The crowd was loud but sober. No one paid particular attention to them, which they considered a good sign.

When they left the inn, the afternoon was still blustery and wet, and they were both glad for their warm coats and the hearty lunch they'd shared. By university tradition, the first meeting of each class was brief and mainly occupied by administrative details and a short outline of the course to come. Still, Lena was both nervous and excited at the prospect of attending her first real classes of the term. Now she would witness first hand the extent to which the rumors were true.

Despite the weather, they enjoyed their walk. They stopped and held each other before Lena walked alone around the corner onto University. Eddie had used one of his six known spells to change the color of Lena's outfit before she walked away. He promised to change it back when she returned.

They agreed to meet at three o'clock at Wells – across University from the Orca. They were both looking forward to an early evening. Eddie moved quickly back through the wet streets to the apartment. Once inside, he shed his coat and boots, got comfortable, and retrieved his book and notes from their hiding place. He was determined to make good on his promise to Mrs. Abellona. Studying was one of the few, obviously useful actions he could undertake while he waited for Joe to make an appearance.

Eddie spent the rest of the afternoon following Mrs. A's prescription for learning to cast spells. To his original list of six, he added a basic understanding of four more; although he wasn't yet confident with them.

His four new spells were:

1.Fumble Fingers – induce someone to drop something (said to work best if subject not paying attention).

2.Heat It Up – make an inanimate object hot. Good for leftovers or to make burglars sorry.

3.Loud Noise – obvious. Good for distractions.

4.Brilliant Flash – likewise obvious. Similar purpose.

Right away, Eddie saw that it would be good to combine simple spells. He thumbed ahead in his text and saw that there were several combination spells. The simplest of these allowed the caster to merge two spells. Later in the text there were more complex combination spells, but he noted that these more advanced spells were not only more difficult but also required more time to cast. He decided that the time needed to set them up would limit the utility of truly complex spells in situations where quick responses were important.

Still, there could be times when he might be able to set up a compound spell and then trigger a complex sequence of paranormal events with one command. Eddie decided it was largely a question of matching effects to circumstances. The more he read, the more interesting the whole field became to him. Although he'd never encountered anything like these books, the ideas and techniques they described were fascinating.

He practiced the spells as best he could in his apartment. Clearly, "Loud Noise" was to be avoided, but even that spell he read over and over. He managed to burn his fingers a couple of times, and he banged into the wall after he completely dazzled his vision with "Brilliant Flash." "Fumble Fingers" made him laugh out loud.

Time passed quickly that afternoon, but after a couple of hours Eddie found that he was profoundly fatigued and extremely hungry. This brought home to him the warnings he'd read in both the *Child's Garden of Spells* and the introductory chapter of the three volume set. These actions took energy. If you weren't careful, they could wear you out and slow your reflexes. Forces and conditions in the natural world resided in a dynamic balance. When you triggered paranormal events, you were really just shifting a balance point, but even small shifts took substantial amounts of energy.

There were ways to mitigate these effects, ways to shift energy between planes so that the overall effects on the caster were minimal. Eddie liked to think of it as a kind of paranormal *jujitsu* in which tiny shifts in energy were amplified by surrounding conditions. It was exciting, but at the same time it was frustrating because the more he read, the more Eddie saw that it would take him years to gain real facility in the practice. And it was clear that they didn't have years to spend.

With a sigh, he recorded a few more key concepts in his notebook and then closed his books for the day. Eddie reminded himself to put his materials back into their hiding place. Afterwards, he rested and ate a couple of sandwiches. He could have eaten more, but by then it was time to rendezvous with Lena.

When he reached the street, Eddie saw that the rain had stopped and the sun was out. The streets were steaming in the cool air and bright sun. He left his coat open as he strolled up Center. The day had become perfect for looking at the sights and the shops and enjoying the sense of potential in the air.

By the time Eddie reached University Avenue most of the moisture in the streets had evaporated. The street was busy and he was a few minutes early, so he crossed and walked up the south side of the street a few blocks past Wells. It felt a little strange to walk past the Orca without going in to work.

At Meridian, Eddie crossed back to the north side of the street. Autumn was far enough along in this northern seaport so that the midday sun barely cleared the awnings to warm the sidewalk. He saw an eastbound trolley roll by. The trolley stopped just a few doors down from where Eddie stood. As Lena stepped off, he smiled and started to call out, but something in her posture made him pause.

She looked up and down the street and their eyes touched. Immediately, she turned away. Then she shook her head just a tiny bit and turned to walk east, toward Wells. Deliberately holding back, Eddie followed in the same direction. He drew even with the trolley just as it started rolling toward its next stop. Eddie glanced up to see university security staff standing inside the trolley. There was even one standing on the stairs at the front of the vehicle.

They were all wearing sunglasses. They scanned the people on the street as though they were looking for someone. The usually crowded and boisterous trolley was mostly empty, and the few riders it carried were quiet, subdued. It was easy to imagine that the cool autumn air lost a few more degrees of warmth.

Making sure that he could see Lena as she continued down the sidewalk, Eddie picked up his pace slightly. He saw her pause at Wells, their agreed-upon, meeting place. She looked in a store window and then glanced back up the street at him. Again she shook her head very slightly and, turning away, continued east on University.

When she passed Center, he guessed that she might be making for the narrow St. Tolemy's. She hesitated but passed that tiny street as well. She finally turned left at Bay Street. By then Eddie had halved the distance between them, so he was only a few seconds behind her when she left University. When she was perhaps halfway up Bay, she stumbled – something Eddie had never seen her do. She dropped her book bag and stood there with her books strewn upon the sidewalk.

Eddie walked up to her. She looked at him but didn't smile or reach for him. "Bend down as though you're a stranger who's stopped to help me pick up my books," she whispered. She barely moved her mouth. They both bent over and gathered the books and papers.

"Just hand me my books and continue on up to Center. Cross and work your way up the north side. I'll take the south side and meet you back in the apartment. Agreed?"

Eddie straightened and nodded. Then, acting as if he didn't know her, he moved on towards Center. As she'd requested, he continued across the street. He paused in front of a window just long enough to watch for her reflection. He saw her reach the south side of the street. Then he continued past Tolemy's Cats.

Minutes later, they were both at the apartment above the bookstore. She was upset and trembling with anger. He held her for a moment. Then she pulled away.

"What is it? What happened?"

"My rooms at the residence hall. When I returned from my classes this afternoon, I found that my rooms had been searched, obviously and messily. Whoever did it dumped all my things out and turned over my furniture. They left the door standing wide open. Several other doors were left open on the floor. I suppose it was a message. Some of my books were taken. Textbooks, mostly, from classes that have been pulled from the curriculum."

"That's terrible. What did you do?"

"I just gathered a few things in my book bag and headed down here. As soon as I got on the trolley, a security guard came up to me and demanded to see my student ID. I refused of course, but he was very intimidating. The same thing happened to all the other students as they boarded. Some were frightened and complied. Others resisted."

She turned towards the window. A moment later she continued. "Reed. I just do not know if I can go back there."

"Well my guess is that's what they want. They obviously want to shut down the university. Did you feel any real physical threat? At any time?"

"No. It was just... terribly unpleasant."

"Yeah. They want to bully people, make people uncomfortable and afraid. Ideally they'll provoke a response at some point, and then they'll have a pretext to shut the whole place down. Tell me, Lena. Do you really need to be there at all? Could you work out something with your advisor to complete all your final classes as independent study?"

"Perhaps. I would have to speak with him, but he is a good man. Very traditional. Very strong on academic freedom. Very committed to the philosophical underpinnings of our society."

She fell silent and shook her head sadly. "This must be terrible for him to see," she added.

Eddie was suddenly sure what he wanted to do.

"Look, Lena, can you call him on the phone – or whatever you call it here – your 'comm'? And propose this?"

"Well, yes. But I still need the rest of my things."

"I'll go up with you and we'll get them."

"Oh, they will not allow you into the residence hall. I saw them turn away several others this afternoon. They are only permitting residents of a given hall inside. There I did have to show my ID. I could not avoid it, but I decided that they knew where I lived anyway."

"Well, then, I'll wait outside. We'll take a cab so that we don't have to deal with the goons on the trolleys."

"Goons? Cab?"

"Yeah, that's what I call people like that. Goons. It's a derogatory term from the vernacular of my world. It means, essentially, hired bullies. Sometimes they do worse than bully. We need to be careful, Lena.

"And a cab is a vehicle that you hire with a driver," he added. "You must have something like that, right? I've seen a few vehicles that looked like that on the streets."

"Oh, yes. That is easily done. It is somewhat expensive, but I suppose it will only be this once."

So Lena got into voice communication with her advisor. She explained in more detail what had happened. Eddie had a difficult time controlling his temper as he listened to her side of the conversation. In an effort to calm himself, the young man decided to focus his attention elsewhere. The best thing he could do would be to review a few of his spells. He got out the first volume of the set and his notes and practiced his memorization while Lena worked out details on the phone.

After she hung up, "signed off," she called it, they made arrangements for a vehicle to haul Lena's things. Using the town's on-line directory service they quickly found a listing for a small electric wagon operated by a driver for hire. The wagon had an open bed. Eddie had seen several similar vehicles on the docks in his first day ashore.

Arrangements made, they grabbed their jackets and went back outside to wait. In less than fifteen minutes, the wagon pulled up in the late afternoon sunlight. They piled onto the bench. The driver was a young man, very local, very "dockside" (Lena's term) in his mannerism.

Young, he was, but big and, by the looks of him, extremely strong. He had massive arms and shoulders and a kind, open face. His thick chest tapered sharply to a slender waist, but his legs looked liked they might hold up the Prince's Wharf pier without much strain. His blond hair was pulled back into a short ponytail and his grin rivaled the width of his shoulders. He introduced himself as "Fleggie."

"So ye wants a ride to-from th' big school? Tha' can happen, true. Cost ye a bit. Not too dear, Fleggie hopes."

He named a sum. Indeed it was not "too dear," but something in his smile made Eddie realize that the young man would probably be offended if they agreed too readily. So they negotiated. It felt interminable, but it was really only a matter of five minutes or so.

The little wagon ran smoothly and was all but silent. It also travelled faster than the big trolleys. By four-thirty, they had pulled into a space near Lena's residence hall. On the way over, Eddie had felt compelled to explain briefly what they intended to do and to mention that there was a slight chance of trouble. This pleased Fleggie to no end. When Eddie used the term "goons" to describe the security guards, the young driver sensed the meaning right away and laughed so hard that he nearly lost control of the wagon.

"Fleggie likes this, he do. If he needed not the plats, he cou' do this for th' lark o' it. True."

"That's good, Fleggie. We're going to need your help, but please remember that our goal is to get my friend's possessions – her 'gear' – and get away without trouble."

"Aye. It be clear. It be clear."

So Eddie and Fleggie waited by the wagon while Lena went inside. She made two trips out to the wagon without incident. She tossed bags and a pack into the back and a big armload of books. As she returned inside, Eddie put the books into one of the bags.

By now they were attracting attention.

Two security guards came up.

"Move along," the shorter one said to Eddie. Students aren't permitted to loiter with townspeople. You are also supposed to use only official university-approved transportation."

"I'm not a student," Eddie replied.

"Let's see your student ID."

"Sorry, I don't have any ID. I'm not a student."

Lena made another trip as Eddie and the guard went around on this. When the guard turned to demand Lena's ID, Fleggie suddenly bent over and moaned, holding his stomach. He made sounds as though he were becoming violently ill. Both guards stepped back.

Fleggie continued to make loud retching sounds. He moaned. He held his head. He leaned against the side of his wagon.

In the meantime, Lena went back inside. A few moments later, she returned. She had six or seven of her school friends with her. They all had their arms full.

"All of you people need to move on. Right now," the shorter guard stood in between the students and the wagon.

The air began to get tense. Fleggie stood up straight and looked warily around. Eddie stepped forward.

"Look, folks, they want to provoke a reaction. Please, *please* just pretend that they are some kind of annoying, moving bits of scenery or decoration. Lampposts, puppets... it doesn't matter what you imagine. The important thing is to ignore and avoid them. Don't touch or confront them in any way. They're looking for an excuse. Please don't provide them with one."

The guards tried to block him as he made this short speech, but he kept backing away from them. He climbed onto the wagon and then jumped off the other side as he finished talking. A couple of the young men in the crowd grumbled, but the rest of the students saw the potential for humor in the situation.

"Oh, I am sorry. I left my ID inside. Here. I will place these books in the wagon and return with it."

"Beg your pardon, sir. Did you see those birds over by the recreation building?"

"Ow. Ow. My eye hurts. Ow. Ow. My eye hurts." A loud belch. "There that is better!"

Eddie could see that the security guards were becoming frustrated. More importantly, the students could see it. The situation was indeed escalating, but not in the way that the guards had hoped.

"How much more of your stuff is there?" he called to Lena.

"One more trip will do it."

"Hurry. Please. This could flash."

"Flash? Flash?" Fleggie wanted to know. He made his voice very loud. "What be 'flash'? Young Fleggie ha' never heard as much. What be 'flash?'"

The guards both looked at him. The students dropped their burdens into the wagon and scampered back into the residence hall. As soon as they were gone, Eddie and Fleggie orbited the wagon. Pretending to ignore the guards, they moved quickly to avoid confrontation. If a guard stepped in front of Eddie, he immediately reversed direction, but he never once acknowledged or even looked directly at the man. Fleggie picked up the strategy immediately. From all appearances, the big man was having a great time.

Now the students were back. The guards were getting dangerously frustrated. One put a communicator to his lips. "Calling for reinforcements at station 212-B. Front of senior residence hall. Situation in progress.

As the students tried to maneuver around the guards, Eddie climbed up to the bed of the wagon. Fleggie stood at the curb waiting. Eddie looked around and felt his heart lurch as he saw a half dozen guards jogging up the hill. They had their batons out. The nearer two guards stepped forward and pulled out their batons as well.

The last of Lena's possessions were now in the wagon, but she was with the other students. The guards were between her and the wagon and Eddie could see that the other guards were coming up behind the students. They'd be here in seconds. He made a quick decision to act.

Staring hard at each guard's baton hand in turn, Eddie tried the Fumble Fingers spell. The guards were looking at the students. As Eddie cast, each guard's hand flailed spastically. Both guards dropped their batons.

"Run, Lena! Up here, Fleggie!" he yelled.

Effortlessly, the young driver swung Lena onto the bench and then hopped up to sit at the controls. Eddie could see that the other security guards were very near the students now. Again he concentrated. This time he used the Heat It Up spell. Either due to distance or his own lack of experience, this had no visible effect.

"Hey, goons! Goons. Yeah. Me. Up here!!!" he yelled at them. They looked up. It was clear that these guards were not particularly well trained. That could cut both ways. They would probably be ineffective in a real crisis, but they also might react violently if pressed too hard.

"What's that?!" he yelled. Casting the Loud Noise spell for all he was worth, he aimed for a spot immediately behind the guards.

The effect was immediate and deafening: imagine a freight car full of china and acetylene landing on a gigantic cymbal and detonating. Invisibly. The guards whirled and tried to look in every direction at once. Eddie quickly followed it with a series of Fumble Fingers casts. The stu-

Michael C. Glaviano

dents scattered. The guards, several of whom had dropped their batons, milled around, confused.

"Go, go, go!" Eddie yelled to Fleggie. The young man complied, and, dumping Eddie into the bed of the vehicle, the wagon jumped ahead. He scrambled quickly to his feet and held onto the back of the seat.

They made it to the edge of campus in less than a minute. Most guards they saw were sprinting towards the cluster of residence halls, but Eddie was sure that before long they'd get organized.

Sure enough. By the time they crossed Biscayne Avenue at the edge of the campus, Eddie could see that guards were fanning out. The guards were as yet nowhere near the quiet electric wagon, but he could imagine that there were others on trolleys already returning up University. These could be called to block their escape.

"Fleggie! Turn left at the first street you can!"

"Aye, mate. Fleggie were thinking same like. No worries. This be not th' first time young Fleggie did a scramble. Hold tight."

Fleggie swung the wagon hard left at Holmes Road. There followed a madcap flight through a maze of streets that Eddie had not yet visited. This led them into the north end of town. Eventually, they turned back south and ended up near Park and Longview. They were several blocks north of the Inn at Three Corners and in a part of town that was mostly empty in the long shadows of early evening.

There were bigger buildings here. Many of the properties had tall fences that faced the street. Some buildings looked as though they might house machine shops or mills. Eddie saw a sign that indicated a furniture maker and another that announced a maker of work clothes. There were a couple of boarding houses and one tiny tavern but little else in the way of residential amenities. Retail stores of any kind were rare in this neighborhood.

Laughter still in his voice, their driver spoke up. "Now mates, we be faced wi' a fork in th' road. We cou' haste us down to where Fleggie picked ye up, or we cou' lay low 'til full dark time. How calls ye?"

"I vote we lay low for now," Lena said.

"Aye. Methinks like," agreed Fleggie. "The goons'll be strutting about for some hours, but sure they be wanting to be at the big school in force sametimes. We ca' wait a bit."

"But where?" Eddie wanted to know. He was looking at the empty streets and industrial buildings that surrounded them.

"No worries, now. No worries. Ken ye this!"

Still heading south, Fleggie turned left at Viceroy. They passed Turnbull. Eddie looked to his right but they were still too far north to make out the Inn. Fleggie pulled over halfway down. There was a board fence along the left side of the narrow street, and the big man leapt down and strode over to the wooden structure.

258

The young driver placed one hand flat on the boards and kicked hard on the fence a couple of times. Eddie was surprised that the structure didn't collapse. Almost immediately, however, a gate opened up in the fence. It wasn't a hinged gate but rather a gap that formed when a portion of the fence simply vanished.

Laughing out loud now, Fleggie ran back to the wagon and clambered aboard. He touched the controls and guided the wagon into something that resembled a cross between a mediaeval wrecking yard and a science lab. There was stuff everywhere. Some items looked modern and slick; other things were ancient. Eddie turned as they passed inside and saw that the illusion of the fence, if illusion it was, reasserted itself as soon as they crossed the boundary.

"See now? Fleggie knows a trick or two. Some folks say it all be gone, but Fleggie's old grand-da' were from early days. He taught that it be harder now, but th' power be here still. The gods dream yet. They weep yet. It be harder, but it be not gone."

Here the big young man looked directly at Eddie and continued. "You be th' first pal me own age who know a bit o' the old. Methinks ye might share. Fleggie reckons that be worth more than a fare."

Now he jumped down and gestured towards a small cottage that lay off to the side of the salvage yard. "It be humble, mates, but it be warm and safe. True now."

Eddie and Lena hesitated for an instant but saw no alternative. They climbed off the wagon. Quickly, surreptitiously, Eddie tried the seeing spell. The aura surrounding the big driver was clear and bright – a real ally! Eddie smiled and took Lena's hand. He began to walk with her toward the tiny cottage, but then his vision swam and grew dark. He stumbled, turned, and clutched at the wagon.

"What is wrong, Reed?"

"Nothing. Or, well, I think it's a reaction from what I did back there. I read that there's a cost to doing spells. I was already tired from practicing earlier. In the excitement, the adrenaline kept me going. Now..." he swayed. Lena grabbed his arm. Fleggie stepped back to Eddie's side and lent a hand. The three young people walked slowly over to the building.

Fleggie waved them inside the cottage. As he'd promised, it was warm, and it felt safe enough. They found themselves in a sparsely furnished rectangle of light. Near the rear and to the right side of the room, a young woman was standing near a stove. She looked up as they entered and smiled. To the left side of the room, a steep, ladder-like stair led up to a sleeping loft. There was a rough bench and a couple of chairs on the wall opposite the stove. The center of the room was taken up by an old table.

Most of the furnishings had been cobbled together from things in the junkyard, but the overall effect was clever as well as being homey and functional.

"So, ye ha' brought more strays home that I might feed 'em, ha' ye now?" the young woman laughed. If Fleggie was big and massive, with strength to match, this young woman was tiny. His wild blond hair was a stark contrast to her dark tresses, which she wore pulled away from her face and wound into a knot at the back of her head.

"That be ma' girl. Call her 'Sweetmaye' if ye please. She's a good sort, if a bit rough about th' edges."

The little, dark-haired woman smiled and her eyes flashed with incipient laughter. Her left fist on her hip, a wooden spoon raised in her right, she spun to face her man. "Not where it counts, me lad. Not e'en a tad rough where it counts! Ye ha' naer complained o' no rough, 'ere now!" Here her laugh grew big, giving the diminutive woman a presence larger than her physical size. The couple were physically different in the extreme, but Eddie and Lena recognized the same spark of good humor and love in both of them.

"Now set ye two. Just set. If me man ha' brought ye hence, why then, ye must be good folk," and with that, both Lena and Eddie felt welcomed.

Eddie was glad to sit down. Fleggie sat across from him and recounted the afternoon's events to Sweetmaye. As they grew more comfortable, Lena or Eddie would occasionally offer a detail or a tidbit of information. The room was filled with good smells and the sound of Sweetmaye's contagious laughter.

Young and fit as he was, Eddie's strength began to return as soon as he sat and rested for a few minutes. By the time Sweetmaye positioned a big bowl of seafood chowder in front of each of them and placed a loaf of heavy bread in the middle of the table, he was feeling better. As they ate, a good warmth filled him and a worrisome, hollow feeling at his core faded.

When they'd finished, Fleggie asked Eddie about his spells. Eddie listed those that he knew. Fleggie was familiar with nearly half of them. They went through the others. Eddie offered to write them out from memory, and there was a minute's embarrassment when it came out that Fleggie could barely read and write.

"Sad, true, but me folks died when I were a babe. Me ol' grandda' did as right as he could by me, but I ha' t' start work an' left school when he took t' sick."

Sweetmaye offered that she "had more letters" and said that she could help Fleggie if the spells were written out simply. She brought paper and a pen from a small cupboard and Eddie wrote out what he remembered. Having practiced it under pressure that afternoon, Eddie was now pretty sure he'd mastered Loud Noise.

Sweetmaye was herself interested in Heat It Up as she thought it might make cooking easier on cold nights. She read the spells and the descriptions of the gestures and focus points that they required. There were a couple of spots where she wrinkled her forehead at an unfamiliar word, but she was able to sound everything out.

Fleggie was very pleased at the trade, but he was also convinced that he would have to hide out for a while. "Methinks Fleggie ought lay low a bit. Business could be off 'til th' goons – he loves that word, mate – 'til th' goons lose th' ken o' him and his wagon. Fleggie cou' lay low here. Or maybe trots elsewhere an' leaves th' yard for a bit. Say, now. Ken ye anything Fleggie might do?"

For a moment, Eddie was taken aback. "Well, what can you do, Fleggie? What are you good at?"

"Oh, Fleggie packs an' stacks an' totes. He's strong. He be clever at fixing the odd machine, an' he buys an' sells. He be a good sort an' hardly ever scraps. Hardly ever," he repeated, laughing. Sweetmaye rolled her eyes.

You know, I wonder. I can't guarantee anything, but if you meet me tomorrow at the Inn at Three Corners, we could try the docks. Fairly early, say at eight o'clock. I know a ship's captain who's a good man.

Sweetmaye spoke up. "What, an' leave poor Sweetmaye on shore by her lone? I think not. I canna' tote an' stack. Sweetmaye be a cook. Used to cook for hands on me da's farm... 'fore th' fancy men took it."

"But that's great, Sweetmaye! I was ship's cook for Captain Thomas. As far as I'm concerned, this dinner is proof enough of your abilities. The crew is already made up of men and women. If the captain hasn't hired a replacement, he'll be interested in meeting you. I'm sure of it."

Then the young woman smiled. "Eight o'clock it is, then, Lamb," was all she said.

Eddie yawned and stretched. It had been another long day. "So much for an early, quiet night," he smiled.

"I think that we will want to move quickly to bring things to the apartment, Reed," Lena said. She turned to Fleggie and Sweetmaye.

"Would you think me rude if I went outside now and spent a few minutes organizing my things so that it will be quicker when we unload?"

"Rude? Ye two be schooled folk, sure. But ye be not too fine in your airs. Sweetmaye'd ne'er think ye rude!"

Lena dipped her head with a smile.

"Say. Let's ha' the men tend t' th' washing up," continued Sweetmaye. "Ye an' me shall pack your things up tight an' be shut of it before they climb off their backsides." She held out her hand and drew Lena from her seat. The two young women went outside. Alley cats lurking at the boundaries of the yard could hear their sweet voices, laughing and talking as they worked in the cold autumn evening.

Michael C. Glaviano

Fleggie and Eddie looked at each other. They shrugged, stepped over to the compact kitchen area and set to work. Soon enough all was done.

When Lena's belongings were packed and tidy in the wagon, it was full dark. After some discussion and more than one invitation, Sweetmaye agreed to join them. Even taking Fleggie's massive shoulders into account, there was plenty of room for all of them on the wide bench. Still, as an extra precaution against recognition Eddie and Fleggie hunkered beneath a tarp in the back among Lena's things.

Sweetmaye guided the electric wagon over to Longview and then south on Anderson. She turned left on Center and in a few minutes' time pulled up in front of Tolemy's Cats.

Eddie and Fleggie threw off the tarp. Moving quickly, they transferred everything from the back of the wagon to the small lobby. Then Fleggie moved the wagon around the side of the building onto St. Tolemy's. The tiny side street was dark and the wagon blended into the shadows.

The four young people loaded themselves with Lena's belongings. Beyond her books and a few articles of clothing there was not terribly much. Now that things were packed in bundles, moving them was quick. Within five minutes they had everything stacked on the landing in front of Eddie's and Lena's rooms.

"Come in, please," Eddie invited.

"Aye, but for a blink only. We mus' be home. Fleggie'd as soon be off th' streets an' snug tonight."

So Sweetmaye and Fleggie were the first guests that Eddie and Lena hosted in their flat above Tolemy's Cats. The young couple stayed for only minutes but promised to return.

"And we'll see you tomorrow at eight in front of the Inn, right?"

"Aye. We'll be there. An' hope for th' best on that. Night, then."

The little apartment grew very quiet in the wake of the other couple's departure. Surrounded as they were by Lena's things, the apartment felt cramped, even smaller than its actual size. At the same time it maintained its atmosphere of sanctuary, a safe, still place in the midst of the forces that circled.

Twenty Nine

Eddie and Lena were up before dawn even though they had stayed up late arranging the apartment. The rooms were uncluttered once books were shelved and Lena's clothes hung in the closet. Since Eddie hadn't acquired anything beyond the most basic of necessities, her remaining possessions were such that they improved the decor and livability of the space.

They ate a quick breakfast and spent a few more minutes organizing things. It was clear that they'd need a small cabinet of some kind for Lena's bathroom gear, but that could wait until they found something workable. Everything else fell easily into place.

Even so, Lena expressed some discomfort at the suddenness of the change.

"Reed, I did not intend to take over like this. We do not have to make this a permanent living arrangement. I can find some rooms near here and we could move somewhat more slowly."

"Well," Eddie admitted, "it is pretty sudden, but you know, I really do love you. It'll be fine. We'll be together, but we'll still have separate interests and separate identities for a while. I'm sure there'll be adjustments. If we're patient, we'll make it work."

She held out her arms. "Come here. Hold me," she told him.

Quiet, they held each other for a moment. As they stepped back, each took a slow deep breath, held it briefly, and let it out. Noticing, they laughed gently.

"But you know, you're going to have to let your folks – your parents – know that you've moved off campus... and in with me," he said. "Otherwise they'll be worried about you. Especially if they hear about the troubles on campus."

"Yes, Reed. I realize that. I hadn't wanted to say anything so soon, but it would be irresponsible not to let them know. I'll contact them this afternoon. But first, we need to see what we can do for our new friends."

"Yeah. Okay, let's get over to the Inn."

The good weather held, but they brought their jackets. As they walked, they saw the shops begin to open on Central Avenue. Shopkeepers were sweeping in front of their stores or putting display tables on the sidewalk. The air was clean and crisp. People were out on two and three wheeled, pedal-driven cycles. Here and there an electric wagon or a compact delivery van glided quietly past.

In less than twenty minutes they were in front of the Inn and just moments later, they saw Fleggie's tall shape striding down Turnbull toward them. He was so big that he stood head and shoulders above the others on the sidewalk. It was another minute before they saw the petite Sweetmaye walking next to him.

"Shall we give it a try?" Eddie asked after the other couple walked up and they had exchanged greetings.

Walking and talking together as though they had known each other for years, the two, young women led the way. Eddie found Fleggie to be a good observer of his surroundings and a great source of information regarding the docks and the people who lived and worked around them. Fleggie stopped several times on the way down to the wharfs and introduced Eddie and Lena to childhood friends and other cohorts.

They basically reversed Eddie's steps from his initial journey uptown. He had forgotten just how long a walk it was, and with the recognition of the distance came a realization of how long it had been since he'd first come this way. He hoped that the *Mother Rose* was still at the dock.

He said as much to Fleggie, who shrugged and replied, "Well, mate, either they will be or no. Depends on if they need refittn' or how quick goes th' findin' o' cargo or what crew signs on. We'll know soon as we may."

The two couples had now crossed Hill and were entering the Warrens, the rougher neighborhoods near the docks. Crowds flowed around obstacles in the cool, bright sunlight. Horse drawn wagons as well as electrics, some heavily laden, some empty, jockeyed for position. Pedal-driven rickshaws wove everywhere. Exotic aromas drifted from the braziers of food vendors. Booths with gaudily-striped awnings sold all manner of herbs, books, and clothing.

Occasionally diving to try to steal from a fishmonger's cart, gulls shrieked overhead. Women – "sailors' friends," Fleggie termed them – called from second floor windows. They were especially, and explicitly, interested in the endowments they thought likely to accompany Fleggie's massive frame.

Sweetmaye heard their calls and turned around to contemplate her man. She wagged a finger at him and arched an eyebrow as if to admonish him against so much as listening to their offers, let alone considering them. Fleggie laughed his big, loud laugh, but Eddie noted that the young man tended to keep his eyes a bit more to himself after the warning.

They finally crossed Water Street and moved out onto Prince's Wharf. At first Eddie couldn't make out the *Mother Rose* and he was worried that they'd missed her. But then, when they were nearly halfway down the wharf, he made out the dark hull and the high tech rigging and his heart rose in his chest. Moments later they could hear Captain Thomas bellowing over the general din of the wharf.

As they walked up to the gangplank, they heard the captain's huge laugh. The big man was helping a longshoreman to his feet. There were several large crates that had tumbled over near the open hatch of the hold. What could have been a real problem had been averted by nothing more than good fortune.

Eddie spoke up. "Ahoy, Captain Thomas!"

The captain looked over and his face broke into a huge grin.

"Reed, lad!! Come aboard! And you've brought friends. Bonny lassies, you have there, Laddies. Best keep 'em secured and stored right against the captain's charms!"

All four young people walked up the gangplank and Eddie did the introductions. Eddie mentioned that his new friends had helped Lena and him out and that he was hoping to return the favor by seeing if they might find work on the *Mother Rose*. As soon as Eddie finished describing the skills Fleggie and Sweetmaye might bring to the ship, the captain looked Fleggie up and down. "Give me your hand, lad," he ordered.

Fleggie reached forward and the captain took it in his own paw, but then stepped past to put his foot behind the young man's leg. Captain Thomas then executed a quick spin and attempted to pull Fleggie off balance, but the big youngster was having none of it. He planted his feet and jerked hard on the captain's brawny arm, and it was the older man who tumbled to the deck.

In a flash, Captain Thomas was back on his feet and he faced Fleggie. Both big men were leaning forward, balanced on the balls of their feet. The captain had a fierce grin on his face and Eddie could see that Fleggie had one that matched.

They grappled and crashed around the deck. Around them, work ground to a halt, and they collected quite an audience from the crew. A short time later, the captain raised his right hand and called a truce. He was still laughing.

"Good lad. I need someone who's not only big and strong, but nimble. And not afraid to scrap should the need arise." This last remark brought a short burst of laughter from the petite Sweetmaye.

The captain turned to her. "And young Reed says that you can cook for hard working people," he observed.

"Aye, Captain, I can. But I'd soon as not have t' wrestle you t' prove it," she replied smartly.

Michael C. Glaviano

This brought a huge blast of laughter from the captain. "No need, Lassie. I'm sure that your man can scrap well enough for any occasion. I think well of young Reed here, and am minded to take you on. The both of you. We're another few days 'til we ship out and there's plenty o' loading to be done... and the gods know that the on-board crew are tired enough of my cooking."

He turned to Eddie and said seriously, "You will vouch for these folk? You say you've only known them a short while."

"Yes, Captain. I've only known them for a day, but they put themselves on the line to help Lena and me when we were in a tight spot. They didn't hesitate. They simply stepped in and helped."

"Well, then. This could be good for all concerned. For some weeks, I'd thought the *Mother Rose* was done for the season. You'll remember that we lost some experienced crew members after the unplanned extension of the voyage. And with the pirate attacks, I wanted time to have all the systems inspected.

But now we have a grand opportunity to haul some expensive cargo north before the truly foul weather sets in. Just two weeks ago I accepted the offer. The *Mother Rose* is tuned up and nearly ready to sail, but I'd not yet found a cook. Your two friends could be a welcome addition to the crew.

"So, suppose you take the lassies down and show them the galley. Give young Sweetmaye a tour; show her where everything in her station is stored... Meanwhile, let's see if this young man can work as well as he can scrap. Fleggie!"

"Aye, Cap'n!"

"Lend a hand to this sorry excuse for a stevedore. See if you can get these crates stowed and secured below decks without any further problems. Mind you, take it slow and careful. There's value in these crates and they're not to be abused... any more than they already have been!"

"Aye, Cap'n!"

Fleggie turned to the dockhand, who was watching warily. While not exactly small himself, the man was easily over-topped by the young man's stature. "I ha' nothin' t' prove. Show me how an' I'll be a' help t' ye," Fleggie offered quietly.

The captain nodded and waved Eddie off. As the young people moved away, they could hear the captain bellowing again. And laughing.

In less than an hour, Eddie had completed the tour of the ship and galley. Sweetmaye had been delighted. She had clapped her hands like a child at the sight of the well-appointed station. She danced as she looked at the stove, the cutlery, the huge pantry and supply cabinets, and all the rest of the resources at her disposal.

266

"True. It were a glad day we crossed paths! This be th' best thing t' happen since I met Fleggie, bless him... an' he th' best thing since me poor da' lost his farm."

They found the captain, and he asked a few more questions of Sweetmaye and Fleggie. Since they were a couple, he offered them the same cabin that had been Eddie's. They were overjoyed at this. When the captain named a wage for each of them. Fleggie literally shook his head in disbelief while Sweetmaye beamed and tears came to her eyes.

"Cap'n, sir. Ye be too kind. We ha' nothing near this our whole lives. We'll do ye proud. True."

Captain Thomas cleared his throat. "I'm sure you both will. Now listen well, youngsters. Listen well. I don't know what young Reed has said to you concerning our last voyage, but it's not all beauty and light aboard a modern sailing vessel these days. Besides work, and there's plenty of that, we've got to deal with brigands."

"Fleggie an' Sweetmaye understand, Cap'n. We been hearin' rumors an' such for months," Fleggie replied. Sweetmaye, eyes suddenly solemn, nodded in silent agreement.

"Well, you've heard true. Now the *Mother Rose* is a powerful, well-armed ship. Not only that, but we're going to be traveling in convoys until these troubles are settled. There will be strike ships joining our convoy. It cuts into profits, but the cities and the merchants understand that it's either that or lose trade entirely."

"So," he continued, "they grumble, but they'll fund us for now. They try to look to the longer term."

Eddie spoke up. "When do you leave, Captain Thomas? I was half afraid that you'd have already gone out."

Now the Captain's usually cheerful visage held a black, stormy look. "Well, first I faced the decision of whether to go out again at all. Then, when this opportunity presented itself, I thought 'Aye, one more trip this season. Why not?'

"But then, I must tell you, for the first time in all my adult life, for all my time in the merchant services, we've had trouble. Trouble with paperwork. Trouble finding stevedores. Trouble with port officials. Storm after storm, I say, and all the while in port. There's something afoot, Laddie, and it means no good for the merchants, the theater troops with their actors, the artists and musicians who travel. It's as if someone... I don't know. I'd as soon not guess."

"It would tie in, Captain. Tie in with what we are seeing at the university," Lena spoke for the first time.

"There is a group that is well-funded and powerful, and they are bent on undermining the whole system of higher education," she continued. "They have all but shut down the school as far as serious studies are concerned."

Captain Thomas was silent, a fierce look on his face. Then he laughed a short blast of defiance. "Well, there's still much arrayed against such, my young friends. We won't know the catch 'til the line's brought in, but I'll continue to fish for as long as I may."

"But to answer your question, Reed, we'd of been gone a week ago but for the delays and the trouble finding crew, but as it stands, we leave in three days on the early tide. I needed a cook and I needed a strong cargo handler. Now, Old One bless me, you've delivered both to the gangplank of the *Mother Rose*. That young Fleggie here can double as a machinist's mate is a bonus."

Then the captain turned towards his two newest crew members. "Can you be here and signed on before sundown tomorrow? That'll give you time to get settled into your duties."

"Aye, Cap'n. That we can," Sweetmaye spoke. Fleggie nodded seriously and rubbed his big hands together.

"We been in th' lot for a fistful o' years now, an' young Fleggie ha' things set up bonny. Like as not, we won' be missed for a good, long while."

The captain looked at the four young people for another minute. Then he shook himself: a big strong sea lion standing on the rocks.

"Be off with you, then! I've got work to do and plenty! See you two tomorrow eve."

He turned to Eddie and Lena, "And you, young uns. You take care. I think there are storms ahead, but, Old One bless you, I expect that you'll weather them well enough."

The captain shook hands all around then and turned back to his work. As the young people moved back up the wharf, they could hear him yelling and laughing for a good, long way.

* * *

"Do you have time to come over and have dinner with us this evening?" Lena asked some time later as they neared Turnbull.

"What think ye, Sweetmaye?"

"Aye. Tha' would be bonny. It would. We ha' jus' made friends, an' now we're to be off. It were good t' spend some happy hours. Wha' ca' we bring?"

"Oh, I think we can manage. This is exciting for Reed and me. You will be our first dinner guests. You have much to do to prepare for your voyage. Just leave the dinner to us. What time would be good for you?"

"Wha' time then? O' say seven o' clock. How be that?"

"That will be fine. See you then!"

So the two couples parted near the Inn at Three corners. Eddie and Lena headed down Turnbull towards Center Street, Fleggie and Sweetmaye up to their hidden lot near Viceroy.

Before long Eddie and Lena neared their neighborhood. It was late morning and the streets were busy. They both kept a look out for university security, but this area was apparently too far away from campus to warrant much attention.

"I think that we should shop for dinner now, while we are out. When we get back to the apartment, I would like to try to contact my advisor and one or two of my friends to see how things stand on campus. Then I would like to study for a while... or try to study anyway."

"Okay. That sounds good to me. I'm glad we're going to have them over tonight. I really like them, and they were a huge help yesterday."

"Yes, Reed, they were. And for some reason, I feel as though I have known that young woman for a long while. Even though her life has not been easy, she is cheerful and optimistic. I am sorry that they will leave so soon, but I agree that it will be safer for them. Fleggie is so... big. He is simply hard not to notice – even in a crowd."

Eddie's brow furrowed. "Lena. I just had a thought. Is there a place where you can call that's away from the apartment? I don't know how your communications system works, but in my world calls can be traced. Probably I'm just being paranoid, but I'd rather take precautions than have problems with these people."

She agreed that this was a good precaution. Unless the majority of the people in the residence hall had left last night, security would have her identity simply by seeing which room had been vacated.

"Let us walk for a block past University Avenue and then I will call my advisor. Afterwards we can loop up to Union and shop for a few things. I may as well call my parents while we're out as well. By moving around and keeping the calls brief, we will be difficult to trace. By tradition and rule of law, manufacturers are forbidden to produce communication devices that make their geo-location known automatically; although they have a locator function available for emergency purposes.

"Although in these times I would not trust tradition, I do still have faith in our laws," she continued. "Still, prudence is a virtue. There is little reason to avoid this simple precaution."

A few minutes later they were on Harbor. They walked west to Union, where there was a small park with some benches. Lena placed her first call there. She kept the call brief. Signing off, she nodded to Eddie.

"Our action yesterday triggered no official response, although my advisor heard rumors of it from some other students. He thinks that RSM's larger plan is to shut down the university, and he shares your opinion that their main goal yesterday was to provoke a violent response

from students. That didn't happen, so they aren't officially acknow-
ledging that the incident occurred.

"I think that I should call my parents next. Would you mind
waiting over there?" she gestured at another cluster of benches at the
other side of the park. "I am sure that the call will go well, but I think
that I should do this by myself."

"Well, sure, Lena. I feel like I haven't had enough exercise since
I've been in town and my legs feel tight. I'll just go over there and do a
few stretches while you talk to 'em."

Eddie moved to the other side of the small park. He used the
benches as props to help him stretch his hamstrings. Then he rested a
hand at the back of the benches so that he could stand on one foot and
stretch his quads. Finally, he stood with his legs hip-width apart, laced
his fingers together behind his back and folded forward from the hips.
Eddie straightened his arms behind him and then extended his arms
above his head so that he could open the spot between his shoulder
blades.

All this time, he could just make out Lena's voice from across the
intervening space, but he couldn't hear what she was saying. After Eddie
stretched for a couple of minutes, he sat on the benches and did some leg
lifts. Then he put the toes of his shoes on a bench and did foot-elevated
push-ups. He did three sets of sixteen. He was starting to get into his
impromptu work and had begun looking around for something he could
use for pull-ups when Lena finished her call and joined him.

"How'd it go?"

Lena laughed a little. "Oh, it went well enough. Father was out.
I spoke with Mother."

"What'd she say?"

"She said that we were young and that we were moving quickly
into a serious relationship."

"Well, yeah, I guess we are. I'm okay with it, though."

"As am I, my love."

"Was she upset?"

"Not really. She even laughed when I pointed out that when she
was my age, she had already decided to get pregnant – pregnant with me,
by the way – even though she and Father had only known each other for
a few months and were not married.

"And there is something else, Reed. Even as a child I was able to
tell when people were suited for each other or when a couple wasn't getting along – often well before any of the adults around were aware of it.
My parents recognized it early on, when I was very young.

"There were several embarrassing incidents before they managed
to teach me to be discreet about my intuition," she laughed. "At any rate,
I can often read the secrets of the heart as easily as I might read a book."

"And you have this sense about you and me? And you told her that?" Eddie asked.

"When we walked together that first night, I knew. Our kiss was powerful, yes, but even before then I was sure. When I told her about that, Mother was quiet for a moment, and then she whispered that she had known it from the first time she saw us stand next to each other. Her voice had tears in it when we finished our call, but I think they were happy tears," Lena added. Now her own voice betrayed a hint of emotion.

She stepped close, and he held her for a few moments. Soon after, they resumed their stroll. They walked through the bright autumn sunlight toward the upscale neighborhood in the southwest part of the town.

"All right. On to more mundane topics. I would like to contact a few of my friends," she said.

She did this as they looped through the wide streets and expensive neighborhoods that characterized this part of Soapstone Bay. In between calls Lena told Eddie that they were in the "Drake Hill" neighborhood. It was unmistakably an upper-class enclave, and the contrast was stark between these houses and the Warrens near the docks or the industrial lots where Fleggie and Sweetmaye lived.

Lena made a handful of brief calls while she pieced together a picture of the situation on campus. It appeared that the administration had essentially capitulated to whoever was behind the push to curtail trade and cultural exchange-related studies. Programs related to the study of magic and cosmology had been cut even more severely. Several friends mentioned that they had been targeted for harassment. Every time they tried to move between classes, they were stopped - sometimes three or four times - and asked for their ID. It made it difficult to get anywhere on time and the tension on campus was rising.

In each case, Lena suggested that people avoid confronting the guards. Taking Eddie's cue, she argued that this would give them an excuse to clamp down and add more restrictions. Some of her friends were more receptive to this advice than others. Worse yet, there appeared to be agitators on campus. They made impromptu, inflammatory speeches. They often disrupted classes and they shouted down and tried to intimidate others who argued for caution. While these people claimed to be students, her friends knew none of them.

The only good news was that the very intensity of what was going on had drawn people together. More students were moving off campus. Those who knew each other well were sharing little apartments and rooms. Older, tenured faculty members were taking on huge loads of independent study classes so that people could continue their education. A feeling persisted that if they could hold out long enough, this wave of problems might pass.

Michael C. Glaviano

"This is pretty nice around here, but I think I'd like to get back to a more crowded area," Eddie remarked as Lena wrapped up her summary. "I feel too exposed walking around this neighborhood."

They retraced their steps as far as Eden Street, where they turned left. University was just two blocks north. They reached the larger street and, turning right, headed back towards the docks. Shops were open and there were more people abroad. Relaxing a little and enjoying the warmth, they walked along the north side of the street.

Just as they drew even with a clothing store, two university security guards stepped out and blocked their way.

"Let's see some ID," one demanded. Each guard had a hand resting on his baton.

Before Eddie could say anything, Lena set the tone of their response.

"We are not on campus. We are not attending any function that requires that we be students. You have no right to stop us or demand anything of us."

The two guards glanced at each other.

"Let's see some ID, girlie. You really don't want to get smart with us, do you? Lack of respect could be a real problem for you and your boyfriend here. Somebody could get hurt."

"I think that we should just ignore these guys," Eddie spoke up. He took Lena's hand and tried to step around the two men. The security guards shifted their positions and again blocked their way.

"I guess you college jerks are just too stupid to get it. You're not going anywhere until we see some ID."

Eddie grew still. He looked carefully at the men accosting them. They weren't very big, and they certainly looked soft around the middle. They were obviously relying on bluster and the fact that they had batons. If not for the batons, he would have been confident that he'd be able to handle them. Still, he was not sure what his move should be.

"Look, we don't want any trouble. Suppose you two just back off. You have no right to..."

At this point the man directly in front of Eddie pulled his baton and raised it menacingly. The one on the right reached forward as if to grab Lena. Eddie moved back a half step, shifted his weight, and prepared to attack.

"Hold it! Hold it right there! What's going on?"

Two other men moved quickly into his field of view. They were wearing uniforms that Eddie remembered seeing from his first day ashore when he'd asked for directions on the docks.

Quickly Lena again spoke up.

"These two security guards have blocked our way and refused to let us pass until we showed them ID. We're not on campus, nor are we

272

attending a university event. Therefore, they have no authority to interrupt our walk. We are not causing any problems."

The town patrol officers looked between the young couple and the guards.

"They have rights of hot pursuit, but you are a long way from the campus. Has either of you been on campus today?" the patrolman replied.

"No, officer, we have not. My friend here works in town and is not even a student."

The lead officer turned to face the guards while his second watched Eddie and Lena. "You appear to be far from your jurisdiction. First of all, you need to put away your batons. These two young people are clearly unarmed. Neither appears to be aggressive. If you were to touch either one of them, you'd be guilty of assault. Now please explain what is going on here."

The guards restored their batons to their belt hooks. The one in front of Eddie spoke up. Eddie could see that he was sweating. His voice, in contrast to Lena's, was aggressive and loud.

"There was a disturbance on campus yesterday. We're not gonna tolerate that. We're stopping all these punks and we're gonna keep up the pressure 'til they learn to behave."

"Yesterday, was it? What sort of disturbance? Was property damaged or taken? Was anyone assaulted? We received no report at the station."

"Some dumb coed bitch got her boyfriend and another guy to help her move her stuff off campus. They got smart with duly chartered security guards when they were told to move along."

At the use of the vulgar language, the lead officer's face froze. In contrast to the agitated security guard, the town patrol officer's voice got very quiet. His eyes were hard and focused.

"I see. So there were words exchanged, and now you are accosting anyone who appears that he or she might be a student?"

"Yeah, and we're gonna keep..."

"You two boys need to move along. Right now. I recommend – in the strongest terms – that you collect the rest of the university security guards who are down here and get them back up to campus."

"An' what if we don't?"

"My partner and I will use whatever force we deem necessary to take you off this street and down to the station. Word is out on you, boys. Unless you're an outworlder, you must know our ways. You must know that citizens' persons are inviolate unless they are engaged in criminal activity. You have been harassing citizens on the public streets, and that will stop immediately."

The second guard spat on the sidewalk. "There ain't no such thing as an 'outworlder.' That's just a load of crap put out by these lying college professors."

"This is your final warning, gentlemen," the officer said calmly. "You need to move along right now. If you stay you will be taken into custody. If you resist, you will regret it."

Finally it sank in that the officers were serious. The security guards exchanged one last glance and then backed off. They mumbled under their breath. When the one nearest Eddie passed, however, he deliberately shoved his shoulder hard into Eddie's chest and said, "Watch yourself, punk. You're not always gonna have no town patrol show up to wipe your schoolie ass."

At this, the officers stepped forward. In literally seconds, both security guards were face down on the sidewalk. Their wrists were fastened tightly behind their backs by a glittering material that expanded to move up their arms and down to cover their hands.

"Whoa. Instant straitjacket," Eddie muttered to himself. He made a mental note to be polite to the town patrol at all times.

The officers appeared completely unruffled. The second spoke to his communicator asking that a wagon be sent to pick up the security guards.

"We're sorry that you two citizens were troubled. We will be taking these two downtown. They will be off the street for forty-eight hours and will subsequently be enjoined against having any contact that implies authority of law with citizens. In other words, they will no longer be able to work as security guards in this city. Would you care to make a formal complaint?"

"Thank you, officer. I don't think that'll be necessary. As long as they leave us alone, I'm good with it," Eddie replied.

"Happy to be of service." The patrolmen actually saluted Lena and Eddie before they pulled their charges to their feet to await transportation.

They continued their stroll down University Avenue. Now Lena had her own communicator out and was contacting her friends on and off campus. She relayed what had just happened. When she finished, she held Eddie's arm excitedly.

"This is just what we were hoping for, Reed. Our regular processes have reasserted themselves. I do not know what triggered the response, but I am glad of it!"

"Yeah, I think we've got ourselves some breathing room," Eddie admitted, "but pulling two pathologically stupid cop-wannabes off the street is one thing. Getting the university back on track, getting trade flowing, all those things. Those are big. They're going to take more than this."

"Cop wanna bees?"

"Never mind. I shouldn't have used that term. It's a derogatory term for security guards. Probably wouldn't use it if I weren't upset by this.

"Hey." Eddie continued, "You certainly were cool under fire. There's no way I could have talked so calmly and rationally like that. You really turned the tables on those cretins."

Lena raised an eyebrow at Eddie's dialect-laden statement and laughed her sweet laugh.

"Well, thank you, I think, Reed. I do believe that I understood most of what you just said."

She took a deep breath. "And now, we had better get our shopping done. Tonight we have guests coming for dinner!"

* * *

Dinner that night was a pleasant end to a long and interesting day. Eddie realized that he missed the Italian food that Joe and he had enjoyed at the Painter Avenue house, so he gathered ingredients that nearly duplicated a favorite: chicken and home-made pasta with red sauce. Salad and garlic bread rounded out the meal. He found a good red wine that was suggestive of a Chianti. Paired with the hearty wine, the food was just unusual enough to be interesting but not so strange as to put anyone off.

Although Eddie and Lena didn't have a table and chairs to seat four, everyone was happy to gather, picnic-style on the floor of the main room. Lena had found a pretty table cloth at a second-hand store, and she spread the cloth in the center of the room. They pulled the cushions from the sofa and the two side chairs. The two young couples sat around the serving dishes arrayed on the table cloth and held their plates in their laps.

Eddie and Lena shared the day's experiences with Fleggie and Sweetmaye, and it was as though a small weight had been lifted. The two couples enjoyed their evening, but that enjoyment was overlayed ever-so-slightly with sadness. They'd only begun to get to know each other, and all got along easily. Soon Sweetmaye and Fleggie would set sail with the *Mother Rose,* and even if there were no delays, they'd be gone for six weeks.

Even so, they all recognized the happy feeling of good company. The food was warm, tasty, and plentiful. The stories and jokes were good, the personal histories interesting and well-told. Sweetmaye kept Fleggie from laughing at full volume in the tiny apartment. After many good-byes and promises of "we'll see you before long," the *Mother Rose's* two newest crew members took their leave to finish packing.

Before they left, however, Fleggie shared the spell of opening for both the lot and their cottage. "Ye ca' never tell. Ye might cou' use a bolt hole some time. An' now it be there for ye!"

In the days that followed, the balance did indeed shift in the town. The university was still under pressure, but the students who moved off campus were no longer harassed. Advisors and faculty members came into the town to meet in coffee houses and, when the weather was good, parks became impromptu meeting places for discussions and lectures.

Equally important, the electronic and print media shook off their torpor and began reporting on the situation. Investigative reporters descended on the little college town. They interviewed students and faculty members. A few brave administrators came forward to risk their careers by describing the pressures that had been applied. Things were still far from normal on campus, but at least the battle was more out in the open.

Lena and Eddie established a routine. She worked mostly in the main room while Eddie took his activities into the breakfast nook in the kitchen. He frequently slipped out to various parks or to the beach to practice spells that needed space or which had side effects such as loud noises or smells.

Work at the Orca continued. Lena finally met Matt and Anna. Sadly, and unlike the case with Fleggie and Sweetmaye, Eddie's friends from the Orca didn't "click" with Lena. This disappointed Eddie to no end and it put a pall over his otherwise enjoyable work time.

Lena, for her part, tried hard to make a connection, but there was always the tiniest bit of friction between her and Anna. When the couples did get together, Anna would invariably wear fancy, revealing outfits that contrasted with Lena's simple mode of dress. Matt's girl-friend rarely spoke directly to Lena. Further, to Eddie's embarrassment and discomfort, Anna lavished most of her attention on him and ignored Matt.

After three or four awkward evenings during which no one had much fun, the two couples tacitly agreed to stop trying. Occasionally, Lena walked Eddie to work at the Orca. When that happened, everyone spoke and exchanged pleasantries, but the tone was always superficial.

On the other hand, Mabel, the manager at the Orca, adored Lena. She immediately began calling her, "sweetheart." She was all hugs and motherly advice and knowing winks. Sometimes Lena referred to the older woman as "Mother Mabel" and this never failed to bring a happy smile to the manager's face.

Matt pulled away slightly from the comradeship of the kitchen as well. This confused Eddie, and he wasn't sure how to deal with it. The feeling was subtle, but Eddie was sure that he wasn't imagining it. Anna continued to be warm and friendly and often arrived a few minutes early, during Eddie's break. When this happened, she'd chat and joke. It was similar to the first days they'd known each other, but Eddie sensed an un-dercurrent of tension.

Anna always asked how Lena was doing and if her studies were progressing, but she rarely waited for Eddie's response before she dove into her own monologue. The whole situation was bewildering to the young man, but he needed the job, so he did his best to remain friendly to all the parties. Also, he continued to value Matt's friendship, so he tried as best he could to keep that going.

Interpersonal drama aside, life was good at the Dancing Orca. The kitchen facilities were well-designed, well-appointed, and a pleasure to work in. The food that Matt and Eddie prepared continued to be a source of pride. Often, when the shifts got busy, the interchange between Eddie and Matt regained it's original tenor. And the money that Eddie brought in was more than sufficient to keep Lena and him comfortable in the tiny apartment.

Every few days, Eddie would return to the Inn at Three Corners to see if anyone had picked up the message they'd left for Joe. Finally, after weeks of waiting, Eddie went in early on a Thursday morning. It was one of those bright, mild mornings that grew more precious as autumn edged toward winter.

Mel, the desk clerk at the inn peered at him for an unusually long time before favoring Eddie with the tiniest of nods. Slowly, the ancient man turned to the pigeonholes behind the old desk.

When Mel turned back, Eddie could see that the old clerk clutched a piece of stiff paper. Gently, deliberately, he pushed a note across the counter to Eddie. "This be what ye seek."

Eddie unfolded the note. The contents surpassed his own in brevity:

Monday. Here. Dinner.

A sense of relief flooding him, Eddie stared at the words. Joe had been here, had received his message. It was going to be a long four days, but the waiting and uncertainty were finally drawing to a close.

Eddie felt Mel's eyes on him and looked up to meet the old man's gaze. "Thank you, Mel. Can you tell me when Joe left this?"

"Joe Tabs tells Old Mel that ye be a trusted friend. Old Mel keeps Joe Tabs' note safe... since night 'fore last."

"And when he is here at the Inn, does Joe take his meals in the common room?" Eddie indicated the doorway to his right.

"Aye. Most-times a' tha' table by th' far wall. Farthest fro' th' door."

"Thank you again, Mel. I appreciate your confidence. I'll return Monday night."

"Be safe, Laddie. Perilous waters an' all."

Silently, the young man held out his hand, and the ancient desk clerk met it with his dry, fragile grip. A sudden, distant clatter in the kitchen trailed into silence. The centuries old stone walls of the Inn surrounded them. The men's eyes met across the gulf that separated them: long memories on one side, great potential on the other. The handshake, the moment passed. Eddie nodded and made his way out to Longview. Bright sun and crisp air met him as he exited the dim confines of the lobby.

So much had happened. It had been only a few months since he had seen Joe, but everything was different. Eddie's mind flitted through the wild ride that those months had contained. Until now, reconnecting with Joe had been a goal in the abstract. Now there was a more definite milestone just ahead, and Eddie realized that there was a real possibility that this life he had cobbled together, this life with Lena, might be swept away.

Eddie paused on the sidewalk and leaned against the stone front of an old building. He breathed in the brisk autumn air and considered his situation. The stillness his time with Lillith had imparted still resided at his core. He was still calm far beyond his years. His strength and determination remained. Even so, the thought of moving on, of turning his back on all this, made a deep ache inside.

Picking up his pace, he resumed his return trip, and his young stride covered the distance back to the apartment in minutes. Eddie charged up the stairs and into their rooms. Lena looked up from her studies and smiled, but then her expression changed to worry as she saw the stricken look on Eddie's face. "What is it, my love?"

"It's Joe. My teacher. He's left word that we should meet."

"Well is that not what you had hoped?"

"Yeah. Of course. It's just that... well, it just hit home... what if he says that I have to leave? Leave you? This world?"

Lena rose and moved to him. She took his hand and held it. Then she pressed up against him and of their own accord, his arms moved to encircle, hold her. "It could well break my heart, Love, but that ending is far from certain."

She was silent for a moment, and then whispered, "We must make a sacrament of each moment."

Eddie inhaled the scent of her, felt the shape of her pressed against him. She pulled back and again took his hand. Silently, she led him back to the bed that they shared. Silently, she guided his hands to her. She wore only a robe that opened at a touch and fell away to reveal again the completeness of her beauty. Eddie looked long at her and, inviting and inflaming them both, she stared deeply into his eyes.

Still silent, Lena helped him remove his own clothing. Then she lay back, reached out to him, and drew him down beside her. Their lovemaking was long and passionate, full of intensity and life, full of the awareness that each moment they were together was precious. She cried out as he entered her and pulled him hard against her, urgency in every line and curve.

Michael C. Glaviano

Thirty

In the subsequent days, the hours they were apart were interminable. The hours when they were together flew past. The remainder of Thursday, then Friday, Saturday, then Sunday marched along, the clocks running slowly or quickly depending on where they were and what they were doing.

Work at the Orca became an ordeal. Anna continued to be chatty, but obviously Matt and she were having problems. The formerly exuberant Matt was distinctly unhappy. In addition, Eddie thought that Anna leaned a little too close to him when she talked. She seemed just a little too friendly, a little too flirty. He tried to be friendly with both of them, but he was preoccupied. His own worries wore on him.

Worse yet, Eddie was pretty sure that Mabel the manager noticed the change in the mood of the restaurant staff. There was nothing overt, but the tension was obvious. Eddie didn't know how to fix it, or even how to make it better, so he was doggedly pleasant to everyone and tried his best to focus on his work.

Monday morning dawned. Reflecting the turmoil the young couple felt, a storm threatened. They stayed indoors, being close. Even though they were concerned about the future, they were strong, and they shared their hopes as well as their fears. Sometimes they were silent, but it was not a silence of brooding. Rather it was a silence of intimacy and confidence. It was not confidence about what they faced – that would have been foolish. It was more a confidence of feeling, a confidence of love.

As the day wore on, the storm that had threatened in the morning came down with a vengeance. It was easily the worst storm that Eddie had experienced since his arrival. Glad now that she could do most of her coursework from home, Lena claimed that the blast was harsh even by deep winter standards. For a time, their thoughts turned to the *Mother Rose* and their friends on board. They hoped that all were safe and were glad that the vessel was so strong and powerful.

Before long, however, their thoughts returned to the evening that lay ahead.

Michael C. Glaviano

"I'd like to bring you with me, Lena. Tonight, to meet Joe, I mean... but I don't know how he'd react to that. And, I'd hate for someone, one of Joe's enemies, to see you. Be able to identify you. So, for this first meeting at least, I think I should go alone."

"I understand, Reed. I really do not like it so much, but I understand. Of course," she added with the tiniest of smiles, "I cannot in truth say that I will be completely unhappy staying in on so cold and wet a night."

Night was falling earlier as winter approached. The shadows were long and dark as Eddie donned his foul weather gear. He kissed Lena, held her close for a long moment, and then went down into the gathering darkness.

He had walked a wet, rainy block and was perhaps halfway to Turnbull, when he heard a familiar voice call out, "Hey Reed! How's it going?" It was Anna Dymond.

"Anna!" What're you doing out here? It's raining something fierce."

"Oh, I needed to get out of that apartment," she said brightly. Too brightly, Eddie thought.

"Matt's turning into an old fuddy... to tell you the truth, I was hoping that I'd run into you. Maybe we could get a drink someplace?"

"Sorry, Anna, but I've got to meet someone. Otherwise I'd be at home."

"Oh. Well." She appeared surprised, taken aback by his abrupt refusal.

"Maybe another time?" she suggested.

"Maybe, Anna. But I have to tell you that I would much rather like to see whatever it is going on between you and Matt get patched up. It was a lot better when you guys were getting along. A lot better for everyone."

"You don't have a clue, do you?"

"What do you mean?"

"What's going on, Reed. You don't have a clue about it."

"Sorry, you've lost me, Anna."

"Guys are just so dense. Okay. I'll spell it out for you. I'm in love with you, Reed. I want you, and I know that you want me too. I'm sick of Matt and me. And I can be more of a woman to you than that big-brained college girl of yours ever thought of being."

Eddie didn't want to hear any of this, and Anna's attack on Lena almost set him off. He forced himself to stay calm on the outside even though he was steaming inside. He took a deep breath and tried to respond as diplomatically as possible, but as he spoke, the tension in him rose up and found its way into his voice.

"Please, Anna. Stop. I love Lena. I have no desire to jeopardize that. You're attractive and funny, and I've enjoyed knowing you. In a

282

sense I'm flattered that you have strong feelings for me, but if that's how you feel... about Lena and about Matt, well, all I can say is that I don't know how you and I can even maintain a friendship. Now please go home and do your best to talk this out with Matt. He's a good guy and he doesn't deserve to be unhappy. And I won't tolerate disrespect directed at Lena."

Anna stepped back as though he'd slapped her. Then her eyes flashed in anger. "Well. I suppose I should of known. Life's just not fair, is it, Reed? You love somebody, you get her. She practically tumbles into your bed. I love somebody and it's 'tough luck, Anna. Be glad for what you've got.' All I can say is that I hope things work out for you and your college girl."

Then she whirled around and stomped off into the darkness and rain. Eddie could hear her footsteps on the sidewalk for a few moments, but they were quickly masked by the sounds of the storm. He stared into the darkness. In many ways this had been worse than facing physical danger. Losing a friend suddenly, witnessing a good relationship go bad and being the unwitting catalyst for its disintegration, these things tore at him. Despite himself, he felt guilty.

He felt an urge to go after her, to find her and comfort her and try to make her understand. But of course that was ridiculous. He had to go try to meet with Joe. Anna and Matt were grownups – even if she wasn't acting like it. And anyway, what would he say to her? They'd have to work this out. Eddie shook himself out of his unhappy reverie. He tried without much success to put the encounter out of his mind. At last he turned and faced towards his goal. Eddie tried to focus on meeting with Joe, to focus on learning what was required of him.

He arrived at the Inn at Three Corners fifteen minutes later. The stiff wind hurled blowing cold and wet up from the harbor, and Eddie had to pull hard on the door to open it. Inside the room was warm and dimly lit. Good smells emanated from the kitchen. To the right, at a table against the far wall, an old man leaned back, rested his head against the wall behind him. It was Joe.

Deliberately, before heading over to Joe's table, Eddie looked around. There were few diners hungry enough to brave the storm, and those present were huddled over their food, intent on their own conversations. A waitress came through the kitchen doors and started over, but Eddie summoned a little smile and waved her off. With a gesture, he indicated that he'd seat himself. Heart pounding, he walked slowly, with what he hoped was a casual, relaxed demeanor.

The room had never felt so big, so exposed, but he finally reached the bench across from Joe. The young man sat down, his back to the room. The old man opened his eyes.

"So, you made it," he spoke as Eddie leaned forward. Joe's voice was barely above a whisper. A pause then, "And I sense that you've grown a great deal in the past months."

"Yeah, well... I guess I have, but it's like the more I learn, the more I need to know."

"Indeed. Well, son, you just have to get used to that. Comes with the territory," Joe chuckled and then winced and pressed his left hand against his side.

"Are you hurt?"

"A little, yes, but I heal quickly. It is nothing for you to concern yourself with at present. I'll be fine... are you hungry?"

"I could eat."

"Good. Call the waitress over. Order for both of us. Soup and bread for me. You get whatever you want." Joe closed his eyes. The old man seemed to withdraw into himself. Eddie had never seen him hurt and found it more than a little alarming to witness, but he did what Joe had requested and caught the waitress's eye.

She came over a few minutes later. This was the first time Eddie had been in during the dinner shift and she was unfamiliar.

"What'll you have?"

"You have any steak and kidney pie or anything like that?"

"Cook got in a fresh turkey. He's baked some turkey pot pies. Will that do ye?"

"Yes, ma'am. My friend here would like some soup and bread."

"Turkey barley?"

"That'll be fine, ma'am."

The waitress glanced over at Joe, and her lips tightened a little but she said nothing. She went off to place their order.

Joe continued speaking softly. At first his remarks didn't make sense, but then the young man figured out that Joe was talking about the events that had precipitated Eddie's flight through the Place and, eventually, here.

"You did well, son. Could have gone wrong, but it didn't. Sorry it took... so long. I realize that they spooked you when I left you alone. Understandable, but it's unlikely that they could actually get past the barriers on their own. Everything they did... everything they seemed to do... lies, illusions.

"I should have been back sooner and saved you from having to make your first transit alone, but the situation became complicated..." he continued. "Anyway, by the time I got back you'd gone. And then other things came up... But you're okay. That's what counts."

The old man fell silent again. He coughed a little, grimaced. This time he reached across his abdomen with his right hand and used the inside of his left arm to press, hold his hand in place. Eyes still closed, he continued to lean back against the rough wall.

"Joe, do you think we should get your injury cared for in some way?"

"Probably not necessary. Not completely sure yet. Where are you staying?"

"I've got some rooms. Over a bookstore. It's called 'Tolemy's Cats.' Run by an old woman. I think she knew you... when... well, years ago."

Joe was silent again. His lips quirked up at the corners. He cracked open one eye and looked across the table. Then he nodded just a little, closed his eye again. "I think I know who you mean. Good. Yes."

"There's something else, Joe."

"What would that be?"

"I'm living with someone. A young woman I met a few months ago. She's good and smart, and..."

"...and you've told her about me and where you're from?"

"Yeah. A little. Like I said, she's smart and she guessed most of it herself. I want you to meet her, Joe, but I didn't want to bring her here."

"Well, that much at least was responsible of you."

"After I left the forest..."

"You met the woman? Of the forest?"

"Maia. Yeah. And Alicia – you remember her, right? Alicia tracked me through the forest. She was hurt trying to run me down. Maia helped..."

Eddie spoke quietly for a few minutes. He'd described the wagon train and meeting Lena and the others and was about to mention staying with the Old One when Joe shook his head. The young man fell silent. A second later the waitress arrived with their food.

Joe focused his attention on his food, so Eddie did likewise. The turkey pie was delicious, full of big chunks of meat, lots of diced turnips, potatoes, green beans, and carrots in a heavy gravy. It warmed him as he ate.

"How's the pie?" Joe whispered.

"Good... the soup?"

"Fine."

They ate in silence. Joe ate slowly as though he could absorb strength better if he took his time. Eddie tried to match him but nevertheless finished eating well before the old man. Eventually, however, Joe mopped up the last of his soup with the last of his bread. Somehow, his movements brought back memories of the kitchen in the house on Painter Avenue in Joe's town. Different place, different world even, but the feeling came back nonetheless.

Joe's color was better and he looked a little more comfortable now. Moving deliberately and carefully, he fished in his pocket. He took out a few coins, looked at them, tossed them on the table. Tentatively, he made his way to his feet. Eddie could see that he was in pain. Joe met his glance.

"Don't fret, son. I'll be okay. Here, shake my hand. As though we've had a nice visit and are parting ways. Meet me outside, on the Longview side. How far will we have to walk?"

"A little more than seven blocks. Don't you think we should call a cab?"

Joe shook his head. "No. I don't want to use any magic outside of healing spells, and I don't dare climb into a cab without taking certain... precautions. Not in this condition. Anyway, I can do seven blocks. Did a hell-of-a lot more than that getting here... damn stairs. Climbing was worse. Anyway, I can already feel myself pulling back together. Healing. Go on. See you in a minute."

So Eddie did his best to turn away casually and walk to the door on the Turnbull Road side. It was full dark and the clouds covered the moon. The wind was still strong and the young man had to push hard against the door. The air was colder and rain still pounded the streets. Eddie was glad for the warm food in his belly. As quickly as he could he made his way around to the lee of the building. A moment later, Joe eased open the door.

"Okay, son. Now I'm going to have to lean on you. You just guide me. I'll be focused inside. Healing things. Staying on my feet. Hiding us. You'll have to be eyes and ears for us both for a while. Just keep me moving. Get us out of this damn storm as fast as you can. Got it?"

"Yeah, Joe. Got it."

Gently, he eased his shoulder underneath Joe's left arm. He reached around to his teacher's uninjured, right side to help support the old man's weight. Joe kept his own right arm folded across his belly, his hand pressed against his side. They walked the distance back to the rooms on St. Tolemy's. It took well over a half hour to walk the distance that Eddie could do in less than twenty minutes. The last few minutes, he could feel Joe shivering. Finally, they were near the stairway.

"I think we're going to have to disturb your landlady," Joe whispered, barely audible above the storm. "She'll know what to do. I don't want to face those stairs tonight."

The bookstore was closed, but Eddie knocked on the door. Somehow, Mrs. Abellona must have been expecting them because she opened the door immediately. She stared intently at the two men.

"By the gods. You haven't changed. And I'm... so... old," she whispered shakily, almost moaned. Then, with a visible force of will, she got her emotions under control. When she uttered her next words, her voice was strong and steady.

"Bring him in, young man. To the back. Don't dawdle."

She turned away. Eddie glanced down at Joe. He was pale again. As gently as he could, he helped his teacher move through the quiet, dimly lit bookshop. When they reached Mrs. A's apartment, she was waiting and motioned them through the living room and little kitchen. Her bedroom was in the back. She'd already turned down the bed. The storm raged outside, but the little room was warm, safe.

"I've never seen him this way. Help me get him out of his clothes and into the bed," she ordered.

So Eddie helped the old woman undress Joe. There was a wound in his left side. Joe had wrapped a crude bandage around it, but the bandage needed to be changed. When they removed the dressing, they saw that the wound was not a clean cut or puncture. The skin had been torn or ripped by the impact of a rough object. A much larger, badly bruised area surrounded the break in the skin. The injured man clenched his teeth and drew breath sharply through his nose as they eased him back on the sheets. He relaxed as they pulled the covers over him.

"Now," she ordered. "In that cupboard. Clean linens. Fold some into a pad. Tear some others into strips."

She stepped through another doorway – into a bathroom, Eddie supposed – and rattled around. A moment later she returned with a washcloth and a basin. She returned to the bathroom and came back with a dark bottle, the contents of which she dumped into the basin. Then she brought a kettle of water from the kitchen. She said a few words over the kettle and poured a stream of hot water into the basin.

"This will probably hurt, but there's no help for it. I can't manage much in the way of healing spells any more," she said. Her voice was quiet, distant, almost as though she spoke to herself. She pulled the covers back just enough to reveal the wound.

At Mrs. Abellona's direction, Eddie tucked a fresh towel beneath Joe's injured side. Mrs. A bathed the wound and Eddie supported Joe's weight so that she could replace the dressing. They covered him again. Joe was silent through the whole process. He had stopped shivering and for the first time he spoke. His eyes were closed and his voice came from a great distance.

"Thank you. Thank you, both. It is good to see you, Iris. Now if you would please leave me, I will be... fine..."

His voice trailed off. Eddie gathered the soiled bandages and the basin and carried them to the kitchen. Softly closing the bedroom door behind her, Mrs. Abellona followed him.

"Just leave them in the sink," she ordered softly. Again her voice shook with emotion. "Go now. I can sleep on the sofa. We will be safe here tonight. Bring your young lady down here tomorrow and we will talk."

Eddie pressed the old woman's hands and nodded to her. Frail as her aged body had become, he could nevertheless sense a deep strength in her. He turned away and walked to the front of the shop. As before, when he closed the door he heard it bolt itself behind him.

He dashed up the stairs to his apartment to find Lena waiting for him, wide-eyed on the sofa. He went to her and sat close by. He picked up her hand.

"I've got him downstairs. He's hurt, but Mrs. A is taking care of him. We're supposed to go down there tomorrow."

Lena looked intently into his eyes. He thought that she looked vulnerable, somehow injured or hurt.

"What is it Lena? What's wrong?" he asked as he returned her gaze.

She shook her head slightly. "Tell me. About your evening, Reed. Tell me everything."

So Eddie described finding Joe in the common room at the Inn and how he noticed that he'd been injured. He went over their conversation and the walk back to St. Tolemy's Cats and how Mrs. A had been waiting, had expected them, and then had taken charge of the situation. When he was done, he fell silent. The air was heavy with silence.

Finally Lena spoke. "So that is all? That is all that happened since you went into the night?"

The way she phrased her question brought Eddie up short. Then he remembered the encounter with Anna Dymond. Meeting Joe and seeing his mentor's physical state, all that had followed, these had driven the incident from his mind.

"Well, yeah... as far as Joe is concerned. There's something else though. Something I need your help with. I don't know what to do about it."

"What would that be, Reed?" There was a tiny catch in her voice.

"Well, right after I left here, Anna Dymond basically accosted me on the sidewalk. I had the strange feeling that she'd been lurking out there in the rain hoping I'd come out."

Lena took a deep breath. "Yes?"

"I don't know how to say this exactly, Lena, but... well, she said she loved me and that she wanted to be with me. She also said unpleasant things about Matt and... and about you. I had to try hard to control myself in the face of her demands."

"Anyway, she was all wound up and when I tried to talk her down, tried to explain that you and I are committed to each other, she blew up and then stalked off into the storm. She said some things that, well, I don't know how I can work with her at the Orca anymore. To be perfectly honest, I really don't want to see her again."

"So there's nothing between you?"

"What?! No, Lena. Of course not. I love you. I only want to be with you. I've always thought of Anna as a friend and co-worker and as

Matt's girlfriend. She's witty and attractive, but she's not the woman I love. You are."

"Reed. Listen to me. She came here less than half an hour after you left. She rang and rang and, when I met her in the lobby, she stood there, sopping wet and hysterical. She claimed that you and she have been having an affair for months. She said that I was tying you down and that I needed to let you go so that you could be happy. With her. Then she slammed the door and stalked off into the night."

Now Lena was crying. The sight of tears streaming down her face was more than Eddie could bear. For her sake, as best he could, he forced his voice to be calm.

"That's crazy, Lena. None of it's true. None of it. I'm worried that our time together will be impacted because of what Joe will need me to do. You know that this world is in danger. Mine is farther along a path to disintegration. We need to focus on what we can do to turn that around. This... fantasy of Anna's is out of control. I don't know what to say. I would never do anything that I thought would hurt you."

She laid the palm of her left hand over his heart. "Oh, Reed. Hold me for a little while. Please."

So he gathered her into his arms and held her close. Wracked by heavy sobs, she pressed her face to his chest and cried. Eddie didn't know what else to do, so he just held her. He didn't try to say anything or do anything. He held her and let her cry.

Eventually, her sobs subsided. She snuggled in closer and he felt her relax. A few minutes later, she started slightly. Then she raised her head and giggled. "I fell asleep."

Lena pulled away slightly and gazed deeply at the palm of her left hand, the hand that had rested over his heart. Finally, she smiled and pressed his cheek with that palm, kissed his other cheek. She got up and went into the bathroom. Eddie could hear the water running. She came out a few minutes later. She had brushed her thick, amber hair and pulled it back from her face. Her bright blue eyes, still puffy from crying, shown in her lovely face, but that was overshadowed by her smile.

"I can tell, Reed. I can tell that you are faithful. Remember, I do have a tiny bit of something akin to magic, you know. Magic in the ways of the heart. But I needed to hear the story from your lips to be sure. We should feel sorry for Anna... and especially for Matt. This likely explains why he has been out of sorts at work."

He rose and went to her. They held each other again.

This time when she pulled back, her eyes sparkled with their usual, sweet humor. Her keen intelligence and wit were restored. "Now tell me some more about that turkey pie," she demanded. "That sounded delicious. I would like to try to make one."

* * *

Although the worst of the storm moved past Soapstone Bay during the night, it was cold and drizzly the next morning. Eddie and Lena went downstairs as soon as they'd eaten. Tolemy's Cats was still displaying its "Closed" sign, but as they approached the door, they heard the heavy bolt slide back. When Eddie tried the door it opened. It locked itself once more as soon as they passed inside.

The overhead lights were off in the store. The smell of the books surrounded them as they went back to Mrs. Abellona's apartment. Lena tapped quietly on the door and Mrs. A opened it a moment later. The old woman looked tired but alert.

"I can't keep him in bed, fool that he is. He's in the kitchen. If he keeps eating like that we're going to have to send you out for supplies."

Indeed, Joe appeared almost back to normal when he glanced up from his huge plate of eggs, potatoes, ham, and toast. His face wore a kind smile as the young couple entered. He blotted his mouth with his napkin, stood, and held out his hand to Lena.

"It's a pleasure to meet you, young woman. Please call me Joe, Joe Tabs."

"I am pleased to meet you, Joe," she replied with a smile of her own. "Reed has spoken much about you. We are both glad that you have arrived safely."

Joe raised an eyebrow at the name "Reed," and Eddie quickly spoke up.

"Er, Joe?"

"Yes?"

"I meant to mention it last night. I'm known as 'Reed' in this world."

"Prudent, that. I should have asked you about it, but I was... not my best."

"You look a lot better."

Joe regarded him with the faraway look that Eddie remembered from the house on Painter Avenue. His mentor looked deeply into the young man's eyes for some time before he spoke again.

"Reed, you know I'm far older than I look. It's time I said it straight out. I'm far older than you could imagine. But I'm hard to hurt and damn difficult to kill outright."

He smiled wryly. "At least it hasn't happened yet... not in all these long years. Oh, I'm human enough. Just enough. Perhaps I'll tell you about it some time. Or not. At any rate, resilience is a helpful attribute in my line of work. I'll admit that when you saw me last night I was hurt significantly, painfully, but I am mending very quickly."

"I must teach you some spells," he added. "We'll talk on that later."

Joe sat back down and returned to his meal. "Iris has been filling me in on the situation here," he remarked. "Suppose you and Lena tell me what you know."

So Eddie and Lena talked for the space of half an hour. Joe peppered them with questions throughout their narrative. Eddie described the problems with brigands who impeded the flow of goods. Lena picked up the story and touched on the mounting isolation of the towns and city-states and the efforts to shutter the university.

Finally they wound down. By then Joe had finished eating. He sipped his coffee.

"Thank you for adding your impressions," Joe remarked quietly. His mood seemed more businesslike, more somber. "This bears serious consideration. I had expected this world, the world of the Old One, of the Lady of the Forest, to be free of the taint of the Locust Queen. But now I learn that the Queen's tendrils reach even here. Yes. We will have to think carefully about this."

Joe was silent for a few moments but then nodded and got up from the table. He glanced over towards Iris Abellona. After a short pause, he stepped closer to the old woman and extended his hands to her. She hesitated and then met his clear eyes with her own. She took his hands, and it was as if a tiny portion of Joe's vast reservoir of strength flowed into her. She stood a little straighter and her color improved.

"Thank you for taking care of me last night, dear friend," he said softly.

When Joe turned away, Eddie noticed that for an instant his teacher looked very sad. It was, however, also discernible that he no longer favored his left side and in fact had regained his usual, robust appearance. Had Eddie not seen him the night before, he'd have never suspected that the older man had been injured. A moment later, Joe returned to more immediate matters.

"So you have a job here in town, eh? But today is your day off. That's good. I need to acquire a change of wardrobe and lay in a few other things. Then we need to decide what we're going to do. We can't take on everything at once. Fortunately, this world is basically healthy. The Queen will not easily gain traction. After all Lillith, bless her, has resided here continuously for most of the past two millennia."

Joe's voice trailed off, and again he gazed off into some great distance. Then, with an effort, he brought himself back. He turned to look at Lena and Eddie.

"Would you both accompany me on my shopping excursion? That way we can get the mechanics out of the way and continue our chat."

He turned back to Mrs. Abellona. "Would you join us for dinner, Iris? You can help us with our plans. Your knowledge of the town will be invaluable."

"Oh, yes. You'll be wanting to run off before you're fully healed. You'll need someone to ride herd on you. That would be me. You've got that much sense at least. Mind that you make sure to speak up when you talk. I can't stand it when people mumble!" The old woman was obviously pleased to be included in the plans, but true to form, she wouldn't say as much.

Eddie and Lena dashed upstairs for their coats. In a few moments they were back on the sidewalk. They spent the next couple of hours getting Joe outfitted. They also did some grocery shopping so that they could have dinner and talk without worrying about being overheard.

Finally, Eddie cleared his throat. "I'm going to head over to the Orca. I've got some problems there with a couple of co-workers. I think I'm going to need to give my notice and start looking for another job."

Joe looked at him, "What sort of problems?"

Lena took the older man's arm. "I will walk back with you, Joe. I can explain. Reed is probably right in that it would be best to move on."

"Well, don't look for another job just now," Joe said to Eddie. "I think we're going to need some flexibility in when we come and go. It's excellent that you rented a flat from Iris. Couldn't be better in fact. My guess is that the Old One wove that into her tapestry. Wouldn't surprise me in the least."

"But what'll I do for money?" Eddie wondered.

"I have an idea," Lena spoke up. "I am going to see if Mrs. A will let me run the bookstore for her in exchange for rent."

"That might work, but I will need to look at her finances," Joe replied. "She will want to help, but she may need the income. In any case, I can cover rent and expenses."

Eddie and Lena exchanged a look.

"Does this mean that I'll be able to stay here? On this world?"

"For now, son. For now. I cannot know what circumstances will arise or what will be required of us, but for the time being this is as good a place as any and far better than most. We will have work enough, and more, to do here."

"Joe! That is wonderful news!" Lena spun around and hugged Joe hard.

"Take it easy, young woman," he chuckled. "Those ribs need a few more hours of pampering before they'll be able tolerate that sort of abuse."

So they divided up the shopping bags and parted company there on University Avenue. Lena and Joe continued on to Tolemy's Cats. Eddie turned back towards Wells and the Dancing Orca. He'd enjoyed his few months there, but it was clearly going to be too awkward to continue.

When he reached the restaurant and went inside, the early lunch crowd was just starting. He found Mabel in the back, in her tiny office.

He knocked on the doorway and she looked up, an unhappy expression on her face.

"Oh. It's you, Reed. Well, you'd better sit down. We've certainly got a mess on our hands. Yes. Matt called me. He and Anna had it out last night."

"I'm sorry, Mabel. I really had no idea that she felt that way. About me, I mean."

"You mean you haven't been seeing her?"

"Of course not."

"Well, that's not what she told Matt."

Eddie sighed. "I guess I'm not surprised. She confronted me on the street last night and wanted me to leave Lena. Demanded it, in fact. I was totally blind-sided, er, surprised I mean, by it. When I said no, she stomped off. While I was out, she showed up at our apartment and told Lena a similar story."

"And?"

"Um, Mabel, without going into too much detail, let me say that Lena knows that I love her and that there is not now and has never been anything between Anna and me. This whole sorry mess has been the result of things going on solely in Anna's head."

"Oh, dear. Well, I'm glad for you. And for your sweet young woman... still, I have a restaurant to run. Matt has been here for a lot longer than you. So. I believe I'm going to have to find another waitress. And an assistant chef."

"I realize that, Mabel. I... can go... there's been enough trouble for you... and for Matt."

"And then some. Okay. Thanks, Reed. I appreciate your understanding and maturity. Let's see. I owe you for last week's work. And I can give you a few days' pay. Let's make it a week. In lieu of notice."

"Well, thanks, Mabel, but I was planning to quit anyway. After last night, I don't see how I could work here. So, I appreciate it, but you really shouldn't feel obligated to pay me anything extra."

Mabel looked levelly at him. "My, you are a decent young man. I appreciate that. Well... if you ever need a reference, I will be happy to give you one."

Then she shook her head. "By the gods, I will never again bend my rule barring romantic entanglements among the staff! Such a mess. And a damn shame. All right. That's enough whining on my part. Meet me out in front. I'll be out with your money in a minute."

So Eddie waited in the foyer near the hostess station. Mabel brought out a small coin purse a few minutes later and handed it to the young man. She offered him her hand and he met it warmly.

"I am sorry this didn't work out, Reed. You're good in the kitchen and you're good with people. Oh, this is just such a mess! Anyway, remember what I said about recommending you. Just give me a call, okay?"

"I will, Mabel. Thanks. Good luck to you. I'm sorry it didn't work out too, but I'm also sure that it'll all settle down now."

A moment later, Eddie was on the sidewalk headed back to St. Tolemy's. A weight slowly lifted from his shoulders. He had liked working in the Orca, but it was definitely time to move on. And of course there was the fact that he'd need to assist Joe as best he could.

Thirty One

"We have one advantage that never deserts us," Joe stated. "You may think it trivial, but it turns out to make a huge difference. We have friends. They don't."

It was early afternoon. The three of them, Eddie, Lena, and Joe, were sitting in Mrs. Abellona's living room. Mrs. A was out in the bookstore. The room was cozy and quiet, a safe refuge where they could meet and plan.

"I do not understand. What do you mean when you say they do not have friends? And how is that so terribly important?" Lena asked.

"The whole class structure of the Blue World, from the Locust Queen all the way down to the lowliest servitor, is strictly hierarchical," Joe replied. "Those in positions of authority assume that their subordinates are trying to undermine their position, to rise in the hierarchy. So they don't share information with the people who work for them. In fact, they often feed disinformation into the system.

"In turn, people fear and despise those above them in the hierarchy. They plot constantly and try to figure out how to bring their superiors down. People who are at about the same level, well, they continually jockey for advantage. Everyone views the society as a zero sum game. No one can get ahead without someone else falling behind.

"So alliances may be formed, but in the end they are always betrayed. Friends, friends who can be trusted to stand by you, friends who will do what they promise to do, who can be relied upon to help, are nonexistent in the Blue World.

"The Queen knows this. She is the architect of it. For all her power, she never sleeps. Never trusts anyone."

"So how do we use that?" Eddie wanted to know.

"Because there are so few of us, the best thing we can do is to open more portals near areas where we detect active agents from the Blue World. The agents won't have effective backup because that would require information sharing, which in turn requires a little bit of trust. Equally important, they will not report setbacks to their superiors. Any result other than complete success is considered a failure, and failure is punished harshly.

"I am sure that they are stretched very thin," the old man contin‑ued, "so they will probably not notice that they are facing resistance at first. And just a slight change in the way society as a whole perceives reality will have big effects."

"Sorry, but how does having a few more portals help?" Lena wondered. "These people are trying to shut down the university."

"Actually, they're trying to convince the people of this world that magic doesn't exist, that the gods don't exist, that there is no Great Hub. The push to muzzle people at the university is just a tactic. So are the moves to disrupt trade and inter-city exchanges of culture and informa‑tion. The more people who have direct experiences with magic, the old ones, the forest spirits, and so on, the better. If you've met the forest lady yourself and somebody tells you she doesn't exist, you're not likely to give their other claims much credence."

"I've met her, and I can tell you... she really exists," Eddie mur‑mured. Unconsciously, he touched the scar on his right cheek. Gently, Lena rested her hand on his arm. He looked at her and smiled.

"Indeed," Joe continued. "And near an open portal, magic is stronger. That applies even to worlds that are as badly injured as ours, son. Here, in this healthy world, the effects will be stronger still.

"So, we need to open two more portals here in Soapstone Bay," Joe wrapped up.

"Two *more*. You mean there's already an open portal here?" Ed‑die wondered aloud.

"Yes. There is a stable, fully-functioning portal deep in the earth below the tower of the Inn at Three Corners. That's how I arrived last night: I made a transit through the Place into that portal. We need to open another near the university and another somewhere else in town. I'm not sure exactly where yet.

"Fortunately, these new openings will not need to be complete portals. Merely having a stable point of continuity with the place between worlds will have the sorts of local effects we desire. We..."

"Wait. Hold it a second. There's a portal here? In Soapstone? If there was already a portal here, then why did I have to come all that way through the Lady's forest and then join the wagon train and... Hey! Ow!" Lena punched him on the arm.

"Not that I would have wanted to miss the wagon train part," Ed‑die added as he grinned at Lena, "and then I stayed with the Old One at her farm and went to sea with the *Mother Rose*. There were just so many things that happened."

"I knew that if you were frightened badly enough to use the portal beneath the Painter Avenue house, you would be on your own, without a guide. You see, Reed, this world and ours lie relatively close to‑gether... you could think of them as adjacent spokes on the wheel whose hub is the Place. Some worlds are completely alien. Some are hard to reach, and some are hostile. But they all have connections with the Place Between. So I had to make sure that you'd be able to find the right world with the simplest of directions. Do you remember what I told you?"

"Sure. Head for higher ground. Keep that foremost in my mind: head for higher ground. You said to make it a mantra."

"Right. I knew that if you followed that single, simple instruction, you'd end up in the Lady's forest. That technique of repetition of a single, clear instruction is one of the most reliable navigation mechanisms when you're in the Hub, the Place Between. And believe me, you don't want to be wandering around there randomly. The Great Hub is not a safe place to linger. The way into the tower at the Inn is not so easy."

"Okay. So how do we open other portals?"

"First I need to spend some time exploring, looking around the town. Just a day or two will do it. I'll decide on some good locations. These will be places where the membrane between the world and the Place is thinnest. Usually, this will be a place where a portal existed in the past but which has collapsed through disuse."

"Reed and I would like to help and to learn more. Can we go with you?" Lena asked. Eddie nodded in agreement.

"Yes, at least for some of the excursions, I think that would be fine, desirable even," Joe agreed. "Depending on what I find, and what sort of moves we attempt, I may request your active assistance. The addition of people who share the same goal can aid the process."

Then he turned to Eddie, "First, however, I want to spend some time determining how much you have learned in the past few months. We'll need to go someplace where we won't bother anyone or draw a lot of attention."

"Well, you could go to Baleen Park on the south end of town," Lena suggested. "It is above the cliffs and very much exposed to the weather. For that reason, few people visit on cold, wet days."

"Yeah, that's what I was thinking." Eddie added. "Sometimes I go out there to practice. It's almost always empty when the weather's bad."

"Baleen Park. So it's still there, is it? Above the cliffs? It's been many years since I visited it, but as I recall it does have the advantage of being wide open. I can set a warding spell on the perimeter so that we can work without being surprised by anyone we'd not want to meet. Yes, that will work. Young Reed and I will spend an hour or two there and return in time for dinner."

"Good. It is settled then," Lena said. "I need to do some work anyway, and I would like to see if Mrs. A could use help in the bookshop. Later, I will cook for us. I look forward to feeding us all."

Plans settled, Joe and Eddie collected their coats and went outside. They ambled down to Turnbull. When they reached the larger street, Joe flagged down a taxi wagon and they rode the rest of the way down to the park. The day continued to be cold and harsh. There was little traffic and few strollers on the streets.

Joe paid the driver. "If you find yourself in the neighborhood in, say, an hour and a half, meet us here. You'll have a return fare."

As they'd hoped, the harsh weather had kept visitors away from Baleen Park. They paced the perimeter of the park while Joe asked the young man about his studies. As he listened, the old man laid a mild spell of warding around the edges of the park. He explained that this spell would do little more than obscure the middle of the park from casual observation. Further, if anyone approached, Joe would know of it. The spell would fade once the teacher and his student had left the vicinity.

Eddie pointed out the benches and the statue of the whale chasing its tail. They walked to the spot and Eddie explained what Mrs A had done so that Lena and he could leave messages for each other. He sat on the bench and showed Joe the secret space in the brick wall.

Joe nodded in appreciation of the work. "Yes, should the need arise, you and your young lady can indeed use this to pass messages."

He paused and stared at the wall behind the bench. "You know, I might also be able to modify the spell so that this space connects to the house on Painter Avenue. In our world."

"You could do that? Cool. That'd be great, Joe! Thanks!"

Joe smiled a little and gestured to Eddie to stand off a few feet. Stooping over, the powerful old man laid his hand on the bricks and closed his eyes. He was still and silent for a few moments. In the shadowless light of the overcast sky, it was not easy to see, but Eddie thought that the bricks glowed beneath his teacher's hands.

Chuckling, Joe straightened. "Not trivial, that. But the modification will work."

He fell silent then, turned suddenly serious and, obviously to Eddie, more than a little sad, "You should have seen Iris when she was young," Joe continued. "She was an amazing woman. 'Lovely' is a completely inadequate term to describe her beauty. Hot tempered in equal measure. But more than that. She had the ability to command huge power, power which she spent profligately... in the defense of this, her world.

"In all my years, all my long, long years, I never met anyone remotely like her," Joe added. Then he grew even more somber. "You realize of course that she didn't have to age so quickly. She simply insisted that she push and push and would never use what she learned to heal her wounds, to strengthen her body. She did so much good for her world, for all the worlds really. Even now she is a force to be reckoned with, but she has become tired. Near her end. May the gods dream her again."

Joe fell silent after this little tribute to Mrs. A. He stared off in the direction of the harbor. Then: "I wonder. Hmmm. I wonder..."

In the distance, Eddie could hear the sounds of the sea. The air was cold and the wind insistent. Exposed and open, Baleen Park was indeed an uncomfortable place to spend a blustery day.

Joe shook himself from some deep place in his memories and sighed sadly. "At any rate, you and your beloved will soon be able to communicate even when you are in your world and she in hers," Joe continued after a moment. "We will need to complete the connection. The easiest, most reliable way would be to place a small object in this niche."

Eddie fished a coin from his pocket. "Will this work?"

"Yes, that will be just right. When we return to our world, I'll pull this through. Then we can send something back, and you'll have what you need: a slender, stable channel between these two worlds. Remember to use it well."

Joe pressed the brick to open the little space behind it. He placed the coin inside and replaced the brick. Then he straightened and faced his young student.

"Now, let's see what you've learned and what I can add in a short amount of time."

So for the next three quarters of an hour, Joe worked with Eddie in their old roles as teacher and student. He tested the young man's new skills and assessed his weaknesses. There were many corrections, many adjustments. On balance, however, the older man expressed satisfaction with the progress that his student had made.

"You have done reasonably well, my young friend. Especially since you were on your own. Of course you need many more spells at your disposal – two hundred times what you've learned and you would reach a solid journeyman's state of proficiency. There is little time for that now, but I'll mark a few things in those books. For the most part, however, you can and should follow the sequence laid out in the texts.

"Master those volumes and you will be glad of it," he added. "In the short term, though, you need to learn how to channel energy so that you can guide and direct its flow without necessarily being either a source or a sink for it. At some point, that skill will be critical for the work you will do. There will be great forces at play, and you must channel the energy without standing in the midst of the flow. On occasion, you may need to manage energy and tap into it but only rarely, very rarely, should you attempt to take it all up at once."

And so Joe worked for another half hour on this one thing: this channeling and "floating" of energy. More than once, Eddie was knocked to the wet grass in the process of learning the technique, but little by little the young man saw how he might stand next to the flow and draw from it just what he needed or return to the flow an excess that had been generated. Finally, Joe called a halt.

Michael C. Glaviano

"That is enough for now." He held up his hand as Eddie started to protest. "We will work on this, on this and more as we are able. You need to rest, to absorb the lesson. You have a foundation. We should be getting back."

Eddie nodded in agreement. With the young man trailing a few steps behind, Joe started back toward Turnbull Road. When they reached the edge of the park, they saw their ride approaching. Eddie was young and strong and eager to learn, but he was also cold and wet. Further, he hurt in more places than he could count. Although he'd been eager to continue his practice, he had to admit to himself that it felt good to rest on the bench of the wagon and ride back to Center Street.

Mrs. Abellona was waiting when they reached Tolemy's Cats. Her arms were folded across her chest and she was tapping her foot. Her bright red hair looked as though she'd been tugging at one side of it for most of the afternoon.

"So you've had your fill of playing in the wet, have you? Two little boys. Even the young one should know better. Your young lady was underfoot for an hour. Finally I had to send her upstairs. I think she's making dinner for us. It better not be too spicy. Or fattening."

"Uh, I think I'll go upstairs and see if I can help," Eddie said.

"What? I can't hear if you mumble. Why don't you go upstairs and see if you can help?" Mrs. Abellona suggested. Eddie smiled and nodded his agreement.

She rounded on Joe. "And you. You were at death's door last night, and today you're out in the weather. Your coat's unbuttoned and you're not even wearing a scarf. What were you thinking when you went out? You go back into my rooms and get warm while I finish things up here. Some people have work to do. And don't forget to leave your shoes in the hall. Don't be tracking across my carpet!"

Eyes sparkling, Joe chuckled a little but Eddie noticed that his teacher didn't argue with Mrs. Abellona. As Eddie left the bookshop to go upstairs, Joe turned and walked to the apartment in the back of the store. If Eddie still had a job, he would have bet a week's wages that Joe left his shoes where he was told.

Later, Lena went downstairs to see about bringing food to the little apartment behind the bookshop. Mrs. Abellona said that she could manage the stairs and that she wanted to see how the young couple had set up the apartment. To this end, she offered the use of a stout folding table and some extra chairs. She kept these in the storeroom next to Eddie and Lena's apartment.

Mrs. A keyed the lock for the storeroom to Eddie's thumbprint. When he went inside to look for the table and chairs, the young man found a space that was, in effect, a mirror image of his own apartment. The main room held some surplus bookshelves from the store and, occupying the center of the space, were several stacks of boxes that ap-

300

peared to contain old books. There was also a numbered collection of file boxes labeled "Financial Records." The place had a lonely, abandoned feel to it.

Eddie located the table and chairs leaning against one wall. He dusted them off and brought them into the front apartment so that they could gather around a comfortable table. Even with the Murphy bed folded up and put away behind its doors, the additional furniture filled much of the small living area. Still with Lena's "new" tablecloth, it made an attractive place to dine.

Mrs. Abellona leaned on Joe's arm and negotiated the stairs slowly but without trouble. The old woman employed her hearing spell so that they could have a real conversation. It improved her mood a great deal. Beneath her frequently astringent exterior lay a sharp mind and a quick wit. She could be funny when she wanted, gracious as well.

Lena started things off with a salad made with autumn greens and a crisp, Riesling-like wine. Then she reprised the turkey pie that Eddie had described from the night before at the Inn. She added some of her own ideas and the result was superb. She'd also made fresh bread and sprinkled rosemary in the dough before baking it. For dessert, she served dried figs that had been reconstituted in Madeira and topped with a dollop of heavy, whipped cream.

They tried to keep the conversation as light as they could, but an undertone of urgency tinged all that they said. Still, the food was plentiful, hot, and delicious. Dinner worked a magic of its own and for the space of an hour or two, they were able to enjoy the warmth of the meal and the company. The weather had turned from blustery to stormy again. The rain pounded the slate shingles and the wind pressed against the windows, but inside the solid old building the room was comfortable.

After dinner, Joe sat with Iris Abellona on the sofa while Eddie and Lena did the washing up. Lena had kept on top of her mess as she cooked, so cleanup was quick. They could hear Joe and Mrs. A arguing – softly for once – in the other room. As the young couple worked, the voices had slowed and then trailed off. A warm heaviness permeated the air, and Eddie nearly dropped the pan he was drying when he turned towards the little living room and saw that it was pulsing with a golden light. A low sound, pitched at the limits of hearing droned in concert with the glow.

Eddie started towards the other room to see what was going on, but Lena restrained him with a hand placed lightly on his arm. "They did not call us," she whispered. "I think this has something to do with whatever it was they were discussing a little while ago. Let us finish and then wait here for a few moments."

So they finished their cleanup. Eddie opened a bottle of Merlot and Lena got four clean glasses. By then, the atmosphere in the living room had returned to normal, so Lena called out, "Shall we bring in some wine?"

"Thank you. That sounds good, dear," came a voice. The voice was familiar but, at the same time, strange, and the young couple hurried in.

They found Joe and Mrs. Abellona where they had left them on the sofa. Joe was still Joe, but Iris Abellona was no longer old. She appeared to be at least forty years younger than when they'd seen her twenty minutes earlier. Worn, frail 70's or 80's had morphed to a healthy and vibrant early-40's. Her skin was clear and unlined. Her hair was a fiery but natural red, thick and wavy. The blouse that moments ago had hung from her aged, stooped shoulders was now filled, stretched across her breasts, loose at the waist. The change was shocking, beautiful in the extreme, but shocking nonetheless.

"Come and sit down," she spoke. Her eyes flashed with strong, complex emotion. Her querulous tone was replaced by a rich contralto.

"Joe has convinced me to allow him to flood my tired body with energy," she continued, "and I have reluctantly agreed to let him do it. Yes. In the interest of the work that we're going to do, I have agreed."

"But know this," she continued, "I am still old. The wounds are salved and masked, but they remain."

She gestured towards Joe. "Even this ancient warrior cannot restore my youth with a few words and secret gestures. He can give me a semblance of it for some weeks, perhaps as long as a year. Then the damage will reassert itself. The decades of damage will demand their due. And I do not know if I can bear losing my strength, my beauty a second time."

"I suspect that age may return quickly, drastically. Oh, Joe says that I will be no worse off for it and that perhaps some benefit will remain, but I've known him for a long while, and he'll say what he needs to say to accomplish his goals."

She paused with an almost fierce, defiant look. "Now, to work. Time is always fleeting. For me, it suddenly feels doubly so. Let us focus on the job at hand."

Joe, silent until now, spoke up. "Yes, to work. We've planning to do."

The beautiful redhead stood and took a seat at the table. She slid her chair in close and leaned forward expectantly. The old man joined her. He steepled his fingers and rested his chin on his thumbs as though deep in thought.

Eddie had been standing in slack-jawed silence during this little speech. Lena possessed far more grace, more resilience in the situation. She rubbed Eddie between his shoulder blades and brought him back to the present. The young couple drew up chairs and handed around the wine.

Joe spoke first. "The first thing to decide is where we want to open portals. We've seen that it is possible to rip open a passage – the woman Alicia did that when I stopped her from entering my rooms. Such a gash reseals itself right away unless a great deal of energy is poured into keeping it open. And, as I said earlier today, we do not need to use these portals to transit between worlds. We need only provide a conduit for the tears of the gods to nourish this world, to admit more magic. In any event, I'd much prefer that we try to identify places that we could simply reopen."

"I have some old documents in the shop," Mrs. A announced suddenly. "Things I've saved from the early times. Some go back to the first settlements of the bay and surroundings. Wait a moment. I'll be right back."

Mrs. A practically leapt from her chair and ran from the room. They heard her hurry down the stairs. The front door slammed. Joe, Lena, and Eddie exchanged looks.

"Will she really...?" Lena asked. Her eyes were soft with worry.

In the absence of Iris Abellona's distracting presence, the young couple realized that Joe looked worn and shrunken. He gave a tired sigh. "It is largely as she said. Oh, there are things that can be done, but they are risky. Very risky, and she knows the risks. Less risky strategies might be applied, but after waiting for so long to do anything to heal her body, energy patterns that would provide real, lasting middle age, let alone youth, would be difficult to establish. For one thing, there would be an extended period of time during which she would have to focus most of her attention on the healing, on repair at the deep levels."

Joe sighed again and sadly shook his head. "And since she wouldn't take the time when she was young, it is difficult to imagine that she'd take the time now. It is terribly unfortunate, but that is her nature. I hope it will be otherwise, and I will do what I can to make it possible. Still, I foresee a battle with her that will be hard to win.

"I... we... We must cherish the time we have with her," he added at last.

Then they heard the front door slam again and the fast, firm tread of Iris Abellona on the stairs. Carrying a large, leather-bound book in her arms, she burst into the room.

"Found it. Did you miss me?" she laughed. There was an edge to her laughter, but it also contained a flash of genuine humor.

She laid the book gently on the table and perched gracefully at the edge of a chair. Eddie noticed that she'd tucked in her blouse and tightened the belt of her trousers across her hips. It was hard not to notice. As Mrs. A opened the book and began scanning its pages, Lena dug her knuckle into Eddie's ribs. They drew their chairs closer and gathered around the book. Joe leaned over the table to peer closely at it.

Mrs. Abellona paged through the ancient volume. It smelled musty and some of the papers stuffed between the bound sheets were crumbling. The book itself was comprised of well-preserved vellum or perhaps parchment bound into a leather cover. The cover, once dark umber, had faded with age and suffered a multitude of spills, burn marks, and cup rings.

"What is this book, Mrs. A?" Lena wanted to know.

The young/old woman looked into Lena's youthful face. Then she turned to Eddie. "For now, while this lasts," here she gestured at herself, "refer to me by my first name, 'Iris.' Afterwards – if there is one – well, we shall see."

Iris took a sip of her wine and then returned her attention to the book. "It contains records, journals, and maps that go back to the earliest days of the settlement that eventually became Soapstone Bay. Here we should find some record of the portals that were open when people first came here."

"May I see that?" Joe asked. When Iris turned the book towards him, Joe thumbed carefully through the document. He paused now and then to gaze more carefully and deeply at something written or drawn on the old pages. Then he closed the heavy tome and laid it on his lap.

"Yes, I think this will be helpful. I will read this book tonight after you've gone to sleep."

"I don't intend to sleep tonight. There is work to be done. You expended tremendous energy to work this change in me," Iris protested.

"Iris. Please. You must rest tonight. Yes, I did expend a great deal of energy, and I would not have my efforts go for nothing. If you rest, then you will be stronger tomorrow. If you can force yourself to take it slow for just a few days, a week at the outside, why you just *might* have years of strength ahead of you. If you last, why at some point, it might even be possible to work a more permanent change. If, however, you insist on stressing yourself immediately..." his voice trailed off.

Iris looked long and hard at Joe. Her eyes flashed dangerously, but he met her gaze calmly, almost blandly. If Eddie didn't know better, he might have dismissed Joe as a kindly, slightly feeble old man. Eventually, it was Iris who dropped her gaze.

"It shall be as you wish. I would be a fool to waste this boon," she agreed finally.

"Thank you, Iris. I think that I understand your feelings in this matter, and I am doubly grateful for your patience. You will not regret a few days' worth of rest, believe me."

The tense moment had passed. Joe took a deep breath and returned to the topic of opening portals that touched the place between worlds.

"There may, probably will be, several opportunities to reopen gaps into the Place. I would like to set up a triangular pattern of portals.

One vertex will be in the basement of the tower at the Inn. A triangular pattern will be stable and strong, hard to perturb."

"What do you plan to do once you have these?" Iris wondered.

"We will need someone to stay here and make sure that we have a good home base. I will return to the world where I've been living, the world where Reed was born – call it 'our world' – and continue what I've been doing for the past few months, traveling all over, looking for places where a gap may be opened and then setting up a portal. Very few are active in our world."

"But I don't understand. You've been living there," Eddie protested. "Why aren't there just the right number of portals open already?"

"For several reasons. First of all, in the past three hundred years or so, the Locust Queen has focused her attention on our world. She has many servants while I have a handful of associates. Further, for many years she cleverly focused her attention on remote areas, so the great places of art and culture – at least those I recognized – persisted. Her minions worked their mischief subtly in the nooks and crannies of the world. So their actions escaped notice. In the meantime, I traveled among many worlds and tried to do a little here, a little there. And all the time, she was chipping away at my own home world.

"Then, five or six decades ago, the Queen's plans began to bear fruit. Within a relatively short span of years, the magic in our world faded. I must confess that I was less vigilant than I should have been. A crushing span of years, of events... wore on me, and brooding, I drew inwards. Years passed before I fully realized what was going on. For much of the past half-century, I have been trying to shake off my lethargy. I've been working to undo her mischief, but progress has been uneven. I have lost touch with many of my old helpers. Some have died; others have become inactive, so I have been working largely alone.

"Now, I suspect a certain complacency in her about the fate of our world," the old warrior continued. "Otherwise, why move some of her resources to this relatively healthy place? After all, Lillith, the Old One dwells here. For nearly two thousand years, she has rarely left and, unlike me, has never become feckless, has never faltered. The Queen must know this.

"Finally, just before things began to fail on our world, Lillith called to me. I answered her appeal, and together with Iris, we fought back an initial foray. Thus, I am not sure what the Queen of the Locusts hopes to accomplish in this place."

"In retrospect, I think that her earlier actions here constituted a feint of sorts," Iris suggested. "This distracted you and helped move her game forward on your world."

She glanced at Lena and then looked seriously, intently at Eddie. "Now, sure of the failure of your world, she moves in earnest to establish a real beachhead here. Of course this may be merely a spasm of evil by one who is overfilled with power and greed. Either way, I agree with this dangerous old man. If we open a triangular pattern of portals here, we will buy time. It may distract her and allow us to focus back on your world."

"Will we be able to return to my world through any of the portals or will I have to go back to the forest?" Eddie wondered.

"We will use the active, stable portal that lies beneath the Inn at Three Corners. I'll be there to help this time," Joe spoke encouragingly.

"As will I," Iris spoke up.

Joe frowned. "I don't know, Iris. It might be better if you stayed here. You have your book shop. You can make sure we have a safe haven."

"Oh, no. I didn't submit to this transformation so that I could sit here and shelve books. Resting for a week is one thing. Sitting by idly is quite another, thank you very much."

"And I, too, would like to help as best I can," Lena added quickly, before the conversation could again escalate into an argument.

"Let me think on this. Please," Joe countered. "I'll try to pull together a plan tonight. It is good to act in concert, but I must make sure that we fit our talents to the tasks that need doing."

Eddie had been thinking of his arboreal trek through the forest. This jogged his memory back to one of his last conversations with Maia.

"Um, Joe? I guess this is sort of beside the point but Maia – the Lady of the Forest? Well, she gave me a sort of packet to take back and plant on my world. It's a long story, but that's how I got this scar," he indicated the fine pattern of lines that marked his right cheek, the pattern that obscured the scar given him by Alicia. "She needed a few drops of my blood to... quicken it. I think that's what she said.

"Anyway, I think it's some kind of seed packet," he added. "She said something about wanting to become a... oh, I don't remember, but it was something about making her forest grow."

"A world-spanning forest?" Joe suggested.

"Yeah. Something like that. Could we do that sometime? When we go back?"

"Could we do that? Of course we could," Joe laughed. "That seed packet could be of great benefit to us all! Do you have it handy?"

"Sure! Hang on." Eddie rose, stepped quickly to the walk-in closet. His pack lay at the back on the floor. After subjecting his camping gear to a good cleaning, he'd stored his things in the pack when he'd moved into the apartment. Now he rummaged through his blanket and other gear. The rabbit fur-wrapped packet lay at the bottom.

"Here it is," he announced as he returned to the room.

Cradling it almost reverently, Joe accepted the little packet and placed it on the table. He carefully unrolled the pelt to reveal a smaller object made of folded leaves. He held this inner packet up to his face and inhaled. "It is viable. This is good; this is very good. It changes everything."

"How so?"

"Her magic is different from ours, son. It is different, but it is a deep and powerful force. If we plant this on our world, the Lady herself will instantly be able to move back and forth. Within a matter of months, the Lady's forest will extend across the Great Hub and link this world with ours. Now her motives are not identical to ours, but the health of her forest depends upon the health of the worlds it spans. Thus, we gain a powerful ally."

"So this seems like it's sort of important."

"Indeed it is, son. And if somehow we could establish a beach-head of the Lady's forest on the Blue World, the stress on the Queen and her minions would be great. It would buy us time. A great deal of it."

"So should we plant it – plant the seed packet – on the Queen's world instead?"

"It doesn't work that way. This was quickened with your blood. It is tied to the world of your birth. Such is the Lady's magic. We'll have to get the Lady's forest going on our world and then ask her if she would be willing to create another of these... this time with the Blue World in mind. Maybe she will be willing, perhaps she will not, but we won't know until we ask."

Joe fell silent again. He stared at the little leaf-wrapped packet in his hands. The cunningly folded leaves were tied with some sort of vine. Through all the traveling and rough handling it had suffered, the packet still looked perfectly fresh and intact. Joe carefully re-wrapped the packet with the rabbit pelt.

"I think this calls for a change in plans. You and I should return to our world immediately. We can establish the Lady's forest and return here within the week. In the meantime, it may be that Iris and your beautiful young woman could discretely investigate where we might open gaps between this world and the Hub...

"I emphasize the word 'discretely,' Iris," he added with a sharp look.

"I can be discrete. You know that. I'm as discrete as they come."

Joe snorted a short laugh, but chose not to comment. Iris glared at him.

"Reed, I am not at all happy at the prospect of being apart right now, but I can see that this is important. Perhaps I might help in the store so that Mrs. A – Iris, I mean – can focus on these plans. That would at least occupy me and keep me from fretting overmuch."

"Iris? Would that suit you?" Joe asked.

Iris beamed at Lena. "Indeed it would, Lamb! We'll start tomor-row morning. I can show a bright girl like you how to run that bookstore before lunch."

Michael C. Glaviano

"Then it is decided," Joe declared. He held up his glass. "*Salud!*"

They echoed his toast and placed their empty glasses on the table. Joe stood, looked around, smiled. Hefting the old book in his left hand, he extended his right to the beautiful, redheaded woman.

"Now, if you will accompany me downstairs, Iris, we can give these young people some privacy. Plan on an early start, Reed. We'll leave at first light."

308

Thirty Two

Lena and Iris saw them off. Breath steaming in the bitingly cold air, the four paused briefly in front of the bookshop. In the glow of the street lamp, Iris appeared to have shed several more years overnight and now looked to be in her mid-thirties. She stood, serene and powerful, with her thick hair unbound. The woman was breathtakingly beautiful, and Eddie could see how her appearance, her mind, and her dedication might have charmed even Joe beyond the boundaries of logic and common sense. Iris radiated an almost divine intensity that was all the more precious for its evanescence.

The good-byes were difficult for the young couple. Pressing her face against his chest, Lena clung to Eddie for a few moments. When Lena finally stepped back, Iris put her arm around the young woman's shoulders and comforted her. In appearance, she could easily have been taken for Lena's older sister. Supported, leaning against that bulwark, Lena straightened and met her lover's eyes. Finally, she smiled and raised her hand in farewell.

Then, the men turned away to walk briskly east on Center Street. The hint of dawn in the eastern sky did little to relieve the gloom as they turned up Turnbull and continued north toward the Inn. Each bundled against the cold, each wrapped in his own thoughts, Joe and Eddie paced side-by-side.

A quarter hour later, they reached Longview, and the massive stone structure that was the Inn at Three Corners loomed ahead of them in the semi-darkness. Avoiding the public room on the Turnbull side, Joe veered onto Longview and headed for the door to the lobby. They found the door unlocked, but it was nearly as dark inside as it had been on the street.

In the dim warmth of the lobby, scents of cedar, citrus, and furniture wax mingled with the breakfast smells wafting from the public room. A single lamp burned on the front desk. Still and silent, Old Mel watched from his seat behind the desk as they entered.

Joe nodded to the elderly desk clerk but said nothing to break the heavy silence. The ancient man met Eddie's eyes for a few heartbeats.

Then he carefully climbed down from his stool. Mel turned to the pigeonholes in the wall behind him and withdrew an old-fashioned key. The key was heavy and ornate and nearly as long as a man's hand.

Ever taciturn, Mel shuffled in the direction of the stairs. Instead of going up to the rooms, however, he led them around to the back of the stairway, where a dark, scarred, heavily bound door waited. The door was half-round and less than six feet in height. The old man inserted the key into the lock, grasped the bow of the key and turned it. Eddie heard the stout bolt withdraw. Mel stepped back. Then Joe grasped the handle and pulled the door open. Narrow, stone steps spiraled down into darkness.

Finally Joe broke the silence. "Count the steps. There are 64 to the first landing. Trail your hand on the wall if you need to keep your balance."

Then, without hesitation, Joe stepped onto the stairway and began his descent. Eddie ducked his head and followed. They had barely started when he heard the massive door close behind them. The lock turned, and the bolt slid into the strike plate with a heavy sound. The darkness was complete.

When his count reached sixty, Eddie slowed his steps. It was a good thing because he must have lost track at some point. The steps ended when he had counted only 63, but he barely stumbled. Joe was waiting.

"We are well below the street and most basements at this point. There are also some very old, very deep spells protecting this place. I have always felt that it was safe to use an illumination spell from here on down, but let's be extra cautious and walk in darkness for one more set of 64. Can you do that?"

"Yeah. I can do it." Eddie's voice sounded ragged to his own ears. He felt a trickle of sweat down his side.

Joe continued downwards. Eddie padded forward. At each footfall he sought carefully for the edge of the landing. Once he located the next flight of steps, he followed the quiet sound of Joe's tread lower and lower into the earth below the Inn. This time he held his focus better, and the steps ended when his count reached 64.

"You did better that time. Focus is everything, but you're learning that. Now. You've been practicing an illumination spell. Can you bring it to bear now?" Joe asked.

"Let me see."

Eddie pulled the words together in his mind. He put his back to the wall on his right and pointed the index finger of his left hand down by his side. Then, pronouncing each word quietly and precisely, he invoked the spell. As he spoke, he made a few gestures with his right hand. A feeble glow fanned out from his left index finger. He concentrated harder, and the glow strengthened and grew steady.

"Good. For the first real try. Now you lead. There are two more sets of 64 steps cut into the rock. Try not to look directly at the light."

Eddie started moving again. It was difficult at first to concentrate on his steps while holding the illumination spell in his mind, but little-by-little he got it. By the time they had reached the bottom of the last section of the stairway, he was getting pretty good at it.

The last section of stairs opened into a round room that, in the dim light resembled the portal chamber beneath Joe's house. There were some candles in a box on the floor and some sconces on the walls. Joe took up two stubs of candle, lit them, and placed them in the sconces nearest the passage through which they'd entered.

"Now, quench the illumination spell. It may take a moment now that you have it going so well. Steady yourself against the wall."

Joe was right. It took Eddie several tries to disassemble the thought sequence in his head. It reminded him of trying to get a popular tune out of his mind. Eventually he did it by concentrating on the memory of Lena's voice. As the spell finally ended, the young man felt a touch of vertigo. He was glad for the wall next to him.

In the flickering light of the candle, Eddie looked more carefully around him. The room was indeed similar to the one beneath Joe's house – at least in the way Eddie remembered it. There was the same curved walkway around the periphery, the same pit at the center. The same polished ceiling that gave the dim glow of the candles back to them. This space was larger, however, and possessed an even more ancient quality.

"Well done, son. Now do you remember how to make the transition?"

"I think so. I walk backwards around the edge three times. When I feel the change in the room, I step backwards off the lip into the pit."

"That's basically it. Remember that you need to walk counterclockwise."

Eddie nodded. "I fell last time and got wet," he said.

"That happens. Try springing up just a tiny bit and flexing your knees. Now that you know what to expect you'll be more likely to keep your balance."

Joe continued. "I'll go through first. There are disturbances in the Place. Wait five or ten seconds after I vanish before you start walking backwards. Remember to go counterclockwise. Got it?"

"Got it," Eddie replied. He realized that he was breathing shallowly and he deliberately slowed and deepened his breathing.

"Stand back in the doorway. When we meet in the Place, we'll head for some standing stones. I'll stand between two of them and cast a spell of finding. That will point us towards the portal back into my world.

Our world. We will need to move quickly and as silently as possible. No talking. I'll point and move. You follow. Now let's get on with it."

Without waiting for a reply, Joe began his circuit around the pit. Eddie quickly stepped back into the doorway to be out of his teacher's way as the man passed. Once, twice, three times, Joe walked backwards. The candles flickered and the strange keening sound emanated from the stones. A glowing, sourceless illumination added a bluish cast to the candlelight. Moving backwards, Joe stepped lightly off the lip of the pit. He vanished before he'd fallen more than a foot or so.

The candlelight steadied, and the sound and bluish light both faded. Eddie swallowed and took a deep breath. The wailing sound made him nervous, ill-at-ease. He counted to five and then began his circumambulation. At the end of his third cycle, the now familiar changes in light and sound rose up.

Trying to emulate Joe's limber, confident movements, Eddie stepped backwards off the lip of the path. He again sensed that instant of icy cold, that brief feeling of resistance. This time he landed on his feet. He stumbled a little, but managed to regain his balance.

The young man peered through the drifting tendrils of fog. Joe stood off perhaps twenty feet to the side. The ground was moist and spongy underfoot. It was warm and humid, just as Eddie remembered from his first visit. There were sounds in the mist too, indeterminate sounds at indeterminate distances. Joe, with some urgency, motioned for Eddie to join him and as soon as the younger man got close, the older man turned and moved quickly away.

Within moments, a large standing stone emerged from the mist. There were two more close by. Without stopping at the first stone, Joe made for the pair of stones. When they reached these rugged megaliths, Joe stood between them. Holding his left hand aloft, he wove a quick pattern with his right, all the while speaking under his breath. A brilliant beam of actinic light shown from his raised palm. The light cut through the fog and illuminated a cairn that stood in the middle distance and slightly off to one side. Something smooth, hard, and conical capped the rough stone cairn.

Joe glanced at Eddie and nodded. Moving with surprising speed, the old warrior sprinted for the cairn. Eddie ran as fast as he could over the intervening fifty yards. Footing was treacherous on the moist ground. When they were just a few feet from the cairn, Eddie saw that it was indeed capped by a sort of inverted funnel made of a silver-gray metal. At that instant, they heard a baying ululation some distance behind them.

It was a sound unlike any that Eddie had experienced. The sound had some characteristics of a human voice, but it was pitched strangely and resonated in a way that made Eddie think it could not have come from a human throat. When the sound reached them, Joe hurled himself forward to the wall of the structure.

Upon gaining the base of the cairn, the older man laid his hands upon it at chest height. He whispered and immediately an outline formed, then an image. It was the image of a door.

The baying ululation came again, clearly closer. The image solidified and became a door. The door swung inwards. Joe turned, grabbed Eddie by the arm, and literally flung the younger man through the open doorway. Eddie spun to see Joe leap towards the door as a large shape loomed in the mist.

Joe crossed the threshold just as the shape resolved into a hideous creature, a perverted combination of human, serpent, and wolf. Naked and rank, surrounded by an evil smell, it loped toward them. Scaly breasts swung grotesquely beneath the deep chest. Its muddy legs pounded against the damp ground as it came on. And above all, frozen in a grotesque, lupine caricature of her former beauty, Alica's face snarled at them as the door slammed to.

The door shook with the impact and they stood in darkness. At a word, Joe brought light to the space around them. They stood at the bottom of a shallow, circular pit. Where the door had stood, there was now an unbroken expanse of stone blocks.

"We're back," Joe announced. "Let's get upstairs."

Michael C. Glaviano

Thirty Three

The beast howled in frustration as it recoiled from its impact on the stone wall. So close! Her hunger new no bounds. She salivated, and great threads dripped from her muzzle. Dimly, she knew that this had been her quarry. Killing them, rending them, feeding upon them, surely would have brought her peace. Instead, her torment grew.

She ran from the place of the stones. She sought something to kill, but most of the easy prey had learned to avoid her. On and on she ran through the hot, moist, mist-shrouded landscape. Each time she crossed the trail of her quarry, she howled her displeasure and frustration. Absorbed by the dense, moist atmosphere, scattered by the shifting landscape, the strange plants and structures, the sound fled before her.

Now she ran further afield. She grew lost and disoriented in the dim landscape. Traces of her quarry grew faint. She ran and ran until her lungs burned and she could run no further. Hurling herself to the ground, she rested. Panting, panting, panting, she gasped for air in the warm, foggy atmosphere. Gradually, she calmed. Her paws were cut from passage over rocks and she licked the wounds.

Eventually, she hunted again, but all she found were small things, prey that kept her hunger at bay but which never sated. She was weaker than she could have been. If only she could feed! She hunted, ate, rested, hunted again. This went on for a long time. There were no days or nights in this misty Place. There was only this warm, foggy, *now*.

She lay again and rested. In her torment, the Alicia creature still possessed a sense of past, a sense of future, and she brooded on the past. She shied away from fleeting memories that brought new anguish and humiliation. With effort, she forced herself to consider future opportunities, hunts that would occur in a time removed from this unhappy, foggy *now*. Next time she would catch their scent sooner. Next time she would be faster. Next time she would leap and strike.

Michael C. Glaviano

Thirty Four

The rim of the pit was at chest height on Eddie, slightly higher on Joe. The older man put his hands on the rim and pushed himself up. He swung his left leg up and easily pulled himself onto the smooth annular floor of the chamber. As he watched, Eddie realized that less than a year previously, he would have been embarrassed at being unable to follow. As it was, he matched Joe's graceful move without trouble.

They trudged up the passage in silence. Eventually, they reached the basement and then the main floor of Joe's house on Painter Avenue. The phone was ringing. Joe went into the kitchen and picked it up. It was Sergeant Driscoll.

"Yes, Sergeant. I realize that I have been out of town, but I've just returned. Eddie is back as well. No, he had to go out of town for several months on business. Oh. Well, I do apologize for the trouble. Again, we've only just returned and I haven't had a chance to check the house, but what little I've seen looks fine so far. We are planning on some more trips, but we will let you know the next time we leave. Yes... Yes... I understand. Thank you, Sergeant. Good-bye."

Joe hung up the phone and turned to Eddie.

"Evidently, the good sergeant has been worried about us. I have come through here from time-to-time over the past several months and have checked in occasionally, but Sergeant Driscoll is who she is. And she worries."

"Uh... does she know about... well, about you?"

"Nothing. At some point, I'll have to move away and live elsewhere until most of the people who know me here are gone. That is sad, but it can't be helped. I do wish that I could take the good sergeant into my confidence, but I have the sense that her personality is such that it would be difficult, likely impossible, for her to accept a reality that is so drastically different from her day-to-day experience."

"Joe. Not to change the subject, but that, that *thing*. That came out of the mist? It looked sort of like..."

"Like the woman we've called 'Alicia?'"

"Yeah. Her."

"Yes. I believe that the ministrations of the Locust Queen and unrelenting fear, coupled with the frustrations of an unfulfilled hunt, drove her mad. She has taken ill-considered actions, made irreversible choices. No longer human, she now lurks in the Great Hub bent on violence. She is, in some ways at least, still intelligent, and she is very dangerous."

"What can we do?"

"To avoid an encounter with her? Not very much. We'll be watchful and quick when we must travel through."

"Can she track us?"

"I doubt that she could leave the Place at this point. She may be able to follow our trail, but the Great Hub is infinite and trails go cold rapidly there."

Joe was silent for a moment. Then he added, "It was she who injured me on my last trip through the Place."

"I wondered about that. How?"

"She picked up my scent and followed me. She sensed me from a distance and ran toward me. I did not suspect her existence and was in the process of moving back to the portal beneath the Inn. Her transformation was incomplete. Her hands could still function as hands. She saw that she could not reach me in time, so she picked up a large rock – nearly a small boulder – and hurled it at me. It was fortunate that I was nearly through. It was only a glancing blow, but afterwards I was in no condition to do battle with her."

"So that's why we needed to hurry this time, right?"

"Well, generally I dislike tarrying in the Place Between. There are too many strange things. Probabilities are wrong. The dreams of the gods can be terribly real while reality can become illusory. No few of my friends and colleagues have met their ends there, may the gods dream of them again."

"But, now especially. With Alicia on the hunt."

"Yes. I don't know how long she will last there or what will become of her, but until we can figure out a defense or some other action, we need to move with extra speed. We must transit between the worlds as quickly as we can."

Eddie nodded. "Okay. So now what? What's next?"

"Well, son, next we get the forest lady's seeds in the ground. I'm thinking that we should locate the nearest protected lands – something like a national forest or national park – and get there right away. There are areas north of here that will suffice, I believe."

"So as soon as Maia's forest is started, we return? To Lena's world?"

"Indeed. I won't separate you and your young woman any longer than necessary. Let's get busy, shall we? You can call the bus station now and obtain information on northbound buses. While you're doing that, I'll get some maps and see what we can find within a day's ride."

So Eddie looked through the directory and found the numbers for Continental Trailways and for Greyhound. He called them and jotted down schedules for northbound routes both departures and arrivals.

He'd just finished when Joe came back holding a map. He pointed to a national forest some four hundred miles to the north. It was bordered on its south by a much smaller state park.

"Here we are. Let's establish the Lady of the Forest here. In this world, our world, her trees will become particularly healthy specimens of native species. They will merge with the forest and strengthen it. Under her care, the forest will nurture all manner of life. She is not a corporeal being in the sense that we are, and her magic is of a different order than ours. As I mentioned last night, she'll be able to travel between the worlds instantaneously. In a sense, this forest and the forest where you met her will become one. Both worlds will be the better for it."

"Are you going to talk to her about extending her forest to the Queen's world? The Blue World?"

"I intend to try, but first let's get this done."

Joe indicated a small circle on the map. "Here's the only town of any significance that's near the forest. Suppose you see when we could reach there by bus. If we have to, we'll make hotel reservations, then get a rental car once we arrive. You take care of that. I'll make us something to eat. Sound good?"

The town nearest to their destination was a place called Furnace Creek. It looked like the population was in the neighborhood of 5000. Eddie could remember pulling off the interstate to cruise through many similar towns during his Drive Away days.

He poured over the bus schedules. Continental Trailways had the soonest bus, but it didn't stop at the town, so he tried the Greyhound people. They had a small terminal there, so he made two round-trip reservations for a bus departing at six-thirty that evening. Unfortunately, it made multiple stops along the way. They'd arrive at Furnace Creek, around two in the morning.

Such an early morning arrival time suggested that they have a place to rest for a few hours before setting out, so Eddie called and made reservations at a Travelodge in Furnace Creek. The woman at the Travelodge guaranteed late arrival and assured him that there was a rental car agency in town. It was called "Warren's Wild Wheels." She looked up the phone number for Eddie, and he was able to speak directly with "Warren."

Warren was a helpful, loquacious person with a hint of a Brooklyn accent. He assured Eddie that he had good cars and that he'd be open bright and early the next morning. Arrangements complete, Eddie hung up. He organized his notes and got times, places, and phone numbers all in order on a single sheet of paper.

Over lunch, they reviewed the plans. Then, as they washed up the lunch things, Joe suggested that Eddie take the bus to a nearby supermarket and purchase some supplies while he looked over the house and made sure that all the protective spells were in order.

Eddie walked to the corner and caught the local bus. On a whim he stopped in for a quick visit with Sergeant Driscoll. She was, in her own way, glad to see him.

"So. Look what wandered in. Lose any expensive cars, kid?"

"No ma'am. I've been out of town doing some things for Joe. We're getting ready to leave and go hiking and relax a bit. Should be fun. I'm going to go get some food for the trip and thought I'd drop by and say hi."

"Well, you look healthy enough. You been keepin' out of trouble?"

"As best I can, Sergeant. As best I can."

"You keep that stayin' out of trouble thing goin'. Got it?"

"Yes ma'am."

"Well. Okay. Unless you have some official business, I better get back to it. Lots of reports. The. Usual. Crap."

"All right then. We'll be gone at most for a day or two. Back by the end of the week at the latest. Just thought I'd let you know. Bye, Sergeant."

The sergeant nodded her head on her short, thick neck. "Bye, kid."

Eddie waved and turned to leave. Just as he was going out the door, the sergeant added, "Thanks for dropping by, kid. Glad you're doin' okay."

That errand accomplished, Eddie completed his shopping. He trundled his bags onto the bus and rode back to the house on Painter. When he got in, he saw that Joe had brought a couple of suitcases up from the basement.

"Here you go, son. Suppose you go up to your rooms and pack. You won't need much. If we get out of here this evening, we should be able to do this as a day trip tomorrow and catch the bus back in the afternoon. I checked the forecast. Make sure you bring a rain parka. While you pack I'll get us a cab."

Eddie dashed up the stairs to his rooms. Everything was undisturbed and not too dusty. He guessed that Joe had had the house cleaners in sometime in the past couple of weeks. Looking around, he realized that he'd missed these rooms and hoped that he'd be able to bring Lena here someday for a visit. Not that the town was great, or even very nice, but these rooms and this house were so comfortable and safe feeling. Eddie wanted her to see them, to share them with her.

It took very little time to throw together some clean things for the trip. Small suitcase in hand, he clattered back down the stairs.

"The cab will be here in a few minutes."

"Okay. I stopped by and said hello to Sergeant Driscoll. Let her know that we'd be back by the end of the week."

"That was considerate. I'm sure she appreciated it." Joe chuckled. "She does think that she needs to look out for me."

"Yeah. Me too, I think. How's the house?"

"Just the usual probes here and there. Nothing serious. No concerted effort since I was here last... Anyway, are you all ready?"

"Yeah. I think so."

"Where is the packet? From the Lady?"

"It's in my suitcase. Think it'll be okay there?"

"Probably, but it might be better if you kept it on your person. Will it fit in your shirt pocket?

Eddie opened his suitcase and took out the packet. With the rabbit pelt around it, the small package was too thick to fit into his shirt pocket, but it slid neatly into his inside jacket pocket.

"That's better I guess. It's also sort of nice knowing it's right there. Over my heart and all."

Joe smiled. Just then the cab pulled up and honked for them. The men grabbed their suitcases and walked out the front door. Joe paused to lock the door behind them.

It was a short ride. The Greyhound station was a block beyond the bar where Eddie had been mugged. Their route took them around the square and Eddie noticed that the bar was now closed. He said as much to Joe.

"It's a sad day when even a bar can't stay open."

"Oh, I don't know, son. Maybe it's a good sign that that particular bar had to close. It didn't exactly function as a healthy anchor for the community now, did it?"

"Excuse me, Driver," Joe spoke up. "Do you know when that bar closed? The one we just passed."

"Oh, yeah. Lemme see. It was four... maybe five months ago. The cops raided it. Word was out they was usin' it to fence stolen stuff."

"Thank you. We just wondered. We'd had a bit of a run-in with some of the people who hung out there."

"Yeah. Bad guys. Bad, but stupid. Like they thought they was big shots. But they was nothin'. Just small time hoods. Real small. None of the drivers liked pickin' up fares around here. Now it ain't quite so bad. Strange times."

"Strange times, indeed. Well, I do believe we've arrived."

"Yep. Greyhound station. Still here."

Joe and Eddie got out of the cab with their suitcases. Joe paid the driver and the men entered the bus terminal. They checked in and located the gate for their bus. They had just over a half hour to wait. The station wasn't crowded but it wasn't empty either. As Eddie had noticed on his previous visit, posted departures outnumbered arrivals by a conspicuous margin.

They found a couple of seats where they wouldn't be overheard and discussed their plans. Eventually Eddie asked Joe if they would have time to complete the "drop-box" between Baleen Park and Joe's house while they were here.

"Yes. We should be able to do that, Joe agreed. "It will take only a few minutes. If I don't mention it, please feel free to remind me after we return to the house.

"Now, I believe they're calling us to board our bus," he added.

Eddie and Joe went over to the line. The queue wasn't very long and they moved to the front of it quickly. The driver and a helper loaded their bags into the cargo area beneath the coach and then the men boarded. The bus was less than half full when the door hissed closed, so they took neighboring aisle seats.

Late autumn shadows were already growing long when, more-or-less on schedule, the bus pulled out of the station. It took only a few minutes to drive through the seedier parts of town and reach the main highway north. Joe and Eddie chatted quietly for another quarter hour, then fell silent. Eddie stared at the overhead rack and wished that he had a book or a magazine. Big diesel engine rumbling, the bus rolled up the interstate.

At some point Eddie must have fallen asleep because it was full dark when, hours later, they reached their first stop. The driver announced the time and the length of the stop. They had already traveled half the distance to their destination.

Joe and Eddie got off the coach and walked around the parking lot to stretch their legs. The air was chilly but enjoyably fresh after the confines of the bus. They considered going into the roadside diner for some food, but neither felt like it particularly, so they opted to snack on the food they'd brought with them.

Before long, the driver came out and opened the bus. The other passengers trickled back onto the bus and settled in. Again the men talked a little, but neither was given to small talk and neither wanted to be overheard discussing their real concerns. As the Greyhound continued to eat up the miles, each of them withdrew once more into his own thoughts. Eventually, Eddie dozed off again and cat-napped for the rest of the trip north.

*   *   *

"We're here. Hopefully we'll be able to find a cab," Joe said as they pulled into the tiny Greyhound station in Furnace Creek.

Eddie struggled out of a fitful half-slumber. The driver cut the engine. The sudden absence of vibration and deep sound left his ears feeling strangely empty. He rubbed his face, then stood and stretched before heading for the door.

It was raining and cold as they stepped from the bus. The air smelled fresh, and a hint of pine from nearby mountain forests reminded Eddie of Lena's world. For an instant, the sense of place was vivid, but then it faded and left behind little beyond his eagerness to finish this errand so that he could return.

The driver had the cargo doors open and was pulling the bags, suitcases, and packs from the belly of the bus. It appeared that most of the passengers were continuing into Canada and had to go through Customs. Eddie and Joe claimed their suitcases and then headed for the front of the terminal. It was nearly two-thirty and there were no cabs, but next door to the tiny bus station was an all night diner.

The diner was warm inside. They took a booth by the windows so they could slide their suitcases on the floor under the table. A tired, middle-aged waitress came over and poured coffee. Her uniform might have looked good on a much younger, more fit woman. On her, it looked merely uncomfortable. When asked about taxis, she said there were usually two or three cabs working graveyard. They were out on fares, but she expected them back within the hour.

"Let's get some breakfast. It'll be something to do," Eddie suggested.

"That sounds fine. Afterwards, we can relax and get cleaned up at the hotel. We'll contact the rental agency when they open."

So they ordered. The food arrived within fifteen minutes or so. Eddie's "Spanish" omelette was slightly on the greasy side, but not too bad. The sourdough toast was okay, the potatoes just so-so. The rain got heavier while they ate.

"Looks like there's a cab at the stand now," Eddie nodded at the window.

They finished their food, retrieved their bags and paid. By the time they reached the cab stand, the first taxi had left, but there was a covered area where they could wait. Another cab turned up within minutes. Eddie pulled out his notes and gave the driver the address of the Travelodge. Furnace Creek was small, and they reached the hotel quickly. If not for the rain and the darkness, they could have walked the distance easily.

Their rooms were waiting as promised. Eddie didn't think he'd sleep after dozing on the bus and eating breakfast, but he decided to lie down anyway. He punched in a seven o'clock wake up call. Then, staring at the dimly lit ceiling, the young man stretched out on the bed. The room was quiet and still. The only sound was the steady rain outside. He turned over on his side and fell asleep within minutes.

The wake up call roused Eddie from a sound sleep. The window faced due east and the tiniest bit of pre-dawn light leaked around the drapes. While he had slept the rain had stopped. A quick shower and a change of clothes brought him fully awake. Joe called as he was tying his hiking boots.

"Let's meet in the lobby in fifteen minutes."

"Right. I'll be there."

Before he left his room, Eddie called the car rental agency. He expected to get a recording and was surprised when a sleepy voice answered, "Warren's."

"Um, yeah. I called yesterday and reserved a car to take up to the forest for a hike? I'm at the Travelodge."

"Yeah. Sure. I remember. I can be over there in about fifteen minutes with a car. Or youse can walk up to my lot. It's right up the main drag from the motel. You don't gotta turn or nothin'. Just walk on up. It'll be on the left side."

"That's fine. We'll walk up." Before he hung up, Eddie confirmed the address.

The lobby was mostly deserted. There were some unappealing food-like items strewn around on a counter top. Nothing looked particularly interesting, and Eddie was still full from breakfast.

"I talked to the rental car guy. Think I woke him up, but he says that if we walk up to his lot, he'll have a car ready."

"That's good. I'd like to get out there, do our errand, and get back to town."

"Same here."

So they checked out of the hotel and, bags in hand, walked up the street. It was cold and the sky was overcast. The streets were wet and rain threatened to return. There was very little vehicle traffic and, except for the two men, no pedestrians.

It was easy to spot "Warren's Wild Wheels." An old gas station hove into view within five minutes. There were a dozen or so vehicles in varying states of repair parked in front. A hand-painted sign announced "cars and trucks for sale or rent."

By the time they walked up, Warren was outside with a cup of coffee and a cigarette. He was perhaps five and half feet tall and wiry. On the phone, Eddie had pictured an older man, but Warren looked to be about 35. He had a heavy beard and his thinning, dark, curly hair was still sleep-rumpled. His windbreaker didn't look adequate to the chill air, but Warren appeared relaxed and cheerful as he watched them approach. He had a dark maroon Subaru Forester waiting in the front of the lot. The tires were good and the car was idling smoothly.

"We'll just need it for the day," Joe said.

"Right. That's what your compadre, here, said when he called."

"So could we pay in advance and just drop the car off this afternoon?"

"Sure thing, Mac. I could use the cash. Things is slow this time of year. Now summers. Summers is great. Lots of fishermen and camper types. But when the weather turns. Bam. Business drops off a cliff."

"Indeed. Well, in any event, we'll be driving up to the state park. We'll look around, perhaps do a day hike into the national forest. Then we'll return."

"Short trip. Youse just checkin' out the neighborhood? If you was gonna be in town for a few days, I could arrange some tours. There's some good places to fish and all."

"If I enjoy the area on this first trip, I expect to return often. At some point, I may want to purchase a cabin nearby. It would serve as a retirement place. My nephew, here, has kindly offered to accompany me on this initial trip, but he must get back down south as quickly as possible."

"Retirement, eh? Furnace Creek is a good town. Friendly and all. There's a couple of real estate guys here. Part time. Lemme know, and I can introduce youse."

"Thank you, Warren. I may take you up on your offer."

As quickly and politely as they could, they disengaged themselves from Warren's banter. They put their bags in the back of the vehicle and drove slowly through town. At the north end of the village, they found the highway that led into the state park.

They turned left at the intersection. Almost immediately, the road began to climb. The two-lane highway wound along the contours of the land. Several times, rain sprinkled briefly and then paused. The Subaru wasn't new, but whatever Warren's other attributes he was obviously able to repair and maintain automobiles. The Forester was clean inside and out, and it ran perfectly. The heater worked and their feet were glad for the warm air.

After an hour's drive, they reached a parking area and a trailhead. There was a map of the park mounted behind glass on the wall of a rustic building that housed the park's restrooms. The parking lot was empty. Overhead, clouds continued to threaten and the air was cold, but the sprinkling rain had taken a break.

Joe pointed at the map of the park. "Let's take this trail," he suggested. "It's six miles each way, and they've helpfully rated it as 'Easy.' It looks like the trail crosses into the national forest at around the four mile mark. If the terrain is flat, I would guess that we can cover the distance to the turnaround point in less than two hours. Do you have the seed packet?"

"Right here," Eddie patted his jacket pocket gently.

They started up the trail. It meandered slightly up and down, but it was not steep. The air was even colder beneath the trees. Joe set a good pace, however, and they were soon warm enough to unzip their rain parkas.

As they walked, Eddie tried to identify the trees and other plants. He'd seen a few of them in Maia's forest; although these specimens included more evergreens while Maia's had been mostly a seasonal forest. Also, the land in this state park had obviously been clear cut at some point. There was more underbrush here and none of the timber had the majesty of the Lady's trees. Still there was more than one species of tree and there were no obvious signs of disease or damage.

After twenty or thirty minutes of steady travel, Eddie realized that he was now in good enough condition to allow some conversation as they walked.

"Do you think she'll like it here? The Lady?"

"Well, I am sure she'll help this wood to grow stronger, and her health and that of her forest are one and the same. If at some point I do take up residence nearby, I will do what I can to help her. Once she is settled in, I am sure she will find this world suitable."

"And that can help this world?"

"It will take time, but eventually, yes. This forest, and the Lady's passage between worlds, these will make the membrane that separates this world from the Great Hub more permeable."

They fell silent again. The trail stayed very manageable and Joe kept up the pace. They took one short break at about an hour in, but neither man really wanted to stop. Shortly thereafter, they crossed into the national forest. They reached a clearing and a trail marker before they'd walked an hour and three-quarters.

"This will suffice, I think. Somewhere around here." Joe looked around.

"What are we looking for?"

"Somewhere sheltered. We want to bury her seed packet so that it won't be disturbed. Once she is established here, she will be able to protect herself from all but deliberate mischief. Since magic is so weak in this world, she will be vulnerable only to a concerted, physical attack."

Eddie remembered the twisted creature that had tormented Maia's trees. He was glad she would not face such attacks in this place.

"What about those rocks?" There were some boulders on the other side of the clearing. They were just visible beneath the trees.

"That might work. Let's look closer."

Eddie started across the clearing, but Joe stopped him. "Let's walk around the clearing beneath the trees. You take one side, and I'll take the other. Look for old campsites or evidence that this place receives a great deal of traffic."

The Locust Queen's Feast

So each walked around one side of the clearing. Eddie tried to muster all of his woodcraft, but he saw nothing that gave evidence of frequent visits. None of the trees had been damaged or defaced. None of the boulders had been tagged. Old nests in the taller trees implied that birds returned to the area in the spring.

Eventually, they met at the boulders beneath the trees. Joe announced that his side looked fine and given the fact that winter weather would soon provide cover, this would be a good place for the Lady's seed packet.

Eddie got down on his knees near the boulders. There were several rocks and three of them were huge. Eddie started to scoop dirt away from the base of the biggest.

"Stand back, son. Even though very little magic remains in this world, I should be able to summon a small spell that will help."

Eddie stepped back beneath the trees. Joe walked over to the rocks and closed his eyes. He stood completely still for a handful of minutes. Then he opened his eyes and looked down. Casting around, he gathered some pebbles. These he fashioned into a small pile where Eddie had scooped away the soil with his hands.

Eyes focused on the little pile of rocks, Joe retreated a step, then another. Eddie watched as his teacher began to chant softly and weave his hands in complicated patterns. Gradually, a humming grew in the area around them. The earth near the boulders began to stir, then roil. At last, looking like nothing so much as a tiny geyser of soil, the dirt rose up. It left behind a very neat hole some two feet deep and half a foot wide.

Joe took out a handkerchief and mopped his forehead. "I am reminded once again of the importance that we're doing this. That spell was many times more complicated and difficult than it needed to be, than it should have been. I believe it took more effort than the entire walk from the car. But the fight is joined, son. Through today's events and other actions, we will heal this world and return magic to its rightful place."

Eddie looked around. The forest held its breath. The light beneath the trees had taken on a surreal quality that slowly faded.

"So I put the seed packet in the hole?"

"Yes. You can put the whole package in there, rabbit skin and all. Just place it gently at the bottom. Cover it with the earth that I have called forth. Smooth it with your hands and then back away. No need to pack the dirt down."

Eddie stepped forward and knelt on the ground near the boulders. He reached inside his jacket and pulled out the little package. He placed the packet carefully at the bottom of the hole and then covered it with the soft, moist earth. Finally, he patted the soil gently and smoothed it. As an afterthought, he went over to some nearby trees and gathered pine needles which he sprinkled over the whole area.

"You have done it, my friends! I can feel this world! It is hurt and needs much care, but I am here!"

Both men turned at the sound. Maia walked toward them holding out her hands. Barefooted and wearing only a plain white shift, she was just as Eddie remembered her. She was completely at home, completely comfortable in the chilly autumn air.

"Reed Woodruff. I remember you! And this man... This powerful man... Yes, from many, many turnings back. My forest was much smaller. Known to my aunt, you were."

Joe bowed his head and spoke, gesturing towards Eddie.

"Lady, this young one has faithfully opened a path for you into this troubled world. May your forest grow and span many worlds. May it bring peace and light to them all."

Maia laughed, and such birds as remained so late in the year flew near and burst into song around her.

"You have done well, and I thank you for it!"

She walked to the place where her seed packet was buried. For the first time, Eddie noticed that her bare feet left no trace or track in the soil. Looking down, Maia smiled and a tear fell from her eye to land on the earth. A tree burst from the soil and as they watched, it grew to a height and shape indistinguishable from those around it.

The forest lady stepped back and again faced the men.

"This will become a deep place. Remember it. For as long as I dwell on this world, you may find me here. My trees will grow strong, but they will grow together, in concert with the life that is already here. Only you will know that this place is different, that I may be found here."

She held her hand out to Eddie. Remembering her power and strangeness, remembering the pattern of scars that marked his cheek, he took her hand gently and tentatively. She smiled once more and spoke.

"You, young Reed Woodruff. You, who will walk the worlds for but an instant. I acknowledge that you have used a part of your precious time to discharge your promise to me. I acknowledge your goodness, your faithfulness. Know this: your children and your children's children, for as long as your line endures, shall find shelter and safety beneath my branches. My waters will quench their thirst. The life of my forest will nourish them."

She released his hand and the young man drew a long breath. His heart was full and happy. He thought carefully for a few heartbeats and then raised his gaze to meet the glowing eyes of the forest lady. "Thank you, Maia. Thank you for the boon you have granted to me and my descendants."

Now Joe spoke up, "One more thing, Lady. When the time comes, I may come to ask if you would extend your forest to the very world of the Locust Queen, to the Blue World."

Instantly Maia grew very still. A tiny furrow formed between her strange, beautiful eyes. She looked back and forth between the two men and drew back a pace.

"In the past, the Queen's minions have hurt me, hurt my forest. She has caused greater forests than mine to be utterly destroyed. I would have to think long on what you ask. I have feelings for you and bear good men no ill will, but my needs are not your needs. My dreams are not yours. Come again in the spring. I will be stronger then. If you truly can strike against the Queen, I may play a part, but you may not rely upon my forest to fight in your stead or to sacrifice its life in one of your schemes."

Joe bowed his head again and said nothing.

When he did not argue or press his case, Maia brightened somewhat, though the tone of her words was more distant now.

"Reed, Old One, once more I thank you for what you have done this day. I hope to feel again your gentle tread on the land beneath my boughs."

"Now, you must fly away," she continued. "You must move as swiftly as your feet may carry you. I call forth a storm to erase your spoor, to hide this place more fully. I call forth a storm to nourish that which you have placed within the sheltering earth. I call forth a storm to see what I may learn of this place and how it fits into the web of the worlds. Now fly! Fly!"

She clapped her hands and thunder rolled off to the north.

"Maia–" Eddie started, not sure what to say.

"I know, young Reed Woodruff. I know of your constancy, your fidelity. I see the love you hold in your heart for the young woman, and I pledge that the boons I grant to you shall be hers also. Now fly! Do not tarry!"

"Let's go, son. She means it." Joe spoke softly. Without waiting for a response, he turned away and started moving toward the trail.

Maia clapped her hands again, and once more thunder rumbled, closer now. Her eyes blazed with a golden light.

Eddie raised a hand and waved. Then he turned to follow his teacher.

This time Joe set a grueling pace. When the trail was broken and rough, he jogged. When the path smoothed, he ran. His eyes were focused and sharp. It was all Eddie could do to keep up. Within fifteen minutes, it was raining. By the time they reached the trailhead, the rain was pouring down and Eddie was very glad for his rain parka.

The Subaru was still the only vehicle parked at the trailhead. They got in and drove out of the park, back down to Furnace Creek. Rain followed them the whole way. They reached the town and returned the car to Warren. Even in the rain it was a short walk past the hotel to the bus station. There was a mid-afternoon bus going south and they confirmed their seats on it.

Each man was busy with his own thoughts and they hardly spoke the rest of the day.

* * *

The next morning, back at the Painter Avenue house, Eddie was all for getting back through the Place right away. He missed Lena. His feelings for her, coupled with the grim surroundings of Joe's home town conspired to weaken the connection he felt with his native world. For his part, Joe argued for caution and at least some kind of plan for safe passage.

"I too would like to return quickly, but it will serve no purpose if we are killed or maimed during our transit. We must have a way to disable, confound, or at very least distract that creature."

"I read about how to do a stun spell. Would that work?"

"It might. If we knew how strong she has become, we would be able to decide that. But I have been doing this work for a long while, Eddie. Let me spend some time on it this afternoon. My thought is that a compound spell would be our best bet."

"That's two spells, right?"

"Two or more. I'm thinking that to be safe, I will want to set up a sequence of a half-dozen or so powerful spells. I will hold them in my mind to be released via a single trigger word."

"Okay, fine. Let's do that."

"Easy for you to say, son. I've got to figure the sequence and map it to the trigger word. And we must consider the effects performing such a spell will have on me. Even with a close balance of endo and exoplasmic forces, performing such a complex event inside the Place will weaken me severely. That means it'll be up to you to get us both through the exit portal."

"Hmmm. Maybe I'll go outside and practice my knife throwing."

"That might not be a bad idea. I've been thinking about that, though. Given what we're dealing with, why don't you see if you can learn to throw a small axe? If I remember right, there are various types of throwing axes in the basement. Look near the back wall. You'll find an interesting collection of old and new weapons."

"Okay. I'll go look. I'm sure I could throw one."

Joe smiled slightly. "Well, yes. Throwing one is relatively easy..."

"Yeah, I know. The trick is hitting what you want to hit. I'll go look... but, Joe?"

"Yes?"

"Well, it's just that before you get going on all that prep work, do you think we could set up the connection so that Lena and I can pass messages back and forth?"

"Of course. Thanks for reminding me. That won't take long. Let's go out to the garden now and take care of it."

"Great!"

The two men walked out through the greenhouse and into the back yard. On the way, Joe picked up a hand trowel and a weed puller. He walked back and forth along the old masonry wall at the rear of the property. The barrier was over two feet thick and a little more than chest height. Eventually, he found a spot near the ground where the mortar around a brick had begun to crumble. He knelt and set to work with the tools. In a matter of minutes he had pried the brick loose. He dug around in the back of the hole to enlarge the space.

"First, I will establish the connection between this small space and Lena's world," he explained.

Joe faced the little space in the wall. He closed his eyes and covered the spot with his hands. Nothing happened for a while, but then Eddie could see light leaking around and through Joe's fingers. Finally, Joe took a deep breath and let it out. He opened his eyes and reached into the space.

"Here's your coin, son. Now, let's send something back to complete and stabilize the connection. Anything small will do."

Eddie pocketed the coin. Then he stooped and picked up a small rock. "That's really something! Thanks, Joe. Okay. Will this do?"

"Yes, of course."

Joe placed the pebble in the space and slid the brick back into place. As he stood, the old man brushed a little dirt from the knees of his work pants.

"That little rock will be waiting for you when you slide the brick out in the wall at Baleen Park. Going forward, the process will be automatic."

"Hey, does this mean that there is a way to go directly between worlds without traveling though the Place?"

"In theory, yes. But it would take a great spell to accomplish that for a corporeal being. It would require a huge expenditure of energy and it could potentially damage the balance of the worlds and perhaps even the Great Hub itself. I would not attempt it unless there were no alternative."

"So why was this so easy? It only took you a few minutes at each site."

"This technique can send a few ounces of inert matter back and forth for you. Nothing alive. Nothing much heavier than that pebble. Nothing with physical attributes that are likely to disrupt the balance. And I should point out that Iris Abellona did the initial setup for this decades ago when she was at the height of her powers. Even this limited capability would have been much more difficult had she not built the foundation for us.

"Again, as I said to you on the other side, in Baleen Park. Use this well."

"I will, Joe. Thanks for doing this. For Lena and me."

Joe nodded and gave the younger man a slight smile.

"My pleasure. Next I must develop a plan to get us through another transit. Suppose you see what you can do with a throwing axe. You have made great progress on many fronts in these past months, but my recommendation is what it would be with any other new endeavor: begin slowly and easily with it."

Eddie picked up the garden tools and followed Joe back through the greenhouse. Then, while Joe closed himself in his rooms on the second floor to develop a plan for getting them through the Place, Eddie rummaged through the shelves and lockers in the basement. He ran across many interesting and bewildering things before finally opening a steel cabinet to find a collection of medieval weapons.

Some of the weapons looked like they had been used in the Crusades. A few, however, were modern updates. Eddie found several double-bladed axes, but most were heavy and obviously suited to close combat rather than throwing.

These weapons were about a yard long and weighed three to five pounds. About half of them had symmetrical blades that were perhaps eight inches in length; others featured a long, jagged point on one side. In the case of the antique battle-axes, many of the blades were notched and dark with stains and rust. Some of the handles were splintered and gashed. They were ugly things, gruesome to consider.

Tentatively, Eddie took up one of the old weapons. He felt the heft of it. With his arm extended, he sited down the handle, turned it. It was quiet in the shadowy basement, and for a moment, the young man lost himself as he imagined the history of the grim artifact.

Whose hand had wielded the axe on the day it garnered those notches? Those stains? Had the weapon been Joe's? The breath of centuries ran down the young man's arm, his neck, and he shivered.

Eventually, Eddie decided that even the smallest battle-axe would be too large and bulky for his purposes. He closed the cabinet and was about to give up his search when he noticed a small footlocker on the bottom shelf of a large metal rack that stood next to the steel cabinet.

Kneeling, he dragged the footlocker from the shelf. The hasp was not secured but was stiff from disuse. Eddie lifted the lid and found a selection of what could only be described as throwing axes. Each was perhaps a foot long. As in the case of the battle-axes, all were double-bladed, but the blades took different forms. Some were symmetrical; others had a sharp point on one side and a curved blade on the other.

Some were forged from a single piece of steel and were black an-
odized. They looked like something from a martial arts film. He hefted a
few of these and liked their feel but, recalling the warm misty conditions
of the Place, he set those aside as too slippery.

Finally, he found three identical hatchets. These had hardwood
handles. Two of them had sheaths that could be hung from a belt. The
axe heads were asymmetrical. One side had a curved edge. The opposite
side featured a triangular point. The edges were sharp and free of
notches.

Eddie gathered up all three hatchets. He'd practice with the one
that was missing its sheath and carry the other two as weapons. As
swiftly as he could, the young man ran up the stairs and through the
house to the back yard. His makeshift plywood target was still near the
wall of the garage.

He was excited to try the throwing axes, but after being unable to
do anything remotely effective with them for fifteen minutes, Eddie
switched to his knife practice. He practiced for a half hour and got into
the rhythm and feel of the familiar weapon. As he concentrated on the
familiar practice, he settled down and dropped into his calm, focused
state. He realized for the first time that this was not unlike the mental
state he'd needed to cast a spell successfully on Lena's world.

Still focused, he picked up his practice axe. He hefted it, raised it
above his shoulder, and flung it. The axe spun perfectly and sailed right
over the plywood to embed its blade in the side wall of the garage.

Eddie stepped closer to the target and tried again. He focused
more on form and release than on strength of the throw. This time he
was able to get the hatchet to stick in the plywood. "Finally. There's one
in a row," he muttered.

Now, Eddie took a break and poked around the yard. Joe had a
pile of scrap lumber on the far side of the garage. Eddie rummaged
through it and found a thick piece of wood that he could nail to the plywood. This made a better target than the plywood itself.

Set up at last, Eddie returned to his practice. At first, the throws
were erratic, but they stabilized quickly. Each time he stuck the axe in
his target successfully ten times in a row, Eddie stepped back a pace.
Each time he missed four in a row, he stepped forward.

The afternoon wore on, and his arm grew tired. It was time to
stop for the day. He spent a few minutes with his knife throwing and
then returned to the house.

Joe was still in his rooms upstairs, so Eddie went for a walk. He
practiced his seeing spell in the park where, so many months earlier, he'd
first encountered Alicia. There were few people out in the cold weather.
He saw no one tinged in red or violet, which, he decided, wasn't surprising. Winter had drawn near enough so that sitting outdoors was uncomfortable, and eventually he returned to Painter Avenue.

It was difficult to sit still. He couldn't keep practicing with the axe and knife; he'd be of no use if he pulled a muscle in his back or his arm or tore something in his shoulder. There weren't any projects that needed doing inside. He grabbed a rake and cleaned up the leaves on the front yard but that only occupied him for a half hour. Finally, at half past four in the afternoon, he went into the kitchen and made dinner.

Joe came down around six. He'd made progress. He thought that he'd be ready to leave in about twenty-four hours. Eddie sighed at the further delay but accepted the need to take precautions so that they would make it through the transit unharmed. After dinner, Joe suggested some readings, and that occupied the evening. Late that night, after a slow and marginally productive day, Eddie lay down, but sleep was a long time coming.

The next morning, Eddie followed the aroma of coffee to find Joe already making breakfast in the kitchen. He had a short list of tasks for Eddie to do in preparation for the next transit. First on the list was to call Sergeant Driscoll and let her know they were going to be gone again, this time for a longer period.

That accomplished, Eddie went through his list and checked things off as he worked his way down the page. He patrolled the perimeter of the property and made sure that the boundaries were secure. He took a bus down to the local post office and stopped mail delivery again. When he returned, he made sure that the front door was latched and securely locked. Finally, he practiced with his throwing axes for a couple of hours. He felt as though he was making progress, but he knew that throwing against a wooden target was very different from throwing at a charging beast on a soggy, fog-shrouded landscape.

Near evening, Eddie came in and washed. He made sure that all the greenhouse windows were securely fastened and locked the back door. He placed his throwing axes near the basement door. Then he went into the kitchen and made himself a light snack. Finally, he could think of nothing else to do, so he paced up and down the hall.

The shadows were long when Joe came downstairs. Eddie thought that his teacher's face looked gray and drawn. Without a word, Joe checked the front and back doors. Eddie gathered up his throwing axes. He hooked the two with sheaths to his belt. The third he carried in his left hand. Finally, Joe handed Eddie a folded piece of paper, labeled with the number "1" and gestured that Eddie should open the paper.

Inside there was another, smaller piece of paper with "2" written on it. Eddie read what Joe had written on the inside of the first sheet.

I am holding a complex, multi-part spell in mind and will not speak during this transit until the moment the spell is needed.

On the second piece of paper, you will find a single word. This is the trigger word for the spell. I've subjected myself to a forgetting spell so that I will not think of the trigger word inadvertently. Memorize the word, but do not say it or allow me to see what's written.

When I say "now," call the word aloud.

Eddie looked up and nodded once. Then he unfolded the second sheet of paper and read the word there. It would be easy to remember. He followed Joe down the basement stairs. At the bottom, he folded back the last few stairs to reveal the sub-basement tunnel.

The men moved quickly and silently down, down through the tunnels. Once again Eddie noticed the transition from newer to ancient construction techniques. Repeating it as he would a mantra, he continued to hold the trigger word in his mind.

Finally they reached the round chamber that had been carved deep in the stone beneath Joe's house. As they'd done in the basement of the Inn, Eddie waited in the archway while Joe made the jump into the Place. Then he counted to five and followed. He walked backwards three times around. Again came the light and the sound. Holding his axe away from his side, Eddie sprang lightly off the lip of the pit.

This time the transition was familiar and smooth. He landed easily and turned. Joe was near. The old man held his hand up for a moment and then moved swiftly through the warm, misty place between worlds.

They had walked for perhaps five minutes when they heard the ululating cry that was the beast's hunting call. It was far off, but fast approaching. Joe picked up the pace. They reached a single standing stone. This one had a triangle etched on its side. Joe counted out ten paces beyond the stone and motioned for Eddie to stand close by.

Then the awful beast that had been Alicia sprang, snarling into view.

"Now!" shouted Joe.

"Raven!" Eddie called in response.

There was a brilliant, blinding flash. Ropes of green fire encircled the beast and dragged her down a shallow depression into the deeper mist. She struggled, but her paws could not find purchase on the spongy, damp ground. Wind blew at her and blinding rain lashed her. The wind and rain pushed harder and harder and finally toppled her back against a large boulder. Another big rock rolled down the hill and pinned her against the first. She was wounded, hurt, and still bound by the green fire, but she continued to struggle.

Joe collapsed against Eddie, who tried to support him.

Michael C. Glaviano

"Three small stones! This big." the older man gasped, holding up his fist. "Make a triangle of them. Surrounding us."

Eddie eased Joe to the ground. The beast was snarling and wriggling, trying to work her way free. Eddie looked around and found three, roughly fist-sized stones lying nearby. One, he left where it was. One he placed a couple of feet from Joe where the older man knelt on the ground. Eddie stepped two paces to stand next to his teacher and pitched the third stone in front of them to complete the triangle. As he helped Joe to his feet, a warm, orange light rose around them in three panels so that they were encased within an amber prism. The Place began to dim and recede.

Alicia worked free of her bonds. She shook herself and howled, and then she sprang. Her claws were outstretched and her fangs bared as she flew at them, but before she could could cover the intervening distance, the scene faded away and was replaced by the transit pit beneath the Inn at Three Corners.

Thirty Five

As the misty illumination of the Place faded, Eddie felt around for the rim of the transit chamber and slid his axe over the lip of the circular path. Next, he called up a beam of light and directed it toward the ceiling. In the reflected glow, he could see that Joe was standing on his own. With his arms bent at the elbows so that his forearms rested on the rim, the older man faced the curving wall of the pit. He leaned forward and rested his forehead against the cool stones. The old man's eyes were closed and his breath came fast, as though he'd run some distance.

"You okay, Joe?" he called.

"Yes. Just give me a minute. I'll be fine."

Eddie hesitated and then pulled himself over the lip of the pit and lit some candles before extinguishing his illumination spell. He stood quietly and watched as his mentor pulled himself together. The older man's breathing slowed, he stood straighter.

"You want a hand up?"

"Yes, son, I think I would like that."

Eddie helped Joe onto the path that ran round the rim of the pit. The younger man stooped to retrieve his axe. Joe still looked worn out but managed a wan smile.

"I poured a great deal of energy into Iris before we left," he spoke softly. "We need her... and of course I care what happens to her. Deeply. I will regain my strength, but I've incurred a deficit and must rest."

"But we made it through."

Joe closed his eyes again and leaned back against the wall. "Indeed, we did... that beast, that poor, twisted thing. You know, before this is over, we must dispatch her somehow. Her presence is upsetting the balance. The situation is not... sustainable."

"How are we going to do that?"

"Son, if I knew, I'd already have done it. It is just... sad."

He was silent then for a few minutes, and then he roused himself. "Very well. Let's get out of here. Do you have everything?"

Eddie nodded. He called up the simple spell that would illuminate the path beneath their feet. Then he extinguished the candles and they made their long, slow way up the 256 steps to the lobby of the Inn at Three Corners.

When they reached the heavy door, Joe passed his hand over it and the latch drew back. Eddie tucked his axe out of site inside his coat with the other two. It made for an awkward collection of handles and blades. The door swung outward and they walked tiredly onto the carpet. The door swung closed behind them and locked.

Old Mel was at his desk. He regarded them without expression.

"Cold out today," he remarked finally. "Be wantin' a wagon ride, Mel expects."

Joe nodded his thanks and walked over to sit heavily on one of the sofas that stood near the front door. Gray light filtered through the windows, but the cold did not penetrate to the Inn's interior.

A few minutes later the cab driver stepped through the main door.

"Is it you two who be needin' a ride?" he asked.

Eddie glanced at Joe who nodded in assent.

"Yeah," Eddie said. "You know where Tolemy's Cats is? The bookstore on Center? We'd like to be dropped off right in front."

Eddie waved at Old Mel who just looked back at him without response. The driver led them out into the cold. Even though they had coats, they were glad that the ride was short. The streets were mostly empty and in ten minutes they were standing on the sidewalk in front of the Cats.

Mrs. A – Iris – must have divined their arrival, for a moment later Lena held Eddie in her arms. Iris, still beautiful and radiant, pulled Joe into the interior of the bookshop. As he allowed himself to be taken inside, Joe spoke over his shoulder. His voice was rough and tired.

"Good work, lad. We'll talk more at dinner."

Lena held Eddie a moment more. Then the young couple went inside the lobby and walked up the stairs to the apartment they shared. Lena raised an eyebrow as Eddie placed his three throwing axes at the door. He shook his head to her unasked question.

"Joe's suggestion. I haven't had to use them; I'm just learning to throw them."

Lena frowned a little at that, but then she came back into his arms and the rest of the world – all the worlds – retreated for a time. They relaxed against each other and were still. Eddie could smell her hair and feel the curves of her body, the touch of her hands on his back as she pressed against him.

"That was a very long four days, my love," Lena whispered into his shoulder some time later. They lay together in the stillness of their room. She had placed a single candle on the coffee table, and the light was dim and flickering.

"Yeah, it sure was. And too much of it was spent sitting in buses and cars. And just waiting while Joe figured out how to get us back. But now we are. Back, I mean. And I'm really glad."

"As am I, Love. As am I," she whispered and snuggled closer.

They went down to the Cats bookshop an hour later. Iris had dinner in the oven. She and Joe were sitting in the tiny living room. He had his feet up and had a glass of red wine in his hand. Wearing a low-cut shift and looking stunningly beautiful, Iris sat across from him. Her fiery hair was pulled back and held in place with a brilliant turquoise clip. Her skin was smooth, her features tranquil, her eyes fathomless.

"Well, the two of you finally made it down here, I see," she laughed as Eddie and Lena walked through the door. Iris' husky contralto played a strong counterpoint to her beauty. Her appearance and poise were hard to reconcile with what they knew her true situation to be. The calm courage with which she faced the future made them admire her all the more.

"Um, can I do anything to help?" Eddie asked.

"Thank you, Reed, but we have everything under control. Our dinner will be ready in half an hour. What would you like to drink?"

Lena and Eddie both opted for wine – a robust, cool-climate red. The four of them made small talk until dinner was ready. Then they sat around the table. The food – a roast leg of lamb with mint, baked potatoes, autumn broccoli steamed with garlic, and a salad – was magnificent. Conversation ground to a halt while they ate.

At last, they pushed back from the table. Iris poured a little more wine.

"While you two have been busy transplanting the Lady of the Forest, we've accomplished several things from our own agenda," she declared. "Would you like to let the 'boys' know what we've done, Lena?"

"Iris has been a kind and effective teacher to me these past days," Lena began.

"What she means to say is that she can run the bookshop perfectly without my interference," Iris interrupted with a gentle laugh.

Lena smiled and continued. "Perhaps of more importance is the progress we have made in identifying the sites of ancient portals into the Great Hub."

"Yes?" Joe encouraged.

"It would be best if I showed you. Please wait. I will return in a moment," Lena said and jumped up. While she was gone, the others quickly cleared the table.

Lena was back in minutes. She had a roll of heavy paper which she smoothed out to reveal a large map of Soapstone Bay. She pointed out dots in various colors that they had added to the map.

"The red dot represents the existing portal at the Inn. The other dots are places where we have seen multiple references to portals or phe-

Michael C. Glaviano

nomena linked to a portal's existence. Green dots represent sites that
have the most recent information, say within the past two hundred years.
Blue dots represent sites that were documented earlier."

"Look. Here and here," she continued. "See? There is a green
dot at the southwest corner of Merryweather Park. That is near the
wealthy neighborhood where we walked the day we were accosted by the
security guards. Remember, Reed? This is a good site. Iris and I found
numerous references to it in that old book."

Eddie nodded. Then Lena pointed to an area on the map that
was closer to the university. "Now if we intend to establish a triangular
pattern of portals, we would hope to find a site around here," she explained. "Unfortunately, there were no recent accounts. Still, we did find
several interesting anecdotes that referred to the area. These were more
difficult to make out, and they faded from the records about three hundred years ago."

Joe stared intently at the map. "Yes," he said. "I think I can recall something here. At Merryweather. If it was there as little as two centuries ago, I know I can reopen it without overtaxing myself or calling
much attention to our activities."

"But where will it be?" Eddie wondered. "The other portals have
been down deep in the ground."

"Oh, those were deliberately opened in hidden places, for security's sake. Others are at ground level. And remember, we don't need
these portals to move to and from the Place. We just want to add connections to it. The portals will let more of the dreams and the tears of the
gods come into this world, to bring more magic."

"Before you make too many plans, there's something else you
might want to know," Iris spoke up.

"What would that be?" Joe asked.

"We found references to other portals in this area."

She gestured gracefully at the map as she continued. " As recently as a 150 years ago, there were entries in the book that mentioned
one portal out at the southwest corner of the university and another, due
north of there. Those two, together with the portal that lies beneath the
Inn at Three Corners, form an equilateral triangle."

"So the inn's name may well refer to the ley lines of the portals
rather than the triangular piece of property upon which it stands!" Lena
added excitedly.

"Not only that, I found an obscure reference to one more portal
at the midpoint of the north-south line at the west edge of the campus.
That would lie within the nature preserve that's west of the university,"
Iris finished with a smile.

"Interesting. And the one out at the southwest corner... could
you tell where it was in relation to the portal at Merryweather park?" Joe
wondered.

"Indeed we could," Iris laughed. "The Merryweather park portal lay at the midpoint of a line connecting the point at the south end of the university with the major portal beneath the Inn at Three Corners!"

"Another midpoint... so if we could indeed open one out there near Holmes Road, that would be six of them. Three points in a large triangle superimposed upon a smaller one," Joe said, more to himself than to the others present.

"Yes," Iris said triumphantly. "If we can open six of them, the whole game changes. Not only that, but the sites at these extreme north and south corners are very well documented. So the midpoint of the leg that goes from north of the school down to the inn gives us an idea where to look for a site in the field near Holmes Road. Even if there was nothing there in the past, it would be easier to open a small connection to the Place if it were the last in a sequence that outlined this geometry."

Now Lena chimed in. Her eyes were bright with excitement. "So you see, this even suggests the order in which to approach the project. We should open the extreme endpoints first. Then the portal at Merryweather Park. That one should be easier. Next, we reopen the midpoint near the nature preserve west of the school. Finally, as Iris says, the energy balances will be on our side as we try to establish the Holmes Road site for the final point in the pattern."

"Uh, excuse me? Sorry, but I've got a question," Eddie interrupted. "I realize that I know almost nothing about all this portal stuff, and the connections with the Great Hub, and all, but this seems weird to me."

"What is it, son? What's bothering you?"

"Well, we're talking about six portals in this one little town. How many are open in all of the corresponding continent on our world?"

"Perhaps four," Joe answered quietly, soberly.

"So what's up with that?"

"Our world is dying, essentially. The connections with the Great Hub, the place between worlds, have fallen into disuse. The tears of the gods no longer support magic. You saw how difficult it was for me to invoke that simple spell when we planted the forest lady's seed packet."

"Well, even though you've talked about it a little, I still don't quite understand how it could have gotten so bad, but I guess that's sort of beside the point right now," Eddie replied. "Anyway, if we have four portals in this whole continent on our world, what's six going to be like in this one little town?"

"Ah, I see the source of your confusion, I think..." Joe replied, but then he trailed off with a distant look in his eyes. After a few seconds, Iris stepped into the gap.

"It is like this, Reed," she offered. "In a healthy world, a world that touches the Great Hub, towns and settlements grow up around connection points – these portals. The portals come and go according to the dreams of the gods. The surroundings are nourished. Natural human creativity and love makes for interesting, powerful dreams for the gods. A healthy feedback loop is maintained."

"So there could be any number of connection points open at a given time?"

"Essentially, yes. Too many is also not so good because the realm can become chaotic. The mad, fevered dreams of the elder gods may be attracted."

"Well, none isn't good and too many aren't good. So what's about right?"

"Oh, in a large city, perhaps a handful would be ideal," the red-head replied.

"Soapstone is hardly a large city," Lena observed, suddenly serious. "Would six portals be dangerous here?"

"Ahh, so that's your concern," Joe nodded, took a sip of his Zin-fandel. "Six is probably more than ideal, but we will do nothing to keep these open. Unlike the major portal beneath the inn, these will not be woven into the tapestry of the Old One. Within a year or two, some of them will surely fade."

"Well what's the point then?" Eddie was becoming frustrated, but he succeeded in keeping his voice soft and even.

"The point is that it will erase the Queen's beachhead here. There will be confusion among her minions. Remember, they spend at least as much effort with their in-fighting as they do in support of the Queen's agenda. Some may try to fight us, but we can be sure that all of them will keep the results of our actions from her ken for as long as they are able.

"Art and science will flow out into the world from this little town," the old man continued. "Eventually, despite the efforts of those who serve her, the Queen will notice the changes here. I know her ways. She is confident of the fate of our world, so she is likely to turn away from it for a time. She is likely to investigate what went wrong here, to question her servants. We can use that distraction to the benefit of our world."

"You're trying to make her take her eye off the ball!" Eddie exclaimed.

Joe nodded. Lena wrinkled her forehead at the colloquialism, but then her brow cleared as she figured out the context. Iris smiled a wry, half-smile.

But once again, Joe had fallen silent. His eyes roved over the map and considered all the marks, the streets, the notes scribbled in the margins. He squinted, pursed his lips, took one more sip of wine.

"Yes, everything you say is correct, but there is one other thing to consider," he said finally.

"And that would be?" Iris challenged.

"There will be a center point as well. If you draw perpendiculars from each midpoint to the opposite vertex, those lines all cross. That means a master point will fall somewhere around here."

He stabbed his index finger onto the map southwest of the intersection of University and Biscayne. His finger moved in a circle and finally came to rest on a street named Harbor.

"Well, okay. There's a center to the shape. What does that mean?" Eddie wondered aloud.

"It means, son, that we could establish a portal at the center point – even if there has never been one opened there in the past. The overall connection between this world and the Place Between would be incredibly stable and rich. That could begin the formation of another major portal such as the one which lies beneath the Inn at Three Corners."

"It is indeed exciting," Iris cautioned, "but fiddling around with that focus point would be dangerous. Magic is already alive in this world. If we were to open another major portal so close to the one beneath the Inn, the membrane between the Place and this world could rupture. People could be sucked through. And things. Things from the Place could come this way. You know what we might face. The realms of chaos could touch Soapstone Bay."

Then it was quiet around the table. The silence lasted, grew uncomfortable, and took on a presence of its own. Finally Joe broke it. The excitement was gone from his voice, replaced by a tiredness that Eddie had never heard before.

"Indeed I do, Iris. I know full well the consequences and the possibilities, and I will not act recklessly. It was just a passing thought, not a proposal. In any case we have plenty to do to reestablish the portals that we know existed in the past."

*　*　*

"Let's begin by visiting the farthest corner points, those north and south of the university. What lies beyond those points in these times?" Joe gestured to the part of the map that represented the areas to the west of the school.

It was the next morning. Joe, Iris, and Eddie were bent over the map in the tiny kitchen. Lena was helping a customer in the bookstore. The weather was cold but clear. Real winter lurked on the horizon.

Iris skimmed her hands over the map. "On the north, sweeping out here and here, there are rolling hills that give way to farmland. I already mentioned the small nature preserve here, directly to the west of the university. It extends well to the west of the location we're interested in. The southern boundary of the university is a forest. It was heavily logged in the early days of the settlement, but it was replanted over 150 years ago," she explained.

"I will want to think about this some more, but yes, I tend to agree that we should begin at these corners," Joe agreed. "They were active in relatively recent times. And we are not likely to be observed while we are busy with our work."

"So what will it take to reopen these things?" Eddie wanted to know.

"Physically, it can be a difficult spell, a tiring spell. It depends on the conditions and the people involved in the opening. Three or four experienced people working together lightens the load. It is more work for one or two. Conceptually, however, it is fairly straightforward," Joe replied.

"At minimum, we'll need a heavy rod of iron. I will stand in the center. Three more must stand around me in a triangle with the same proportions as the large triangle we are trying to form with this set of portals. I will lead a call-and-response spell. If we are undisturbed, it is a matter of five to ten minutes. Since I will draw power from the fabric of the cosmos down through the rod at the same time I pull energy from the place between worlds, the balance must be precise. Working alone as I will be, I expect that it will be taxing."

"At ten minutes per spot, we should be able to get these all done in a morning!"

"Hardly. I will rest for at least 24 hours after each opening."

"Well, I've done this before. I can certainly do at least one per day," Iris said confidently.

"Iris, Iris. I know that you're capable, that you have the knowledge. And I know that in the old days you would not have hesitated to perform this spell two or even three times within a 24 hour period. But there is no need for you to drain yourself. In fact, I will need you to be alert and to keep watch."

"We should still be able to do one each," she argued.

"I'd rather not. You will have to make sure that Reed and Lena are standing exactly where they should stand. You must make sure that their responses are precise and timed correctly. I must rely on you, Iris."

"I have the strength! You have given me the strength! Why should I not use it?"

"Iris, please. We need your knowledge as well as your strength. I must be able to rely on you to guide these young ones. Please understand. We must make sure that you retain this semblance of youth for as long as we can. If something goes wrong, we will all be in your hands."

The beautiful, proud redhead was visibly angry, but she slowly calmed herself. Her eyes flashed, but, with one adjustment, she agreed to do what Joe asked.

"So, Old Man. As usual, you win. But do you have any objection to my leading the call-and-response while you manage the center point? Would that not take a slight amount of pressure from your oh-so-able shoulders? Surely that much would not over-burden me!"

After a short, slightly tense pause, he assented. "Yes, Iris. I think that would be appropriate."

"Good. Now," Iris continued, "do you have any idea where we can obtain a stout rod of the earthen metal?"

Just then Lena walked into the kitchen.

"Things are slow, so I thought I would check in with you for a moment. Are the plans progressing?" she asked.

"In a manner of speaking," Iris replied, obviously still tense.

"Um... I have an idea... about that metal rod you mentioned," Eddie spoke up.

"Lena and I have two friends, Fleggie and Sweetmaye," he continued. "They have a sort of salvage yard north of the Inn. I'd be surprised if they didn't have what we need. What do you think, Lena? They have all sorts of scrap metal at their yard."

"Well, yes. Even if they do not have it in their lot, they would be able to get it for us. They should be back from their voyage soon."

"Right. If they weren't delayed, it should be any day now. The *Mother Rose* was supposed to be going out for six weeks and it's been just about that long. Let's go down to the docks and see if they've returned!"

"You are sure that you can trust these two?" Joe asked.

"Yes. I am quite sure that Sweetmaye and Fleggie are trustworthy. When Reed helped me move off campus, Fleggie stepped in and helped. He had no obligation; we had merely hired his wagon to carry my things. But when he saw the need, he simply helped. Also, I have spent some time talking with Sweetmaye, and although I could be wrong about anyone, I came away from our conversations with the strongest of impressions. I am sure she is a fine person." Lena answered.

Eddie nodded in agreement. "They are good people. I know you'll judge for yourself, of course, but I'm pretty confident that you'll like them. And they'll have just finished a six week voyage working for Captain Wyndham on the *Mother Rose*. He'll know them very well by now.

"So, can you describe what you need?" the young man added.

"We need a rod of a ferrous metal or an alloy that is mostly ferrous metal. It should be perhaps as big around as your thumb and at least a head taller than the tallest of us. We call it a 'grounding rod' and will use it as the focal point as we try to reopen each portal. I'll explain more later."

"Well then, shall we go down to the docks and find out about the *Mother Rose*?"

"You two go, but if you encounter your friends, please say little about this. Iris and I need to discuss some things and make more detailed plans and decisions regarding individual roles."

It was obvious that Iris was still agitated, but she nodded shortly and said nothing.

"All right then. Do you have time to do this now, Lena?"

"Yes. As long as Iris can let me take off for a couple of hours. I made good progress with my university studies while you were gone and would enjoy a walk in the fresh air. As changeable as the weather is this time of year, we should go down there as soon as we can. If the *Mother Rose* is not in yet, we can go to the port administration office. They will have an updated arrival time."

"That's fine, dear," Iris smiled at Lena. "You two run down to the docks. As you've noticed, things are slow in most of the shops when the weather gets bad. We merchants have learned to live with it."

Eddie and Lena grabbed heavy coats against the cold and walked down Center Street to Turnbull.

"Let's do a detour over to Baleen Park and pull the pebble through from my world," he suggested. "It'll only take a second, and then we'll have closed the loop. We'll be able to send notes back and forth any time."

"That sounds fine, my love. Although I will never be completely happy when we are apart, it will be good to have that capability when circumstances separate us."

So they took a taxi wagon down Turnbull Road to Baleen Park. Eddie stayed with the driver while Lena ran to the center of the park and retrieved the small rock that had been transported from Eddie's world to hers. She was flushed from her run through the cold when she returned. Her mouth turned up slightly at the corner, and her eyes sparkled as she took her seat next to him in the cab.

Once the cab was moving, she turned her hand over and opened it. Eddie saw the small stone lying in the palm of her hand. Then she closed her fist over the stone and held it for the rest of the ride up Turnbull.

It took little time to ride back up Turnbull to Prince's Wharf Road. They jumped out of the cab, paid the driver, and began walking down to the wharf. As always when he came this way, Eddie was struck by the contrast between this part of Soapstone Bay and the more affluent areas south of University.

The streets were narrower here. The smooth, high tech paving material gave way to cobblestones. The buildings pressed in on the sides and it was clear that most of them dated from the earliest periods of the settlement. No urban amenities were visible: no benches or plants or attractive public spaces. There were few indications of community.

This was the only part of the town Eddie had visited where poverty was in evidence, and it wasn't due simply to the age of the buildings or the way the streets were paved. It had something to do with the state of maintenance. The sidewalks were cracked. There were boarded-up windows. There were people sitting and looking out of windows, too. Some of these people – not too many, but some – evinced a hollow, haunted look.

"Can you tell me why this part of Soapstone is run-down?" Eddie wondered, careful to keep his voice low.

"It has always been this way. For as long as I can remember and in all the local histories I've read, the Warrens have been rough," she answered.

"It's kind of strange. Even in the industrial area where Flcggic and Sweetmaye have their salvage yard, the surroundings are neat and well-kept. It's not affluent, and it's utilitarian and no-nonsense, but it has none of this decrepit, badly-maintained look."

"Yes, these narrow streets are different. I grant you that. Much research has been done on the subject, and many articles have been written on the results of the research. It puzzles our scholars. The best explanation I have heard is that societies need to have some sort of escape valve. The neighborhood that we call 'The Warrens' serves that purpose for Soapstone Bay. There is no institutionalized under-class – no one is trapped here. Still, there are people who crave this life. And whatever its other flaws, when the weather is fine it can be a lively place!"

"I'll bet it is. Probably more lively than we'd like after dark," Eddie laughed.

He looked around again. The frigid weather kept casual visitors indoors. The people they passed were bundled against the cold and bent upon completing their assigned tasks. A few stood and talked but not for very long. The worn shop fronts struck Eddie as being especially forlorn in the cold, wet wind that marched up from the harbor. This would be a good place to avoid on a January day.

By now, the young couple had walked most of the way down to the wharf proper. The *Mother Rose* was not in evidence, and though they listened, Captain Wyndham's booming laugh or bellow of command never reached their ears. Eventually, they walked all the way down to the end of the stone quay without seeing the ship.

They stood for a moment at the end of the wharf. Barely visible in the mist, a distant breakwater sheltered the moorage from the heaviest of waves. Even so, the water was choppy and windblown, the color of slate. Raw wind chilled their faces and hands.

Before long they'd had their fill of the harsh, exposed terminus. They turned their back on the water and retraced their path. Stacked cargo, covered with tarpaulin and heavy netting; rusty utility sheds; cranes; huge cleats and hawsers; and ships, restless in their slips, gave way to stone buildings as they reached the place where the wharf ended and Prince's Wharf Road began. The port administrator's office straddled this boundary.

Lena indicated the weathered, two story stone structure. "We can go in here and check on the status of any ship that travels in or out of Soapstone Bay. There are information kiosks and people to help. Let us see what we can learn regarding our friends."

The cold was keeping casual visitors to a minimum and there were few people inside the public space of the main floor. As was the case with most of the buildings on the road, this one was old, most likely as old as the wharf itself. Inside, however, it was reasonably clean. The floors obviously benefitted from regular attention. The simple furniture was in good repair.

Unbidden, the image of Sergeant Driscoll's desk and the room where she worked rose in Eddie's mind. For all its age and hard use, this port office was in better condition than that bleak police station. He shook off the memory and looked around the room.

Near the back of the public area was a counter, staffed by a bored looking clerk. Mail slots adorned the wall behind the clerk. Beneath those squatted a heavy, worn table that was covered with stacks of forms and other objects vaguely evocative of things maritime. In the left, rear corner of the room, stairs led up, presumably to offices on the second floor.

Most of the middle of the room was occupied by information kiosks. The three furthest from the draft of the door were in use, but the fourth kiosk was free, and they stepped up to it. Lena pressed her thumb to the scanner. Immediately, the system recognized her and displayed a prompt. Using the touch screen display, she gained access to the public records of the shipping database and queried for the status of the *Mother Rose*.

"Oh, this is not too bad, Reed. See? It says here that they are a day-and-a-half out. They will probably arrive tomorrow evening or the morning after at the latest."

"I suppose we could come back down here tomorrow to check back, but is there a way to receive notification at the store when they arrive?"

Lena stabbed at the touch screen as she tried a few options. "There must be a way to do that... Oh, wait. Here it is. Yes... That does it! We will receive notification at the bookstore when the *Mother Rose* comes in. It will be good to see Sweetmaye and Fleggie again, will it not? I wonder if they will want to stay in for a while or if they will want to ship out again. Of course fewer and fewer ships go out as the weather worsens."

"I wouldn't want to be out there during winter storms," Eddie agreed. "The *Mother Rose* is a high tech ship, but it's still no good to be on the water in a big storm. Of course Captain Thomas will try to talk them into whatever he wants them to do.

"Still, wouldn't it be nice for them to spend some time each year out and some time each year here in town?" he added. "I wonder if they could make something like that work. When I was aboard the *Rose*, I gathered that a lot of the semi-professional sailors do that."

"Yes. For now, though, let us simply hope for a safe return and that we are able to enjoy visiting with them."

Eddie nodded in agreement. "What do you say we head back uptown? The afternoon's getting along. I'd like to talk some more with Joe and Iris."

"That sounds fine to me, my love."

As they made their way up Prince's Wharf Road and through the Warrens, the wind picked up and made the sad streets even more dreary and empty. It also drove more local denizens indoors, which in turn made the young couple feel more visible and exposed. It was a relief to pass Park Street and then LeRoy.

By the time they reached Turnbull Road, the wind had blown dark clouds overhead. The already chill wind grew colder and it began to drizzle. They walked quickly down sidewalks past shops. Here, as down in the Warrens, the weather had driven people indoors, and shopkeepers were enjoying little in the way of commerce. Eddie and Lena took advantage of what shelter was available from shop-front awnings and trees and so were protected from the worst of the wet.

At first the rain was little more than a sprinkle, but as they turned onto Center Street, the drizzle became real rain. They were not soaked through, but they were very glad to reach the bookstore a few minutes later. It was warm inside, and the smell of the books added to the pleasant, welcoming atmosphere.

Iris was behind the counter. There was a big stack of books on a cart next to her and a couple of empty packing boxes on the floor near the counter. She looked up as they entered and smiled at them. Apparently she had let go of her disagreement with Joe, and now her radiant beauty lit up the store.

"Well, you two look more than a little bedraggled. Why don't you run upstairs and change into dry clothes? Joe is back in my apartment. He's brooding over his plans. I'm sure he'll want to hear what you found out."

"I'm taking advantage of the scarcity of customers on this cold, dreary day and getting some inventory logged in," she added.

"That sounds good, Mrs. A... sorry, I mean Iris. We checked on the *Mother Rose*. She's not in yet, but Lena arranged to have information sent here to the store when they arrive. The ship should be dockside tomorrow night or soon after."

Iris nodded and smiled again, this time adding shooing motions with her hands. Eddie and Lena ran upstairs and changed into dry clothes.

They were back in a quarter hour. Iris had opened the last of the packing boxes and had more books piled on both the top and bottom sections of her cart.

"Could you use some help with those books?" Eddie offered.

"Oh, that would be grand. Do you know how to shelve them? I'm sure that your sweetheart can explain it to you."

Lena smiled at her. "And if you would like to take a break, I will watch over the register while Reed puts the books on the shelves."

"Well, yes. I would enjoy a break. Mostly, I'd like to go check on that old rascal to make sure he's setting things up properly. I'll give him the news regarding your friends' ship as well."

"It's nearly closing time. If there are no more customers in the next half hour, why don't you turn the sign around and lock the door?"

Lena agreed and turned to the inventory display. She motioned to Reed to join her so that she could explain Tolemy's Cats shelving system. After watching them thoughtfully for a moment, Iris thanked them and left them in charge of the shop while she walked back to talk with Joe.

Eddie and Lena enjoyed themselves for the rest of the afternoon. A couple of customers actually did brave the elements to visit the bookstore. One said that he was stocking up some reading material for the winter season. The young couple ended up closing the store on time, a few minutes after their last customer paid for her purchases and walked into the rainy evening shadows.

While Eddie finished shelving the books, Lena reconciled the register and closed out the daily receipts. Then they shut off the lights and started back to Mrs. A's apartment where another argument was in full swing.

"You say it would be better to have more people involved, but you don't want to confide in more people. You won't let me take up the slack because you want me to 'save my strength.' Do you have any idea what you *would* like to do?"

"Please, Iris. Try to calm down."

"I'll show you calm. You want calm?! I'll show you calm!"

Mrs. A nearly crashed into Lena and Eddie as she slammed the door and marched up the aisle at full speed.

"Whoa, Iris! What's going on?"

"Ask *him*, why don't you?"

"Please. We need to work together on this. We need your help, Iris. I... I know this whole situation must be terribly difficult for you..." Eddie started.

"Difficult? *Difficult?* It's humiliating, that's what it is! I am neither young nor old. Neither in charge nor able to sit by while *he* makes the decisions."

At that moment, Lena stepped between Mrs. Abellona and Eddie. Gracefully, gently, she moved close to the beautiful, angry redheaded woman – who was at least a full head taller than she – and without speaking, wrapped her arms around Iris, hugged her. At first, Iris made as if to push herself away, but suddenly she broke down and sobbed. Lena held fast and turned her head to raise an eyebrow in Eddie's direction. He took the hint and moved away quietly to join Joe in the apartment at the back of the store.

Eddie stepped into the apartment and closed the door softly behind him. He could hear Joe moving around in the kitchen, so he walked back there to find the older man pacing back and forth, muttering. Joe looked up as Eddie walked in.

"Do you know how old I am? Do you? No. How could you know? I'm... well, suffice it to say that I've lived and fought and loved for a good long while, and in all my years I have never met a woman half so exasperating as Iris Abellona."

"Joe..."

"What?"

"Nothing. Just remember that you've had to hose me down a time or two. None of us has your perspective. You know more and have seen more, but that doesn't mean that the rest of us are completely clueless."

Joe started to respond, but Eddie held up his hand and shook his head. He took a quick breath and continued.

"It also doesn't mean that you're infallible. I was there when you asked Maia for help. When we planted the seed packet in our world and right away you asked her if she'd extend her forest to the Queen's world. You didn't handle that very well, Joe. We didn't talk about it afterwards, but it was clear that you jumped the gun. You should have waited. Sometimes you need to take it a little easy with people... even with forest goddesses."

Joe glared at Eddie, and for a moment the younger man thought that he might have taken it too far. He remembered suddenly that Joe was more like a force of nature than a normal human being, but he stood his ground and met the powerful old warrior's glare with as calm a look as he could muster.

All of a sudden, Joe appeared to shrink slightly and pull into himself. He took a deep breath and let it out with a sigh.

"Nobody said that you were clueless, son."

"I know that, but..."

"But what? She's thinking that I think she's clueless? I doubt that."

Eddie let that pass. "Joe... Would it be such a mistake to let her take the lead in setting up the details of the plan?"

"It's got to be right, son. There's little margin for mistakes."

"So step in if there's a real flaw in her plans, but wait and see what her plans really are before you try to correct them."

At this, Joe again looked hard at Eddie for several seconds, but then his look changed and he sighed once more. And now he smiled. There was a little wistfulness in that smile, Eddie thought, but the old man's face had softened. The tension had receded.

"By the gods, son, it was a good day when Sergeant Driscoll dropped you on my doorstep. You have changed much in the past year. Changed and grown into a man. You are right. Please excuse me while I go try to make amends for my arrogance."

Joe stepped around Eddie and walked to the front door of the apartment. Eddie could hear him speak to the women in the hallway. Although he couldn't make out the words, Eddie could at first hear unmistakable anger in Iris' voice. This soon subsided.

Moments later, Lena came into the kitchen and took Eddie by the hand. Silently, she led him out of Iris' rooms, through the darkened bookstore, and upstairs to the apartment they shared. As they passed through the store, they could hear Iris' and Joe's voices speaking softly in one of the other aisles.

The next day, the rain continued unabated. Rather than a violent storm, this had all the earmarks of a steady soaker. Lena wanted to stay in and work on her studies for a few hours. Eddie left her working in the apartment and went down to the bookstore. He found Iris at the counter. She appeared calm and happy enough. Her fiery hair was pulled back somewhat severely and she was dressed in conservative business attire. She had some papers on the counter and was in the process of reaching for her communicator when Eddie walked through the front door.

"Morning, Iris."

"Good morning, Reed. Why don't you go back and talk with Joe? He and I have agreed on a plan. Oh, and the store's data system received a message from the port administration. Your friends' ship should dock tonight."

"That's great!"

"Yes... Joe and I will want to meet your friends before we bring them into our full confidence, but if things work out we will ask them to help us. You haven't said anything about your origin to them; is that right?"

"Yeah, that's right."

"Good. Let Joe know that the ship is arriving, will you? I have some things I need to take care of, so if you'll excuse me..."

"Oh, sure."

Eddie made his way back to the apartment. He found Joe in the kitchen poring over a map of the locale. The older man gestured to a seat at the table and then pointed to the map.

"It is obvious that Iris has been devoting a significant portion of her formidable skills to this problem. No wonder she was angry when I presumed to take over," he added with a rueful smile.

"Glad you two worked it out. So, what are we looking at here?"

"She's taken into account the historical record and what is known regarding these spots and her sequence of the portal openings makes sense. I can find nothing wrong with her assumptions or her reasoning. And at this point I am also inclined to accept the wisdom of including two more people in our effort."

"That reminds me, Iris just told me she received word that the *Mother Rose* will dock tonight."

"Good. I will send my own message to the good captain. Iris and I would like to accompany you to the docks tomorrow and meet your friends. You say they know something of the old magic?"

"Fleggie does definitely, and Sweetmaye clearly accepted its reality. He even knew a handful of practical spells. Things that help him secure his salvage yard, for instance. And, since Fleggie left school before he mastered reading, she volunteered to help him learn others."

"Well, that's something anyway. At least we won't have to convince them of the reality of what we are doing. Now, returning to Iris' plan. Would you like to see how we intend to approach this?"

So Joe and Eddie went over the map. Joe explained that they wanted to sequence things to keep the pattern of portals as evenly distributed as possible. As they'd discussed before, they would save the effort in the area north of Holmes Road, the only one where they had been unable to find a record of prior existence, for last. The rationale was that once five of the six portals in the double triangle were open, the last one should be easier. Also, having the pattern nearly complete would let them use ley lines to calculate a precise location for the last one.

For his part, Eddie saw that this was in essence the plan that Lena and Iris had outlined when Joe and he had first returned from establishing Maia's forest on their world. All the argument had been unnecessary. The young man chose not to remark on his observation.

"In the spring, when the Lady of the Forest is better established in our world," Joe continued, "we will have more latitude, more power on our side. Until then, however, we'll be improvising.

"One thing's sadly clear: I waited too long to return to our world. Too many allies grew old or were lost in the meantime. I became distracted, my energies deployed elsewhere. Someday, perhaps, we will not be spread so thinly, but now we have to catch up.

"We do not have to make final plans yet, however," he continued. "First we'll see how things unfold in this world. Then, as we learn more, we can decide our next steps. I've been careful to consult with Iris and she agrees with me."

The older man went on to explain his views on the balance of forces and how long they might expect to operate before the Queen detected changes that stemmed from their activities. He discussed the relative merits of staying in one world and working versus moving among two or more worlds and acting here and there in an attempt to frustrate the Queen's plans. The ideas he described were confusing and seemed in Eddie's mind to spin around and fold back on themselves. There was always one more thing to explain, one more weird constraint on them, one more detail to take into account. It sounded to Eddie almost as if Joe were arguing with himself. Finally, the young man decided that he had absorbed about as much confusing information as he could stand for one day.

"Uh, well, thanks for explaining all this, Joe. It makes about as much sense as it possibly can, I guess. If you don't have anything else for me to do, I think I'll go back upstairs and see how Lena is getting along. I'd like to spend some time with my studies too."

"That sounds like a good idea, son."

Then Joe looked up suddenly, sharply. He appeared to be staring through the wall. The image came to Eddie's mind of a hunting animal of some kind. The old warrior stared intently for a few moments and then relaxed. He glanced at Eddie again.

"When you walk through the store, you will notice that Iris has changed her appearance for her business meeting. It would be best if you acted as though you noticed nothing."

"Well, okay, Joe. Thanks for warning me."

Joe nodded. "Unless you hear otherwise, let's plan to meet out in front of the bookstore tomorrow morning at nine."

"Okay. Sounds good to me."

Eddie left the apartment and made his way to the front of the bookstore. As he neared the front counter he could hear Iris Abellona's voice. It sounded exactly as it had when he first met her, loud, grating, and querulous. As she came into view, he saw that her appearance had been altered to match the voice. She looked for all the world like the testy elder who had rented him the apartment. The clothes that had looked so good on her earlier now hung from her stooped frame.

She was in the process of haranguing a middle-aged gentleman in a business suit. He had a harassed, but patient look. There were papers strewn across the counter, and he leaned forward as if to study them more closely. As he pulled one from the pile, Mrs. Abellona looked up and met Eddie's eyes. Warning him, apparently, against a visible reaction to the tableau, she shook her head ever so slightly in his direction.

"Young man! Did you get that shelf installed properly? I don't want to have to call your supervisor to complain of shoddy work when my books fall."

"Er, yes ma'am," Eddie answered. "It's, um, all done now."

"What?! Speak up, young man. Oh, I hate it when people mumble!"

"I'VE FINISHED WITH IT, MRS. ABELLONA," Eddie yelled as he got into the spirit of the scene.

"Well, good. Mind, you don't slam the door as you leave!"

Eddie waved and left the shop. He looked back through the windows before stepping into the neighboring lobby. Iris had returned her attention to the well-dressed gentleman.

Lena was deeply engrossed in her schoolwork when he got back upstairs. Eddie rubbed his head. Listening to Joe's confusing discourse on guerilla tactics as applied to the place between worlds had given him a headache, and he went into the kitchen and made himself a cup of tea. As he sipped the hot brew, he thought back over their latest conversation.

The basic concepts weren't all that complicated. Yes, the Locust Queen's agenda was evil and must be resisted. Yes, there was the place between worlds and the cosmology of the Great Wheel and the conditions under which magic could be made to work. All of that made sense, was easy to follow. Where it got confusing was when Joe talked about more immediate actions. Eddie wasn't sure, but he sensed that Joe was leaving something out of his explanations. This business about opening portals seemed obtuse. Why? He shrugged and, for the afternoon at least, gave up the struggle.

After he finished his tea, Eddie quietly gathered his notes and a text from the hidden compartment beneath the Murphy bed. He claimed a corner of the sofa and settled in to read. It felt good to be in that warm, quiet space with Lena. It was pleasant to spend an afternoon studying material that had been laid out in a logical and organized fashion. For a few hours at least, he could pretend that the world made sense.

*　*　*

The next morning at nine o'clock, the four of them met outside on the sidewalk in front of the bookstore. Iris Abellona had reverted to her youthful appearance and behavior, and she turned heads as they strolled along. It took them most of an hour to walk down through the Warrens to the docks. Although the rain and blustery wind had passed, winter was drawing near, and there were many people out working in the clear, cold air.

As they walked, Lena explained the sense of urgency that underlay the bustling scene around them. "From now until spring, people will take advantage of every mild day to do what needs doing. The severe storms of deep winter often paralyze this whole district."

They reached Prince's Wharf and looked for the *Mother Rose*. Her new berth was three quarters of the way down the quay. As Eddie had come to expect, he could hear Captain Wyndham well in advance of actually spotting the vessel he commanded.

The captain spied them as soon as they reached the ship and invited them all aboard. He showed Joe great deference and uncharacteristic seriousness, and he bowed low over Iris Abellona's beautiful hand. He embraced Eddie and flirted with Lena before calling out to his first mate to find Fleggie and Sweetmaye to let them know they had a welcoming party awaiting them.

As they waited, they learned that this, the final voyage of the season had been successful. Yes, they had encountered raiders, but now that the merchants were prepared, the raiders had suffered serious setbacks. Many had been captured and no few of their vessels had been sunk.

Now they would stay in port and do heavy maintenance on the *Mother Rose*. They would make sure that she was seaworthy and well provisioned for her next voyage in the spring. As always, the captain stayed aboard. Eddie was surprised to learn that he rarely set foot on land. "There's no need," Captain Thomas maintained heartily. "My ship is my life. I've no family apart from my crew. This is where I belong."

Fleggie and Sweetmaye finished their duties and joined them on deck. There were smiles all around and real joy at homecoming. The captain shook hands solemnly with each of them and said they'd be welcome to ship with him again come spring. The couple was pleased and excited at the prospect even though they appeared glad in equal measure to return to port.

Eddie performed introductions. "Joe, Iris, I'd like you to meet our friends, Fleggie and Sweetmaye. Fleggie and Sweetmaye, these are people who are important in Lena's and my lives. We hope that you'll have some time to get acquainted."

"It be very good to meet ye. It were a grand time on the sea and it be a grand thing to be home again!" Fleggie spoke up.

"Fine thing it is, to meet ye," Sweetmaye added.

"Pleasure to meet you Fleggie... Sweetmaye," Joe responded.

Iris shook hands with each of them and smiled her dazzling smile.

"Iris and I would like to stay behind and visit with Captain Wyndham. Would you four like to start your trek back uptown? Perhaps we could meet for dinner later tonight. Would that suit you?"

"Well... we been out t' sea for six weeks, sir, an' me girl an' me here wou' like t' check in at our yard. Still, Fleggie ca' make out tha' ye have something serious to talk on, so we'll do our best."

"Would you like company back to your place?" Lena offered.

"Aye. We ca' catch up an' then see how th' wind blows once we be settled in," Fleggie agreed.

"We'll be needin' nourishment later anyways." Sweetmaye added, "An' after six weeks o' non-stop cooking, I'd not mind a few mealtimes' worth o' holiday for me homecoming."

So the two young couples strolled up the wharf. Iris and Joe stayed to talk with the captain. Eddie was sure that the purpose of this was to gather Thomas Wyndham's impressions of his newest crew members, but in any case he was looking forward to catching up with Fleggie and Sweetmaye.

Lena spoke first. "Oh, it is so good to see you both. Do you feel up to talking? We would certainly understand if you would prefer to rest and be alone."

"Oh, and 'tis good to see ye both as well. We be a tad worn, but ready enough to gab a bit," Sweetmaye replied with her warm smile.

"The *Mother Rose* be a fine ship, and th' crew were a pleasure. Come spring me girl an' me cou' might sign on again! Th' work were right enough. No' a burden," Fleggie added. He shifted their sea bag upon his broad shoulder as he strode along beneath the bright, cold sky.

"Glad to hear that it went well."

"Aye," and here Fleggie dropped his voice and bent close in to his friends, "an' th' pay were good! Cap'n added a wee might at th' end o' th' voyage. An' what he promise at th' start were good and more enou'. Aye. It were a fine day tha' ye brought us to meet Cap'n Thomas. Fleggie remembers that."

"True enou' said," said Sweetmaye.

"An' Cap'n Thomas. He knows o' the old magic an' th' old ways. It were an honor t' serve under him. He be a fair man," added Fleggie.

"So, what ha' befallen ye these past weeks?" Sweetmaye wondered. "Be ye still at th' big school?"

"Yes, Sweetmaye. The situation is slightly better at the university. The RSM people are still interfering with the curricula, but they had to back off after their private security guards tried to extend their territory into the town. The city patrol pushed back firmly. So, I am basically meeting with professors and other students off campus. We discuss readings and submit papers. It is not terribly convenient, but it is manageable. Best of all, this is my last semester."

"We've been involved in some work with Joe and Iris. I think you'll get to know them better later on," Eddie added.

"He an' she be powerful an' tha's true," Fleggie spoke in a subdued voice. "About her I canna' say, but there be somethin' that be... I dunno what exact-like. Fleggie has just enough o' the Sight t' tell tha' much."

"An'... well, Fleggie thinks he cou' might be an Old One," the big man added in a whisper.

"You guess well, Fleggie. More than that I'd rather not say. It would be best for them to talk to you directly."

"It be strange times when th' likes o' them needs t' be meetin' wi' th' likes o' Fleggie. True enou' tha' be."

The two young couples walked in silence for another half a block and then Sweetmaye suddenly spoke up, a laugh in the lilt of her voice.

"Say! It be near on time for midday meal. Thanks t' th' good cap'n, Fleggie an' me purse were near fat as er' ha' been. We be comin' up on th' Inn. Would ye care t' break bread? It'd please Fleggie an' me t' treat."

"Why, thank you very much, Sweetmaye! Reed and I would love to join you for lunch."

The four friends reached the Inn at Three Corners a few minutes later. Despite the cold weather, the place was doing a decent business. As usual, it was cozy in the public room, and the smells from the kitchen were inviting. They found places at a large table near the door to the kitchen.

Eddie saw Margaret, the cheerful, middle-aged waitress that he'd met on his first visit for breakfast months earlier, but until she spoke, he wasn't sure that she recognized him.

"Where ha' ye' been keeping yourself, young man? An' yer' beauty o' a girl?" she asked as she handed around menus.

"Hi, Margaret. I've been out of town. Just got back last week. These are our friends, Fleggie and Sweetmaye. And you remember Lena."

"It be a joy an' more t' see ye," said Lena.

"An' ye, darlin," came Margaret's easy rejoinder. Fleggie and Sweetmaye's eyes grew round to hear Lena match their style of speech so smoothly, but they recovered and smiled at the friendly waitress.

After Margaret took their orders and bustled off, Sweetmaye leaned forward and whispered to Lena.

"Ye talk th' dockside way as if ye cut yer milk teeth here! Why do ye tha'? An' how ca' ye manage it so handy?"

Lena's eyes shone as she replied, "'Tis a bonny way o' talk, an' pleasin' enough. Me ma's family ha' lived here past time's knowin'. She were raised in th' south, but ne'r forgot th' good speech o' her aunts an' th' like. An' she passed it on t' her little daughter – tha' be me – as best she cou'."

"What be yer las' name then?"

"It be Graysmith, but in th' habit o' th' south, me ma took me da's name. Her name were Bonham."

"Bonham, is it? Me da' had Bonhams in his line. Oh it were a sunny day if we two be cousins, true?" Sweetmaye laughed.

"True, Sweetmaye. It would be a sunny day indeed."

"But why do ye' tha' here? Ye also speak th' fine talk o' th' big school an' all."

"It were better t' blend in wi' th' place, think ye not? An' one other thing. Were some bad sort t' come 'round askin' after us, me speech cou' might throw 'em off th' scent, true?"

Fleggie and Sweetmaye nodded at this, understanding and sobered by the thought. But then Fleggie's natural good humor took hold.

He cleared his throat and spoke slowly and deliberately, "Indeed. Perhaps I should practice a more refined manner of speaking myself. It were... Oh, blast! Fleggie near' pulled it off!"

They all laughed hard at this. "Th' shadow ne'r strays far fro' th' cat. True enou', me darlins," added Sweetmaye as she wiped tears of laughter from her eyes.

They were still chuckling when Margaret brought their lunch. Conversation – conversation in all manner of dialects – trailed off as they enjoyed their food.

After lunch, the four friends walked up to Fleggie and Sweetmaye's salvage yard. As they approached the fence, they heard sounds of a vicious dog running around inside the yard. Snarling and barking, it was jumping, hurling itself at the fence.

Startled, Eddie stepped back from the fence. "Whoa! I didn't know you guys had a dog! Good thing we didn't need to hide out here. That thing sounds bad!"

Fleggie just chuckled. "Look o'er th' fence."

"Er, no thanks."

"Ha' faith, friend, an' look o'er th' fence."

Reluctantly, Eddie sidled up to the fence. The sounds grew louder, closer, and more frenzied. He gritted his teeth and jumped up to grab the top of the fence. Expecting to have his fingers bitten any second, Eddie pulled himself up and looked over. There was no dog or any other animal visible. A pattern of rocks lay in the dirt a few feet from the fence. The sounds emanated from the rocks.

Eddie laughed and jumped down. "That's pretty good, Fleggie. What do you call that spell?"

Fleggie was laughing and practically hopping from foot to foot with amusement. "Yer a brave un', true enou'. Fleggie doubts he'd a done th' same. I calls it 'bad doggie.' Me grand-da' taught Fleggie tha' one!"

Fleggie performed his gate-opening spell. He went over and kicked the pattern of rocks apart and the dog sounds cut off.

"Meant t' let ye know 'bout tha'. Forgot in all th' rush an' excitement o' shippin' out wi' th' *Mother Rose*."

"No harm done. Maybe you could teach it to me some time."

"Aye, an' sure enou'."

Michael C. Glaviano

The salvage yard looked as they had seen it last. Sweetmaye's and Fleggie's tidy cottage was undisturbed. They invited Lena and Eddie to stay and visit, but it was obvious that they were tired.

"We should let you two rest and get unpacked. Do you still feel up for meeting tonight with Joe and Iris, or would you rather that we set another time?"

"Nah. Fleggie be ready. Give him an' hour or so in th' kip an' he'll be right. How 'bout you, ma' girl?"

Sweetmaye nodded her agreement and added, "Aye. A pair o' hours' rest will put us right. Sweetmaye be fair thrilled t' meet wi' th' wise folk. An' 'twill be a rare chance for fancy dress, methinks. Say we come by your place 'round six?"

"Sounds perfect. Come to the bookstore. Iris owns it and lives in an apartment in the back. We'll meet you inside and talk for a few minutes before we go out."

The four friends said their good-byes and Lena and Eddie began their walk back to Tolemy's Cats. They'd walked the half a block or so up Viceroy to Turnbull when Eddie looked over his shoulder. The tall, apparently unbroken fence was back in place.

Out on the street, the frigid afternoon air barely stirred. Traffic continued to be sparse. Eddie and Lena walked down Turnbull and past the Inn. Twenty minutes later they they were upstairs in their apartment. It was warm and comfortable after being out in the weather.

"It was good to see Fleggie and Sweetmaye, was it not, my love?" Lena said as she hung up her coat and placed her shoes near the door.

"Yeah. It's funny how some people we just connect with and others don't seem to... I don't know... There's no resonance," he replied.

She went into the bathroom and Eddie could hear her running water in the sink. A few minutes later she came out. She was patting her face dry with a towel. Her auburn hair was brushed and shiny. She had left her pants in the bathroom. Her blouse was mostly unbuttoned and her shapely legs extended from beneath her shirt tails.

"Indeed. You and I resonated right away, however," she said as though there'd been no interruption in their talk.

"Yeah, we sure did," he agreed. "And I'm really glad of it."

"Do you want to go downstairs right away, Reed?"

"Not particularly."

"Me either."

"Um... I guess we could, ah, study."

Lena stepped lithely over to the wall bed, opened the doors and drew the bed down. She turned and smiled at Eddie. "Yes, I suppose we could. Perhaps you could study me. Closely."

Thirty Six

Eddie and Lena went down to the bookstore just before its nominal closing time of five o'clock. They let Joe and Iris know that Fleggie and Sweetmaye would be there within the hour.

"That's good. Do you happen to have their comm ID?" Iris asked.

"Well, yeah. Why?"

"I'd like to hire a wagon to bring them over."

"Um, okay, I guess. They've got their own utility wagon, though. That's what Fleggie uses for his salvage yard."

"I think it would be nicer to pick them up in a warm, enclosed vehicle. That way, after dinner, we can all ride together to drop them off."

While Iris called to make those arrangements, Joe had a question of his own.

"What did you say about us? About Iris and me and what we're up to?" he wondered.

"To be perfectly honest, Joe, we spoke little about either of you and nothing at all about our plans," Lena responded. "From his remarks, I gathered that Fleggie has what some call 'the sight.' At any rate, he is aware that there is something unusual about Iris and he flatly said that he thought you, Joe, are what he termed an 'Old One.'"

"Interesting. And neither he nor his young woman friend were put off by any of this?"

"Not at all, as far as we could tell," added Eddie. "But you know we really didn't discuss it."

Joe nodded. "Probably best."

"So, I assume that you spoke with Captain Thomas about Fleggie and Sweetmaye?" Eddie prompted.

"Of course. The good captain appears to share your positive impression of them."

"A group of six would be very good. It would make the process go somewhat more quickly," chimed in Iris. "I believe that we have overcome Joe's reticence."

"I am leaning that way, but I intend to make up my own mind."

Iris looked at him sharply and he quickly added, "not regarding your overall strategy, Iris. I have accepted that. I just want to be comfortable that Sweetmaye and Fleggie are the right ones to round out our group."

Eddie and Lena were both confident that Joe would come around to their point of view about Sweetmaye and Fleggie and they said as much to him. Joe held up his hands as if to call a time out.

"Please. I have heard what you have to say. Let me take the lead in this. I'm sure your friends will be fine, but I want to have a chance to speak with them before I give my approval. That's all. Now, I'd like to change the subject slightly. Here is the map of the portals. As before, it shows the order in which we'd like to proceed..."

The tone of Joe's voice was noteworthy. Eddie realized that he had in a sense forgotten who Joe really was. He'd gotten used to thinking of the ancient warrior as a mentor and then even somewhat as a friend. It must have taken a huge effort of will on Joe's part to remain patient and accommodating. Eddie resolved to be quiet and do his best to listen and learn.

The next half hour was occupied with technical discussions of the work that lay ahead. Both Iris and Joe agreed that the first and second re-openings would be relatively easy. The only real issue would have to do with their proximity to the university and the security guards on campus.

The third re-opening would be simple as well. It was the most recently active portal to which they had found reference in the historical records. The only problem there was its proximity to the wealthy neighborhood of Drake Hill.

The fourth might be tricky because it was due west of campus and in an area frequented by students. The fifth portal was the biggest question mark. Despite continuing investigation, Iris had been unable to find a record of anything in that area. But they were both confident that they could calculate an ideal location for it from the overall geometry of the pattern.

"If at all possible, Iris and I would like to tackle the first one of these tomorrow night. If we are successful, we will have two portals open to the place between worlds."

Iris spoke up. "And now I sense that Reed and Lena's friends are only a block from here. Even though we met briefly at the docks, they are excited but somewhat nervous about getting acquainted with Joe and myself. That much is obvious. I would like to welcome them to my shop."

She turned to Lena and Eddie. "Perhaps it would be less intimidating if you met them and exchanged pleasantries. Then I will make my appearance. Joe, gruff old trooper that he is, can be rolled out last."

Lena smiled slightly and stood. She reached her hand to Eddie and they walked to the front of the store. True to Iris' prediction, Fleggie's substantial form appeared moments later. His silhouette cast a wide shadow on the blinds that covered the front windows of Tolemy's Cats.

The door opened, and their friends from the salvage yard came inside. Fleggie, who had treated the confrontation with the security guards in front of Lena's residence hall as an afternoon's lark, did indeed appear to be nervous. Sweetmaye was also subdued and more serious than her usual buoyant self.

Eddie could tell immediately that Fleggie and Sweetmaye had worn their best clothes for the occasion. The big man wore a long, leather frock coat over a light colored sweater and dark wool trousers. He'd replaced his usual work boots with clean, polished shoes. Sweetmaye had on a simple black dress. She wore a bright red sash around her tiny waist. She had a heavy wool coat and black leather boots that reached her calves. Her wavy hair was wound into a knot atop her head.

Fleggie's worried look broke into a smile when he saw Eddie and Lena. Lena went over and quickly hugged both of their friends. Eddie shook Fleggie's hand and hugged Sweetmaye. The atmosphere took on a sense of gravity, almost a feeling of ceremony or ritual, but the nervousness withdrew.

"Welcome, both of you. We're glad that you could come and meet with us. We'll go out and have some dinner in a few minutes, but first Iris – Mrs. Abellona – would like to meet you and welcome you to her bookstore. Iris?" Eddie called out.

"I'll be right there!" came an answer from the back of the store.

The sound of her footsteps proceeded Iris up the aisle. She stepped around the corner of the tall row of shelves. And the four young friends each drew an involuntary breath as she came before them.

Somehow, in a matter of seconds, she had traded her nice but plain workday outfit for a deep green dress and a long coat. She wore formal boots that were both elegant yet perfect for the cold and wet season that was upon them. As a beautiful frame enhances a painting, her fiery hair curled back from the radiance of her face. The term "transcendent beauty" surfaced in Eddie's mind. The woman's smile was nothing less than stunning.

"Welcome! Welcome, to both of you! I hope and expect that we will someday be comfortable around each other, but I realize that the first few meetings are often stiff and awkward. This will quickly pass."

She held out her hands and clasped Fleggie's huge paw with her left as she took Sweetmaye's in her right. Her smile continued to dazzle, but warmth and acceptance flowed from her.

"Thank-ee, ma'am. We be glad," Fleggie managed. His voice was hoarse.

"'Tis a pleasure an' more to see ye again," Sweetmaye added, dimpling.

"Now I would like to introduce my old friend, Joe," Iris continued.

She looked serious for a moment. "Lena tells me that you have the sight, Fleggie. That you can tell something of our nature. Please understand, please *believe*, that we are as human as you. Yes, you have guessed correctly that Joe is old beyond what you could imagine. At the same time, he is a man. A strong and good man who wishes you well."

Fleggie nodded solemnly and swallowed. There was a little bit of perspiration at his temples. Sweetmaye looked watchful and alert but, unlike Fleggie, was not visibly nervous. Iris gazed intently at them for just a few more seconds. Then her expression relaxed. She radiated a sense of approval and satisfaction with what she had seen.

"Joe!?" she called. "Please join us and become better acquainted with our new friends. Our brief exchange at the docks this morning bears elaboration."

A few seconds later, Joe stepped around the corner of the bookshelves. He wore a dress shirt, open at the collar, with a vest. Dark slacks matched a soft wool scarf that he wore lightly draped over his shoulders. Joe wore a coat similar in cut to Fleggie's, although darker in color.

Joe strode forward and shook hands with Fleggie and Sweetmaye each in turn. In each case, he clasped their right hand with both of his. He held each handshake for a few seconds and then released his grasp. Then he stepped back and let out a sigh.

"Thank you both," he said. "I... required... the chance to see you carefully in a quiet, protected place. It was necessary to look deeply inside you. Please excuse that. But yes, in your hearts you are as our young friends, Reed and Lena, as our experienced Captain Wyndham, and as our fierce angel, Iris have all claimed. You will be a boon to us."

Sweetmaye smiled slightly. Fleggie stood a little straighter. The big man's eyes flashed suddenly bright, as if filled with unshed tears.

Joe rubbed his hands together and laughed his infectious laugh. "Now, let's go see if we can find something to eat!"

"What about the Running Tortoise over on St. Zeno's?" Eddie asked.

"Oh, I've heard that place is pretty good from my friends at school," offered Lena. "Let us at least go by there and give it a look."

So it was agreed. It was a twenty minute walk to St. Zeno's and the night had grown colder. Iris suggested they hire a wagon to take them to the restaurant. "There will be one along in just a moment," she offered with a tiny smile at the corner of her mouth.

Indeed, a comfortable cab rolled up within moments. They piled in and Eddie gave the directions. The six of them chatted as the vehicle rolled along. A short ride brought them to the front of the restaurant.

As they emerged from the wagon, Joe and Iris suddenly hesitated, exchanged glances. "Driver. Would you mind waiting for just a moment?" Joe spoke quietly to the cabby.

They walked up to the window and looked at the menu posted there. The food looked good enough. There was a fine variety. Eddie was just starting to reach for the door when Iris spoke up.

"Reed, do you or Lena know anyone who works here? Someone who might... experience strong feelings upon seeing us all together?"

"Gee, not that I know of. You, Lena?"

She shook her head.

"There! Who is that woman?" Joe asked, pointing through the window into the restaurant.

Eddie's heart fell. "Oh... that's Anna Dymond. She and I used to work at the Orca."

Just then, Anna looked up to the window. Her face hardened as she saw them looking at her and then she turned abruptly away.

"Wow, I didn't expect to see her here. Maybe we'd better find someplace else to eat."

"Yes, we need neither the attention nor the bad feelings," Lena added.

"Not to worry. Fleggie be fine anywhere."

"Let's get back in the cab." Iris suggested. I think I know just the place.

So they had a longer drive, but in the end it was to a better restaurant. The place was called "Morgan's Pub." It was a restaurant in a slightly more upscale part of town near the intersection of Harbor and Meridian.

"Good choice, Iris," Joe smiled as they stepped inside. The entryway was warm and quiet.

"This is one of the oldest, continuously operated restaurants in Soapstone Bay," Iris explained to their young guests. "It is very nice but not terribly fancy. It has been in the same family for at least seven generations. The only place I know that is older is the Inn at Three Corners, and unlike this establishment, the Inn has changed hands many times over the years."

"Iris and I have eaten here... before." Joe added. He took Iris' hand, and met the woman's steady gaze. Her lovely face was unreadable in the soft light of the restaurant. The lighting and the decor came from a much earlier age and the overall effect amplified Iris' beauty.

The maitre d' materialized from the depths of the dining room. "Dinner for... ah, six?" he asked. His voice faltered just slightly as he cast

Michael C. Glaviano

his eyes across the party and rested for just a second on each of the three beautiful but very different women.

"Yes. And we have some business to discuss. If at all possible, could you seat us somewhere where we might speak without being over-heard?" Joe asked.

Their host recovered and focused his eyes on the eldest of the group. "Certainly, sir. We have a large table near the back of the restaurant, and we are not terribly busy on such a cold night. Please follow me."

The maitre d' turned and the group followed him into the interior of the restaurant. As he had claimed, there was a large table that would be ideal for their purpose. A coat rack stood adjacent to it, and half walls jutted out from the rear of the room to render the space reminiscent of a private dining room. Comfortable chairs surrounded the table, and what few other diners had braved the cold night were seated well away.

"This will do nicely. Thank you so much," Joe spoke softly. Naming a specific label and vintage, he requested that wine be brought. The maitre d' smiled in a bemused sort of way and went off to fetch the wine.

The six of them seated themselves around the table. Looking at one another, they sat in silence for a moment. The younger four relaxed slightly.

Iris made small talk and helped the newcomers feel more com-fortable. "We will move to serious topics soon enough," she announced. "I believe we shall find the food here satisfying and enjoyable. And it will be a pleasure to pass the evening meal in such good company."

As if on cue, the maitre d' returned with a small wine cart. He had three bottles of the wine Joe had selected. He went through the wine ritual with Joe, who found the offering to his liking. The host poured the wine around and then withdrew.

Raising his glass, Joe stood. The others followed suit.

"To friends. To the worlds. May all that is good thrive. May the gods dream well," he spoke softly, but distinctly. It was a scene of great dignity and beauty. The hands that held the glasses, the lips that tasted the vintage, spanned an enormous gulf. The weight of the moment es-caped no one.

As the six stood, the maitre d' had started to approach but found that he was rooted to the floor halfway across the dining room. He heard not one syllable of Joe's words, but the sight of the six people standing for the toast filled him with a powerful emotion. With amazement, the man realized that he was weeping, and when he was again able to move, he turned away and passed through the kitchen and on to a private corner of the restaurant. There, he wiped his eyes and composed himself before returning to carry on with his duties. For the rest of his life, he carried that image at the center of his heart. He never spoke of it to any-one.

366

Dinner was indeed a pleasure. The restaurant was quiet. During the meal, the six of them existed in a scope outside the normal flow of space and time. Restaurant staff came and went, but always at the right time, always at an ebb in the conversation, when it was convenient to pause and admit others into the sphere that surrounded them.

At one point, Joe remarked casually, "So, Fleggie. Reed here says that you have a salvage yard."

Fleggie, suddenly laser-focused attention, nodded in assent.

"Do you think you might have or be able to acquire a stout rod of metal? The metal must be of the type to feel the effects of a magnet. The rod should be the diameter of my thumb and be longer then you are tall by at least a head."

Fleggie stared long at Joe. He looked to the left and right; although no one was near to the six.

"So ye mean t' open doors, sir. Fleggie wondered as much. Hoped as much. An' me an' Sweetmaye are t' help."

"If you are willing."

"We be willing. We be honored t' help ye," spoke Sweetmaye in a soft voice.

"Aye. Fleggie can get what ye need. When?"

"Tomorrow evening if possible. Sooner is better in this instance."

"An' Fleggie is t' bring it t' th'... place we met tonight? Or some other?"

"If we can use your wagon, it would be best to meet somewhere else. This time at least."

"Aye. Tha' be fine. Fleggie will lay upon th' rod a thick blanket and then a net of metal. A heavy wire fro' th' net shall trail over th' back of th' wagon, t' th' ground. Prying eyes will see less then. True?"

"Very good, Fleggie. That is perfect. Your grandfather knew much."

"Too much died wi' him, sir."

"Much will return if we succeed."

Joe turned to Iris. "Where should we meet?"

Iris looked far off. If she was pleased at his deference, she showed it only in a momentary softening of her eyes. She was silent for a few seconds.

"If one of us accompanies our young friends, we can offer some protection and defense on this first... action. What say I start out from the yard with Sweetmaye? I shall walk from the bookstore to the yard. Fleggie will walk in the opposite direction. He and I will cross paths at the southern tip of the Inn. He will continue on to meet Lena and Reed at the bookshop. From the shop, Fleggie, Lena, and Reed can walk together up to Meridian and then over to Harbor. We will pass by in the wagon and collect them as they walk west. We will meet you at the site."

"Yes, Iris, that will be fine," Joe agreed. "For this first opening, we should orchestrate everything beforehand, separate at the start, and then come together for the action. That will obscure our trail. Something similar may be appropriate for the second. After that, we shall see."

Dinner passed in this manner. There were plans presented and questions asked. Some questions were answered, but that was not always possible. In between, there was fine food and wine.

When it was time to go, the maitre d' – although he could not have said why – attempted to refuse payment for the meal. Joe and then Iris graciously and gently but firmly insisted that the restaurant be paid. The host stared long at the door that closed behind the six of them.

Another cab pulled up just as they left the restaurant and stepped onto the sidewalk. The night had become even colder, but the vehicle's cabin was large and comfortable. They rode across the quiet town and let Fleggie and Sweetmaye off in front of their salvage yard.

"Until tomorrow evening then. Six o'clock at the south point of the Inn. Oh, and bring your stoutest foul weather gear. A serious storm threatens," Iris called.

"Aye. An' tomorrow it be."

The remaining four rode back toward the shopping district. The cab let them off in front of Tolemy's Cats. The next day the driver had no recollection of that particular fare or how he came by the large tip he found in his jacket pocket.

*　*　*

Sunrise was obscured by leaden clouds and drizzling rain. As before, it started out more of a steady soaker than a violent storm, but by midday, strong gusts of wind buffeted the awnings and storefronts uptown. Reinforcing Iris' statement of the previous night, the weather service indicated that a major storm was heading in from the northeast. It was unclear when it would make landfall. They gathered what rain gear they had. Lena already had most of what she needed, but she and Eddie went out early and purchased some additional pieces for Joe, Eddie, and Iris.

"Couldn't you use some sort of spell to keep the weather from getting bad?" Eddie wondered aloud when, mid-afternoon, they checked in with the older couple.

"We could do that, but the spell of opening must be performed precisely, and it's best not to risk perturbing it. Also, if conditions are right, I may use some of the storm's energy to help us punch through. Most importantly, the bad weather is likely to keep prying eyes indoors," Joe explained.

"So, it is better to leave the weather alone and make the best of it," he concluded. Joe stepped back and fell silent. The old man locked eyes briefly with Iris and then sat in one of the chairs in her little living room. He withdrew into some deep place.

"Yes," Iris spoke up. "Soon Joe and I will make our own preparations, but here is what we will need from you two. First of all, from the time we pick you up in the wagon, try not to speak except, once we reach the site, to repeat your parts of the spell. In fact, Joe and I will be concentrating deeply, so it would be helpful if you did not so much as try to make eye contact."

"Will we know what to repeat?" Lena asked.

"I will make that clear. Once I have you positioned you must stay where I place you. Then I'll stand where you'll be able to see me. I will gesture, like this, to you when I want you to repeat."

Here Iris reached both hands out, palms up, just above waist high. Her hands curved gently, as though she expected to catch falling rain in the palms of her hands.

"When I let my hands fall to my sides, you will fall silent. Watch the rise and fall of my breath and try to synchronize your own breathing. I will let Sweetmaye and Fleggie know these things as well."

Iris insisted that Lena and Eddie be able to repeat these instructions back to her.

"This evening at six, moving in opposite directions, Fleggie and I will walk past one another at the Inn. Allow perhaps a quarter of an hour and then go outside and wait for him. When Fleggie arrives, walk down St. Tolemy's and cross University. I think you should get off University as quickly as possible, so just walk as far as Union and take that to Harbor. Walk slowly up Harbor until Sweetmaye and I come by in the wagon."

"We will pull past you perhaps a block – I intend to cast about to ensure that we are not observed – and wait for you to catch up. Scramble aboard as quickly as you can. Again, do not speak. Fleggie is big enough so that he should sit on one side of the wagon and you two on the other. Balance is key. Balance and concentration. Focus your gaze on the metal netting and steady your breathing."

"Now, when we arrive at the site, I will leave the wagon first. I will point to each of you in turn. When I point to you, climb from the wagon and walk to where I stand. Place your feet where I have stood. Once you are positioned, I will take my place and turn to face you."

"Finally, once we are done, Joe and I will return the rod to the wagon. Step back, out of the way and do not try to help. Do not touch either of us or the rod itself. Even if one of us stumbles or the rod slips from our grasp or some other interruption occurs, just stand and watch. We will take care of it. Once I am on the bench in front, return to the wagon and take your places. Try to move quietly but quickly."

Now Iris insisted that the young couple repeat this as well, and then the first set of instructions once again. Satisfied at last, Iris held her hands out to them and smiled. The gesture was much the same as what she'd used to greet Fleggie and Sweetmaye the previous evening. They held hands briefly. Then she asked them to go upstairs and eat some good, solid food. And wait.

Lena and Eddie returned to their apartment. They were glad for the warmth and the quiet of their place. They ate and then snuggled next to each other on the sofa. They laid a small, plaid blanket across their laps and held hands. As the afternoon wore on, the storm grew in intensity. Rain lashed the windows, and whistling wind tugged at the stone corners of the building.

Even though they were keyed up, the buffeting of the storm outside and the warmth of the apartment, together with the comfort of being near one another worked a simple magic on them. Slowly, they relaxed and, eventually, dozed off. A crash of thunder woke them just after five o'clock. The heavy clouds darkened the sky and made the time appear later than it was. They stretched and snacked and made themselves ready.

Eddie practiced his simple spells for casting light and for illuminating the area beneath his feet. He didn't expect to use them, but he needed to do something while they waited. At last it was time. They pulled on layers of clothing for warmth and then their outer layers of rain gear and locked the door behind them as they left the warmth and comfort of the apartment. The young couple held hands again as they stepped quietly down the stairs.

They waited for a few moments inside the tiny lobby at the bottom of the stairs. The wind and rain continued unabated. They fastened up the last of their gear, stepped outside, and were immediately glad for the heavy raincoats, boots, and hats. Hands inside gloves that were jammed inside pockets, they looked down the street, toward Turnbull Road. It was only a minute or two before Fleggie's large frame emerged from the rain and mist.

Grinning broadly in the face of the storm, he strode up to them. "Great night fer it. True enou'? Ye can scarce see more 'n a block, an' tha' be a good thing, thinks Fleggie."

They walked along the side of the building and out to University Avenue. Visibility was poor, but from what they could see, the street was completely deserted. The rain came down and the wind snatched at their words to make talk difficult. Quickly they darted across the wide thoroughfare and walked up the south side of the street to Union. All the shops they passed were closed. All the windows were dark.

At Union they turned left and walked the two blocks to Harbor. Union was dark, but Harbor had street lamps. Each pool of yellow light was streaked with rain that slanted in the heavy wind. As on University, the storefronts were dark. The shadows beneath the awnings were deep and impenetrable.

The storm drove them into their individual thoughts and they leaned forward slightly as they walked. As Iris had instructed, they kept their pace deliberately slow and steady. They walked for perhaps ten minutes when, barely discernible beneath the bluster, the chatter and hiss of the storm, they heard the quiet electric hum of a wagon just behind.

They let the wagon pass without turning their heads. It was indeed Iris and Sweetmaye perched on the bench of Fleggie's wagon. The women were bundled beyond recognition, but the wagon was familiar. And they could just make out the fat wire that extended from the metal net to trail upon the pavement.

The wagon trundled past without pausing. It passed through one, two, then a third cone of rain-streaked light as it drew even with street lamps. It was now dark enough so that the wagon all but vanished in-between the shining pools. Barely visible at the edge of illumination, the vehicle drew to a stop in the next block.

It felt like a long, exposed walk, but it was really just a matter of a minute or so before they reached the wagon. They hastened aboard, Lena and Eddie on the street side and Fleggie on the sidewalk side. Then the wagon continued on.

Eddie sat hunched over in the back of the wagon. He could feel Lena pressed against his side. The windblown rain was cold on his face but he was warm inside his rain gear. He glanced across the wagon at Fleggie. Peering alertly into the murky night, the big man was huddled within his own foul weather gear.

It was full dark by the time they reached Biscayne and turned south. Few lights were visible on the campus at their right. Biscayne marked the western boundary of the upscale Drake Hill neighborhood. As he craned his neck around to look behind him, Eddie could see a few lights glimmering through the drapery-shrouded windows of the large homes.

Gradually, they all settled down. As Iris had instructed, they focused their attention on the object that lay in the bed of the wagon. The rod itself was wrapped in a tarp and was visible only as a dim shape in the darkness. The wire mesh that overlay their cargo was visible in the light of the occasional street lamp. Fastened to the mesh, a heavy wire trailed over the side of the wagon to drag on the pavement.

They passed the southern boundary of the campus. It was marked by an ornamental section of wall and a final street lamp. Had it been daytime, they would have noticed immediately that the groomed lawns of the university gave way to a well-stewarded, new-growth forest. A short time later, the wagon slowed, and then, following a narrow, unmarked track, it entered the woods.

The wagon crept forward in the rainy darkness. Continuing west, roughly parallel to the southern edge of the campus, they moved deeper into the young forest. Eventually they made out a dim glow among the trees. Iris pulled to a stop. Then she carefully maneuvered the wagon around so that it pointed back the way they had come. She extinguished the running lights. The sound of the rain and the wind pressed in on them.

As Iris leapt from the wagon, Joe emerged from beneath the trees. He was cowled and wrapped in a dark, heavy cloak, and he pulled his hood back to look at the four young assistants who waited in the wagon. He nodded at them solemnly before tugging the cowl back in place.

Joe and Iris clasped hands briefly, then strode quickly to the rear of the wagon. They drew off the mesh and unwrapped the heavy rod. Joe dragged the grounding rod from the bed of the wagon and together they carried it over to the place where light glowed among the trees. Finally, holding the heavy rod in a vertical position, Joe stood as still as the sturdy boles of the trees that surrounded him.

Iris stood a short distance to the side. She planted her feet carefully. Now she looked up and gestured to Lena. The young woman sprang lightly down and moved quickly to where Iris was standing. From his vantage point in the wagon, Eddie could see that footprints glowed where Iris had stood, so it was easy for Lena to place her feet precisely.

Next, Iris beckoned to Sweetmaye. Then she got Fleggie into position. Eddie felt alone and exposed for those few moments during which he waited, alone in the wagon. Finally Iris gestured to Eddie. He jumped down and walked to his place in the pattern. He placed his feet within the glowing outlines she had left for him.

Standing as they were, beneath the trees, they were sheltered from the brunt of the storm. It rained, but the water that reached them had dripped down through the living forest canopy. The rich, loamy floor of the forest was deep and it absorbed a great deal of water, so where they stood was wet but not muddy. The smells that reached them were the aromas of living things, vibrant and wild: pine and oak and birch, fungi, birds and forest animals both large and small. The night around them was alive.

Now they could sense a pulsing, golden light emanating from Iris. They realized that it pulsed in time with her breath and they easily matched their own breathing with hers.

Finally, her rich contralto began to chant:

May the gods dream
May they dream of us
May their dreams delight them

A low humming sound rose up in the surrounding darkness. From where Eddie stood, he could make out that the rod had begun to glow. This time gesturing for them to repeat after her, Iris continued:

We come here reverently
We come here to open a door to the place between worlds
We seek to heal this world, all worlds
We wish peace and happiness for all living creatures

The rod sang out several octaves higher than the low hum that emanated from the forest. The rod's glow had intensified to a bright green, almost fierce color. Iris paused as the sound and the light both grew more intense. Again she indicated that the four young people should echo her words:

Now the door opens
Now the door opens
Now the door opens!

At the third repetition a bolt of green lightning hurtled up from the grounding rod. It was met at the treetops by an electric blue flash of lightning from the sky. There was a sizzling sound and a whiff of ozone, but no thunderclap. In the afterimage, Eddie thought he saw the misty landscape of the Place Between stretching off in all directions.

Iris gestured, and the running lights of the wagon came up while the golden glow surrounding the site of the new portal faded. Eddie could see that Joe was struggling to remain standing and his first instinct was to jump forward to support his mentor and friend. Then he recalled Iris' words of warning and held steady instead. His other friends did the same. Each of them drew off to the side as Iris came forward.

She took over the support of the rod. Joe stepped back and dropped to his knees. He rested there for several minutes. The forest returned to normal. The rain fell through the trees to drip around them. At last Joe took a deep breath and got to his feet. Iris tipped the rod towards him and the old man reached up to grasp it. Together, they returned the grounding rod to the wagon and wrapped it in its tarp. Then they covered the rod with the mesh and made sure the metal lead touched the earth behind the wagon.

She and Joe climbed onto the bench in the front of the wagon. Once they were settled, Iris gestured for the four young people to climb into the back. Then, their passage masked by the darkness, the rain, and the wind, they trundled along the narrow track to emerge from the forest. Turning north, they retraced their path through the town, all the way to Fleggie and Sweetmaye's salvage yard.

They pulled up in front of the fence and Fleggie jumped out to open the invisible gate. As they pulled to a stop inside the yard, Sweetmaye spoke in a low, gentle voice.

"I've left mulled cider on me stove. Come in if it please yer, an' rest a bit before ye return home. Ye'll be th' better for it. True, now."

"Thank you, young woman," Joe agreed softly. "I think that is a fine idea. Do you agree, Iris?"

"Yes, I do."

So the six of them gathered around Sweetmaye and Fleggie's rough, homey table. Sweetmaye spoke the heating spell she'd learned from Eddie and soon served them each a large mug of hot, strong cider. In the dim lamplight, Eddie was shocked to see the heavy lines on Joe's face.

The cider was full of cinnamon and orange and carried a hint of cardamom and more exotic things. It restored and warmed them all. They were very quiet, each content to sit with his or her own thoughts. Eddie glanced once or twice over towards Joe and was relieved to see that the older man's vitality was quickly reasserting itself.

Eventually, Joe set his mug on the table. He sighed contentedly.

"Well, I think we should be getting home now. I for one need to rest. We should repeat this process tomorrow evening at the northernmost vertex of our field of portals. Are you willing to do this again?"

There were nods all around. Joe smiled. "Good. You did well this evening. Iris and I have talked about this and we've agreed to vary the sequence slightly tomorrow evening.

"Reed and Lena will come here tomorrow at half past six. The four of you should take the wagon up Longview. Look for Iris. She'll be waiting in a safe location. Once she joins you, take up the same positions in the wagon that you used tonight. Iris will drive to our rendezvous."

"After tomorrow evening, we will suspend these activities for a few days," Iris added. "We will have completed the outer of the two triangular patterns. Soon after, we'll meet and decide our next plans. Now, we should make our way home."

Joe stood and Iris took his arm. Whether it was a companionable gesture or an unobtrusive way to provide physical support, Eddie couldn't tell.

They thanked their hosts and said their good byes. It was still raining and despite the foul weather gear, Eddie was not excited at the prospect of a wet, cold walk home. As they reached the sidewalk outside the salvage yard, however, a vacant cab pulled up and stopped. The driver appeared to be sleeping. Iris smiled her secret smile. They rode home in silence.

*　　*　　*

Lena and Eddie slept deeply and did not wake until midmorning. The weather outside was unchanged, and the storm continued to hammer the solid old building. They slipped from their warm bed and made breakfast together. Then they brought it back to bed to eat it: a little nest in the eye of the storm.

Sometime later they got up to face the day. Eddie offered to clean up while Lena signed onto the school network to check on the status of the papers she'd submitted for her degree. All appeared to be in order. Lena wondered aloud if having her final semester so watered down had devalued her degree and whether it was worth the effort to wrap things up. Eddie encouraged her to finish. He reminded her that both Iris and Joe had brought it up as well. In any case, it was more-or-less done and Lena was unequivocally glad of that much.

More to the point of their immediate concerns, the reports from her friends on campus indicated nothing, no awareness of the events of the previous night. That relieved some of the tension that both felt. She was careful not to ask any but the most casual-seeming questions.

"What's been going on? Any news? Anything interesting happening?"

They read and talked and relaxed a little. About an hour after lunch, they went downstairs to check on Iris and Joe and found them up and active, engaged in mundane tasks. Iris was helping a customer who had braved the storm to pick up the latest novel by a favorite author. Joe was repairing some worn fixtures in the kitchen. He appeared for all the world as though he were in his own house on Painter Avenue.

"How are you feeling, Joe?"

"Oh, I'm more-or-less back to normal now, thanks. I've done this sort of thing many times in the past. It is wearing but my constitution is such that I bounce right back. I will be ready in time for this evening's work."

"And then we will leave things alone for a little while?"

"Yes, I think that is for the best. As I believe Iris mentioned last night, we should all rest for a few days.

"Also, at some point we must return to our home world and do some work there," his mentor added. "Here, we are preventing the Queen from gaining a solid footing; there, we must see what we might do to reverse the damage. There are a few others on our world whom I can and should enlist to help."

"We'll have to pass through the Place Between."

"Of course."

"What are we going to do about that... that *thing*?" Eddie hadn't mentioned it to Lena or his friends, but he'd dreamed a few times of the beast that had pursued them in their past two transits. He couldn't bear to call it Alicia.

"I don't know yet, son. For now, all we can do is move quickly and try to avoid her. At this point, she's far more beast than human. She started out bent on some kind of vengeance, but now, in her present state, she will surely wander."

Eddie was disappointed that his mentor had no better solution for the situation and of course Joe sensed this. "Look, son. We'll do what we can, but we can't upset the balance. We don't own the Great Hub. We transit it by the sufferance of the dreams of the gods."

"I understand that. At least I think I do. There just should be something I can do to help." Then Eddie had a thought, "I guess there's one thing," he added.

"What would that be?"

"As soon as the storm passes, I'm going to spend some serious time practicing my axe throwing."

"As long as you don't get overconfident, I think that's a very good thing for you to do."

"Overconfident? That's pretty funny."

The rest of the afternoon crawled past. By evening the storm had weakened. Even so, Lena and Eddie donned their rain gear for the walk up to Fleggie and Sweetmaye's place. Their friends were ready and waiting for them when they arrived. They all piled in the wagon and set off up Longview. The wind had died down and the heavy rain had dropped to a steady drizzle.

Unlike the illumination on Harbor, which bounded a wealthy neighborhood, the street lamps on Longview were widely spaced. They drove slowly on the nearly empty streets. The wagon moved quietly through the rain and darkness as they looked for Iris. They were three-quarters of the way up the street and starting to get worried that they'd missed her when a light flared off to the right.

It flashed again and they saw that it illuminated a figure. They slowed down to a crawl. They drew nearer. Iris, her face clearly visible in the running lights of the wagon, stepped from the curb. As Iris climbed up to the bench seat to join Sweetmaye at the controls, Lena climbed back into the bed of the wagon to lean against Eddie. Lena worked her hand inside the pocket of his raincoat and they held hands as the wagon continued up Longview.

The street intersected Biscayne at an angle that marked the north end of the university campus. This was the beginning of some low, rolling hills that extended north into farm country. During harvest time and in the summer, this road was used throughout the day and night by farmers from outlying areas. Their stout, heavily laden wagons brought produce to markets in Soapstone.

During the summer months, visitors from small, outlying villages added to the parade of wagons and electric carts. This time of year, however, people stayed close to home. The road was rarely used, and only an occasional vehicle made the journey into the town for supplies or social events.

Just past the intersection, a smaller road angled off to the left. This slender byway ran parallel to the northern boundary of the campus.

Longview continued and eventually crested the rise of the first hill. They turned off Longview and took the narrow road west.

This road was slightly better than the track through the forest, but the terrain around was largely open, and they didn't want to rely on more than their running lights, so they travelled slowly. After several minutes, they could just barely make out a dim glow off to their left. Iris pulled the wagon off the road and inched carefully toward the glowing light. When she got close they could see Joe's figure, dressed as on the previous night. As before, Iris swung the wagon around so that it would be quick and easy to get away once they had finished their work.

Joe joined them at the wagon. He and Iris again unloaded the heavy grounding rod and set it up. Then, one at a time, Iris called them from the wagon. The spell went as smoothly as it had the first time; although Joe had to rest for a longer time before he was able to get up and help return the rod to the wagon. Without the surrounding forest, Eddie was sure that the brilliant beams of light had been visible for miles around, so he was on edge until they were packed up and well on their way down the road to the salvage yard.

Once more, they stayed with Fleggie and Sweetmaye and drank hot mulled cider. Joe looked far more worn this evening than he had the night before, and he barely spoke as he sipped his cider. He withdrew into himself and kept his eyes closed for much of the time. His breathing was labored, as if he had to force air into his lungs consciously.

Later that night, as Lena and Eddie lay together in the darkness, Eddie wondered if all was as they'd been told. The changes in Joe's energy and appearance were so drastic that they were both worried.

"Do you think there's something else going on?" Eddie whispered.

"I do not know, Love. How *could* we know? We are relying on Joe and Iris for all of our information."

"Well, at least they've said that this is the last portal for a while," he whispered.

They whispered back and forth for some time as they held each other. Eventually, Eddie realized from the way she was breathing that Lena had fallen asleep in his arms. He shifted his weight slightly to turn on his back. Without waking, she snuggled in closer with her head on his chest.

*   *   *

Joe was weak after the second portal opening and didn't appear the entire next day. Eddie and Lena hung around the bookshop. Iris said that Joe continued to sleep. For most of the day, they filled in for Iris so that she, in turn, could care for Joe.

On the afternoon of the second day, Joe called them back to Iris' apartment. He looked more himself, but he was still tired. He tried to reassure them and explain away his condition.

"Look, I appreciate everyone's concern. I overdid it. Nothing more. These portals hadn't been open for a long time, so it was difficult to get them open and stable. It took a lot of energy, and I suppose I haven't yet fully recovered from my efforts to reverse Iris' aging."

"So what are you going to do?"

"Just what we decided in the first place. We'll wait here for a few days and then see about opening the portal at Merryweather Park."

"Oh, and in the meantime, you can practice with that axe of yours," he added.

Eddie gave a laugh. "Well... okay. Lena and I are glad you're taking it easy."

"Indeed we are, Joe," Lena spoke quietly but earnestly. "My studies are all but complete. I have learned that there will be no graduation ceremony, but that is nothing compared to the actual finishing of the work. In the days ahead, I will help Iris and visit with our friends."

"You can do something else," Joe replied. "Maintain communication with your friends from the university. See if there is any change. Is the softening of the barrier between this world and the place between worlds having an effect? We are entering the depths of winter. Going abroad will be more and more challenging for at least the next two months. More people will stay in this vicinity than at other times of the year. We'll be looking to see a burst of creativity in the local arts community. That would be a good sign."

"I can do that. Iris and I will discuss what I learn. It may even be possible to return to campus at some point."

"I don't want you to take any unnecessary risks, Lena," Eddie cautioned.

Lena swiveled her head and met his eyes. Her voice was calm and level but her blue eyes flashed in a way that reminded Eddie of Iris at her fiercest. "Excuse me? You travel through the realm of the tears of the gods. You dodge ravening beasts. Your dreams are troubled by what you've seen – yes, I have noticed that, Reed. You feel compelled to learn to throw an axe, may the gods dream happily!"

Here she paused and took a deep breath before continuing. "Yet you worry over my inquiring whether it might be feasible to return to a university campus? That is almost amusing, Reed. Almost, but not quite."

"I'm sorry, Lena. I didn't mean to imply that you couldn't handle yourself. I just... worry."

She looked at him for another few seconds and then, unable to maintain such a serious demeanor, she dimpled slightly. "It really is sweet, and I appreciate it on one level, but do try to remember where you first met me. Should the need arise, I am capable of defending myself."

Joe cleared his throat. "In any event, I suggest that you both enjoy the break in our efforts. Visit with Fleggie and Sweetmaye. Read. Practice. Learn. Spend time together just being a couple. Enjoy this time while you may. One never knows what will come next."

The next few days were indeed a welcome respite from all the darkness and strangeness. The four young friends spent a lot of their free time together. Eddie found that he enjoyed helping Fleggie at the salvage yard. They sorted things, sold things, bought and traded things.

Fleggie was fascinated by Eddie's axe throwing. He watched Eddie practice for a few hours and then asked to hold the axes and look closely at them. Quietly, almost lovingly, he turned the axes over and over in his huge hands. Fleggie carefully traced their outlines on some heavy paper before he handed them back to his friend.

"They be beautiful. True enough," was all he said.

Then the big man found some hardened steel plates and fashioned handles for them. He ground the edges of the heads to a rough shape and then filed them and finally honed them with a stone. His axes were proportioned to the size of his powerful frame, and although he was wild at first, he quickly developed a feel for the weapon.

As his accuracy developed, the effects of Fleggie's throws were truly something to behold. The young men obliterated a couple of targets before securing a huge tree trunk (which a homeowner up in Drake Hill paid them to remove) that could stand up to the punishment.

Having someone to practice with also helped Eddie tremendously. At first, the young women were amused by "their boys," but that initial feeling passed as the results of the hours of competitive practice became apparent. All four of them knew that danger lay around them. It was good to take some action.

Of course they didn't spend all of their time destroying things with their throwing axes. The four friends ate many meals together. When the weather was decent, they went for walks. They visited Captain Wyndham down at the *Mother Rose*. They were especially interested in walking the boundaries of the university and looking around.

Whether it was a coincidence or a result of their actions, change was indeed in the air. Despite the time of year, audiences were braving the weather to attend performances of several experimental plays. There were musicians in the clubs, attentive listeners at the tables. Review articles in the local newspaper remarked on the sudden resurgence of art and music in the usually sleepy town. Quietly, when no one else could hear, the two young couples discussed opening the other three portals. They were excited and wondered what effects those changes would bring.

* * *

A week later, Joe and Iris showed up at Sweetmaye and Fleggie's salvage yard. It was a Tuesday, a sunny afternoon. The air was cool and crisp, but the sky was a bright, robin's egg blue. The four young friends were enjoying the novelty of fine weather when the gate illusion faded briefly and Iris and Joe walked into the yard.

Fleggie stood and smiled happily. "Welcome be ye! Come, ha' a seat! What would ye like to drink? We ha' beer, mulled cider, an' maybe a bit o' wine."

Iris smiled. Her health, power, and youthful appearance were proving to be resilient. It was difficult for Lena and Eddie to look at her and remember how she had been just a few weeks earlier.

"Hello, everyone!" she called.

"Hey, Iris!"

"Hello, Iris!"

"It be a pleasure t' see ye' out an' about."

"You have Sweetmaye's wonderful mulled cider? I'll have that, please," her voice was musical and full of life.

Joe seemed rested. He looked more himself than he had appeared of late, more the vigorous middle-aged man that Eddie had known on his own world. "Good afternoon to you. Are you drinking beer? That sounds perfect on this sunny day."

Fleggie strode over to his tiny home and returned momentarily with drinks. He took the opportunity to refill everyone else's while he was up.

"Thank you, Fleggie. That's good," Joe said after tasting his beer. "Well, I've rested enough. It's time to open the portal at Merryweather Park," Joe added, casually. From the tone of his voice, he might as well have said, "I bought some socks yesterday."

"Well, when?"

"As soon as we can. Tonight, if possible."

Fleggie and Sweetmaye nodded. Fleggie rubbed his big hands together and looked decidedly pleased at the prospect. Lena and Eddie looked at each other and shrugged. "Sounds fine to us. Will this be the same as before?"

"Not quite. My, that *is* good," Iris sipped her cider again.

"It is different in two essential ways," she added. "First, this portal was open and active relatively recently, so it should not be so difficult to reactivate. That's the good news."

"And the not-so-good news?"

"We've just come from there," Joe spoke up. It's completely open and visible. And completely surrounded by homes. We are going to have to get there, reopen the portal, and get out of there very quickly."

"We think the best time to do this will be around three in the morning. I realize that's not the most convenient hour, but we want to have the best chance of escaping notice."

"Folks'll not be using th' park overmuch a' tha' hour, Fleggie thinks."

"Yes," Joe nodded, "but that's a well-to-do neighborhood. If anyone does notice us, they're certain to call the town patrol."

"Indeed. Reed and I have both seen how effective they are."

"No kidding. I'd just as soon not mess with them."

Iris took the lead in the conversation. "Joe and I have given this some thought. It's likely that we'll have at least ten minutes, and that's if someone notices us and calls the authority within minutes of our arrival. We might have as much as twice that, but we certainly can't count on that much time."

"With your permission, Sweetmaye and Fleggie, we'll all stay here tonight. The weather is fine, and Joe and I have secured camping gear for us and for Reed and Lena."

"T'would be our pleasure to host ye. True," smiled Sweetmaye.

"Thank you," Iris smiled in return.

"Now, we will get everything set up later this afternoon," she continued. "Joe will go to the park at two o'clock tomorrow morning to prepare the site. He can do that without being noticed. At two-thirty, we'll leave here. We will drive around the park in a wagon while I cast a sleep spell on all the houses that are close to the portal point."

"We have rented a wagon for the day. Joe will take that over to the park. After we open the portal, I'll take him back to the bookstore in that wagon. I can cast an invisibility spell over it."

Now Iris paused for a few seconds. "So, Reed?" she asked.

"Yes?"

"Have you been practicing your spells?"

"Well, yeah. I have. Some."

"Some." She looked at him with an unreadable expression. "Can you do invisibility?"

"A little."

"How little?"

"I can make things disappear. And I've sat on a bench uptown and made myself invisible to the people walking around. But, well, I haven't been able to cast it over a wide area. I haven't been able to get that part right."

"That will have to do. It will be dark, which makes it easier. You'll only need to keep the spell going for ten or fifteen minutes. Once you're part way up Turnbull, you'll be able to drop it. Joe will coach you this afternoon. Perhaps it might help to sit in the wagon to practice."

"Now, we would like to get going on the preparations. Joe and I will go back and get the camping gear and some heavy coats for Lena,

Reed, and us. I'd also like to pick up some things for dinner. So we can all eat together."

"Oh, I can feed us, tha' be true," Sweetmaye objected.

"We don't wish to impose any more than we already are," Joe spoke up.

"'Tis not an imposition t' share a meal wi' friends. We be friends, true?"

"Of course we are."

"Then 'tis settled!" Her eyes sparkled as the tiny, black-haired beauty laughed her outsize laugh.

Suddenly, the sunny and relaxing afternoon became busy as the salvage yard turned into a hive of activity. Joe and Iris left to pick up the rented wagon, camping gear, and warm coats. While they were gone, Fleggie and Eddie cleared some spaces for tents. The older couple re-turned within three-quarters of an hour. Then Joe joined Lena and Sweetmaye inside to help with the dinner preparations.

Iris, Eddie, and Fleggie set up two nice tents along with camp cots and sleeping bags in the recently-cleared, flat area near the little cot-tage. Fleggie had a sink mounted to the side of the cottage so that after working in the salvage yard he could clean up before going inside. This was conveniently next to where the tents were pitched.

Camp setup complete, Iris went into the house to relieve Joe so that the older man could work with Eddie. Joe came out a moment later and they prepared to practice. Fleggie hovered nearby. He was ill-at-ease, as if he wanted to say something but wasn't sure how to broach the topic. Eddie noticed first.

"What's up, Fleggie? I mean... what's on your mind? Er..."

"Fleggie takes yer' meanin', mate. He wonders. Does ye suppose Fleggie cou' learn this spell? It be a real spell. From th' old times. Me grand-da' spoke o' such as this."

"It's a fine idea, lad!" Joe agreed heartily. "Reed said that you'd learned some spells. The two of you performing the same spell at the same time will make the effects that much stronger."

The big man's face broke into a huge smile. The three of them started to work. Joe explained the words, the necessary mental image, and the hand motions appropriate to the invisibility spell. Fleggie quickly overcame his initial shyness. In this, as in many other things, Ed-die's friend possessed a natural affinity. And, as Joe had predicted, working together, Eddie and Fleggie were able to cast an effective, if basic invisibility spell over an area even bigger than the wagon.

"Good work, gentlemen. Let's let it be for a while. Then we'll practice again after dinner."

Laughing, Eddie and Fleggie shook hands spontaneously. They shared a new feeling of friendship, akin to that experienced by the members of any solid team. A few minutes later, the women called them to dinner.

Dinner was good and hearty, another seafood chowder that was balanced by Sweetmaye's home-baked bread. Of course, even with the food and companionship, the evening ahead of them overlay everyone's thoughts. Joe did his best to keep the mood relaxed by telling a few stories of worlds he'd visited and people he'd met over his long, long life. That helped a little perhaps, but everyone knew that tonight's effort would be the most exposed thus far, and the possibility of discovery weighed on them.

They cleaned up and the three men returned to the yard to practice. Within a half hour or so, it was clear that both Eddie and Fleggie had mastered the spell. Either one could cast a respectable invisibility spell. Together, they were even more effective. That was one less worry.

It was deep twilight when they returned to the cozy little house. The women were chatting and sipping mulled cider. The six of them sat together. At first they were keyed up, but they gradually settled down. Eventually, they were yawning. It had been a fine day, punctuated by good activities and useful results.

"I think I'd like to turn in. What do you think, Lena?"

"Yes, Reed. That sounds good. Will someone wake us at the right time?"

"Oh, indeed we will," Iris assured her. "Sleep well and soundly. Joe will keep watch on us all, and I can set my internal alarm clock. We'll wake you in plenty of time."

The three couples said their good-nights and moved to their various sleeping arrangements. Eddie and Lena pushed their cots together and zipped the two sleeping bags into one. The side bars of the camp cots made it difficult to snuggle, but Lena managed to get her leg over the impediment so that she could rest a foot on Eddie's leg.

In the small hours, they were awakened by Iris. Once that she saw that they were up, she moved to the little house and roused Fleggie and Sweetmaye. Joe had already gone to prepare the site. Eddie and Lena dressed in the cold darkness. Eddie needed a few moments of illumination spell so that he could find his shoes and socks.

It was the time of the new moon and so was full dark in the yard. Eddie splashed his face at the outside sink. They bundled up against the cold. Sweetmaye came out with mugs of hot chocolate. Soon it was time to go.

They took their usual places on Fleggie's wagon. Iris and Sweetmaye were on the front bench, Eddie and Lena on one side of the wagon bed, Fleggie on the other. The streets were dark and silent as they left the yard. Heading toward the docks, a couple of stray dogs cantered past. As they passed the Inn at Three Corners, a few stragglers stumbled from the common room to disperse into the darkness.

Their way took them far down Turnbull Road. A couple of blocks before Baleen Park, they turned right to head west on Spruce Street. The night was very still; the drive up Spruce was quiet and peaceful. Ornate, decorative street lamps lined the pavement of the neat neighborhood, but when they neared Merryweather Park they saw that the lamps had all been extinguished. They could just barely make out the wagon that Joe had used. It waited at the southwest corner of the park.

Iris guided the wagon around the park. She made the same hand gestures over and over, as though she flung something at each house they passed. She did this at a handful of houses on both Spruce and the cross street, Meridian. Finally, she drove back to the southwest corner.

Joe stepped up as they pulled to a stop behind the first wagon. They doused the running lights. He and Iris got the rod positioned. Then, Iris turned to face the two couples who waited in Fleggie and Sweetmaye's wagon. They all sensed that the clock was ticking rapidly.

Just as they were about to begin the ritual, a wagon came up the street. The vehicle lurched from side-to-side, and they could hear drunken voices raised in song. That set the neighborhood dogs off.

Joe steadied the heavy rod in his left hand. Quickly, he held up his right hand and made a complex gesture. The world around them faded behind a shimmering glow. The passing wagon grew fuzzy and dim. This was obviously very different from the simple invisibility spell that Eddie and Fleggie had practiced in the afternoon. The dogs gradually settled down again.

Joe nodded his head and Iris began again. This time the opening ritual went off without a hitch. The brilliant green light was connected to the beam that flowed down from the sky. Slowly the lights faded. Again, dogs barked in the yards of the big houses nearby. A few lights flickered on in the houses.

Joe recovered quickly, but he moved slowly. He and Iris got the rod back into Fleggie's wagon and then she motioned to Fleggie to help her get Joe into their wagon. That done, she waved the big man back.

Fleggie and the others climbed onto their vehicle. Working together, the two young men cast their invisibility spells. Iris must have done something at about the same time because the streetlights flared and regained their steady glow. As they started rolling, Eddie glanced past Sweetmaye to see Iris' and Joe's wagon fade from view.

With Sweetmaye now at the controls, the two couples rode back down Spruce. As they turned onto Turnbull, they saw the bright flashing lights of approaching city patrol vehicles. Eddie and Fleggie both reinforced their invisibility spell while Sweetmaye pulled into the darkness between pools of light cast by the street lamps. They all sat very still as the official vehicles passed.

They pulled out onto the street again, but a moment later another wagon came rushing out of Maple street and swung onto Turnbull. It held a half-dozen men and this new vehicle gained rapidly on the wagon from the salvage yard.

"You people need to pull over. Right now!" the driver yelled, voice somehow amplified.

"How can they see us?" Lena whispered. You are both keeping up the spell, are you not?"

Fleggie and Eddie both nodded as they concentrated on the invisibility spell. Now there was a sharp *crack!* of a firearm.

"I said pull over! The next shot takes out the driver."

"Fleggie guesses they be on our trail. Pull over, me girl."

Sweetmaye nodded and again pulled the wagon over to the side of Turnbull. She moved slowly past the glow of a street lamp and stopped. She turned slowly in her seat to face the second wagon. "These be not town patrol," she whispered.

Their pursuers stopped about fifteen yards behind and four men climbed cautiously from the wagon. They were armed and held their weapons at the ready. The men first fanned out and then slowly approached the wagon. The other two stayed on the driver's bench.

Sweetmaye spoke very quietly. "Reed, lad. Can ye do the heat-it spell wi' little Sweetmaye? She be thinkin' tha' th' charge jars in yonder wagon may no' like bein' bro' to a boil."

"Yeah. I can do that. Fleggie, you keep up the invisibility spell. Maybe only one or two of them can penetrate it."

"Aye, mate."

"Together, then. On count o' three," the tiny woman whispered. "Aim jus' 'neath th' driver's bench."

"One... two... three!"

At first nothing happened, but Eddie kept repeating the spell. He could hear Sweetmaye doing the same. Moving slowly and cautiously, the armed men had covered about half the distance to Fleggie's wagon. In the dim light of the nearby street lamp, Eddie could make out that they all wore a tan or khaki uniform that featured high, black boots and a red armband.

When the men were about fifteen feet away, Fleggie suddenly dropped the invisibility spell and joined the other two repeating the heat spell. Now the results were sudden and dramatic. A bright glow spread with frightening rapidity on the bulkhead beneath the driver's bench. Flames leapt. The driver and the other man yelled and jumped from the bench.

There was a terrific, ear-shattering explosion. A glowing cloud, studded with flames and sparks enveloped the second wagon. The men who had jumped from the wagon screamed. All the gunmen spun to see what had happened and Eddie quickly shifted from the heat spell to fumble-fingers. Three of the nearer men dropped their rifles.

"Go, lass. Go, go, go!" yelled Fleggie.

Sweetmaye spun on the bench and got the wagon moving at full speed, but the big man's voice had attracted the attention of the fourth attacker. This one possessed more presence of mind than the others. Ignoring the weapons that lay on the ground, he drew a pistol from his belt, turned on his heel, crouched and aimed. Fleggie stood to shield Sweetmaye's back. Sweetmaye swerved the wagon from side-to-side. Eddie pushed Lena to the floor and dove on top of her. Another *crack!* and then four more in quick succession. Eddie heard Fleggie grunt in surprise, felt the wagon lurch as the big man sagged to one knee.

"Fleggie took one, lass. No! Do no stop!" he gasped. "This'll no do for Fleggie. Run me wagon full on. Mate, ye bes' bring up tha' invisible spell again."

Far off, now but rapidly approaching, they could hear sirens. Eddie took a deep breath and reached inside himself to summon as much stillness as he could muster. He began the invisibility spell. Within a minute, approaching from both directions on Longview, they could see the lights of town patrol vehicles coming on fast.

With an effort, Eddie squinted his eyes, drew his attention away from the commotion, and concentrated on the spell. From far off, he sensed Lena squirm out of his arms, rise, crawl to Fleggie. A moment later, he felt her fumble for the knife at his belt. He kept up the spell for all he was worth as two patrol cruisers screamed past to be followed a moment later by a fire control vehicle.

Fifteen minutes later they were back in the salvage yard with the gate spell closed safely behind them. It was just past four in the morning. Eddie dropped the invisibility spell and looked up. Lena had used his knife to cut large pieces of material from her sweatshirt. She pressed pieces of thick fabric against an entry wound in Fleggie's abdomen, and a larger, exit wound just to the right of the big man's spine.

With Eddie's help, Fleggie eased himself off the wagon and into the little cottage. Once indoors, Sweetmaye brought up the lights. Fleggie's face was pale, but he grinned through clenched teeth.

"Fleggie thinks, tha' wee slug missed most o' th' good parts." He ventured a small laugh, but then gasped.

"The bleeding is not subsiding," Lena cautioned, "and the bullet may have punctured something vital. We must get him medical attention," she insisted.

"Right. We've got two choices. Either we contact Joe and Iris or else we get him to the hospital."

"Fleggie votes fer the Old One an' his fiery witch," the big man insisted. Sweat beaded his face. Now he looked terribly pale.

Eddie looked at Sweetmaye. She nodded, reached for the comm, and established the connection.

"Iris, dear one? It be little Sweetmaye disturbin' ye. Some bad 'uns tried t' waylay us. Fleggie's shot. Ca' ye' do somethin', or shou' we try t' bring him t' hospital?

"Aye. He be awake an' talkin' an' tryin' a joke or two, but th' bullet took 'im in th' belly. It'll be more 'n needle an' thread t' patch th' oaf. He be bleedin' out some. More 'n Sweetmaye likes. True now... A grace be on ye, darlin'. We'll abide ye, an' thanks."

Sweetmaye severed the connection and returned to Fleggie's side.

"Iris say she'll be here. Oh, Fleggie. Ye may no' leave me! Sweetmaye'll no' stand for it!"

Eyes closed, Fleggie smiled a small, grim smile. "Iris'll set it right. Ye'll see, me angel," he managed, his voice weak.

The four friends looked at each other. Lena still held cloth pressed against Fleggie's wounds. Sweetmaye held Fleggie's huge hand between her two.

A moment later, the cottage door flew open. Sweetmaye and Lena looked up. Eddie whirled around and reached for his knife, which he realized was still in the wagon. Fleggie opened his eyes. Everyone relaxed as Iris strode into the room.

"Sorry to startle you all. It sounded serious, so I moved... across. Please. May I see?"

She stepped to the wounded man. Lena withdrew the blood-soaked cloth, and Iris bent to look at the wound. She made a clicking sound, tongue against teeth, looked around the cottage, then up at Eddie.

"We need to get him upstairs to the sleeping loft. Help me."

Eddie didn't see how they would manage to negotiate the steep, ladder-like stairs, but he knew better than to argue with Iris. He swallowed, nodded.

"Please drop to your knees. Take his feet."

Puzzled now, Eddie bent down and eased Fleggie's feet off the floor. "Don't try to help, Fleggie. I've got you, man."

Kicking the table out of the way, Iris stepped around behind the bench where Fleggie rested. She stooped behind him, slid her slender arms beneath his massive ones, laced her fingers across the broad chest.

"Now. Fleggie, Reed. Close your eyes. Reed: drop gently to your knees. It will help if you hold your breath. Ready?"

Eddie felt a spinning in his head, a sudden spasm of vertigo. It passed before he could figure out what was happening.

"Good. Help me get him in bed now. Sweetmaye, dear? Bring clean cloths. Quickly!"

Eddie opened his eyes. The three of them were in the sleeping loft. Dazed, Eddie shook his head.

"Right now, Reed."

"Oh. Sorry."

Iris waved her hand and the bed turned itself down. Sweetmaye appeared with a bundle of clean linen. Iris made a pad of some of it. Carefully they got Fleggie lying down.

"Thank you, Reed. You can wait downstairs now. And Sweetmaye. Please stay and help me with your man."

Eddie watched his friend for a moment. He assured himself that the big man was still breathing. Then he rejoined Lena downstairs.

"What happened?" he whispered.

"It was very strange," she replied. "One second you were here. Then you all seemed to... fold, somehow, into a small space, and then you were just... *there*." She pointed up to the loft.

"That's pretty cool. I don't think I could've carried even half of Fleggie's weight up those stairs."

They heard the injured man gasp then moan slightly. Eyes worried and serious, they went over to sit on the bench that Fleggie had lately vacated. The young couple held hands and waited. Up in the loft they could hear Iris and Sweetmaye talking quietly. Then they heard Iris' musical contralto begin to chant. A pulsing light filled the little sleeping loft. Unknown syllables drifted on the still air.

Lena got up, went to the cooking niche in the back of the cottage. She bustled around the stove and got it going. "It's cold in here. Do you think you could make a fire for us, my love?" she called softly to Eddie.

Glad to have something to do, Eddie nodded and went to kneel in front of the wood stove. There was kindling and some dry wood. In minutes he had a fire going. Soon after, Lena brought over a pot of tea. Gradually the cottage got warmer.

Quietly, they restored the big table to its accustomed place and pulled up the benches. Lena poured a little tea and they sipped the hot liquid while they sat and waited. A quarter hour passed, then another.

At last they heard Iris' voice. "Good. He'll be fine. He'll sleep for a little while now. If he wakes up, try to make him rest. He'll be sore, so I doubt you'll have too much trouble with him. You can feed him whatever he likes."

"Thank ye, kind woman. Ye be good t' care for him as though he were yer own babe," came Sweetmaye's soft reply.

A moment later, Iris joined them downstairs. She went to the sink and washed her hands. Then she crossed to the table where she yawned and stretched, poured herself a cup of tea. Eddie thought that beneath her beauty she looked tired and worn.

"You did well to call. I could heal in hours what would otherwise take weeks to mend. Suppose you tell me what happened."

So Lena and Eddie explained what had happened when they had been overtaken on Longview. Iris was silent during their story. When they wound down she asked a few questions.

"So there were, what, six of them? And they were armed and wore some sort of military-style uniform."

The young couple nodded.

"Well. The RSM jackals are coming out to play. My guess is that the town patrol didn't take too kindly to finding a uniformed paramilitary group on the streets carrying semiautomatic weapons. When they see that at least one of the weapons has been fired, there will be many questions."

The red-headed woman smiled tiredly. "That was quick thinking of Sweetmaye's. I wonder how hot the power cells got with all three of you working in concert. Hot enough, evidently.

"Well, I'm going to go back now and see how Joe is doing," she added. "Unless I'm there to ride herd on him, there is no telling what he'll be up to."

"Thanks, Iris," Eddie said softly.

"Yes. Thank you Iris," Lena added.

"Nonsense. We are together in this. We have now finished three of the five. That is grand. Not only that, but our adversaries have tipped their hand. So we will watch for them, be ready if they strike again.

"Anyway, you should let your friends rest. Stay for a little longer to see if they need anything, but then get back home and take some time for yourself."

The young couple nodded. Iris stood, stepped to the door and was gone.

Eddie and Lena finished their tea. Moments later, Sweetmaye joined them and poured herself a cup.

"Fleggie sleeps easy, may th' gods dream sweet. Little Sweetmaye liked tha' no' a' all. True now. Still, th' bonny red witch be a powerful an' good force."

"Indeed, Iris is powerful. And good," agreed Lena.

Eddie drummed his fingers on the table. He reached over and took up Lena's hand, laid his other hand atop Sweetmaye's. "Why don't you guys stay in here for a little while longer. I'm still really wired up from all this. I need to do something. I think I'll go outside and strike the tents, pack away the camping gear, and all that. Would that be okay?"

Sweetmaye nodded and mustered a small, tired smile. Her pretty face was open and vulnerable. "Sweetmaye hears Iris tell ye to go, but true now, little Sweetmaye'd as soon not be alone i' th' next hours."

Lena stood. Moving softly and gracefully, she crossed to the other side of the table to sit beside Sweetmaye. Lena wrapped her arms around the smaller woman and pulled her close, comforted her. Quietly, Eddie retrieved his coat from where he'd dropped it upon entering the cottage. He opened the door and stepped outside. The sky to the east was light. His breath fogged in the chill air as he stepped to the campsite to sort out all the equipment.

First he located and re-sheathed his knife. Then, he unwrapped the grounding rod that lay shrouded in the back of the wagon. He dragged the heavy rod off the wagon and carried it to its hiding place in the yard. He folded the tarp and the metallic netting and hid them as well.

Next he turned his attention to the camping gear. He rolled the sleeping bags, folded the cots, and repacked the tents. An hour later, Eddie had everything packed and stowed neatly on the bed of Fleggie and Sweetmaye's wagon. He looked around the yard. All was neat; all was back to normal. He'd burned off his nervous energy.

Now it was full light. Eddie was tired and hungry, but there was one more thing he wanted to do. He searched around and found, stuck in the backrest of the driver's seat, the slug that had wounded his friend. It was a small caliber round and had spent most of its momentum by the time it hit the stout, wooden backrest. It took Eddie only a minute or so to pry it out.

Thinking to collect Lena and walk back to their apartment, Eddie poked his head inside the warm cabin. He looked and then closed his eyes and looked again. Fleggie was up and sitting at the table. He had a huge platter of food in front of him and an equally big grin on his face.

"Hey, mate! Fleggie got too hungry an' cou' no sleep. Me girl's made us a wee morsel of a snack. Come in and wash up 'fore it be all gone."

"Fleggie, man. Should you be up?"

"Aye. Fleggie feels good enou'. A bit sore here an' there. But good enou'."

"He ha' no sense an' that's the truth." Brandishing a spatula, Sweetmaye stood next to him. Her pretty face looked like thunder, but even standing at her man's broad shoulder, she barely overtopped him.

"Sweetmaye were fixin' him somat to eat an' she turns around t' find th' fool's clawed his way down t' table!" She shook her head.

The big man's smile grew broader. "Fleggie'll rest. He promises ye' true. Jus' grant 'im a bit o' nourishment," the big man laughed, grimaced, pressed his hand to his belly.

"Aye! See then?! Yer' 'bout to tear that wound open. True, now."

"Set. Just set ye' down, darlin' an' be calm."

Sweetmaye looked at Eddie, half scowled, half laughed. "Well, do no' be standin' there. Come an' eat. Then mayhaps th' oaf'll take himself back up t' bed."

"Excuse me, Fleggie," Lena added with a soft smile, "but can you imagine how Iris would react if you were to undo her work?"

At the suggestion of Iris' disapproval, Fleggie's smile vanished.

"Oh, aye... Fleggie din't reckon on tha'... Iris... Fleggie wou' no wan' t' cross tha' 'un... Uh, mate?"

"Yeah?" Eddie answered.

"Say ye' help ol' Fleggie back up th' ladder. Mayhaps ye' cou' sit wi' me an' we cou' chat a bit as we eat."

"You bet, man. Let me get out of these wet boots."

So Eddie helped his big friend negotiate the ladder-like steps back up to the sleeping loft. Then the two young women brought up plates and the three of them sat on the floor around the bed. The smell of eggs, sausage, potatoes, and hot bread worked its own magic and Eddie's stomach rumbled in response. The three of them kept watch over their injured friend, cheered him.

Eddie fished the flattened slug from his pocket and held it out. "Here's a souvenir, man."

The big man reached out and Eddie dropped the slug in the wide, outstretched palm. "Tha' be it? Tha' wee mite near' did fer Fleggie? It be hard t' fathom."

As if he might crush it, Fleggie clenched his huge fist over the bullet. Then he sighed and dropped the slug on the small crate that served as a night stand. He turned back to his food.

As they finished eating, Fleggie began to yawn. His eyes grew heavy. Sweetmaye helped him lie back and pulled the covers around her man. "Ye' mus' promise now, t' stay abed 'til afternoon," she spoke soothingly, softly. Fleggie nodded once, twice, and then drifted off to sleep.

While Sweetmaye sat her vigil, Eddie and Lena gathered the breakfast things and took them downstairs. As quietly as they could, they washed them up and put them away. Sweetmaye came downstairs as they were getting into their coats.

"Thanks be to ye' both fer yer' kindness an' help in managin' him."

"Sure thing, Sweetmaye. Thanks for that breakfast!"

"You must be exhausted too, Sweetmaye," Lena added. "Please try to rest. We will talk this afternoon. Call us on the comm when you feel ready."

Finally, Sweetmaye's emotions overtopped her reserve. Tears streamed down her pretty face while she struggled to regain control. With a fierce, wiry strength, the diminutive beauty hugged both of her friends. She nodded and smiled through her tears and kissed them both. Then she pulled the door softly closed behind them as they went out into the cold morning.

Tired as they were, Lena and Eddie enjoyed the stroll down the now-familiar sidewalks. The early morning air was chilly, but the brief interlude of clear weather held. At the corner of Turnbull and Center, there was a small greengrocer. The owner was out in front getting set up for the day. He smiled and waved as they turned the corner.

"It is still early. We should allow Iris and Joe to rest undisturbed," Lena suggested as they neared their destination. "Let us go upstairs and try to rest."

By now, Eddie was exhausted, but he was also sure that he wouldn't be able to sleep. The images from the previous night continued to flash in front of his eyes. They both had hot showers and lay down. The room was quiet and warm, but indeed, neither of them slept much.

They got up around ten o'clock. Enjoying the quiet time, they sat on the couch and sipped tea. Their energy level improved as the morning wore on. Lena and Eddie had just sat down to a light lunch when there was a knock at the door. It was Iris.

"Come in. We didn't want to disturb you. How are you and Joe doing? Would you like some lunch?"

Iris looked a little bit haggard but basically healthy. Her hair was still a vibrant red. Her eyes still sparkled. Eddie noticed some fine lines on her face that could have been merely fatigue. Or not.

"Just ate, thanks. Joe's up, but he's taking it easy. We both are. That was harder on both of us than we expected. That opening should have been fairly easy, but all the peripheral spells took effort. And then needing to go out again to tend to Fleggie... that was especially fatiguing.

"Was he resting comfortably when you left?" she added.

With an economy of words, Lena described the scene back at the cottage. Iris sighed. "What is it with you men? It's the same thing with that old scoundrel downstairs. You can't be trusted to take the simplest precautions..."

Hoping to forestall Iris before she became wound up, Lena nodded, smiled gently. She laid her hand atop the older woman's. "I think he was a little bit hungry, Iris, but I think he mostly needed to have his friends around him. As soon as we gathered around his bed and had a bite to eat, he relaxed and went to sleep."

Slightly mollified, the redheaded woman looked off into space for a moment, shook her head slightly. "Oh, we'll all three bounce back quickly enough. Joe assures me that if he hadn't needed to cast that large illusion and then hold it while he managed the grounding rod, he wouldn't feel worn out at all." She was silent for a moment, and then continued. "And I know I'd feel fine if I hadn't had to go out again. Thank the gods' happy dreams that none of you were killed!

"At any rate, your oversized friend should feel well this afternoon. He'll be sore, but the spells will hold him, heal him. If at all possible, he should avoid doing anything overtaxing, but the bullet did little serious damage. It is very good that it was a small caliber weapon. The RSM relies mostly on fear and intimidation.

"So, we will rest and recuperate while we monitor the weather forecasts," Iris continued. "The next big storm can cover our efforts. That will make things easier. And we will stay together afterwards. Count on that. You shouldn't have had to face those jackals alone."

They chatted a little longer, but everyone felt a strange mixture of nervous energy, subdued mood, and fatigue. Promising to check back in later in the day, Iris smiled and left the apartment to return to her shop downstairs.

Mid-afternoon, Fleggie called. He sounded slightly weak but in good spirits. He allowed that he couldn't sit still anymore. He'd convinced Sweetmaye to peek beneath the bandages to verify that the wounds were closed and not at all inflamed. Now he wanted to get out of the cottage. Sweetmaye had reluctantly agreed. They arranged to meet in front of the shop.

Lena and Eddie finished their lunch and went downstairs. Lena spoke to Iris and confirmed that the rental gear should go to a store just up the street. The day was growing more overcast, but it was still dry and the temperature was reasonably mild. A few minutes later, Fleggie and Sweetmaye drove up with the wagon. The camping gear was in the back.

"Fleggie and I can take care of this stuff. Do you two want to stay and visit for a little while?" Eddie asked.

"I were hoping to spend a bit 'o girl-talk-time wi' yer darlin.' Truth, now," Sweetmaye replied.

"That sounds good. I can show you around the store, Sweetmaye, and we can go upstairs and chat over tea."

The tiny, black-haired woman turned to favor Fleggie with a fierce look. "An' ye' gave yer word t'carry nothin' o' consequence, t' do no damage t' yerself. That were th' promise! True, now!"

"Aye, lass. That were th' deal. Fleggie'll keep t' his promise."

"Well, ye'd best be on yer way then."

Eddie jumped up onto the bench next to Fleggie. The big man manipulated the controls and pulled the electric wagon out into the road. Traffic was light. In a few moments they were in front of the camping goods store. They brought the tents and sleeping bags into the store. The clerk was busy with another customer so Fleggie and Eddie browsed the shelves.

They located the ice axes and regular, wood cutting axes and tried the heft and feel of them. There were several interesting types and styles, but it was clear that none was designed specifically with throwing in mind.

"Fleggie likes his own pieces, well enou' now. He keeps tryin' an' changin' things. Mayhaps he'll think on these when he builds his next set o' blades."

"Yeah, these are kind of cool looking, but I don't think they'd stand up to the kind of stress we put on 'em."

"You thinkin' you cou' get away for a couple o' hours throwin' this afternoon?"

"I'd like that. But I think it's a really bad idea. You need to rest for at least a day, man. A few hours ago you had a gunshot wound in your stomach!"

"Oh, aye, aye, mate. We don' want t' cause no home strife, true enou' eh?" Fleggie chuckled.

"You got that right, man. Let's just go sharpen the axes. I know that mine haven't had any real attention since I got them."

"That'd be good enou' mate."

By then the clerk was ready. He checked in the gear and gave the young men a receipt. In five minutes they were back at the apartment. Lena and Sweetmaye said that they'd be happy to stay upstairs for the afternoon. They'd sip tea and chat and let "their boys" go play with sharp things.

"How about this? We'll work on our axes for a couple of hours. They all need to be sharpened. Then we'll swing by and get some groceries. Fleggie and I can fix dinner," Eddie offered.

"Oh, you are sweetening the deal!" Lena laughed. "I cannot turn that offer down. What say you, Sweetmaye?"

"O. Let Sweetmaye think on this," the petite, dark-haired beauty giggled. "On th' one hand, we girls talk in a nice, cozy room an' th' men cook dinner. On th' other hand, little Sweetmaye goes back t' th' yard whilst her man broods, complains, an' paces about th' cottage. 'Tis a clear enou' choice t' this lass.

"Still... ken ye yer promise t' sharpen only! No throwin' today. None... an' tha' means *none*! Agreed?"

"Oh, aye, lass. Aye. Fleggie'll keep t' tha'.''

So Fleggie and Eddie drove back to the salvage yard and got in nearly three hours of work. They sharpened and buffed the weapons. Eddie was delighted to see that his axes would hold a well-honed edge.

As they worked, Fleggie described his idea for an overhead, two-handed throw. He'd been practicing it a little and thought that if he could improve his accuracy, the results of the throw would be huge. For his part, Eddie revealed his thoughts about a left handed throw. His eventual goal was to throw two axes with no break between. They discussed these and other ideas. Neither man could have said precisely why he felt such an urgent need to improve his skills, but they both felt compelled to approach these weapons in a serious and focused manner.

Both men enjoyed the quiet camaraderie, but they were careful to break in time to keep up their end of the bargain. As Fleggie and Eddie washed up at the basin outside the cottage, they realized that they were again hungry. This prompted them to select dinner supplies to match their hunger.

After a brief shopping trip, they returned to the apartment over Tolemy's Cats. Lena and Sweetmaye laughed when they saw how much food the men carted into the kitchen. The men waved them back to their tea and set to work in the tiny kitchen. Eddie hadn't applied his culinary skills all that often since he'd left the Orca, and he wanted to go all out.

Eddie got the main course, which consisted of two, heavily spiced capons, into the oven to roast. The birds barely fit into the stove's pint-sized oven. While Eddie worked on those, Fleggie sliced mushrooms and sauteed them along with some ground lamb in olive oil and garlic. When the mushroom and lamb mixture were done, the big man added it to a large pot of rice.

The grocer had two giant squashes that reminded Eddie of zucchini. He sliced these lengthwise and scooped out the seeds. When the capons were done, they removed them from the oven and kept them covered on the stove. They used the oven to bake the squash for about 15 minutes. Then they laid the squash on a platter and heaped the mushroom-lamb-rice mixture on top and returned it to the oven.

Fleggie carved the capons while Eddie made gravy from the juices left in the roasting pan. They brought out two bottles of white wine. Although they'd originally planned to make a rich dessert, the young men had been unable to resist a fresh-baked berry pie that they spied at the nearby bakery, so that rounded out the feast.

Fleggie ate until he groaned and had to push his plate away. Eddie tried but failed to match his big friend in sheer volume consumed. Sweetmaye and Lena showed more restraint but enjoyed the meal nonetheless. They laughed and told stories.

Dinner helped them move past the frightening events of the previous night. They relished not only the food, but the tiny apartment that sheltered them from the elements and the voices that pushed back the darkness. Most of all, this evening of friendship reminded them that the struggle in which they were engaged, for all its discomforts and dangers, was worth it.

Michael C. Glaviano

Thirty Seven

The next day, the local news services were full of reports about the mysterious, early-morning explosion on Turnbull Road. Reports surfaced that investigating patrol officers had been fired upon by RSM paramilitary elements. There were casualties on both sides and the surviving RSM forces were in custody.

Three days later, there was a raid on a secret RSM center in the Warrens. Records, computer equipment, and a huge cache of weapons were found and confiscated. Ten more jack-booted, RSM thugs were arrested when they started a brawl with uniformed patrolmen. Most importantly, two self-proclaimed leaders were taken into custody. A third was killed when he directed automatic weapons fire at the arresting officers. For a time the threat of RSM-borne violence receded.

For his part, Fleggie called to assure them that he was completely mended by the following afternoon. By Friday evening, Joe had rebounded and appeared to have regained his usual vitality. Iris recovered even faster. They monitored the weather forecasts and although Sunday was beautiful, rain was expected sometime Monday as the leading edge of a storm came ashore. There was a strong likelihood that Tuesday night would be wet and cold.

A gray dawn awaited them the next morning. It was already raining and the temperature had not risen substantially from the nighttime low. They were cleaning up the breakfast things when Joe knocked on the door.

"Good morning, son, Lena," he said quietly. "Sorry to disturb you so early. Iris and I would like to open the portal in the nature preserve tomorrow night. The conditions will be right for it. Would you please contact Sweetmaye and Fleggie to let them know? See if they can come over this evening to go over the plans."

"Sure thing, Joe."

"Oh, and Lena. Iris wanted me to ask if you would mind the store today so that she and I can make sure that we have everything planned out."

"Of course. It probably won't be terribly busy. I can read or tidy things up in between customers."

Joe nodded and left them to return downstairs.

They finished straightening up the little apartment and Lena ran downstairs. Eddie activated the comm link to talk to their friends. Fleggie picked up.

"Hey, there. Fleggie here."

"Fleggie. Joe and Iris want to try again. Can you and Sweetmaye come over this evening? To go over things?"

"Aye. We ca' be there. True enough. Be a time set?"

"Joe said after dinner. Let's say seven o'clock. Will that work?"

"Aye. Think ye' may make it over t' the yard today for some throwin'? Be good practice in the wet an' all."

"That sounds good. I'll see if I can break away in the early afternoon, okay?"

"Good enou', mate. Cheers."

"Bye."

That done, Eddie got out his spell books and studied. It was hard going at first, but the subject matter was incredibly interesting and potentially life-saving, so little by little, Eddie was drawn into the material. It seemed particularly appropriate to sit in the cozy apartment on a cold, stormy day and study spell casting.

During the opening at Merryweather Park he and Fleggie had put the invisibility spell to good use. It was obvious that their RSM adversaries included some whose abilities allowed them to penetrate his simple spell. Still, he had the sense that their efforts had helped. He reviewed that spell a few times and was confident that he had it well in hand.

Since it had proven to be a lifesaver, he also practiced the Heat It spell. He'd recently been looking at other spells such as "Freeze It," "Find Lost Object," "Slippery," and "Tanglefoot." There were also "Sleep" and "Electric Shock" to consider. Clearly, "Stun" would be useful as well, but that spell was complicated and needed to be performed quickly if it were to be effective.

Over the next two hours, Eddie cycled through these spells. Reading them, reciting the keywords, and practicing the gestures, he sensed an underlying pattern to the knowledge. The exact nature of that pattern and how he might use it were beyond his fledgling ability, but the dim glimpses he caught were motivating. His small successes fueled his efforts.

Outside, there were periods of heavy rain and wind. It was as though the storm held a steady position above Soapstone Bay and had no desire to pass. Just before noon, Lena came upstairs and sat with Eddie for a few minutes. They heated some leftovers and shared another quiet meal.

"It appears that I will continue to mind the store for Iris this afternoon. What would you like to do, my love?" Lena asked.

"Well... if you need me to help out, I'll do that of course. But Fleggie thinks that practicing in the wet weather would be good for us. I sort of agree with him, especially since I missed practicing yesterday. Still, given a choice between staying indoors with you and standing in the rain throwing axes, I'll pick you anytime."

Lena smiled a little bit at this but shook her head slightly. "I would rather we spent the day together too, Reed, and I am not particularly happy with the prospect of you throwing axes in the rain. Still, Fleggie has a point. You should spend the afternoon practicing. I think I will call Sweetmaye to see if she would like to come over again and help me in the store. It will surely be slow with this weather."

So after lunch, Eddie bundled up in his foul weather gear. Lena had added some loops inside the big coat so that the throwing axes could rest across his chest as well as hang from his belt. Of course the axes weren't particularly comfortable, but they fit inside his coat and kept his hands free.

About the time Lena called to invite Sweetmaye over, the rain had picked up considerably and Fleggie offered to bring Sweetmaye down and give Eddie a ride back. Eddie thought it would be good to stretch his legs, but the notion of a quick ride through the wet as opposed to a long slog through it won out. He kissed Lena in front of the bookstore and waited under the awning for their friends to arrive.

They pulled up a short while later. Sweetmaye hopped off the wagon and, with a smile and a wave, disappeared into the bookshop. Eddie climbed aboard the wagon.

"Ye have yer' axes with ye?"

"Yeah. The two with sheathes are on my belt. Lena sewed some heavy loops inside this coat so I don't have to carry the other one in weather like this. It's also a little more discreet that way. I'll show you when we get there."

"Sounds good, mate."

The two men rode in silence up to the salvage yard. Eddie hung his coat inside the cottage and showed Fleggie the loops that Lena had added for the axe. Fleggie liked that.

"Mayhaps I cou' get me girl t' do something close t' tha' in me greatcoat. O' course I'll ha' t' mind th' handles. They could catch Fleggie 'tween th' legs."

"Ouch!"

"Aye. True enou'."

They went outside and took turns warming up. It was immediately apparent that slippery handles precluded the hardest throws. Without a good grip and a clean release, both men found that their accuracy suffered dramatically. After missing the target completely several times, they took a break and discussed what to do about throwing under bad conditions.

"This isn't working, Fleggie. Maybe we should take a different approach."

"Fleggie be open t' ideas, mate. We jus' got these blades polished. Soon as not break an axe-head on a stone."

"Well, when I first started, I got up close to the target and focused on good, clean throws. If I hit ten in a row, I took a step away from the target. If I missed several times in a row, four I think it was, I'd step closer to the target again."

"Aye. Like startin' over, we are. It be a new skill, throwin' in th' wet an' all. Fleggie be game t' try."

So they took turns again, but this time they were merely trying to find a range at which they could throw well consistently. First they cut their distance to the target in half. Then in half again. Eventually the men were nearly on top of the target, but finally they could hit it consistently with solid throws.

They practiced through the afternoon in a steady rain. Water got in their sleeves and in their boots. After a couple of hours, their hands were cold, wet and muddy, but they were hitting the target well and had recovered perhaps half of their distance. Wet conditions were a significant handicap, but on balance they both felt that the practice had been worthwhile.

"What say we go inside an' see 'bout thawin' out a wee bit, eh mate?"

"Yeah. I'm starting to feel pretty cold. We're going to be out in it again tomorrow night. No sense getting sick."

So they went inside. They removed their sodden boots at the door and hung their jackets up to dry. Fleggie built up the fire and they brought their boots over to dry. Even though they were cold at first, they'd been exercising, and once they had toweled their heads and hands, their internal heat combined with the warmth of the stove to make them comfortable.

"Care for a bit o' tea then?"

"Sounds great, man. Thanks."

"Let's see. Hey! Me darlin' Sweetmaye's left some bits o' this n' tha' for us t' eat."

So they chatted over tea and snacks until Sweetmaye called to say that she was ready to come home. By then their boots were at least warm if not completely dry, so they bundled up again and made the drive down to Tolemy's Cats.

As they pulled up, Sweetmaye and Lena came out of the bookstore to stand beneath the awning. They were bundled up in their heavy coats. "We've decided that you ought to take your hardworking women out for dinner this evening," Lena called, with her eyes sparkling.

Eddie and Fleggie exchanged glances. "An where wou' ye lovely lasses care t' dine?"

It turned out they had already picked out a casual restaurant over on University. The others waited while Eddie dashed upstairs to deposit his axes in the apartment. Minutes later, the four friends were seated inside a restaurant just a few blocks west of St. Tolemey's. Despite the storm, the place was bustling. It was warm inside and smelled of good food.

After dinner they returned to the bookstore. Joe and Iris were waiting near the front desk and led them back to the little apartment. They had brought a couple of extra chairs from the kitchen so that everyone could gather around the living room.

Her vibrant beauty all the more vivid against the backdrop of her serious, almost somber demeanor, Iris spoke each name as she looked around the room. "We think we have worked out a way to proceed tomorrow night. All the weather forecasts – my own included – indicate that the storm will strengthen over the next day or so. We doubt anyone will be out in the forest preserve tomorrow evening."

"As before, I'll make my own way up to the site in advance to prepare," Joe added. "We think it will be fine if Fleggie and Sweetmaye come here to collect Iris, Reed, and Lena. That will simplify things and keep anyone from needing to walk around in the storm."

"What if they are being watched?" Lena wanted to know.

"That is very unlikely," replied Iris. "After the Merryweather Park incident, Joe and I placed some very sophisticated watchers around our friends' yard. There is no indication that they are being observed."

"Well somebody attacked us!" Eddie countered.

"Indeed. And I presume that you've been following the news broadcasts. Those responsible for that particular attack are no longer at large. According to the reports, their organization has been further thinned in the past week. I doubt they have enough forces to trouble us at this point."

"Yeah, we've been following the news. Still, how'd they know to go after us?"

Iris nodded. "That is problematic. We agree. Our guess is that they had some spotters. Perhaps they noticed the flash when we opened the portal north of campus. It was rather exposed.

"They must know that the portal at Merryweather was open fairly recently," she continued. "That much is well-known. So the most-likely explanation is that they had someone posted. Someone keeping watch for another flash."

"Yeah. So they could keep another lookout... and there was somebody who could penetrate an invisibility spell," Eddie added.

"While it's obvious that our adversaries are aware of our actions, they cannot know precisely when we will make our next move," Joe countered. "Further, only the portal at Merryweather Park was commonly known in recent times. Unless they have access to the historical record and manage to duplicate Iris' and Lena's research, they will not know of the much older portal whose existence we suspect. They clearly made their move too soon. Their ranks have been curtailed as a result of their precipitate actions."

Now Lena spoke up again. "Excuse me, both of you, but is it not prudent to assume that one's adversaries are both capable and intelligent? We do not know how many of them remain at large. It seems to me that the risk lies on the side of underestimating their abilities rather than assigning them excessive skill. The outer triangle is in place. Now that the portal has been reopened at Merryweather Park, these people need only notice that it lies at the midpoint of one side of that triangle. If they see the pattern, they could easily be waiting for us."

It was obvious from the silence that ensued that neither Joe nor Iris enjoyed being challenged. After a weighty pause, however, Iris admitted that they were assuming much.

"Here is our reasoning, Lena. If the Queen were directly involved, we'd be hard-pressed to succeed, but we've managed to open three portals and only had trouble during the most recent activity. From past experience, we know that the Queen's agents operate in small teams. They coordinate no more than they absolutely must. They try to jockey for position, try to undercut each other. We've seen these behaviors over and over.

"As for your notion of a map, well, you are correct that if they have the idea of it, they could conceivably reproduce our plan," she continued. "Even so, Joe will precede us to the site as he has on other occasions. They will not catch us unawares. Of that much we can be sure. What say you all?"

"Fleggie, for one wants t' finish this. He takes ill a' bein' shot."

"I want to finish as well," agreed Lena. "I merely want to make sure that I understand the thought behind this plan. Given what happened last time, it seems only prudent."

"Look. I have no way to guess if this is a good plan or not," Eddie said. "I just think we need to be careful. Lena and I have the benefit of location. After all, we live over your bookstore, Iris. Fleggie and Sweetmaye are more exposed."

Sweetmaye looked between Iris and Joe. Visibly summoning her courage, the small woman locked eyes with the old warrior. "Little Sweetmaye wonders if there be a way t' strengthen the spells abou' the yard. If th' bad uns canna' see us, if they see nothin' worth their frettin'... well, it be worth th' risk o' it."

Joe nodded at this, smiled kindly. "Certainly, Sweetmaye. I'd be happy to increase the warding around your salvage yard. In truth, I should have offered that myself. When you leave tonight, I will go with you. I will employ all my skill and knowledge to make you as safe as I possibly can.

"Thanks be t' ye, sir."

"And afterwards, after the opening, we'll go back with you and ensure that you've not been followed," Iris added. "Now, with these added assurances, shall we proceed?"

"Aye."

"Yes."

"Aye."

"Yeah."

Iris nodded, picked up the thread. "Once you've collected us in front of the store, we'll drive up Center Street and turn right at Meridian. We will wind through the Holmes Road area and join University just before Biscayne. At that corner, Fleggie and Reed will put an invisibility spell on the wagon and all its contents. I will add a different sort of shielding spell as well. Between the three of us, we will be well-cloaked as we travel through the middle of the school."

"Tha' be brazen enou'," Fleggie observed.

"Yes, I supposed it is," Iris smiled slightly, "but if the forecasts are right, the weather will be miserable. Few people will be wandering around outside. And again, we have no indication that campus security will be expecting us."

"An' when should Fleggie an' Sweetmaye get here?" Sweetmaye asked.

"Let's say around eight o' clock in the evening," Joe replied. "It will be full dark then. Most people will be indoors. The exact time is less precise since I am the only one who will be waiting outside, and I can create an invisible shelter for myself easily enough. Once we're at the site, we'll proceed as on the other occasions. Just follow Iris' lead. Take care not to interrupt the flow of the spell once it's started."

"At this stage, I think everyone knows what to expect," Iris remarked. "We should be there and back within an hour and a half. This is our second opening at the midpoint of a segment. Only one more to go after this one is open. Any questions?"

Although nervous, no one suggested any modifications to the plan. Accompanied by Joe, Fleggie and Sweetmaye returned home. Later, Eddie and Lena talked upstairs in their apartment.

"This one that we're doing tomorrow night shouldn't be that hard. At least I hope that it won't be. All this is obviously taking more out of Joe than he said it would. And we've asked him to do more in the way of protecting our friends."

"I agree. We must do our parts, but we must also be watchful. I continue to suspect that we are missing something."

Outside the rain persisted. Over the next hour, the storm gathered force. The young couple stayed up for a while longer. They read. They talked. They even laughed a little, but as before, the weight of their circumstances was never far from their minds. Neither of them slept particularly well.

After breakfast the next morning, Lena went downstairs to run the bookstore. Iris was already at the desk, but it took little effort for Lena to persuade the older woman to go back and rest. As on the day before, Eddie stayed upstairs for the morning to study and practice. Around noon, Lena came upstairs and they had lunch.

Eddie felt that he had done enough study during the morning and asked if he could come down and help in the shop. Lena was obviously grateful for the company. "You can dust the shelves and perhaps mop the floors," she assented. "They get very dirty when people track in the mud and the wet. In this weather, half a dozen customers is all it takes to make the entrance messy and unwelcoming."

There was a rush of customers in the early afternoon, but then things tapered off. They closed on time and returned to the apartment to prepare. They tried to rest a little. Neither was very hungry so they just snacked. Mostly they just sat together and waited for eight o' clock to roll by.

Eventually, they bundled up against the storm and went downstairs. It was dark, and they could see the rain streaming through the light of the street lamp in front of the bookstore. The rain looked like tiny sparks that winked out as soon as they reached the shadows. A few minutes later, they saw a wagon emerge from the darkness to stop in front of the store. Iris came out the front door to join them. The sound of the lock was loud above the hissing drone of the storm.

As if she could pierce the gloom, Iris peered into the surrounding shadows. They waited, and finally, the older woman nodded her assent. They stepped into the wind and rain to climb aboard the wagon. As she had on other nights, Iris sat on the bench next to Sweetmaye and took the controls. Fleggie sat on one side of the wagon's bed, Eddie and Lena on the other. No one spoke.

Iris moved the wagon away from the curb and headed west on Center. At the end of the street she turned right onto Meridian. Now the wind and rain blew directly into Lena's and Eddie's faces. The pools of light beneath the street lamps did little to relieve the darkness as they picked their way along, so there wasn't much to see. The young couple leaned forward and turned their faces toward the bed of the wagon so that the water dripped off the visors of their waterproof storm hoods.

Their way led west again for about a block on Long's Peak. Then they turned left once more onto Holmes. The road zig-zagged south and west toward University Avenue, and this narrower lane featured big, mature trees. Although most of the branches were bare they provided some shelter from the worst of the wind. Finally, the wagon approached University. The illumination was greater at the intersection. Iris pulled up just outside the first pool of light. She turned back and met Eddie's and Fleggie's eyes. Iris nodded and the young men both cast their invisibility spells.

A moment later, she wove a pattern with her hands and the world around them withdrew behind a rippling curtain of shadows. Smoothly, quietly, the electric vehicle rolled forward into the glow cast by the street lamps at the corner. Had spying eyes been there to see, they might have noticed that the rain fell strangely beneath the lights for a few seconds. More than anything else, it looked like a trick of the wind.

They crossed Biscayne and entered the campus. The street lamps were perched on taller poles here and they cast their light farther but not much more brightly. They saw no one as they traveled almost due west through the campus. It took only ten minutes to reach the western boundary of the campus.

The gate leading to the nature preserve was closed but at a gesture from Iris it swung silently back. They passed and it closed behind them. Now they were on a small, gravel track that led among the trees. In contrast to the plantings of the town streetscape, most of the trees in the nature preserve were large evergreens. Iris drove slowly, and they were grateful for the windbreak the trees provided. The rain continued to fall heavily.

Some minutes later, they spied a light off to the left among the trees. Iris turned the wagon around and doused the running lights. As on previous occasions, Joe stepped from the darkness. Iris climbed down and helped Joe set up the grounding rod.

The opening spell came off as planned. At the end, Joe fell to his knees, and once again it took him several minutes to get back up. Iris replaced the grounding rod herself and then quietly ask Fleggie to support the older man as Joe climbed into the back of the wagon. Eddie hoped it was only a trick of the light, but in the lightning flash that accompanied the instant of opening, he thought that Iris' flawlessly smooth features were overlaid with a deeply-lined, haggard look.

They retraced their way through the university grounds. Eddie and Fleggie stayed focused on maintaining the invisibility spell until they were in between street lamps on Meridian. There was no traffic on the side streets.

When they pulled up in front of Tolemy's Cats, Fleggie helped Iris get Joe inside. Eddie, Lena, and Sweetmaye waited near the doorway of the shop. As they watched, Joe stood up straighter and thanked Fleggie for his help. In the brighter light of the bookstore, Iris looked fine. Eddie decided that the flickering flash at the instant of portal opening had confused his sight.

Iris returned a moment later. They again climbed aboard the electric wagon, this time with the purpose of seeing their friends safely back to their salvage yard. Fleggie, Eddie, and Iris maintained the invisibility spell all the way into the yard.

Once inside the yard, Eddie and Fleggie stowed the grounding rod. Sweetmaye invited them all into the warm shelter of the cottage, but Iris wanted to return to the shop so that she could watch over Joe. Still as a statue, she gazed out into the night. A few moments later, she motioned that Eddie and Lena should join her on the street. They said their goodbyes, and Iris warned Fleggie and Sweetmaye to stay within the boundaries of their salvage yard until the sun's morning light shone on their front door. Their friends stepped back inside the yard.

A minute later, an electric carriage idled to a stop. Slumped at the controls, a somnolent driver snored softly. Iris made some passes at the fence. Her hands danced in the soft light. Crawling over the worn boards of the fence, tiny sparks of light coruscated and the warding spells once again surrounded and protected their friends.

No one spoke as the carriage made its own way back to the bookshop. Eddie and Lena were lost in similar thoughts. They'd assisted in four, apparently successful opening spells, but the only thing they knew for sure was that the nights' activities took a toll on their older, more experienced friends. Despite the rumors of a tiny, local renaissance, they could see little concrete difference in the world around them. Despite the RSM's recent setbacks, no strong sense of security or safety comforted them.

Later that night, in the quiet of their bed, Eddie and Lena wondered if the fifth and final portal opening would result in unmistakable, perhaps dramatic changes. The pattern would be complete: a huge triangle with portals at each vertex and at the midpoint of each side. Would this really change things for the better?

* * *

The rain continued through the night but the worst of the storm had passed when Lena and Eddie got out of bed the next morning. They made ready for the day, but they were somewhat at a loss as to what they were going to do. Eddie was particularly troubled.

"I need to work off this feeling, but I just don't feel like throwing axes in the rain today," Eddie admitted. "It feels weird to be sitting around but I can't think of anything to accomplish. Probably I should just get over it and study for a few hours.

"The thing is," he added, "I miss my job at the Orca. I don't miss the drama, the interpersonal problems, but I enjoyed the work. Oh, I realize up here," he pointed to the side of his head, "that we're fighting some kind of battle against evil forces... but it's all so... abstract."

"Yes, Love. I think I know how you feel. It is difficult to believe we are doing anything of consequence. All this sneaking around in the dark and the rain. All of these incantations. Perhaps they are making things better for this world. I truly hope so of course, but we cannot really tell."

"And I think it's knocking the stuffing out of Joe and maybe Iris too."

"Indeed, I agree; although Joe is obviously the more severely impacted."

They mulled this over but could reach no conclusion. Late in the morning, Iris knocked at their door and asked if she could speak with them. As she walked in and sat on the little sofa, Eddie thought that she looked basically okay, but the fatigue lines that he had noted after the night at Merryweather Park were more pronounced than ever.

"Joe and I are well enough," she began without preamble, "but something is making this harder than I, for one, expected. It was not an idle boast when I said that in past times I have performed this spell many times without problem. Joe is much more fatigued than I, and given his usual strength and power, this is both strange and worrisome."

Iris sat silently for a few moments. She looked down at her hands. They were folded in her lap with unconscious grace. Now she looked up at her young friends and helpers. "It surprised us and, frankly, we're both a little bit depressed over it."

"Is there a way that we might help, Iris? Some way so that you might rest more?" Lena asked. Eddie too expressed concern.

Iris nodded. "I stayed up most of the night and sought for signs of detection by our adversaries. I am convinced they did not see us last night and that they, for whatever reason, are not looking for us. Joe and I are sure that you two, as well as your friends at their salvage yard will be safe as long as you stay close to home and limit your nighttime excursions.

"So, with that preamble, we have a favor to ask. Would you mind terribly running the shop for a few days? Joe and I would like to go off together for the rest of the week. I know of a place a half day south of here where we can settle in and recharge in advance of the upcoming work."

"Iris, we would be delighted to fill in. We will treat your shop with care – as though it were our own business," Lena replied. Eddie agreed wholeheartedly.

"I know that you will," Iris replied seriously. Then she summoned a wan smile. "Well, then. I should get back down and confirm our reservations. A coach will come by for us. We will leave in a couple of hours. Expect us back late this weekend. Sunday night, probably. Thank you both again. Take reasonable precautions and all will be well." Now she stood up as if preparing to leave. Lena and Eddie stood facing her.

"It will be fine, Iris. Please try not to worry. We will do our best for you."

The beautiful woman just nodded and smiled again. Then suddenly she stepped forward and gathered them both in her arms. She hugged them tightly to her for a few moments and then released them. She turned away quickly and waved as she darted out the door. Eddie saw that her eyes were filled with tears.

Eddie and Lena looked at each other after Iris' abrupt departure.

"What was that about?" he wondered.

"I suspect that before last night, Iris was denying to herself the reality of her situation. Despite her remarks to the contrary, she felt young enough inside to pretend she really was young. Also... I think something else is going on."

"What? Tell me!"

"Well, it is clear that Joe and she were romantically involved something like a half century ago."

Eddie nodded at this and Lena continued. "My suspicion, and it is only a suspicion at this point, is that Joe tapped far more of his strength than he admitted to accomplish this transformation in Iris' vitality. His explanations for his condition are not consistent with what we are seeing, Reed. We have evidence that the man has lived for centuries, perhaps millennia. He claims that he has cast countless spells of opening in the past. Now he cannot stand after performing even one, and he has the assistance of five other people."

"You don't think that Joe could have done some kind of permanent damage to himself, do you?"

"I am trying not to reach a conclusion with regards to that. Of course I hope that it is not the case, but obviously something is not right."

Eddie wrinkled up his forehead. "You remember when he first got back here and he was badly hurt? And how overnight he had mostly recovered and wanted to go out to Baleen Park and have me demonstrate what I'd learned and all?"

"Yes."

"Well... I'm trying to remember exactly what he said, but it was something like, 'you should have seen Iris when...' and then he said, 'it didn't have to be this way,' or something like that. And then he kind of trailed off like he was considering, or weighing possibilities, and it was that evening he did whatever he did to restore her."

"Well, perhaps they will work this out, whatever it is, when they go away this week. I certainly hope they do. As much as I respect Joe and Iris, I confess that I am uncomfortable with our dependence upon them. And if they are suddenly incapacitated, or worse, we could find ourselves in a very bad situation."

"Yeah. I've started worrying about that too. At first they seemed so powerful and confident, but now... sometimes Joe looks, well, frail. I've never seen him like that.

"And we've involved Sweetmaye and Fleggie," he added.

"Indeed we have, Reed."

He walked into the kitchen and poured himself a fresh cup of coffee. "Want anything?" he called.

"No, thank you, Reed." Eddie came back out. He took a sip of his coffee and sat down.

"Come here and sit with me for a little while, will you, Lena? I think we need to analyze some things. Perform some thought experiments."

"Such as?"

"Well, we have evidence that the bad guys – the 'Locusts' – aren't just going to go away. They have a pattern of behavior, and they have turned their attention to your world and mine. If no one pushes them back the end results for countless people will be terrible."

"Most of that evidence comes from things that Joe, and to some extent Iris, have told us, however," Lena argued.

"Sure. But these RSM people who attacked us and who are behind the troubles at the university are real. The censorship and the aggressive security guards are real too. The RSM people are getting their support from somewhere."

"Somewhere, yes, but not necessarily from off-world."

"Well, but Maia has at least corroborated what Joe has said to me. When we established her forest on my world she specifically said the Queen had caused the destruction of great forests. Then there is the woman that we called 'Alicia.' She has definitely gone mad and transformed herself into something hideous. I've seen that with my own eyes..."

Eddie stared off into space. Then he started ticking things off on his fingers. "And of course there's my own world. You haven't seen it, Lena, but it's really pretty far gone. It's hard to imagine it just got that way by itself. Then there are the things the Old One said to me, taught me when I stayed with her. And the remarks Captain Thomas made. And the pirate attacks. Those were real enough."

"No, something's going on," he concluded. "It might well be that Iris and Joe are less capable or weaker, somehow, than we assumed – but if we take what Joe said at face value, then opening the portals on this world will have a shielding effect. If it works out the way he said, our actions here could buy us some time to do something for my world."

"Yes, Reed. Let us grant all of that, but the line of reasoning leads us to the Queen herself. If we are effective, then at some point she will become aware of our actions. Once she becomes aware, she will act. I cannot imagine her allowing our ragtag bunch to thwart her intentions."

"Yeah, you're right. I guess the only thing I can ask is 'What would we do differently?'"

"I do not know, my love. I do not know."

*   *   *

So the remainder of the week offered a variation in routine if no real answers. Each day Lena and Eddie got up early and went to work in the shop. If things were slow in the afternoons, Eddie would go over and practice with Fleggie at the salvage yard. It felt good to have something mundane and well defined to do.

The four friends got together for lunch once, but they all agreed that with Iris and Joe out of town, their safety would be best served by staying indoors at night. They used the comm to check in each morning. Fleggie had some salvage work to do and Eddie helped his big friend a couple of times. Mostly, though, he alternated between his studies and working in the shop with Lena.

Wednesday was reasonably nice, but Thursday, the weather turned cold again and it rained on and off through Friday and much of the weekend. There were a few hours of clear weather on Sunday afternoon, and the sudden crowds on the street created the impression that everyone in the town who had been hiding from the rain and the cold came out to shop and enjoy the sunshine. The bookstore did a brisk business for much of the day, and Eddie had to call Fleggie to beg off their plan of several hours of afternoon practice.

Whenever weather and their responsibilities permitted, the two young men had worked diligently, and their practice was starting to bear fruit. Fleggie's two-handed, overhead throw was frighteningly powerful. When he hit the tree trunk target solidly it sometimes took ten minutes of prying and wiggling to free the axe from the target.

Eddie's left handed throw was becoming reliable. On Saturday he'd for the first time held an axe in each hand, thrown one immediately after the other, and buried them both in the target. His throws didn't have anything like the power of Fleggie's, but he was accurate and fast. When Eddie realized he wouldn't be able to practice on Sunday, he tried not to let his disappointment show, but it was easy to see that he seriously missed it.

Around closing time on Sunday, Joe and Iris returned from their trip. They walked in from the street as Eddie and Lena were closing the shop for the night. Their appearance drove any thoughts of bookstores or throwing axes from the young peoples' minds.

Joe had returned to his usual, vigorous self. He stood straight, and his eyes were clear and piercing. His hair was thick and wavy. His stomach was flat and he moved with the easy grace that Eddie remembered from the days at the Painter Street house.

Iris was not so fortunate. In the few days they were gone she had regressed from her youthful appearance as a beautiful woman in her late 30's to become a pretty but worn and tired woman ten years older. Her fiery hair was not quite as thick, not quite as shiny. Her eyes were still sharp and clear, however, and her voice still strong.

She didn't flinch from discussing the change and without preamble, launched into a concise explanation. "It took me several tries to pry it out of him, but now I understand what has happened. When Joe convinced me to agree to the transformation he neglected to mention that he would have to pour energy into me continually to keep the reversal of damage going. While I appreciate that he cares for me and would willingly accept damage to himself that he might heal me and restore my youth, we simply cannot afford this right now."

"Iris, please," Joe began. Despite his renewed strength and vigor, he looked stricken and ill at heart.

"No. They have a right to hear this, my dear one. They are involved in the struggle, as are their friends. So we went off and had a couple of days together and then we put the energy balance back to where it belongs. Joe will no longer starve himself to support me. Depending on how things go, I may fade quickly. Or not. We cannot know."

"All right. All right. Let me tell the rest, anyway, please?"

So Joe explained some of the history that Iris and he shared. He openly admitted what he had done. He talked of their love and how in all his long centuries he'd never felt about any other woman the way he did about Iris. He realized that he hadn't made a wise move, but he said that he had a hard time regretting it nonetheless.

"We've succeeded in opening four portals. Only one remains to be done on this world. Then we shall see about moving our efforts to Reed's and my badly damaged home world.

"At any rate, if we can all make it through this, Iris has agreed – has given me her solemn word – that this time, unlike the situation all those years ago, she will allow me to heal her. To take her to the Old One and let Lillith minister to us both. Remember, please. I am old, yes, and very strong, but I am still human. I still feel. It is so hard to bear, going on and on, fighting. And being alone as those I care for fade into memory."

After Joe fell silent, Eddie and Lena hardly knew what to say. They tried to understand and to offer compassion. They realized that these proud, powerful people did not desire sympathy from two who were still in their first flush of youth. Finally, Eddie hit on the words he wanted to say.

"Look, you guys. Lena and I care about you and respect you. All we have to offer, really, are our help, our loyalty, and our genuine affection for you both," his voice trailed off.

Joe came over and shook Eddie's hand firmly. "I know that, son. And it means something precious to us. Thank you both."

Joe took a deep breath and let it out in a sigh. Iris pulled out some handkerchiefs. She offered one to Lena and dabbed at her own eyes with the other. Then she straightened and took a deep breath of her own. When she let it out and spoke, she was all business again.

"What's the weather report for the next few days? We need to finish this. We still think that it's best to take advantage of the weather as much as we can. So we're going to look for rainy nights when fewer people are likely to be abroad."

"There is some chance of rain, but is not forecast to be as fierce as the last storm," Lena said.

"That might be enough," Joe said. "Now that I am back to normal, I may use the rainy weather to create a dense fog that will shield us from view. It takes little energy to set it up and once in place, the fog will remain in place for perhaps a half hour in the absence of strong winds."

"Yes, that might do," agreed Iris. "Let's plan on Tuesday night or, depending on the weather, Wednesday or Thursday. Not even two weeks from our most recent effort. It seems much longer."

Iris leaned a little on the counter as if she were tired. "Well, I am going to go rest. This old scoundrel here has convinced me that it's the best thing I can do for myself for the next few days. And I've promised to cooperate. Can you continue to handle the store for me, Lena?

"And you, young man. You need to split your time between spell practice and that axe throwing fetish you and Fleggie have developed. It may tilt the balance when the time comes. And it may save your life during some transit."

"I can handle the store, Iris," Lena tried to reassure her. "We ran it last week and enjoyed it. Occasionally, if things get busy, I may need a little help, but I really can take care of it at this point."

Eddie spoke up. "Yeah, and I've been practicing. I admit I've spent more time with the axes than I have with the spells, but I'll balance the work more. Count on it."

Iris nodded. She kissed everyone on the cheek and pressed Joe's hand for a few silent moments. Then, looking for a brief instant as though she hurt deep in her bones, she walked between the shelves back to her apartment to lie down.

When Iris was gone, Joe looked seriously at Eddie and Lena. "I'm going to try to remain as objective as I can, but that woman means more to me than a thousand worlds. I let her go once and have regretted it for half a century. If we win this battle, I'll never let her go again."

He sighed again. "Now you two go on upstairs. I'll lock up. Tomorrow I'll rethink the next opening and see if there is a way to shield Iris from the worst effects without breaking my promise to her. Let's plan on meeting tomorrow night after dinner, shall we? Come down here. Ask Fleggie and Sweetmaye if they can join us. I will spend tonight scanning, looking for signs that we are under observation. We'll finalize the details of this week's work."

There was nothing more to say. Solemnly, Eddie held out his hand and Joe shook it once more. Lena placed her hand on Joe's arm for a moment. Then she took Eddie's hand and they walked to the door of the shop.

They didn't see Iris during the daylight hours of the next day. Fleggie and Sweetmaye came to the shop after their dinner on Monday evening. Lena called them in advance and made sure that their friends understood the situation with Iris so that they wouldn't appear shocked when they saw the redheaded woman later that evening.

They met once again in the tidy front room of Iris' apartment. Joe began the moment everyone was seated and comfortable.

"Thank you, Fleggie and Sweetmaye. I presume that Lena and Eddie have explained the situation to you. At this point we're just waiting for the weather to help hide us. Then we'll try to open the final portal. This one will complete the pattern. I suspect that changes in the fabric of the Great Hub will resonate with our actions. Energies will flow, visible to those who know how to look for them. We must assume the Queen herself will learn of our activities. It is likely this will be the last thing we can accomplish in this world without serious resistance."

"That means it will be important to do our work and then, as soon as possible, move our efforts to Reed's and Joe's native world. The Queen may be – probably will be – distracted. We should take advantage of it," Iris added.

They went over the location and the route to reach it. Once again, Joe would make his way there on his own to prepare the site. Later, Fleggie and Sweetmaye would come to the bookstore and pick up Iris, Lena, and Eddie. They only needed a night with conditions that would either directly help them avoid notice or conditions that Joe could employ to mask them from view.

Everyone agreed to be ready to act as soon as Joe and Iris gave the word. The group was somber as it broke up. Eddie and Lena went out to the front of the store to chat with Fleggie and Sweetmaye a little before their friends left.

"Iris, the good red witch, she were not lookin' all tha' well, Fleggie thinks," the big man spoke softly, sadly.

"Yes. We are not sure what will happen to her this time," Lena said. Her arms were folded and pressed over her stomach against the cold. "I am worried about that and am actually hoping that we wait for another day or two so that she can rest as much as possible."

"Yeah, but we also need to wrap this up," Eddie added. "I keep thinking that it's just a matter of time before somebody beyond the local

RSM contingent notices the changes – somebody that none of us wants to meet. Joe and Iris said as much tonight."

"Well, I shall work the store for her for a day or two at any rate. That might help. Reed and I have been talking. And there is something else. We are worried about what might happen to you and to us if a serious mishap were to befall either Iris or Joe."

"Aye. Me man an' I ha' thou' much th' same. Mayhaps we'd lay low a bit... or more than a bit. Wouldna' be th' firs' time, sad t' say."

Fleggie nodded and added, "But we be wi' ye' on this. Ne'r fear tha', friends. Fleggie an' his girl both."

Lena hugged the big man and the small, pretty woman. "You know. Whatever happens, I am so glad to have become friends with you both."

Eddie didn't trust his voice just then and only nodded. As soon as he could, he cleared his throat and spoke softly. "Lena-love, I think you should get inside. You're not dressed for this weather."

So the four friends parted. Secure in their trust for each other, they were, on the other hand, less clear than ever about what lay ahead. In the days that followed, they stayed in close contact.

Joe prowled the streets and back alleys of Soapstone Bay. He sought evidence that they were being watched but came away with nothing of substance. He also visited the site out near Holmes Road where they would attempt to open a brand-new portal to complete the pattern. After careful measurements and close study of town maps he decided on a precise location for their final attempt.

Lena spent most of her time helping Iris in the store. Business in the shop remained spotty and tied to changes in the weather. In truth, Lena did most of the work, but she noticed right away that Iris derived support and comfort from her presence, so the young woman was happy to help. They spent many hours talking together.

Eddie studied and practiced. Occasionally, when Fleggie needed an extra pair of hands, he helped his friend on salvage jobs. Through Tuesday, the weather stayed mostly clear and mild, and Wednesday morning was bright and sunny, albeit cold. The forecasts called for a new storm front to hit the coast late Wednesday night.

Joe and Iris sent word that they wanted to try for the final portal opening late Thursday night. Even though they all knew their roles, they decided to get together one last time on Wednesday evening. They sat in Iris' living room with mugs of hot cider as they reviewed the plans. They agreed on a rendezvous time of ten o'clock in front of the bookstore. Outside, the weather was changing, and they could hear rain starting to fall.

Joe went back into the bedroom to get his coat so he could accompany Fleggie and Sweetmaye home and recheck his warding spells. While they waited for Joe's return, Iris looked at the young couples and spoke softly, hesitatingly. "One more thing," she said. Eddie thought that her voice sounded unnatural, a little bit strained.

"We are making some... changes in the ritual. To reduce the stress on me. I have agreed to this – reluctantly, I'll add," she looked around at each of them. Then she shook her head slightly and dropped her gaze.

"At any rate, your responses will be unchanged," she added. Please remember that once we've started, you must not interrupt the process. Everything must flow according to the prescribed sequence."

The four young people nodded their assent. "I am sure it will work out, Iris," Lena added. She was sitting next to Iris on the sofa, and she placed her hand atop the older woman's and let it rest there. Iris looked at her and smiled slightly but said nothing.

Joe came back in as he buttoned his coat. "Well, then. If no one has any questions, I suppose that's it. Shall we go, my young friends?"

As the others prepared to leave, Iris stood, rested her hand on the back of the sofa. For a moment, it looked as though she were going to say something, but after a few seconds she just shook her head slightly and then sat back down. Leaving Iris resting on the sofa, the others filed out of the shop. They parted company on the sidewalk.

That night, Lena was particularly passionate in her lovemaking. She clung to Eddie fiercely and drove her body hard against his. Outside, the rain and wind increased in intensity and it was as though the storm drove the young woman as well. Again and again, she aroused him and drew him inside her. She cried out in the candlelight. Her movements were urgent and almost violent. And more than once, Eddie was sure that her tears wet his face and chest. Each time he tried to speak, to ask her what troubled her, she covered his mouth with hers.

At last, she lay against him, partially atop him. She trembled for a long while, but gradually that subsided and she slept. The storm crashed around the ancient stones of the building. Eddie listened for a time in the warm, close darkness before following his beloved into a deep, dreamless sleep.

* * *

The next morning, by the time a crash of thunder dragged Eddie from his slumbers, Lena had already gone down to work in the bookstore. She had left a note in the kitchen and some breakfast in the oven for him. The note was intimate and loving and encouraged him to take his time as he prepared for the day.

The young man showered and shaved. He lingered over breakfast as the storm continued. His body still tingled with the way she had thrust against him the night before. The flesh of him remembered in a more vivid, a deeper way than his mind was able. Sighing, he got up from his meal and cleaned the kitchen.

He found a sweatshirt and pulled it over his head. He settled himself on the sofa and reviewed his spells, especially the invisibility spell. He practiced casting it around himself, which was frustrating because he couldn't really verify how well it was working. He had a better sense of its effectiveness when he practiced on other objects. Eventually, he found that he could keep four objects located in different parts of the room invisible at the same time.

After a half hour of attention on that single spell, Eddie went over the rest of his repertoire of spells and rehearsed each as best he could. Even though he needed some guidance and expert feedback with some of them, he could detect progress. Finally, he reviewed both the heat spell and the invisibility spell again.

Around noon, he heard Lena's feet on the stairs. He set his notes and books aside and went to the door to greet her. Looking both radiant and at the same time fragile, she stepped inside the apartment. She held out her arms and smiled. He held her close.

"What's going on, Lena? What's wrong?" he whispered.

She just shook her head and pressed her face against his chest. Then she pulled back and smiled. Her auburn hair was pulled back in a tight braid. Her bright blue eyes looked slightly gray in the light that filtered through the storm. It was a smile that held secrets. She took his hand and asked if he were ready for some lunch.

"Oh, gosh, Lena. I've just been sitting here, studying all morning. I'm still kind of full from breakfast... which was good, by the way.

"Hey," he added. "How'd you cook that and get ready to work downstairs without waking me up?"

Now she laughed. "You were snoring so loudly that you drowned out any little sounds I could make with pans and a stove!"

She stayed up in the apartment for her lunch break and they chatted. While Lena was her usual warm and sweet self, she was also slightly distant and withdrawn. It was clear to Eddie that she didn't want to discuss whatever it was that was on her mind, so he didn't press her. In the end, he ate a little of the lunch she had made and let her know that he'd have dinner ready when she got off work later.

They walked downstairs together and Eddie donned his foul weather gear to go out for a few things to fix for dinner. She kissed him and then darted inside the bookstore. He made his way down Center to the greengrocer at Turnbull. The storm continued to dump water on Soapstone, and there were few people on the streets.

Weather and season had conspired to limit the selections available, and few customers were in the store. The grocer was glad for any business. It was too early for the main winter crops and in any case, the farmers didn't want to drive all the way into town in such weather. Still, there was enough to make a good, warming supper for the two of them. Eddie put his purchases in his pack and trudged back up the street. It was good to get back indoors.

Food put away, Eddie went back to his studies. He reviewed what he'd done in the morning and practiced the invisibility spell several more times. At one point he took a break and got out his throwing axes. He held them and tossed them end over end a few times like a juggler, but there was no real way to practice with them and it was asking for trouble to play with them indoors. Eventually he contented himself with getting out his file and sharpening stone and touching up the edges.

Around four o'clock, he started to prepare dinner. He had ingredients to make a good casserole and the grocer had had some fresh bread. Eddie figured they'd want to eat something substantial and warming before venturing out into the storm for the night's activities.

The casserole was nearly done when Lena appeared. Business had been very slow and Iris had suggested that she go upstairs early. The older woman had wanted to close up shop herself. Before Lena had left the store, Iris promised to be upstairs a few minutes before ten. Outside, the storm was, if anything, growing stronger.

They ate a quiet dinner. Afterwards, Lena wanted to sit on the sofa next to Eddie. He put his arms around her and held her close. Listening to the storm, they stayed that way for a long time. He smelled the sweet scent of her hair. She felt his strength and his love for her.

At half past eight, they rose and stretched. Eddie felt a little bit drowsy and went into the bathroom to splash some cold water on his face. When he came out, Lena was up and moving around the apartment. Straightening and cleaning here and there in the already tidy space, she seemed unable to sit still. Every movement betrayed a tense, nervous energy. It was a relief when Iris finally knocked on the door.

Iris looked better for having rested through much of the week. She was no longer young looking but she had less of the frailty that had so shocked Lena and Eddie upon her return. As she had done on other occasions, she clasped both of their hands, one in each of hers, and held them for a moment. Then she reminded them once again that they must not interrupt the spell once they arrived at the site.

"I will see you downstairs in a few moments," she said. Her voice was very quiet, almost a whisper, and Eddie thought that the woman's voice shook just a little.

Once again, Lena and Eddie donned their foul weather gear. They made their way down to the front of the store and waited beneath the awning. Once again, wind drove the rain almost horizontally and they were glad for their waterproof pants and boots.

Iris walked out of the store just as Fleggie and Sweetmaye pulled up in their wagon. Fleggie hopped in the back and Iris took a seat at the controls next to Sweetmaye. As usual, Eddie and Lena sat across from their big friend. The storm held steady. Bad as it was, the weather wasn't as harsh as it had been when they opened the portal in the nature preserve.

As they had the week before, they drove west on Center to turn right on Meridian and then west again on Long's Peak. This time, however, they continued on past Holmes Road. A few blocks before Long's Peak crossed Biscayne, they turned left onto a narrow lane called "Drew."

They could see lights from a handful of widely-spaced houses in the first block of Drew, but then the narrow street assumed the character of a country road. Modern pavement gave way to macadam. The road curved around and followed the contours of this patch of undeveloped land that was encompassed by the town. Without visual landmarks it was difficult to keep the cardinal points in mind. They passed one more house on their left. A dog barked but didn't want to leave the shelter of its house to investigate closer.

The road became a muddy track and they saw a dim light to their right. Iris turned the quiet electric wagon around and Joe came over. She brought the wagon lights down to their lowest setting. The falling rain visible all around him, Joe stepped into the soft glow. Holding his left hand straight out at the shoulder, he began to chant softly, just at the threshold of hearing. As he chanted, he made a series of complex gestures with his right hand.

Now he fell silent. He brought his right arm up and pointed at the clouds overhead. He turned slowly in place and drew the rain from the sky. A whirling thread of moisture spun down to his right hand. A dense fog streamed from his left as he spun. The dank, chill breath of the fog enveloped them and then passed them by. Joe completed three turns before he dropped his hands.

He stood still for a moment. Concentrating on distant thoughts, he might have been carved from stone. Eventually, he opened his eyes, looked up at Iris, and nodded to her. Slowly, she climbed from the wagon to assist Joe in setting up the grounding rod. They pulled it from its wrappings and carried it to a place that Joe had determined. Reflected at some distance by the dense, enveloping fog, the dim glow of an illumination spell augmented the soft light from the wagon.

Once Joe was in place, however, Iris did not step to the head of the pattern. Instead she trudged slowly back towards the wagon. She paused there in the glimmer of the wagon's running light. Eddie thought that she looked terribly sad and careworn.

As Iris approached, Lena clutched Eddie's hand. She brought it to her lips and pressed her mouth against it. Then she released his hand and sprang from the wagon. Iris continued over to lean against the side of the vehicle. Rain and fog masked all other sounds.

Now Lena stood at the head of the pattern, at the place Iris had occupied on previous nights. She met Eddie's shocked, stricken look and shook her head ever so slightly. She begged him with her eyes to remain silent, not to break the spell. Then averting her glance, she gestured to Sweetmaye and Fleggie and they took their places on one side. Finally, Lena looked at Eddie and Iris and gestured for them to take their places on the other side. The pattern was complete.

Just as Iris had done on previous occasions, Lena now led the invocation. She had the cadences, the words, and the gestures down perfectly. At the end of the opening stanzas of the spell, the now familiar low humming sound rose to surround them. Tonight it competed with and over-topped the sound of the storm.

At the final *"Now the door opens!"* the green lightning leapt up from the brightly glowing, singing staff that Joe supported at the center of the pattern. As before, the green lightning was met with an electric flash that descended from the clouds.

This time Joe's arms jerked slightly as if he'd received a jolt of electricity, but he did not fall to his knees. Still grasping the rod, the powerful old man spun easily to face Eddie. Joe held one hand, palm out, to warn the young man back, and it was all that Eddie could do to comply. He could see that Lena was frozen, riveted where she stood. Quickly, easily, Joe carried the rod to the back of the wagon. Iris moved to his side and took over the shrouding of the rod.

All this time Eddie's eyes were on Lena. She swayed in the dim light where she stood. Joe sprang to her side and made complex motions with his hands. Lena collapsed, crumpled into his arms like a limp doll. "Now! Take her!" Joe hissed across the way to Eddie.

The young man hurried forward and gathered his beloved into in his arms. She, who had always been so full of life and energy had become suddenly inert, shrunken and frail, and she did not respond to his urgently whispered call to her. Her eyes, unfocused, vacant, opened just the tiniest bit. Eddie felt her throat. Her pulse beat there but it was weak and fluttery. Fleggie and Sweetmaye stepped to Eddie's aid and together, they got Lena into the back of the wagon where Eddie could support her head.

Iris and Joe climbed onto the bench and they headed back the way they had come. As they entered the surrounding ring of dense fog, Joe spoke softly over his shoulder. "I will mask the wagon from prying eyes. No one will discern us or bother us. You see to your woman." He was silent for a few heartbeats and then he added, "As soon as I saw her take the position at the head of the circle, I feared this would happen. Whisper her name. Call softly to her. Ask her to return to you. Beg her. Do not stop."

Eddie bent close to Lena's face. As he was told, he begged her to come back. As they reached the town streets and began to pass near brighter street lamps, Eddie could see that her eyes remained lost, focused at infinity. His heart sank as he looked into her still face.

Although they drove quickly, the return trip went on forever. Eddie tried to shield Lena from the brunt of the storm, but now the wind and rain were fierce. Fleggie came over. The wagon lurched beneath his weight. The big man stooped and opened his coat. He held it aloft to shield them.

Finally, they reached their building. Fleggie jumped down. "Let Fleggie take her, mate. Ye' run ahead an' get th' door open."

Gently, Eddie handed Lena over to his friend. He ran to the door, thumbed the lock, and held it open as they followed. Then he ran to the top of the stairs and unlocked the door to their apartment. Moments later they had Lena's rain gear and boots off and she lay on the bed. She was pale, her breathing shallow. Eddie leaned close and brushed her wet hair away from her face.

From what felt like a great distance, Iris' trembling voice reached his ears. "She insisted on taking my place, Reed. Do not blame Joe. He realized too late what we'd done... what I'd agreed to let her do. Lena made me swear an oath not to speak of it."

Although he still stood straight and strong at Eddie's shoulder, Joe's voice was tired. "She took such a risk. At one point in this spell, you dangle by the finest of threads, far above the infinite. You are unable to ignore the hideously unbalanced relationship between the individual and the cosmos. For one so young and inexperienced it can be... difficult... to find one's way back from the edge of the Abyss."

Eddie wanted to rage at them both, but he swallowed his anger. "And... all I can do... is talk to her? And try... to call her... back?" His voice shook with emotion as he focused his desperate gaze on his beloved's beautiful, still face.

"Do not discount that. It is indeed the best course, the best you can do. She is young and strong, son, as is the love you have for each other. Stay with her. Perhaps your friends will help you keep your vigil. I must tend to Iris. I'll check back in a few hours."

Eddie looked up finally, and his anger drained from him. Iris looked dead on her feet. She was pale and shaking and crying openly. She sagged in pain, unable to breathe comfortably. Tiny Sweetmaye was struggling to hold her up. Joe stepped across the room to put his arm around Iris. He relieved Sweetmaye of her burden and half carried the older woman from the room.

"Fleggie, go t' th' kitchen an' see if ye' cou' find a bit o' somethin' hot fer us t' drink. Try not t' break things, hear?" The big man looked relieved at being given a job to do. He moved with his innate, powerful grace to the tiny kitchen where he began rummaging around.

Sweetmaye turned to Eddie. "Now, dear friend, go ye' t' help me great oaf of a man. Just an eyeblink. I'll tend t' yer' darlin' an' get her 'neath th' covers. Go, now. Go."

Eddie hesitated, but yielded beneath Sweetmaye's steady look. He joined Fleggie in the kitchen. They made tea and Eddie found some cinnamon bread that he toasted and brought into the main room of the tiny apartment. By the time the men returned, Sweetmaye had Lena undressed and in the bed. The tiny woman had put a towel beneath her friend's head and combed the wet hair from Lena's beautiful, still face. Lena looked comfortable, if terribly fragile. Eddie held her hand and spoke her name.

In the hours that followed, he whispered to her. He talked about when they had met during the previous summer. He told her how he had loved her so quickly and so thoroughly. He reminded her of how the recollection of her face had saved him from the harpy's deadly, nocturnal embrace.

After a time his voice grew hoarse. Fleggie came over and knelt on the floor beside the bed. "Take a bit o' break, mate. Have a cup o' tea. Fleggie'll spell ye'."

Then the big man cleared his throat and, hesitating just briefly, sang. He sang softly, his voice surprisingly sweet and high. He sang lullabies and sea shanties and drinking songs. All the while he held Lena's delicate hand in his great paw. Eddie realized that he had never had such a friend in his life as this gentle mountain of a man.

The hot tea soothed his throat, and Eddie rested for a short while. Fleggie finally ran out of songs, and Eddie returned to sit next to Lena and speak to her. This time he spoke of what he hoped for their future together, the dreams that he'd not yet had the courage or wisdom to share. It went on.

Growing fiercer now, the storm raged outside. It crashed against the windows and dumped rain on the slates. The wind tried to find purchase on the ancient stones of the building, but as it had for hundreds of years, the stout structure shrugged off the onslaught and enveloped its occupants within sheltering warmth. Lightning flashed and thunder rumbled across the little town of Soapstone Bay as three young friends kept their vigil over a fourth.

Finally, in the small hours of the morning, Lena's breathing changed. It became stronger, more like the breathing of someone deeply asleep. She turned over in bed and Eddie's heart leaped with joy. In another half hour or so, Lena coughed gently in her sleep. Her eyes fluttered open.

Outside, the worst of the storm finally passed. The crashing violence faded. Torrents of rain tapered to a steady flow. The blustery wind became a breeze and then fell still.

At first Lena's eyes focused at some distant point. Frightening in their remoteness, they were almost like the eyes of the dead. But as her friends watched, the young woman drew back from that brink and be-

Michael C. Glaviano

came aware of the room, the people around her. She smiled and stretched.

"I heard you, Reed. And you, too, Fleggie. All the way out there... at the... edge of everything..." she shuddered and her sight began to drift away again. Then she blinked hard, shook her head. Holding the covers in front of her, she sat up.

"I was aware of you all," she continued with a gentle, sweet smile. "I remember that dreadful ride back in the wagon. I almost lost my way then. But next I felt Sweetmaye get me undressed and into bed. I heard her whisper and felt her comb my hair. You watched over me. I heard you talking and singing. It was the thread that I followed back. It was such a long way."

She smiled again. "I am really back now. I can feel it. Thank you all."

Sweetmaye moved close and took Lena's hand for just a moment. Then she turned to Fleggie and lit up the room with her outsize smile. "Time we made ourselves scarce, me big man!" she said.

Leaving fingerprints on the ceiling, Fleggie stood and stretched. "Aye, lass. Fleggie cou' use a bit o' sleep himself. True now."

Dawn hovered just beyond the wings of night's dark stage when Sweetmaye and Fleggie bundled into their foul weather gear and took their leave. They walked arm-in-arm down the stairs and out to the street where their wagon waited. Tired but confident, Fleggie spoke the words of the invisibility spell. They and their wagon faded from view. Quietly, passing as shadows in the dark, they rode back to their own tiny cottage.

Thirty Eight

The grounds and exterior walls of her castle were coated with sheets of crystalline water. Magnificent icicles hung from galleries, depended from vaulted ceilings. Illuminated by a million glowing lights, glacial stalactites formed ever-changing chandeliers of ice.

At the very center of her power, the Locust Queen reclined upon her icy, jewel-encrusted throne. Suddenly, the dreadful monarch tensed, sat up abruptly. The chill air hissed with whispers. Something had happened. Something unexpected. The dangerous, cold woman cast the featureless blue orbs that were her eyes toward the courtiers. As usual, as she demanded, her attendants stood, scrawny, ill-clad and shivering. Their whispers ceased, replaced by an atmosphere of dread. That was better.

Moving languidly in the blue twilight, the Queen raised one shapely arm. She gestured and vanished, leaving behind all manner of speculation. Her minions would jockey for position. They would fabricate stories and seek ways of betraying each other. At some point she would descend upon one or more of them while the others watched. That would restore authority, restore order; reinforce that they must, above all, fear her.

But first, she must determine what had changed. Something had perturbed her web of sensors. That would never do.

She materialized in a brightly lit room. Partially but not totally masking other, less pleasant odors, a strong smell of disinfectant permeated everything. There were a dozen shallow, stainless steel basins in the room. Perhaps three quarters of them were occupied by... things. Things that had once been human. Things that wanted only to die. But only rarely did she allow that.

These were her sensors. Gelded, dismembered, eyes plucked out, auditory nerves cauterized, they lay in the icy brightness. Their nervous systems had been altered, modified to suit the needs of she who would rule all, who would consume all. Sensory inputs were tied together and fed from probes that rested in the place between worlds. The signals terminated deep within the pain centers of their brains. From time to time,

423

one or more of her sensors screamed or moaned, but the sounds were in-articulate for their tongues, too had been removed at the root.

Weaving a tapestry of pain and degradation, wires and tubes led from form to form, around and around. These wires and tubes were inserted here and there. Some wires were coupled to nerves; others were connected to sources of great heat or cold. Tubes supplied something like nutrients, carried away wastes. Strong electrical shocks were administered in the event that a sensor managed to come in contact with the barbed, metal rails that surrounded the periphery of each basin. Connected as they were, all would bask in the brilliance of pain initiated by the transgression of any.

The Locust Queen caressed the nearest of her sensors. The blind, hairless thing trembled, quivered beneath her touch. This displeased her and she dug the perfect fingernails of her perfect hand into the sallow skin of the thing's sunken chest. All of them screamed then, and their screaming soothed her.

Again, probing with her thoughts, she caressed another of the hapless things. She sought to know the source of the disturbance.

An image swam before her cold, featureless eyes. It was an image of a world, one where she had only begun her work. Her agents had been dispatched to begin the standard program, but this was a world whose Old One, curse them all, had never faltered, had continued to nurture and protect. And now, some... other... meddler had opened a stable pattern of portals to the Great Hub. The pattern was indeed *very* stable, yes, but perhaps not irreversibly so.

So she must begin anew in this world. An irritation. A setback. Someone, better yet a multitude, would suffer as a result. And she would, of course, prevail. She would not be denied. Ever.

Then she vanished from that place of pain and defilement. Careless as always of the cost, the power she expended, she slid, blinked in-*between* and reappeared in her throne room to select a new agent. He would be sent to this world to learn in more detail what had disrupted her plans. He was made to understand that he must contact those already established and receive their intelligence. He was made to understand that he would next gather what other impressions he might and finally report back. Of course the Queen knew the only way to believe his report would be to question him. Thoroughly. She smiled then, secure in the knowledge that the questioning would add to her enjoyment of the game.

The agent bowed his way out of her presence to prepare for his mission. Gazing once more upon the vermin that comprised her subjects, the Locust Queen took her ease. She reclined comfortably, beautifully upon her throne. She cast her mind in the direction of that bright, icy, machine-filled chamber: nothing disturbed her sensors. They lay, once again calm. Wrapped in their world of humiliation and pain, they lay still. The place between the worlds settled back into its infinite, ever-changing sameness.

Her earlier sense of urgency faded, replaced by an appreciation of her own beauty and strength. She knew the agent would return when he felt he had something with which he might curry favor. That was something to anticipate. Then she would enjoy the questioning.

Michael C. Glaviano

Thirty Nine

Recovering from trip through Place Between. Hate it there. Big thing there, hunting. Hungry. Familiar but not exactly. Almost caught, but got through.

Town. Skulking around. Asking questions here and there. Not much to find. No one says much. People here sense, know, understand... something about motivations. Not inclined to rat each other out, damn them.

Contacts agents already on-world. Incompetents, they. Hired even worse to do the Queen's bidding. Fools. Fools, all. Ham-fisted in town; pushed back by local authorities. Unable to hamper learning. Unable to unravel the fabric. Whine. Claim off-worlders involved. Whine, whine, whine, whine. Laughs. Queen will eat them. Laughs.

Try downtown. Poor. Other agents. Hungry. Sneaky.
Try uptown. Fools. Little is locked up. Lots of things to steal, sell.
Watch. Look. Sneak.
Watch. Steal. Sell. Eat.
Watch. Watch.

Find. Unhappy. Bitch.
Follow her, following others. She stalks them! Why? Follow her. What does she care? Happy couple. Pretty she. Strong he. Stay away. Stay far back. Watch Unhappy Bitch. She hates her/loves him/hates him for loving her. Crazy hates. Almost like back in Blue World. She stalks, watches, curses, broods.

Interested, hungry, he follows.

Michael C. Glaviano

Forty

In the aftermath of the final portal opening, things slowly returned to a more mundane flow. The winter solstice passed. Despite the terrible fright it caused, Lena's experience left her unharmed if not completely unchanged. She was a little quieter than she had been, a little more given to deep silences, but she was no less loving in her heart and no less enthralled with the beauty of her world and the pleasure she found in her friends. She began to display an interest in magic and, after hesitating for a day or two, asked Eddie if she might begin reading his texts on the subject.

Iris, on the other hand, emerged from the experience very ill and weak. Joe tended her, but she insisted that he take no extraordinary steps to restore her. Mostly she kept to her bed and tried to regroup. Lena and Eddie naturally stepped into the gap and ran the store for nearly two more weeks. Finally, Iris emerged from her rooms. Her beauty had faded to a distant reflection of what it had been, and her demeanor suggested damage at some deep level.

She did take some pleasure in working the shop with Lena. It was almost as though the loving acceptance of the younger woman allowed Iris to function, allowed her to lay aside a portion of the guilt she so obviously carried. Looking at them, one might assume that one was the beloved granddaughter and the other the doting grandmother. The work was not demanding, and Lena knew she would welcome it as a diversion when it came time for her lover and his mentor to carry the struggle back to their native world.

Fleggie and Sweetmaye, Lena and Eddie spent as much time together as they could. Their shared experiences had forged a powerful bond between them. The atmosphere in Soapstone Bay remained tense, but the four were still young, still given to boisterous activities and, more recently, even a few late nights out. They also could be observed sitting together quietly and comfortably around a table speaking in muted but glad tones.

They were watchful when they went abroad, and they took care as to where they went and by what means. Within days of the final opening, the four of them visited the focal point, the center of the six portals. All of them sensed the effects of their actions. On bright days, the air was clearer, the colors more vivid. Other times, the fogs were more shrouded in mystery and potential.

Joe, and when she was able, Iris toured that special area with them. They pronounced it stable and secure. Iris appeared to be comforted by this and, despite her fragility, was on occasion seen to smile and even laugh a little.

Even though it was now deep winter, and despite the tension engendered by the RSM, it was clear that something was afoot in the town. Creative energy was building. The situation at the university changed for the better. The detractors of learning found that their influence had waned. Bona fide faculty and administration stood shoulder to shoulder and drove out the poseurs whose agenda had been to stifle intellectual life.

In town, the clubs were open late. There was great music by local and visiting performers. Galleries had show after show. Word moved out through the world that this little seaport town had an amazing music and art scene. Travelers braved the storms, the cold, and the occasional spasms of RSM-induced violence to visit and experience what some claimed was nothing less than a renaissance in the creative and intellectual realms.

Of course this renaissance didn't happen immediately. It also didn't happen without a struggle. The agents of the Locust Queen knew better than to return to the Blue World and admit failure. For a while, they attempted to recruit more mercenaries to restore the ranks of their front organization, the RSM, and for a while, the RSM operatives maintained a presence uptown. Gradually, however, people banded together to fight back against the brand of intimidation practiced by the RSM operatives with their scarlet armbands and their jackboots.

Merchants carried products that their customers wanted, products that often were not blessed by appearing on the RSM-approved vendor list. The merchants supported one-another and could be relied upon to show up on a moment's notice if the RSM goons attempted to coerce or bully. The town patrol supported the merchants' desire to pursue commerce and trade and pulled RSM people off the streets anytime they attempted to use physical force or intimidation. The comm system was upgraded so that the citizens and merchants could request immediate help from the town patrol.

An uneasy balance of forces permeated Soapstone Bay for the better part of a week. Then, on the first bright, mild day in January, two dozen RSM troops marched up the middle of University Avenue. They stopped traffic during the mid-day rush. They bullied and, occasionally, assaulted citizens. They used bullhorns to blare their demands. Shops would carry only RSM-approved goods. The university would be closed.

All students who were not local citizens were to be expelled from the town. Labeled as purveyors of smut and discord, art galleries and performance venues would be closed. The list went on.

Near the university the RSM forces were met by town patrol and told to disperse. The first minutes of the confrontation contained little beyond shouting, posturing. During this apparent standoff, another dozen RSM troopers used the landscaping at the edge of campus as cover. They crept as close as they could to the unprotected backs of the patrol officers. At the height of the tension, this second force charged across Biscayne Avenue.

About 20 students had gathered nearby and they witnessed the onset of the charge. Several called out to warn the patrol. Half of the RSM troops split off and went after the students with their batons. Ten more guards appeared and attempted to surround the students. A general melee ensued.

The patrol called in reinforcements and quelled the riot. Eighteen RSM troopers were arrested and charged with serious offenses, but no known leaders of the movement were found among those taken into custody. In the end, three students were hospitalized with severe head injuries. Ten more had broken bones.

The next morning, local media blasted the city government and the town patrol for mishandling the situation. The citizenry was outraged at the inability of the government to restore order and peace in the town. Obviously pre-written letters to the editor laid the blame for the disorder at the feet of students and the impoverished people who dwelt in the Warrens.

At the same time, pro-RSM comm net stories began circulating. These portrayed the Rational Science Movement as noble vigilantes who were acting in the best interests of the people. They further claimed that the elected government in Soapstone had lost touch with the true needs of the people and had become soft on crime, immorality, and disorder. For a day, all appeared bleak, but this unhappy circumstance was temporary.

The city government had realized early on that they must break the organizational center of the disturbances. Over and over, the town patrol had pulled violent perpetrators off the streets. Occasionally they had arrested lieutenants but had never been able to crush the actual leadership structure of the paramilitary group. The city council knew full well that the RSM's goal was to frighten the populace and to sew discord among various groups. They understood that if the center failed to hold, people would eventually succumb to unrelenting propaganda.

Quietly, they had begun to prepare for a violent standoff and so had been ready for the riot at the west end of town. At the height of the riot, specially trained patrol sharpshooters took command of nearby rooftops. They fired into the melee. Their weapons emitted neither lethal projectiles nor rubber bullets. Instead, they fired tiny radio transmitters. These embedded themselves in fabric. The two dozen or so RSM forces who were allowed to escape carried those transmitters back to their hideouts.

Now the patrol went on the offensive. In a coordinated action, the RSM hideouts were surrounded and raided. This time senior RSM leaders as well as foot-soldiers were rounded up and questioned. This led to more arrests. The city government shared intelligence with regional authorities and within weeks, the Rational Science Movement as a regional socio-political force was broken.

During this period, the handful of RSM operatives who escaped arrest fled the uptown district and began haunting the shadowy corners of the Warrens. The agents of the Locust Queen, their erstwhile employers, went to ground. The agents stopped paying their mercenaries, and the RSM dissolved in the absence of coherent leadership.

For a short time, individuals and small gangs of thugs thought to prey on the residents of the Warrens. This was a serious and, ultimately, fatal mistake. The long-time denizens of that rough district lived by a code of justice unto themselves. They tolerated much in the way of hardship, and they suffered the commerce that passed among them as a necessity of life, but they dealt harshly with any outsider who presumed to violate their turf.

A month after the opening of the final portal, Lena's world – at least the corner of it around Soapstone Bay – began to feel secure. The town had pulled back from the brink, taken a breath, and looked with clearer eyes at the world. In another six weeks, the spring thaw would start and that would bring with it even more visitors. It appeared likely that science, art, music, and other intellectual pursuits would continue to flourish.

It was against this backdrop that Joe reached a decision. He and Eddie could delay no longer. They must return to their home world to see what they could do. It was too early to count on lasting effects in Lena's world, but the trends were finally moving in the right direction. Momentum was on their side for now and Joe sought to take advantage of the situation. While the Queen's agents were in disarray, Joe would shift the terms of engagement.

Fleggie and Sweetmaye had their friends over for dinner on the night before Eddie's departure. It was a somber affair, with lots of heartfelt words and no few tears. Fleggie was particularly hard-pressed to accept that Eddie would be gone for an indeterminate period of time.

"Mate. It be a hard thing. Fleggie feels he shou' go an' help ye'."

Sweetmaye put her hand on his arm and shook her head, "A' think not, me great lamb. Thing's still be touchy here. If you be gone then who is t' look ou' fer' us?"

"She's right, Fleggie, as much as I'd like to have you with us. For me to function, I'll need to know that someone I can trust is here in Soap-stone."

At a slightly intense look from Lena, Eddie hastened to add, "That's not saying that Lena and Sweetmaye can't take care of them-selves, of course, but there's the situation with Iris. And Lena may want to take some graduate classes now that the university is up and running again. And she's been blasting through my magic texts too..."

"No, Fleggie," Eddie shook his head. "We need to divide our forces now." Eddie paused for a moment as he thought about the situ-ation on his native world. "And there's something else, man."

"What be tha'?" The big man looked at him intently.

"You've never been to my native world," Eddie replied. "It's a lot less... free... than this one. And even in places of relative affluence it's crowded and tense. You have to be careful, very careful not to draw at-tention to yourself. For you to visit the world where I was born we'd need to have documents created for you. Documents that you could use to fend off interference by the authorities. Remember, the Queen and her minions have been busy in my world for years.

"If you had the same accent as I," Eddie continued, "maybe we could acquire such documents. But in Joe's town – or anywhere else on the continent – you'd be tagged immediately as someone born elsewhere. Believe me on this one, friend."

The big man mulled this over. Finally he nodded, "Fleggie sees it, mate. It still be a hard thing, but Fleggie sees th' right o' it."

Then conversation passed on to other topics, some serious, some light. The night wore on. They shared dreams they had for the days and years ahead. They talked about the adventures they'd been through to-gether. Around ten-thirty, Lena stifled a yawn and said she'd like to go home.

Even though the night was clear, it was cold, and their friends in-sisted on giving them a ride back to the bookstore. They said their good-byes under the awning in front of the shop. Eddie and Lena stood watch-ing as the electric wagon looped around and hummed its way back down Central towards Turnbull.

Fleggie and Sweetmaye held their hands high and waved as the wagon receded into the night.

In contrast to their fierce coupling on the night before the final portal opening, Eddie and Lena were tender and gentle on this night. Af-terwards, they held each other and whispered in the dark for a long time. They drifted off to sleep in the small hours to wake when the sunlight brightened their room in the morning. Surrounded by that beautiful morning light, Lena and Eddie made love once again.

At noon, Joe and Eddie were ready to go. Iris wanted to accom-pany the men to the Inn, and Lena also liked the idea of seeing them off.

Joe insisted they hire a cab so that Iris wouldn't be out in the winter cold. She had recovered somewhat, but obviously she would not regain her strength and youth. She was angry and embarrassed about needing to ride where a few weeks earlier she could walk, but she could not argue with the wisdom of it.

Joe and Iris held hands all the way to the Inn. Lena and Eddie did the same. No one spoke. When they reached the Inn, Eddie asked the driver if he would wait for the women to accompany Joe and him inside. The driver was glad for the return fare and only too happy to comply.

They climbed from the cab in front of the Inn at Three Corners. Eddie swung his pack onto his back and again took Lena's hand. He held the door open for Iris and Joe, and then Eddie and his beloved followed the older couple inside. Once inside the door, the men shed their heavy coats. Eddie put one sheathed throwing axe on his belt and hung the other over his shoulder. He'd left the axe that was missing its sheath in the apartment.

Mel was at his usual post behind the desk of the dark lobby. He looked up but said nothing. The two couples said their good-byes as they crossed the quiet room to stand near the door beneath the stairs. Eddie and Lena hugged. She laughed, but she cried, just a little, at the same time. Eddie handed her his coat and her breath caught in her throat for a second, but she swallowed and mustered a half smile. For each other's sake, they put up brave fronts, but they were both miserable.

Iris clung to Joe for a few moments. She said nothing at all as she stepped back. She looked at Joe and then at Eddie and again back at Joe. Then she nodded once and reached for Joe's coat, which she pulled over her own shoulders as though it were a heavy cape. She took Lena's hand and turned away to walked swiftly towards the door and the waiting cab. When they reached the door, Lena looked back to meet Eddie's gaze. She smiled and waved a hand in farewell as they left, but Iris left the lobby without another glance.

After the women were gone, Mel climbed down from his perch and shuffled slowly over to the door with his heavy, ornate key. "Safe journey to ye'. Mayhaps Old Mel 'l be a waitin' when next ye' pass this way. If ye' pass."

They made their way down the stairs quickly this time. Eddie had mastered the spell to illuminate the space beneath his feet, and he could count the steps easily enough. It was but a handful of minutes before they reached the round room at the bottom of the stairs.

"Do you need the candles, son?"

"Well, I'm not sure, but I don't think so."

"Good. You go through first. Step off to one side. Not far, just a few steps. I'll follow quickly."

Eddie nodded. Joe waited up the stairs just out of sight, and the younger man cast a slight nimbus of light around himself to illuminate his circuits of the room. He heard the keening sound that flowed down the tunnel towards him and saw the light that accompanied the sound. He pulled one of his throwing axes – the one at his belt – free. Then he faced the wall and, with his back to the pit, stepped off the edge. He landed gracefully, with his knees bent.

Quickly he looked around. Nothing moved but tendrils of mist. The ground was soft and spongy with moisture. The air was warm and humid, and he was immediately glad that he'd left his heavy coat in Soapstone Bay. Eddie stepped off to one side. A few seconds later, Joe materialized a couple of feet above the soft earth and dropped to a crouched position.

Joe gestured for Eddie to follow him and then strode rapidly through the mist. Moving confidently, Joe found and passed the first standing stone. He quickly moved to stand between the nearby pair of stones where he once again created a brilliant beam of light to illuminate the cairn they sought.

This time they reached the cairn undetected and Joe cast the spell to open the portal into their native world. Seconds later, they stepped through the open door and slammed it shut behind them. They were in the portal chamber that lay deep in the earth beneath Joe's house.

They pulled themselves from the circular pit and walked up the long, subterranean passageway. Eddie left his throwing axes on the table at the mouth of the tunnel. Finally, they climbed the stairs to reach the entry hall of the house.

As soon as they assured themselves that the house was undisturbed, Eddie continued out into the back yard. There was snow on the ground and it was chilly. The back yard looked sad and neglected.

Eddie drew a note from his pocket. He'd written it earlier in the day. It simply told Lena that they had reached their destination safely. He reached the back wall and located the loose brick. Once he worked it free, Eddie could see that there was already a note waiting for him. Lena and Iris must have gone directly to Baleen Park after leaving the Inn.

My Love,

Hasten to your work so you may return to me as quickly as possible. Be safe. Know that you are always in my heart.

Lena

Eddie replaced Lena's note with his own and returned the brick to its place. He felt heavy and incomplete, and the cold was seeping into his body. He returned to the house. Joe had already called Sergeant Driscoll and let her know they were back. He looked up as Eddie came into the kitchen.

"First off, we'll need to get in touch with some of my old compatriots. I realize now that it was foolish to work alone as much as I did. While I do that, would you mind going to the store and laying in some supplies? We should get the fundamentals established so that we can move forward quickly."

"No problem, Joe. It'll give me something to keep busy. I'm feeling sorta down, so I want to do as much as I can to work myself out of it."

The old man nodded. "I think I understand your feelings. There will be plenty to do soon enough, I suspect. Physical activity is a good prescription to combat melancholy, so once you return from the store, you could clean the place and tend to the yard and greenhouse. If you feel like it of course."

"Sure. I'll be glad to do something useful. And I know up here," he pointed to his head, "that staying busy is my best bet."

So Eddie went back down to the basement and found a large, canvas pack. Then he pulled a warm coat from the hall closet and ventured out into the late winter cold of the Painter Avenue neighborhood. About an hour later he was back. Joe was on the phone. It sounded like he was arguing with someone.

Eddie put the groceries and other supplies away. Next, as Joe had suggested, he tended to the greenhouse and the yards. This mostly involved cleanup work. Trash had accumulated in front of the house in their absence. Wind had blown refuse down the alley. In the greenhouse, last autumn's pots needed emptying. What remained of the winter vegetables had languished and could go into the compost. This work occupied him for another hour.

As he knew would be the case, Eddie began to feel better as he worked. After finishing outdoors, he climbed the stairs to his rooms and began cleaning. The only thing his rooms required was basic housecleaning, which took little effort and passed quickly.

Out of habit he left Joe's private rooms alone and after vacuuming and dusting the hall on the second floor, Eddie went after the main floor rooms. Joe moved his operation up to his quarters to be out of the way. By late afternoon Eddie was hungry and dirty but was in a better mood. He washed up a little in the kitchen sink and started some dinner.

Joe's mood, however, did not match his own. The old man was scowling heavily when he came down the stairs and entered the kitchen. Eddie was heating some pasta sauce and had water on the stove for spaghetti. He'd already made a salad and had a bottle of Pinot Noir breathing on the counter. Garlic bread was ready to go into the oven and fresh grated parmesan waited on the kitchen table.

"Well this is not going as well as I'd hoped," Joe grumbled. "Not well at all. I suppose it's my own damn fault. I know it is. I've waited too long. Most of my old compatriots are too old or too frightened to do more than whine at me. Several of them have died. Not a few of them said that they were surprised I had not!"

Eddie stirred the sauce. "So what are we going to do? How many people do we need?"

Joe sat down and splashed a taste of wine into his glass, tried it. "That's pretty good, and the sauce smells fine... for pre-made stuff. Did you happen to get any kalamata olives?" When Eddie nodded, Joe smiled just a tiny bit. "Would you mind chopping some of those into the sauce?" He fell silent for a moment. Then he picked up the thread of his thoughts again. "I suppose we don't really need that many helpers – or any at all, if it comes to it. It's just that I was foolishly hoping that I'd be able to get things going quickly so that we could return. Clearly, that's not going to be the case."

"Well, can we bring new people in?"

"In principle. But consider the intellectual climate on this world. Finding and recruiting the right people would take time. Also, whom could we trust? The consequences of betrayal are grave. And, of course, recall your own initial reaction to forces and events at odds with your view of reality."

"Right, right. I remember... Okay, so what are we going to do?"

"Well, my afternoon's efforts were not completely in vain. Three of my old friends are willing and able to help. I've invited them to join us here. They'll be arriving within the week."

"From where?"

"They're scattered across the west. One lives just outside Albuquerque, out past the Rio Grande. Another lives in a college town a couple of hours north of Santa Barbara. The third has settled up near the Canadian border, south of Vancouver."

"And they're all old men?"

"Yes, but these three have kept active. We won't know for certain until they arrive, but they definitely conveyed the impression of vitality on the phone. They have learned how to maintain their health and energy. And unlike Iris, they didn't insist on ignoring their own bodies. If they have been keeping up with the spells they've learned – admittedly that's not an easy task in this world – we'll find them to be capable, alert, and reliable."

Eddie finished slicing the kalamatas. He scraped them into the sauce and stirred it again. The water was boiling, and he added the pasta. Then he slid the garlic bread under the broiler. "Okay, so there will be five of us. What'll we do?"

"First of all, I'll need to teach you how to manage the staff – the grounding rod. We will be able to use a different spell from what we have employed recently. Then, when they arrive, we'll have to see how much stress they can take. Here's the thing, son: if we have three or four strong, experienced people performing the spells while you focus the energies moving through the grounding rod, the whole process will go much faster and be much easier than it was on Iris' world.

Here Joe looked terribly sad for a few moments. Then he shook himself and poured glasses of Pinot for them both. "Better check that garlic bread, son."

"Joe. If you don't mind me asking. Why won't Iris let you help her? I mean if you can truly restore her..."

"It's the same as it has always been. She won't put herself before the struggle. Even though she'd be more effective if she had full command of her skills and her knowledge, she keeps coming back to the place in her mind that asks, 'what must I do today?' and the answer is always something other than take care of her own needs."

"And she's fading again. Even I could tell."

Joe nodded. "Yes she is. She has promised me that if we return in time, and things remain stable, she will allow me to help her."

"That's something, I guess."

"Precious little, actually. That narrowly averted tragedy... where we almost lost Lena. That would never have happened if Iris hadn't been failing. If she'd been thinking clearly, she'd never have allowed Lena to take that risk. We don't have much time to save her."

They dished up their food and conversation dropped off for a while. Then Joe repeated that he needed to evaluate his old friends' condition when they arrived. "The most prudent thing would be to go out and back three times," he said after a minute.

"I could let each of them lead short excursions to other worlds. See what they can do. Watch them. That way I'd only be traveling with one person each time."

"Yeah, Joe, but that would mean three trips. And the beast is still out there."

"Indeed she is. And we don't have that kind of time anyway. Even if she hasn't already, the Queen will soon learn of our activities. I cannot tell when that will happen, but I have no doubt it will.

"Her usual pattern is to operate through intermediaries. I tell you, son, if she had a real organization, the situation would be hopeless. Her paranoia, her habit of doling out tiny bits of information, and her elimination of her most powerful and talented subordinates... these form our only basis for optimism. Of course if we make progress here, then at some point she will decide to take a direct role. I only hope we're ready by then."

Eddie changed the subject. There was something that had been nagging at him for weeks. "Joe. If I needed to get back to Soapstone Bay quickly, right now I'd have to rely on you. Do you think you'd have time to coach me so I'd have a good chance of reaching there on my own?"

"We just arrived here, son. We need to get some work done."

"Yeah, I know that. But just in case. As it stands now, if I had to go by myself, I'd have to go via Maia's forest and then do the long hike and then try to get a ride south. It would take weeks. Longer if the weather's bad. What if you were out of commission? Or just needed to be somewhere else for a while?"

Joe picked at his food for a minute. Then he wiped his mouth with his napkin and took another sip of wine. "All right, you have a point. As soon as you've mastered the handling of the grounding rod, I will teach you the two transits that go between the Inn at Three Corners and this house. Fair?"

"Sounds good to me." Eddie agreed. "That makes me feel better. Just a little more autonomous. Okay, now where are the portals that we're going to open in this world? Do you know yet?"

"Indeed. I've been thinking about that. In the interest of staying hidden from view..."

"Staying under the radar."

"Yes, that. In the interest of staying under the Queen's radar, I think we should look for opportunities to open portals near each of my friends' homes. That way the new portals will be widely separated and less likely to attract attention. In addition, their presence will support the efforts of our colleagues to stay vital and enjoy maximal lifetimes."

"Oh, yeah... I guess that's the least we could do," Eddie mused. "but then why have them all travel here? Why not just have everyone meet at one of your friends' places?"

"Well, we could do that, but, again, we need to do something to see what shape they're in when they arrive. They haven't been active for decades. They may have forgotten things. Talking on the phone is one thing. Traveling here on short notice, interacting with people they haven't seen in many years, meeting you for the first time, being in unfamiliar surroundings... these are all challenges of a sort. We can see how they manage these challenges.

"And remember, son. We'll use the time until they arrive to train you in the use of the grounding rod. You'll be glad of that, believe me."

"Okay, but this sounds like we're going to open, what, three portals total? Those, plus the one under your house here makes four. You said there are maybe four functioning portals in all of North America. So we add three more connection points. How's that going to do anything?"

"Of course by themselves these three won't do much. These are merely good places to start. Our work won't stop there. We'll begin with these three and see how they go, see if there's a response from the Locust Queen. I anticipate continued activity for some time."

"So there's no telling when I'll be able to go back... to be with Lena and the others."

"Sorry, son. Oh, we'll go check in from time-to-time. Perhaps we can even bring them here to visit. Lena and Iris could fit in well enough. Your other friends..."

"Yeah, I know. Their dialect would give them away. We already talked about it. But honestly Joe, I'm not all that keen on bringing Lena through the Hub with the beast still around."

"Agreed. So for now, let's just take it step-by-step. We'll get my old friends here and see what shape they're in. We'll establish a few more connection points. Then we'll decide our next steps."

"Okay. I guess that makes sense," Eddie sighed.

Joe pushed back from the table. "I'm full. Thanks for making dinner. I'll take care of cleanup. If you feel up to it, would you see to the guest rooms upstairs? They haven't been used for a long time. The hall bath could use some attention too."

So Eddie grabbed his cleaning kit and the vacuum cleaner and returned to the second floor. He'd never entered the guest rooms. They were simple. Each had a double bed with a foot locker at its base, a dresser, a side chair and a small closet. The back of each door featured a full length mirror. All the furniture was covered in dust cloths.

The room nearest the bathroom had one exterior wall with a window. The other two rooms were at the end of the hall. Each of these had windows on two sides.

First, moving from room-to-room, Eddie folded the cloths carefully in on themselves to minimize the distribution of the dust. These he placed in the hall. Then he vacuumed the rooms, turned and vacuumed the mattresses, dusted and waxed the furniture, and finished up by polishing each mirror and cleaning the inside of the windows. He pulled fresh linens from the hall closet and made the beds.

Finally, he spent twenty minutes or so on the bathroom. In just over two hours, the second floor was ready for guests. As he was wrapping things up, Joe called up the stairs, "Just leave the cleaning supplies up there, will you? I'll want to have a go at my rooms as well."

"Sure thing," Eddie called. He gathered the folded dust cloths and headed for the stairs. Joe was standing in the living room when the younger man reached the main floor. He had a fire going. He held several sheets of paper in his left hand and a tumbler of Pinot in his right.

"Here you go. I've written up some notes on the use of the staff in the spells of opening. This is by no means a complete description, but it will give you what you need to know for our purposes. In the next couple of days I'd like you to commit this material to memory."

Eddie took the offered sheets of paper. There were five pages covered on both sides with Joe's neat handwriting. Several included diagrams that showed hand and foot placement. "Thanks, Joe, for doing all this. It'll help me get started without taking a bunch of your time."

"Of course. There is an old grounding rod in the basement. We can practice with that. We will need to have a staff available at each site. That complicates matters somewhat because for a staff to be used most effectively, the caster should practice with it. Unfortunately, it's impractical to ship this one around to the various sites. It's over eight feet long and was hand wrought a couple of centuries ago in Eastern Europe. The rod is nearly two inches thick and quite heavy."

"So what will we do?"

"I've been thinking about it. I believe we'll have the best result if we have one fabricated in each of the three towns. For the ferrous core, we can use three pieces of re-bar and have them arc welded together. Re-bar is a standard product, so each piece will be very much like the others. We will have the ends bound in brass coils and alternate copper and steel bands in the center section. With a combination of brazing and arc welding any competent welder will be able to handle the project.

"I will draw up the plans tonight and get them overnighted to our friends. As soon as they have the projects ordered, they can come here. We'll schedule our visits based on the delivery schedule for the grounding rods."

"And then what do we do with these staffs after we're done?"

"That's almost the best part of this approach. We will leave them with our colleagues. It may be that they will be able to make use of them in the future. Having such a set spread out like that across the western part of the continent could be a good thing. Almost like a network of sorts.

"The possibilities are interesting. At the very least having three very similar grounding rods would allow us to meet anywhere within driving range to open subsequent portals. We could fan out from each place and add connection points as we go."

"Joe. I just had a thought. These are going to be sort of strange projects for the welders to tackle. Do you think that we should have some kind of cover story?"

"Well, I don't see how a single project is going to attract attention, but I suppose it can't hurt. Do you have something in mind?"

"Um, how about something along the lines of saying that the pieces will be focal points in upcoming garden competitions. I've heard that some retired people are very serious about their gardens. And in a sense, these truly are a form of yard art."

Joe laughed. "Yard art it is! I'll make sure to suggest something along those lines. That will also give our friends a plausible reason to ask for firm delivery dates. Yard art!" He chuckled a few more times at the thought.

Eddie yawned. "I think I'd like to go upstairs and get some sleep. If the weather's good, maybe I can do some more yard cleanup tomorrow. After I study of course," he hastened to add.

"Yes. You should get some rest. I think that we've made good headway for our first afternoon back. I'll have the plans drawn up and duplicated by breakfast. Also, before it gets any later, I want to touch base with our friends out west and tell them to start looking for experienced metal workers for their yard art," he chuckled again.

Eddie bent to pick up the dust cloths. "I'll take care of those, son. Just get some rest." Joe assured him. Eddie nodded his thanks and climbed the stairs to his rooms. He enjoyed a hot shower and slid into his bed with a sigh. Once again hoping that he would someday be able to show Lena this place and sleep with her in this bed, he fell asleep.

*   *   *

First thing in the morning, Eddie wrote a short note to Lena. Then he tucked that into his shirt pocket and ran down the stairs. Joe already had breakfast ready. He had his plans for the grounding rods ready as well. They were very detailed drawings done using a CAD system.

"Unless you have something else that needs doing, after breakfast, I'd like you to spend some time reading the notes I wrote up for you. I'll take these plans downtown and FedEx them to our friends. I think you're going to enjoy meeting them when the time comes. They're all intelligent people who've led interesting lives."

Eddie nodded and swallowed his food. Then he had a sip of the strong, black coffee Joe invariably brewed when he made breakfast. "Aack! Dang, Joe! Sure that's safe to drink? Anyway, I'm sure I will. Enjoy meeting them, that is. Let me finish eating and clean up the breakfast things. Then I'll study, okay? Maybe we can go over your notes when you get back to see how much I'm absorbing."

Joe was pulling on his coat and had taken a battered hat from the counter and crammed it on his head. "One thing I like about this world is my collection of old hats," he said to himself. "They're so familiar... and they keep my head warm this time of year."

He turned to Eddie. "And, yes, of course. When I return we can review what you've read."

Eddie finished his breakfast and poured about a third of the big mug of coffee down the sink. Then he filled the mug the rest of the way with hot water. He took the coffee into the living room and read through the notes Joe had left for him. There were several scenarios described in the notes. Each scenario was accompanied by detailed instructions on what spells and precautions were appropriate.

He read them all the way through and then reviewed the more complex parts. Then he read through them all again. Since Joe wanted him to memorize this material, he kept at it and soon entered an enjoyable mental state in which the handful of pages became the true center of his attention. By the time Joe returned, Eddie could recite most of the material on the sheets.

Joe was happy to see his student's progress. "That's a good start, son. A very good start. Of course you realize that memorizing and truly internalizing knowledge are different things, but I am pleased at this. Let's bring the grounding rod upstairs and have you get used to holding it while we go through some of the spells together. That will help put what you've learned so far into context."

The two men worked through the rest of the morning. After lunch, the sun came out so they went outside and did a couple of hours' worth of yard work. Late winter was turning towards spring, and it was time to prune the dormant shrubs and tress. Eddie bundled all the trimmings and stacked them near the garage.

Eddie found that Lena had written him another note. She was pleased that he'd returned and was in contact. He replaced her note with the one he'd written upon waking. It felt almost like they were exchanging postcards between towns instead of sending notes between worlds.

After dinner that evening, they studied a little more. Both men enjoyed the mentor-student relationship and the rapid learning such an education model provided. Before bed that night, Eddie wrote a longer letter to Lena that outlined in general terms what they were doing. He decided it was prudent to focus more on feelings and impressions than on details of the work.

The next few days fell into a good rhythm of study and work around the old house. Eddie was learning the use of the grounding rod and how to focus the flow of subtle energies that ran through it. Equally important, he was learning how to stand outside that powerful, potentially dangerous flow.

This spell, while similar to what he had seen before, was different in detail. The obvious difference was that Eddie would be surrounded by people who were experienced in this work. In Lena's world, Joe had done all the heavy lifting of the spell while simultaneously holding the grounding rod steady and managing the energy flow.

In this world, however, Eddie's focus would be limited. He would steady the heavy staff, channel the energies it conducted, and try very hard to stay safely outside the flow. Those around him would perform the actual spell. They would stand together at the rim of the Abyss. Eddie would not.

Since all of the players would be wrapped within the field of the spell, any of them could help Eddie set up or carry the grounding rod. There would be no discontinuity in the energies. There would be no danger to passive helpers. The end result would be the same, but effort of the spell was distributed more evenly.

They received confirmation that the packets containing the engineering drawings had reached their destinations. After a few days, one of Joe's old colleagues called to say he'd found an experienced metal worker and had contracted him to build a grounding rod. On the following day, one more project got underway and the day after that, the final piece of "yard art" was commissioned. All three men booked flights to Joe's town.

John Sullivan was the first to arrive. Joe met him at the bus station at three in the afternoon. The day was bright but cold, just the sort of day where a greenhouse is a great blessing to a gardener. Eddie was working on a vent window in the greenhouse when he heard the men in the nearby kitchen.

"You indoors, son?" Joe called from the kitchen.

"Out here. Working on that sticky window in the greenhouse."

John Sullivan came around the corner as though he'd been launched from a catapult.

"Hello there, young man!" he smiled up at Eddie, who was perched on a stepladder. Eddie climbed down and offered his hand as Joe did the introductions.

"Eddie, this is John L. Sullivan. Named for the famous 19th century heavyweight boxer."

"Good to meet you, Mr. Sullivan."

"Call me Sully, Eddie. Everybody else does." Although Eddie knew that he was older, Sullivan appeared to be a robust man in his late fifties. His hair was gray at the temples, his face lined but not deeply creased. The man's handshake was firm, his hands large and powerful. Eddie noticed right away that although he was slightly taller than Sullivan, the older man's shoulders and arms were broad and powerful. While not the size of Fleggie, Sullivan's upper body would not have looked out of place on a much taller man.

In fact, despite the differences in age and height, Sullivan's open friendliness and good humor reminded Eddie a little of Fleggie. The mental image of his big friend, in turn, drew his thoughts toward Soapstone Bay and Lena. With an effort, he pulled himself back to the present. Sullivan was commenting on the arrangement of Joe's greenhouse.

"Nice greenhouse, Joe. I see that you can close it off from the kitchen when the weather's warm. That's a good design feature. Probably makes the back of the house comfortable on cool, bright days like this. We don't get many days like this up Bellingham way.

"Anyway, what are you up to, young man?" he looked back at Eddie. "I heard you say something about a sticky window."

"Well... Sully. That window..." Eddie pointed to a window just above the stepladder.

"I can see that it's used to vent the greenhouse when the weather's warm. Yes."

"Well, it sticks when you try to open it, and then it doesn't always stay open. See how it's stripped the stops off this brace?"

"Let me climb up there, okay? I'd like to take a closer look." Without waiting for a response, Sullivan stepped agilely around Eddie and up the ladder. Eddie noticed that, like Joe, Sullivan moved with the loose confidence of a much younger man. Sullivan appeared to be a little older than Joe, but Eddie knew that had nothing to do with their true relative ages.

At the top of the ladder, Sullivan pulled some reading glasses from his shirt pocket. He inspected the window and the failed brace. Then he turned and looked over the top of his glasses down at Eddie and Joe.

"The window's too heavy for this brace. You either need to beef up the brace or else put a counterweight on the window. Since young Eddie here has already observed that the window's hard to open, I vote for taking the counterweight approach."

Joe was chuckling at this point. "You may as well learn this right away, Eddie. Sully's an engineer by training. A mechanical engineer. He and I used to have a business together, oh forty-five years ago. He's an inveterate tinkerer."

Smiling, Sullivan climbed down from the ladder. "Indeed I am. That's why I was able to find a metal fab shop to build that grounding rod right away. I know most of the active metal workers in Bellingham – at least the ones worth knowing. But you should have had me look at the design before you distributed the drawings, Giuseppe. I thought of several improvements right away."

Now Joe was laughing outright. "Sully, Sully. I knew that you'd want to improve the design, but we don't have time for three iterations and two prototypes. This will work. I've done it before, remember?"

Suddenly more serious, Joe threw his arm around Sullivan's broad shoulders and continued, "By the way, no one calls me that anymore, but I do enjoy hearing that name once in a while. Thanks, Sully."

John Sullivan acknowledged Joe's remarks with a nod of his head and a smile of his own. Then he turned back to Eddie. "What say you show me my room, lad? Joe here has promised me a good glass of wine and a fine dinner tonight. I'd like to settle in." Here he paused and glanced back at Joe with a twinkle in his eyes. "Then I'll sketch a couple of designs for a better window setup and we'll see what materials Giuseppe has in the garage and that famous basement of his!"

Eddie led Sullivan back to the entry hall. He reached for the bag that lay near the front door, but the older man insisted on carrying it himself. "Thanks, Eddie, but I'm still able to do for myself in most things. And I intend to keep that up as long as I can. Lead the way, if you please."

A few moments later, Eddie had shown Sullivan upstairs and the older man was happily setting up his room. "This looks comfortable. It's good to see Joe and to see that he's connecting with someone younger. He may be able to go on forever, but the old guard can't..." Here he paused for a second with a serious look on his face as he stared into the distance.

Then he brightened. "Anyway, I'll just get set up here and rest a bit. It's a long trip from Bellingham down to SeaTac and then the flight here. I've been traveling since six this morning and I lost two hours due to the time zones... It'll be good to relax and regroup. Do you know when the others will arrive?"

"Joe said they'll be here tomorrow. Take your time, Sully. I think I'd be wiped out if I'd been traveling since six. Come down and join us when you're ready, okay?"

Sullivan nodded and waved Eddie off. "Thanks, again, lad. I'll see you in an hour or so."

Joe was waiting downstairs in the living room when Eddie returned. "Take a seat, son. I poured you a glass of wine. White Zin. It's pretty good. What do you think of Sully?"

Eddie settled into one of the big chairs. "Thanks. Well, I think he's great. Smart, upbeat. He's got real energy. Why?"

"Oh, nothing. Just curious. Sully's going to do fine for us. I can already tell. He's had some pretty hard knocks, but you'd never know it to meet him. Was in the US auto business for nearly twenty years. Tried to champion quality and efficiency at a time when hubcaps and chrome were all that mattered. He was poor at reading corporate politics and it ended up costing him his career." Joe's voice trailed off.

Joe took a sip of his wine and picked up again, "Anyway, he and I met in St. Louis in the early nineteen-sixties. He was down and out. His wife was working as a librarian. They had a little girl. It was a tough time for Sully, but he came through it without losing his spirit. His wife was a good woman and she stuck with him. Eventually he and I set up a light manufacturing business. We worked well together and we prospered. I set it up so he could buy me out around '65. Later, I helped him invest in some commercial real estate. He's not rich, but he's comfortable and doesn't care too much about wealth."

"So he's married and has a grown daughter."

"Well, he was married. Cindy, that was his wife's name, died more than ten years ago. Cancer. Sully lives close to his daughter and her husband up near the Canadian border. He likes it up there and seems to have kept interested in the metal working business for all these years. That's worked out to our advantage."

Eddie was quiet as he digested this background. "But he also worked with you like I do, right? To try to protect this world? To fight the Locust Queen and all?"

Joe nodded. "That, yes. And other things. Sully's smart. And very observant. It took him a while, but he worked out that I was much older than I looked. By then he knew me and trusted me. One afternoon, he walked into my office at our shop and closed the door. He looked me straight in the eye and asked me how old I was."

"So just how old are you, Joe?"

"Doesn't matter, son. After long enough it doesn't matter at all. It just becomes a long march. You put one foot in front of the other. You just keep going because somebody needs to. But we were talking about Sully."

"And is that what you told Sully? That how old you are isn't what matters?"

"Something like that. Then I showed him a few things. We came down here and I took him through on a transit. He's a data-driven sort of man, so I knew he'd need to see something for himself. Then he did what he could to help me. We opened a few portals. One in the jungles of Peru. In an Incan temple that remains undiscovered to this day. Another 'way up in Scotland. In a burrow near some of those standing stones that the ancients of this world left. About eight degrees south of the arctic circle, that one was. We could have done more, but..."

"But, what?"

"Well, Sully's wife was a very good person but also very conservative. Very religious in an austere sort of way. Her beliefs stood their marriage in good stead during the bad times, but when Sully told Cindy about me and tried to explain how the cosmology of the Great Wheel works, she couldn't accept it. She forbade him to have me in their home or near their daughter. I think it was the only ultimatum she ever laid down. He loved her and did as she wanted. Mostly."

"What do you mean, 'mostly?'"

"Oh, only that she didn't want him to have anything to do with what she called the 'devil's work' or with me. That's why I set up the company so he could buy me out. I felt responsible for causing those problems. But he and I stayed in touch discreetly after that."

"And she never knew that you guys stayed in touch, so she just let the whole thing slide. Wow. That's kind of a trip."

"Indeed. I'm pretty sure she suspected, but she never knew for sure, and she could practice denial as well as the next person. Over the years, I wrote Sully. We got together when we could, and I showed him a few things so that he could preserve his health and vitality without being too conspicuous. That's more-or-less it. I was somewhat surprised when he agreed to pick up the fight so readily. It makes me wonder how his life has been in recent years. It is fine to see him, though. I must say that."

"So these other guys who're coming? Do they know Sully too?"

"The three of them know each other to some extent. They're all roughly contemporaries. Born in the first third of the twentieth century. Very different backgrounds. Different personalities. I've known them all for different lengths of time." Joe fell silent then and took another small sip of his wine. He appeared lost in thought.

Eddie leaned forward. "If it's okay, I'd like you to tell me about them. This might sound kind of strange, but I feel like I'm part of a line. A line of people who've worked with you. I get the sense that this line stretches back in time and I'd like to know about other people in the line – especially about these guys that are coming here."

Joe looked up with a distant, unreadable expression. Slowly, he focused his attention on his young helper and student. "Yes, young man, that's exactly what you are. You are part of a line." He paused a moment before continuing. "Yes. I think that is appropriate. I'll give you a little bit of background. I'll move back in time."

He took another small taste of wine. "Let's do this over dinner preparation, what do you say?"

"Sure. That sounds great."

So they moved their conversation to the kitchen. Joe was going to be the main cook for the evening, but he wanted to cook something that required a lot of prep work. So Eddie collected a pile of vegetables and a cutting board and started to work. Joe busied himself with herbs as he began making a marinade and some sauces that would go with the main dishes. As they worked, Joe picked up the thread of the narrative.

"The man I became acquainted with prior to Sully is named Fred Wilkins. He was an optometrist by profession. Spent some time in the army medical corps. By the early 1950's he was well off and semi-retired, just worked in his practice a couple of days each week. He did a lot of charity work for farm workers on the coast of California at a time when few people recognized how harsh their lives were.

"Now Fred also loved art. As far as I know he still does. Fred's personality was always on the intense side. He never did anything tentat-ively, always threw himself into his ideas and projects. He and I met at an art show in the fall of 1952 in Hollywood, and by the next spring he had a small gallery in a little farm town on the central coast. A place called San Luis Obispo. Today, it's very much a university town and has become quite upscale, but back then it was a sleepy little place that catered mostly to the needs of the agricultural community.

"People traveling between LA and San Francisco would often stop in San Luis for a day, and some of them would visit Fred's gallery. Fred had a little studio in the back and he'd paint. His studio featured what he liked to call "emerging artists." There were some very abstract and surreal pieces. Things that pushed the edge of what mainstream audiences were used to seeing. Fred was also fond of erotic art. I visited the gallery many times, and although I never saw anything that was even vaguely pornographic, some of the pieces he featured were shocking to the local people. That caused talk around town.

"Over time, word of his charity work spread, and with his connection to the art community in Los Angeles, he ended up attracting the attention of Joseph McCarthy and his minions. They subpoenaed him. They called him before congressional committees, intimidated, and harassed him. Fred, being Fred, fought as best he could and resisted for several years, but eventually, the pressure became unbearable and he sold what remained of his practice and closed his gallery.

"We'd been in touch throughout the whole ugly affair. I was keeping a very low profile during those years. I was working in a machine shop in the LA area. Just learning the trade and keeping to myself. When Fred called me to tell me that he'd shut down his practice and closed his gallery, I arranged to meet him up in Santa Barbara.

"I drove up and we had lunch. We went for a hike in the hills above the town. I listened to Fred as he raged about censorship and the importance of intellectual and artistic freedom. It wasn't hard to see that despite the differences in our origins and lives, that in this area at least, we were congruent in our thinking."

Eddie spoke up now. "So you told him about yourself and recruited him to help, right?"

Joe shook his head. "Remember, these were difficult times, son. Harsh times. People were harassing him already. He was afraid and angry, and I couldn't afford to be noticed. I was taking a risk just to meet with him. So I didn't say anything then. I mostly listened. That first time, all I did was to ask him if there were anything I could do to help."

"What'd he say?"

"Oh, I remember that clearly. He said, 'Just continue to be a friend. So many of my friends have run for cover.'"

"Well, then what did you do?"

"Over the subsequent period, the second half of the 1950's, we stayed in touch. Even though Fred no longer ran a gallery, he continued to be an avid and knowledgeable collector. By late in the decade, the hysteria was fading. Public opinion was moving a little more to the center; although many people had their careers and lives ruined through what eventually came to be seen as the most cynical type of political manipulation.

"Eventually, during one of my visits to the central coast, I felt comfortable asking Fred if he could act on his beliefs. I made sure to preface my question with an assurance that I was not suggesting anything un-American or pro-communist or even against the law. I think Fred took it as some kind of rhetorical or theoretical question. He was sur-

Michael C. Glaviano

prised when I suggested that we come here, to this house, so I could show him something."

"But he agreed?"

"Yes. As I said, he'd gone into full retirement by then. He painted. He cooked. He read, and of course he had women friends. But he was no longer tied to a daily routine, and he could afford to travel a little. At any rate, he was cautious, but in the end he agreed. We came by different routes and arrived on different days. We sat in this room and had a talk that was not too different from what you and I had last year. In the end, I took him on a transit. He met the Lady of the Forest too, by the way, but she didn't seem to trust him the way she did you.

"After that, he and I worked together for many years. Occasion- ally he worked in concert with Sully and with my other friend 'Harry.' I'll tell you about him next."

"So that's Fred's story. Is there anything else I should know? I hope he's gotten a little more relaxed in recent times."

Joe laughed shortly. "Relaxed. Well, we'll see. That's most of his story. You'll learn more of him as you get to know him and you work together. We haven't spoken in years, but I expect that Fred remains passionate where intellectual freedom is concerned. He too learned how to prolong his middle years; although he tends to go a little soft. You see, Fred also likes to cook. And he likes women quite a lot. He's been mar- ried three times that I know of. When it suits him, Fred can be very charming, and he tends to flirt with the young ones. Although they are very different people, I hope you'll like him just as you think well of Sully."

By this time Eddie had finished cutting up the vegetables. Joe had a couple of pans going on the stove. He started prepping a roast for the oven. As he worked, he began describing the third person that Eddie was soon to meet.

"I suppose that brings us to the man I met first of these three friends, Haruo Ikeda."

"You called him 'Harry.'"

"Yes. I am sure he'll want you to call him that, but his name is 'Haruo.' It means 'Man of the Spring.' He was indeed born in the spring. It was the spring of 1935. By the time Harry was born, I already knew his father somewhat. Harry's parents were Japanese immigrants and they had a small shop in Los Angeles. It was a grocery store that catered to the Asian community. I always called Harry's father, 'Mr. Ikeda' and his mother, 'Mrs. Ikeda.'"

"Of course the Ikedas were impacted by the anti-Japanese hys- teria of the war years. They lost their business and their savings. Harry spent most of the time between his 7th and 10th birthdays in the Man- zanar internment camp. I don't know how much you know about that, son, but it was a harsh place. It was out in the desert northeast of LA.

450

Being a child, Harry adjusted to his situation, but I don't think his parents ever recovered from the experience. They never spoke of it, but I think they spent the rest of their lives being afraid at some level.

"At any rate, after the camp closed in 1945, I was able to get Harry's father a job at a grocery store in Fresno. A year later I purchased the store and asked Mr. Ikeda to manage it. I visited whenever I could. Mr. Ikeda did very well at the store and saved as much as he could. Eventually I set it up so that he could buy the store outright.

"All this time, young Harry was showing signs of a strong intellect and an energetic nature. He became interested in Aikido when he was around eleven and worked hard to find resources so that he could learn the form. He pursued that all through high school. Harry was a serious student and earned excellent grades. Later he was able to secure a scholarship to attend UC Berkeley.

"He met his wife, who was a real beauty by the way, when they were both in graduate school. They've been together ever since. By then Harry was very advanced in Aikido. After law school, he had a long career as an expert in human rights issues at the US State Department. They have one son, Jason. Their son specializes in cardiovascular medicine at the University of Maryland Medical Center."

"So does his wife know about you?"

"Yes, Hiroko knows and approves. Both Harry and Hiroko are deeply spiritual people, but they see no conflict between their beliefs and the cosmology of the Great Wheel. After he retired from the State Department, Harry opened a dojo in Albuquerque. The last I checked, he continued to teach special workshops for very advanced students."

Joe fell silent again. Now the roast was in the oven. Joe opened a bottle of Cabernet Sauvignon and set it out to breathe. Eddie could hear water running upstairs. Their guest was most likely up from his nap.

"Let's have a little antipasto, shall we?" Joe asked. "How about some olives and some of those carrots you've sliced and maybe a few artichoke hearts. Is there any salami? Slice up a little of that too, will you?"

"Sounds great, Joe." Eddie put the vegetables and the olives on some small plates, which he laid on the kitchen table. "Your friends are all totally different from each other."

"Yes, I suppose they are in some ways. Different backgrounds, certainly. But you know, son, they all share a deep commitment to the dignity of the individual. Each, in his own way, is creative and intelligent. Each was successful in his career; although their careers were certainly varied. So there are other similarities as well. I'd like you to get to know them as best you can."

"Well, we're going to work together. That'll help."

Again Joe fell silent for a moment. He smiled slightly. Then he turned and checked the oven timer. "I believe I'm going to go upstairs and roust Sully. It's time he was down here."

Just then John Sullivan walked through the doorway from the living room. "Well I am here. I may not be tan, but I'm rested and ready. Is there a glass of wine to be had?"

"Well it took you long enough," Joe laughed. He wiped his hands on a dishtowel. "You want red or white?"

"Whatever you gentlemen are drinking will be just fine, I'm sure."

A few minutes later, the remaining dishes were in the second oven and the three men were relaxing in the living room. "I've been filling Eddie in just a bit on your history and that of Fred and Harry."

"Then he has me at a disadvantage," Sully replied. "Where do you come from, young man? How did you come to be embroiled in this most excellent of projects?"

So Eddie spent the next few minutes talking about himself. It felt more than a little strange to talk in this way with these much older men, but that feeling passed as John Sullivan displayed a sincere interest in him. Besides finding him easy to talk to, Eddie sensed in Sullivan a strong, perceptive intellect.

After a few minutes, Eddie relaxed enough to speak a little bit about the tragedy that had struck his family. Sullivan expressed sympathy but in an unforced, respectful way. The conversation moved on, and Eddie gave an abbreviated account of the past year.

"And now you have friends and are in love with a woman from another world. It is truly an amazing thing, isn't it?" Sullivan remarked when Eddie finished.

"Yeah. I guess it is amazing, but you know most of the time, I just don't think about it. I just try to do what needs doing. I have come to feel that Lena's world is where I want to live though. When the time is right I would like to make my home there."

Joe had been silent during Eddie's narrative. Now he spoke up. "Indeed, that often happens. Many of my old colleagues from this world have found other worlds where their hearts told them to stay. These three, Harry, Fred, and Sully here are rare. In ancient times, more stayed in this world."

Eddie had a thought then. "So are any of your more... ancient colleagues still around? On this world or some other where we could maybe get in touch with them?"

Joe looked levelly at Eddie for some seconds. Then he glanced over at Sully. "Let me think on that for a moment. Excuse me while I check on dinner." Joe stood and went into the kitchen. Delightful smells were emanating from the ovens and cookware. The sounds of lids being lifted, contents being stirred, casseroles being checked formed a sort of accompaniment to the aromas that wafted into the living room.

In a minute, Joe was back. "After my first few calls the other day, I reached the conclusion that I should focus on people I worked with over the last half century," he said. "Remember, magic is not strong here. It is difficult for someone to stay vital for centuries if one does not visit other worlds. Worlds where magic is strong." Now his voice trailed off and he drew away, lost in memories.

Eddie started to ask another question, but Sullivan held up his hand for silence and, his eyes on Joe's face, shook his head slightly.

"But in every world where the Locust Queen's power is not absolute, a few, out-of the-way corners remain, and so even in this world, a venerable scattering of former associates still dwell in deeply hidden places," Joe's voice continued quietly, just above a whisper. "There is a tiny monastery in a deep valley at the roof of the world. Whispers of rumors of it gave rise to stories of lost cities and immortal mystics. The reality is that a monk there has watched over a functioning portal for centuries.

"In the Theban Necropolis, a very holy Islamic scholar currently assumes the mantle of an Egyptian professor of antiquities. He watches over another active portal into the Great Hub. He makes sure that the tomb which contains it is always at the bottom of the funding list for exploration. Taking various roles in the local culture, he has lived there for the past thousand years.

"And there are a handful of others: in the jungles of Cambodia, in the Australian sub-continent. They watch and care for their charges... but there is little that remains on this continent. Here is where we must act. Here is where we must avoid detection.

"Remember, also, foreigners must have visas. There are travel restrictions and security checkpoints. Government offices are easily infiltrated by the agents of the Locust Queen. No. Sadly, I can think of no one among the handful of my oldest helpers who remain that might be able to travel freely and thus join us here to help. We are on our own."

"These places you have selected, Giuseppe. If we open them, what will they do? What changes will we see? This isn't some stone circle in northern Scotland we're proposing now, correct?"

"Indeed they aren't. I haven't really picked them. All I know is that I'd like them to be near where you three − Harry, Fred, and you − live. I'd like you to be able to visit them."

"Yes, yes, Giuseppe. That's all well and good, but you didn't answer my question. What will happen?"

Joe chuckled. "Same old Sully, I see. Hard to distract. Latches onto an idea or a question and won't let go until he's satisfied. So. How about this? I'm not a hundred percent sure. I can tell you what I hope."

"Okay. What do you hope will happen?"

"First, I hope we can get at least two of these done before we're noticed. The chances of all three are minimal. After all, this world is very much under the Queen's sway. Even so, her agents are unlikely to report back to her of their own accord. They will much prefer to deal with our interference themselves.

"Of course, she will be on her guard as a result of our recent activities in the world of Eddie's friends. Still, I hope that we will avoid her – Eddie calls it 'staying under her radar' – for some time.

"Second, I'm hoping that after a time, say six months or so, in the areas immediately adjacent to the portal openings, we'll see a softening of the membrane that separates this world from the Place. Such a softening will allow some magic to be performed in the vicinity. That, in turn, will allow you to practice more of the life extending and health enhancing spells I have taught you.

"Third, and this is longer term, I assume that certain creative personalities will be drawn closer to these spots. That could engender mini-renaissance-type changes in each locale. To counter the Queen's influence. In the meantime, we can branch out, open connections in other parts of the continent. Satisfied?"

Sully nodded. "Yes. Everything you say sounds reasonable, Giuseppe. What do we do if there's a response?"

"Well, obviously that depends on the nature and intensity of the response. Best case, we provoke a limited response. If the Queen's agents do keep it secret and try to take care of it themselves... well, we can handle them."

"And the worst case?" Sullivan asked.

"Worst case... well, I can think of two things," Joe replied. "One would be an overwhelming, coordinated response. Another would be direct intervention by the Queen."

Sullivan whistled. "By the Queen herself, huh? Damn. I agree: dealing with her would be a worst-case scenario."

"Actually, I think it's unlikely," the old man continued. "In recent decades the Locust Queen has absorbed so much power that she has changed. I strongly suspect that little of her original humanity remains. She has become, in a sense, a twisted creature of her own arrogance and pride. In her vanity, she has assumed a goddess-like form... or what she conceives a goddess-like form to be. At any rate, this world has become so devoid of magic that she would be hard-pressed to manifest here for any significant period of time."

"Well, that's something, anyway." Sullivan paused in thought before continuing. "You haven't picked the particular places you say?"

"Right. I was hoping to get feedback from you."

"Hmmm. Let me think on that. I'll have to get back to you." Here Sully paused for a moment and directed his eyes to the ceiling. "Of course it's terribly difficult to come up with creative ideas on an empty stomach."

"Keep your shirt on, Sully. Dinner will be ready in a half hour."

"Hey, Joe had me put together a little antipasto. Shall I get it?" Eddie offered.

"Now you're talking, young man!"

As it turned out, the antipasto first course segued into dinner. By the time dinner was done and the kitchen cleaned up, it was late. Sullivan was ready to call it quits for the day. Joe suggested they wait until the other two men joined them before they got into the real details of a plan.

Eddie stayed up and wrote a note to Lena. When he went out to place it in the wall he found that she had sent him a longer letter. He sat in the kitchen to read what she'd written. Her words brought home to Eddie once again how much he missed her.

Lena wrote that Iris had experienced a setback. Lena suspected it had been triggered by Joe's departure. In the last twenty four hours, Iris had stabilized somewhat but was still very frail. It was difficult to tell with confidence whether the woman's state was truly rooted in physical causes. Iris still dwelt on her feelings of guilt over what had happened at the final portal opening. Lena was trying with only modest success to get the older woman to acknowledge the ultimate success of the endeavor.

In happier news, Fleggie and Sweetmaye had come to visit every evening. The couple's presence cheered, or at least distracted, Iris a little. When the commitments of her own life permitted, Sweetmaye came to the shop and helped Lena.

For all its drama and danger, the final portal opening lent support to the gathering momentum of creativity and commerce in Soapstone Bay and the surrounding region. Spring weather arrived early. Ships were out already. Soon they would return, and they would bear trade goods from up and down the coast. The university was slowly shaking off the bad times of the previous year. The townspeople seemed finally to have put the troubles with the RSM behind them.

Clearly Lena was trying to reassure Eddie that she was managing the situation around her in her usual, competent manner. She wrote of her love for him and sent everyone's heartfelt wish that he finish his work and return quickly.

Lena reminded Eddie that their building was secure and emphasized that he should not worry about them. The spells Iris had developed over the years were still strong and effective. She did not feel they were in any kind of personal danger.

Eddie folded the letter and looked off into space. The last bit had worried him, which was certainly the opposite of its intended effect. He wondered why Lena had felt compelled to mention the building's security. Was it just a further attempt to reassure him, or was there something she wasn't sharing?

He drummed his fingers on the table. He got up from the kitchen table and drank a glass of water. Finally, he went to look for Joe and remind his mentor of his promise to train him to make transits by himself.

Forty One

Late the next morning, Haruo Ikeda turned up at the Painter Avenue house. Eddie answered the door to see a slender, wiry Asian man waiting in the cold. At his feet, stood a single suitcase. He wore a parka that was unbuttoned to reveal a down vest worn over a flannel shirt.

"Mr. Ikeda? Please come in." Eddie offered his hand.

Ikeda clasped Eddie's hand with a firm grip. He offered a slight bow and then straightened before retrieving his suitcase and stepping into the entry hall.

"Yes. You must be Eddie. Joe spoke of you. Please call me 'Harry.'"

"Yes, I am. Thank you, um... Harry, for joining us. Please leave your bag here. I'll take it upstairs. Can I take your coat?"

"Certainly. Thank you."

Eddie hung the heavy parka in the entry hall closet.

"The others are in the living room."

"Excellent. Who has arrived?"

"Just Sully – John Sullivan," Eddie replied. "Fred Wilkins should be here in a few hours."

"I hear Sully's laugh now. It is both unmistakable and welcome."

"Shall we go in and say hello?"

Ikeda nodded his assent and strode ahead to the living room. When Sullivan saw Harry Ikeda his face broke into a huge smile. Joe and Sully both stood. Harry Ikeda bowed more formally to Joe. "*Sensei*. It is good to see you after all these years. You look well." Now he turned to John Sullivan and offered his hand. "And you, Sullivan. The years have treated you well."

"You could have called, Harry. I'd have been happy to pick you up at the station."

"An unnecessary disturbance, *Sensei*. I enjoyed the ride over. The town has not thrived as well as one might hope, however."

"Yes, sadly, your observations are as accurate as always. The town is far from thriving. Still, we are very happy to see you. Sully and I were just chatting, trying to come up with a plan. Would you join us, Harry? Would you like anything to eat or drink?"

"Some *o-cha* if it is convenient, *Sensei*. Otherwise plain tea or just some water."

Eddie had followed Ikeda into the living room. "We do have some pretty good green tea," he said. "It's not *o-cha*, though. Joe says that's difficult to obtain here. If it's okay I will put water on and then take your bag upstairs."

Harry Ikeda smiled gratefully and nodded his head in Eddie's direction. "Yes. That would be welcome. The flight from Albuquerque was... stressful."

Something about Ikeda's quiet and dignified demeanor made Eddie want to seek approval. He excused himself and put the water on to boil. Returning to the foyer, he took the suitcase up to the room Ikeda would occupy. That done, he ran back down the stairs, passed through the living room, and returned to the kitchen. When the water was ready, he scalded the pot and brewed the tea.

The young man monitored the steeping time carefully. When the tea was ready, he removed the infuser and brought the pot and a cup into the living room. He placed these on the end table near Ikeda. He noted that the older man had left his shoes near the entry hall door and was sitting on the sofa with his feet tucked beneath him.

"Would anyone else like anything?" he asked.

"We're good," Sully answered. "Sit down and join us for a few minutes."

Now there were four of them. They chatted for another hour and then moved to the kitchen for lunch. Joe had made a pot of lentil soup and sliced some fresh bread. Winter did not want to release its grip on the region, so the warm soup was welcome.

They continued visiting through lunch and gradually, Eddie grew comfortable with Ikeda. As Joe had said, he was different from the more outgoing John Sullivan, but he had a very kind way about him that quickly put the young man at ease.

Around two in the afternoon, the phone rang. Joe took the call. It was Fred Wilkins. They chatted for a couple of minutes and then Joe hung up.

"Fred's bags didn't show up," Joe reported when he returned to the living room. "I offered to come and get him, but he said he wants to get a cab at the airport. He wondered if he'd need to stop at the store on the way over for toiletries or other supplies. He sounded pretty frazzled and was relieved when I told him that all he needed was to get himself here. Knowing Fred, I think we might want to have a glass of wine ready when he gets here."

An hour passed before the doorbell rang again. Eddie jumped up and ran to the door. He opened it to see a man who had a cell phone jammed against his ear. An argument was underway.

"No. That's not all right. In fact, that's completely outrageous. You charged me to check my bag. Then you lost my bag. Then you say that if you happen to locate it, you won't bother to let me know. Instead, I will have to call to 'determine the status' of my bag. For pity's sake! I had to follow a push-button maze of touch tone options to reach you. You're telling me that I'm going to have to do this over and over?"

The older man looked at Eddie and shook his head. Eddie held the door open and the man stepped into the warm house. Eventually the argument wound down and the man hung up the phone.

Eddie offered his hand. "Mr. Wilkins? Hello. I'm Eddie."

"Yes. Yes. Good to meet you." His handshake was perfunctory.

"I'm sorry that your luggage was lost," Eddie offered. "But I think we'll be able to make you comfortable tonight."

Wilkins nodded. He was stooped slightly and more than a little soft around the middle. The contrast between Fred Wilkins and the earlier arrivals was noticeable. He brightened faintly when he walked into the living room and saw the others, but he remained preoccupied. They had all stood to greet him. There were handshakes all around. The newcomer relaxed ever so slightly. Joe offered Wilkins a glass of Sauvignon Blanc.

"Welcome Fred. Sorry about the hassle. We'll get you set up. But now we are all here. We can begin in earnest. *Salud!*"

Wilkins' cell phone went off at that moment. The man turned away, opened it, and spoke into the instrument.

"Wilkins. Yes. Yes. Good. Tonight? No, I don't have a car. You should deliver the bag. I have to pay for it?! You've got to be kidding!"

At this point, Joe set his own glass down and came over to his friend. "Give me the phone, Fred."

Wilkins looked startled, but after a short hesitation, he handed over the cell phone. As Joe took the phone, the timbre of his voice changed subtly. It became deep and hypnotic. A cold voice. Eddie had never heard Joe use that tone before and decided immediately that he'd hate to be on the other end of the call.

"Hello? Yes, this is Mr. Wilkins' host. Please deliver his bag to this address." Joe gave the address of the house. "Yes, I will cover the delivery charge if the bag arrives tonight. Please do your very best to ensure it arrives safely. I would consider it a personal favor if there were no further difficulties. Thank you for your help. Good-bye."

Joe hung up. He looked down at the phone that lay in his palm. Then he pushed a button to turn it off. He looked back to his friend. "Can I rely on you to leave this shut off, Fred, or shall I mind it for you while we are together?" he inquired mildly. His voice, Eddie noted, was again warm and friendly. "It could prove disastrous if it were to ring at the wrong time."

Fred Wilkins looked for a moment as if he might object. Then he looked around the room, took a deep breath, and shrugged – a little sheepishly Eddie thought. It was as though the man had just then actually arrived. "Yeah. I guess I'm kind of wired into the whole 24/7/52 thing. Just a habit. Keep it for me, Joe. It's been too long since we've seen each other, hasn't it?"

"Indeed it has."

Wilkins took another deep breath. "Well, it's good to be here." He looked around at the men gathered around him. "Yes. It's good to be here. Good to see you all. And to meet you, young man. Please call me 'Fred' or 'Wilkins.' I'll answer to either."

He shook Eddie's hand again. This time the grip was firm and sincere.

"Are you hungry? Would you like something?" Eddie offered. "Or perhaps I should show you to your room so that you could relax a little?"

"A little something to eat would be welcome. I'd like to cook dinner tonight, of course. Let's see what Joe has in his kitchen, shall we?"

As Eddie watched, Wilkins rummaged around in the kitchen. He seemed to know instinctively where to look to find what he wanted. Wilkins ended up slicing some French bread and building a sandwich that consisted of mortadella, dry salami, a slice of provolone and another of cheddar, pepperoncini, lettuce and olive oil. Thus fortified, he returned to the living room and the others.

"Okay. I think better when I've got some nourishment to sustain me. What's up?"

"You look pretty well sustained there, Wilkins." Sully laughed.

"What? Oh. I know, I've put on a few pounds. But there's solid muscle underneath. No worries."

"That's good to know, Fred. Good to know," Sullivan replied.

Harry said nothing, but Eddie noticed that he and Joe met each other's glance for an instant.

"All right. It would be fine if you'd like to cook this evening, Fred," Joe agreed. "But let's eat early and keep it simple, shall we? Now that you've all arrived, I want to get our plans in place. We need to decide what to do and then act."

"Fine. Fine." Fred turned to Eddie. "If I give you a shopping list, can you get what I need to cook? Ordinarily I'd prefer to do my own shopping, but I expect that Joe here will want to talk." Wilkins took a small notepad and pen from his pocket, thought for a minute and then scribbled several items. He tore the sheet from the pad and held it out. "Here you go."

"Well, sure... I can do that," Eddie set his wine down, accepted the paper and read down the list. He was slightly put off by Wilkins' tone, but he tried not to show it. "Let me get my coat and I'll take care of it."

Fred didn't respond. After an uncomfortable second, Harry Ikeda spoke up. "Young Eddie. May I join you on your shopping excursion? There are a few things I would like to purchase, and I have not visited here for many years. It would be a pleasure to see even a tiny bit more of this fine old city."

"Well, Mr. Ikeda... um, Harry, it would be great if you wanted to come with me, but if you'd rather stay here, you could just add your things to the list and I'd be happy to pick them up for you."

"That is gracious of you, but I would enjoy the company of a young person," Ikeda replied. "Now that my son has moved to Maryland and I am no longer active in the day-to-day operation of the dojo, I find I am around the energy of youth less than I would like."

"Well, okay. Sure. Do you need to do anything before we leave?"

"I need only don my parka and we can make our way to the bus stop."

"Let's go then."

Eddie and Harry got their coats and went out into the late afternoon cold. The wind had picked up. Eddie was quiet at first. He was glad for the company, but as he looked around, he found it difficult to avoid the comparison between this town and the beauty and charm of Soapstone Bay.

Eddie shook himself loose from his funk. "Thank you for coming with me, Harry. I appreciate the company."

Harry nodded. "You noticed the glance which *Sensei* and I shared. We may speak of this now. We fear that our old friend, Fred Wilkins, may not be up to what we require of him. Wilkins-san may have become too... settled in his patterns of living to break away. That would be unfortunate, but we must remain in balance. While we are out, Sullivan and *Sensei* will engage him in conversation."

"He does appear, well, more self-absorbed than you and Sully."

"Indeed. Let us pass to more pleasant topics for now. May I see the grocery list?"

Eddie handed it over. Ikeda looked it over and then folded it and put it in his pocket. Then he asked Eddie if there were any supermarkets nearby. "My feeling is that this town's economic fortunes have been such that we would do well to emphasize efficiency over the pleasurable aspects of leisurely shopping for one's foodstuffs."

"Sure. There's a Safeway and a QFC on bus routes we can catch at this stop. It just depends on which bus comes by first."

They reached the bus stop and stepped out of the wind. An elderly woman waited on the bench in the bus shelter. Harry nodded to her but she eyed them both suspiciously. Her ankles were swollen above her scuffed shoes, her coat barely adequate for the bleak afternoon. Her gray hair was jammed into a knit cap that looked badly in need of some Woolite and warm water. A cane leaned against her left side. A wrinkled shopping bag huddled near her right foot.

Harry stepped out onto the curb and looked down the boulevard. "I can see the twenty-five coming up the street."

"Oh. That'll take us to the QFC."

A moment later the bus pulled up. It was about half full. The doors hissed open. Clutching her cane and shopping bag, the elderly woman groaned herself to her feet. She shuffled toward the open doors. Eddie and Harry stood aside and let her board first. It was warmer on the bus.

Eight blocks later, they got off at a stop near the supermarket. Some of the fluorescents that illuminated the yellow QFC sign needed to be replaced. Inside, however, it was clear the employees were doing what they could to keep the store clean and tidy. The floors were swept. The goods visible at the front of the store were arranged neatly.

Harry pulled the list from his pocket and glanced at it again. "Here, my friend. Let us each take a basket. I will locate the items from the top of Wilkins-san's list. It will take me but a minute to select what I wish to purchase. Shall we meet in the produce section?"

"Oh. Sure." Eddie was impressed that Ikeda had obviously memorized the list so easily. "See you in a few minutes."

They met up and compared what they had bought. Harry had added some shampoo and other personal products to his basket. They were done and back outside in under twenty minutes. "We'll need to cross the street to catch the bus going back to Joe's neighborhood," Eddie remarked.

"Lead on, young friend. Oh, I presume that *Sensei* has instructed you in the spell of seeing?" Ikeda added in a casual manner. When Eddie nodded, he continued. "When we reach the crosswalk, please turn and look casually over your right shoulder, back towards the store. Not now. When we reach the crosswalk."

With an effort, Eddie controlled his urge to turn. They reached the crosswalk and Eddie did as Harry had requested. There were three seedy looking men loitering near the Presto Log display at the front of the store. They were obviously staring at Eddie and Harry and the auras surrounding them were a brilliant, angry crimson. As Eddie glanced their way, the men moved away from the store and started across the parking lot toward them.

"Do you see them? Please look back at me."

Eddie nodded.

"Well the bus will arrive before the situation becomes unpleasant. You see? It is not a half-block distant."

Not sure what to say, Eddie nodded again. Ikeda was unperturbed.

The twenty-three, on its return loop to the neighborhoods, pulled up just then. Going this direction it was slightly more full. Some people were getting off work downtown and were making their way home.

Eddie and Harry boarded the bus. The driver closed the doors and prepared to pull away from the curb, and Eddie felt a sense of relief. Then he noticed that the three men sprinted for the bus. The driver stopped the bus and re-opened the doors.

"Let us move to the rearmost empty seats," Harry spoke quietly.

They got up and moved to seats near the back of the bus. They were just behind the rear doors. As they sat down, the three men got onto the bus. There was a moment's argument as one tried to board without paying his fare. Then the three of them took seats.

One, a blond man who looked to be in his late twenties, turned in his seat and stared openly at Harry and Eddie. Occasionally, he made a comment to his compatriots, but he mostly watched. The blond man's bloody red aura was far brighter and intense than those of the others.

"Do you think those guys are agents of the Queen?" Eddie muttered under his breath.

"We cannot know. Probably, hopefully, they are simply unfortunate and angry men. We shall see," Harry replied. Now he continued in his mild, conversational tone. "Forgive me for noticing, but I observe that you are right side dominant. I am left. That could prove to be useful. When we leave the bus, please hold your grocery bags in your left hand and walk on my right side.

"We have not yet fought together, and of course I hope that we will avoid confrontation, but somehow I think we will be tested shortly. Please remain calm and centered. *Sensei* tells me that you are capable, and I have noticed that you are fit and that you carry yourself well. As long as they do not have firearms, we will be fine."

Ikeda fell silent at this point. Eddie's heart was pounding with the fight-or-flight reflex, but he focused on his breathing and did what he could to stay relaxed and loose. As the bus traveled the eight blocks to their stop, he thought back to the lessons that he'd practiced the year before. He recalled Joe's patient voice and the gentle wisdom of Lillith. He recalled his own clarity amidst the difficult encounters with RSM forces on Lena's world. The young man tried for, nearly reached, a sense of alert balance and calm.

While he did not succeed in becoming completely still inside, Eddie's mental state had begun to clear by the time they reached their stop. Harry stood and moved towards the rear doors. Eddie followed suit. Near the front of the bus, the men elbowed each other and laughed. They stood and crowded near the front door of the bus. It appeared that the driver noticed the tension, but he said nothing.

When Eddie and Harry left the bus, Eddie transferred both of his shopping bags to his left hand. He and the older man began walking down the sidewalk towards Joe's house, but they could both hear the men behind them. Now one called out.

"Hey there! Yeah. You two! Where you off to?"

Standing on Eddie's left, Harry sighed. "It is as I feared. I will turn where I stand. Please walk behind me and stand to my right side. Give me perhaps three feet of space if you are able."

The older man stopped walking. He spun slowly around. As instructed, Eddie stepped behind Harry and stood to his right. Now they faced the three men. Behind them, he could see that the bus driver had poked his head out of the front door. The driver watched the developing altercation for a few seconds and then returned to the bus.

The blond man was clearly the leader of the trio. He was flanked by the other two, much larger men. As they approached, Eddie got a good look at them and decided that they were probably not too much older than he was. One had a large beer belly and was already losing his hair. The other had pittted skin and was heavily muscled.

Now they stepped close. Eddie caught a whiff of unwashed bodies and alcohol. "So where're you two love birds off to?" the blond demanded. "What? No response? That's not polite, old man. You like 'em young, old man? This your butt-boy?"

Eddie felt anger rise in him at this, but he knew that was the purpose of the remarks, so he focused on keeping his shoulders down and relaxed, focused on his breathing. The blond turned to him, but the next taunt had less effect, and he managed to remain silent.

"You like being this old chink's butt-boy, do you? What? You don't talk either? For a couple of stinking faggots, you don't talk much. Maybe you squeal good though. Yeah. I bet you squeal real good when this old chink slams you in the butt."

Now Harry spoke up. His tone was mild and polite, and he may have been talking to a stone for all the effect it had. "It would please us both, if you three went on your way and left us alone. We have no wish for trouble. No wish..."

"Well, you got trouble, old man. You got a shitload of trouble right in your face. Hear? Billy! Go stand by butt-boy!"

The heavily muscled one with the bad skin swaggered over to stand near Eddie. Eddie balanced his weight as the big man moved closer.

"What? Still no words outta the butt-boy! Okay, old man. Give us your wallet. And that watch. That looks like a real good watch you got there." A sense of calm descended on Eddie. In contrast, the blond was obviously working himself up to a frenzy.

"I prefer to keep my wallet and my watch, young man," Harry's voice was now very quiet, very still.

"Well, I don't give a shit what you perfer! Maybe you perfer this!"

Now the man stepped forward and swung his fist at Harry. It was a hard, fast right, and had it connected it might have done serious damage, but the blow did not connect. Ikeda shifted his weight slightly and reached towards his attacker. A second later, the blond man lay on his back upon the sidewalk, his eyes unfocused.

The big man stepped behind Eddie and tried to grab him around the throat. Simultaneously Eddie stomped hard on the man's foot and elbowed him in the stomach. He turned, but before he could move, Harry laid that man on the ground too. The third man, the balding one with the beer belly, pulled a knife.

"Please move farther to my right, Eddie," Harry spoke quietly. "And watch the two on the ground."

The third attacker charged, but Harry stepped aside at the last second. The man with the knife appeared to levitate for a second before he crashed face first into the sidewalk. Sliding on his face, he skidded to a stop. Despite himself, Eddie felt a pang in his stomach at how much that probably hurt.

Just then, the blond moaned a little and rolled to his hands and knees. He shook his head and looked up. Quickly, the man jumped to his feet and moved closer. Eddie sidled to his right so that the man's back was facing Harry. He could hear a siren and see in his peripheral vision the flashing lights from an oncoming patrol car. The blond man was oblivious. Again he shook his head and now he glared at Eddie.

"You're gonna be real sorry, butt-boy. For maybe five seconds. Then you're gonna be real dead." The blond reached into his pocket and drew a gun just as the patrol car skidded to a stop.

Time slowed down. Eddie watched as the man raised the weapon. He could see the man's knuckle whiten as he began to squeeze the trigger. Eddie lunged farther to his right, away from the line of fire. His assailant tracked his motion with his weapon.

"DROP THE GUN!" a voice bellowed from the blond man's left. Eddie's assailant hesitated then and glanced toward the police car. Then he looked back towards Eddie. His eyes were empty, devoid of anything but blind rage.

"DROP THE GUN! THIS IS YOUR LAST WARNING!" the voice bellowed again. The voice sounded familiar, but there was no time to listen.

The man ignored the voice and squeezed off a shot, but Eddie had moved far enough and the first shot grazed his left arm. It felt like fire. Now Eddie was off balance and falling to the sidewalk himself. He landed and tried to roll away. The shooter took aim again.

Michael C. Glaviano

There were three shots in quick succession from near the patrol car. The blond man spun out of Eddie's field of view. His gun went off again, but it was pointed at the sky.

Eddie continued his roll and started to stand. "STAY DOWN, KID! STAY DOWN!" the voice came again. Eddie dropped flat on the sidewalk. He watched as the blond man kicked two or three times and then lay still. Pressed as he was onto the gritty, cracked concrete, Eddie could see the soles of the man's shoes. They were worn nearly through.

A second later, Eddie heard heavy feet on the pavement and saw Sergeant Driscoll and another officer run up to handcuff the other two assailants. Then he felt a hand on his arm. "Up you go. You okay, kid?" Eddie looked into Sergeant Driscoll's heavy, scowling face and thought he'd seen few such beautiful sights.

"Yeah. I'm okay." Eddie felt something wet on his arm. He looked down and winced. The arm was bleeding slightly, staining his coat. "Where's Harry? Is he okay?" His voice was a little shaky in his own ears.

"Indeed, young man, I am fine," came the quiet, calm voice. Harry stepped closer. "Age has taken its toll. I failed to move far enough to the side, and that one managed to nick the right arm of my coat as he fell." He indicated with a slight tilt of the head, the man who lay face down on the sidewalk. That man was just beginning to stir, to strain against the handcuffs.

"WHAT ARE YOU DOING?! LET'S GET A FIRST AID KIT OVER HERE!!" Sergeant Driscoll yelled at the other officer. Then she looked at Harry and Eddie again. "Sit down. Both of you. I don't want either of you passing out on me," the sergeant ordered.

Ikeda and Eddie met each other's eyes and shrugged. They hunkered down and waited while the other officer ran up with a battered plastic box. He tore open sterile gauze packages and handed them to Eddie. "The paramedics will be here in a few minutes. In the meantime, direct pressure on the wound," he said. "If you start to feel dizzy, put your head down."

Eddie drew his left arm from his coat and pressed the bandage to the wound. His arm hurt but it was easily tolerable. The shallow wound was about two inches long.

The sergeant turned to the big, heavily muscled man, who had regained consciousness and had managed to sit up. He looked rapidly around the scene and, hampered by his hands, which were restrained behind his back, was trying to struggle to his feet. "Okay. That's enough. Don't even think about standing up, scumbag. Face down on the sidewalk. You're already in big trouble. Wiggle around and I'll put manacles on you!" she ordered.

She looked over at the dead man. Eddie might have been mistaken, but for a second, he thought her face betrayed a terrible grief, a

466

pain beyond bearing. When she turned to the other officer, however, Driscoll's face was carefully devoid of emotion.

"Get some tape up. And get these gawkers out of here," she ordered the other officer. "And bring over the bus driver. I want to take his statement myself."

She turned back to Eddie and Harry. "You two okay now? Damn. I'm glad that driver had the sense to call this in. What the hell were you doing out here?"

"We went to the grocery store to get some things for dinner, Sergeant," Harry spoke up. "Thank you for helping us. These men were sadly bent on mayhem."

"This is one of Joe's friends, Sergeant Driscoll. Joe has a couple of old friends in town for a visit," Eddie added. He was still shaky from the adrenalin. His arm hurt where he pressed the gauze pad against it, but the bleeding had subsided.

The sergeant looked closer at Harry Ikeda and wrinkled her forehead. "I recognize you. I haven't seen you for a long time, but I remember. You sure have aged well, I'll give you that."

"Uh, Sergeant, would it be okay if we gathered up our groceries?" Eddie asked as the silence lengthened uncomfortably.

Driscoll brought herself back with an effort. "Can you do it without passing out?" she demanded.

"Yes, ma'am."

"Then do it."

She called to the officer who was walking up with the bus driver. "See that house there? That one. The one that looks neat. Yeah. Run across and tell the guy who lives there to come out here."

Backup arrived just then. Moments later, an ambulance and a van from the coroner's office also pulled up to the scene of the incident. The coroner staff took photos and then loaded the body into a bag. Their van was gone within fifteen minutes.

Meanwhile, harried paramedics looked at Eddie's wound and pronounced it minor. Although they offered to take him to the emergency room for treatment, Eddie could tell they didn't really think it was necessary. The paramedics looked relieved when he declined their offer. They suggested that he make sure his tetanus vaccination was up to date. The paramedics had just closed the doors of the ambulance when another emergency call came in. Siren blaring, the ambulance roared away from the curb.

The officers began taking statements from the bus passengers and the driver. Several of the passengers had gathered on the sidewalk and were complaining loudly about the delay. The surviving assailants were stuffed in the back of the second patrol car and carted off to jail.

Joe crossed the street and spoke with the sergeant. He nodded and then came over to Eddie and Harry. "The good sergeant says you will survive, son. Of course you'll both have to make statements, but I've convinced her that you should come out of the cold.

She'll come over to take your statements after she finishes here. This is more attention than I wanted, but of course that can't be helped. She says assaults of this nature are on the rise. The police force is putting everyone possible out on the streets."

"I am saddened, *Sensei*. Had the police not arrived so quickly, I could have disarmed the blond one. I failed in that, and he is now beyond our help," Ikeda spoke softly, but Eddie could hear a real note of sadness in the usually cheerful voice.

"Yes, I am sure you are sad, Harry, but this could have been much worse. You are uninjured and Eddie's wound is superficial. Now, let's get you both out of this wind."

A patrolman halted traffic on Painter Avenue so the three men could cross. In the ugly glare of the sodium vapor street lamps a young man, an older but vital man, and a man who appeared to be of vigorous middle age but was in fact ancient beyond measure crossed the street and climbed the steps to enter the well-kept house.

Indoors, it was warm. As they closed the door behind them, Fred Wilkins was complaining about the lateness of the hour and the time it would take to prepare a proper meal.

"You know, to cook chicken and keep it tender you have to use a slow oven. Now dinner will be like something thrown together by a midwest housewife. It's just hard to abide, I tell you." He looked up from his chair as Joe, Harry, and Eddie entered the living room. "What kept you people?"

Now it was Joe's turn to look sad. "I told you a few moments ago, Fred. When the policeman came to the door, remember? Harry and Eddie were attacked across the street from the house. We are fortunate they were not seriously injured."

Joe turned to John Sullivan. "Sully, would you help Fred in the kitchen? I know cooking isn't your favorite pastime, but I'd like you to help while we discuss something in here. Here you go, Fred. Here are your groceries. Try to keep it simple. We just need a healthy dinner. Nothing fancy. Can you do that for me?"

Wilkins looked put-out, but he accepted the grocery bags. Harry withdrew the few items he'd purchased for himself. When the other two went into the kitchen, Joe turned toward Eddie and Ikeda with a serious expression darkening his features.

"It is as we feared when he first arrived then, *Sensei*?" Harry spoke first.

"Yes it is." Joe spoke softly. "Of course I'm not qualified to make a medical diagnosis, but Sully and I are afraid that Fred is suffering from some type of dementia. He is irascible and forgetful. He still remembers big events from his past, but frequently things that happen fifteen minutes earlier don't stick. It is clear that he won't be able to help us. The four of us will have to make do."

"Who will care for him?"

"I will make inquiries tonight and tomorrow morning. I believe there are good facilities on the central coast of California, but until and unless I can get Fred to sign himself up..." Joe trailed off.

"What will we do to open a portal there? Will we drop that?" Eddie wondered.

"Oh, I think not. I know of a place that will work. There are cliffs at some of the beaches near San Luis Obispo. I'll show you when the time comes. We'll make that trip first and try to get Fred squared away while we're out there. Then we'll go up to Bellingham and wrap up in central New Mexico."

The three men chatted for a few more minutes. There were noises from the kitchen, and good aromas began drifting into the living room. Another quarter hour passed. The doorbell rang. It was Sergeant Driscoll and the rookie patrolman who had been driving the car during the incident. Now the young officer was functioning as her assistant. Joe got up to answer the door.

"Come in, Sergeant, Officer. They are in the living room. Can I get you some coffee or tea?" Joe offered.

"Yeah, Joe. Coffee'd be good about now. Thanks," Sergeant Driscoll agreed. The other officer gratefully accepted as well.

Joe headed off to the kitchen. Sergeant Driscoll looked between Eddie and Harry. "Well, for once we got a lucky break. Of sorts," she said.

"Good news?"

"Yeah. The bullet that grazed the kid's arm? It ended up taking out the windshield of a parked car. We found the slug in the back seat. And the gun is the same caliber weapon that we've ID'd for several other crimes. Including three homicides. If anybody asks, you didn't hear that from me. Got it? Anyway, we'll get a ballistics report back in a few days that'll confirm it, but it prob'ly means we've got a bad one off the streets. Permanently.

"And miracle of miracles, most of the witnesses – the bus driver and several passengers – have actually given statements that are mostly, sorta consistent. That's rare.

"So, if you two can remember what happened, maybe we'll be able to close this one down. After all, you both survived and can be called as witnesses. And of course Officer Warren and I both witnessed the assault from the patrol car," she craned her neck at the police officer who stood nearby.

"Thank you, Sergeant," Eddie said. "I'm really glad you guys showed up. I'm sorry that you had to shoot that guy, but..."

"Yeah. Me too, kid. On both counts."

Eddie thought she worked hard to control her features for a second or two. She cleared her throat before continuing. "Now I'll be back flyin' a desk while the mandatory paperwork grinds its way through the department. I can use the break, but the city needs feet on the street.

"And I'm kinda surprised you've stuck around," she added. "This town hasn't exactly been kind to you, kid."

The remark caught Eddie by surprise. "Well... I'm learning a lot working for Joe. It's a good opportunity... and better than doing the Drive Away thing," he finished a little lamely.

"Humph. Whatever. Okay, let's do this as quick as we can. How about Officer Warren here takes your statement in another room? I'll take this gentleman's statement here," she craned her neck in Harry Ikeda's direction. "Then we'll be outta your hair for this evening. But we're gonna want you to stick around for a couple of days while we check all the statements. If everybody's stories line up, we're golden."

So Eddie and Officer Warren went into the rarely used parlor. The officer sipped his coffee and interviewed Eddie in some detail. Eddie thought the officer was barely older than he. The young man was trying hard to do his job well. Eddie suspected that Sergeant Driscoll wasn't particularly easy on her subordinates.

As he answered the questions, Eddie sensed a sad irony in the situation. It was hard not to reflect upon the fact that the assailants, the police officer, and he were all of similar ages. Different circumstances; different lives. And in one unhappy instance, a life cut very short.

Once his statement was taken, Eddie stood and offered his hand to the young officer. The man shook his hand with a firm grip. "Perhaps we'll see each other in better circumstances someday, Officer Warren," he offered.

"Maybe so. Thank you. If you have anything else you would like to add, please call and ask for me at the station. Here's my card." The of-ficer handed Eddie a simple business card that displayed his name, rank, and a voicemail number.

After the police left, Eddie and Harry washed up. Joe treated the gouge on Eddie's arm with some of his herbal concoctions and replaced the bandages. Dinner was ready by then.

Dinner was a subdued affair. Now that Joe had put the pieces to-gether for him, Eddie could see that Fred Wilkins was indeed suffering from some sort of mental impairment. He lost track of the conversation several times. More than once, he interrupted the others with enthusi-astically offered irrelevancies.

Still, Fred's kitchen expertise appeared to be in top form. The main dish consisted of chicken breasts, pounded flat and lightly floured before being wrapped around Italian sausage and baked. There were French cut green beans with slivered almonds and a very nice wild rice pilaf that featured dried cherries. With a flourish, Fred presented an impressively rich chocolate tort for dessert.

He appeared to have used every pot, pan, mixing bowl, and utensil in the kitchen. Eddie's arm throbbed and his head ached, but he gamely volunteered for cleanup. Sully and Joe said they'd pitch in as well. Harry took Fred off to converse in the living room.

With the three men working together, it took only forty-five minutes to return the kitchen to order. They talked as they worked.

"Sergeant Driscoll wants Harry and me to stick around for a few days at least. I hope that doesn't screw up the plans."

"I'm sure it'll be fine, son," Joe assured him. "Sergeant Driscoll is nothing if not efficient. In the meantime, Sully and I will go out to California and make arrangements. We'll take Fred with us of course. You and Harry can join us as soon as you're able."

"I'll want to check on the staff that Fred ordered anyway," Sullivan added. "That is, *if* he actually ordered it. He was vague on that part."

The retired engineer shook his head sadly, "Time is the harshest teacher of them all."

"I beg your pardon?" Joe asked, puzzled.

"Oh. Sorry. I'm getting maudlin. As time passes, we learn from our experiences. Ideally we are better for it. But then time weakens us. Robs us of our strength. Our loves, the very experiences that define us."

"Try not to let it get to you, Sully. I'm grateful to have you and Harry on my side. It is just plain good to see you... and to see that you two, at least, have remained vital and strong," Joe replied.

"And young Eddie here has been a huge help," he continued. "Never fear, my good man. You and Harry are in better shape than I could have hoped. The four of us will be enough. We'll make things work. You'll see. And we'll do what we can for Fred."

They joined Harry Ikeda and Fred Wilkins in the living room. Fred brightened when they walked in. "I was just telling Harry that I'll make an early Easter dinner tomorrow evening. What do you say? It'll push back these winter weather blues."

"Perhaps, Fred," Joe replied. "But remember we are planning to go out to California as soon as we can. I'll try to make flight arrangements tonight if I can find available seats for tomorrow."

"Oh. Yes. I... I guess that slipped my mind," Wilkins replied.

The doorbell rang again. This time it was the courier bearing Fred Wilkin's lost luggage. Joe paid the man and left the bag in the entry hall.

"Well, gentlemen. The day did not wrap up as I'd planned, but at least we have a sequence and the rudiments of a plan. Try to get some rest. I'll see what I can do about travel arrangements."

"Yes, *Sensei*. I would like to go upstairs and sit for a while. My mind is troubled. It wants stilling."

Eddie stood and stretched. He was tired but didn't think he could rest. "If it's all the same to you, I'll show Harry and Mr. Wilkins here up to their rooms. Then I'll come back down and look at the fire for a while. I'm still kind of wound up."

"I'll wait down here for a bit myself," Sully added.

Joe nodded. "Suit yourselves, gentlemen."

Wilkins agreed eagerly. He followed Eddie and Harry upstairs. They got him and his bag into a room. Outside the Aikido master's room, Eddie shook hands with Harry Ikeda.

"I just wanted to thank you, Harry," he said. "I realize that I probably wouldn't be alive right now if you hadn't been with me this afternoon."

"One never knows, young man. Had you gone alone, you would have taken longer to shop, or perhaps you would have gone to a different store. Or those young predators might have chosen another victim. In any case, thanks are unnecessary. We do what we are able.

"And it is good to know you. You fight well for one untrained and young. It was an honor to stand shoulder to shoulder with you. Joe has chosen well. I see potential if you are willing to remain humble and learn.

"Now, if you will excuse me, I must sit," Harry finished with a slight bow.

Eddie did his best to bow in return. It felt like the right response. The older man went into his room and softly closed the door. Then, his arm throbbing in time with his steps, Eddie trudged slowly down the stairs. As he descended, he passed Joe who was on his way up.

"Try to get some rest, son."

"I will. I want to check to see if Lena wrote today." He looked earnestly at Joe and forced himself to look directly into the disquieting depths of his mentor's eyes. "...and remember I still want to learn how to do transits between here and the Inn by myself."

Joe sighed. "I haven't forgotten. If you feel well in the morning, we'll go over the technique. If there is time, we might make a pair of quick transits. Just there and back so I can watch you do it."

Eddie's heart lifted. "That'd be great, Joe. I'd like that a lot. Thanks."

Joe merely nodded and continued up the stairs. Injured arm forgotten, Eddie continued down to the first floor and grabbed a jacket. Sully looked up from one of the chairs in front of the fire.

"Be right back, Sully!" Eddie called as he dashed through. It was full dark and there was no moon, so he flicked the porch light on before going outside. He ran across the winter-dormant grass and felt for the loose brick. There was a note! Quickly, he pulled it out and replaced the brick.

Inside again, Eddie sat at the kitchen table to see what his beloved had written. This was a shorter note. It was more consistently cheerful than the previous letter. After the traumatic events of the late afternoon, Lena's loving words and good news were all the more welcome. Eddie read the note several times and then pulled a sheet of paper and a pen from one of the drawers.

After a short hesitation, he dashed off a note that omitted mention of the violence that Harry and he had encountered. Instead, he let Lena know that all of Joe's friends had arrived and that they would be setting out for various locales soon. He tried hard to keep his words lighthearted and optimistic.

When he was done, Eddie folded the note and returned to the wall. As he bent to draw out the brick he was struck by a powerful sense that he was being observed. Half afraid at what he might see looking back at him, he stood and looked around. There was nothing but blackness beyond the walls of the property, blackness and the feeling that something he couldn't see was looking back at him. Something malevolent.

He bent again and put his note inside the niche. After sliding the brick into place, he stood and again looked around. Now his heart was pounding. He forced himself to stand still and peer into the darkness. He walked around the perimeter. Nothing. Nothing but darkness and a sense of being watched.

Eddie returned to the house. He shut off the porch light and locked the back door. He passed through the kitchen and doused the lights there too. Now Sully stared into the fire with a brooding expression on his face. Eddie stepped quickly and quietly past.

Leaving his jacket in the entry closet, the young man continued up the stairs to Joe's rooms. He rarely bothered his mentor when the older man was in his rooms, and almost never when the doors were closed. He could hear Joe's voice. He tapped quietly at the door. There was a pause, and then Joe called, "Come in!"

Eddie opened the door. Joe was sitting at his desk. He cradled the telephone in one hand. He looked at Eddie's face and gestured that he take a seat. Then he turned back to the phone.

"Listen. Something has come up. I'll call you back to complete the reservations. Will that be all right? Thank you."

Joe hung up the phone and looked back at Eddie. He stood up at his desk. "What happened, son? You don't look well. Is it Sully? Is he okay?"

"No," Eddie shook his head. "Sully's fine. Sorry to bother you. I... I just went out in the back yard. To send a note through to Lena. I had the strangest feeling somebody or some*thing* was watching me. Something that meant us harm."

"Oh, that." Joe sat down. "Well, you're getting more sensitive. That's a good thing, I suppose."

"So you already sensed that... whatever it is?"

"Well, let's just say I'm not surprised. The Queen's minions are abroad. They often test the boundaries of this house. You know that. They are attracted to violence. Some of them feed on it."

"And this evening..."

"Indeed. There was violence that culminated in a death, and it happened right in front of the house that obsesses them. The house whose occupants fight against their hold on this world.

I would be surprised if they hadn't shown up. Still, I am glad that you mentioned it. I will take certain precautions tonight. They will withdraw."

"Okay. Well, that's good to know, I guess. It's been a lousy day hasn't it, Joe?"

"Not the best. But, sadly, I've seen much worse. Again, thank you for mentioning this. The sooner I learn of these things the more effective my response can be.

You said you sent a note to your young woman. Has she sent any word of her circumstances?"

"Uh, yes. She did. Iris wasn't doing too well right after we left, but Lena says she was a little better today. The weather's good. The situation in the town is looking up. In fact, the whole note was good. I was pretty excited for a few minutes there. Otherwise I probably would have noticed even sooner."

"Well, son, it could be much worse. It's not going to take us all that long to wrap things up. Even if it's only for a visit, I think you'll be able to get back there soon. I know we haven't moved quickly enough for you so far, but the pace will pick up now. You realize that I want to be there too, don't you? I want to take care of Iris. Really heal her this time."

Eddie swallowed and nodded a little. "I know. Well... I think I'll go down and sit with Sully for a little while," he said finally.

"Probably a good idea, son. Try not to fret. I already have plane reservations set up. I'm in the process of securing rental cars and, should Fred's house prove inadequate to our needs, accommodations."

The young man stood. His arm was throbbing again but he didn't want to show it.

"Okay... thanks." Eddie went out. As he pulled the door closed, Joe was already entering a number on his phone.

Eddie returned to the living room. John Sullivan had barely moved, but when the young man came in this time he looked up and mustered a wan smile. "I was just thinking of putting another log on the fire."

"Too bad Joe's upstairs. When he's tending the fire it just keeps going. Anyway, I'll get it," Eddie offered. He opened the doors of the fireplace and added a piece of wood from the stack near the hearth. He poked the logs around a little and the new piece caught. He closed the doors and took a seat in one of the comfortable old chairs.

Sully looked at the empty glass that sat next to his chair. "What're you drinking?" Sully asked.

"Nothing, thanks. I just want to relax for a few minutes."

"Don't blame you. I think I'm done for the night myself. Relax away, young man."

So the men sat in companionable silence and watched the fire. Once in a while one would get up and stir the logs a little. Sully added another log a half hour later. Finally, Eddie felt himself nodding off. He stood and stretched.

"Okay. I think I can turn in now. Thanks, Sully."

The older man nodded. "A pleasure. I appreciated the company myself."

Eddie walked up to his rooms in the garret and got ready for bed. He was exhausted and emotionally drained but awake again. The day's events continued to replay in front of his eyes. The violence, the sudden finality of death, and the lack of resolution conspired together to push rest away. His arm continued to ache and he lay there for a long time before blessed sleep finally embraced him.

*　　*　　*

Once finally asleep, Eddie slept deeply. He awoke around seven and enjoyed five minutes of forgetfulness before recollection of the previous day's experience drove him from the bed. In less than a half hour, he was showered and downstairs. His arm was slightly sore to the touch, but it no longer throbbed and there was no inflammation around the wound. Joe's healing herbs had done their job.

Fred Wilkins was holding forth in the kitchen. He was speaking to Joe about the importance of a long and pleasurable breakfast. He stood at the stove and had both flapjacks and an egg scramble ready in copious quantities. The aroma of food lifted Eddie's spirits.

"Well, who's this?" Fred looked at Eddie in surprise when the younger man entered.

"That's Eddie, Fred. You met him yesterday. You remember," Joe explained patiently.

"Oh. Right. Yes. It just slipped my mind for a moment. How are you, young man? Sleep well? Grab a plate!"

"Thanks, Fred. Yes. This smells great." Eddie loaded his plate with food and decided that despite the sad fact that Fred was losing his short term memory and general faculties, the man was still a fantastic cook.

Sully and Harry joined them a few minutes later. Harry made himself some tea to go with his food. Sully took modest amounts of breakfast and poured himself some coffee.

"Well, Giuseppe, what's the plan?" he asked as he sat down and took a sip of coffee. "Gak! You realize, old friend, that coffee needn't always be able to function as paint stripper don't you?"

Joe laughed his big, hearty laugh. "If it doesn't try to wrestle your arm back to the table as you lift the cup, it's not worth drinking!"

"Indeed," Sullivan grumbled. He went to the sink and poured out some of the strong brew. Then he topped up the cup with hot water left over from Harry's tea.

Eddie nodded. "I do the same thing all the time, Sully." Then he turned to Joe.

Before he could speak, Joe held up his hand to forestall the question. "Yes, son. We'll do as you wish this morning. Sully, Fred, and I have a flight out tonight at six o'clock. We should have plenty of time."

"Cool. Thanks, Joe. Hey, when's Harry's and my flight?"

"You and Harry have a flight scheduled for Tuesday of next week."

"That long huh? That's a bummer."

"Yes. It is unfortunate," Joe agreed with a chuckle. "As soon as we've finished breakfast, I'm going to call the police station and see if Sergeant Driscoll can expedite things in some way."

By then, Eddie had a mouthful of pancakes so he only nodded.

A few moments later, Joe convinced Fred to stop cooking and sit down to have some food himself. The men talked and joked their way through breakfast. Harry had regained his equanimity. Eddie was still troubled from the previous day's events, but he felt his steadiness returning.

By nine o'clock they had restored the kitchen to a semblance of order. Joe called the police station and spoke with the sergeant. Eddie listened to Joe at his diplomatic best as his mentor alternately cajoled, commiserated, supported, sympathized, and negotiated with Sergeant Driscoll.

Finally, Joe hung up. He was smiling. In the end, Sergeant Driscoll committed to having all the paperwork wrapped up in time for Harry and Eddie to fly out to California on the following Tuesday morning. They would have to go into the courthouse prior to their departure so they could make formal statements in front of a judge. She thought she could get them a time slot on Friday.

"Okay, son. Now let's go out in the back yard and talk about those transits."

"Need any help?" Fred offered.

Harry cleared his throat gently. "I could use your assistance, Fred. I seem to have misplaced my down vest. Could I impose on you to help me look for it?"

"Sure. I can help you," Fred agreed. "As long as we finish up in time to make lunch," he added. Harry and Fred walked upstairs.

Sullivan stared fixedly into his coffee. A moment later he muttered something about needing to pack and followed the other two. In the silence that followed, Joe repeated that he wanted to practice the transit steps outside. Eddie went to the entry hall closet and pulled on his jacket. Then he joined Joe in the back yard.

The air was still cold, but the sun was shining and the wind had died down. Eddie looked around the yard. There was no evidence of the feeling of being watched that had been so strong the night before. He turned to Joe with an inquiring look.

"I promised you that I would take certain steps to discourage those who lingered last evening. When you and Harry follow us out to California, even stronger measures will come into play. The house will remain undisturbed in our absence. Only you or I will be able to gain admittance. You can count on it, son.

"Now, tell me what you remember of the transit from here to the portal beneath the Inn at Three Corners," Joe demanded.

"Um, okay. Well... I remember we walked for a little while. And there was a tall standing stone. Just one. It had something carved on it. Sorry... no! It was a triangle. We walked a little further. Things were confusing then because the Alicia creature had attacked and your spells triggered and all, but I think I made a triangle of fist-sized stones around us and that was it. The Place just sort of faded out and we were in the basement of the Inn."

"Not bad, son. Not bad at all," Joe said with approval. He pulled a piece of paper from his pocket and unfolded it. It was a beautiful artist's rendering of a standing stone with a triangle etched on the side. Joe handed it to Eddie.

"Just as you held the thought of moving to higher ground in your mind to reach the Lady's forest, to reach the basement of the Inn, you must focus your mind on this image. You will walk slowly as you concentrate. Once the image is strong, the stone will emerge from the mist.

"You must observe the triangle that's carved on the side of the stone. One vertex will point off to one side. That indicates the direction you are to walk. Once you're sure of the heading, you walk ten paces in that direction. Find three, good sized stones. They needn't be big or hard to move, but they must be substantial – not pebbles. You surround yourself with these stones and the transit will occur."

"That seems pretty easy," Eddie observed.

"Yes, going that direction is fairly straightforward. That world, the world where our dear friends dwell, is not so cut off from the Place as is this. Now, repeat the instructions back to me."

Eddie did as he was requested. Joe had him do it over and over. Then they went in and Joe had Eddie trace the rendering of the standing stone. He practiced and practiced the drawing until he could fashion a fairly good copy from memory. Finally, Joe said that he was satisfied.

"Very well. I think you have it. It will be easier once you've done it a few times. Do you have any questions?"

"Well, yeah. Each time I go through, I find some rocks and put them in the shape of a triangle. I always walk ten paces past the standing stone. So who moves the rocks?"

"Ah... Yes, I could see how that might puzzle you. There is still so much that we have not had time to discuss. Suffice it to say that although you always visualize the pillar with the triangle glyph, the Place is never the same. It continues to be washed with the tears of the gods as they dream and, caught in the emotions of their dreams, weep. So it's never the same pillar. Never the same rocks. That is the way of the Place."

Joe handed him another sheet of heavy paper. This one was covered with Joe's careful handwriting. "I think you have this transit well-in-hand, but here, for reference, are some notes that describe the whole process."

"Now let's try the transit back," he continued. "What do you remember about that one?"

"Should we go back outside to talk?"

"Our guests seem settled in upstairs. Harry and Sully will keep Fred occupied. We might as well stay here."

Eddie nodded. "Okay. That one included a spell, I remember. You held one hand up and made gestures with your other hand. You projected a beam of bright blue light that showed the way to a big pile of rocks with a sort of funnel perched on top. Kind of like the tin man in the Wizard of Oz.

"Oh, wait... I remember more," he continued. "There was another spell. You put your hands on the rock pile and said a few words and then a doorway formed. It opened and we came through."

"That's pretty good. You omitted mention of the three standing stones. That image is the trigger image, the image you must first hold in mind. Here."

Joe produced another detailed rendering. It showed a single standing stone with two more that were nearby but partially shrouded by the mist. Eddie nodded when he saw the picture.

"Right. I remember that. I'll need to memorize the spells too."

"Indeed you will. The first spell is a simple combination spell. It is called 'Showing the Way.' Once you've found the three stones and are standing between the two stones with your back to the first, you cast the

'Showing the Way' spell to locate the cairn and illuminate the way to reach it.

The problem is that the beam you produce will be visible all around, so you have to move fast. Basically, you should run for the cairn. When you reach it, you place your hands at chest height and cast the 'Spell of Opening.' That's just a generic spell to open locked or hidden doors."

"Got it. At least I think I do," Eddie said.

"We'll see. Now the key here is the Showing the Way spell. You've already held the image of the stones in your mind. That gets you to where you need to stand and shows you which direction to face. Then you change your focus to rest on the image of the cairn."

Joe handed Eddie three more pieces of paper. One contained a final rendering, this time a detailed drawing of the cylindrical cairn topped with an inverted metal funnel. The other two pages held detailed instructions for the two spells that Eddie would need for the transit.

"I suggest that you go up to your rooms and memorize these. Review everything. I'm going to my rooms for a little while. Once you are confident you can perform these two transits without assistance from me or anyone else, come to my rooms. I'll test you and if I am satisfied, we'll try it."

"Cool. Can we...?"

"I'm sorry. I'd like to spend some time with Iris and I know you would like to be with Lena and to visit your other friends, but we need to hurry. The Queen's agents may try to observe us from a distance. They may try to follow us. The sooner we make our moves the less time they'll have to prepare."

Disappointed but hardly surprised, he agreed without argument and headed for his rooms. On the second floor, he saw that the doors to all the guest rooms were open. All three of Joe's old friends were gathered in Harry's room and talking. Eddie hurried past and up to his garret apartment.

Once inside, he closed the door and sat at the small desk. Eddie laid out the papers to correspond to the sequence of steps he would follow during the transits. He cycled through several activities: reviewing the drawings, holding the images in his mind, tracing or copying the images, reviewing the spells, and so on. Over and over, he reviewed the material that Joe had given him.

At first the going was rough. He was impatient and didn't feel like studying, but he knew that he needed to master the transits if he were to have more autonomy. Gradually, as he forced himself to practice, his state of mind shifted. He let go of his impatience and moved into the flow of the work itself. Time passed.

Finally, Eddie felt he'd internalized the material. He looked at the clock on his desk. He'd been at it for over two hours. If he were go-

ing to do this, now was the time. He organized his materials and put
them in his bookshelves. Then he hurried down to Joe's rooms. The
door was closed, and he knocked softly. Joe opened the door immediately. He looked at Eddie.

"Are you ready?" he asked.

"Well, yes, I think I am."

"Good. Let's go."

"You're not going to test me? You said you would."

"I just did. You are telling the truth. You do indeed believe
you're ready. Don't get a big head about it, but I know you well enough
by now, son, to have some confidence in you. You think you're ready.
That's the test. Let's go."

"Okay..." Eddie swallowed. "Uh, great!" he nodded and tried to
reassure himself.

The house had become strangely quiet, the atmosphere of the
place somehow altered. The guest room doors were closed, the voices behind them muted. The two men went down the stairs to the entry hall.
Joe opened the door to the basement and led the way down the stairs.
When Eddie reached the bottom, Joe undid the hidden latch and folded
the stairs away.

Eddie had left his throwing axes on the table, and he reached for
them now. Joe nodded in approval. Eddie shrugged. Clearly it would be
better if they were able to make the transits quickly, but the young man
felt better with the heft of the axes slung over his shoulders.

They worked their long way down the tunnel, deep into the earth.
At the portal chamber, Joe lit the candles. "I'll go through first and then
step to one side. Count to five and follow."

They went through the portal and into the Place without mishap.
The moist warmth surrounded them. Veils of mist drifted on the unfelt
breath of the sleeping gods. Indistinct shapes studded the eerie landscape. Muted sounds murmured at indeterminate distances.

Eddie glanced at Joe and then called up the image of the single
standing stone, the standing stone that held the glyph of the triangle. He
concentrated and walked slowly forward. Joe followed. The damp
ground absorbed the sounds of their footsteps. In moments, the stone
loomed in the mist. The triangle was clearly visible on its side.

Eddie stepped close to the stone and looked up at the triangular
carving. The glyph pointed off to his left as he faced the stone, so he
turned to walk in that direction. He counted ten paces and looked
around. There were stones of various sizes scattered among the fleshy
plants and patches of soft, damp earth.

Eddie motioned for Joe to step near one of the fist-sized stones.
Then the young man turned away and found two more stones that were
about the same size as the one near Joe. He placed one a few feet off to
the left of his teacher. Finally, standing near the older man, Eddie

reached out and dropped the stone an approximately equal distance to the right.

Almost immediately, the panels of amber light rose up in the spaces between the stones. Once the light reached above their heads, their view of the Place faded, to be replaced with the stones of the portal chamber that waited in the earth far below the Inn at Three Corners. The moist air of the Place was replaced by the dry, dusty air of the ancient chamber. The stones pressed around them.

As Joe cast an illumination spell, Eddie turned towards his teacher. Joe favored him with a slight nod and climbed up over the rim of the pit. "This time, you go through first. Step off a few paces and wait for me. Begin holding the image of the three stones in your mind as soon as you're in position."

Joe walked up the tunnel and out of sight. Eddie brought up an illumination spell of his own. Slowly he made the three circuits of the pit. He faced the tunnel opening, heard the keening and saw the glow begin to form. He stepped backwards off the lip and again dropped through into the Place.

He looked around. Nothing had changed. Everything had changed. The ground was moist, the air warm and full of mist. Eddie walked off to the side and began to hold the image of the three stones in his mind. He concentrated and felt rather than heard Joe join him a few seconds later.

They began walking, Eddie continued to focus on the image. There was the first pillar, the largest of the three. There were the two smaller ones. Eddie moved confidently over to stand between the two smaller stones. He faced away from the large pillar.

Now Eddie became slightly disoriented. He tried to call up the image of the cairn that he knew came next, but there had been too much concentrating. Too little time had passed in his practice. The images were not second nature. He tried to still his mind, to focus on his breathing.

Eddie glanced over at Joe. His mentor was looking at him expectantly, confidently. Eddie closed his eyes and reached into his memory. This time he called up the image of the large, cylindrical cairn that was capped by the incongruity of a inverted metal funnel.

He clutched the image securely as he raised his left hand and made the passes with his right. He spoke the words and the bright beam sprang from his left palm to illuminate the cairn. As it emerged from the mist, Eddie realized that the cairn had materialized farther away than it had on other transits, and he started running toward the structure. The illuminating beam persisted and he and Joe moved closer.

They had covered perhaps two-thirds of the distance when they heard the sound that Eddie dreaded. The beast had caught their scent or seen the flash of light. The strange ululating cry sounded again. She was headed toward them. The men piled on all the speed they could muster.

Now they were close, but so was the beast. "Cast the spell of opening!" Joe ordered. He turned to face the onrushing creature.

Eddie placed his hands and called up the words. He heard Joe cast a spell behind him. There was a sizzling sound and a yelp of pain. The outline of the door began forming, solidifying. Joe cast again, another cry of pain and frustrated rage. Finally, the door swung inwards.

"Now, Joe!" Eddie jumped into the blackness of the yawning doorway. Joe followed and slammed shut the door. Outside, the cries of rage continued and then slowly faded. Eddie took a deep breath and called up an illumination spell. They were surrounded by the stones of the portal chamber that lay beneath the Painter Avenue house.

"That was good for your first try, son." Joe spoke sincerely. "You had a bit of trouble there, but you recovered. You'd better keep practicing, but I think if worse came to worse and you had to perform a transit by yourself, you'd stand a good chance of making it through. Of course it will help if luck is on your side."

Eddie felt wrung out. His shirt was drenched with the mist of the Place and with his own sweat. "Thanks, Joe. Thanks for showing me how to do this. I really appreciate it."

"Okay. Just keep practicing. You've got a few more days before your flight. Keep at it. Alternate between practicing with those axes and memorizing the images and the spells. Now let's get upstairs and see what the others are up to. I need to get packed myself."

Eddie hiked up to the basement. Once there, he left his throwing axes slung over his shoulders and waited for Joe to stand next to him so he could fold the stairs back to hide the sub-basement. At last, the young man trudging, the old one moving easily and swiftly, they continued up to the main floor.

When they reached the entry hall, they saw that the other men had already put their bags near the front door. Sullivan's was a small, compact bag, while Fred Wilkins' suitcase was much larger. They could hear voices in the living room.

As they walked in to join the others, Sully was talking about possible sites near his town of Bellingham. Conversation ground to a halt as Eddie appeared in the doorway. He clearly looked worse for the wear. And of course he still had his throwing axes with him.

Alarmed, Fred stood up quickly. "Who is this? Who is this, and why does he have those... those *things* strapped on his shoulders?"

Harry spoke into the embarrassed silence. Gently and patiently, without a hint of condescension or annoyance, he reminded Fred of who Eddie was. He explained that the young man helped Joe and that the throwing axes were of use to help protect Joe.

Fred put his hand up to his head. "Oh. Yes... I'm sorry. You've all noticed. I'm... sorry. I've been holding it at bay, mostly, but it's getting worse... quickly." His face crumpled then. He sat back down, buried his face in his hands. Now Sully came to stand nearby. The engineer placed his big hand on Fred's shoulder.

"Don't worry, old friend. We're here. We're going to make sure you're okay. We're going to fly home tonight and get you settled."

Joe nodded. Eddie thought his teacher looked sad and worried and even a little tired. "Sully's right, Fred. Try not to worry. We'll see to your needs. Now hang in there a little longer. It'll be easier when we return to your familiar surroundings. I need to dash upstairs for my bag. I'll be right back.

Harry, will you call a cab for us? Three for the airport; six o'clock flight."

"Certainly, *Sensei*."

Joe was true to his word. He was downstairs well before the cab arrived. Fred's old friends gathered around him, chatting about old times, and about art and food. Eddie felt a little superfluous and moved around the periphery of the living room to pass into the kitchen. He left his throwing axes in the greenhouse and went outside to see if Lena had written.

A short note lifted his heart. Things were largely unchanged in her world. Iris' condition had stabilized. Lena was glad they were beginning to act in his world. He realized that it was not so much the information but rather the sight of the words she had written that gladdened him. He could imagine her sweet voice as he read the note.

He replaced Lena's note with one of his own. Then he went inside and washed his hands and face. He realized he was hungry and rooted around in the refrigerator for something to eat. He found some leftover chicken, green beans, and rice and heated them in the microwave.

As he ate, Eddie listened to the older men in the living room. Obviously, they were simply keeping Fred Wilkins occupied and engaged while they waited for the cab to arrive. Eddie heard the man's hearty laugh a few times and decided that their efforts were sad but, at the same time, worthwhile. Eventually, announcing the arrival of the taxi, the doorbell rang.

Eddie set down his fork and wiped his mouth. He got up to see the others out, but Sully walked into the kitchen and suggested that he wait.

"We've got Fred calmed down and comfortable now, son. It'd probably be best if he sees only Harry at this point. Explaining the cab driver may be challenge enough. We'll call you when we reach San Luis Obispo."

"Oh, okay. I understand. I just wish I had known him when he was..." Eddie's voice trailed off as he realized that he didn't know exactly how to complete the sentence, but Sully caught the sentiment.

"Yes. It's a terrible thing. Fred was sharp and witty and tough. Now... well, I suppose we should be grateful if we're merely able to see that his needs are taken care of. It is nonetheless dreadful to witness this decline."

Eddie nodded his head. "Well, Sully. Um, it has been great meeting you. And we'll see you next week in any case." He extended his hand. John Sullivan straightened, shook off his gloom and took the young man's hand in his own, sure grip.

"Indeed we will," he replied. "Indeed we will." Sullivan turned and walked out to join the others. Eddie returned to his meal. He heard the front door open and then close as Joe, Fred, and Sully left. A moment later, Ikeda joined him in the kitchen. The Aikido master poured himself some tea, heated it and sat at the kitchen table facing Eddie.

"Well, that is done. They are on their way. They will look after Wilkins-san."

"Hmmm. I guess we should call down at the police station and see when our appointment with the judge will be."

"I took the liberty of doing that while you and *Sensei* were gone earlier today. The soonest we could get on the docket turned out to be next Monday morning at ten. I suspect that the good sergeant had to call in quite a number of favors to obtain that appointment for us," Harry added. His eyes had regained their spark of good humor and there was again joy in his voice.

"Oh. So we've got a few days. What do you think we should do?"

"If you are willing, young Eddie, I would be very grateful if you would demonstrate your skill with your weapons of choice."

"Me? The throwing axes?"

Harry simply smiled and bowed his head slowly and gracefully.

"Well. Sure. I'd be glad to, but I'm sure that, well, you know..."

"Try to stay centered, my friend. You do well under difficult circumstances. I have witnessed that myself.

"You have placed your weapons near the door. I assume you intend to practice. I fancy that I am not yet so old as to prevent my appreciating a form that is new to me," Ikeda added.

"Um, okay. When?"

"Why not after you finish your food?"

So Eddie finished eating and cleaned up. He picked up the sheathed weapons and carried them to the back yard. The afternoon sun had emerged from clouds that had shrouded it in the morning, and the air carried the tiniest tang of spring to his nostrils. The makeshift target still leaned against the side of the garage. With the martial arts master accompanying him, Eddie carried his throwing axes to the opposite end of the yard.

"May I inspect one of the weapons while you warm up?" Harry asked.

That simple question stopped Eddie in his tracks. He hadn't thought about warming up. Generally he just started throwing, but he didn't want to say that.

Silently, he offered one of the sheathed axes to Ikeda and turned away. Somewhat at a loss, Eddie focused on his breathing for a few moments as he tried to get used to the fact that his audience of one had been a master of Aikido for longer than he had been alive. Then, inspiration struck.

Eddie walked up close to the target. Gently, he lobbed the axe. It flew, spun once, and stuck easily in the target. He walked over and freed it from the deeply scarred board. He returned to his spot and threw again. Alternating hands, he did this several more times. He took a handful of steps back and repeated the process.

While he missed a few times, Eddie quickly realized that this urban back yard was much smaller than Fleggie's huge salvage yard. This realization improved his confidence, and he began to relax. By degrees, he dropped into his practice. Gradually, the axe became an extension of his hand, his arm, his eye.

In this way, he worked his way back across the yard to Ikeda. By the time Eddie reached the old man, he was warmed up and feeling a little less self conscious.

"I can see that you have practiced this form for many hours. May I try?"

"Of course. And I would be grateful for any insights you might share," Eddie replied. He offered the axe that he held so that Ikeda could have two to practice with.

Ikeda faced the target. He walked closer and threw an axe. It stuck. He threw the second. It also landed solidly. He retrieved them and threw again. More perfect hits.

The Aikido master began to pace. The afternoon sun shone brightly. A few of the nearby trees showed tiny buds of life. Here and there one could observe minute green shoots, more harbingers of the spring to come.

Now the weapons flashed and flew. Ikeda walked, threw, retrieved, walked, threw again, all around the yard. Even though he threw in a relaxed manner with only moderate force, the axes embedded themselves deeply into the thick board. Even though he barely glanced at the target, the axes invariably struck at the center and at an optimal angle.

Eddie thought back to his first attempts with the knife and later with the axes. He realized then the true meaning of a master. He was in the presence of a man who had focused on martial arts for his entire, long life. The man was amazing. He possessed unaffected grace. He was powerful without strain.

And abruptly, the realization came that the man he observed with such awe was over 70 years old. Yes, Ikeda had held weakness at bay with the knowledge Joe had shared, but even so, the ability and energy of the master were overwhelming. Eddie stood in awe of the perfectly harnessed power of the older man's skill.

An expression of quiet joy illuminating his face, Ikeda walked up and returned Eddie's throwing axes with a small, formal bow. "Thank you. You have selected a good form and are progressing well. Continue to practice."

Ikeda began to return to the house. "Wait. Please. Do you have any advice? Anything that I should change?" Eddie called. "You just spent ten minutes with the axes. I've been working at this for months, yet I can't throw like you."

The older man turned back. "Under the present circumstances, I think it is best for you to continue as you are. If we lived in peaceful times, if we had years of study ahead of us, I might suggest changes. But I fear that at some point you may confront an adversary far more dangerous than a board propped against a wall. At your present level of skill, you stand a good chance of hitting that at which you aim.

"You will advance along your current path. If you would permit me, I would like to suggest some readings. It is now nearly four o'clock. You have perhaps another half hour of good light. While you practice, I will see if I might acquire the books."

"Do you want me to go with you? After last night and all..." Eddie offered.

"Thank you very much. I will be fine. Please practice. And I caution you against trying to emulate my style at this time. We will speak more at dinner.

"This has been a pleasure," Ikeda added with another slight bow. Then he turned and walked toward the house.

Eddie stood and watched the master's retreating back. In a moment he was again alone in the back yard. With Ikeda's departure, some of the light drained from the afternoon sun. After a moment's reflection, however, the young man shook himself from his reverie, took a deep breath and resumed his practice.

Of course, he couldn't completely follow Ikeda's advice. For a few minutes, Eddie tried to walk around the yard and throw the axes at the target without looking at it. The results were disastrous for the side of the garage. After an axe bounced off the target and struck sparks against the masonry wall, Eddie was reminded that if he broke a blade, he would cut his armament in half. At that point he settled down and continued practicing in his usual fashion.

Thinking of the dim, shifting light of the place between worlds, Eddie continued practicing as late winter afternoon gave way to evening. By quarter past five, however, it was too cold to be outside without a heavy coat. Eddie carried his gear into the house. He got some rags and wiped down his axes. Then he sheathed them and left them on a shelf in the greenhouse before going up to his rooms to shower and change.

When he came back down at six, he found that Harry Ikeda had returned and was in the kitchen preparing dinner. There were four slim volumes sitting on the table:

The Art of War
The Book of Five Rings
Zen and the Art of Archery
Zen Guitar

"These are all for me? Thanks! Is this one really about playing guitar?"

Haruo Ikeda laughed his merry laugh. "Indeed it is. In fact Philip Sudo's delightful book on guitar is where I suggest you start. You may discern some parallels between the forms.

"That talented man died far too young," Ikeda added more seriously, "it is good to respect his memory and his effort to contribute something of value.

"Following that, I suggest you read the other three lightly. Glance here and there, read more where something catches your eye. In the future, if things go well, you may want to study them all in more depth."

"Well, thank you, again. This is very kind of you."

"Indeed. It is my pleasure. Now, I have prepared some little thing for us to eat. I fear that I have neither the culinary grace of our unfortunate friend, Wilkins-san, nor the penchant for hearty comfort that *Sensei* so ably demonstrates. And of course my dear wife, Hiroko, can do wonderful things with the simplest of ingredients."

The "some little thing" turned out to be a very nice teriyaki chicken with stir-fried vegetables and rice. And somehow, Harry had even managed to secure some Sapporo. The presentation was simple and elegant. They ate well and long.

After dinner, Eddie insisted on cleaning up. The kitchen showed few signs that it had seen use, and wrapping up was the least he could do after being treated so kindly by Ikeda. After a brief, polite argument, Harry graciously assented.

While Eddie made short work of the dishes and the cookware, Ikeda took the opportunity to phone his wife. They chatted and joked as Eddie worked. After the kitchen was clean, Eddie waited in the living

487

room until Ikeda had finished his phone call. He began reading the Sudo book and found it immediately engaging.

"I see you have wasted no time in getting started," Harry said, when he came in from the kitchen.

"It's really good. I can sort of see how the approach this guy suggests for guitar players would apply to what I do."

Harry nodded his head and smiled. "I thought you might see the similarities. If you will excuse me, I will leave you to your reading. I would like to go upstairs and sit. This night is peaceful and suited to the pursuit of one's own thoughts with the hope of stilling a few of them."

"Thank you again, Harry."

"And you, my friend."

Eddie stayed up and read perhaps half of Sudo's book. Then he wrote a note to Lena describing Ikeda and the gifts he had given him. Finally, he went upstairs. He too, tried to sit for a time, tried to still his thoughts in their unceasing, reeling dance. There was perhaps a second of stillness, which fled upon recognition.

Forty Two

Where'd he go? Strong, happy boy with pretty girl? He has left? Why, where, when? Is this news for Queen? Is this nothing of importance? Be sure. Better to be sure. Must be sure.

Watch more, hide in deep, dark place, creep more carefully. Other agents stupid, stupid, stupid. Failed in all ways. Queen will eat them. Fear.

Watch more. Must not fail. Happy town, happy people, happy town, happy ships, happy school. Happy, happy, happy. Stupid. Boring. Stupid. No power. No ruling class. Who to infiltrate? Who to control, to manipulate? Watch more.

Hide.

Wait.

Watch.

See Pretty Girl again. Alone now, mostly. Sometimes with Old Woman. Old Woman has power, but tired now. Weak now. No threat. Hide, watch.

Oh.

Unhappy Bitch hides, spies, follows.

Something to do now.

Follow Unhappy Bitch following Pretty Girl. Hide, watch, wait.

Every day now, Unhappy Bitch follows Pretty Girl. Watches. Back and forth. All around town. To stupid park. Back. To stupid park. Back. Over and over. Good weather, bad weather. Why this same, stupid park? Always same bench. Always.

Oh.

Watch carefully. Something there. Something.

Something to tell Queen? Something to hide? Must return soon. Must have something to say. Something to keep back. Queen will expect that. Fear. Fear.

Michael C. Glaviano

Forty Three

The next days could have been dreadful in their waiting. Instead, they provided a brief but welcome respite in between actions. Whenever the late-winter weather cooperated, even a little, Eddie practiced with his axes in the back yard. He rummaged around the garage and found a file and a stone and was able to hone the blades, to restore and polish their edges.

As Joe had suggested, Eddie studied the transits. He reviewed the spells and practiced tracing the images until he could reproduce them from memory. Little-by-little, his confidence improved, and he was tempted to try some transits on his own, but the thought of encountering the Alica creature prevented him from taking the risk.

He read too. As Ikeda had suggested, he read Philip Sudo's book straight through. It was so engaging that Eddie was tempted to re-read it immediately, but he set it aside and looked at the other volumes. He read here-and-there and tried to get a sense for the subjects that were covered. Sometimes he skimmed; other times he dug more deeply. The Aikido master was both a steadying influence and a pleasure to be around.

And of course he and Lena continued to exchange short notes and longer letters. Eddie looked forward to his return to her and to his other friends. Even so, interesting and valuable studies kept his mind busy, and many hours of throwing practice focused his youthful energy in a constructive direction. So the time passed readily enough.

Sergeant Driscoll called on Saturday. She asked that they come in at eight o'clock on Monday. She had arranged it so that attorneys from the prosecution and the state-appointed defense would take their depositions prior to their going before the judge.

Eventually, Monday rolled around. Eddie found the whole legal process both mystifying and, at times, frustrating. Some of the attorneys' questions bordered on hostile, but he was mostly unfazed by it. He simply did his best to move through the day without fetching up on some unperceived snag in the current.

The time before the judge was actually easier than dealing with the attorneys. The jurist was an experienced, no-nonsense professional.

He had obviously read the police report and the witness statements and remarked on the clarity and consistency of the reports.

The attorneys made brief statements. The hearing ground along. The judge told Eddie and Harry they were free to go. It was possible that they could be called to testify at some point in the future, but given the amount of consistent witness testimony, it was likely that the accused would attempt some kind of plea-bargain.

After the proceedings, Sergeant Driscoll told them that both of the surviving assailants had been out on parole. They were already back at the state prison. The most likely outcome was that whatever plea-bargain their attorneys would be able to negotiate would be tacked onto their already significant sentences.

"So chalk one up for the good-guys. We were due, overdue even," the sergeant remarked as they walked out of the court.

"Thanks again, Sergeant Driscoll," Eddie said sincerely. He held out his hand and was surprised when the gruff, middle-aged woman knocked his hand away and wrapped her arms around him. She held him for just a moment and then shoved him abruptly away.

"Go on. Get out of here. And you," she rounded on Harry. "You see if you can keep this dumb kid outta trouble, hear?"

Without waiting for a response, she spun on her heel and strode away into the depths of the halls of justice.

Harry and Eddie met each other's gaze. Even the unflappable martial arts master was slightly taken aback at the sergeant's brief display of emotion.

"I believe that she has some genuine affection for you, my young friend. I sense that such feelings do not come often or easily to that woman. They are to be cherished all the more for it."

"Yeah. It surprised me too. Funny thing. I *do* like her. She's grouchy has hell and really tough on everybody around her – especially herself – but she just won't give up on this falling-apart mess of a city. I don't think I've ever met anyone like her, but I'm glad to know her."

"Someday, if it is appropriate and you have the opportunity, I suspect it would mean a great deal to Sergeant Driscoll if you were to let her know your feelings.

"Now, let us return to the house and begin our preparations for tomorrow's journey."

*   *   *

Upon return to the Painter Avenue house, Eddie spent two more hours practicing with his throwing axes. His form was good and he felt relaxed and accurate in his throws. He figured he wouldn't have any practice until his return, so he poured himself into his work. At the end of each session, he carefully wiped down the blades and touched up the edges.   Finally, on the evening before their journey, he carried the sheathed blades to the basement and left them at the base of the stairs.

After he cleaned up and packed, he and Ikeda shared a simple, quiet meal. Eddie thought that he might turn in early and went upstairs to read. He lay on the bed with the books. At first he skimmed here and there but after half an hour or so, he became absorbed in *The Art of War* and ended up reading until late. He woke up when the book slipped from his hands and fell on his face.

Eddie stowed the texts on the shelf next to the notes that Joe had created to teach him the portal transits. It wasn't a full bookshelf, but what was there had value and personal meaning to him. He fell asleep with his head full of new ideas and barely-glimpsed possibilities.

Michael C. Glaviano

Forty Four

The central coast of California enjoyed a climate rivaling the best parts of the Mediterranean. Winters were mild. Summers were hot and sunny. Wine grapes were the region's biggest cash crop, but there were also small farms that produced a wide variety of fresh food.

The State University at San Luis Obispo was not generally viewed as being at the forefront of academia. Nevertheless it enjoyed a solid reputation as a place where one might obtain a credible four year degree in the arts or applied sciences. A notable exception was the school of architecture, which stood out even among the top tier in the United States. Cal Poly also had a fine chamber orchestra and an excellent stage band called "The Collegians."

Over the years, the influence of the University in general and, in particular, the architecture department made itself felt in the neighboring communities. Botched facades that were tacked in place on commercial buildings during the 1950's were removed forty years later to reveal attractive architecture. By the late 1990's downtown San Luis Obispo had been largely restored. Zoning laws were enacted to slow sprawl. The city council walked a delicate, contentious balance between development and preservation. Progressive moves were balanced by an influx of wealthy retirees. They brought a strongly anti-regulation, anti-tax, and anti-education perspective to the debate.

The influx of money combined with the attempt to preserve the natural beauty of the area drove up property values. The lack of a solid industrial or high tech job base made it difficult for young people to find good paying jobs. The result of all these forces was an area that remained beautiful but which did not truly demonstrate a normal distribution of wealth, income, age, and education.

There was no major airport for two hundred miles in either direction. Therefore, to reach this oddly skewed paradise on the Central Coast, Harry and Eddie first flew into San Jose on Southwest Airlines. There, they boarded a small, dual engine turbo-prop operated by Sky West for the shorter flight down the coast.

Michael C. Glaviano

A few minutes before boarding, they phoned Joe from the amazing, money-centric, multicultural jumble that characterizes San Jose International Airport. They let him know their expected arrival time, and this allowed Joe to meet them at the little airport east of San Luis a couple of hours later. He was driving a rented Nissan Sentra.

The San Luis Obispo County Regional Airport lay southeast of the town. Highway 227 (aka "Broad Street") provided direct access into San Luis. They turned right on Buchon, right again on Johnson, and after entering a quiet residential neighborhood near the French Hospital, they finally pulled up in front of a substantial, 1920's bungalow on Cosentino Drive.

Harry and Eddie got their bags from the trunk and followed Joe to the front door. Joe unlocked the door and showed them in. The house was warm and tidy. A hallway led to the back of the house, and a stairway gave access to a second story with two more bedrooms and a bath. At one time, the upstairs bedrooms had functioned as art storage and extra studio space for Fred. Now they were mostly empty, unfurnished apart from single beds.

"Sully is out, and we're not leaving Fred alone, so he's gone too. As we'd feared, Fred didn't do anything about the grounding rod, so Sully has taken on the fabrication work. He found a welder down in Arroyo Grande who rented him shop space for the project."

"I've got bed linens and towels in the wash. There's plenty of space, so you'll each have a room. You might enjoy one of the upper story rooms, Harry. There is very nice light and one room has a built-in bench where you could sit."

"Gosh. I wasn't expecting this," Eddie remarked. "I thought from how Fred acted last week that the house would be... I don't know... not like this, anyway."

"Oh, it was a mess when we arrived. Sully and I had to stay in a hotel for the first three days. It appears that Fred hasn't been able to cope with basic housekeeping for the past several months. I found some people to come in and haul out the piles of trash. Then I got housekeepers in to clean the place. It took two solid days of work. It's livable now, but it won't stay that way if we leave him alone."

Eddie looked around and tried to picture the beautiful home filled with piles of trash. "I'm surprised he could make it all the way to your house by himself, Joe," he remarked.

"I think that for a number of years, he performed the spells of vitality and health that I taught him," Joe replied. "Over time, he let that practice slip, but residual effects remained. My suspicion is that he has been unable to perform the spells in recent months... or perhaps for years. So while he can muster himself to action for short periods, the deterioration is never reversed. It is merely held in abeyance for a time."

496

"Perhaps, at some level, he knew that he was failing. He sensed that he needed help, and when you called, he rose to the occasion for one final trip," Ikeda suggested.

Joe nodded and then continued. "Something like that is possible. In any case, Fred is happier now that he's back in familiar surroundings. I've tried to minister to him a little. I doubt there is anything that I could truly do at this stage, but he had several very lucid hours on the day after our return. We talked calmly and rationally and he mostly stayed on-topic. He expressed an understanding of his situation. Eventually, he went to one of his bookshelves, pulled out a large binder, and handed it to me."

"A living trust?" Harry Ikeda asked hopefully.

"Indeed. And there's a durable power of attorney, instructions for various scenarios involving Fred's death or incapacitation, and so on. It was drawn up by a lawyer who specializes in estate law and, blessing of blessings, is still in local practice."

"And who has power of attorney?"

"His second ex-wife. At least I think it was the second one. I think you might have met her once or twice. As was the case with most of his ex's, she's much younger than Fred. Evidently this particular parting was amicable, because the legal documents were signed well after he parted company with a subsequent spouse or two.

"The attorney has been very gracious and helpful. His legal secretary located the woman, who evidently runs some kind of high-powered consulting company in southern California. Anyway, Fred's ex is driving up from LA and promised she would be here tomorrow.

"In the meantime, I've called around town and found Fred's physician. He came over and chatted with Fred for a little while. In the past twenty-four hours, Fred has gotten worse. You'll notice right away when you see him. Although he would of course not discuss the case with us, the doctor was obviously alarmed. Less than an hour after he left, his office called to let us know that they had arranged for the necessary psychiatric evaluations. That will be tomorrow morning."

"You have been productive, *Sensei*. Clearly, Wilkins-san has been both wise and fortunate in his choice of community. We should be grateful for that."

"Yes, I suppose we should, Harry. Once again, however, I feel we're racing against a clock. The Queen has many tendrils of control in this world. We need to act and then we need to move along."

Eddie finally felt it was appropriate to ask the question that had been on his mind since their arrival. "Okay then. So, when will we try to open the portal?"

"If Sully can do his own special brand of metal working magic and brings a grounding rod back this evening, I'd like to try for tomorrow. We can do it after we drop Fred off at the psychiatric clinic. Do you remember what you need to do as you hold the grounding rod, son?"

"Well, I'd like to go over it a few more times, but, yeah, I think I remember.... The key is to stand outside the energy flow while at the same time steering and focusing it. We've never done a real portal opening in the daytime, though."

"Day or night makes no difference. I want to do this out at Montaña de Oro state park, on some cliffs that overlook the ocean. The place is a favorite of students at the university, as well as long-time residents, and having a portal open there would help more creativity flow into the community."

"If it's such a popular place, won't it be crawling with people?" Eddie wondered.

"I'd be more concerned about that if this weren't the end of winter, but I think we will be fine. The weather forecast isn't great, and classes are in session. We'll just park in the lot, cart the rod out onto the cliffs and cast the spell of opening. If no one bothers us we'll be out of there in fifteen minutes."

"And if someone bothers us?"

"That will depend on who it is. If there's a serious problem, we'll come back here and open a portal in Fred's back yard or a neighborhood park. But again, I think we'll be fine.

"Now why don't you put your bag away, get your room set up, and relax for a few minutes?" Joe added. "Sullivan should be back soon and we will be able to rehearse with the grounding rod that you'll hold tomorrow. I can put a gentle sleep spell on Fred if need be."

An hour later a minivan pulled into the driveway. It was Sully and Fred. Sully had some bandages around the fingers of his left hand, but he proudly hefted a seven foot long rod from the back of the rented vehicle. The powerful muscles in his shoulders and arms bulged beneath his shirt, but he lifted the heavy rod easily. The waiting men went out to the front yard to see what Sully had accomplished.

It was a beautiful piece of work. Three rods of re-bar had been welded together with flawless seams. The ends were bound in brass bands that had been brazed onto the re-bar. Near the center, where Eddie would hold the rod, there were alternating bands of copper and steel.

"I got a little excited and laid my hand on the rod before it was cool. Apart from that it was a piece of cake," Sully said proudly.

Fred walked around from the passenger side of the van. He appeared to be alert and happy as he looked at the others gathered in his driveway.

"May I see it?" asked Joe, reaching for the rod.

Still beaming, Sully stood the grounding rod on end and held it for Joe to examine closely.

"Still have the touch, I see. This is very fine, Sully."

Harry was smiling happily as well. "It is excellent work, my friend."

As Ikeda spoke, Fred turned and focused on his face. Fred's forehead wrinkled for a second or two and then cleared. "Harry? Harry Ikeda? My goodness! I haven't seen you in years! When did you get into town?"

Fred stepped forward and clutched Harry's hand in both of his. Then he turned towards Eddie. "And this young man! Is he a friend of yours?"

Silence shattered the celebratory feelings of a moment earlier. Joe recovered first.

"Yes, Fred. Harry's come to visit for the afternoon. He's brought a friend and student of mine with him. The young man's name is 'Eddie.' They'll both stay tonight... if it's all right with you, of course."

Fred stepped forward and offered his hand to Eddie. "All right? Of course! I'm always happy to have guests. We'll cook a big meal tonight. Something special!"

At a loss, Eddie returned the handshake. "It's a pleasure to... meet you, Mr. Wilkins," he managed.

Joe nodded his head and then turned back to Fred. "Eddie will be using this staff that you and Sully built today.

"Here, son," Joe offered to the young man. "See how it feels in your hands."

Eddie stepped forward and gripped the heavy rod, one hand above the other on the polished bands of the center section. Although it was different from the antique grounding rod that he and Joe had used for practice, this new one was solid and felt good to hold.

"I like this! It feels real now. What we're going to do tomorrow. I can hardly wait!" Eddie said enthusiastically.

"Okay. Let's get it inside. We can practice with it in the living room after dinner."

Sullivan helped Eddie maneuver the heavy rod into the house.

If Fred had been unusually lucid two days earlier, it now appeared that he was having a setback. The evening was difficult. While attempting to be unobtrusive, either Harry or Sully stayed close at hand all the time. The former gourmet chef now had a tendency to wander off with things turned up high on the big Wolf commercial stove.

In the living room, Joe and Eddie did their best to review the delicate task of managing energy flows. It was very good that they had practiced extensively in the first days back at the Painter Avenue house. There were constant distractions, and the gathering was tainted with a pall of embarrassment and sadness.

Fred came out to the living room several times as he took a break from cooking to ask if someone preferred red or white wine with his meal. Twice, he had to be re-introduced to Eddie. Once, he stared at Joe for several seconds before he was able to say his name.

Under the watchful team of Ikeda and Sullivan, dinner preparations proceeded without serious injury or property damage. The results were far from gourmet, however. Fred's former mastery of herbs, spices, and delicate sauces had abruptly deserted him. His sense of timing was AWOL. Result: The chicken was dry, the vegetables were overdone, the risotto bland. Dessert... well, Fred forgot about dessert.

The evening was not entirely devoid of joy, however. For one thing, Fred appeared to be happily oblivious to his condition. He was surrounded by patient friends who treated him with respect and kindness.

For another, Fred's former wife called while Eddie and Joe were tackling the mess in the kitchen. Before gridlock had clamped its usual hold on the southland's freeways, she'd gotten out of LA and driven up the coast as far as Santa Barbara. She had checked into a hotel, would stay the night and get back on the road early the next morning. She promised that she'd be in time to accompany Fred to his appointment with the psychiatrist.

Later that evening, Joe put Fred under a light sleep spell. Sullivan and Joe had noticed that Fred was more lucid when he rested well, as though his brain used deep sleep to push back the onslaught of plaque and damaged tissue. This did nothing to stem the tide of decline, but as a temporary measure, it offered some relief.

With Fred sleeping comfortably, the other four men were able to rehearse the opening spell without interruption. It took four practice runs before Eddie was confident of his part, but the others were patient. Joe and Eddie carried the grounding rod out and locked it in the minivan. The late winter night was cool and still. A hint of frost made the air clean and sharp in their nostrils.

*　　*　　*

Highway 1 hugged the coast. Where the terrain permitted, Interstate 101 ran along the same route. Where that was impractical, 101 moved inland to wind among rolling hills that were covered with low grasses and scrub oak, small farms and large vineyards. Santa Barbara was two hours south of San Luis Obispo.

Nadine Goodman was true to her word. She phoned from Santa Maria, just as the men were finishing breakfast. Forty minutes later, she swung her late-model BMW into the driveway next to the minivan.

"Now who could that be?" Fred wondered aloud when the doorbell rang a few minutes past nine.

"Relax, Fred. I'll get it," Joe said as he rose and strode toward the entry hall.

From his seat in the kitchen, Eddie could hear them conversing, but he couldn't make out individual words. Fred, now unconcerned, shifted in his seat and gazed out the window. A moment later, he got up from the table and poured himself another cup of coffee. He looked rested and acted slightly clearer in his thinking this morning.

Fred looked up expectantly as Nadine walked into the kitchen. He appeared confused and stood awkwardly.

"Hello, Fred. How are you? Do you remember me?" she asked in a kind, soft voice.

Fred looked and looked. His eyes filled. "Nadine? Nadine... is that you?" he asked.

"Yes, dear. I'm here. I've arranged to stay for a few days. I understand we're going to see a doctor in about an hour."

"Oh. Don't you feel well? Can I get you anything? I've missed you," Fred offered.

Now it was the woman who teared up. She quickly composed herself, however. "Don't worry, Fred. You're going to have a check up and I'm going to go with you. Just to make sure that you're comfortable."

She stepped forward and hugged Fred. Initially at a loss about how he should respond, he tentatively returned her embrace. Holding his shoulders, she stepped back and looked into his eyes.

Fred smiled back at first, but as they watched he began to drift. "I think I'd like another cup of coffee," he remarked. Eddie saw the nearly full cup waiting near Fred's plate. Fred turned away from Nadine's gaze and returned to his seat. She looked ever-so-slightly hurt for a second, but she pressed her lips together and nodded to herself.

Nadine Goodman was a trim brunette who projected an image of calm self-assurance. She had obviously been a beautiful woman when she was young, and she was moving gracefully into her late forties. Her features were kind and her eyes clear. Her clothes were tasteful and expensive looking.

She turned back to Joe. "It is good that you got involved. We'll get things sorted out for him. Now, please introduce me to your other friends."

Joe began by introducing Harry Ikeda, and Nadine brightened immediately. "I believe I met you once or twice, Mr. Ikeda. And your wife? Is she well?" Nadine remarked as she shook Harry's hand.

"Yes, thank you. Hiroko is very well. Please call me 'Harry,' if you would be so kind."

Nadine nodded and smiled.

"I don't think we ever met. Sully's my name," John Sullivan offered when he was introduced.

"It is a pleasure to meet you, Sully," she replied. "Do you live around here?"

"No. I live up in Washington State. Near the Canadian border. A place called Bellingham."

"Indeed. I know the area. Although I haven't spent much time in Bellingham, I do recall that it has a very nice historic district."

"Well, yes, it does," Sully responded with a smile.

"I like the Pacific Northwest a great deal. It's beautiful, and I find the climate serene and soothing."

"Even the storms?" Sully wondered.

"Yes, Sully, even the storms," Nadine assured him with a relaxed, musical laugh. Then, she turned to Eddie. "And I know I haven't met this young man. What are you doing hanging around with the geriatric set?" Nadine laughed.

He felt himself redden a little. Joe stepped in to rescue him.

"Eddie works for me, Nadine," the older man offered. He graciously agreed to come out to help with the situation here. He's anxious to get back to his fiancée of course, but in the meantime, he's remarkably patient with all of us geezers."

"Oh? And what's your fiancée's name?" Nadine asked.

"Lena," Eddie responded.

"A lovely name. What does she do?"

"Well, right now she's working in a bookstore. She just finished her University studies."

"Really. What was her major?"

"Um... well, it's a degree in.... applied history of commerce and economics."

"My. That sounds serious. She must be very intelligent. What school?"

"It's a small... school back east. I'm sure you haven't heard of it."

"Try me."

Eddie was at a loss. He'd never actually paid attention to the name of the school where Lena'd pursued her studies. He thought fast. "It's called 'University of the Northeastern Seaboard," he improvised.

Behind Nadine's back, Joe was grinning broadly. He was clearly amused by Eddie's discomfiture.

"Well, you have me there, Eddie. I haven't heard of it. What town did you say it was in?"

"Um. I didn't," Eddie took a breath. "The town's called Soapstone Bay."

"Hmmm. Soapstone Bay," Nadine mused. Now that sounds vaguely familiar. I have a mind for details in most things. It seems to me that Fred might have mentioned that to me..."

Smoothly coming to Eddie's rescue, Joe finally intervened.

"Well, Nadine, I think that it's time to get Fred to his appointment. I'll ride over with you. The others will follow in the van. Do you need to freshen up before we go?"

"Yes, please. But we're all going to the appointment? That is a little odd, overwhelming even," she observed.

"Oh, no. We've got an errand of our own. I want to take some... measurements at the coast. Atmospheric readings. It's a hobby of mine. If it's okay, we'll meet you back here after Fred's appointment."

Nadine agreed easily. A few minutes later they were all ready to go. Fred started to leave the house without so much as a sweater. Nadine stopped him with a hand on his arm. She looked in the hall closet and found a jacket for him.

The low-slung, black sports sedan contrasted starkly with the bulbous, white van. Joe guided Fred into the back seat of the BMW and then got in the front next to Nadine. Sully got behind the wheel of the van. Eddie was going to get in the back, but Harry invited him to ride shotgun.

"Hmmph. No offense, gents," Sully remarked as he backed out. "But it's hard not to notice that I'm driving this POS minivan with a couple of men in it, while our old buddy Joe is in the front seat of a nice set of wheels being chauffeured by a fine looking woman."

Harry and Eddie both burst out laughing. "Sullivan, my friend," Ikeda countered, "did you not notice that Nadine-san's eyes repeatedly drifted in your direction throughout her dialog with young Eddie?"

"Pretty funny, Harry," groused Sullivan. His affinity for all things mechanical evidently extended to his driving skills. With the engineer at the controls, the awkward minivan easily tracked the black BMW through early morning traffic.

"You know, I think Harry's right, come to think of it. She was sort of checking you out, man," Eddie added a minute later.

"All right. Don't you start."

"All kidding aside, my friend. Do not discount yourself. You are intelligent, fit, and personable. You could easily be taken for a healthy man twenty years your junior. The woman was indeed looking at you," Harry insisted.

Sully shrugged as he drove. "Whatever."

Ten minutes later, they pulled into the parking lot of the Central Coast Psychiatric Clinic on Higuera Street. Sully parked the minivan next to the BMW and shut off the engine. Joe helped Nadine get Fred inside. A few minutes later Joe came out and climbed into the back next to Harry.

"Everything, okay?" Sully asked.

"Oh, as well as we can hope," Joe replied. "I think Fred's in good hands.

"By-the-way. I think you made quite an impression on Ms. Goodman," Joe continued.

"Okay. Don't you start too."

"Excuse me?"

Michael C. Glaviano

"Never mind. Where're we headed, boss?"

"Get back on Higuera."

"Which way?" Sullivan asked, still rattled.

"Well, it's a one-way street. You could follow the direction the traffic's going. That's usually a good bet."

"Oh. Right."

They pulled back into traffic. Just past South Street, they merged onto Madonna Road. Eddie was fascinated by the glimpse he caught of the Madonna Inn, which Joe described as one of the great architectural calamities of the second half of the twentieth century. Traffic thinned on Madonna Road as they passed Laguna Lake park and then turned right onto Los Osos Valley Road.

"None of this development was out here when I last visited," Joe remarked. "By the time you reached this spot, you were out of the city."

The road continued west-northwest. Eventually, less-developed countryside reclaimed both sides of the road. Twenty minutes later, they reached the bedroom community of Los Osos. They took the gentle left to follow Pecho Valley Road. The sky darkened as they neared the coast.

The tract housing developments around Los Osos receded as the road narrowed and groves of eucalyptus trees pressed close on either side. Dense fog crept among the trees as the road wound through the stands. "Hey," Eddie noticed. "These trees are all planted in rows!"

"Indeed. Early last century, somebody had an idea to farm these trees," Joe answered. "I don't know the details, and I've heard multiple, conflicting stories about it. At any rate, whatever use was planned for the trees never materialized, so here they remain. It is interesting to wander among the groves on a moonlit night. The rows make it look as though every direction is 'the path.'"

The trees thinned and they reached the gates of Montaña de Oro state park. They passed a campground and the ranger's station on the left. A parking area and restrooms were to the right. A small cottage for the resident ranger snuggled into the hillside just behind the station.

"Let's continue on to one of the more remote areas. The road goes for quite a ways yet. There used to be a place to park and turn around farther along here. Go slow."

"Got it."

Sully slowed down and they took in the scenery as they drove. Several hundred yards away on their left, roughly east, they could see rolling hills. Eucalyptus rapidly gave way to well-established stands of scrub oak. Eddie rolled down his window. He could smell the trees and the ocean. On the right side of the road, tall grasses carpeted flatter terrain beyond which the sea was visible. The temperature was in the mid-fifties, Fahrenheit, but the dampness and mist made it feel a lot cooler. Even though it was mid-morning, visibility was limited. Far off to the right, a dense fog bank lurked off the coast.

"Slow down some more, Sully. Yes, this is the place I re-membered. Oh, and I just recalled something else, gentlemen. When we get out of the vehicle I suggest you stay on the ocean side of the road and watch for poison oak. The park's loaded with it, but it's much worse on the inland side of the road."

There was a small, gravel parking area and an official looking, state park-type restroom. Split rail fences funneled visitors towards trails that were described on adjacent wooden signs. There were a couple of other cars, but there was plenty of space in the lot and no other visitors were immediately apparent.

"Okay. Let's get on with it. We'll take this trail towards the cliffs. You want to help me with the staff, Eddie?"

"Sure."

They climbed out and went around to the back of the minivan. Sully popped the latch and the slender compressed air cylinders hissed as the hatch rose. Gradually feeding the weight to Eddie, Joe pulled the grounding rod from the back of the van. The rod glinted strangely in the subdued light. Faint colors and shadows appeared to chase each other along its length. Off to the west they could hear waves crashing on the cliffs. Seabirds complained overhead.

The men balanced the rod between them. They had just started toward the trail when a state park truck came around the bend. The ranger did a double take and pulled the truck to a stop. He got out but stood back by his truck.

"Good morning, gentlemen," he called.

"Good morning. How are you?" Joe answered. Eddie tried to look pleasant and harmless. He glanced over at Harry and Sully. Sully bent to tie his shoe. Harry smiled gently in the ranger's direction.

"Well, I'm fine, thank you. What do you have there?" the ranger gestured at the grounding rod.

"Oh. It's a mock-up for an antenna. I am planning to take some measurements of the electromagnetic fields along the coast. These are my associates: Mr. Jones, Mr. Takahashi, and Mr. Ross."

This was the first time Eddie had heard these names, but he nod-ded as Joe gestured in his direction.

"Are you from Cal Poly?"

"No. We're from a school back east. We were riding up to San Jose. We stayed with friends in town and they suggested we come out to look at the park. It certainly is beautiful here."

"These are public lands. You have to stop in at the ranger station to get a permit before you do any experiments or set up any apparatus," the ranger remarked. He had relaxed slightly but was still maintaining his distance.

"Oh, we're not going to take any measurements today. Again, this is just a mock-up. It is roughly the same size and weight as the actual instrument. We had it in the van and thought that since we were here, we might as well walk it out to the bluffs and see if we could manage the weight. Would that be okay? We weren't planning to set it up or leave it or anything like that."

"Well, I guess if you're just going to walk around with it, that would be okay," the ranger relented.

Harry produced a small camera from his jacket pocket. "Could we trouble you to take a photo of us? Standing around the instrument?" he asked.

"Yes, I could do that," the ranger agreed with a slight smile.

Moving slowly, Ikeda walked over to the ranger. He pointed to the top of the camera. "Please press this button halfway down to focus. Then, line us up in the view-finder and depress the button fully. Go ahead and take two or three photos, if you'd be so kind."

The ranger accepted the camera from Ikeda as Joe and Eddie got the grounding rod pointing up to the sky. The men gathered around the heavy rod with its polished metal bands. The ranger snapped a few photographs and then returned the camera.

"Okay, gentlemen. Be careful. Stay away from the edges of the cliffs. Most of them are undercut and you never know when one is going to collapse. If you decide to do any measurements or set up any apparatus, please come by the station and fill out the requisite paperwork."

"Thank you very much, sir," Harry said as he retrieved his camera.

The ranger retreated to his truck. Joe and Eddie got the rod oriented horizontally and headed toward the trail. The men waved at the ranger as they moved out. The ranger nodded back to them. "Nice touch, Harry," Sullivan commented with a short laugh.

Fifteen minutes later, they were out on the bluffs. The wind had gotten stronger, but it drove the fog toward them rather than clearing the air. The temperature fell and the air grew more damp. Eddie wished he had some gloves. The metal rod sucked the heat from his hands.

Finally Joe looked around and called a halt. Visibility tapered off to become a featureless gray wall fifty feet away in every direction. Surf hammered the cliffs below and produced a muted, powerful sound. The tall grasses of the bluffs were bent by the wind. Above them, birds called as they rode the air currents, but no other visitors were visible. The scents of salt air, eucalyptus, and damp earth underlay everything else.

"This'll do. Let's get it over with. We'll want to get out of here as soon as we finish. If the ranger sees the light flash, he'll probably be back over here to see what we're up to.

With his usual economy of movement, Joe helped Eddie stand the grounding rod on end. "Yes. That's it, son. Keep your hands roughly an arm's length apart on the staff. Focus your thoughts on how you will manipulate the flow of energy from the outside. Keep concentrating on the technique. Eddie's arms and the space between his hands formed a rough, equilateral triangle. The long, heavy object was difficult to manage, but Eddie slowed his breathing and the rod held steady.

Now Joe motioned to the other two men. Ikeda bowed solemnly. Sullivan stood still, his expression attentive and uncharacteristically serious. Each standing perhaps five feet out from him, they flanked the younger man. Joe stood in front, forming the third vertex of another triangle with the grounding rod at its center.

Joe made some passes with his hands. The sounds of the surf, the wind, the birds, all seemed to recede to a distant point beyond the cliffs. The air immediately around them grew expectant, hushed. Next, Joe reached out with his hands. His palms faced towards Sullivan and Ikeda. From the corners of his eyes, Eddie could see that the palm of Sully's outstretched right hand faced Joe's left. Similarly, Harry's left hand faced Joe's right. He assumed that their opposite hands completed the invisible circuit around the periphery of the larger triangle.

On an unspoken cue, all three of the older men chanted in unison. The words were the same as those he'd heard used in Lena's world:

> *May the gods dream*
> *May they dream of us*
> *May their dreams delight them*

The now familiar, low humming rose up around them. Directly in front of Eddie, the rod emitted a soft, barely-visible light of its own. He could feel the tingling of a subtle current in his hands. He concentrated and the current extended no further than his wrists. It was as though he had dipped his hands into a warm fluid.

The chanting continued, and Eddie fancied that he could detect a pulsing of golden light passing between the palms of those standing around him:

> *We come here reverently*
> *We come here to open a door to the place between worlds*
> *We seek to heal this world, all worlds*
> *We wish peace and happiness for all living creatures*

Now the rod was singing out several octaves higher than the low hum that emanated from the windswept bluff. The rod's glow had intensified to a bright green color. Eddie could feel the current more strongly now. He continued to concentrate, to keep the feeling in his hands and out of his arms.

Joe paused for a breath, began the final lines of the spell. Although they stood close by, Eddie could barely hear their voices as the three men continued. They chanted in perfect unison:

Now the door opens
Now the door opens
Now the door opens!

The tingling in Eddie's hands rose to a peak. The warm fluid feeling abruptly expanded into a cylinder that reached to his elbows. He sensed rather than saw the bolt of green lightning leap into the sky as a golden flash rushed down to meet it. Now he could no longer feel his hands, but he held his concentration. His eyes were closed to slits.

Eddie was disoriented at the end, unaware that the spell had finished. Gradually, he heard Joe's voice speaking in a normal tone, albeit with some urgency. The wind and the sound of the coast slammed back into them.

"Well done, gentlemen! Okay. Let's get out of here. Eddie! Come out of it, son!"

Joe shook Eddie's shoulder gently and then a little more forcefully. The young man's eyes opened fully and he let go of the rod involuntarily. With characteristically fluid grace, Harry Ikeda stepped forward and steadied the rod before it tipped more than a few degrees.

Eddie shook his head and took a deep breath. "Okay. Okay. Sorry. I'm back now. Whew! That was some charge there at the end."

"You did well, young man," Sullivan complemented him. "It'll be more straightforward the next time... Although I keep thinking that there really should be some kind of optimization we can do with this process."

"Always the engineer, Sullivan-san," Harry Ikeda added. The note of good humor and joy back in his voice.

"Okay. I repeat. We really should get out of here," Joe insisted.

Eddie nodded, but he didn't move. He looked around, drew air through his nostrils and deeply into his lungs. The air was sweet and fresh. The subdued colors of the bluffs were slightly more vivid. The aromas of life and the sea were slightly more intense. The young man stooped down and gathered a handful of the sandy soil at his feet. It was warm to the touch and it sparkled slightly in the gray light. He poured the soil from his hands back to the earth and wiped his palms on his thighs.

"There's magic," he whispered. "Not a lot, but you can feel it. There's magic in this place that was absent before."

With an effort, he brought himself fully into action. He reached for the rod. On the return to the van, the four men each supported a section of the rod. Jogging back along the smooth, flat trail, they covered the distance in a few minutes. They had the rod stored back in the minivan and were chatting quietly when the ranger came driving quickly back around the bend in the road.

"Casual. That's the tone to strike, gentlemen. Casual," Joe muttered under his breath. The ranger's truck slid to a stop in the parking lot. The man rolled down the window of the truck.

Eddie leaned against the side of the van. This time Harry bent down to tie his shoe while Sullivan waved at the ranger.

"Were you out there? On the cliffs?" the ranger called, concern in his voice. "When the lightning struck?"

"There was lightning?" Sullivan deadpanned. "I didn't hear any thunder."

"Oh. Well. Come to think of it, I didn't hear any thunder either, but it sure looked like a lighting stroke from back near the station," the ranger replied. He sounded a little unsure.

"Maybe it was just a trick of the light. The fog and all. This doesn't feel much like thunderstorm weather," Joe commented as he looked around. "Anyway, we just walked out and back a short distance. We've been relaxing here enjoying the view of the hills."

"I saw some kind of raptor. Up over that hill," Eddie added. He gestured inland. "We were hoping to see it again. Do you know what it is?" The ranger was visibly relieved, and Eddie felt a slight stab of regret at the deceit they were practicing and the worry their action had caused.

"Oh, that could be a turkey vulture," the man offered. "We see quite a few red tailed hawks too. That's the most common bird of prey around here. Did you see the tail feathers?"

"Sorry. No. There was a moment's gap in the fog just as the bird passed between those two tall hills."

"You know, we should probably be getting back to town. We want to meet Wanda and Ernie before we head north," Ikeda stated blandly.

"Oh, right you are," Joe replied. He smiled again at the ranger. "It's very pleasant out here, isn't it? Even on a gray day, there's a great deal of beauty. You notice these things as you get older."

Now the ranger relaxed into his element. "Yes, sir. We try to distinguish between entertainment and enjoyment in our parks. It is good to see people enjoying the natural beauty. So many people expect to be entertained. There's a difference."

"Indeed there is. I couldn't agree more." Now Joe sighed – a little overdone, Eddie thought to himself. "Well, I suppose we should do as Mr. Takahashi suggests and get back to town to meet with our friends. Thank you for being concerned about us."

"No problem, sir. No problem. I hope you're able to come back when you can stay longer. There's quite a nice cove up near the ranger station. People often overlook it because it's so near the gate."

"Yes, I hope we are able to see that cove as well some time. Thanks again."

Eddie and the others took the cue and moved around to climb aboard the minivan. The ranger smiled and waved as he drove back up the road. Sullivan backed the van around and they retraced their drive through the park and out to Pecho Valley Road.

Later that afternoon, the ranger drove out on his regular rounds. He stopped for a few minutes and got out of his truck to stand near where he'd had the encounter with the four men. The ranger looked around with new eyes and noted to himself that the area was particularly beautiful. The light, the sound, the breeze, all fit together remarkably well.

In later years, that area of the park enjoyed an increase in popularity. People would come and picnic and linger through long summer afternoons. Even with greater use, the area remained unusually pristine and free of trash or other refuse.

Elderly residents from the surrounding communities visited, sometimes two or three times per week. They returned to their homes feeling rejuvenated, more at peace. Many young people requested permission to marry on the bluffs, and many others hiked in on moonlight nights to make love near the spot where an unseen portal had been opened into the place between worlds.

*   *   *

The men were quiet on the ride back into town. Each dwelt within his own thoughts and feelings in the aftermath of the portal opening. Eddie again rode shotgun. He enjoyed the drive as they followed Pecho Valley Road back out to Los Osos Valley Road. When they turned briefly onto High Street and then picked up Buchon on the final leg of the return to Fred's neighborhood, he shook himself from his reverie.

"So what's the plan? What do we do next?" he wanted to know.

"I would like us to get up to Bellingham as soon as possible," answered Joe. "Again, I feel our time is limited. Ideally, we should leave tonight; although my guess is that we must wait until tomorrow."

"Fred?" Sullivan asked.

"Yes. I feel a strong obligation to stay long enough to make sure Nadine has things covered."

"I too feel that we should discharge our obligations to Fred," Harry Ikeda agreed. "He was part of our group. It is appropriate to acknowledge and honor that. And executor or no, it would be callous to drop all responsibility for resolution upon Nadine-san's shoulders."

It was about half-past noon when they pulled into the driveway at Fred's two story bungalow. Nadine's black BMW was already there. They went inside and found her sitting alone in the living room. She had nestled, one leg folded beneath her, into the cushions of the big rattan sofa. Nadine stared through the windows into the back yard but looked up and smiled at them as they arrived. It was a pretty smile, a kind smile, but it was tinged with sadness.

Joe spoke first. "So how is he?"

"Intermediate stage Alzheimer's. Entering late stage," she replied. "Somehow, he managed to hide it. The psychiatrist was quite surprised that Fred was able to function for so long. He said that it was 'really rather unprecedented.' As if that somehow made the whole thing less tragic."

Silence weighed heavily on them for a few moments.

"Where is he?" Sully asked finally.

"Oh. He's lying down. The psychiatrist gave him a sedative. From what I could gather, the testing went very badly with Fred. They only permitted me to be present at the very beginning of it, but they told me there were some parts during which he was lucid. Very lucid. Lucid enough to recognize what was happening to him. But after perhaps an hour, he broke down rapidly.

"I can't say for sure, but I suspect he didn't really know who I was on the drive back over here. Anyway, he's resting now. Which is something, I suppose," she finished.

Silence again. Finally, Joe cleared his throat.

"Well, Nadine. Thank you for taking him. With you having power of attorney and being willing to help... well, that made things go much better than they could have otherwise. The doctor would not have been able to discuss Fred's situation with any of us."

"And what is the prognosis?" Harry asked.

"The doctor isn't a hundred percent sure. Because Fred seems able to draw on some reserve inside himself and rouse himself for brief periods of clarity, it's possible that he could last a little longer before moving irreversibly into late stage. Personally, I think Fred's just been holding on until he sensed at some deep level that he could let go. I'll be surprised if things don't deteriorate quickly now."

Gracefully, Nadine stood and smoothed her dark business suit. Staring briefly into each face as if it might hold some solution to a problem or puzzle, she looked at each of the men in the room. Then she looked away, rolled her shoulders up around her neck and down her back in an effort to relieve tension that lay there.

"At the end, the doctor let me know about the best place in town – 'off the record,' of course – for Fred to be at this point," she added after another silence. "I called and made arrangements as soon as I got back here and got him to lie down. We can take him over there tonight."

She fell silent again. For just a moment she looked lonely and vulnerable. Sullivan stepped closer, held out his hand. "Thank you for taking care of him, Nadine," he said softly.

She took the proffered hand and smiled a little. "Thank you all for being his friends. I hate to think what might have happened if you hadn't called to set up this little reunion," she replied. She looked across the room at Harry and Joe as she placed her well-manicured left hand atop Sullivan's right. Lastly, she looked up into the engineer's kind face. A single tear rolled down her cheek and she stepped forward. He wrapped his free arm around her and she pressed her face to his chest.

Joe caught Harry's and Eddie's eyes and tilted his head towards the kitchen. They made for the doorway as quietly as they could, but Nadine recovered her composure quickly. She stepped back a pace.

"I'm fine. Really I am. Thank you, Sully. I just needed to be held for a moment."

"Uh, anytime... Oh, I mean... That's not exactly what I meant..." Sully stumbled over his words.

Nadine laughed then and the sad mood was broken. "I know, Sully. Thank you, again."

"Now we have work to do," she announced in a different tone of voice. This was a businesslike voice, a voice used to setting goals and having those goals met.

"Joe. Suppose you put some things together for Fred to take with him to the facility. Pack as though he were going on a vacation. Two weeks or so.

"Harry. Would you please call the attorney and let him know the status? I've already told him that if the diagnosis were bad, I'd want him to prepare papers that will allow us to get Fred's house sold. We'll place the proceeds, along with any other savings or assets, into a fund that will pay for his care. His attorney should get that going as well.

"Fred has no living relatives, no one to complicate things," she added. "From what I gather he sold much of his art collection some time ago."

She looked at the floor, or perhaps, at her hand, which still held Sullivan's. Then she raised her eyes to meet Eddie's.

"And you, young man. Can you cook? Whether or not Fred is lucid, I think we should have a final meal together with him. Something moderately celebratory but not too fancy. Can you manage that?"

Eddie nodded, as did the others.

"What would you like me to do?" Sullivan asked.

Nadine's voice softened just a little. "Truthfully, Sully, I'd like you to sit here with me for a few minutes. I don't need you to say any-thing or do anything. Just sit with me."

She paused and then added, "Then, you can see if you can find a real estate agent. We need to get this place listed as quickly as possible."

John Sullivan, named for the famous boxer, with his strong shoulders and arms and his quick wit, looked just a tiny bit like a deer in the headlights for a couple of seconds. He recovered quickly though and met the slender woman's eyes with his own straightforward, open look.

Gently, he passed her hand from his right to his left and drew her down to sit next to him on the sofa.

The others, even the ancient and powerful Giuseppe Tablarasa, scurried off to perform their appointed tasks.

Eddie spent a few minutes exploring Fred's well-appointed kitchen. It was a place to behold. Despite his own experience as a cook, he felt very much the apprentice let loose in the master's studio. He took a brief inventory of the contents of the refrigerator, the deep freeze, and the pantry. After a few moments' thought about ingredients and flavors, he began planning a menu.

Ten minutes later, Joe came in and sat at the kitchen table. He leaned on his forearms. "Well, that's done," he remarked quietly. "Is there any coffee?" he added.

Eddie had begun pulling things from the pantry. As he came back with some cans of tomato sauce and a box of lasagna noodles, he glanced in Joe's direction and was surprised at how tired he looked.

"What happened, Joe? You look really tired all of a sudden. Is this some kind of reaction to opening the portal?"

"Ah... no, son. Nothing to do with that. I'll be fine in an hour or so."

An old stainless steel drip coffee maker sat on the stove. Eddie frowned as he lifted the lid and looked inside. "Only dregs. I'll make some fresh... Oh." He had a sudden thought. "Did you do something so that Fred...?"

As if to warn Eddie off that line of inquiry, Joe gave a tiny shake of his head. Just then Nadine walked in.

"Any change in Fred?" she asked.

"Not really. He is still resting comfortably. I've packed a suitcase for him and put it by the front door."

She leveled an appraising look at Joe. Eddie was glad that he didn't have to sit beneath that gaze, but Joe just looked blandly back at her.

Nadine looked more closely. "You look exhausted. You looked fine a few minutes ago. What happened?"

"Nothing. Really, Nadine. I'll be fine in a few minutes. I'll take you up on that coffee, son, if you don't mind."

Eddie was pretty sure he knew what Joe had done and that, as a result, Fred would have another evening – perhaps his last – of lucidity. Not trusting himself to hide his suspicions, the young man busied himself with the coffee. While the water was heating, he pulled a package of ground round and another of sweet Italian sausage from the deep freeze.

"These won't be as good as fresh, but I'll defrost them gently in the microwave. We can have some lasagna. There are some nice winter greens in the fridge. There isn't any bread for garlic toast though. That sound okay?"

Joe nodded enthusiastically. Eddie couldn't tell if he was trying to distract Nadine's attention away from himself or if he was just excited about the menu. "Yes indeed. Lasagna on a winter night. I bet Fred has some good red wine too. I'll go to the store and pick up some bread. Does he have olive oil and garlic?"

"Yeah. I found all your favorite food groups, Joe," Eddie laughed. Joe chuckled in response.

"And there's some really nice looking, artisan mozzarella," Eddie added. "The only thing that's missing is the bread. If you're going to the store anyway, though, see if there are any decent tomatoes. And maybe some ricotta, okay?"

"They'll be hothouse tomatoes this time of year," Joe observed, "but they'll be better than no tomatoes at all. So bread, ricotta, and to-matoes. Got it."

The water boiled and Eddie poured it into the top section of the coffee maker. The aroma of fresh coffee drifted through the air.

Harry Ikeda came in as Joe got up to pour himself some coffee.

"The attorney said that he already has the forms made up and just needs to have his secretary fill in the blanks," Ikeda said. "You will be able to go to his office and sign the papers tomorrow at your convenience. The legal secretary will have them ready for you.

"I took the liberty of asking the attorney if he knew of any real estate people who had experience in these matters. Wilkins-san certainly has retained excellent legal counsel. The attorney transferred me to his secretary who provided us with a list of reputable brokers.

"Sullivan-san is calling them now," he finished.

Nadine nodded at this and Harry turned towards Eddie.

"Tell me, my friend. In your explorations of this well-appointed kitchen, did you chance upon any tea?"

"Yep. I just made some hot water too. Fred has some bulk tea and some bags on the counter in the pantry. What would you like?"

"I will see what is to be had."

After a quick scan of the pantry, Harry made himself some tea and was staring peacefully into the cup when Sullivan joined them.

"Well that wasn't difficult. I made a few calls. A broker will be available tomorrow. Here's the name and phone number." He handed a neatly printed note to Nadine. She glanced at it and set it aside.

"Thank you all. That went very smoothly. Now I suggest we relax and try to have a pleasant evening. I think I would like a cup of coffee myself."

Joe finished his cup and took it over to the sink. "The sooner I get to the store, the sooner I can get back and relax." He paused and then glanced around the room before continuing. "You obviously have a plan, Nadine. Do you need anything from us, or do you feel comfortable taking it from here? Harry, Sully, Eddie and I have business to transact in

Bellingham and Albuquerque. At the same time, we don't want to drop this all on you."

"Oh, please. I'm fine. As long as you're okay with it, I'll wrap things up," Nadine replied. She sipped her coffee and looked back at Joe. "Once we have Fred checked into the facility, the rest is just mechanics. I'll need to sign some papers and provide a key.

"Based on my earlier conversations with Fred's attorney, I decided to retain an estate auction service," she continued. "Some people that I know are reputable. When we got back from the psychiatrist, as soon as I got Fred to lie down, I called the auction service. They'll be here tomorrow. We won't get top dollar that way, but I don't need the emotional turmoil of running though Fred's personal belongings. Anyone have any objections to that?"

Joe was still standing near the sink. He cleared his throat. "Just a slight one. I think Fred would appreciate it if any journals or papers of a personal nature were either given to one of us or disposed of in a discreet manner."

"I can see that. Yes," Nadine agreed. "We can all look around. Perhaps we'll find something, perhaps not." Again, however, she leveled an appraising look at Joe. He either did not notice or else chose not to show that he had.

"Good. That's settled then." Joe stretched. "I guess I'll go to the store and get those items. We don't want to hold up our chef here. I think you'll be pleased at what Eddie can do in a kitchen, Nadine. He has more experience as a cook than you might realize."

She smiled then, but Eddie still thought that there was a look behind the smile. Next, Nadine turned to Sullivan. "Sully. I'd like to get out for a few minutes. Would you take me to the store? We can chat a little and do the shopping."

"Sure thing... I'd like to see the inside of that fancy set of wheels you've got parked in the driveway."

"Would you mind driving? I rarely get to relax in my own car," Nadine asked with a slight smile.

"Mind? Me? I'd love to drive that car," Sully answered with a smile of his own.

"Do you know what Eddie needs?" Joe asked.

"Sure. I was paying attention. I generally do. Tomatoes, bread for garlic toast, and ricotta. Will low fat ricotta work, Eddie?" she asked.

"Oh. Yeah. Low fat's fine," Eddie replied.

"Well then. If you'll excuse us, we'll go in search of a grocery store," Nadine stood.

She and Sullivan left a few minutes later. As if he were pondering something, Joe was quiet for a while. Then he abruptly announced that he wanted to look through Fred's books and left the kitchen.

"Do you need any assistance with dinner?" Ikeda asked.

"Oh, I can handle it, thanks. If you really want to help, I can give you some things to do, but it's not necessary, and I like to cook," Eddie replied.

"Actually, my friend, I would enjoy the peaceful movements of food preparation. You mentioned lasagna. That would imply onions and garlic. Shall I chop an onion?" Ikeda obviously wanted to participate.

"Of course, Harry. It'd be great if you wanted to chop an onion. Then we'll see what else we need to do. I'm going to begin by trying to defrost this meat gently enough so that it still tastes good."

The two men spoke quietly as they worked.

"I think Nadine suspects something," Eddie offered after a minute or so.

"Indeed. I agree with you. That is for *Sensei* to deal with, however. We merely need to wrap things up here and take ourselves to Bellingham as soon as we're able."

"Yeah. I guess you're right. Hey, what do you think we'll do with the grounding rod?" Eddie wondered.

"Now that is an interesting question. It is unfortunate that there is no one here to be its caretaker. I propose that we ship it ahead. It can go to any of our homes. Even though it would be painfully expensive to express ship it, we can send it by ground. That implies some delay in its arrival of course.

"Yeah. That'll work," Eddie nodded. "If we ship it tomorrow, we'd beat it to Bellingham, and anyway, Sully's staff should be ready and waiting when we arrive there.

"But if we ship this one tomorrow, maybe it'll get to Albuquerque in time for us," Eddie observed. "And you could always just keep it there or ship it to Joe's or back up to Sully if we needed it later."

Ikeda bowed his head in acknowledgment. The conversation passed on to other, more mundane things: the sauce, the grating of mozzarella, the preparation of salad dressing.

The sauce was simmering on the stove and the meat was cooking gently among the perfectly chopped onions and garlic when Sullivan and Nadine returned with the remaining ingredients. After the pasta was cooked and cooled, Eddie combined all the ingredients. The lasagna went into the oven, and perhaps half an hour later, Eddie began assembling the salad.

"Dinner will be ready in about twenty minutes!" he announced to whoever was in earshot. The others were having a glass of wine in the living room. He could hear Nadine say that she wanted to check on Fred. She walked down the hall, looked in on her ex-husband, and returned a moment later to say that Fred was sitting up in his room and appeared to be awake and clear headed.

"It's remarkable. He recognized me," she said. "It was almost like the 'old Fred' I knew fifteen years ago. Anyway, he says he'll be out in a few minutes."

True to his promise, Fred joined them soon after. Eddie could hear the four old friends talking in the living room. A short time later, the whole ensemble migrated to the kitchen.

"Well now. Take a little nap on a winter's afternoon, and some young hotshot takes over the kitchen!" Fred joked as he saw Eddie at work on the salad.

"That smells good. Very good. It's Eddie, right? I met you at Joe's last week." Fred held out his hand and Eddie shook it. The contrast between this and Fred's earlier condition was dramatic. Eddie glanced towards Joe. The older man was standing behind Nadine. He glanced at Eddie before turning his attention to another bottle of wine.

"We'll eat soon. Can someone set the table?" the young man requested.

"I can do that. It's the least I can do after you've taken care of feeding us!" Fred declared with a friendly smile.

The lasagna came out of the oven and rested on the stove top for fifteen minutes, during which time, Eddie wrapped up preparations by basting the sourdough French bread with olive oil and sprinkling it with garlic powder and a little salt. He watched the bread toast to perfection beneath the big broiler. A short time later they all gathered around the dining room table.

"I'd like to propose a toast to you," Fred spoke solemnly as he raised his glass. "I know that I'm failing." He gazed around the table, held Joe's eyes for a long moment before continuing. "I suspect this will be my last truly lucid evening. I've held this at bay for as long as possible and I'm grateful beyond saying for the gift of being able to say good-bye to you. A man's success is measured by his friends. I am truly rich. Thank you all."

"Well-said, my friend," Sullivan replied, his voice hoarse.

"Well-said and well-met. You have fought ably," Joe added.

Nadine swallowed. She opened her mouth but closed it again and shook her head from side-to-side. Then, for a moment, she seemed to study the clean expanse of her plate. When she raised her head, she brought her napkin up to dry her eyes and blot her cheeks.

Ikeda stood and stepped to Fred's place at the table. Solemnly, silently, the two men shook hands. Then the Aikido master returned to his seat.

"All right then. Enough of that," Fred ordered. "Let's see what young Eddie has wrought in my kitchen."

Dinner was as Nadine had requested. It was celebratory but simple. They all ate well and the robust Hearthstone Cabernet matched the hearty food perfectly. Eddie was pleased that everyone enjoyed his offering. Even Nadine helped herself to multiple servings. No one forgot the somber undertone of the evening, but the gathering remained joyful.

Near the end of the meal, Fred turned to Eddie.

"Ah... I'd like to say that I am glad that you are here this evening, Eddie. Beyond this fine meal, it comforts me to see the line continue. I am glad to see who will take up the gauntlet that I lay down. It gives me a peace you cannot know, and I salute you, young man." Fred raised his glass again and everyone around the table faced Eddie and echoed the toast.

Eddie hardly knew what to say. "Well, thank you, Fred," he managed. "I'll do my best to... to honor everyone who has gone before."

Joe cleared his throat but didn't speak. Nadine sat to Eddie's left and out of the corner of his eye, the young man saw the puzzled glance she flung in his direction. Then she gazed around the room at each of the older men. Nadine ended her survey at Joe. Serious appraisal overlaying her delicate features, she paused there before looking back at Fred.

Ignoring the unasked questions, Joe stood. "Fred, we've made arrangements for your care going forward. Even though you are feeling pretty well right now, it really would be best if we were to get you checked in this evening. Nadine will stay in town for a few days to wrap things up, but the rest of us need to get up north as quickly as we can."

"I understand completely, old man," Fred agreed. He mustered a smile. "I am holding my own right now, but I can feel the waves undercutting the cliffs."

Joe nodded. "Whom would you like to accompany you? Any or all of us would be honored."

Fred was quiet for a moment as he looked around the room. "You know, if it's all the same, I'd like to have young Eddie drive me over. That way the rest of you can remember me walking out of here, out of this house, under my own steam."

"We can make that happen," Nadine spoke, a slight catch in her voice.

"Good. It's settled then. Also, that way the rest of you can clean up," Fred added with a spark of humor in his eye. "The chef shouldn't have clean up duty after a feast like this.

"Now. Just give me a few moments will you?" he said more seriously. "You can wait out in front to see me off. I'd like to walk around, say goodbye to this house. It's been my home... for a long time."

"Of course, Fred," Nadine agreed. "Come, everyone." She led the way out the front door. Eddie stopped to grab his jacket at the entry hall.

"That's your bag in the entry, by-the-way. Joe packed it for you," she called back inside as they gathered on the deep front porch of the bungalow.

She explained the location of the assisted living and long term care facility to Eddie as they waited. It was very close by, on Laguna Seca

Drive near the French Hospital. A quarter of an hour later, Fred joined them on the porch. He had his jacket on and he carried his bag easily in his left hand. He set down the bag and one-by-one embraced all of his old friends. Then, retrieving his bag, he turned to Eddie.

"Shall we?" he asked.

"Here, Eddie. Take my car please," Nadine offered. She held out the keys to the black BMW.

Eddie nodded and took the keys. Fred walked to the car and looked back. He waved one last time and then got in. Gazing straight ahead at his home and friends, he sat in the front passenger seat. Eddie backed the car out and headed down the quiet residential street.

Fred was silent for a moment. Then he bent down and pulled something from the bag that lay on the floor between his feet. "Here you go, son," he held out a worn journal. "I don't have anyone else to give this to. It's got some of my favorite spells. There are also some notes on things I did over the years working with Joe. I think you should have it. Anyway, I hope it'll be of use to you at some point."

"Thanks, Fred. I really appreciate that. I'll look forward to reading it. Maybe someday I'll be in a position to pass it along."

"I'd like that, young man. I doubt you can imagine just how much." He fell silent again. Then he spoke one last time. "Listen. If you get a chance, tell Nadine to look for a secret panel in the base of the kitchen cupboard to the right of the sink. It just lifts up. There's a packet of letters in there for her. I owe her that much." He chuckled. "I owe her a lot more, actually. Anyway, I didn't want to say anything about it. Already too much emotion and all. Can you do that for me?"

"You bet. I'll let her know," Eddie assured him. Fred nodded then and turned away. He looked at the quiet streets of his home town for the rest of the short drive. When they reached the facility, Eddie accompanied him inside. Nadine had called ahead and the staff was ready for them.

There were of course some papers to sign. Fred waited patiently, his eyes still clear, while Eddie initialed the forms. Yes. Nadine would have to come back tomorrow to finish things up. He would let her know. No. Fred was not prone to violent or aggressive behavior. Nadine should inform Fred's physician and psychiatrist that he was now in the care of the specialists of the facility. There were a few other details.

In the end, it took only a few minutes to transform an independent adult into the ward of an institution. Meeting his eyes but saying nothing, Fred nodded one more time and shook hands with Eddie. His grip was firm, warm, genuine. Then, flanked by a nurse and an orderly, he turned and walked into the interior of the facility. As the swinging doors closed behind Fred Wilkins, Eddie caught one last glimpse of the man's back. His spine was straight and he walked with a firm step.

*   *   *

When he returned to the bungalow on Cosentino Drive, Eddie was pleased to note that the others had indeed cleaned up the kitchen. In truth, during his time aboard the *Mother Rose*, Eddie had developed the habit of keeping his galley orderly and neat while at work, so he hadn't left much of a mess beyond the dishes and utensils. Still, he felt drained by the day and was glad to sit in the living room and relax.

The room's walls were finished in a heavy plaster, and dark, polished woodwork surrounded and warmed them. The red, gray, and black geometric designs of the large, antique Navajo Klagetoh rug were accented by the amber of the original fir flooring. A few pieces of fine art, all that remained of Fred's collection, added to the beauty of the room. Overlaying all was the strong sense that they were enjoying the surroundings by the leave of an absent but gracious host.

The night was quiet. Talk was sparse and for a time centered on memories they had of Fred. The feeling of a wake permeated the mood and the tone of their voices. Eddie listened and found the stories compelling and oftentimes funny.

Eventually, however, the topic turned to what lay ahead. After a long silence, Joe looked over at Eddie. "While you were out, I made travel arrangements. There are only two flights out tomorrow, and connecting flights up to SeaTac were crowded. It took some doing, but we can all be up in Bellingham by tomorrow evening. Sully and I will take the first one out in the morning. Harry and you are on the afternoon flight."

"Oh, okay. What time do I leave?"

"Your flight out of here is at one o'clock. You have an hour and a half layover at SFO. Sully and I, on the other hand, will get to cool our heels in the south bay for three hours, so we should all arrive at SeaTac within the same hour – if the flights are on time."

"Several shuttles run between the airport and Bellingham," Sullivan added. "If traffic around Seattle isn't too much of a disaster, we can get from the airport to my house in about two hours.

"...of course it's nearly always a disaster," he sighed. "At least I can put us all up. I've got a guest room with a couple of twin beds in it, and the sofa in the living room makes up into a bed. It's a little spartan, but it'll do for the short time we're there," he finished.

"It appears that tomorrow will basically be a travel day," Ikeda summed up the plans.

Nadine sat on the big rattan sofa next to Sullivan watching the back-and-forth between the men. Finally, she spoke up.

"So, I have to ask. What's the rush? Do you *have* to get to Bellingham tomorrow?" she wondered.

"We don't have to exactly," Joe answered, "but I would like us to get to Harry's place near Albuquerque before too much more time passes."

She nodded at this. Clearly she wasn't satisfied with Joe's answer, but she chose not to pursue the topic. She stood and stretched a little.

"Well, I'm going to check into a hotel for the night. I suppose I should get busy on that."

"A hotel? Why don't you stay here?" Sullivan asked.

She smiled tiredly at him. "Under other circumstances, perhaps, Sully. But there are too many memories here. Fred's absence is itself a presence, if you know what I mean."

"Oh. Of course. I'm sorry. I didn't think... sometimes, I'm so clueless," looking embarrassed, Sullivan trailed off into silence.

"Don't worry about it, Sully. We'll talk tomorrow."

As she turned to go, Joe stared intensely at Sullivan and angled his head in Nadine's direction. At first Sullivan looked bewildered. Then his face cleared.

"Um, can I walk you to your car, Nadine?"

"Yes, please, Sully. That would be good," she replied.

When they had gone outside, Joe picked up the thread of the conversation. "Okay then, gentlemen. First thing tomorrow we'll get the grounding rod shipped to Harry's. Then we'll return the minivan. I've already arranged with the rental car agency for Harry to turn in the Sentra tomorrow."

"I cannot know what Nadine-san has learned regarding the nature of the cosmos and the situation of this world, but she was close to Fred for some time, *Sensei*. She clearly suspects something," Ikeda spoke softly, with the tiniest undercurrent of mirth in his voice.

"Indeed she does, but she'll be occupied here for a couple of days at least. Best case, by the time she's freed up, we'll be in Albuquerque at your place, Harry. We might even be back at our respective homes by the time she gets out of here."

They heard the sound of the front door opening and closing then and Sullivan came back into the living room. "She is one fine woman. I hope I can get to know her better when things settle down again."

"I hope you can too, Sully, but don't count on things settling down too much," Joe replied. "I think we're going to be pretty active for a time."

Harry Ikeda shook his head. "My friends. I feel we bear some responsibility for this state of affairs. We were inattentive. We withdrew into our comfortable corners of this world. Now we must make amends."

"It is I who was remiss," Joe argued gently. "I see it now. I became tired... or perhaps complacent. Yes, I can go on and on, but there is a danger in that. I began to realize it last year. It is clear that I..."

Just then the doorbell rang, followed by heavy pounding on the front door. Joe looked up sharply, squinted in the direction of the front entry. "Stay out of direct view from the door, gentlemen. All of you," he ordered.

He got up and went to the door. The voices were loud, and Eddie, Ikeda, and Sullivan could hear most of the conversation.

"Are you Fred Wilkins?"

"No. I am a friend of his, he –"

"We need to speak with Fred Wilkins."

"I'm sorry. He's not here."

"Then what are you doing in his house?"

"We came here together. Fred became ill shortly after our arrival. Tonight he checked himself into a custodial care facility near here. I can provide you with the name of the facility."

"You didn't answer my question. If the owner is not here, then what are you doing in his house? Is anyone else here with you?"

"Yes, officer. Some of his friends are here. His ex-wife has power of attorney over his estate and control over Fred's medical treatments."

"Is she here?"

"No, she is staying in a hotel. We're watching over the house until tomorrow. Then she will stay until she can wrap things up with his estate and make sure –"

"This is pretty convenient. Wilkins is not here. Neither is the person you claim should be in charge. How do we know that you're not planning to empty this house out tonight? Do you have anything to say that will convince us that we shouldn't bring you all in for questioning?"

Eddie, from his vantage point in the living room, could see a deep golden light begin to pulse from the entry hall. Simultaneously, he heard Joe's voice call out.

"Eddie! Call 911. These aren't police!"

Sully stood and began to edge silently toward the front door. Ikeda waited as Eddie dashed through the dining room and into the kitchen. Then the Aikido master quickly followed and took up a position in the kitchen doorway across the entry hall from Sullivan.

Eddie grabbed the phone off the wall and punched 911. The dispatcher answered on the second ring.

"Hello. We're taking care of a house for a friend. Some people just showed up claiming to be from the police department. We think they're impersonating officers to gain entrance. Yes. Consentino Drive. Yes, Fred Wilkins' place. That's it."

Eddie hung up and took a deep breath. Now there was a deep humming sound emanating from the entry hall of the house. Alert and still, Ikeda stood with his back to the young man. Eddie glanced past the Aikido master to where Joe stood in the entry hall. Beyond Joe, Eddie could see Sullivan at the mouth of the hall that led to the bedrooms. Only Joe was visible from the front door, but Sullivan and Ikeda both had their hands outstretched. It was similar in some respects to the portal opening, but there was a lot of power flowing out, towards the front door.

Now, in the distance, Eddie could hear a siren. It was getting nearer.

"Hold, gentlemen. They can't move while we keep this up. That's it, hold," Joe's voice was mild, almost conversational, but Eddie could see sweat beading at his temples with the effort of the spell.

"We'll release these men the instant the real police pull up," Joe continued, voice still calm. "Hold. Stay shielded behind the walls, please. There will be a couple of seconds during which they may be able to move. Keep holding... a little more... Okay. Now! Release."

The pulsing light stopped and the sound trailed off as Eddie heard a car screech to a halt at the foot of the driveway. A second later another car pulled over across the street. Doors slammed.

"Hold it! Everybody freeze! Don't move!"

Heavy footsteps ran up the driveway.

"I said freeze! Watch it! That one's got a gun! Damn!"

There was the sound of a shot from a heavy caliber hand gun and then another. Then there was a soft impact and the sound of a body hitting the pavement.

"Get back, sir. Get back!"

Joe stepped back and moved around the corner to stand near Sullivan. More heavy feet, closer now. Then some scuffling and loud cursing. Eddie was dying to see what was happening, but he knew better than to step out into a potential line of fire.

An engine revved and tires spun as a car accelerated. A siren blared again and a second later there came the crunch of an impact. Then the sounds of more struggling and cursing came from the street.

Eddie could hear the police in the second car calling for more backup.

"Okay. We got 'em! Are you all right sir?"

Joe looked tentatively around the corner. "Certainly, officer. Thank you for getting here so quickly."

"Who called us in?"

"Oh, that would be my assistant, Edward. I asked him to place the call. Something was just not right with these two."

"Your suspicions were correct. These guys are packing some heavy weapons. There's a third one that was waiting in a car across the street. Definitely not one of ours. We got him when he took off after ramming our second patrol car. You took quite a risk knocking that one out!"

"Well, I didn't feel that I had a choice. When he turned toward you and raised his gun, he gave me a clear view of the back of his head. It

523

really was just a matter of hitting him as hard as I could," Joe remarked. "I was concerned that you would be reluctant to return fire with me standing there, and I knew that he could turn back around and fire in my direction at any second. So I hit him."

To Eddie it sounded as though Joe were describing a play at an afternoon baseball game. He wondered if the police found it odd that the older man was so cool under fire.

"So may we come in? We'll need to get statements."

"Of course, officer."

The San Luis Obispo police officers were professional and thorough. They impounded a white Ford Taurus that the three police impersonators had used. They asked questions of all four men independently.

As soon as they learned of her role in the situation, the officers called Nadine on her cell phone. Looking worried and exhausted, she returned a few minutes later. She had barely reached her hotel. When Nadine arrived, the police took down the numbers of Fred's attorney and the facility where Fred was receiving care.

Finally, they brought everyone back together in Fred's living room and the OIC at the scene asked if anyone had an idea why they had been targeted in this way. Nadine spoke up clearly and authoritatively.

"Well officer, San Luis is a small town. I suspect that word has already gotten around about Fred's condition. This is a nice house with fine furnishings. That rug alone," she indicated the roughly ninety square feet of hand-woven Navajo art that lay near their feet, "is worth over $16,000. Fred is known in the community as a collector of fine art. Most likely, they have been watching the comings and goings and decided to make a move."

Now the OIC looked thoughtful. "But why not wait until you all had left?"

"Perhaps it is a coincidence, but an auction company is coming tomorrow to clear out the home. The art, the collectables, and the expensive furnishings will all be gone," Nadine answered.

"Makes sense, I guess," the OIC agreed. "Okay. This gives us some leads. Whoever these people are, they're well organized. Since one of them actually fired on us, all three resisted arrest violently, and all three were wearing fake uniforms, we'll almost certainly be able to get convictions at the felony level. So even if we can't track down the organization, we'll at least get these three off the street."

Finally, the officer stood. "Well, I believe we have enough information for this evening. We will post an officer outside for the rest of the night. He can get someone to follow you back over to your hotel if you like," he said to Nadine.

"Here's my card. If you have any other ideas, I hope you'll contact me," he added.

Nadine stood and took the card. She shook the OIC's hand. The rest of the men also stood up.

Joe escorted the officer to the door and returned to find Nadine still standing.

"So, this isn't about art is it, Joe?" she asked.

"I beg your pardon?"

"This isn't about art, and I really doubt the police are going to find that any of those leads turn out to be fruitful."

"Well, Nadine, I can't say for sure."

"Oh, please. I was married to Fred, remember? He and I stayed in contact for years after we split up. Yes, there were problems due to Fred's womanizing... and of course I couldn't pursue my career in this little town. That was the story we agreed to tell. But underneath everything else, I knew, I *knew* something was going on that smacked of metaphysics.

"And I don't mean your garden-variety, county fair type of mumbo-jumbo either. Something real. Something powerful. That was okay, but he wouldn't trust me. Wouldn't tell me what was going on. And after a while, I became frustrated with the whole thing, so I left.

"Then tonight at dinner there were those cryptic remarks Fred made about 'picking up the gauntlet' and the 'line continuing.' What's that about? Now I've probably committed a felony by sending the authorities on a wild goose chase so you'd have more space to do whatever it is you four are doing. So what is it?"

"Nadine, I don't think you'd believe me if I told you."

"So try me."

They stood there, eyes locked. The woman was not angry, but she was clearly very determined. Joe considered her for what seemed a long time. Then he shrugged.

"Very well. I've... checked up on you. I know I can trust you. And Sully, here is a great judge of character. I know he's in your corner. He's been arguing on your behalf every time we've been alone for five minutes today."

"Indeed I am, Joe. I recommend her in the strongest terms. I –"

Joe held up his hand. "I know, Sully. I know, and I value your judgment." He turned to the Aikido master. "And you, Harry. What do you say?"

"*Sensei.* The decision is yours, but I am confident that Nadine-san is an honorable, strong, and intelligent woman. You said yourself that you must begin to hand over the defense of this world to others. Why not include her?"

Joe sighed a deep sigh that translated into, "So be it."

He continued to hold Nadine's gaze, but now there was less intensity in his look.

"It's late. Come back first thing tomorrow. Be here early. We'll talk, and we'll see if you really want to get involved."

Nadine nodded, satisfied for the moment. "That will work. I'll be here first thing. Anything else for tonight? Anything you'd care to tell me?" The woman picked up her coat and draped it over her shoulders.

Joe shook his head. He glanced at Eddie. "Do you have anything to add, son?"

Suddenly Eddie remembered Fred's last instructions. This was as good a time as any to mention it.

"Um, Nadine. I just remembered. When I was driving Fred over, well, he said that he left some letters for you. Said he owed it to you. You may as well take them tonight. Maybe there will be something in it that explains... all this... Or not. Anyway, if you want I can show you."

She turned her head to meet Eddie's eyes. "Okay. Let's see what he left. Is it close by?"

Eddie went into the kitchen with the rest of them trailing behind. As Nadine and the others watched, he knelt in front of the kitchen cabinet that Fred had mentioned and opened the doors. There were several casserole dishes and baking pans on the bottom shelf. Once he had pulled the dishes from the cabinet, he could see that the shelf had been notched so someone could grip it and pull it out of the cabinet.

He drew the shelf out and saw there was indeed an oilskin packet lying on the exposed sub-floor.

"Here you go. It's even got your name on it."

She looked down at the packet. Eddie was standing close and he saw a shadow pass across her face as she read her name, scrawled in Fred's handwriting, on the cover.

"Thank you, Eddie," she said quietly after a moment. Sullivan stepped up to help as she pushed her arms through the sleeves of her coat. Nadine hugged the packet to her chest and strode towards the entry hall.

"I'll see you all in the morning. Would you walk me to my car, Sully?"

A few minutes later, Sullivan was back. The men stood around the kitchen.

"I would like to take the precaution of phoning Hiroko. I shall suggest that she check into a hotel at least until we can assure ourselves of her safety," Ikeda announced.

"I agree. They may have simply noticed our activities today and acted without planning or coordination, but it's equally likely that they traced us here, so they probably have some idea who is involved."

"And tomorrow will be filled with activities. It will be tiring. After I speak with my wife, I think I shall sit for a time and then rest," Ikeda added.

"Good idea," Joe replied. "I have a great deal to consider. Clearly, the Queen's agents are abroad. They have detected us, but the hapless three who came here tonight will be out of commission for a while at least. The big question is whether they have reported back to her or not.

"I think we must figure out a way to move faster, to keep them off balance if possible... And Sullivan..."

"Yes, Giuseppe?"

"As soon as you can, please turn that formidable intellect of yours onto the problem of figuring out an excellent place to open a portal in your town... and in getting us back on airplanes and on our way to New Mexico all in the same day."

"Got it, boss."

"Oh, and Eddie. Fred told you about that packet of letters for Nadine. Did he say why he didn't mention it himself sooner?"

"Yeah. He said there was enough emotion already... or something like that."

"Makes sense. Did he give you any indication of other documents?"

"Well, he gave me an old notebook of his. Said it had some of his favorite spells and he wanted to pass it along. Why? Do you want to see it?"

"As long as you have it that's not necessary. I just don't want anything like that to be left behind. Keep it safe, okay?"

Eddie nodded. "I plan to do just that, Joe."

"I'll look around tonight while the rest of you sleep, but I suspect that Fred took care of everything else himself.

"Well. That's more than enough for now, gentlemen," Joe observed. "I'll see you all bright and early."

Eddie realized that the events of the day had wiped him out. He took himself to bed. For a while, the evening's events spun around in his head, but even the excitement of the confrontation with the agents of the Locust Queen could not keep him awake for long.

*   *   *

The next morning, Nadine rang the doorbell at seven o'clock. She looked fresh and rested. Joe let her in. The night had erased any signs of fatigue in the old partisan, and he looked the same as usual. Eddie, Sullivan, and Ikeda were in the kitchen finishing up breakfast.

She had Fred's packet of letters in her hand and gestured with it as she followed Joe into the kitchen. "So is this all true?" she wanted to know.

"Well, I haven't seen it, so I can't say for sure, but my guess is that whatever Fred described was the truth as he understood it," Joe replied.

"I'm talking about this 'Cosmology of the Great Wheel,' this notion of parallel worlds, this 'place between worlds' that is like some kind of hub with an untold number of earths all touching it to varying degrees."

"Yes, that's all true," Sullivan answered.

"Thank you, Sully. And this 'Locust Queen?' She's real too?"

"Sadly, yes. She and her minions do great damage. Their appetites are insatiable. They practice evil for evil's sake. And they are abroad in this world," Ikeda replied.

"And it was most-likely the Queen's agents who were at the door last night."

This time Eddie replied. "Yeah. It was them."

"Okay then. Thank you all for your candor. This... 'world view,' I'll call it is a lot to accept all at once. A lot to digest. But assuming it's all as you say it is, what do we do about it?"

Joe held up his hands, palms out. "Stop. Hold on just a moment, please. There is much to learn. You cannot merely 'do something.' We took an action yesterday that drew the attention of some of the Queen's agents. They may or may not have reported back to her home world before acting."

"What action did you take?" Nadine wanted to know.

"Let me try to explain, okay?" Eddie requested. "Each time I go through it, things become clearer in my mind. It's helping me learn."

"Of course, son. You talk. We have to get the grounding rod down to the UPS office anyway. They open at seven-thirty and it's down on Lower Higuera. Harry and I will take it. You two stay here and answer Nadine's questions."

Eddie nodded. Joe and Ikeda left.

"What are they going to do?" Nadine asked.

Sullivan spoke up. "Oh, we use an artifact to help focus the energies and punch through to create a little connection to the Place. We call the artifact a 'grounding rod.' Harry, Fred, and I were each supposed to have one made. Fred wasn't able to make that happen, so I took care of it when we arrived. Now we can't leave it here, so we're going to ship it to Harry's home in New Mexico. We'll figure out what to do with it when we get there."

"So that's what you all did yesterday when I was at the psychiatrist with poor Fred."

Eddie nodded. "Yeah. We went down to the state park and opened a portal on some bluffs that overlook the ocean."

"A portal? That sounds like a 'door.' Can you use it to move between worlds?"

"Uh, no. I don't think so, anyway. Well... I guess Joe could. He could probably just punch himself through anywhere, but I couldn't. This is just a tiny gap that'll let magic flow back into the world."

Eddie began describing the connections between the Place and the worlds on the hub of the Great Wheel. He explained why those connections were important and why the Queen tried to cut them off.

Nadine listened to Eddie for a few moments before she spoke again. "That portal you opened yesterday. Will it last, or will the Queen's agents seal it off?"

"Oh, it doesn't work exactly like that," Sully explained. "Once the portal is established, it withers or thrives largely due to what goes on around it. I mean they could seal it off, I suppose, but it would be harder than what we did yesterday. This place is popular with students at the university. Campers, hikers, and picnickers all visit the area.

"It's perfect," Sullivan continued. "It was already a beautiful spot. Now it's also got this magical feeling. In fact, things you would consider to be 'magic' will soon begin to work in its vicinity."

"What next?"

"We're going to go up to my town. I've figured out an appropriate place to open another portal, I think," Sully continued.

"I want to help, Sully. What can I do?"

"I'm not sure yet. Joe will think of something."

"So what about him?"

"Joe? Well, he's sort of the leader, I guess you'd say. And a teacher to us all. He's..." Sullivan's voice trailed off.

"I think we should just tell her, Sully," Eddie spoke up. He looked earnestly at the woman. "This part is pretty weird, Nadine, but well, Joe is really old."

"Old? What do you mean? He looks healthy enough."

"No. I mean really old. Several hundred years at very least. Lots of times I think that estimate's ridiculously low."

"Oh. And the rest of you?"

"I'm what I look like. I turned twenty-one last May," Eddie offered.

"And I'm, well, I'm a little older than I appear, Nadine. You see, Joe has taught Harry, Fred, and me certain techniques. If we practice them regularly, we can hold old age and senescence at bay for a long while," Sully admitted.

"I see..." Her voice trailed off. Then she spoke sharply, "So. What happened to Fred? Is it something to do with these... activities?"

Sullivan shook his head. "I'm not sure what happened, but my guess is Fred didn't follow the practices rigorously. You know how he is. Undisciplined; hates routine. And there's something else."

She smiled wryly and a little sadly at this. "And what's that?" she wondered. "What else is there?"

Michael C. Glaviano

"Well, for example, I have a grown daughter, you see. Married. Has a family. Things are starting to get strange."

"Strange? How so?"

"Well I haven't aged significantly in twenty-five or so years."

"That's a wonderful thing."

"Ah, from my point of view, certainly. But you see my wife –"

"You're married?!"

"Widowed. More than ten years ago."

"Oh, sorry, Sully. I didn't mean that the way it sounded –"

"Never mind now. If we work together, you'd learn about it sooner or later.

"Anyway, my wife was devoutly, conservatively religious. When she learned about Joe, she almost left me over it. She was a good and kind woman, but in this there was no reaching her. In fact, the trouble Cindy and I had might have factored into Fred's own secrecy with you. He sure was aware of the problems.

"Anyway," Sullivan continued, "my wife was adamant. She forbade me to see Joe or to speak with him. My daughter knows nothing of him or of my work with him.

"Now my daughter has adopted her mother's world view. She and her husband follow a very strict code of beliefs that has no flexibility. Has no way of admitting a truth that lies beyond doctrine. Even though there is ample room for religious belief to fit within the context of the Great Wheel, certain groups will not learn. Will not ask the right questions. They simply reject.

"Sadly, such people are ripe for manipulation by the minions of the Queen," Sully finished. He fell silent and looked down at the floor.

Nadine considered all this for a few moments. "I think I see. At some point, you're going to have to fake your own death, aren't you? It's either that or simply let yourself die in actuality."

Sully swallowed and nodded. He covered his unhappiness by taking a sip of his coffee.

Eddie picked up the thread. "Joe stayed up and thought about this last night. He hardly ever sleeps, by the way. Anyway, we guess that Fred just loved this place, loved this life he'd built for himself so much that he didn't want to let it go. Didn't want to let go of the community of friends."

But for the sound of the dishwasher, the kitchen became silent for several minutes. Finally, Nadine spoke up. "Well. Again, this is a lot to digest. It sort of takes your feet out from under you at first, doesn't it?"

"Yeah. But you get used to it. It's strange, but at the same time, you meet all these great people."

"Your girlfriend?"

530

Eddie nodded. "She lives on another world. Near this one on the hub. Her world is in a lot better shape though. I have other friends there too. We opened a big, stable pattern of portals there that we hope'll set the Queen back for a while – maybe a long time. Then Joe and I returned to try to make things better on this world."

"So now you're going around in this world, opening these portals?"

"Right. We're going to Bellingham tonight. And then we're going to meet in New Mexico near where Harry lives with his wife."

"You'll recall I mentioned meeting her. Does she know?"

Sullivan nodded. "Hiroko knows and understands. And accepts. She sees how her and Harry's beliefs fit into the way things are. Sees the battle for what it is. I don't know about their son, though. Whether or not he knows, that is."

"Very good. Thank you both. I think that's enough information for now. I'll see if I can pull this whole thing together in the next couple of days and meet you at Harry and Hiroko's house.

"In the meantime, Sully, would you be so kind as to walk me around the garden? It's still slightly cold out, but the sky is clear."

"I'd be delighted, Nadine."

While Sullivan and Nadine walked together in the back yard, Eddie finished packing. Shortly after, Harry and Joe returned.

"Where's Sully? Is he all packed?" Joe asked as he came in.

"Sully's right here. I'll be packed in a couple of minutes," the big engineer answered as he and Nadine came in from the back yard.

"Good. I want to get over to the airport and get the van turned in as soon as we can."

The rest of the morning became a flurry of activities as phone calls dealing with Fred's estate, final packing, and another visit from the San Luis Obispo police department all vied for attention.

Soon enough, however, Sullivan and Joe were ready. Nadine walked them out. "Unless you hear otherwise from me, I will see you in New Mexico day after tomorrow," she assured them. "I'm bringing my staff in on this business with Fred's estate. My priority for now is learning how I might fit into the struggle that occupied so much of Fred's life."

"Be sure, Nadine," Joe cautioned. "This can consume your life. And I cannot guarantee your personal safety."

The woman looked levelly at him. "For my whole life, I've pushed and pushed," Nadine replied. "I've built a successful business. So successful that I have a constant stream of companies that want to buy me out. I can afford to take a couple of weeks and see if this is something I want to take up. If it is, you can be sure that I'll bring something to the table."

"I'm sure that you will. But as I told young Eddie last year. Once you've had a taste of this, you'll find it hard to go back. Just be as sure as you can be."

"Indeed. I will see you in a few days. We can discuss this more at that time. Have a safe trip, both of you."

Joe nodded finally. "Very well. We'll look forward to seeing you. In the meantime, please be careful. Vary the ways you travel to and from your destinations. Don't stay in the same hotel two nights in a row. Just assume you're being watched. I sense no nearby threat, but that can change."

"He means it, Nadine. Please be careful," Sullivan added. Nadine stepped forward and hugged the big engineer one more time. She released him and nodded.

"I understand... and will be careful. See you soon."

Joe and Sullivan climbed into the minivan and left for the airport. Nadine drove over to the assisted living facility to sign the remaining papers.

There was little to do for the next couple of hours. Eventually Nadine returned. She got on the phone right away with her offices in southern California to bring her considerable resources to bear on the problem of making sure Fred's remaining years would be as comfortable and trouble free as possible.

When she hung up the phone, she came into the kitchen. Eddie and Harry were all packed and were having a snack before leaving for the airport. She joined them at the table.

"It's going to be strange here once you two leave," she remarked.

"You know I asked to see Fred when I went by the facility," she continued. "It took him a few minutes, but he managed to remember me. At least I think he did. I couldn't be completely sure, and I have no doubt that he won't by this time next week. I probably shouldn't have done it, but I just couldn't go over there and not look in on him."

"That is understandable, Nadine-san. It is fortunate that you will be able to finish these obligations soon. This house is full of ghosts."

"Yes." She glanced at her watch. "Well, if they're on time, the auction people will be here any minute. Shouldn't you be heading out?"

"Yeah. I guess so. Shall we go, Harry?"

"I think so." Ikeda turned back to Nadine. "We will look forward to seeing you soon," he added. His voice was calm and encouraging.

Nadine walked with them to the door. "Oh. This is good timing," she remarked. A large van from Fransen's Estate Auctions drove past the house, stopped, and backed up. They walked out to the curb as the driver came up the driveway.

"Is this the place?" he asked.

"Yes, indeed it is. Let me move my car and you can back in. Then we'll go through the home and mark everything you are to take. Will you be doing the estimates yourself?"

"Naw. My supervisor should be here in a minute. He's the one you probably talked to on the phone."

"Good."

After a final good-bye to Nadine, Eddie and Ikeda got into the Sentra. As they prepared to pull away from the curb, a silver Cadillac CTS pulled up and parked across the street. A portly gentleman wearing a somewhat rumpled brown suit climbed out to waddle across and shake hands with Nadine. Instinctively, Eddie used the seeing spell. The man was no more than he appeared.

"Yes, you grow cautious. That is prudent," the ever observant Ikeda commented. "Look around, my friend," he remarked as they drove away. "It is not likely that we will have occasion to visit this neighborhood again soon if ever. So flows the stream of time."

Michael C. Glaviano

Forty Five

In the subsequent hour, they returned the car and checked in for their flight. The security checkpoint was not very crowded in the small regional airport. Then began the start/stop/hurry/wait sequence of events that defined air travel in that time and place. Some hours later, tired but not too worse for the wear, they met up with Sullivan and Joe at SeaTac.

"Flight uneventful, I take it?"

"Yeah. It was okay. What's the plan?"

"Well, I've secured a rental van for us," Joe announced. "That'll work better than a shuttle if the goal is to finish our business and get out of here ASAP. If at all possible, we're going to take care of our activities early in the morning and catch a flight out of here tomorrow afternoon. Sullivan called the machine shop from the San Jose International. They promised to deliver the grounding rod to his daughter's house. So if we can get up there in a reasonable amount of time we should be able to take care of this before the Queen can track us."

"Did you make reservations?"

"No. That's the next thing on the list. Shall we proceed, gentlemen?"

They collected their bags and wound their way through the crowds to the Southwest Airlines counter. The mid-afternoon flight out of SeaTac had plenty of empty seats, so they made their reservations on the spot before returning to the Avis desk. They completed that transaction, collected their paperwork and followed the skyway over to the lot where their vehicle waited.

"This'll do. It's nondescript and new. They just aren't that much fun to drive though," Sullivan remarked. As usual, Joe had made the engineer the primary driver.

"Sit back and relax, gentlemen," Sullivan continued. "Depending on the degree that Seattle traffic imitates the lower realms of Chaos, we should reach Bellingham sometime in the next two to four hours. If anyone needs potty or food breaks, talk to the management."

Joe snorted a short blast of something that passed for laughter as Sullivan guided the van out onto the airport access road. Fifteen minutes later, they were heading north on I-5 towards Seattle. Ten minutes after that, they were sitting in bumper-to-bumper traffic.

They stopped in Edmonds for some questionable pizza before continuing up to Bellingham. Sullivan called his daughter's house and spoke to his son-in-law. Yes, the metal thing had been delivered. It would be waiting in the back yard.

It was nearly eight o'clock when they finally pulled up at the house where Sullivan's daughter lived with her husband and their family. Most of the street-facing side was taken up by a three car garage. A Ford Expedition and an F-250 long-bed consumed the driveway. Eddie jumped out of the van and accompanied the older man up to the front door. They edged around the back of the massive vehicles and followed a narrow walkway up to the front door. The glow of a big screen television shown through gaps in the drapes of the front room of the house.

Sullivan rang the bell. A moment later the porch light came on. A man, Eddie guessed it was Sullivan's son-in-law, opened the door a little and peered out at them through the screen door.

"Oh, it's you," he said. He glanced in Eddie's direction and then back at Sullivan.

"Yes, Ted. I've come for my metal work."

"Like I told you on the phone. It's in the back."

"I just wanted to let you know I was here. Are you all doing well?"

"Yeah. We're fine. Now we're sorta busy, so if you don't mind...?"

"All right. Good night, Ted. Please give my regards to Darlene and the children."

The man closed the door and shut off the porch light. Sullivan sighed a little and turned away. He motioned to Eddie to follow him. They retraced their steps with only the glow of the street lamps to guide them and then worked their way past the big vehicles to the opposite side of the garage. The night sky was cloudy, and it was hard to see along the side yard. Eddie tried casting his beam of light spell, but it didn't work.

Sullivan tripped as he negotiated a cluster of trash cans. With a clatter and a whispered expletive, he recovered his balance. A dog began barking across the street. They reached a gate and Sullivan fumbled around to find a latch.

"The gate opens out, Eddie, so we'll have to step back." The gate sagged against the hinges as Sullivan pulled it towards him. They moved into the back yard. There were various indistinct shapes in the dim light. These resolved themselves as the moon came out from behind some clouds: play equipment, plastic toys, patio furniture, a huge gas barbecue.

"Ah! There it is," Sullivan observed.

536

The grounding rod located, the men each took an end of it and quickly maneuvered the heavy object out of the yard and onto the drive-way. The rod glistened in the dim light.

Eddie set his end down on the cement. "I'll catch the gate, Sully."

He got around the trash cans and lifted the gate on its hinges. Then he pushed it against the latch and returned to the driveway as quickly as he could. The dog across the street continued to bark. It took only another minute to get the rod stowed in the back of the van.

"Okay, the usual, warm homecoming complete, we can now drive across town to my place," Sullivan quipped. Despite the show of humor, it was clear the older man was both embarrassed and wounded by his son-in-law's rudeness.

"No improvement?" Joe asked.

"None. I don't expect it at this point, Giuseppe."

"Sorry, nonetheless, old friend."

Sullivan shrugged and drove in silence. A few moments later, Joe spoke up again.

"We should assume at this point that Sully's house is being ob-served. I propose that you drop me off a block or so away. I'll walk over. You drive around for fifteen minutes or so before actually bringing this vehicle within sight of your home."

"If you have no objection, I would like to accompany you on this little walk, Sensei."

"Thank you, Harry. I will welcome it."

A short time later, Sullivan pulled over at a Park 'n Shop conveni-ence store. "This eyesore was added since your last visit, boss, but if you walk to that corner, you'll be in the neighborhood. I think you'll recog-nize it well enough. Eddie and I will drive up the way here for a bit and then we'll see you at, say roughly quarter to nine?"

"That will be sufficient," Ikeda agreed calmly. Joe merely nod-ded. They exited the van and walked to the corner. Sullivan drove out of the parking lot and continued along the boulevard.

"We'll just drive for five or ten minutes and then turn around."

"Sully. Um, I'm sorry your son-in-law was so..."

"What? Rude?" Sullivan sighed. "Thanks, Eddie. Darlene and Ted have their good side. With the people they consider their friends, they are gracious and warm. The trouble is, I don't fit into their model of what I should be. They can't get past that."

"Well, it's their loss."

"Mine too, actually. I would like very much to be part of my grandchildren's lives. But I appreciate the sentiment, my friend."

Sullivan drove in silence for another minute. Then he laughed a short, rueful laugh. "You know, young man. I've missed this. I've been too isolated, too much going through the motions. Just treading water.

Now Giuseppe's back. Harry's here. And we've got somebody young on the team – that'd be you, kid. It's just good."

"Thanks, Sully. And there's Nadine."

"Indeed there is. I don't know where that's going. Maybe nowhere. But I know it's past time I moved forward with my life.

"Okay," he continued. "Let's turn around at the light."

About ten minutes later, they pulled up in front of Sullivan's home. As was the case with Joe, the retired engineer lived in an older part of town. His house was a modest frame structure, reminiscent of an early 20th century farm house. A winding brick path led from the side-walk across a small lawn to the steps of a deep front porch. A pair of huge madronas graced the parkway in front of the home. Two chest-high junipers shielded the deep front porch and provided some privacy.

"Nice place, Sully."

"Thanks. It's a double city lot. I've got a three car garage in back, off the alley. I keep one bay for my car and the other two I use for a shop."

Harry stepped from the shadows of the front porch and waved to them.

"Let's see what they've found."

When they neared the porch, they could see that there were several people lying on the grass in the shadow of the juniper.

"*Sensei* was correct. Three were hiding around the property. A forth waited in that car across the street," Harry gestured at a light-colored Chevy Cobalt.

"Are they...?" Eddie stood gazing at the still forms.

"Oh, they are uninjured," Joe assured him. "Which is better than they deserve. You'll see some pretty nasty weapons up on the porch. They weren't planning to have a friendly chat with us.

"Anyway, we'll give them something to occupy themselves. Three of them will sleep for 24 hours. The forth was the leader. He will drive. He'll be alert, completely unable to so much as doze. And he'll feel utterly, totally obsessed with driving. He won't rest until they reach Bakersfield. Then, after an hour or so, he'll want to continue onto Las Vegas. When the others wake, they'll be puzzled, but they are trained to follow orders."

"Bakersfield? That's as in Bakersfield, California, right? Why Bakersfield?"

"Why not? Best case, traveling non-stop, it's the better part of an 18 hour drive. They'll have to stop for gas. The important thing is they won't be able to track us. We should be out of here well before they get themselves organized.

"And remember," Joe continued, "these are minions of the Queen. They won't report failure willingly. They'll make up some story or, better yet, try to disappear once they emerge from the compulsion I've cast over them."

"*Sensei*. Perhaps we should get them off the street and on their way."

"Yes, we should. Bring their car around, will you, son? Here are the keys," Joe held out his hand and Eddie took the key ring.

Eddie darted across the street and started the Cobalt. He turned the car around and pulled up in front of the van. He left the little Chevrolet idling and joined the others.

Next, Ikeda stepped into the shadows to keep watch. One-by-one, Joe spoke quiet words to the unconscious men. He ordered them to get into the car and fasten their seat belts. Five minutes later, they had driven off to their appointment in Bakersfield and points east.

In the meantime, Eddie and Sully brought in their bags and the grounding rod. Finally, they collected the weapons from the front porch.

"Let's take these out to my shop. I can disassemble the firearms and re-use the parts. For now, I'll stash them in one of my hidey-holes."

By nine-thirty, the men sat around Sullivan's comfortable living room. His home was, without a doubt, the abode of a single man. Unlike Fred, who had loved art and visual beauty, Sullivan was an engineer who loved things mechanical and electrical. The furniture tended towards the functional and well-worn. The kitchen was completely utilitarian. It reminded Eddie just slightly of the compact galley aboard the *Mother Rose*. Several of the walls were covered with bookshelves. There were three, beautifully constructed model steam engines on display stands in the living room.

"Do these work?" Eddie asked.

"Indeed they do!" Sullivan answered with a quiet pride. "That one right near you is a type alpha Stirling engine. And that one is a simple, reciprocating steam engine."

"That's pretty cool."

"Well, thanks, young man. I love to build things in my shop. I'd have built the grounding rod myself but for Joe's insistence that I farm out the work."

"I know you too well, Sully," Joe laughed. "Unless you've got someone to ride herd on you, you'll tinker with designs. We didn't have time for that. The rod you built in that shop in San Luis Obispo was the fastest I've ever seen you finish a project!

"Of course you should feel free to start your own line of 'yard art' after things cool down. Imagine if there were hundreds of grounding rods in peoples' gardens all over the country!"

Sullivan's eyes sparkled with the prospect. "Oh, I like that! I could have several designs. Of course none would actually open a portal by itself, but they do draw the eye, don't they? The light plays on the different types of metal. You can almost feel the energies gathering around it."

"But I'm getting ahead of myself," Sullivan shook his head ruefully. "We've got tomorrow's activities ahead of us. I've been thinking about this, and I am pretty sure what we should do."

Sullivan then proceeded to outline the plan for the next day. They'd be operating in a public area, but they'd be out early, before the morning crowds. As Sullivan laid out the plans, Eddie once more found himself impressed by the way the older man's mind worked. The big engineer's personality was all warmth and humility, but his thoughts were rigorous, logical, and orderly. An unusual combination. An admirable combination.

Joe asked several questions before he was satisfied with Sullivan's plan. Gently, Ikeda suggested that they leave slightly earlier, let him off near their destination, and drive at least one circuit around the area. He could thus assure himself of their safety.

By the time everything was settled, all questions raised and answered satisfactorily, it was nearly eleven o'clock. Eddie was yawning. Sullivan showed Harry & Eddie the guest room they'd share.

"I will stay up and sit for a while yet, my friend," Ikeda noted. "If you have no objections, I would prefer this bed by the door. I will wake you in time for us to move out," the Aikido master added.

"Fine with me," Eddie stifled another yawn.

"The bathroom's down the hall," Sullivan gestured. "Towels in the hall closet."

Eddie was showered and in bed by midnight. He turned over and closed his eyes. It seemed only a moment later that Ikeda shook him gently awake. It was still dark.

*   *   *

Eddie rolled out of bed and shivered a little as his feet touched the cool floor. He stood and stretched. He'd laid his clothes out the night before and he dressed quickly in the pre-dawn darkness. Even with a quick detour to the bathroom, he was in the kitchen within ten minutes, drawn by the welcome scent of freshly brewed coffee.

Joe and Ikeda were already there. Sullivan joined them a moment later. Except for the light over the kitchen table, the house was dark. The men hardly spoke as they stood and readied themselves. Eddie came fully awake.

"Well. Shall we, gentlemen?" Joe spoke softly.

They placed their cups in the sink and filed into the living room. The grounding rod lay on the floor near the door. Apparently identical to the one they'd employed in San Luis Obispo, the unusual combination of metals and finishes gleamed in the dim light and drew the eye into suggestions of patterns. They donned their coats against the morning chill.

Joe opened the front door and after looking around, came back inside and motioned for Sullivan to take the lead. The big engineer pulled keys from his pocket and stepped onto the porch. Ikeda came out and glided silently into the shade of the junipers.

Joe and Eddie picked up the heavy staff and walked to the front yard. Sullivan locked the door behind them. Quickly, the four men moved across the grass and stowed the rod in the van. Dawn came late this time of year, and there was only the tiniest hint of light in the eastern sky as they drove down the street.

They traveled south on Marinedi Avenue. Traffic was light and they reached the gentle curve that merged onto Broadway in ten minutes. In five more, they turned left onto West Holly. Traffic grew heavier as they neared the central business district. The air was calm, the setting moon obscured by overcast.

Eddie could smell the water, and it reminded him of Soapstone Bay and Lena and his friends there. On the heels of the image, he felt the weight of the separation that lay on his heart. With an effort, he pulled himself from his reverie as they made another left, this time onto West Champion Street. Seconds later, they made a sharp left onto Prospect Street and pulled into a parking space in front of a large, official-looking Victorian building.

"This is it? It looks like a courthouse," Eddie remarked as he scanned the edifice. It was constructed of red brick and stone and had an air of dignity and permanence.

"Well, it was the city hall for this area a hundred or so years ago. The town of Whatcom was absorbed by the neighboring community of Bellingham. Now this building houses an art museum... and is itself a real architectural treasure," Sullivan answered, obviously proud of his town.

"See the trees and shrubbery up ahead?" Sullivan pointed out the window of the van. "You can't make it out from here, but those trees surround a couple of stone benches. People come here to eat lunch or just to enjoy good weather. There's a beautiful view of the old building from the benches."

"Yes, Sully. That looks just right," Joe agreed.

Traffic was less heavy here, but there were a few people on the sidewalks. Ikeda climbed quickly out and walked off into the dim light. They circled the block and returned to the same parking space. Alert and relaxed, their friend stepped from the shadows as Joe rolled down the passenger-side window.

"It is acceptable. The site is somewhat exposed, but few are abroad once one leaves the sidewalk. An unfortunate man, homeless I suspect, sleeps on the ground in the shelter of the trees. Let us move quickly and take our position. I will meet you there," the Aikido master spoke in his usual calm, quiet tones. Then he turned and circled off to the right.

Trying to project a relaxed demeanor, the men unloaded the grounding rod and walked onto the museum grounds. Joe and Sullivan took the grounding rod between them and moved towards the small grove of trees at a fast walk. Eddie brought up the rear.

Ikeda was waiting when they reached the grove. Silently, he indicated the dim shape beneath the trees where the homeless man had sheltered for the night. With Eddie supporting the staff and flanked by Ikeda and Sullivan, the men stood in the same pattern as before. They all faced Joe.

As on the previous opening, the older men began chanting simultaneously at some unspoken signal. As before, Eddie worked silently to stand outside the flow of energies that coursed though the heavy rod he grasped. As before, the young man struggled as the feeling of immersion expanded past his wrists and up his arms, but this time he arrested the sensation sooner and more effectively.

And as before, at the final "*Now the door opens!*" there came the brilliant flash of green lightning that rose from the earth to be met by the gold brilliance that flew down from the sky. As before, there was no report, no thunder that accompanied the flash.

This time, however, there was a silent witness. The homeless man had heard them. At first he blearily wondered what was happening, wondered what new insult or hardship was being levied upon him. But then his mind cleared and he watched silently as the four men finished their strange task and melted into the dawn.

The last one to leave turned and met the homeless man's eyes. He raised a hand in silent salute. The homeless man, huddled in his filthy sleeping bag, did not respond, but some time later he climbed to shiver and stand where the others had stood. He felt the thrum of strange energies, and the old, familiar suffering eased slightly but perceptibly. He looked around him and stood a little straighter, breathed a little deeper. Then he returned to his nest to gather his things and go before the crowds came.

Within seconds, Eddie and the others were back at the van. They drew a few odd looks from passers-by but no one challenged them. Sullivan started the van and drove north on Prospect, away from the business district. Under his expert guidance, the ungainly vehicle wove through the lettered streets smoothly and easily. They reached Marinedi Avenue and headed north back towards Sullivan's neighborhood.

At Sullivan's house, Eddie and their host unloaded the grounding rod and placed it in the workshop. There was plenty of time for a good breakfast before the quartet headed into the ordeal of the traffic that clogged the arteries of Puget Sound's eastern shore.

Traveling on major roads, it was roughly one hundred miles from Bellingham to SeaTac. In mid-day traffic, it took nearly three hours to reach the rental car return lot. Fortunately, the check-in went smoothly. The the tank was full, and there were no delays.

Unlike the regional airport near San Luis Obispo, SeaTac served the entire greater Puget Sound area, and the security checkpoints were busy. It was very good that the four men arrived early. As it was, they reached the gate for Southwest Airlines flight 216 to Albuquerque about fifteen minutes before boarding started.

Michael C. Glaviano

Forty Six

Flying time between SeaTac and Albuquerque was slightly under three hours. The Boeing 737 touched down just after seven o'clock. Because it was late winter, the evening turbulence over the Rockies hadn't been terrible, but the descent over southeastern Utah and northwestern New Mexico was bumpy enough to upset children and keep adults pointlessly alert.

Harry and Hiroko lived in a semi-rural area west of town. The area was dotted with *"ranchitos"* – little ranches – that fanned out around the Rio Grande. Artists had studios and independent galleries in their homes. Musicians had created recording and practice studios and even performance spaces. Medical and legal professionals raised llamas and buffalo. Everyone grew chile.

Twenty minutes after crossing I-25, when they were about a quarter of a mile from the property, Harry asked the driver to stop. The four men got out and collected their bags. Shaking his head at the *calabasas locos* who would prefer to walk on this cold night rather than ride to their doorstep, the driver made a U-turn and sped back toward town.

The air was bracing after the closeness of the cab and the stifling fumes of the airport. Ikeda and Joe left their bags and disappeared into the night to check the area for signs of their adversaries. Taking the bags with them, Sullivan and Eddie stepped softly into the deeper shade of some large boulders to wait. Cold had crept into their feet and up their legs by the time the two scouts returned.

"Perhaps our enemies were confounded by the disappearance of our would-be assailants, coupled with our abrupt departure from the Pacific Northwest. Or, as is more likely, the Queen has few agents in this sparsely populated part of the country," the martial arts expert spoke softly as he and Joe returned and reclaimed their bags.

"Anyway, we're unobserved," Joe chimed in. "This peace probably won't last, but we should be okay for the night. Come on. It's a short walk."

The moon rose into the clear skies above the Sangre de Cristos, and the landscape was flooded with silvery light. The four men emerged from the shadows of the boulders and onto the road.

"Someday I hope you may return for a social visit. This place is truly enchanting. Nowhere else are there skies to compare with those over New Mexico," Ikeada remarked as they walked. "And we can feed you such *chile verde* and *chile rojo* as to make the gods themselves jealous," he added with laughter in his voice.

They stepped onto the deep, low porch of a well-proportioned adobe and, seconds later, into the cozy interior. Just inside the front door, there was a tiled entry with racks for street shoes and a box in which slippers of various sizes, neatly stacked, waited for visitors.

The men removed their shoes and followed Ikeda into a central living room. Vigas supported the ceiling. The walls were thick and solid, with deep niches set here and there in the white plaster that lay over the adobe. The windows were recessed and the frames had been painted a vivid turquoise. Doors were painted turquoise, coral, and sometimes other, more subdued colors. Pieces of split piñon lay stacked near the kiva fireplace in the corner of the room. The effect was both striking and tranquil.

"Welcome. Please make yourselves comfortable while I phone Hiroko at the hotel to let her know of our arrival. Then we will see what we can find to eat."

A short time later they were gathered around the table in the kitchen enjoying steaming bowls of posole. Eddie had never experienced New Mexican cooking and was amazed at the combination of flavors and the heat of the chile.

He drew the sleeve of his shirt across his forehead and laughed. "I'm sweating from the chile, Harry, but this is so good."

"Indeed. I am pleased that you enjoy it. In the southern part of the state, posole is invariably made with red chile. Farther north, either red or green is used. A variety of meats may be included, and some people favor a vegetarian form of the stew. Hiroko and I both enjoy this combination of green chile, hominy, and shredded chicken.

"Again, someday, if you are able to come for a social visit, we may make a pilgrimage to Hatch."

"Hatch?"

"Yes. A small town in the south. Known by chile aficionados worldwide. When a farmer parks a pickup truck at the side of the road and leans a sign reading 'Hatch Chiles' against the vehicle, people will line up in order to buy burlap bags filled with the treasure."

"Wow. That's really cool, Harry. Sign me up."

Joe cleared his throat and set down his spoon. "Sorry, gentlemen, to interrupt, but we have a world to save."

"Spoilsport!" Sullivan muttered as he ladled more posole into his bowl.

A twinkle in his eyes, Harry leaned forward in his chair. He made a slight bow in Joe's direction.

"I have given the situation some thought, *Sensei*, and would presume to suggest multiple courses of action for us to consider."

"Yes?"

"First of all, there is the small question of what to do with the grounding rod that should arrive later this week from California. I propose that I present it as a gift to the head of security at the Isleta Pueblo."

"Interesting. Why?"

"Over the years, he and I have become... not close friends, precisely, but let us say associates who greatly respect each other's traditions. I have trained many of his officers at the dojo in Albuquerque. He has on occasion consulted with me on matters of law enforcement strategy for the village proper.

"His spirituality, steeped as it is in the traditions of the indigenous people, is largely congruent with the cosmology of the Great Wheel, and I suspect that he has observed more about our life here than he has let on. He says little; yet my instincts tell me that he would recognize the grounding rod as an object of power and, as such, would deploy it to the benefit of this world."

Joe considered this in silence. His eyes gazed into deep places. Watching his mentor, Eddie observed that the ancient man's eyes no longer reflected the warm light of the kitchen. Those "windows of the soul" had become passages to other times, to remote thoughts and memories.

At length Joe roused himself. His eyes became merely eyes. He again assumed the aspect of the middle-aged leader of a group of men bent on a task.

"As usual, my friend, your insights are sound. I have looked for connections and found them. We should meet this man. I would shake his hand and look upon his face, but yes, I am inclined to agree with you on this.

"Now. What other counsel would you give?"

"Just this, *Sensei*. South of here, about 50 miles, there is a small range of mountains that stand alone. Looming, brooding over the surrounding grasslands, these mountains are called '*Sierra Ladrone*' – the 'thieves' mountains.' As recently as the early twentieth century, bandits, rustlers, raiding parties and the like hid in the canyons and secret places there, hence the name. The locals often refer to the whole area as 'the *Ladrones*.'

"But the ancient history is much richer," Ikeda continued. "There is evidence of human habitation going back at least 10,000 years. More recently, perhaps a thousand years ago, the 'Old Ones,' the *Ana-*

sazi, and others lived there. It is a rugged, harsh place at lower elevations; although the peaks receive enough precipitation to support forests
on the upper slopes. There are bears, mountain lions, pronghorn antelope, and desert bighorn sheep. Birds of prey circle overhead.

Now the excitement in Ikeda's voice grew. "We should go there,
Sensei. We should perform many spells of opening in a tight pattern. We
must establish a major connection to the Place. A connection that could
eventually be developed into a full passage, such as that which lies beneath your home.

"This, *Sensei,* is my counsel," Harry finished.

Again, Joe fell silent, but only briefly.

"You would risk this?" he asked. "Yourself? Sullivan? You are
both strong, yes. You have performed the spells of vitality as faithfully as
you are able in this injured world, but you are not as I. You are not born
of the bones of a world. You could be hurt, perhaps beyond calling back.
It would tire even me to do this. And our young friend here... he has
strength and talent in plenty. And he is faithful, but he has little experience. A mistake... would have... consequences."

"For what it's worth, I agree with Harry," Sullivan chimed in.
"You said it yourself, boss. This world is injured. I suspect that it's failing. What we did out on the coast and up north were all well and good,
but we need to do something bigger if we are to turn the tide. This would
be such an action."

"Yes, Sully, it would be. It would also attract the attention of the
Queen herself. You could count on it. Our experiences in San Luis and
up in Bellingham demonstrate that her agents are already abroad, and
she has other ways of gathering information."

"Forgive me, *Sensei,* but I must ask you. How much difference
can we make by taking small actions? And as for our strength, I can only
say that each passing year brings with it more difficulties. The spells become harder to perform and produce a weaker effect. This action has the
potential to reverse that – at least for this vicinity."

"And can we gain access to this 'thieves' mountain?' And crawl
back out afterwards?"

Harry bowed his head. "The mountain range is a combination of
private and Bureau of Land Management lands. My wife and I have
hiked there many times. And hunted desert antelope as well. I have a
place in mind. Hiroko and I own an appropriate vehicle. She can operate
it adequately. Expertly, even."

"So you would even involve your wife in this?"

"Is she not already involved, *Sensei*? Is she not hiding in a hotel
as we speak? She has a stake in this as well. And clearly, the woman
Nadine will also wish to participate. Remember that she plans to join us
here. I sense she will not be put off easily."

Joe's nostrils flared and his eyes flashed. He stood abruptly and glanced back and forth at the men sitting in front of him. Ikeda and Sullivan both met his gaze calmly, openly. Joe moved his regard in Eddie's direction and the young man steeled himself to meet that powerful look.

The moment passed. Relenting, Joe shrank into himself. "Yes. You are right of course," he spoke barely above a whisper. "I have been at this too long, I suppose. I have grown inward, obsessed with moves and counter-moves, obsessed with minute degrees of balance. It is almost timid, and it is to the detriment of us all."

Sullivan laughed his big laugh. "Somehow 'timid' isn't exactly how I'd describe you, boss. You've just been operating alone for too long. We need to bring in more people."

"If we bring the wrong person in, we may as well write this world off, not to mention that we'd be wiped out. Bugs on a windshield."

"Come on, Giuseppe. I know you've looked inside Nadine's heart. And you know she can be trusted. And Hiroko has been in this for decades, even if she's chosen to stay on the sidelines. She can be relied on as well as any of us. I repeat: we need more help. We can move slowly on the recruitment front, but six of us are better than four."

"And keep in mind, *Sensei*, that in all these years, Hiroko has witnessed little beyond the actions, the spells she and I practice to main- tain our vigor," added Ikeda. "Nadine has heard nothing but words, seen nothing, really, with her own eyes. Even if they are not called upon to act, their direct experience will bring home to them the gravity of their decision to become involved."

Tentatively, Eddie spoke up. His thoughts circled around some- thing that the others had barely touched upon, something that he scarcely wanted to speak aloud, yet felt compelled at the same time to ut- ter.

"Excuse me, guys, but if we don't do something big... what else is going to matter? Talk about 'bugs on a windshield.' If the Queen has her way, won't everybody be wiped out anyway? Won't there be terrible, un- imaginable suffering?"

No one responded at first. The refrigerator clicked on. The posole on the stove simmered. Outside, the wind blew down the Rio Grande valley. Burning in stoves and fireplaces upwind, the faintest scent of piñon, reached them. Further afield, coyotes hunted among the rocks, sage and creosote.

Finally, Joe nodded his head and returned to his seat.

"Very well, gentlemen. Let's do this. Now that we've decided the what, let's figure out the how."

They talked long into the night. They proposed and discarded plans. They drew diagrams. Harry went briefly to another room and re- turned bearing topographical maps of the area in question. They con- sidered and rejected the idea of bringing more people in right away.

Finally, well after midnight, they settled on the outlines of a plan. Ikeda showed Sullivan and Eddie to guest rooms. When he shut off the light in his room, Eddie could see dim shapes in the room: the furniture illuminated by the silver glow of the New Mexico moon. As his eyes became more dark-adapted, the glow grew brighter, the shapes more distinct. He fell asleep while gazing into the enchanted light.

* * *

The previous day's activities had worn them out. Everyone but Joe slept until nearly eight o'clock in the morning. It was just as well. Little could happen until they gathered the equipment and people that would be needed.

At ten, Sullivan called Nadine's mobile number. Yes, she had wrapped things up sufficiently so that her staff could carry forward the organizational details of Fred's care and the disposition of his estate. She had arisen early and, driving south on Highway 101, was well beyond Thousand Oaks.

Yes, she was still planning to join them and in fact had reservations for an early afternoon flight to Albuquerque. To avoid the delay of driving into LA, two of her staff would meet her at the Burbank airport with warm clothes appropriate for winter in the southwest. She would hand the car over to them as well. Nadine planned to arrive around four-thirty in the afternoon.

Ikeda called his wife and suggested that she wait at the hotel until he could meet her there. The Aikido master spoke several sentences in rapid fire Japanese before hanging up. "Please excuse my not speaking English," he said as he hung up. "I thought it prudent to employ ambiguity available in the language of my parents. In this way, I could warn Hiroko to take care without saying anything that might arouse suspicion.

"From here on out, I believe we should at very least travel in pairs," Ikeda added.

"Yes. I concur," Joe agreed. "Our quick stop in Bellingham coupled with the sudden disappearance of the Queen's unfortunate agents, may slow them, but they will certainly pick up our trail again."

Ikeda turned to Eddie. "Would you care to accompany me? We can join Hiroko and then go to a sporting goods store near her hotel. I hope it turns out not to be necessary, but we should acquire ammunition."

"Yeah. I'd like to get out a little. Do we have time for you to show me around your place before we leave?"

"I would be pleased to do so."

The Ikedas' ranchito was situated on a beautiful, three-acre parcel. Huge cottonwood trees, bare in the winter months, would shade the west side of the house from the summer sun. A vegetable garden lay behind the house. This time of year the garden was planted in a cover crop of winter rye. Nearer the house, Harry had fashioned a rock garden with meditation benches that were shaded by pergolas and smaller trees. The landscaped portion of the property faded into native plants near the southern boundary.

In a manner reminiscent of Joe's home on Painter Avenue, the back of the Ikeda's adobe faced south and featured a large, attached greenhouse. Eddie remarked on the similarity.

"That is a sound observation. It was *Sensei* who first suggested the greenhouse to me. You will notice, however, that the size of the connecting area is much smaller here than at his house. The New Mexico sun is very intense. We can open that single sliding door into our kitchen to admit sun-warmed air. The rest of the greenhouse heats the exterior adobe wall. In the winter, the heat diffuses through the bricks and stabilizes the temperature indoors.

"In the spring and fall, we open vents at the top of the greenhouse so the heat can escape. In the summer, I have a large awning that extends on tracks to cover the entire roof of the greenhouse. The sides and back of the space all possess screened openings so we can maximize ventilation. In this way, the sun becomes our ally year around.

"Our friend, Sullivan designed the whole system. It has functioned perfectly for many years."

"It's beautiful. You and your wife must enjoy it here a lot," Eddie remarked.

"You are kind, my friend. Yes, we do. Now, I fear we must return to the realities of our present situation."

Ikeda led the way to a garage at the side of the property. Inside was a modern Toyota FJ Cruiser. The four wheel drive vehicle had been repainted to blend with the colors of the high desert. It featured a large, heavy duty storage rack on the roof and a swing out bar for the spare tire.

"Cool ride, Harry."

Ikeda acknowledged the young man's compliment with a small bow and a slight smile. "My wife and I use this vehicle to camp and hunt in remote areas – areas where reliability and ruggedness are important. It has proven itself to be adequate if not pushed too severely and has had several modifications that are less visible than the paint. The clutch and suspension have been enhanced. These are race-qualified tires and rims. Hiroko says it is a symptom of my vanished youth, but I think, when the time comes, we will be glad to have this vehicle.

"And although she will never admit as much, my dear wife loves to drive it. She can get very enthusiastic – very nearly aggressive – when she is far from the pavement," the Aikido master added with a chuckle.

The day was glorious in the way a late-winter morning can be in New Mexico. It took them about forty minutes to drive to the hotel, every second of which was a feast for the eyes. Even in the midst of the city, Eddie could see the wall of the Sandia Crest looming above Albuquerque.

Harry pulled into the parking lot and found his wife's Prius. A moment later, Eddie met the Aikido master's wife of nearly fifty years.

Hiroko Sato was a very petite, pretty woman. She wore jeans, a black turtleneck, and a rust colored down vest. She appeared to be about Harry's age, which Eddie by now realized meant little. Harry spoke the English of an educated, native born American, but Hiroko had been born in Japan and lived her early years there. She had attended college and graduate school in the U.S. and lived nearly all of her adult life there. As a result, her accent had receded to the limits of detectability.

She shook Eddie's hand firmly when Harry introduced the young man. "I am very pleased to meet you," she said. Her voice was deeper than Eddie had expected.

"Would you please follow us in the Prius, Eddie?" Harry asked. "That will allow me to bring Hiroko up to date on the situation and our plans. We need drive only a dozen blocks up Central Avenue to the sporting goods store. Then, we must visit the artisans I have commissioned to build the grounding rod.

"After we collect the staff, we shall stop at a service station. This beast of a vehicle is regrettably and constantly hungry, which is why it spends most of its time in the garage. Finally, we will retrace our way back home. You will have an opportunity to see much of western and a little of southern Albuquerque."

"Sure thing. I'd be happy to follow you around in the other car."

They had to wait for several minutes while Hiroko checked out of the hotel. Traffic on Central was heavy, so they pulled out of the parking lot onto a side street and then drove around the block to take advantage of a stoplight. It took them another fifteen minutes to reach Lonnie's Sporting Goods and Outdoor Gear in the 3600 block of Central Avenue Southeast.

Lonnie's was a cavernous old building. It gave the impression of a previous life spent as a warehouse. The parking lot was half full and they were able to park the two vehicles side-by-side. As he shut off the FJ Cruiser, Ikeda held up his hand and met Eddie's eyes briefly in an obvious signal to wait.

The Aikido master got out and walked around the lot before gesturing to his wife and Eddie to join him. "From here on, we must emphasize caution," he explained shortly.

It was chilly and quiet inside the big building. Sodium vapor lamps suspended from a high, shadowy ceiling provided the interior illumination. This lighting arrangement produced a few areas of bright glare near the center of the store while much of the periphery of the space was less well-lit. Only the ski and snowboard equipment sections bustled with noise and activity. Suddenly remembering the store in Soapstone Bay, Eddie asked if they could visit the camping equipment departments.

Sure enough, there were several types of hand axes and rock hammers available. Eddie held several of them. The rock hammers – they looked like small picks – were interesting, but Eddie felt that he needed to stay with an edged weapon. He eventually selected three hand axes. They didn't feel as good as those he'd left at Joe's, but he thought he would be able to throw them with fair accuracy. Harry nodded his approval.

Next, Ikeda led the way to the department that sold ammunition. He purchased several boxes. Eddie looked at the full bags and swallowed. The seriousness of what they faced suddenly came home.

Again, Ikeda led the way outside and then motioned for the others to join him. Eddie left the uneven lighting of the warehouse and blinked in the bright New Mexico sunlight. He found himself trying to look in all directions at once. Eventually he fell back on his spell of seeing, but he detected nothing out of the ordinary.

The next stop was the metal workers south of Central. Harry called before driving over. Yes the rod was finished. There had been some problems obtaining the exact mix of metals specified, however, and they had improvised somewhat.

It took nearly a half hour to reach the metal shop. It was in a small strip of concrete industrial buildings near the tracks that led back towards I-25 and the Rio Grande.

The owner, a thin man in his thirties was apologetic. "Will this work? If not, my brother says he knows somebody up in Española who could maybe get what you want. Maybe next week."

The rod was the right length, but the copper bands were missing. They were replaced with strips of hammered aluminum and wrought iron. The design was visually attractive, but Eddie had no way of knowing what would work and what would not. Ikeda looked at the rod carefully.

"I cannot say for sure if these metals will have the right properties, but perhaps it will suffice. I must speak with my client and see what he says. What do I owe you?"

The man named a price. Eddie thought that it was too high given the fact that the work had not been done to the specifications requested, but Ikeda was disinclined to haggle. He paid cash and they slid the rod into the back of the FJ Cruiser.

Three quarters of an hour later they were back at the Ikeda's home. Joe was waiting in the back yard. When she saw him, Hiroko bowed formally and then stepped forward to offer her hand. Like her husband, she referred to Joe as, "Sensei" – teacher.

Stopping to leave their shoes in the greenhouse, they carried their purchases inside. Sullivan was standing at the sink, and when he turned around, Hiroko launched herself in his direction and hugged the big engineer with a fierce energy that belied her stature. "Whoa, there!

Who's this? I didn't know you had a daughter, Ikeda!" Sullivan asked in mock-surprise.

"You know damn well who I am, Sully, and it is wonderful to see you. It has been too long. Far too long." She stepped back and held his big arms in her small, beautifully shaped hands. As if to imprint his kind features more securely in her memory, she looked intently at the burly engineer's face. She hugged him again before releasing him.

Hiroko turned away briefly and wiped her eyes. Finally, she turned back to the men standing around. "Don't just stand there. Go do something. I'll make lunch."

"*Sensei*, Sullivan-san, did UPS happen to deliver the grounding rod from California?" Ikeda asked.

"Not yet. Why? Did you pick up the rod from town?" Sullivan asked in return.

"Yes, we did, but as often happens, what was done was not precisely what was requested. Shall we see if this will work for us?"

They all filed out to see. When Eddie and Ikeda pulled the rod out to stand it, Joe and Sullivan came over.

"This might work, but the lack of copper will make it harder to control," Joe observed.

Sullivan reached out to grip the heavy staff in one powerful hand. "Hmmm. Do you have any heavy gauge copper, Harry? Anything at all? Plumbing? Perhaps some heavy copper wire?"

"It is possible. Let us rummage around in the garage and see what may be had."

In fifteen minutes, they had returned. Sullivan was carrying a spool of wire and a utility knife. "Here's what I propose, Giuseppe. I'll strip the insulation from this stranded copper wire. Then I'll braid it around these bands they've substituted in place of what we specified. I know a way to splice the wire in place. It won't look the same, but we'll end up with quite a bit of copper wrapped tightly around the rod. What do you think?"

Joe looked thoughtful. "Well, let's hope for the UPS truck, but yes. Go ahead, Sully. Do your own brand of magic."

Eddie walked back to the greenhouse and returned with his shopping bag. "I want to see if I can throw these things," Eddie reached into the bag and drew out the three camping axes. Sullivan whistled.

"It's easy to throw them, son..." Joe began.

"Yeah. I know. Throwing's easy. It's hitting what you're aiming at that's tough," Eddie laughed at the oft-repeated caution. Joe smiled in response.

"We should all go about in pairs from now on," Ikeda reminded them.

"I can work on the grounding rod outside here as well as anyplace else. It's just a matter of weaving a splice around and around," Sullivan offered. "I can watch while I work. I want to see this."

Ikeda nodded in assent.

"That is good. You will find a stump just beyond the garden. We took out a large cottonwood so that the garden would have adequate sun. There is a scrap pile behind the garage. Feel free to prop anything you find there against the stump so that you will have a target," the Aikido master offered.

The engineer found an old chair in the greenhouse and dragged it out to sit in the sun and watch while he worked. At first Eddie's throws were wild. Nearly a week had passed since he'd practiced, and the new axes had a different feel from what he was used to. And, as always, he found practicing in front of an audience, even an audience of one, distracting.

As had happened on so many other occasions, however, the rhythm of the practice drew Eddie into a calm, still mental state. He looked, aimed, threw. Over and over. He started near his makeshift target and gradually worked his way back until he was standing in the middle of the dormant garden plot.

Over the next three quarters of an hour, Eddie's throws got stronger and more precise. He sensed and compensated for the differences in feel and balance. Like a guitar player moving from an electric to an acoustic instrument, the superficial differences melted to reveal the underlying similarities.

By the time Hiroko called them to lunch, Eddie was hitting nearly all his shots, and the target was splintered to kindling.

"That's really something, Eddie. Really something indeed," Sullivan said. "I'm glad to have you with us."

"Thanks, Sully. That means a lot. How'd it go with the rod?"

"Here, take a look. What do you think?"

Somehow the engineer had woven the stranded wire tightly around the grounding rod. While the rod didn't have quite the same look as the others, it did have a certain beauty. Eddie stood the rod on end and gripped it with outstretched hands. He thought that he sensed a subtle flow of energies deep in the metal.

"That's impressive, Sully. I'll be interested in hearing what Joe has to say."

Eddie held the heavy grounding rod out so that Sullivan could take it and lay it gently in the back of the FJ Cruiser. Then the young man trotted over and pulled out his axes and laid them on the stump.

He carted what was left of his target out to the scrap pile, came back and sheathed the weapons. He and Sullivan walked through the greenhouse and into the kitchen where Hiroko admonished them to wash up before lunch.

Michael C. Glaviano

Amazingly, Hiroko in just over an hour, had produced a wonderful enchilada casserole. She put out side dishes of black beans and rice. They ate and ate and talked, and then ate some more. Unlike the posole the night before, the casserole used a robust red sauce. It was fiery and full of flavor.

"I had no idea that this type of Mexican food even existed, let alone that it was so good," Eddie said as he carried his plate to the sink. "Let me clean up, okay?"

"Thank you, young man. That is considerate. I will accept your offer," Hiroko replied. "I will put everything away after you've done. That will save having to show you where I hide my cookware and utensils."

Joe and Sullivan went out to the SUV together to inspect the grounding rod. They came back to report that while Joe was concerned with the strength of the woven copper under the stress of repeated spells, he thought what Sullivan had done was wonderful. In the end, he pronounced the grounding staff usable.

Shadows were lengthening by the time Eddie finished washing the dishes. He joined the others in the living room where they were enjoying coffee and chatting around a fire in the kiva fireplace.

The UPS shipment had still not arrived. Joe had called UPS and been informed that their shipment had "had an exception" and was now on time for its new delivery date. Unfortunately, the UPS clerk had not been able to say exactly what that new date would be.

"We'll leave soon to pick up Nadine," Sullivan announced as Eddie entered. "How about Joe, you, and Hiroko stay here, while Harry and I go to the airport? What do you think?"

"I'm fine with that. I wish we could go out tonight and do this, though," Eddie answered.

"We were just talking about that. Even if we left now, it would be dark well before we reached the canyon where we have decided to set up," Ikeda replied. "The moon is near full, and it will be bright. We could do this but for one thing: the Queen will surely detect our efforts before we are done. If she acts against us, we will be tired, cold, and at a disadvantage in the moonlit landscape. That is not the best way to meet the wrath of the Locust Queen.

"Then there is the matter of the grounding rod. What Sullivan-san has done is beautiful, but it is still not solid copper that has been brazed in place. We must perform the spell of opening six, possibly nine times in quick succession. The rod we use should be the best possible. What I have supplied, even augmented by Sully's mastery, is less than ideal.

"And of course, we can use Nadine's help," the Aikido master continued. "The more lookouts we have the better. As it is, we won't get back from the airport until half-past five or six at the earliest. No. I sug-

556

gest patience as our best course. We will explain the plan to Nadine-san. Then we will try to rest and leave tomorrow. During daylight it will be easier for us to detect pursuit."

"I agree with Harry," Joe added. "Reluctantly, of course. I'd prefer to act immediately, but it is risky. Getting out there early tomorrow is our best bet. What is the weather forecast for tomorrow?"

"I will check," Hiroko answered. She pulled a handheld computer from a nearby bookshelf and studied it for a few minutes. She looked up, puzzled.

"This is odd. There is snow in the forecast. That is rare so late in the winter. I checked the forecasts for central New Mexico. A storm approaches from the north.

"It should hit Santa Fe around ten tonight, Albuquerque before midnight. Socorro, the town nearest the Ladrones, is south of the mountains. The forecast calls for heavy snow in Socorro early tomorrow. That means places both north and south of the Ladrones will get snow. The forecast doesn't guarantee it of course, but it is likely we will have to contend with snow."

The wind began to pick up. Dust blew across the road in the afternoon light. Sullivan leaned forward to pour himself another cup of coffee. He sipped it and set the cup down on the table next to him. The cup made a surprisingly loud sound as it touched the ceramic coaster.

"This changes things. Do you suppose that the Queen is manipulating the weather in the hope of forcing us to make a move?" Ikeda wondered.

"She has no way of knowing what we intend to do. No, my guess is that at most, her agents know only of our presence," Joe answered. "They may not even have reported back to the Queen. This could be the work of a group of her senior agents. Perhaps they are monitoring flights. They might well be able to do that.

"They hope to use the cloud cover in some way. Or, once the storm starts, they will try to direct it... as a weapon of sorts. That will be extremely difficult since they've weakened magic so much in this world, but the Queen cares nothing for the lives she spends to reach her goals. And punishment for failure is both swift and cruel. Her agents know these things and will act accordingly."

"Maybe this is just a coincidence?" Eddie suggested. He doubted it even as he said it, but the others gave it serious consideration.

"It is possible of course," Joe said finally. "But we lose little if we consider it otherwise. No. Now we must reopen the question: Is it better to wait until tomorrow or to act tonight?"

"The grounding rod is imperfect. Remember that," Ikeda cautioned.

"Yes, yes, yes. Maybe the whole thing is wrong. Maybe we should just drive downtown, pick a spot and open a portal like we did before," Sullivan offered. That brought everyone up short.

Finally Eddie spoke up again. "Look, I know I'm the weak link in this, but I'm willing to try. If we have Nadine and Hiroko both keeping watch and we work fast... well, I just think it's our best shot. Speaking of which, who will be holding the guns?"

"Haruo and I each I have a small rifle – Winchester .30-30's," Hiroko spoke quietly, matter-of-factly. "Although I would hardly consider myself an avid practitioner, my husband and I have hunted desert antelope. I hope I will not be called upon to fire, but I will be with you and I am willing to do what is required."

Abruptly, Joe stood and began pacing the room. Everyone watched as he paced back and forth, back and forth. On his third pass, he stopped and threw up his hands. "We are beyond making a rational decision at this point. Here is what I propose. Sully, Harry. You two go get Nadine at the airport. The rest of us will prepare. And think. When you get back, we'll make our final decision, but I am leaning more towards acting tonight than waiting. They know we're here. We do not know if the storm is their best trick or if they have something else planned."

"Got it, boss."

"Yes, *Sensei*. It shall be as you say. We will take the Prius so that you may load the FJ while we are gone. That will save time."

Joe nodded his approval.

As the shadows deepened, Ikeda and Sullivan left for the airport. Hiroko, Joe, and Eddie discussed what to bring on the trip to the Ladrones.

"We'll be six in that vehicle. It will be crowded, and things could get busy. We should keep it simple," Joe advised.

"I can ride in the back," Eddie offered.

"It is not a short ride, and we will be off-road for some of it. You will bounce and be uncomfortable," Hiroko objected.

"It'll be okay. If you have a pad or something I could sit on, it'd help, but I'm sure I'll manage."

Now Joe spoke up again. "We should bring some drinking water, Hiroko. And, if you have anything handy, something to eat that can supply us with calories. Doing that many spells is going to take a lot out of us.

"Apart from that, we'll need clothing appropriate to the weather," Joe concluded.

"And the weapons and ammunition. Yes, *Sensei*, let us move to the kitchen. I will gather the things. Then we will organize what we have and load the vehicle."

"Won't we need flashlights?" Eddie wondered.

"We keep several flashlights mounted beneath the rear seat of the vehicle. The moon is very bright, but we will have those if we need them."

Hiroko brought out two rifles and leaned them against the back wall of the kitchen. Eddie stepped into the greenhouse and retrieved the boxes of ammunition. He placed these on the floor. Hiroko looked at the cardboard boxes and then turned to rummage beneath the utility sink of the laundry room that lay off to the side of the kitchen. She returned with a stout wire basket and handed it to Eddie.

"Please put the ammunition boxes in here. That will keep them together."

She found water bottles and set them out to be filled. Then she went back down a short hall to the bedrooms. In a few minutes Hiroko returned to the kitchen bearing an armload of outdoor clothing.

"Haruo and you both are of a close enough size. I sometimes complain he owns too many down vests, too many coats. Now I am glad. What shall we do about Sully, though? He is so big across here?" she drew her hand across her own shoulders.

"He brought a coat with him. Do you think he'll need another layer?"

"It gets very cold at night in the high desert, *Sensei*."

"Well, then, do you have an old blanket?" Joe asked from the sink where he was filling the bottles. "Something he could use as a serape?"

"Ah! Indeed, yes. I know just the thing... and what of this woman, Nadine? I believe I may have met her once, years ago, but I do not remember her size. Is she large or small?"

"Oh, um. Well, she's thin, but taller than you, Hiroko," Eddie answered. "And she told Sully that she would bring appropriate clothes."

The older woman's face creased in a sweet smile. "Nearly every adult in my adopted country is taller than I, young man. It is an interesting vantage point, being the shortest grownup in every gathering. She may not require it, but just in case, I will see what I can do for her."

Hiroko left again to return a moment later laden with a heavy blanket and another vest hugged against her chest. She also had a first aid kit balanced precariously at the top of the pile.

Eddie stepped over to relieve her of the kit. "That's probably a good idea, but I sure hope we don't need it," he said as he set the plastic box on the kitchen table.

"Now I will cut a hole in this old blanket so that Sullivan may slip it over his head," she announced as she went to the laundry room. She returned with a pair of heavy scissors and a length of rope. "And he can wrap this rope around his waist to hold the serape closed against the cold," she added.

She cut a slit in the middle of the heavy blanket. Then Hiroko re-folded it and held it up to show him. "Will this do as a pad?" she asked.

"Sure. That'll be fine. Thanks."

Hiroko smiled at him. "One last thing now: food. I believe there is something adequate to our needs in the pantry." A moment later she returned with a large bag of trail mix. She slid that into a heavy canvas shopping bag and added it to the other things on the kitchen table.

"Okay. That looks very good. Thank you, Hiroko," Joe spoke into the quiet of the kitchen.

"It is not so much. There are snack bars in the pantry as well. Let us add those," she replied. She went back to the pantry and returned with several food bars. Then she put all the snacks and the filled water bottles in a cardboard box from the greenhouse. "I only hope that it proves to be adequate," Hiroko said as she stepped back and surveyed the supplies.

Joe cleared his throat. "Hiroko. I just had a thought. We will be out very late, and it will be cold. Do you have thermoses? Could we trouble you to fill them with something hot to drink?"

"Certainly, *Sensei*. What would you prefer?"

"Well, I'll always choose coffee if it's to be had, but that's not necessary."

"Coffee it shall be, *Sensei*."

"Thank you very much, Hiroko. Now I think I should take a few moments to scan the perimeter of your property. I don't yet sense any close presence, but it is best to be certain."

"Want some help?" Eddie offered.

"Thanks, son, but it'll be quicker if I just do this myself. Relax. I'll be right back."

Joe was true to his word. He was back within minutes. "It's still clear. Perhaps they're counting on us doing something close by and are just waiting for the snow. Whatever. We can't count on it staying this way, but I'd say we can load the vehicle now without being observed."

They gathered the food box, the firearms and the ammunition and carried it to the garage. Joe suggested that they wrap the grounding rod in a tarp and place it on the roof of the vehicle. It took five minutes to find a tarp and bungee cords. Then the two men maneuvered the heavy rod to the luggage rack on the roof and fastened the bundle securely.

The rearmost window on the driver's side had a gun rack mounted inside, and they secured the matching .30-30's in the rack. There were tie-downs beneath the gun rack and they used these to attach the ammunition and food containers to the side panel. Eddie wedged his sheathed throwing axes between the two crates. Hiroko brought the first aid kit from the house and slid it beneath the front seat.

It took a little more than a quarter hour to get everything stowed inside the FJ Cruiser. They locked the side door of the garage and returned to the house. The moon had not yet risen and the sky was dark. The high desert was fast losing what little heat it had gathered from the winter sun. Eddie wished he had his hat with him, but he'd left it at Joe's house.

"Hiroko, is there a hat I could borrow?"

"Certainly. My husband has many knit hats. I will get some for whoever wants one." She went to the back of the house and returned with an armload of warm-looking knit ski-hats.

"Thanks, Hiroko. That'll help a lot."

She smiled and nodded slightly in response.

"It would perhaps be best if we took the clothing articles and the coffee out at the very last, when we are ready to leave," Hiroko suggested.

Joe sat at the kitchen table. "Yes. I agree. Now we wait."

A few minutes later, the phone rang. When she saw the caller ID display, Hiroko punched the speaker button on the kitchen phone. It was Sullivan. He spoke briefly and cryptically. "It's all good here. On our way back. Expect us soon."

Hiroko went to the front room and shut out the lights. She stood in the dark near the door where she could observe the road. It was perhaps fifteen minutes before a car passed, but it continued on without slowing. Then, about five minutes later, she saw the Prius slow in front of the house and turn into the drive. "They're here," she announced as she returned to the kitchen.

After pausing to remove their shoes in the greenhouse, Ikeda, Sullivan, and Nadine came in from the garage. Briefly, Nadine shook hands with Joe and with Eddie and then turned to Hiroko.

"Nadine-san, this is my wife, Hiroko."

Nadine extended her hand. She was more than a head taller than the older woman. "I think we met once, perhaps twenty years ago," she said with a smile.

"Yes. Now that I see you, I remember. Welcome, Nadine," Hiroko replied, taking the taller brunette's hand in her own.

Nadine had indeed dressed appropriately for winter in the southwest. She wore jeans, a heavy turtleneck, and a down vest. She carried a heavy parka over her left arm. Her hair was pulled back and confined by a scarf. A knit cap protruded from the pocket of her vest.

"Well, are we ready?" Sullivan asked into the brief silence.

"As ready as possible, I think, Sully. Have you briefed Nadine?" Joe wanted to know.

Nadine answered for herself. "Sully and Harry told me a few things. I understand we're going out into the desert tonight to do *something*. Although I had a discussion with Sully and Eddie back in San Luis about portals and such, I'm not precisely sure what to expect. I understand it may be dangerous. I expect I don't need to know much more at this point."

"And you are sure? Sure you want to get involved?" Joe spoke up. He looked very somber.

The slender brunette's eyes flashed and she met Joe's gaze directly. "Thank you, yes. I know you maintain some reservations about me. That is perhaps understandable, but you should know that I have taken risks all my life. I weigh my odds as best I can and then make my move. I have read and reread Fred's letters and have decided I must see the truth for myself. Please count me in."

Joe nodded briefly. "Fine. From what Harry says, you'll have plenty of time to ask any other questions that come to you on the way out."

Now he looked around at everyone gathered in the tidy kitchen. "Anybody have a compelling argument that we've not yet heard? If not, we should get moving."

"Remember, we're going outdoors in the high desert on a winter night. It will be cold out there. Here are some warm clothes in case you need them," Hiroko offered. "We have fashioned a serape for you, Sully," she added.

"Ah. Excellent. Thank you, Hiroko. I think I'll appreciate that once we're out in the cold," the engineer replied gratefully.

"It is time. If we are to do this, we must be on our way," Harry stated quietly.

Pausing in the greenhouse to step into their outdoor shoes, they all filed into the back yard. Eddie noticed that Nadine had brought stout hiking boots. She pulled gloves from the pocket of her parka and slipped those on as well.

Once back in the garage, the six of them quickly sorted themselves into the FJ Cruiser. Eddie wedged himself into the very back. Facing the rifle racks and crated supplies, he sat cross-legged on the folded blanket that would later function as Sullivan's serape. The two women shared the back seat with the broad-shouldered engineer. Harry was at the wheel and Joe rode shotgun.

"All ready?"

"Let's go."

Harry backed the four wheel drive vehicle out of the garage, pressed the remote to close the doors and pulled onto the road. He drove east to I-25. By the time they reached the interstate, the rising moon glowed just beneath the eastern horizon.

Eddie did okay for the first several miles, but it took nearly three-quarters of an hour to reach the interchange at Bernardo, some 50 miles south of Albuquerque. Highway 60 came in from the east there. Old Highway 85 headed west, off into the desert. By then, the moon had cleared the horizon and Eddie was carsick and uncomfortable. He tried to stretch his legs across the cargo area.

"Anyone need a break?" Harry spoke quietly as they turned off the interstate. No one else said anything, so Eddie just swallowed, took a deep breath and continued to tough it out.

Tough indeed was the rest of the trip. The road became rough and then petered out altogether. After about eight miles, Harry stopped the FJ and then turned due west.

"It would be helpful if someone would walk ahead of me for the next mile or two. We do not want to become high-centered out here. I will direct you using the turn indicators."

"I'll do it," Eddie volunteered.

"I think I should join you, son. Two sets of eyes and all," Joe added.

Harry cut the headlights and the two men got out. After the closeness of the interior of the FJ, the icy air cut into Eddie's nostrils. Glad for his borrowed knit hat, he pulled up his collar and snapped the down vest closed before zipping up his jacket and jamming his hands in the pockets.

The brilliant, high-desert moon had climbed a third of the way up the eastern sky. No clouds obscured the silvery light. Their eyes adapted quickly and Eddie could clearly make out the central peak named *Sierra Ladrone*. It loomed above them, mostly barren in its lower elevations but crowned with a wreath of conifers. Far off to the south, coyotes hunted. The landscape came into focus all around them.

Eddie and Joe stood ten feet apart and led the way west. Their job was to look for small drop-offs that might trap the Toyota. The vehicle idled as they walked ahead. Harry knew the landmarks and would occasionally use the turn indicators to keep them on course. Despite the cold, Eddie was grateful to be out of the back and into the fresh air. Even in the icy air, his legs loosened and warmed quickly. Grudgingly forgiving him for its earlier mistreatment, his stomach took longer to settle down.

They walked for perhaps twenty minutes, and as they progressed, the ground began to rise. They wound into a steep-sided canyon. Another quarter hour passed, and the walls closed in. They faced a precipitous incline. Now Eddie was warm from the exertion. Harry leaned out of the driver's window. "This is the place. I will turn the vehicle around here."

Everyone piled out. Harry turned the Toyota to point back the way they'd come. He cut the engine and the sounds of the high desert at night closed around them. Everyone spoke quietly, as if they might disturb someone, as if they might be overheard by some unseen listener.

Joe bent down and gathered a few small pebbles. He put them in his jacket pockets. "Start unloading the vehicle. I want to establish a perimeter right away."

He moved off twenty or thirty feet to the side. He drew out a pebble and blew on it. Then he dropped it to the ground and moved on. In this way, he surrounded the party with small stones. Then he moved out to a greater distance and repeated the process. Finally, he moved out near the tall canyon walls and completed a third circuit. Then he returned to the group.

"Everyone, please do your best to stay inside this inner circle. Now, Harry, Sullivan. Let's lay out a pattern for the spells. We'll do three sets of three, triangular patterns. The first, innermost pattern will point northwest, the second northeast. The outermost pattern will point due north."

They fanned out. Joe used his uncanny sense of the compass to state his preferences. At each of the nine points, they put a stone and scribed a circle in the sandy soil. While they did that, Eddie unrolled the heavy grounding rod and lugged it to the first, northwest-facing vertex.

In the meantime, Hiroko and Nadine carried the firearms and ammunition over to a waist-high, flat topped boulder near the vehicle.

"Do you have experience with these?" Hiroko asked.

"Rifles? Sorry, no. I've never fired one."

"No matter. I hope we will not need them. Still, would you mind loading for me, should that become necessary?"

"I'd be happy to. Just show me how to do it. Now that we're out here I feel strange and nervous. I need something to do. Something to occupy my attention," Nadine replied.

"Thank you so much. Each magazine will hold twelve rounds. They go in like this, do you see? Now you try it. Yes. That is perfect. Take your time. I will watch this time, but it is really very simple."

Eddie came over. He set an unsheathed hand axe next to the ammunition basket on the rock.

"I want to leave one axe with you guys, okay? I can drape two over my shoulder with my belt, but three are too heavy."

"Oh. Perhaps we should have looked for some kind of strap. I did not think of it."

"No, it's fine, Hiroko, thanks. I've put a bungee cord around my waist for a belt. Even with a strap, I think three would be too much. If my hands were free, I'd hold one and carry the other two, but I'm going to be holding that grounding rod.

"How's it going here?" he added.

"We are set up. Next we will get food and water ready in the back of the Toyota," Hiroko answered.

"Great. Now if I call for that axe, just underhand it in my direction, okay? It's not going to hurt me if you lob it. Just toss it at my feet."

"I can do that," Nadine agreed.

Now the other three walked up.

"We're ready to go, son. Are you ready to start?"

"Yeah. I think I'm good to go."

"I think we should be okay for at least the first four or five spells. We'll take a short break, then, before continuing. When we hit the sixth, we will have established a symmetric pattern and the Queen will almost certainly sense it. She will try to search among the worlds for the source of the disturbance. The seventh portal will perturb the symmetry and make it difficult to trace us, so if we can move quickly to that one, we should be left alone until we do the ninth and final opening.

"I cannot imagine that she will *not* respond then, though there is little she can do once the ninth portal has opened. We will have established a new connection, a major connection between this world and the Great Hub. Within moments, magic will work in this place. Better than it has for centuries.

"I do not know what form her response will take, but she will be insane with rage. You can count on it," Joe finished.

Hiroko and Nadine sat in the open back of the Toyota and watched wordlessly as Joe completed this little monologue.

The spells began. They started at the northwest vertex of the inner triangle. When they completed the final part of the chant, and the sizzling, green and gold lightning slammed together above the four men, Nadine gasped. Despite the brightness of the moon, the afterimage was visible for several minutes.

The second and third spells went off flawlessly; although Eddie wobbled on his feet at the last and was glad for the support of Sullivan's strong arm. The young man shook his head and stood up straight. He nodded at the others and moved to the position of the next vertex, the northeast-pointing triangle.

After the fourth spell, Eddie sagged again. Joe called a halt.

"I'm okay. The wire braiding just got hot that time."

"Let me see. You go get a sip of water and maybe a little coffee," Joe held out his hands for the grounding rod. He bent his face to examine it closely in the dim light.

Eddie walked back to the Toyota where Nadine and Hiroko waited. Hiroko offered him a water bottle and the young man gratefully accepted a drink. He was surprised at how thirsty he'd become.

"Thanks," he whispered, his voice slightly hoarse. He cleared his throat and walked back to the cluster of older men.

"Sully's splices are holding, but the pattern of manual weaving cannot be as uniform as a piece of solid metal. You must concentrate very deeply, son. Breathe into it. Follow your breath deeply into the metal and observe the flow of energies. Observe and focus, but do not allow yourself to be drawn inside."

"Yeah. I know. I sort of lost it that last time. I'll do better," Eddie insisted.

Michael C. Glaviano

The wind picked up. It reached into the blind canyon and sucked heat away from them. The moon was high now, and gathering to the north in that silvery light, clouds were visible. Eddie took off his make-shift axe holder strap and laid the hand axes gently on the hood of the Toyota. He felt lighter as he returned to the southeast vertex and lifted the metallic grounding rod. The staff felt heavier now, but it was still warm in his hands and he was grateful for that little bit of comfort.

"Come on. Let's keep going," he said.

Eddie focused on his breathing as Joe stood in front of him and Harry and Sullivan flanked him. He struggled for a moment but then found his concentration. He dropped into the same feeling that some-times awaited him inside his practice with the throwing axes. His breath steadied. The fifth spell was much like the first. The feeling of immer-sion moved barely past his wrists. His hands stayed comfortable.

"Okay, gentlemen. This sixth opening will cause a discernible change in our surroundings. Remember, we must move immediately and confidently to open the seventh connection point."

Again Eddie tried to move back into that zone of concentration, but this time it was slippery. Perhaps he was too aware of the importance of the symmetry they were building. For whatever reason, as the spell progressed, the sense of immersion surrounding his hands expanded all the way to his chest. He fought it back by visualizing the flow of energies, but his hands became numb and unfeeling.

At the final, "*now the door opens!*" the heavy staff came alive in his fitful grasp.

"I could use a little help, here," he managed as he slipped to the ground.

Forty Seven

The Locust Queen had been uneasy for the space of an hour. The room, usually so delightfully cool and still, had become annoyingly warm. Here and there, ice crystal chandeliers dripped. The enveloping shadows had drawn back. Dim light and flickering shadows had become harsh, stark.

The Queen had grown uncomfortable and risen to stand in front of her carved throne. Something pressed, ached. The emptiness that lay at her core sucked at her. She paced back and forth before her throne.

Gradually, the matrix of stolen energies that lay beneath her form shifted and her body became bathed in sweat. Her gown grew clingy and irritating. The courtiers retreated to the very edge of the expansive chamber. The Queen's discomfort was ever a thing to dread.

Now, without warning, the Queen threw back her head and screamed. Deafened, eardrums shattered, those nearest the fell monarch collapsed in agony. She glared into the cowering forms before her and strode forward. She became taller, crossed the space in but two strides. Faster than the eye could follow, she reached out, snagged two unlucky ones and shook them as she hurled questions they could barely understand, let alone answer.

Enraged, she dashed them together and cast their broken, lifeless bodies aside. The featureless sapphires of her eyes blazed upon the courtiers who cowered and cried in their fear. Stupid, helpless, disgusting cowards, her few remaining advisors also shrank from the divine power of her gaze. She could well imagine killing them all.

Instead, she vanished from the chaos of her throne room to materialize in the bedlam of the chamber that housed her web of sensors. These at least were loyal. Altered as they were, they could be nothing else. With immense self-control borne of necessity, she resisted the urge to silence their screams permanently.

Ignoring the shuddering that her ministrations invoked, she probed deeply but gently with her mind. What world? What world had dared? It must be near. Where were her agents? Why had they not prevented this... nascent connection? Why had they not reported? Did they not know that she was Queen? They would surely pay for their failure. Yes.

But first she must find them. And to find and punish these miscreants, she must first find the world that so audaciously wriggled within her grasp. What world was the source of this outrage? Which, among the myriad that touched the Great Hub had dared to trouble her divine hunger? Where? Where?

Forty Eight

"Quick! Get him on his feet!" Joe called urgently.

Sliding his massive shoulders under the younger man's limp arms, Sullivan lifted Eddie as if he were a child.

"C'mon, kid. Come back to us. You can do it!"

Eddie fought his way back. He shook his head. "Thirsty!" he got out. Indeed, he felt completely drained and dry inside.

Hiroko hurried up with a water bottle. Eddie reached for it, and Sullivan helped him drink a little. That brought him back.

He looked around. There were now six, faint lines of green light arching into the night. Reaching for infinity, striving to be seen against the glare of moonlight, each line extended from a vertex of the pattern of portals they had opened.

"Could I have a sip of coffee? Maybe half water and half coffee?" he croaked.

"Certainly."

"Bring him to the next vertex while she gets that, will you, Sully? We have to do the next spell right away," Joe whispered urgently.

Eddie began to regain feeling in his arms and legs as the engineer helped him to the north vertex of the final, outermost pattern. Hiroko ran back up with some weak coffee, which Eddie gratefully swallowed. He felt it move down into the emptiness that lay inside him. The feeling of it restored him a little more.

"Okay. That's it. I've got it now," he said to the concerned faces around him.

"This one is critical, son. The odd number, the asymmetry of seven connections, will confound her search for us. Give us time."

"I'm ready," he said shakily. "I can do this. Then we can take a break, right?"

"Right."

Eddie reached deep into himself. He focused his thoughts. The cold desert night receded as he held the warm grounding rod. It felt heavier still, and he needed Sullivan's help to position the staff at the right point. The braided copper was now a familiar texture beneath his

Michael C. Glaviano

hands. He lifted his head and stared at the moon, so far away, so cold and silvery.

He drew the frigid air into his lungs and the shadows cleared from his mind. He slowed his breathing deliberately. He forced his hands to steady themselves, forced the quivering from his legs. The calmness came. The feeling descended around him as the spell commenced.

This time he kept his focus all the way through. He wobbled slightly as the final line was chanted, but he held himself up until Sullivan could relieve him of the heavy grounding rod.

"Okay. You all should grab a snack. Get off your feet. Rest as best you can. I want to look around for a few moments," Joe announced. He took a step back and faded into the deep shadows of the rocks that surrounded them.

Forty Nine

"WHERE ARE THEY?!!" her shriek exploded in the minds of all who dwelt within the confines of the Queen's castle. She had nearly been upon them, but they slipped from her web of sensors and eluded her. They had sunk back, submerged into the infinity of worlds that radiated from the Hub. Now the Locust Queen screamed and tore at the pattern of energy that was her thick hair.

Her sensors were no use now, and she killed one of them and reached for another before she regained a measure of composure. She consoled herself with slamming the controls for the circuits that drove their pain centers to the maximum settings. She watched, a half smile curving her beautiful, full lips as the remaining sensors writhed and screamed their blind, inarticulate pain.

Once again, this calmed her. She discarded the still form of the sensor whose service she had terminated in the first bloom of her rage. Soon she must replace that one. Now, however, events were afoot. Events that demanded a reasoned response.

With some longing, real effort, and no little hunger, she readjusted the controls that fed impressions to the pathetic things that writhed in their stainless steel basins. The screaming receded, became a whimpering whisper of its former music. The agonized writhing became mere spasms of affliction and then twitches of discomfort.

The Locust Queen considered the situation. She contemplated her next step and decided that she must learn more. Was this ripple a mere anomaly? She thought not. Was it, as she strongly suspected, a serious perturbation, a challenge to her will? She required more knowledge, but knowledge was not flowing towards her. A short pause... then a decision was reached. She must seek that which would answer these and other questions.

Resolute now, she drew upon the reservoir of the lives, the worlds she had consumed. The great Queen immersed herself in deep oceans of power. Such effort had long been unnecessary, but she still knew the ways into the furthest recesses of the twisted wrinkles of Chaos, the lowest circles of the Hell Realms. The pattern of her power had been bought at great price and, once purchased, would never desert her.

Dusty, silent galleries of possibility unfolded at her will. Shadows, nightmarish shapes, the fevered clutch of the elder gods, and more witnessed the wake of her passage. This vexation, she saw, was not done. This affront would continue until she authored its cessation. She must ready a response.

So. She would, therefore, immerse herself within the web of her remaining sensors. She would lie still, quiet, and aware at the center of their web. When external disturbances next invoked their distress, she must follow their pain to its source and hurl her response at the miscreants.

Knowing, reckoning, secure in her foreseeing, she departed from those grim corridors. Withdrawing from those arid places, the Queen wound her way back through the maze of probabilities. She shifted past the notice of hungry things that hissed and brooded among the shadows. Footprints had marked her passage through the endless, dusty hallways, and as she retraced her steps, she took care to ensure her track was erased.

At last, she stood once more in the comfortable chill of her chamber of sensors. The featureless sapphire orbs of her eyes considered her environs, her own form. She saw that her gown was soiled, ruined. At a glance it vanished to reveal her unblemished, full, porcelain beauty. The matrix of energy that represented her hair was disheveled, and so she drew her fingers through the thick, waving blackness of her tresses and coerced the coiffure into electric perfection.

She extracted a minute fragment of her own beauty to fashion a frame for her exquisite shape and then wrapped her divine loveliness in a new gown. Once more tranquil, again perfect in her own regard, the Locust Queen considered her response. Her riposte must be forceful, definitive. It must bear her mark.

But what specific form should her action take? Her agents had proved themselves feckless, her advisors incompetent. Her sensors were reliable but could do no more than feel, perceive, and suffer. The courtiers were nothing: snacks to relieve bored cravings.

Ah, but what of her hounds? Yes. The next time she caught wind of this... *transgression* on her intent, she would follow the thread that led to it and set her hounds upon those who dared raise their puny wills against hers. The beauty, the hunger, the strength and speed of her hounds would erase this insult.

She would be ready.

Fifty

Eddie dragged his feet back to the Toyota. Offering simple comfort, Nadine came over and put her arm around his waist. "I've never
seen anything like this," she said. "It's simply unprecedented for me,"
she added and then laughed at the tautology.

"Until tonight, I was willing to admit the possibility of other-
worldly forces, of magic, of things beyond everyday experience. Now that
I've seen it first hand... well, I guess I didn't truly believe it until now."

She shook her head. "Anyway, what can we get you, Eddie?" she
continued.

The young man realized that he was extremely hungry as well as
thirsty. "Let me grab a couple of handfuls of trail mix and a food bar.
Then I'd like some water and some coffee!"

That brought a round of gentle laughter from those gathered
nearby. Hiroko offered the bag containing the trail mix and Eddie pulled
out a large handful. No scrumptious, five course dinner had ever been
more welcome.

Eddie had just about finished his snack when Joe emerged from
the shadows.

"So far so good," the ancient warrior announced. "Obviously, we
got that seventh portal open in time. Are you feeling better now?"

"Yeah. I'm good for two more, I think," Eddie assured his ment-
or.

"As soon as you're ready, we'll get busy. I think I should describe
what will happen when we open the final portal in the pattern. I assume
you all noticed how after the sixth spell finished, the green lines of light
persisted for several minutes.

"Now. Know this: after the last opening, you should expect a
column of green and gold light. It will reach up fifty or sixty feet. It will
be pretty bright if you look directly at it, so try to face away from it. Rapidly, a pool will form at the base of the column. Tears of the gods, yes.
These phenomena will last until dawn.

"As quickly as possible, stand with your backs to the column of
light. I expect the Queen's response to come up the canyon, but there's

no guarantee of it. Hiroko and Nadine. You should ready an armed response. Eddie. As soon as you get your feet under control, get to your
axes. As soon as you can hold one, ready it.

"Sullivan and Harry. You should be spotters at first. Try to look
in all the directions. Again, here in this canyon, magic will work better
than it has for centuries on this poor, injured world. Your advanced seeing spells will work. Better yet, many of your other spells, including
spells useful in combat, will work. Perhaps they will not perform in precisely the same way as they would in a truly healthy world, but they will
indeed work.

Eddie finished his food bar and drank deeply from a water bottle.
Next, he poured himself a cup of coffee and sipped it as he stared into the
night. He stretched and felt the kinks in his back and neck settle away. It
was late and they were all getting tired.

Soon they were ready to finish the evening's work. Joe, Ikeda,
Sullivan, and Eddie returned to the pattern. Now they stood at the eighth
vertex of the series.

"Just two more," Eddie told himself. "Just two more."

The young man stooped and, with Sullivan's help, took up the
grounding rod. The staff continued to grow in apparent mass. Eddie saw
that the copper braiding was beginning to fray and loosen, but the contact was good when he gripped it tightly. The others took their places.
He again stilled his mind and focused on the task at hand. The spell
began.

It was easier this time. The break had calmed and restored Eddie, as had the knowledge that they were nearly done with this part of the
work. Also, the feeling of reaching deep into something warm and thick
was no longer quite so strange, no longer quite so distracting. As those
around him entered the final stanza of the chant, the feeling reached his
elbows and then pulled back slightly. Manageable. Not frightening.

At the end of the spell, he shifted his hands on the grounding rod
and the copper weaving came the rest of the way loose. It fell to the
ground. There was a brief spark, then nothing. Joe stooped and picked it
up.

"Well, that's too bad. You're going to need to wrap it around and
hold it tightly for this last one. We can give you a minute or so to get it
right. You're probably able to feel it at this point."

"Yeah. I know how it should feel."

Joe took the heavy staff and walked the distance to the ninth and
final vertex of the pattern. He positioned the grounding rod carefully and
then handed it off to Eddie. This last spell would complete the connection between this hidden canyon in the *Sierra Ladrones* and the place
between worlds. The tears of the gods would moisten the soil of this
place. Magic would come.

Eddie wrapped the braided band around the rod. Working his right hand in a circle around the three pieces of welded re-bar, he shaped the copper braid and tucked its edges together. Once the copper braid felt right in his hand, he gripped the bar on the second braided band with his left. It was also coming loose but would be secure enough for one more spell.

"Okay, I'm ready,"

The final spell of opening began. The tingling, the low sound, all returned. The chant moved inexorably forward. Eddie focused and focused, intent on the energies that flowed deep within the ground and above in the sky. He focused on their meeting point near the center of the metal staff.

The flow was uneven now, and he struggled to keep it steady. He went deep inside to see, to stand very near to the flow and pressed *here* and *there* with his mind. The focus held. At the final "*now the door opens!*" he was rocked back on his heels, but he stayed up.

He could feel warmth on his face and sense bright light through his closed lids. Eddie took a deep breath and opened his eyes to tiny slits to see a column of green and gold light swirling before him. The bright column reached up into the New Mexico sky. He stepped back and tried to shift his hands on the grounding rod.

"My hands! They're stuck," he whispered.

Taking the weight from Eddie's hands, Sullivan leaned forward and gripped the metal staff. Joe stepped closer and looked intently.

"Yes," Joe said. "You've welded the copper in place. That's very good. Some day you may be able to do it deliberately, consciously. Now, however, we must get your hands off without permanently damaging them."

Joe wiggled Eddie's fingers and got them to relax. Little by little, he worked. All the while, he chanted a strange set of syllables under his breath. At last, Eddie was able to pull his hands away. The skin felt sens-itive, as though it were sunburned. Later, he would see that the pattern of the braid had been imprinted on the palms of his hands. It would re-main that way for years.

He flexed his hands and looked around the strangely illuminated landscape. Far away, he could hear a howling, a baying. He remembered Maia's forest and the Queen's hounds. Here, however, there were no great trees to offer protection, no giant elk to trample the hounds under-foot.

Michael C. Glaviano

Fifty One

There! There they are! How *dare* they interfere. This world was nearly ready to be consumed! Now it might take years to undo their meddling. Who are these pathetic creatures? Oh. That ancient one. His callow help-mate. Others.

The Locust Queen recognized their scent: the scent of foolish busybodies. Well, the scent of fear would soon overlay all else. And be-fore the sun rose again on this hapless world, the scent of blood would wash away all traces of these interlopers.

She perceived that this interference had festered for too long. She contemplated the pleasure of setting the hounds upon them. Her lovely, hungry hounds would feed well tonight. And these trespassers upon her intention would know fear and despair before death released them.

How many beauties should she send on this errand? The annoy-ing fools stand outside, in the open air. There is no shelter. There is nowhere for them to hide. Three, beautiful, hungry hounds should do. Five might be too quick. Quick is bad. But uncertainty is worse. No. She would sacrifice the pleasure of their suffering for the certainty of the result. It shall be nine. She would send all nine of her ravenous beauties!

"Fly, my children!" came her command. "Fly down this thread! Do you see? It leads to the throats of those who would transgress upon the beauty, upon the will of the Locust Queen."

The great Queen closed her eyes then to observe the battle to come. It would be short, truly, but it promised to be pleasurable. She re-gretted slightly that she would not witness the battle in person. She re-gretted somewhat more that these meddlers would not perceive her grace and power as their lives bled into the ground. With a world so damaged, however, that was sadly impossible. The pattern that sustained her beauty, her strength, and her power could not remain coherent in such a world. In such a world, she would be unable to hold at bay the fragment of the Abyss that gnawed at her core. This limitation was unavoidable. It was the cost of her power and must be borne.

Michael C. Glaviano

She must be satisfied to witness at a remove the elimination of these vermin. She would watch. Then she would begin anew. These events, after all, constituted nothing more than an interruption.

In time, this world would fall. In the end, the life of this world would feed her, sustain her, add to her glory and power. The beauty of this world would be absorbed into her beauty. The strength of its storms would augment her strength. She would suck the depths of the night sky into her heart and would leave behind a lifeless cinder.

Fifty Two

The baying came again. It was still distant, but it drew rapidly closer. "I know that sound! It's the hounds!" Eddie called hoarsely. "They chased me in the forest. You remember? When I met Maia."

Joe's reply was all quiet reassurance. "Be calm, son. Everyone, settle down," he said. "Yes, I know the Queen's hounds. They are great beasts and are indeed ferocious. But they are still merely beasts. Ikeda has chosen this spot well. We hold the high ground. The hounds will have to run uphill from the mouth of the canyon to reach us. If we fight well together, we will stand against them. Quickly, now. Listen to me.

"Hiroko. Focus on stopping the wolves as they first appear. Shoot quickly, but make your shots count. Nadine. You must make sure that Hiroko has a loaded weapon in her hands at all times. Eddie. You must stand over them and be ready to throw your axes. Some hounds will undoubtedly get too close for the rifle. Save one axe for close-in fighting.

"Sullivan, Ikeda. You're with me. We'll put our backs to the column of light and draw on the energy to illuminate the landscape. Then we'll use what spells we can to slow the onslaught of the Queen's hounds."

"What spells do you suggest, *Sensei*?"

"One of you should do Beam of Light. Aim for their eyes. They hunt with their sense of smell, but the bright light will still bother them."

"I can do that, boss."

"Fine. Then Harry and I will try spells to impede the hounds physically. I'm not sure what will work. Tanglefoot, Stun, Slippery, Sleep, Electric Shock... we'll try them all and see what works."

"It is many years since I have used those, *Sensei*. We shall see how good my memory is tonight."

Now the sounds were much closer. Individual, baying and howling voices echoed over nearby hills. The three older men moved back to the column of light. Trying to regain full use and sensation, Eddie flexed his hands as he strode as quickly as he could to the Toyota to retrieve his throwing axes. He joined Nadine and Hiroko at the rock just as Sullivan cast a searchlight beam over the terrain to the east.

The temperature dropped and the sky darkened as clouds blew over the face of the moon. The snowstorm had arrived. The pillar of light illuminated snowflakes as they fell. Shining through the sparkling snow seconds later, Sullivan's beam of light caught the first of the great, shaggy beasts as it appeared. Then another and another hurtled past the mouth of the canyon. They were visible, but they moved fast. With a speed and agility that belied their size, they dodged sideways into shadow as the light hit them.

Hiroko fired three times before she brought the lead beast down at just over one hundred yards. It took four more shots to stop the second. By then, five more of the hounds were running toward them. Harry and Joe began casting spells in the direction of the oncoming animals. Sullivan continued to illuminate the landscape and try to blind the beasts.

At first, the spells had no discernible effect, but then one of the hounds fell with a yelp. It skidded forward, struggled to get up, and then lay still. That gave Hiroko time to bring down another that was just behind it. She fired again but missed. One more shot dropped still another. Now the rifle was empty.

The snow fell more heavily. Snow on the ground reflected the dazzling green and gold column of light that stood at their backs. Hiroko handed the empty Winchester to Nadine and took the loaded repeater. Nadine bent, opened the magazine and began to refill the first weapon. The hounds were at fifty yards when they began to have trouble making headway against Joe's and Harry's spells.

The onrushing animals ran up against the perimeter that Joe had established upon their arrival. Lightning flashed and burned the animals as they tried to pass. Snapping at each other and howling, they yelped and spun in the falling snow, but they threw themselves against the barrier over and over. Gradually, visible in the flickering light, the hungry beasts began to make headway.

The animals fell and got up and fell again. Hiroko was able to shoot two more, but now the beasts were very close. Hiroko emptied the Winchester as quickly as she could but there were still two wolves facing them. All at once, the animals ceased their baying cries. They broke off their headlong charge, and using deep pockets of shadow, began circling.

Sullivan tried to keep the beams of light on the beasts, but it was getting harder to see in the blowing snow. Crafty and smart, the hounds dodged the light as they wove nearer and nearer. Now, apart from the sounds of their panting, they were nearly silent. Adding to the alien scene, the innermost circle of the perimeter flared brightly.

"Let me in there now," Eddie spoke urgently. "Take the rifle that Nadine's loaded."

Eddie's hands were still tingly and sore, but he gripped the cold handles of the axes as best he could. He tried to drop into his zone, but his mind was foggy and tired and the pain in his hands was a distraction. He took a deep breath.

There was a sudden burst of movement from the right. One of the hounds leapt from the snowy shadows to run directly at him. Eddie threw and missed. Now the huge animal was just fifteen feet away. A spell caught the beast and made it spin and yelp. That gave Eddie his opening. The axe flew fast and hard and struck the animal's side before it could turn back. It cried and fell and a shot from Hiroko's weapon finished it off.

The remaining hound sprang into view. Eddie bent to grab the third axe from the rock in front of him, but there was no time to throw. The animal lunged at him and he jumped to the side. The young man's tired legs were slow, but he raised the axe as the beast spun to face him. It's eyes glowed eerily and it's powerful jaws yawned as it lunged again. With all the force he could muster, Eddie slammed the edge of the axe into the animal's mouth.

The hound was badly hurt, but the momentum of its leap carried it forward. It knocked him down. The yawning vice of its jaws tried to find his throat. Eddie got his hands under the animal's muzzle and pushed the great head up. The hound clawed at him and tried to force his arms away.

Suddenly the animal snarled and tried to turn. The weight was gone. There was a sickening, wet impact, a yelp, then a final shot. Eddie sat up. Sullivan stood over the beast, breathing hard. His hands were still locked around the animal's hind legs. Hiroko had run up and put a bullet through its head.

"Heavy bastard, that one," the engineer observed in a matter-of-fact voice. Just then, another of the great hounds leapt to the top of the Toyota and jumped at Sullivan's back. Ikeda appeared out of nowhere to grab the heavier man's arm and swing him out of harm's way.

With perfect grace, the Aikido master rolled back to his feet and faced the hound. The animal was badly hurt. It's sides heaved, and blood flowed from the wound in its powerful chest to spatter the snow-covered earth. The man and the beast stared at each other across a space of ten feet. Everyone froze. Where he sat on the ground, Eddie could see his bloody axe lying next to him.

The young man's vision narrowed to a sharp field centered on the crouching hound. Eddie wiped his hand on his pant leg, reached for the axe, and threw it just as the animal sprang one last time. Ikeda began to turn from the hound's trajectory. Covered by snow and hidden in the shadowy, flickering light, a rock lay unseen. The Aikido master's foot came down upon it.

The injured beast's leap carried it forward and the axe took it in the side. The animal cried in pain and it seemed to curl on itself as it flew. Ikeda recovered but was unable to turn quickly enough. Even so, the lunge that should have reached the man's throat was instead blocked by his outstretched arm. Snapping jaws worked their way up the bottom side of Ikeda's arm and the animal sank its teeth into the muscles around his armpit and chest. The hound kicked spasmodically and finally died, but its huge jaws were locked upon Ikeda's shoulder and ribs.

Joe dashed to his friend. Amidst the scattered snow and blood, he knelt on the cold ground. He pried the hound's muzzle open and, as though it weighed nothing, hurled the huge beast into the darkness. Then he tore open the man's shirt. In the glow cast by the portal, Eddie could see blood welling up with terrifying speed.

Haruko ran up crying, "Husband! Husband!" Sobbing then, she fell to the earth and cradled her husband's head in her lap. Ikeda lay deathly still in the cold. The snow continued to fall around them.

"Quick!" shouted Joe. "The tears. The tears of the gods. Bathe the wound. Everyone." He jumped to the base of the glowing pillar of light to cup his hands and scoop up some of the liquid gathered there. He ran back to his friend and poured the water of the tears onto the wound.

Harry gasped with pain as the tears of the gods touched the gruesome wound. Then he took a shallow, ragged breath. Sullivan and Eddie ran to the pool and carried what they could back to pour on the deep gash in the man's body. Nadine paused and removed the cups from the tops of the thermoses before joining the others. Over and over they ladled the tears of the gods as Joe whispered strange syllables, as Hiroko wept softly, as the injured man struggled to live.

Now Joe made a pulling motion above the wound. A cloud formed above the largest, most horrific gash. The cloud glowed with the color of a bad bruise: purple and a putrid green-yellow. The cloud clung to Ikeda's chest as Joe pulled and pulled. All at once, the cloud came away and Joe gathered it into a ball which he threw towards the pillar of gold and green light. The ball burst into flame and disappeared before it had covered half the distance.

Ikeda's breathing grew easier. Joe ran back to the pool and made a few more trips to bathe the less severe bites along the arm. Then he began to chant as his hands wove a complex pattern over the man's injuries. Joe drew light from the shining pillar and cast that light upon his injured friend. Finally, he stood still. "That's all we can do for him now. Let us hope it is enough. Eddie took off his coat and laid it over Ikeda's torso to help shelter him from the falling snow.

Then the ancient warrior sprang lightly to his feet. "Time passes and we are not done here," Joe continued. "Sully, Eddie, Nadine. Help me with the grounding rod!"

The men lifted the rod up. Joe pointed to the pillar of light. "Set it up there. Hold it in place, Sully, right in the middle of the light. Straight into the sky and very still." His face craggy and serious, Joe turned to face Nadine and Eddie. "You two: we need rocks to pile around the base."

They gathered stones quickly. Eddie's hands throbbed and his back hurt but he looked around in the flickering light to find rocks that he could carry back to the pillar. At first, all three of them carried rocks back to where Sullivan stood. Then, once there were a dozen or so, Joe told the others to keep at it. Nadine moved gracefully; Eddie staggered back and forth.

Joe knelt in the pool that surrounded the pillar of light. Rivers of sweat ran down Sullivan's face as he held the metal staff straight up within the green and gold column. Joe began to stack rocks at the base of the rod. As he worked, he chanted. Some syllables were unrecognized and strange, others familiar: *rock, stone, seal, perfect, forever...*

Eddie and Nadine continued to carry, drag, and roll the stones they found back to where Joe knelt. Finally Joe stood up and motioned them back. He reached out and touched Sullivan's powerful arm just above the elbow.

The engineer opened his eyes and looked around. He nodded his head and stepped back. The base of the grounding rod was embedded in a single, rough cylinder of fused rock about three feet high. Sullivan sloshed back through the pool and Joe stood at his side. They gazed into the light. At a gesture from Joe, the liquid that soaked their clothes steamed away into the night and left them dry.

"Stand back a bit, everyone," he ordered quietly.

Sullivan, Eddie, and Nadine backed up and waited near where Hiroko still cradled her husband's head. Eddie glanced down. Ikeda's eyes were open and he looked up at the young man with a weak smile.

Eddie looked up again as Joe began a new chant in another strange, unfamiliar language. Even with Maia's gift of tongues, Eddie was able to make out very few of the words. The ground around Joe was free of the snow that blanketed much of the landscape, and Joe began to stoop and pick up stones that lay near his feet.

The ancient warrior continued to chant as, one-by-one, he cast the stones into the light. Each one landed atop the rough cylinder of rock that lay at the base of the grounding rod. As a stalagmite grows up from the floor of a cave hidden deep in the earth, each rock added to the cylinder's height and girth.

Faster now, the rough cylinder waxed taller in the center of the flickering light. Finally, a standing stone rested there. It completely encased the grounding rod. The stone thrust into the night to perhaps three times the height of a man. Eight feet across at its base, the megalith appeared to grow from the earth.

Michael C. Glaviano

Finally Joe stepped back and reached toward the rough cylinder. With passes of his hands and ancient words, he gathered light to himself, molded it and cast it back upon the rocky pillar. The cylinder spun slowly and screwed itself into the earth. It gave up half its height before it ground to a stop.

"Now it is settled, a new portal on this earth, a new doorway to the landscape that is watered with the tears of the gods. Perform a transit spell at this standing stone and you will find yourself in the Place. By dawn, the glow will fade and the tears will sink into the earth, but magic has returned to this place." he finished.

He looked tired then but roused himself and looked about him to give more orders. "Sully, my friend. Help Hiroko get Harry into the vehicle, will you? We need to get out of here."

Eddie remembered the first aid kit and retrieved it from the Toyota. Nadine held out her hand as he trudged to where Harry lay on the ground.

"I'll take care of the bandaging," she offered. "Then Sully can help us get him inside."

"Sure thing," Sullivan answered. His voice betrayed his exhaustion, but he moved quickly to her side to help.

Joe continued. "You've done well. All of you. Now, we must dispose of these carcasses and be on our way before dawn finds us. Can you help me, son?"

Eddie nodded. He and Joe dragged the closest of the dead hounds back to where three more of them lay. Nearby, Eddie found the axes he'd thrown and he lobbed them towards the vehicle. As quickly as their exhaustion would permit, the old man and his young helper worked their way toward the small rise where the beasts had first appeared. Eventually, they dragged all nine of them into a pile.

Then Joe sent Eddie back to the Toyota to wait. Eddie watched from there as his mentor faced the grisly pile, walked around it, stepped back, and made as if to cast something into its midst.

A nacreous light rose up around the dead hounds. Their bodies began to crumble and collapse. Then the whole ugly mess faded and was gone. Snow continued to fall. It would soon cover the place where the remains had been piled.

Fifty Three

In her throne room, the Locust Queen witnessed the defeat of her beautiful hounds and was enraged beyond all rational thought. As the outcome of the battle turned against her, she threw things. She hurt those around her until all the courtiers who were still capable of escape fled in terror. Then she sat in her elegant, cold room and brooded. And thought. For the first time in hundreds of years, a hint of worry touched her, brushed her divine form.

The emptiness that lay at her core must be fed. That was the bargain she had negotiated when she trapped that demon all those centuries ago. She had power, beauty, life, but she was always hungry. She must feed upon the stuff of worlds lest she herself be consumed by the fragment of the Void that fueled her majesty.

Now, these miscreants had deprived her of her feast, and the hunger gnawed at her. Oh, she was far away from danger. She knew she would prevail, but even so, the delay was disquieting. How had these puny beings survived? They were evidently far stronger than they appeared. How could that be? What was their secret?

She must think. She must control her desire to strike in favor of planning. There must be a weakness that she could exploit. Again, what was their secret? All but the meddlesome Old One was puny, weak. But working together they had killed not merely one or two, but *all nine* of her beautiful hounds.

She raged again at the memory and it was some time before she became calm enough to resume coherent thought.

Reluctantly, she recognized, she admitted to herself their strength. The Queen saw that they cooperated, supported, and protected each other as none of her puppets ever would. She had encouraged infighting and paranoia for centuries. Divide and conquer had always worked to her favor.

Could she sew discord among these interlopers? Perhaps. But that would take time. And during that time, they might continue their meddling. What was available to her? She could not attack them directly while they huddled in this damaged world. Even if they continued their meddling, it would be decades before sufficient magic returned that she might manifest there and visit her wrath directly upon them.

In the meantime, what tricks, what illusions could she bring to bear? She must think. What did she know? She must call in her agents. She would bring in many of those who had been so busy on this world. And others. Fewer agents dwelt in the world these wrongdoers had lately vacated. She must question all of those who remained. Learn what they had learned. See what they had seen.

And, yes, the questioning would itself be pleasurable. Her thoughts drifted, then, in anticipation of their fear, of the texture of their pain. She became distracted. Yes. She needed a new sensor or two anyway. Others she could question... thoroughly. To the point at which they'd be fit only as food for the pups she would raise to be her new crop of hounds. Yes. That would be best.

Now she stood and stretched and drew the illumination of the throne room to her. She called forth an icy, blue glare and cast it upon herself. Her admiration of her own beauty and brilliance waxed without bound. The light wrapped her in all the garments her perfect form required.

At ease once again, she reclined upon her icy throne and began calling agents back from the worlds these meddlesome gnats had visited. One or two at a time, she summoned her minions that they might relate what intelligence they had gleaned. Enjoyment beckoned and she began to smile. Ever sensitive to the Locust Queen's mood, her courtiers began to trickle back, to fawn at her feet.

Fifty Four

Joe hurried up to the Toyota. In an attempt to keep him warm, Nadine and Hiroko were sitting in the back seat on either side of Harry. "Gather everything. Let's move."

Sullivan gathered the rifles, checked the safeties, and leaned the firearms against the side of the vehicle. Eddie was very cold as he pushed the remaining food back into the box and slid the box against the back seat. Then he trudged over to the basket that contained the unused ammunition and carried it back. He fastened everything in place.

Finally, he collected his axes and his belt. Two of the axes were fouled with the blood of the hounds. He cleaned the weapons as best he could by wiping them in the snow. Shivering now, he sheathed them and put them in the back of the vehicle.

"Hiroko," Joe spoke gently, "I know you would rather stay with Harry, but we will get back faster and easier if you drive."

Hiroko shook her head as if to argue, but then Ikeda spoke for the first time since he had been hurt. "I feel you are not rid of me yet, dear wife. And *Sensei* is correct in his opinion. I will be fine here. Drive us home, please."

Reluctance in every movement, Hiroko climbed out of the back seat. "I will sit with him, Hiroko," Joe said. "During the ride back I will direct all my skill toward his well-being."

"Here, son," he added. "You look cold. Take my jacket."

Eddie gratefully shrugged the jacket over his down vest. He was still cold inside, and his feet were freezing, but the added layer helped reduce the shivers.

Now Sullivan spoke up. "Eddie and I will walk ahead and lead us back out, okay Hiroko?"

As if she did not trust her voice, Hiroko simply nodded once. She took the wheel, adjusted the seat and started the FJ Cruiser. As they set out, the brilliant light of the moon was obscured by heavy snow clouds, so Hiroko turned on the headlights. The snow continued. It had piled up in sheltered places. The falling snow sparkled and danced in the beams of the headlights.

Sullivan and Eddie each picked up a .30-30 and, cradling the weapons, walked to the front of the vehicle. Here and there, where the wind had kept the ground mostly clear, they could see the track of their way in. Looking out for places where the vehicle could get stuck, they walked ahead. Progress was slow and miserable, but eventually they reached old Highway 85 without further incident. The snow was a few inches deep there, but the surface beneath was reasonably flat and free of deep holes.

Sullivan took charge of the rifles. He ejected the live ammunition and stowed the weapons in the gun rack. Eddie blew on his hands and jammed them into the pockets of his borrowed jacket.

"Can I use your poncho to sit on in the back, Sully?" Eddie asked.

"Sure thing. But you want me to take a turn back there? You can ride shotgun," the broad-shouldered engineer offered.

"Thanks, man. You'd fit worse than me. I'm so wiped out that I'll probably fall asleep anyway."

Sullivan pulled off his poncho and folded it into a rough cushion for Eddie. The young man shoved it into the space behind the back seat and crawled in after it. Sullivan closed the back hatch and returned to climb into the front passenger seat. They bounced along for a few miles until they reached the onramp at Bernardo.

They headed north on I-25. Eddie shivered for about fifteen minutes, but he gradually warmed up. He was dozing by the time they passed Belen. When Hiroko finally pulled into the driveway at the ranchito west of Albuquerque, Eddie fought his way back to wakefulness. Through the foggy glass of the side windows, he could see that everything was blanketed in snow.

Hiroko pushed the remote for the garage door and pulled the Toyota inside. She shut off the engine and closed the garage door. They started climbing out of the vehicle, but Joe insisted they wait while he run around to verify that nothing more hostile than the weather awaited them outside.

In a moment he was back. "I feel a change. The strings of the world sound a new note," Joe announced. "The minions of the Queen withdraw from this world. Many of them, anyway."

"Well, that's something, isn't it, boss?" Sullivan grunted as he climbed out of the front seat. He went around and opened the back hatch for Eddie. Then he turned to open the side door. Sullivan reached his strong arms inside and helped Nadine ease Ikeda out.

Ikeda was conscious but very weak. "I fear it will take me some time to walk to my bed," he joked softly. "Have patience with this feeble old man, friends."

"Baloney. You saved my sorry hide out there, Harry. Get ready for a ride," Sullivan countered. He stooped slightly with knees bent and lifted the wiry Aikido master as he would a child. "Just don't get used to this sort of treatment," he added gruffly, gently.

They returned to the warmth of the house. Feelings of safety and of refuge surrounded and sustained them. As quickly as gentleness permitted, Sullivan and Hiroko helped Harry to bed. Joe followed them down the hall. The retired engineer returned first and, with a huge yawn, joined Nadine and Eddie at the kitchen table. The rear yard light shown on steadily falling snow.

For a time, the tick of the clock on the wall was the only sound that accompanied their tired breathing.

Eventually, Joe came back. A few minutes later Hiroko followed. The small woman spoke in her surprisingly husky voice. "My husband rests comfortably. He has no fever and, thanks to all of you and to the magic you brought, the terrible wound he suffered has already closed and begun to heal.

"I thank you," she continued, "but I fear I have been a poor host tonight. May I show you to your beds, or would you prefer some breakfast?"

"I'll tell you what, Hiroko," Joe offered. "You find beds for Sully, Nadine, and Eddie. Then you tend to Harry and I'll rest here at the table. That will be sufficient for me. When everyone gets up I'll cook breakfast."

"Thank you, *Sensei*. You are most gracious."

Nadine yawned. She stepped back and leaned her head against Sullivan's broad chest. Gently, tentatively, he wrapped his powerful arms around her and pulled her closer. She laid her slender hands atop his and snuggled in.

"I have so many questions," she said. "What I witnessed tonight... if I told anyone about it, well, they'd think I was crazy. But I am exhausted now.

"Hiroko, dear?" Nadine added after a short pause.

"Yes?"

"Is there a place where I could lie next to Sully? I don't want to be alone right now."

Hiroko smiled. "Of course. Please, both of you, come with me."

The kitchen was even quieter with only Eddie and Joe occupying it. "We've done well, son. The battle's not over by a long shot, but have no doubt: tonight was a turning point."

"That's great, Joe." Eddie yawned. He glanced at the clock on the kitchen wall. It read twenty minutes shy of five o'clock. "I want to rest, but I think I'm too keyed up to fall asleep. I think I'll look for a shower and then maybe we can eat something.

"And you know I'd like to get back to Soapstone Bay and Lena as soon as I can, right?" he added.

Michael C. Glaviano

"Yes, I know that, son. And I want to see how Iris is doing. But we can't leave these people just yet. I must make sure they are as safe as possible. As soon as things settle down a little here, we'll head back. I promise."

About thirty minutes later, Eddie had showered and changed into fresh clothes. Wrapped in a blanket, he dozed for a while on a couch in the living room, but wild images from the battle kept him from true sleep. The aroma of coffee drew him back to the kitchen by seven.

"Eggs, potatoes, and toast?" Joe said by way of greeting when the young man walked in. "I'm sure Hiroko and Harry have some more of that great green chile that we can scramble into the eggs. Maybe there are some tomatoes and a little bit of sharp cheddar as well."

Eddie's stomach rumbled. "You bet! Need some help?"

"Relax. Have a cup of coffee."

"Cool. Thanks."

Eddie felt better after he'd had something to eat. He was still tired and a little disoriented from being awake for essentially all night, but solid food in his stomach had a restorative effect.

As Eddie enjoyed his breakfast, Joe let the young man know how he'd spent the previous two hours. "I've been trying to detect some trace of the Queen's hand, her agents, anything. From what I can tell, she has pulled away, turned her attention elsewhere."

"Lena's world?" Eddie asked worriedly.

"Well, that's a possibility of course... but she wasn't making good progress there, right? When we set up that stable pattern around Soapstone, we made it hard for her to seal off that world. Maia's forest, the Old One with her spinning wheel... the openness with which magic is accepted and practiced, all of those things are barriers to the Queen's goals."

"So... what, then?"

"I really don't know. We're just going to have to watch and wait."

"Is there something else we can do?"

"We might bring a few more people in, younger people especially, but we've got to regroup a little. We nearly lost Harry last night. We have to let everyone heal and regain strength before we act again."

"Well, what about planning? Coming up with ideas?"

"Yes, son. Of course, we can do that."

"And as soon as possible, we should get back. To Soapstone. Let's at least check return flights."

Joe nodded his agreement and Eddie returned his attention to his coffee. After they'd cleaned up, they went outside together and walked the perimeter of the Ikedas' property. Joe could detect nothing that hinted of observation or untoward attention.

After the episode of intense action and danger, the subsequent twenty-four hours were torture for Eddie. Joe insisted they stay put

590

while they made sure their friends were safe. In the afternoon, the bright New Mexico sun drove away the piled snow in all but the shady places. Carrying with it the unseasonably late snow, mist rose from the ground and rose into the air.

Throughout the day, Nadine and Sullivan sat close to each other. Once the sun came out, they walked around in the back yard. They talked quietly together. They held hands often and surrounded themselves with a bubble of intimacy.

By the afternoon, Harry was definitely on the mend, and Joe offered to make plane reservations for anyone who wanted to leave. Hiroko and Harry invited everyone to stay as long as they liked. After another quiet chat, Sullivan announced that he and Nadine would be pleased to accept the invitation and stay for a few more days.

Joe made flight reservations for the following afternoon for Eddie and himself. Eddie was relieved that he would finally be able to get back in touch with Lena but chafed at having to wait for another twenty-four hours. It was a struggle, but he did his best to wait gracefully and be considerate of those around him.

In the evening, Harry felt much better and came out to sit in the living room. He was still pale, but his eyes were filled with life and good humor. His spirit was strong and he was healing quickly. Hiroko made him some miso soup and steamed vegetables, and this restored him further.

At dinner, everyone but Harry dug into stuffed sopapillas and cold beer. Eddie's mouth was on fire. At first he'd been skeptical of pouring honey on top of the green chile, rice, and bean mixture that filled the fried bread. After one bite, he was convinced. After two bites, he decided he needed to start growing chile himself. After three, he began considering a pilgrimage to Hatch, New Mexico in the following autumn.

As he finished his plate, Joe looked across the table at the wiry martial arts master. "It is good to see you up and around," he remarked seriously. "That was too close, my friend."

"Indeed, *Sensei*. Last night, for a moment, I began to gaze into the west, but now I can feel my strength returning. I am grateful. We fought well and victory was ours this time."

"In this battle, yes. And it was an important battle, but the war is not won."

For the first time during the meal, Nadine spoke up. "I just want to say that I am so glad to have connected with you all. Of course Sully and I feel especially close, but all of you... well, I feel part of something worthwhile. I have a desire to learn, to make greater contributions than I have so far."

"What are your plans, if I may ask?" Joe wondered.

"I have decided to contact my offices in LA tomorrow and instruct them to accept the latest buyout offer. One of the big management consulting firms has been trying to buy us for nearly a year. They made their latest offer three weeks ago. It's a good offer – an excellent one, actually – but I think they'll be surprised when I accept it. Anyway, it will take some time, perhaps as long as six months, to wind things down completely, but I am hoping to join Sully up north as soon as I can.

"He claims he's willing to put up with a headstrong businesswoman. I'm sure he doesn't quite know what's in store for him, but I'll do my best to make the transition... tolerable," she ended with a smile.

Sitting next to her, Sullivan's face reddened with something other than the heat of the chile. He cleared his throat and reached for his beer.

The six friends chatted and joked for a while after dinner, but there were many yawns and sleepy eyes. Talk wound into silences that lengthened. Before long, sleep claimed all but Joe. As was his habit, he stayed awake to watch over the others, to plan, and to walk in his ancient memories.

*　*　*

The next morning, the brilliant New Mexico sun woke them early. Everyone was up well before the morning was halfway gone. Breakfast consisted of huevos rancheros with more green chile and sourdough toast. The meal was merry and punctuated by laughter.

The grounding rod they'd shipped from San Luis Obispo still had not arrived. Joe announced that he would accept Ikeda's suggestion about its disposition. Despite his injury, the Aikido master bowed low at this and replied that he was honored by his *Sensei's* expression of trust but had another thought he would like to discuss.

"My forced inactivity has given me more time to think about this, *Sensei*. I have a new suggestion. The rod we used to open the new portal in the *Ladrones* lies embedded within the standing stone. When the grounding rod finally arrives, I propose that we retain it here for a time. We could use it to open more small connections to the Hub, such as those in Washington and California. I would build on the momentum we have established."

Sullivan was enthusiastic about the idea. "I totally agree with Harry on this. If we had a few more openings established our spells of regeneration and vitality would be more efficient. I was thinking about proposing we open one here in Harry and Hiroko's garden and, when it's convenient, another in my back yard."

"So, you're determined to become active again," Joe observed with a smile. "I'm of course pleased to hear that. Ideally, we might fan out from all three of our new portals."

Ikeda smiled gently. Hiroko sat next to him with her hand resting on his arm. She nodded her assent. "Yes, that would be helpful," the Aikido master agreed. "Very helpful indeed.

"I would still like to give one of the grounding rods to the head of security at Isleta Pueblo. I am confident that it would be beneficial to this world as well as to the residents of the pueblo. I propose we open a few more portals. Then I will have another grounding rod made – this time with the leisure to make sure it is done properly – and present that as a gift."

Eddie tried to be patient, but he was excited to get back to Joe's house. He hoped to return to Lena and to Soapstone Bay soon. Failing that, they'd at least be able to write back-and-forth. He didn't like the thought of hanging around longer, but he kept quiet during this conversation.

At the same time, he was sad about leaving these people. He especially liked the Ikedas and Sullivan, the big engineer. For months he had felt no connection with his home world; now he had friends. They weren't friends his own age as he had in Soapstone, but they were good friends nonetheless.

His relationships with Sullivan and Ikeda were different from the mentor-student relationship he had with Joe. Although with Joe there were some aspects of friendship, the strangeness and complexity of the ancient man's life presented a barrier. With these two, however, Eddie felt that over time, real connections of respect, admiration, and friendship would evolve. The difference in ages would matter less and less in the years ahead.

Then a new thought came to the young man. "Uh, Joe? Why can't we use the *Ladrone* portal, the one we just opened, to go back to Soapstone for a visit? Then we wouldn't have to fly to your place. We could just go and check on Lena and Iris and then come back and then continue the work here."

"Well, son, I could perform the spells to activate it, but it's a new portal and it's of a different form than what you're used to. For a time, transits will not be easy or comfortable. Someday you'll know how to use it and will be able to come and go from there, but it's premature now. For the time being our best bet would be to go back to the Painter Avenue house while we plan our next moves."

"Oh, okay. I was hoping..."

"I think I understand, son, and I know you're anxious to get back."

"Well, I am and I'm not. That's why I was hoping that we could get to and from the Hub without leaving New Mexico. I miss Lena and my friends, but... well, I'm going to miss everybody here too."

Everyone around the table smiled at this. In silence, they shared a strong feeling of connection, almost a feeling of family. Then, after a little more gentle conversation, the six of them straightened the house, cleaned the kitchen and made ready to say farewell to two of their number.

Eddie walked outside with his coffee and sat in the sun. A few minutes later, he heard the door open, close. Ikeda had followed him out. "Leave taking is sad, my friend, but I sense that we will meet again. Rejoice in the memory of our shared struggles. Learn. Become stronger. There will be another time."

"Thanks, Harry. I've enjoyed getting to know you and Sully. And meeting Hiroko and Nadine was great. But everything was so intense and fast. Sometime maybe we can just hang out... Anyway, I'll look forward to seeing you guys again."

"And, wherever you are, you may always think of this place, this garden. The land and the sky endure. Call up their images and they will comfort you."

Eddie stood then and offered his hand. The agile, wiry martial arts master met his handshake firmly. "Well, I guess I'd better go finish packing," the younger man said in reply.

Ikeda simply nodded once and then looked in the direction of his rock garden. "I shall sit for a while. Then Sullivan and I will drive you and *Sensei* to the airport."

Half an hour later, Eddie and Joe were ready to leave. The day continued to be bright and clear, perfect traveling weather. Nadine and Hiroko hugged them both and extracted promises of visits in the near future. They stood in front of the Ikeda's house and watched the Prius drive up the road toward town. It took 40 minutes to reach Albuquerque International. For the most part, the men passed the time in silence.

It was moderately busy at the curb. They all got out to stand for a moment beneath the Air Alaska sign. Sullivan and Ikeda shook hands with their departing friends and got back into the Prius. Eddie waved, and the older men pulled back into the swirl of traffic that surrounded the terminal building.

"Let's get checked in," Joe suggested.

The self check-in kiosks accepted Eddie's reservation, but Joe's kept coming up with a message that said, "See agent." Eddie went over to the newsstand to see if he could find something to read while he waited. Joe got in line at the Air Alaska counter.

Eddie found a selection, a mystery from the *New York Times* bestseller list, and paid for it. He went to wait outside the newsstand. Perhaps ten minutes later, Joe came up. Eddie could tell something was wrong as soon as he saw his mentor's face.

Joe held out his hand and smiled a cool, professional smile. Puzzled, Eddie took the proffered handshake. "Smile. We're business acquaintances, meeting by chance," Joe muttered sotto voce.

"Got it. What's up?"

Joe withdrew his hand. "Well, it appears the Queen's agents were busy before they left. I've been put on the 'No Fly List.' No one can tell me how or why that happened of course. I just am not allowed to travel by air."

"What're we going to do?"

"Well, we shouldn't stand around talking. If it hasn't started already, I'm sure to be under surveillance soon, so we should definitely split up. The feds pay attention to people on that list. You go on ahead, son. I'll get a bus or a train if I can't sort this out in the next couple of hours. Worst case, I'll go back to the Ikedas' and get them to take me to the new portal. I'd rather let it settle for a few months, but I can wriggle myself through there if I have to.

"Anyway, just get to the house and stay put," he continued. "I'll call my attorney and get him going on this. I'll be in contact as soon as I learn something."

"What about the protections around the house? Will I be able to get in?"

"Oh, right. I guess in some ways this has flustered me more than I realized," the old man admitted. "Here's what you do: palm of left hand, shoulder height on the front door. Right hand on the knob. Put a little bit of pressure on the knob as though you're going to turn it to the left. Not the right, mind you. Counterclockwise. Say the name you go by on Maia's world aloud. Say it three times. No need to yell it, just barely aloud will do the trick. In a manner of speaking, the house knows you by now.

"Anyway, if the door clicks then, you're in. Got it?"

"Yeah, sure. I've got it. You'll be all right?"

"Of course. This is just foolishness. I'll get it straightened out. My guess is they intended to block us all from air travel and had just started at it when the Queen recalled them. Now shake hands with me. Smile. Wave casually and walk away."

Woodenly, Eddie moved off to the security checkpoint. He showed his ID, ticket, and boarding pass three times. Each time he expected to be turned away or pulled aside, but he sailed right through. He got to the gate for Air Alaska flight 251 an hour before his flight was scheduled to leave. The board said the flight was on-time.

He sat in the uncomfortable plastic seat and opened his paperback. After reading the first page four times without remembering any of it, he gave that up and jammed the book into his carry-on. Eddie looked around and spotted a place where he could get some tea.

The clock crawled along. He imagined people were looking at him. He expected to be confronted by TSA personnel or law enforcement at any time, but boarding for his flight began without incident. Eddie finished his tea and walked over to join the crowd that loitered near the tail of the boarding line.

Eventually his row was called and Eddie moved through the last bit of line to hand his boarding pass to the gate attendant. "Have a pleasant flight," she intoned as she fed his pass through the machine. He gathered the stub from the slot and walked down the stuffy jetway to board the plane.

He found his seat and retrieved his paperback before stowing his carry-on in the overhead. Again he thumbed through the book. The scent of the paper and ink contrasted with the stale airplane air. Until the door was sealed and the plane began to taxi into position, Eddie expected to be taken off the plane, but it didn't happen. Finally, the plane took off. As the aircraft climbed to cruising altitude, he began to relax.

Questions rattled around in his head, but he did his best to set them aside. The flight was expected to last just under three hours. Weather was good in the midwest. He was in the belly of the transportation system, and his whereabouts were completely the responsibility of the flight crew. There was nothing to do but wait and hope that Joe would be able to catch a later flight.

Eventually, Eddie calmed down enough to sit with his book. He could tell he'd enjoy it under other circumstances, but today it didn't engage him. For the duration of the flight, he'd manage to read a few pages and then look around, read a few more, and so on.

Finally, the pilot came on and, amidst static and engine noise, mumbled that they were beginning their descent. A short time later, the flight attendants started the multistep process of collecting trash, answering questions, and preparing for landing. The flight landed almost on time. Eddie waited in the crush of the center of the plane for his chance to exit. Finally the aisle cleared and he made his way toward the cockpit.

He stepped through the door and into another jetway, this one dirtier and more beat up than the one he'd walked down in Albuquerque. With his emergence back into the crowds of a terminal, Eddie again expected to be confronted, but no one so much as looked at him. He followed the sign for "Ground Transportation" and eventually collected a ticket for a shuttle bus.

He just managed to catch the shuttle, and one final hour of travel time got him to the sidewalk in front of Joe's house on Painter Avenue. The combination of travel time and an hour's worth of time zone had brought him here at early evening. Although the worst of winter had passed, Eddie was glad for his jacket.

The street lights were on – at least those that still functioned. Everything looked the same: cracked sidewalk, street in need of repair, beautiful old trees. Eddie looked around and satisfied himself as best he could that he was not being watched. He walked up the steps.

Left hand placed so, right hand on the knob. Counterclockwise pressure. The name, "Reed Woodruff," three times. The click of the door: it all worked. The door swung open and he stepped inside.

Eddie locked the door behind him as he entered. He set his bag at the foot of the stairs. Everything was as they'd left it.

Michael C. Glaviano

Fifty Five

The Queen had regained her high, good humor. So simple. A little pressure in the right places, and she separated the youth from the care of the meddlesome ancient. Now the young one would become prey of the creature Alicia. And bait to trap his teacher.

Yes, so simple. In addition to his youth and inexperience, the Old One's callow helper had a fatal weakness: he was emotionally linked to a young woman. Pathetically, the two youngsters felt compelled to ex-change notes. Of course one of her agents had observed the process. What a simple matter: exchange the young woman's note for another! The writing would be the same, but the effect would be oh, so much bet-ter.

The Queen laughed aloud and vanished from the cool shadows and murmuring that filled her throne room. The courtiers puzzled at her behavior. Let them. They knew nothing. The agents who were directly involved had experienced her questioning. They remained... to the last... her loyal servants.

Ensuring their loyalty had added to her pleasure, and of course they were rendered quite speechless through her ministrations. Oh yes. Thus her strategies were complete, secure. She appeared in the chamber that lay at the center of her castle. The guards prostrated themselves be-fore her radiance. Here, always guarded, was the one, fully-functioning portal that she permitted to exist.

She employed the portal to materialize in the warm dampness of the Place. The Queen was uncomfortable there and disliked tarrying. She preferred the cool confines of her throne room or her various cham-bers of pleasure. More to the point, she much preferred to be the unseen puppet mistress. Circumstances, however, forced her to act directly. Oh, well. This too had its pleasures.

The Locust Queen thought a spell and the mist roiled around her. A great light fanned out and, in the distance, she spied a perverted form that lay astride a smaller creature and fed. In a blink, the Queen halved the distance separating them. Halved it again, and that which had once been the woman Alicia turned feral eyes away from her kill to look upon the beauty of her mistress. A low growl rumbled deep within the scale-encrusted chest.

By this time, Alicia was little more than a tormented beast. There was no flash of recognition, and this displeased the Queen. It was not right that her creation failed to recognize the power of She who had been and would always be the author of her fate. The Locust Queen raised her hand and did what she might to restore consciousness and self-awareness to the beast. The cost of doing so was great, but that was nothing to count against the pleasure the creature's self-awareness brought to the Queen.

The Alicia creature gasped as her eyes regained the spark of intelligence that had been mercifully buried by the horror of her existence. The Queen laughed and caused her own beautiful form to be illuminated as by the flickering light of a thousand fires. She pointed to the marshy ground at her feet, and the thing that had been Alicia struggled awkwardly to crawl forward through the mud, to lie face-down while the Queen surveyed her handiwork.

Then, out of light, the Queen fashioned a leash. She slipped it over the head of the hapless creature and turned to stride through the mist. Her creature shuddered but had no will to rebel. Trotting at the Queen's heel, it followed. The warm dampness closed around them. They made little sound as they covered the moist ground. Vaporous tendrils drifted, obscured their passage.

At each step, icy blue fire flowed down the perfect legs and feet of the Queen. The fire killed all it touched. It instantly desiccated and hardened the marshy ground so the Queen's shoes were not soiled. In contrast, the beast's paw prints immediately filled with the tears of the gods and soon faded, melted away.

At the right place, the Queen stopped. *HERE. STAY!* Her thoughts rang painfully in Alicia's mind. The leash faded. Alicia's tormented eyes looked out from the ruin of her face to gaze on the misty, shadowed landscape that surrounded them. She whined deep in her throat and crouched on the boggy ground.

A great pile of rocks stood nearby, the lair of the snake thing upon which Alicia had fed so long ago. Alicia recognized the place that had witnessed her ultimate metamorphosis and again shuddered. It was not precisely the same spot of course, for this was the place between worlds. But this was nonetheless as she remembered it.

For, she did remember... and regret. She looked up at the Queen. For a brief instant, Alicia pictured herself springing at the perfect throat of the form that stood in front of her.

The Queen knew her creature's fitful urge and laughed. Her full, unblemished figure moved rhythmically with the humor of it, and the scent of the Queen filled the damp air around them. *YOU ARE WELCOME TO TRY*, laughed the Locust Queen inside Alicia's brain. *YOU*

ARE ALWAYS WELCOME TO TRY... BUT WE HAVE SOMETHING ELSE TO TEMPT YOU, LITTLE ONE...

Once more, Alicia hunkered down in the moist earth and trembled with rage and humiliation. And fear.

YOU WILL SEE THAT YOUR QUEEN CAN BE GENEROUS. YOU WILL EXPERIENCE OUR WISDOM. YOU WILL WAIT HERE AND FEED UPON HE WHO WILL SOON COME THIS WAY!

The Locust Queen knew she had won, knew she would prevail. The young one would come and be killed. He was no match for the killing machine that Alicia had become. The troublesome Old One would soon follow. Then, at her leisure, her remaining agents – there were always more of those fools to be recruited – could be directed to deal with the Old One's few remaining assistants. In the absence of his protection they were insignificant and would be swept aside.

Yes. Only she would go on in her beauty and power. She would undo this meddling. Her hunger, never truly sated, would at least be assuaged. She would pour the lives of multitudes into the void that gnawed at her core and then would move her attention to the next world... and the next. Worlds without number awaited her.

Already she was bored and desirous of something else upon which to focus the brilliance of her skill. The Queen sought to quit this warm, damp landscape and return to her favored surroundings, her chosen pastimes and pleasures. With a final look about her, a final great expenditure of energy, she vanished from the Place to step directly to the sapphire shadows of her throne room.

Tormented, the Alicia creature stared at the misty space lately vacated by the Queen. Alicia now retained full awareness of what she had been, what she had become. She remembered, and remembering, she no longer sought vengeance or even to fulfill hunger. No. She desired only oblivion. Still, the Locust Queen had commanded and Alicia knew better than to fail, so she crouched there and waited.

Michael C. Glaviano

Fifty Six

Upon arrival, Eddie's first thought was to go to the wall and see what message Lena had left. He passed through the kitchen and noticed the light blinking on the phone. Someone had left a message. Probably Sergeant Driscoll. He'd call back later.

He was thirsty after the long flight, though, and stopped for a glass of water. As he set the glass down, the phone rang, and he picked it up.

"Hello?"

"That you, kid?" Sergeant Driscoll's unmistakable voice came through the receiver.

"Yeah. It's me. Just got in."

"Joe with you?"

"No... There was... some kind of screw up with his reservation. He's going to get here as soon as he can."

"Huh. Okay, well. Stay outta trouble, you hear me?"

"Sure thing, Sergeant. I'm glad to be back."

"That's a laugh. Where you been, Hell?"

"Hardly. Saw some nice places, actually. California, Washington, New Mexico. Great food there, let me tell you. It's just good not to be traveling. Airplanes, terminals, and all. You know," he finished.

"Yeah. I know, kid. Well, listen. I gotta go. To protect and to serve and all. Glad you made it back."

"Thanks, Sergeant. Talk to you soon."

Eddie hung up the phone and reflected for a moment on the way the tenor of his relationship with the sergeant had changed over the course of a year. Then he shrugged and headed for the back yard. It must have snowed since they'd left, because the dormant lawn was covered with an inch or two of crust-covered slush.

It was mostly dark now, and he flicked on the back porch light before stepping into the yard. In the dim light, he could see his throwing target over near the garage. The wall was ahead, near the limit of visibility. He sensed no feeling of being watched, no sense of malevolence as had greeted him before the trip west.

Hurrying now, Eddie walked over to the back wall and stooped to feel for the loose brick. He worked it out and felt inside. There was a piece of paper! Quickly, he retrieved the folded sheet and replaced the brick. It was too dark to read outside, so he dashed back into the house before unfolding the paper in the kitchen.

Lena's note was scribbled, as if written in haste.

All is in ruins, dearest. Come as quickly as you can!

Eddie stood and looked at it. In the quiet of the empty kitchen, the note stared back at him. What was in ruins? The town? Iris? Something wrong with Fleggie or Sweetmaye? Surely not Lena herself. Not that.

Trying to remain calm, Eddie reviewed the transit he had learned from Joe. The image of the single standing stone came to him. He must picture the stone with the triangle etched on its side, hold the image in his mind while he walks until he finds the standing stone. Then count ten paces. Then place the three stones in a triangle around himself. That was it.

Eddie took a deep breath. He could do this! Where were his throwing axes? Oh, right. He'd left them downstairs, after his last practice session before traveling with Harry Ikeda to California. What else would he need? He was a little bit hungry, but damned if he was going to stop and fix a snack at this juncture.

He thought of calling Joe's mobile phone but decided that his mentor would probably try to get him to put off going, and he could not bear to wait. He had to know what had befallen his friends in Soapstone Bay.

Eddie rummaged in a drawer to the left of the sink to find a pen. He scrawled a brief note in the margin of the paper he had pulled from the wall. Just to explain to Joe where he had gone. Then he ran to the basement stairs.

He flung open the door and clattered down the stairs. At the bottom, he stooped to pick up his throwing axes. With shaking hands, he threaded one sheathed axe onto his belt. Then he discarded the other sheath and held the second axe in his right hand. He knew it would be hot in the Place so he left his jacket open.

Once again, Eddie folded back the bottom three stairs. After stepping into the sub-basement tunnel, he reached up and carefully replaced the stairs behind him so the way he'd gone would be less obvious. Momentarily grateful that magic worked in the immediate vicinity of the portal, he called up a spell to light his way. As he walked down the long tunnel, he swung the unsheathed axe. Around and around, the axe spun. He passed it from hand to hand.

He wished for daylight to practice, to warm up, but he couldn't wait for a whole night to go, to seek news of his friends. He contented himself with the feel of the axe in his hands. He reached the transit chamber in minutes.

Although he wanted nothing more than to hurry to Lena's side, the long walk had cooled the first rush of his urgency. He forced himself to stop and think. They had encountered the Alicia creature on multiple transits. Joe said that as time passed, she would be likely to wander, but Eddie realized that he would do no one any good if he were killed during this transit.

He breathed deeply, slowly. He reviewed spells: Stun, Sleep, Tangle-foot, and so on. Especially Stun. As he went over this vital knowledge in his mind, he passed the axe from hand to hand, over and over. Finally, Eddie could think of nothing else upon which he was willing to spend time. Now he held his unsheathed axe in his left hand. He held his right hand out from his side for balance and so that he might cast a spell quickly.

In this position, he felt as prepared as he was likely to be. He extinguished his illumination spell and in the darkness began his backwards walk around the perimeter of the pit. At the third circuit, the now-familiar sound and light arose in the chamber. He stepped off the edge and endeavored to land with knees bent.

Eddie fell through the membrane that separates the Great Hub from each world it touches. He landed well-balanced with his knees bent. It was warm. There was nothing in his field of view but dim shapes. Nothing reached his ears beyond the indistinct sounds of the Place.

He detected a slight change in the air currents. It was no more than a tiny vibration, but Eddie flung himself to the right. He rolled on his shoulder and scrambled to gain footing on the damp ground. The Alicia creature had been waiting for him!

Eddie raised his right hand and cast a stun spell. She cried out in pain and whirled. She crouched to sprang at him again as he cast tangle-foot, and she stumbled. Eddie used the second to look around him. There was a pile of rocks perhaps a dozen feet off. He ran for it, but she was faster than he and he knew that he couldn't reach the comparative shelter in time.

He spun again and cast another stun spell. She cried out, but it barely slowed her charge. She was almost upon him when he slung his axe in a fast, underhanded throw. The blade took her near her right shoulder and buried itself in the flesh and muscles there. The beast that had once been a beautiful woman was checked in her headlong rush.

With a cry of pain, she fell and slid in the mud. She struggled and tried to paw the axe free from the deep wound. Dark blood welled up and flowed.

Now Eddie turned again to sprint for the pile of rocks. He saw that it was both larger and farther away than he'd first judged. He poured on as much speed as he could risk while treading on the slippery ground.

As he reached the huge, jumbled pile, he looked over his shoulder and saw that Alicia had climbed to her feet. She was working her way towards him in a painful, three-legged jog. Blood flowed down her leg to trail behind her. She was seriously hurt, but she was only seconds away.

Now Eddie saw and smelled a mephitic crevice near the base of the rocks and, pausing to hope it was not already occupied, dove for it. He scrambled inside just as his pursuer caught up with him. The crevice opened into a small cave that had once been some predator's den. It was filled with bits of bone and noisome fragments. Here and there he caught images, brief glimpses, of wet places where moisture had pooled.

The light extended a few feet in and Eddie groped forward to seek the back of the cave just as the light was blocked from behind. Alicia reached far inside with the claws of her uninjured arm. Before he could move far enough into the dark, he felt a burning pain as she raked his right leg from the mid thigh down to his ankle. He gasped with the agony of it.

She slammed her shoulder into the rocks behind him. Loose stones rained down and Eddie was afraid the ceiling might fall. Desperately, he cast Beam of Light into the way ahead. There was a narrow, low tunnel in the rocks and he got onto his belly and crawled into it.

He gritted his teeth against the pain and dragged his injured leg behind him. The leg throbbed and felt hot and he wondered if her claws had contained some kind of poison. Eddie crawled as far as he could into the confining space. Behind him he could hear Alicia crashing against the rocks again and again.

Moments later, what he had most feared happened. The ceiling of the cave behind him was dislodged by her repeated impacts. He continued his wriggling forward as rocks rained down. Dust rose around him and it became difficult to breathe. A few small rocks landed on his injured leg with agonizing pulses of pain.

Finally, the sound of falling rock tapered and stopped. She could not reach him, but now he was sealed into a tiny space in the rocks. He could advance no further. The way behind was blocked. He was wedged in, barely able to move. Turning around was out of the question. Eddie's concentration fled and he lost the spell of illumination. Coughing, struggling to breathe, he lay there, panicked, in the fetid darkness.

*　*　*

Alicia pulled her uninjured forearm from the crevice after the first few rocks fell on it. This arm was bruised and the paw was perhaps broken. She bled from the deep wound in her right shoulder. Slowly, painfully, she scrabbled to the top of the great pile of rocks and lay there panting.

She rested. Perhaps something would come along that she could kill and eat. Feeding would help. Yes.

She looked down at what had become of her body. The ruin of her filled her with disgust, but she also remembered the Queen's last command. She must stay here. She must feed upon the young one. Death was preferable to life, yes, but even a twisted life was markedly preferable to the Queen's reward for failure.

*　*　*

Slowly, slowly, the dust settled around Eddie, but as the dust settled, his panic rose. Now he could breathe a little better, but he could not so much as turn over. He could draw his hands beneath him and then down to his sides, or he could pull them forward and raise them above his head. He could move his left leg a little. He thought maybe he could move his right leg, but it felt puffy and numb, so it was hard to tell for sure.

From the painful shape beneath his left side, Eddie could tell that he still had one of his axes. He couldn't pull it out and couldn't imagine what use it would be if he could. How long could he last this way? He was already thirsty. He tried to get a grip on his panic, but the blind fear continued to build inside him, continued to stampede rational thought before it.

His mind flashed over times in the past year when he thought he might die, but those times death had always manifested itself as a relatively quick and clean possibility. The possibility of being buried alive in the dark was beyond anything he'd considered. It was beyond his ability to make sense of it or grasp it to wrest control of his mind away from it.

He tried to calm himself, but the panic kept welling up. Over and over he fought down the feelings of claustrophobia. Over and over he breathed as slowly and deeply as he could and tried to consider possibilities or strategies. Nothing of use presented itself.

Time passed and his thirst became the center of his consciousness. All lines of thought led back to it. It bested all mental exercises and attempts to distract. Eventually, alone and thirsty and in pain, Eddie lost all semblance of rational thought.

He struggled blindly in mad panic for a time. He began pounding his face on the rocks. The pain brought him back to his senses, and then, hurting in the darkness, he lay still. Finally, exhausted by terror and his fruitless exertions, he lost consciousness.

How long he slept, it was impossible to say. In the place between worlds, the Cosmic Hub of all places, time flows according to the dreams of the gods. An hour in the world of Soapstone Bay or Bellingham, Washington, could be any amount of time in that Place. It could be a second or a thousand years. Few beings willingly slept in the Place. Inescapable madness sometimes lay waiting.

Even so, Eddie slept. This was not the sleep of fatigue but rather a delirium of stress and exhaustion. And as Eddie slept, he did indeed dream. These were not dreams of places or people he knew but rather a series of disjointed images, fragments, perhaps, of the dreams of the gods.

Storms blew across islands and the islands became mountains. Trails clung to the sides of the craggy slopes, and tiny, indistinct silhouettes crept along the trails. Distant sounds of chanting welled up from the canyons into a red sky. The vague shapes moved endlessly along the treacherous paths.

Laden with brightly colored packs, animals followed one-another across a trackless waste. No one guided them, but they followed a constellation that coruscated in a never-changing night sky. Crows hopped from beast to beast and bent to peer closely at the colored parcels. With first one eye, then the other, the birds investigated and moved on. The great pack animals trudged through the endless night.

In a cloister, nuns were pursued by demons bent on mayhem. The nuns screamed and tried ineffectively to fend off their attackers. Suddenly, the Mother Superior crashed in to brandish a whip and a cross. Rampantly tumid, hands on hips, heads thrown back, mouths yawning wide, teeth flashing, the demons laughed. Pandemonium reigned.

Gardens grew and were harvested of dreadful fruit. Shrouded figures carried baskets and gathered the terrible shapes from bushes whose colors were wrong. Bats perched on the shoulders of the figures and whispered secrets.

With barely a ripple to disturb the surface, a calm ocean extended for thousands of leagues. A tiny ship was becalmed at the exact center. The image panned out and the ocean became the surface of a teaspoon of some syrupy liquid.

Demons were chased by nuns bent on back-arching, high-heeled revenge. Eyes rolling and popping with terror, the demons were forced onto their backs. Habits opened to reveal figures of profound sensuality. The formerly terrified nuns rode their mounts to a remote, satiated country of exhaustion.

Eddie awoke with his face sputtering in some warm liquid. During his minutes or centuries of mad dreams, the tears of the gods had misted upon the great pile of rocks. The tears traced through cracks and tiny fissures to collect and flow to the bottom where they formed a pool in the tiny space around him.

In his delirium, Eddie had unknowingly drawn this liquid into his lungs. He coughed mightily and light flashed around him. Again and again he coughed and the tiny cave around him came alive with light.

In the dim glow he saw the liquid puddled all around and his thirst overcame all caution. He tasted the liquid that had pooled near his mouth. Eddie discovered that unlike the tears of men, those of the gods were not overly salty. The moisture soothed his dreadfully parched throat. He dipped his face, and the wounds of his earlier, crazed thrashing were healed.

At some point, Eddie realized that his body had expanded to fill the tiny space. Panic welled again but then was replaced by the knowledge that within that deep place, he needed only to imagine his strength for it to be sufficient to his needs. He drank one last time and felt the full measure of his strength upon him.

He readied himself to shake off the stony prison but paused for a moment. The sounds of a struggle reached his ears! Near it was, perhaps off to the side, perhaps on the pile above him. Then he resolved to break free. He gathered the power he needed, the power imbibed from the tears of the dreaming gods. Eddie breathed deeply and drew his arms beneath him.

Elbows tucked to his sides, he forced his hands to press down at the space beneath his shoulders. He pushed mightily and felt his shirt tear around his neck, back, and arms. His tattered jacket split. The rocks slid from his back. It became obvious that the tiny crack in which he had been wedged lay right at the boundary of the great pile of rocks.

Eddie pushed and kicked himself free and stood. Looking around at the misty landscape, he sensed that the perspective was wrong. Gradually, he realized that he had grown significantly taller. His feet were pinched and he kicked off his shoes to stand barefoot on the damp ground. His trouser legs reached just past his knees. His jacket bound his arms. He tore that away as well and stretched.

As he put more weight on his right leg, he felt a flash of pain. Looking down in the dim light, he saw the huge, puckered weal left behind by Alicia's claws. The ugly gash ran down the leg. Carefully, he knelt and forced his hand back into the crevasse from which he had so lately escaped. He cupped his hand and dipped it into the pooled tears. Two, three times, he ladled the precious liquid onto the painful wound. The inflammation retreated; the injury began to heal.

The belt that held his remaining axe cut into the skin at his waist. He pulled the axe from the sheath, discarded the strap. He rolled his massive shoulders and swung the axe in a great circle. The sharp weapon was small in his hand.

A yell brought him back from his reverie. He recognized that voice. Quickly, he scrambled to the top of the rocks and looked around. Joe was there, ten yards to the side of the heaped stones. The old warrior fought the Alicia creature. She must have surprised him, caught him unawares, for he was injured. His left arm hung limply at his side and he dragged his left leg as he tried to turn and face his attacker.

Eddie flexed his knees and felt the strength in his legs. In one great leap, he sprang from the top of the pile to land near the struggle. The force of his impact distracted Alicia and she spun to face him.

Still tortured with self-awareness, her eyes looked deeply into his. Her lips drew back and she bared her teeth. The result of their earlier encounter was painfully visible. Caked with dried blood, her right foreleg dangled uselessly from her shoulder.

Eddie raised his axe and she hesitated. "You have suffered too much. Do you understand me? I do not wish to kill you," he said softly.

She shook her head at this, snarled, and lunged at him. He brought the axe down hard, splitting her scaled body from shoulder to mid-section. For an instant, she stood, eyes locked upon his, and then with a brilliant flash, she crumpled and shed the grotesque form that she had assumed. The energy of Alicia's multitude of kills, the huge surge of power that the Queen had used to restore Alicia's self-awareness, all of this flowed up the axe handle into Eddie's arm. It rushed, coursed through him and he dropped to one knee. Momentarily dizzy, he allowed his head to hang. He felt his strength multiply a hundredfold. He felt his body grow larger still.

He looked up as Alicia fell towards him. She was human again. Naked, dirty and ragged, she was... and very near death from the terrible wound he had inflicted. But her madness had fled. With one immense hand, he caught her as she fell and he eased her to the damp ground. She looked up at him and managed to nod once before the light left her eyes. Sadly, gently, he withdrew the axe that had released her.

Eddie stood as Joe hobbled up. "You have absorbed the energy she stole from lesser creatures with her kills," the old man whispered hoarsely. "In her, the energy was tainted, perverted by her mad cruelty. You may use it for good and thus restore the balance."

Eddie saw the wounds his mentor had suffered. "Can I heal you?"

"Yes, but we may need that energy to battle the Queen. She is sure to act now. You realize that it was her trickery that delayed me in Albuquerque, that led you here alone?"

The pieces all fell together in Eddie's mind and he nodded. "She must've found out about the message wall and inserted that note. Almost got me, didn't she?"

"Indeed. But she knew nothing of your skill with the axe. It's not something she'd notice or consider in her plans. And finally, I think the

Alicia creature wanted no more of what she had become. She could not defy the Queen, of course, but Alicia's heart was no longer in the hunt.

"So much waste. So much suffering. It becomes unfathomable." Joe shook his head. "Here. Give me your hand. I will take only what I need so that we can move quickly."

Eddie reached out his hand and Joe took it. The younger man could feel strength and power flow down his arm and watched as his teacher and friend stood straighter.

"That will do for now. As always, I will heal quickly. Come. Let us focus on finding the pillar."

"Not yet, Joe. We can't just leave her lying there. It's not right."

Joe looked tiredly, sadly down at the still form.

"Yes, son. Something must be done, of course. May her spirit be at peace in the brightest, gentlest reaches of the Great Realm. Stand back. I can at least commit her body to the cleansing flames."

Joe made a complex series of passes with his hands. He spoke strange syllables in the tongue of the elder gods. Light shown in the mists above them. One by one, glowing brands drifted down to settle upon Alicia's body. When the pathetic, broken form was completely covered, Joe stepped back and made one final pass. The glow became fire and the pyre raged. They turned away and felt the warmth of the flames at their back as they walked from the place where Alicia had finally laid down her burden of torment and madness.

A short time later they were in the deep chamber beneath the Inn at Three Corners. Eddie gestured at the shreds of cloth that draped the huge expanse of his chest. His pants, shorts now, were unbuttoned and stretched across his hips. "Look at the size of me, Joe. I'm going to attract a lot of attention going out in public like this."

"Mel will have something we can wrap around you. A large blanket will do."

"Yeah. Just like what we did for Sully. Okay."

The tunnel could barely accommodate him, and Eddie had to crouch – crawl, nearly – all the way up the stairs. His legs and back ached fiercely by the time they reached the door that led to the lobby. He'd stubbed his toes more times than he could count and his head hurt from where he'd repeatedly banged it on the ceiling.

Joe opened the door and stepped into the lobby. "Wait here," he said quietly.

Eddie knelt down to take the load off his back and legs. Five minutes later, Joe returned. He held a large blanket.

"Here you go. I've made a serape of it. And by the way, son, you might want to keep that axe out of sight, okay?"

Eddie looked down. He still held the axe he'd used in his last battle with Alicia. The weapon appeared tiny, ridiculously toy-like. He drew it inside the makeshift serape and walked into the dim lobby of the

Inn. Mel was at his usual station behind the desk. The aged desk clerk looked at him and, with barely a raised eyebrow, nodded once before returning to his work.

Out on the street, it was midday. Clouds were scudding on a strong wind. Heads turned at the strangely clad giant and the old man who limped by his side, but no one challenged them.

They walked as quickly as they could down Turnbull and up Center. Eddie's heart began to pound with nervousness. He was gigantic, grotesque. What would Lena think when she saw him? Would she be horrified?

Fifty Seven

The Locust Queen felt the death of her servant, her creation in the Place. All traces of good humor evaporated in a paroxysm of anger. She raged, brought carnage all around her. It was time for direct action. No more intermediaries. These meddling insects would know the true wrath of the Queen. She vanished from the scene of chaos and death that she'd meted out in her throne room...

...and reappeared in the chamber of her web of sensors. The smells, the lights, the machines and cables surrounded her. The forms in their basins beckoned. She had to find where her adversaries had gone, the Old One and his youthful assistant. She had to track them before she could crush them and feed on their remains. Only then could she start anew.

She began her ministrations, her caresses. The sensors responded as was their wont. She was focused on her goals this time and so refused to be distracted by the usual diversions their suffering offered. Nearly gentle, she remained calm and centered.

Where? First the world. Where? Surely not the hurt, damaged world where they had bested her hounds. She could not go there. That world would not support the magic that she required to maintain her form, to do battle.

Ah! It was as she had hoped! They had returned to the world where they'd first opened the stable pattern of six portals, the world of the young woman who had served as the initial bait for her failed trap. Well, that settled the destination, the location of the upcoming confrontation. Magic was still alive and vibrant in that world. Magic would support the matrix of energies that she had woven into her power, her brilliance.

Now, where should she enter that world? The only active portal of which she was aware was the slimy, filthy tunnel through which she pushed her agents. It terminated deep in the Warrens near the harbor of that little town. Even if she could fit within its confines, she was unwilling to subject her glorious form to the indignity of crawling through that dirty passage.

Surely there was a better way. Of course! The very pattern that her puny foes had established would do! How just! How perfect! The Locust Queen resolved to use the artifact of their meddlesome behavior to exact her revenge. Course of action now determined, she set about her work.

Fifty Eight

Eddie and Joe reached Tolemy's Cats as the wind began to pick up. Eddie took a deep breath and pulled the door open. Joe limped inside. Eddie stooped and got his head under the top of the door frame, passed across the threshold.

Lena was at the front desk. She looked up as the bizarre duo came in and closed the door behind them.

Her eyes grew wide and her mouth made an "O" as she recognized the men standing in front of her. "Iris!" she called. "Joe and Reed have returned. They need our help!"

Then she ran from behind the counter to press herself against Eddie's massive body. Her head was just above his midsection. He let the axe drop from his hand and carefully reached around to hold his beloved. She felt like a child in his huge arms.

She looked up and her face was streaked with tears. Recovering quickly, she smiled at him through her tears. "What has happened, my love?"

"Too much to say," he whispered, his voice deep and resonant.

"Well, you are back. That is wonderful."

"Even... even as I am now?"

"You are back. That is enough. Anything else is mere detail."

Just then Iris came walking up the aisle. Her apparent age had settled in her mid-sixties. She moved well enough, but she no longer radiated self-assured power. She no longer commanded the grace and beauty that had made her so striking.

"And what's this darkening my door? Two vagabonds looking for a port in a storm?"

Joe hobbled over to take Iris' arm. "I could use some help. We've had quite a battle during the last transit. The Queen's creature has been... dispatched..."

"Ahhh. And the magic of the Place has had its way with our young friend. Well, it may be set right over time."

"Indeed, Iris, but I suspect we have little time. The Queen will know we have destroyed her handiwork. With the help of friends there, we pushed her back in Reed's world, my world. She will be be insane with anger. I know that for a fact, but I do not know where or how she will manifest her wrath."

Lena spoke up from where she stood holding Eddie's huge hand in both of hers. "We should contact Fleggie and Sweetmaye. Perhaps they might help. They must at least be warned."

Joe nodded. "Do that, please."

Then he turned to the woman he had loved beyond his ability to make right choices. "Dear Iris. It is so good to see you. We may yet prevail. I may yet be able to heal you. Stay with me.

"Now, though, I need food and water..." he continued, "and I expect Reed here will have an appetite that matches his stature. We must gather our strength. I need to cast spells of healing on myself. And most of all we must determine the point of the Queen's attack."

Lena sidled around to the desk and activated the communicator.

"If you're going to talk to them, would you please see if Fleggie has some axes I can use?" Eddie asked. "He was experimenting with several designs. As long as they're big and have a handle and an edge, I'll try 'em. I lost one in the Place, and this other one... well, it's too small now."

She nodded and smiled her beautiful smile. Her hair was pulled back. Her brilliant eyes sparkled without a hint of reservation. Eddie was grateful merely to be in the same room with her. That her eyes shone upon him with love filled his heart with gratitude.

"Hello, Sweetmaye, dear. They are back. Yes. Reed and Joe. Reed has suffered some kind of... transformation though. Oh, no. Nothing as bad as that. He is well, merely large. Very large. Much bigger than Fleggie. What?"

Lena laughed and blushed to the tips of her ears. "I cannot say as yet, but I shall let you know as soon as I am able."

Then more seriously. "They think the Queen will come here. To Soapstone. Please meet us at the store right away. Can you do that?"

Here Eddie stooped and picked up the throwing axe he'd dropped. He held it between his thumb and forefinger and the axe looked like a toy in his hand. Eyebrows raised in silent reminder, he waved the weapon back and forth.

Lena nodded and smiled again. "Wait! Sweetmaye? If at all possible, Reed needs to borrow some of Fleggie's axes. The one he has here looks ridiculously small in his hands. Yes, that big. Please have Fleggie bring all the axes he can. Thank you, dear one!"

Lena cut the connection. "Let us get you upstairs and see if we can at least clean you up a little, my love. Then we shall see about getting you some food and proper clothing."

Iris turned the shop sign to read "CLOSED." "No sales this afternoon, I expect," she sighed.

"Now, you old scoundrel, once again I bring you into my home and see what may be done to make you fit for your next battle."

She glanced once in Lena's and Eddie's direction. "Shall we meet back here in half an hour?" Without waiting for an answer, the older woman took Joe's arm and led him back to her apartment.

Eddie and Lena got up to their apartment. Eddie had to go through the doorways sideways and could barely stand up straight in the tiny living room. He stripped out of his bizarre costume and carefully wiggled his way into the bathroom. He crouched down in the tub and Lena did her best to wash him down.

While he was drying himself off, she went to the kitchen and made him a sandwich. There was fresh bread and she simply sliced a loaf horizontally. Then she layered it with meat and cheese and peppers and doused it with olive oil. Finally, she put the whole thing in the oven to warm.

Eddie had returned to the living room. "Maybe I could make some kind of loincloth or a kilt from another blanket. Then I'd at least have top and bottom covered in something that doesn't bind... I know, Lena, that I've become a monster of sorts." There was frustration in his deep voice. Frustration and worry.

"Never doubt for a moment that we shall manage," she replied. "Do not fret. I love the you that still lies within that great exterior. When we are done with this, perhaps Joe will be able to put things right. Surely he will. And if by some chance this is the form you are destined to wear from now on, my love, we shall make do in that case as well."

With quick confidence, Lena stripped a blanket from the bed they had shared. "This one was always too big for our bed. Now its size will make it serve all the better."

She folded the blanket in half and cut a hole for Eddie's waist. That done, she cut a slit up the middle of the folded blanket to create big flaps for his legs. She poked holes up the outside and inside of the flaps.

A moment later, she darted to the kitchen and came back with a spool of heavy twine and the gigantic sandwich she'd made.

While Eddie ate, Lena threaded the twine in the holes to fashion pant legs. "We'll need some kind of belt, but these are almost pants, and they'll let you move freely and keep you warm!"

Eddie was pleased and surprised. He set his sandwich carefully on the plate. Then he pulled on the pants. In a matter of minutes, Lena had turned an oversize blanket into a pair of rough but serviceable trousers. Eddie wriggled back into the poncho. He was still far larger than the tallest people he'd ever seen, but at least he was wearing clothes that covered him.

"Thank you, Lena. Thank you! This feels so much better!" even to his own ears, his voice rumbled in his chest.

"I cannot think of what we can do for your poor feet, though."

"Oh, it'll be fine. I'm not cold at all."

"Well, then. Let us return downstairs. The urgency in Joe's voice has me worried."

"Yeah. Me too."

Awkwardly negotiating the tile steps and inadequate ceiling height, Eddie followed Lena down the stairs. The wind had picked up by the time they reached the sidewalk. It was not a cold wind but rather a breath both damp and warm. It would have been a strange wind at any time of the year in a northern seaport. It was stranger, still, in waning days of winter.

Lena and Eddie went inside the bookshop. Eddie was reluctant to try to move between the bookshelves, so he waited in the front of the store and finished his sandwich while Lena went back to Iris' apartment to announce their return.

Lena came back a few moments later. Iris was with her. The older woman looked levelly at Eddie for a long time and then nodded as if she'd figured out the solution to a vexing problem or difficult puzzle. "What, Iris?" he asked.

"Nothing. You're the same callow youth. Just bigger. Well, that great size may be of use. We shall see. Tell me. Did you think to bring your throwing knife?"

"Well, no. It's too small for me to hold now. I'm hoping –"

"Lena, dear. Will you please run up and get his knife? We don't know what we'll need when the time comes. We certainly can't leave it to the men to figure these things out."

"Yes. I can do that, Iris," Lena agreed and dashed outside and up the stairs.

It was quiet when she left the store. Iris was looking intently at him again. "Uh, where's Joe?" he wondered aloud.

"He's resting. Actually, he just says he's resting. I know him better than that. He's casting about. Trying to figure out where the Queen will come into this world. I'm letting him occupy himself. I've already figured it out."

Lena returned a minute later. She'd hooked two belts together and carefully slid the sheath, which held Eddie's throwing knife, onto the combined length. "Here you go, Love. We needed to add a belt anyway. Let me help you."

She looped the belts around his waist and made sure that the buckles were snug. Perched there on his hip, the knife looked tiny and useless, but he didn't think it could do any harm. In any case, he didn't feel like arguing with the short-fused Iris.

Joe joined them a moment later. His face was deeply lined and there were dark circles beneath his eyes, but he was smiling. "I've figured it out. I'm nearly certain."

"The stable pattern of portal openings we created... the Queen will use that. She will emerge at the central point, will she not?" Iris crowed.

Joe was taken aback. "Why didn't you say so if you figured it out?"

"I know you. If I had suggested it, you'd have only wanted to debate it. This way, there's no question. We both reached the same conclusion. The Locust Queen will enter this world at the focal point on Harbor Boulevard, up near Biscayne!"

Joe looked stormy then and Eddie worried an argument was about to erupt. Just then Fleggie and Sweetmaye pushed their way into the front of the store to join them.

"Hey there, mate! Me girl sez' ye ha' grown a wee tad an' there be truth t' it. Be it th' food on that home world o' yours?" The big man grinned broadly and pounded Eddie's back.

Slightly embarrassed, Eddie noted that his tall, strapping friend had to reach up to do it.

"Great to see you, man!" Eddie recovered and said wholeheartedly. He grabbed Fleggie in a bear hug and lifted the big man off his feet.

"Take care, mate! Fleggie needs his ribs!"

"An' is tiny Sweetmaye too small to notice? She still be a force in this battle," the diminutive woman laughed and danced about the big man who was her lover and the giant Eddie had become.

"Take care, girl. We'd not like t' step on ye!" laughed Fleggie.

"Okay, friends. We are glad to be back, but time is fleeting. Both Iris and I..." and here he paused and glared for a second at the older woman, "both Iris and I are convinced that the Locust Queen will manifest at the focal point we established with those portal openings. We should go there immediately and keep watch."

"Aye, so be it," nodded Fleggie.

"Fleggie. Did you happen to bring any spare axes?" Eddie asked hopefully.

"True now. Sweetmaye tells Fleggie an' Fleggie does it. There be four each for us. In th' bed o' Fleggie's wagon. Some ha' better balance than others, but they'll serve."

"Great. Thanks."

"Shall we go then?" Lena suggested.

The six of them left the store. Eddie crouched on one side of the wagon. Fleggie, Joe, and Iris sat opposite and still the wagon sagged slightly beneath Eddie's mass. Sweetmaye took the controls and Lena sat next to her on the bench.

Heads swiveled to watch as they swung around the corner of Center Street to turn right at St. Tolemy. They turned right again at University Avenue. People stopped what they were doing at the sight of the two men in the wagon. "They notice ye an' wee' Fleggie, true now," laughed Fleggie. Eddie tried to smile in return, but his face felt stiff and awkward.

Sweetmaye turned left on Wells and then, two long blocks later, she turned right on Harbor. Far ahead, they could see clouds gathering in the sky. There were fewer people on the street here, but those who were out definitely noticed their passage.

The mid-afternoon sky grew dark as they headed west on Harbor. Traffic thinned and they made good time. It took only ten minutes for them to pull into a parking space near the intersection of Harbor and Biscayne.

The clouds spiraled above a point just ahead. Fleggie and Eddie each pulled four large axes from the bed of the wagon and began walking the last block or so toward the intersection. The unseasonably warm and moist air flowed toward them from the eddy of the clouds.

"Excuse me, gentlemen. Where do you think you're going with those weapons?"

It was the town patrol. Eddie hadn't thought about the possibility of interference from official authority. "The Queen, uh, she... well..." he stammered. He was all too aware of the image he presented to the uniformed officers. Carefully, slowly, he laid the axes on the pavement and showed the officers his immense, empty hands. Out of the corner of his eye, he saw Fleggie do the same.

Fortunately, Joe and the others stepped to his rescue.

"Officers. Please listen. It is vital that you keep crowds away. Perhaps some of you will be able to help us, but we have reason to believe the Locust Queen is bent on attacking this world."

"Beg your pardon?"

"Do you know to whom I refer when I say 'the Locust Queen?'"

"We all know the stories about the cosmology of the Great Wheel and the hub. And the evil Queen who is the nemesis of all. These are stories from our youth. You are saying this is real? That she is bent on coming here?" There was no little skepticism in the patrolman's voice, but he hesitated as he looked back and forth between the giant Eddie had become and the brawny, blond Fleggie, who was merely huge. The officer glanced more than once at the whirling clouds in the sky behind them.

"It's not a story, young man," Iris snapped. "It is the bald-faced truth. A battle is about to be waged. Here. The Locust Queen comes."

Now Lena joined in. She spoke softly and calmly and her beauty shone out with a magic of its own. "Sadly, yes, officers. This has moved well beyond the realm of stories. You will remember last year's troubles at the school and the security forces that tried to take control of Soapstone Bay. They were nothing more than opening salvos. We need your help. We need it badly... and if you cannot see your way to help us directly, then we beg you simply to keep innocent people as far away from here as you can."

"An' if tha' be not enou' fer ye', think on th' stories yer own grand da' tol' you on his knee. Think on it, lads, an' decide if yer grand da' were telling ye true," added Sweetmaye.

The patrolmen looked at them silently. The wind increased. Now a vortex began to form in the sky. A column of intense blue light extended downwards from the tip of the vortex. The phenomenon in front of them was clearly unique in their experience. The cloud looked neither natural nor benign.

"Well something unprecedented is happening here. That much is clear," one of the officers stated the obvious. He turned to his partner. "Call for backups. Get as many troopers as can be spared up here. Take half of the force to cordon off the space for a block around and have the rest of them meet me.

"Worst case, I lose my job," the patrolman added as he turned back towards Iris, Joe, and the others, "but something tells me we'll lose much more than that if we don't act."

Michael C. Glaviano

Fifty Nine

From her vantage point, the Queen could now perceive the world that would bear the brunt of her wrath. She could sense the point of contact, the life force of those near. She experienced disappointment at the scarcity of bystanders. There was so much more to be gained by extensive collateral damage.

A few moments more and the great cylinder would connect with the light that she cast aloft from her position in the warm mists of the Place. Then these fools would indeed plumb the depths of hopelessness.

Michael C. Glaviano

Sixty

The town patrol cleared civilians away from the immediate danger of the focal point. The patrolmen arrayed themselves around the deserted street. Joe nodded in approval of their forces.

Next, he turned to move quickly to stand near the spot where the vortex was directed. He said a few words under his breath and cupped his hands. His voice rang out as though amplified, and the gathered forces murmured at the obvious evidence of something beyond their experience.

"Thank you for being here. You shall serve as both witnesses to great events and as defenders of your world. The Locust Queen comes. She will appear soon. You will be enthralled by the beauty of her form, but do not let her appearance deceive you. She is evil. She is the very definition of evil. If you hesitate, you will be lost.

"When she appears you must fire on her. Aim for the place where a human heart would beat. Aim for her eyes. Your weapons by themselves cannot bring her down, but they will cause her discomfort and will make it more difficult for her to focus her attack. We will be scattered among you and add our own weapons to the fray.

"If we hold true, we may prevail. You stand near the place between worlds, the Great Hub that connects everything. The Place is perched above the lower realms that descend, in turn, to the planes of chaos which spawned the elder gods. And beneath all else, lies the Abyss. It yawns, hungry, always empty. This world, all worlds, hang by a thread.

"Now, we wait," he finished. "Ready yourselves. The wait will not be a long one."

His instructions to the thirty or so members of the town patrol complete, Joe fell silent. He turned to Fleggie and Eddie. "Stand well apart. Fleggie, lad, you throw first. Then Reed. Throw hard and fast, but be accurate. Aim for the center of her chest.

"Throw one axe at a time, alternating sides. Fleggie, after your second throw, hurl a third without waiting for Eddie. That will break the pattern just as she senses it.

"Pray you each hit more than once. It will take at least that much to kill her. I will face her and try to draw her attention and do what I can to weaken her, but cold steel is our best bet."

Now Joe turned to Sweetmaye, Lena, and Iris. "Please. All three of you. Draw back between the buildings. We will fight better if we know that you are out of sight."

Lena stepped forward and hugged Eddie fiercely. Sweetmaye did the same with Fleggie. Eddie expected an argument from Iris, but she merely looked intently at the men before her.

Wordlessly, Iris gathered the young women to her. They followed Eddie has he made his way off to the left but then dropped back behind him. He looked over his immense shoulder to see where they'd gone. They had taken shelter within a gap between buildings. They were nearer than he liked, but they could see what was going on and they would be hidden from casual view.

Eddie looked across the street. He could see Fleggie towering over the town patrol who stood nearby. Eddie laid three axes at his feet. Holding the fourth, he raised his hand in salute. As his friend answered with a raised axe of his own, the wind grew in intensity.

Seeking edges to snag, shrubs and trees to uproot, the warm wind roared. The brilliant light at the tip of the vortex was now at the level of the buildings. Another, even brighter light rose up from the pavement in front of him. The light grew in brilliance and became hard to bear. It rose to perhaps twice Eddie's enhanced height.

The light began to have form, shape, structure. Clouds and mist whirled about the brilliant light and obscured the shape within. The clouds grew thicker as the light sucked energy from the wind. Brighter and brighter, the shape in the light glowed as the wind died. A thrumming resonated deep in the earth. Teeth were set on edge. Eyes darted around the street with the expectation of an earthquake. Finally, the wind was still and all eyes were focused on the brilliant, glowing shape. The thrumming grew in pitch and volume and became deafening.

Now the glow began to fade, the clouds to dissipate. Within a moment, the shape resolved itself into the form of a giant woman. Her skin was icy, blue-white. Her hair was black as the Abyss. Her eyes were featureless cobalt orbs. She was draped in diaphanous ivory, trimmed in silver, indigo and black. A band of blue fire circled her waist.

She stood, beautiful and terrible in front of them and laughed. "See me! Know your end. Know the end of your world, of all that your puny lives hold dear."

Joe's voice rang out. "Fire, damn you all. Fire!"

And the town patrol shook themselves from their trance and fired upon the lovely, terrible form. At first the Queen merely laughed. Blue fire sprang from her fingertips to find targets. She ripped apart pavement, stone, and flesh with that fire.

Then Joe's first bolt struck, and the Queen's laughter stopped. Fleggie threw and the Queen turned the blade aside. Then Eddie threw and she did the same. Now Joe struck again, and again Fleggie threw. This time, the axe touched her before she batted it away. Something like blood and blue fire welled up from a wound in her breast. Fleggie hurled one more axe, a devastating two-handed throw. The blade buried itself in her arm. She screamed, and the sound of her scream drove all other sounds before it.

The patrol fired and fired. The terrible eyes provided the best target. Now Eddie threw. Again the Queen batted the axe away. She began to turn towards Eddie, and the full force of her face was terrible to behold. Joe struck again, and the Queen's gaze shifted. Fleggie threw his last axe and it bit deeply into her chest.

The Locust Queen reeled back. She howled deafeningly. Eddie threw and this time his axe found its mark. He had one last axe and he put all the force he had behind his final throw. It took her full in her chest and vanished into the writhing body.

The Queen was gravely, perhaps mortally injured but she still stood. Joe sent bolt after bolt her way, but he was weakening. As they watched, the Queen seemed to realize she had already borne the brunt of the attack, and with that realization, she smiled horribly. Blue fluids dripped from her mouth to roll down her chin and onto her body, but still she stood and gathered strength from the fear of those arrayed around her.

Again destroying fire flowed from her outstretched hand. A building collapsed and masonry buried the patrol forces at its base. Dust rose up. Eddie could no longer see Fleggie across the street.

At some point the town patrol must have called in heavy reinforcements, because now Eddie heard a sound familiar from his home world: helicopters! Suddenly, two of the machines hove into view above the buildings. They fired heavy caliber machine guns and the Queen fell to her knees.

She fell, but she was not done. She ripped huge blocks of pavement from the street and hurled them at the hovering, tormenting aircraft. First one and then the other patrol helicopter was struck to explode and rain fire and wreckage onto the troops below.

Now the Queen staggered to her feet. She began to make passes with her hands and chant strange syllables. Her injured form began to glow and the street became icy, terribly cold. Weapons fire became sporadic and then stopped altogether. Still dripping with cerulean fluids, the Locust Queen smiled her terrible smile. "I shall suck this world into the icy realm from whence I sprang," she declared in a deafening, unnatural-sounding voice. "There it shall nourish me that I might rise again and return to my glory!"

Then, emitting a stentorian blast of sound, she screamed as brilliant fire rose along her sides. The Queen spun and Eddie turned to follow her gaze. Lena and tiny Sweetmaye had emerged from the alley. They were using a heat spell to burn the hateful figure. Fleggie must have noticed, because now the Queen whirled yet again as more fire climbed up her left leg to consume her gown. Taking the lead from his friends, Eddie readied his own spell to add.

Then Eddie saw the fire die back and felt the cold return. Joe's bolts of energy sputtered and ceased. Once more, the icy monarch, the devourer of worlds, smiled. She had managed to staunch the flow of blood from her wounds. The Queen drew back a massive fist as though she might crush them all.

Eddie felt something at his side. It was Iris. In a move almost too fast to follow, Iris lunged at him and pulled his knife from the sheath at his side. Then she placed a hand on his arm and drew and drew and drew the energies that had been stored inside him. "Iris? What are you doing?" he had time to ask, but then he fell to his hands and knees.

Drained of the strange power that had coursed through him, Eddie felt himself shrink to his normal size. Dizzy, weak, he looked up. Iris stood there, radiant, her beauty restored. Her strength and power were again at full flow. With the knife extended in her outstretched hand, she flung herself at the injured Queen. As an arrow is loosed from a great bow, Iris flew straight at her mark.

The knife took the Queen just beneath the chin. Iris' hand was buried to the wrist in the Queen's neck. Ichor flooded down then. The razor sharp blade, honed by the magic of Lillith, the Old One, came to rest deep in the terrible monarch's brain. Like some dreadful lover, Iris twisted and turned the knife with her right hand and hugged the Queen's neck with her left arm, as she wrapped her legs around the Queen's slender waist.

The Queen staggered back. A shining rainbow of light surrounded the struggling forms. Framing a vast expanse of nighttime sky, a great gap opened in the air behind them. The light of unknown constellations, distant galaxies blazed into the afternoon sky above Soapstone Bay.

"IT IS DONE!" the Queen shrieked. "YOU WRETCHED... I... " but she fell back then into that gap. Iris clung to the last. The rainbow glow closed around them and the figures faded from sight. All was silence.

The Queen's blood had spattered the pavement. The pools of it began to seethe and burn. The smoke of the burning was foul, but the pall rose into the pure air above Soapstone Bay and was blown into nothingness.

Eddie struggled to his feet. He was swathed in blankets that hampered his movements. "Lena!" he called. There was no answer. He hitched up his unwieldy garments. Then he worked his way back towards

628

the cranny between the buildings where the women had sheltered before emerging to take their part in the battle. Hiding behind a huge pile of up-rooted street pavement and crumbled masonry, Lena and Sweetmaye huddled together for warmth. They were still shivering from the effects of the Queen's final, withering blast of cold.

At his clumsy approach, Sweetmaye sat up and looked around. "Be the battle won? Were the Locust Queen bested? True now!"

"Yes, Sweetmaye. She is gone. Iris finished her off."

"And Iris? Where is she? We could not see at the end," Lena asked worriedly.

"No one can know that, lass," Joe spoke. He'd come up just then, Fleggie was close behind. The big man was covered in dust and blood, but he had escaped serious injury.

Eddie looked at his teacher, his mentor, his friend. A complex array of expressions played across Joe's face. Pain, sadness, pride, all battled in that fierce visage. Tears poured freely from the eyes that could laugh, could flash fire. Eddie could see that the ancient warrior was hurt badly. He was wounded in battle and distraught at the loss of his love.

Barely able to speak, Joe cleared his throat and forced out a few words. "I should have known. Iris. She would never stay on the side-lines. Now, she falls through worlds without end. She will draw from the dying Queen's life force and be restored, but she is unlikely to find her way back. Ever."

His shoulders slumped then, and Joe turned away to vanish into the milling crowd that had begun to form at the scene.

Fleggie stooped and scooped up Sweetmaye. Lena came over and looped her arm around Eddie's waist. The way her curves fit into his side felt very good.

Sweetmaye buried her face in her lover's chest and cried a little. Then she squirmed in his arms. "Put me down, ye great oaf! We must be away from this place. True now."

Moving with his usual speed and grace, Fleggie scrambled around the square. He gathered five of his axes. The remaining three had fallen out of the world, embedded in the dying body of the Locust Queen.

Eddie gathered his makeshift clothing around himself and made his way back to the wagon. The four friends rode back to Tolemy's Cats. Wrapped in the comfort of each other's presence, none felt the need to speak.

"You want to come in?" Eddie asked, finally, as they pulled to a stop in front of the empty store.

"Thanks, mate, but Fleggie be done in, an' ye looks na' better. True now. Let's meet at the Inn for breakfast. Tomorrow, nine. Sound fair?"

"That sounds perfect. Thanks... Thank you both so much."

Michael C. Glaviano

With a smile, the big man turned away, then paused and turned back.

"Ye know, mates, Fleggie thinks mayhaps we won on this day."

"For now, yes. I believe we have indeed won," Lena spoke, her voice simultaneously joyful and somber. "Of course Evil is never truly eliminated, and one such as the Queen will someday trouble the worlds again, but we have set the dark forces back for a time. Perhaps a long while."

"Until tomorrow then, darlings," Sweetmaye called from the wagon.

"Until tomorrow, friends," Eddie replied.

* * *

When he did not wish to be noticed, the Old One could pass unseen. Silent and still, eyes closed, barely breathing, Joe hunkered here and there in the days that followed. He rested beneath metal fire escapes or in hidden alleys or in old shipping containers during the daytime. Moving silently, wrapped in his long, brooding thoughts, he wandered the streets in the small hours.

Thus, Giuseppe Tablarasa, ancient warrior, preserver of worlds, captain, teacher, friend vanished into the shadows of Soapstone Bay for the better part of a week. Then, with many sighs and regrets, he roused himself to action once more. He made another transit back to his home on Painter Avenue where he arranged for an extended absence. He gathered a few items and returned to Soapstone Bay. He took a room at the Inn at Three Corners. There he rested again and made preparations.

Finally he could bring himself to return to the bookshop on Central Avenue. Arriving a few minutes after opening, he appeared, unannounced, on a sunny morning. He carried a substantial parcel beneath his left arm. Silent, he stepped into the warmth, comfort, and memories of the store.

"Joe!" Lena called when she looked up from her work at the front desk. She ran around and hugged the tired old man, for thus he appeared at this juncture, and cried for the joy of seeing him. He produced the hint of a smile and ran his hand gently down the side of the young woman's head. He patted her upper arm as he would a sweet child. Then he placed his package near his feet.

"Please. Do not vanish again," she begged. "Wait. I shall fetch Reed. He is in the back."

She turned and moved with her unconscious grace up the aisle to the back of the store. Outside, in the tiny space behind the building, Eddie was cleaning a downspout that had become clogged with debris. "Reed! Oh, Reed! Joe is back... He has come back!"

630

The two young people hurried to the front of the store where they found Joe standing quietly. Eyes closed, face to the sun, he leaned heavily against the door frame. As they came up, Joe turned slowly to face them. His face creased in a smile. It was a tired smile, a sad smile as well, but it held more than a hint of the old, familiar strength and humor.

"Joe! Where've you been? We looked all around," Eddie demanded.

"It is good to see you both," Joe replied after a short pause. "And Fleggie? Sweetmaye? They are well?"

"Yes. They're fine. You want something to eat? Some coffee?"

"Thank you, no. I will leave in a moment."

"Leave? But where?"

"Oh, here and there, son. I have booked passage with Captain Thomas and intend to sail north with the *Mother Rose*. I've a mind to spend some time with my sister. At her farm."

"You have a sister?!"

"You've met her, son. Lillith is my sister. Or cousin. Whatever. The relationship is... complex. They call her 'the Old One' in this world. She weaves. You gained strength and no little wisdom beneath her roof. In all the worlds, she is the one best suited to help me heal."

"When I feel ready, I shall travel west from Lillith's farm. Whether by horse or afoot, I have not yet decided. At any rate, I shall travel west and come to the forest of the Lady.

"Remember, I must still induce her – as well as help her – to extend her forest into the Queen's own Blue World," he added.

Her eyes welling, Lena protested. "You cannot stay even for a day?" she asked.

"The good captain intends to sail on the tide. I would not keep him waiting.

"But there are things you should know," he added. His tone now more clipped and businesslike.

"I wanted to let you know that Iris... Iris has deeded this place to you, Lena." Joe's voice choked off and he swallowed and took a deep breath before looking at Eddie and continuing. "I believe, you saw the lawyer here at one point, son. Iris was... haranguing him here at the desk."

"Yes, I remember that."

"You should expect to hear from the lawyer in the next day or two. You needn't feel tied to this property, but if you rent out the two apartments upstairs and live in the back..." his face worked for a minute.

"Anyway," he continued finally, "I need to get moving." Joe turned to go.

"Joe. Joe. Wait for just a second, man. Will we see you again?"

The old spark flared within the ancient warrior's eyes. "You think, perhaps, your work is done? I promised you would be marked for

631

life, and you are. Believe it. The Locust Queen was one threat. There are – will be – others.

"And you have made a start, but there is a great deal more to learn. Didn't Ikeda tell you as much? Study. Stay in touch with him. With Sullivan. The house on Painter Avenue is open to you. Do not yearn overmuch that I darken your doorway too soon.

The spark faded and the gentle old man again stood before them. "And of course, you really must bring Lena to meet Sergeant Driscoll," he added, softly, with the smallest of laughs. Then he gently kicked the parcel that stood at his feet.

"Oh, and here are a few things I've brought for you. Just a few things you might find useful."

Eddie retrieved the box and carried it over to the counter. The package contained three, beautiful new throwing axes, the books that had been Ikeda's gift, and the notes that described how to do the transits between the Painter Avenue house and the Inn at Three Corners. At the bottom was the worn notebook that had been Fred Wilkins' bequest.

"Thanks, Joe. These are great!" Eddie hefted one of the sheathed axes. The handle fit his hands perfectly. Next, he picked up Ikeda's books and smiled in gratitude. His smile changed and became more thoughtful and tinged with complex feelings as he touched the frayed cover of the notebook. Last, he held Joe's beautiful, hand-written notes and shuffled through them.

"I'm sure you can do the transits now," the old man added, "but you'll want to review those notes again before you take your friends visiting... Very well. I think that's it... for now."

Then he held out his hand and Eddie took it in his own. The two men looked deep into each other's eyes.

Her calm, happy demeanor abandoning her for the moment, Lena hugged Joe again and wet his shirt with her tears. The old man stepped back, smiled slightly one last time, and raised a hand in farewell. Then he stepped from the shop to melt into the bustle of the bright morning.

Made in the USA
Lexington, KY
08 July 2010